Dance of Life

Dance of Life

Popular Music and Politics in Southeast Asia

Craig A. Lockard

University of Hawai'i Press

Honolulu

03 02 01 00 99 98 5 4 3 2 1

Library of Congress Cataloging-in-Publication Data

Lockard, Craig A.
Dance of life: popular music and politics in Southeast Asia / Craig A. Lockard.
p. cm.
Includes bibliographical references (p.) and index.
ISBN 0-8248-1848-2 (alk. paper)—
ISBN 0-8248-1918-7 (pbk.: alk. paper)
1. Popular music—Asia, Southeastern—History and criticism. 2. Music and state—Asia, Southeastern. I. Title. ML3502.A785L6 1998
306.4'84—dc21
96-39802
CIP
MN

University of Hawai'i Press books are printed on acid-free paper and meet the guidelines for permanence and durability of the Council on Library Resources

Designed by Jennifer Osborn

Contents

Introduction

You have made your home
In the streets of life
You'll take whatever . . . will come . . .
Then you put on your shoes of blue
And you immediately dance
Dance of life . . .
So you follow this song.
Malaysian rock group Kembara, 1984[1]

This book explores the connection between popular music and politics in Southeast Asia over the past five decades, with particular emphasis on Indonesia, the Philippines, Thailand, and Malaysia/Singapore. An examination of Southeast Asia constitutes part of a larger analysis of the relationship between popular music and politics throughout what is often rather imprecisely termed the "Third World." In another study I address the subject matter in non-Asian contexts such as Jamaica, Trinidad, Chile, Brazil, Nigeria, and South Africa.[2] Considerable attention is devoted in both works to the relationship between popular music and politics generally (including the expression of political protest and commentary), the role of the singer or musician as a political actor, and the way certain of these performers have used music as a weapon or tool—even sometimes as a call to arms—with the goal of changing, challenging, or overthrowing governments or socioeconomic systems that they consider unjust. The studies also examine their songs to determine the sort of messages they are trying to convey and the specific issues that preoccupy them.

In recent years anthropologists have been encouraged to more systematically address issues of popular and mass culture.[3] Historians, including those specialized on Southeast Asia, have generally neglected popular music and other mass-mediated cultural developments, even perhaps the crucial role of mass communications generally, in their writings on the twentieth century. The scholarship on sociopolitical change in Southeast Asia also tends to ignore the role of popular music and culture—unlike the literature on countries such as Jamaica, Trinidad, and Brazil.[4] A major goal of this study is to rectify that lacuna.

Popular music can generally be distinguished from other types of music by two essential features: It is disseminated largely by the mass media, and it is the by-product of the mass basis for marketing commodities. But the role that popular music plays in the modern world is a subject of considerable debate. There is no agreement as to who ultimately controls the production of popular music, and consequently, depending on your answer, whether it can actually play a significant role in society. A study focused on Southeast Asia can help to answer several relevant questions in this hitherto essentially Western debate. For example, does popular music have (or possess the capacity for) a potentially revolutionary and liberating influence, empowering or stimulating or educating people to reflection or action? Or, contrarily, does it largely play a conservative, institution-maintaining role in the sociopolitical order, diverting or pacifying them so that they accept the status quo? Does popular music chiefly challenge or reaffirm the social order? Or is it simultaneously challenging and supportive? Is heavily commodified and commercialized popular music essentially a matter of pure resistance by the people or of clear superimposition by corporate and other elites? Or do both the elites and the public influence the music? Should it perhaps be seen as an arena for negotiation and expression of societal conflicts and patterns? Is music a double-edged sword, both escapist and dynamic?[5] These questions are challenging and not easily answered, even if some themes are becoming clearer.

Various students of mass-mediated culture have analyzed its role as a mirror of society. For example, sociologist I.C. Jarvie wrote that the Hong Kong film industry "is not of interest because of contributions to the art of film. Its interest is sociological: what the films and their industry tell us about the society in, and for which, they are made."[6] Cinema has also been viewed as a major vehicle for the creative expression of cultural identity, not the least in major filmmaking Asian nations like China, India, and Japan.[7] Likewise, literature is the product of social process and hence cannot be separated from society and politics; perhaps the same claim can be made for music. Most popular music also derives from déclassé origins and consequently offers a proletarian appeal, allowing us to use it as a vehicle in studying "history from the bottom up."

Some observers doubt that popular music any longer plays a progressive role in Anglo-American society—if it ever did. Recently Simon Frith, a renowned British sociologist and pop music expert, has even contended that the colonization and co-optation of rock music by capitalism has undermined the genre: "I am now quite sure that the rock era is over."[8] Another British observer agrees that it has become a spent force in many parts of the world:

> Rock as the sounds of rebellion, as the mythological soundtrack of youth-as-opposition, as hipster and liberation *engagé*, as teddy boy, mod, hippy and punk, or, more simply and likely, as suburban romantic, has now apparently metamorphosed into the musical wallpaper of the ten thousand lifts, hotel foyers, shopping centres, airport lounges and television advertisements that await us in the 1990s.[9]

On the other hand, there is an anarchic quality to some of this music, especially to rock, that has seemed to encourage—perhaps even sometimes to incite—youth to rebel against societal constraints. Or at least, so it has seemed to some critics. This quality was most pronounced in the United States and Western Europe from the mid-1960s through the early 1970s, but it can be seen as a continuing thread from the mid-1950s onward. Robert Pielke, an American philosopher and playwright, even argues that rock music has been at the center of a profound cultural revolution in the United States and perhaps elsewhere, constituting an important catalyst for change. He believes this cultural revolution has embodied a fundamental challenge to some prevailing values of Western culture. "I'm convinced," he writes, "that music not only reflects cultural consciousness but also participates in creating, stabilizing, and changing it."[10] In other words, popular art, when in serious conflict with art preferred by those with political, social, or economic power, represents a potentially revolutionary set of values.

This may be even more true in the Third World, where neocolonial forms—as well as the sociopolitical influences—of capitalism differ in many important respects from the industrialized capitalism of the Western world. The situation in many Third World societies seems to have been more complex than in the West. Jamaican singer Jimmy Cliff once characterized reggae as "the cry of the people."[11] As the late Victor Jara, one of the standard-bearers of the progressive New Song movement in Chile, sang:

I don't sing for the love of singing
Or to show off my voice
But for the statements
Made by my honest guitar
My guitar is not for killers
Greedy for money and power
But for the people who labor
So that the future may flower.[12]

During the 1960s, some of those involved in the anti-Vietnam War movement in both the United States and South Vietnam were inspired by the poignant, bitter songs of South Vietnamese protest singers/peace activists like the often arrested Trinh Con San, such as "Love Song of a Woman Maddened by War":

I have a lover ... who died in the dark covered jungles
Who died in the cold; his body burned as charcoal
I want to ... love Viet Nam
As soon as I grow up my ears are accustomed to the sounds of
Bullets and mines
My hands are now free. But I forget from now on
The human language.[13]

Hence, popular music genres and musicians, like their counterparts in literature and film, have sometimes reflected and articulated themes of cultural decolonization, empowerment, neocolonialism, cultural confrontation, disillusionment, despair, widespread inequalities, subcultural nationalism or identity, nation building, and anti-imperialism. They have also provided alternative channels of communication in societies characterized by illiteracy and government-controlled media.

Sometimes music played a direct political role.[14] For example, Bob Marley and other reggae musicians were closely connected to the triumph and rule of the Peoples National Party in Jamaica during the 1970s, just as Jara and the New Song movement were identified with the Allende years in Chile. Brazilian pop stars Chico Buarque, Gilberto Gil, and Caetano Veloso challenged through song the repressive junta in the late 1960s and early 1970s, providing at considerable personal cost one of the major vehicles for expressing popular dissatisfaction. The superstar Fela, one of the most provocative musicians in the world, has long been a flamboyant thorn in the side of Nigerian governments and a focus for oppositional sentiments. His controversial music and lifestyle, as well as his overtly critical lyrics and statements, have earned him chronic harassment, and sometimes even physical assault or incarceration. Few popular musicians anywhere can match Fela's radical stance and talent for incurring official wrath while also becoming a hero to millions in the urban underclass and frustrated student populations.

Still, in Southeast Asia the music of superstars like Thailand groups Caravan and Carabao, Indonesia's Rhoma Irama and Iwan Fals, the Filipino Freddie Aguilar, and the Malaysian rock group Kembara inevitably reflected and articulated the views of many while also providing an oppositional or critical discourse on national or international affairs. As we shall see, some were identified with mass-based sociopolitical movements seeking change. For example, Caravan helped spark and sustain the student democracy movement in Thailand during the early 1970s, Aguilar's culturally nationalistic music provided a rhythm for the agitation that brought down Ferdinand Marcos in the mid-1980s, and Rhoma's music advocated a more Islamic tone in Indonesian life as well as challenging some prevailing political and economic values during the 1970s and 1980s. At the same time, there were clear limits to the political influence of music. In Malaysia popular music had a less militant tinge, although musicians like Kembara and P. Ramlee addressed societal realities. Much of popular music is escapist in orientation—characteristically dwelling on romantic feelings or relationships, such as the light pop formula in Malaysia. In many countries political interference or control helped shape mass culture.

It is clear that popular music has become a significant sociocultural force and enjoys extraordinary influence all over the world. While scholars have long analyzed the roles of folk and classical music, the value of studying popular music or even popular culture generally has been more controversial. That is now changing for Southeast Asia, with a growing literature on topics like films, soap operas, and such popular writing forms as comics, humor magazines, and women's magazines. When I first sojourned in Southeast Asia in the mid-1960s, the growing role of popular music (imported and local) seemed obvious. Many of my youthful acquaintances avidly followed the pop charts, and a few even sported names (given or adopted) such as Elvis or Ringo. Western popular music from Radio Malaysia (including the ubiquitous request programs) and the U.S. Armed Forces Radio in South Vietnam, as well as the BBC, Voice of America, and Australian broadcasting, was easily picked up and widely followed throughout Sarawak, even in remote villages. I fondly recall an ethnic Kenyah teenager from deep in the Sarawak interior (and now a prominent government official) who knew the lyrics to most of the Beatles songs and could do a passable imitation of John Lennon.

Yet the study of popular music and sociocultural change in Southeast Asia developed very slowly (certainly in comparison to Africa and the Caribbean) and has only just begun to produce some important scholarly work in the past decade or so. Some of the pioneering work has perhaps even become obscure. In the early 1970s Australian historian Heather Sutherland made the case for studying such neglected lower-class hybrid Indonesian cultural elements as *komedie stambul* theatre and *kroncong* music, both highly popular in the late nineteenth and early twentieth centuries, arguing that the issue of cultural borrowing and adaptation was a major force in artistic and social development.[15] A mid-1970s article on the disco way of life in Jakarta, as well as several short studies in that period on kroncong's history, further suggested the increasing importance of popular culture.[16] American historian Bill Frederick's stimulating 1982 essay on Indonesian superstar Rhoma Irama demonstrated how to study the relationship between popular music and social change, and marked the first step toward analyzing for Southeast Asia the sort of trends that had long been discussed in African and Caribbean studies.[17] By 1988 Peter Manuel, an American ethnomusicologist, was able to offer some preliminary remarks on the various popular music traditions in the region in his comprehensive overview of Asia, Africa, and Latin America.[18] In the past few years scholars and writers including James Chopyak, Eleanor Elequin, Doreen Fernandez, Martin Hatch, Norma Japitana, Peter Manuel, Randell Baier, Pamela Myers-Moro, Tan Sooi Beng, Ubonrat Siriyuvasak, Anderson Sutton, Sean Williams, Deborah Wong, and Philip Yampolsky have considerably deepened our understanding of Southeast Asian popular musics, making this more ambitious study possible.

Clearly the overall context of modern Southeast Asian history was crucial in shaping the emerging popular cultures of the region. This includes the patterns, going back millennia, of creatively assimilating or absorbing the influences and peoples emanating from outside with the indigenous structures and values, and creating out of them a new synthesis. All of the region experienced the destabilizing influence of Western imperialism. All except Thailand were colonies through the first half of the twentieth century. Effectively a neocolony of the West, Thailand was transformed in many of the same ways as her neighbors. As with sub-Saharan Africa, the colonial interlude imposed both artificial boundaries and extractive economies geared to commodity production for the world market, subjecting many Southeast Asians to the vagaries of world commodity prices. Commercialization of land and agriculture created a situation of progressive economic marginalization for many. These years saw the roots of rampant urbanization that would eventually draw many rural peoples—as well as immigrants—into the growing cities. Nationalism emerged and controversies over national identity erupted. By the twentieth century most of the countries contained diverse populations riven by ethnic, sociocultural, linguistic, and religious divisions. Frequently the marginalized "outsiders," whether highlanders or cultural and ethnic minorities, resented governments controlled by majority, privileged, secular, or "Westernized" groups.

The postcolonial years witnessed considerable economic growth and movement toward the creation of national cultures from the "plural societies." As a major history text argues, "in societies that have lost the momentum of historical continuity, new sorts of [unifying and legitimizing] symbols must be found."[19] Both social and labor mobility grew as rural migrants crowded into burgeoning cities, many surrounded by shantytown slums, where they came into more regular contact with members of other ethnic, racial, regional, or religious groups. As in Africa, this mixture often generated syncretic cultural patterns that crossed ethnic or subgroup lines. Many urban workers became proletarianized with the growth of skilled labor employment and industry. Expanding educational systems created national consciousness and contributed to the growth of an urban middle class.

But, as in other parts of the Third World, a new privileged class of political, bureaucratic, military, commercial, and technical elites monopolized a large share of the wealth, while the gap between the few rich and many poor generally intensified. Western and Japanese economic (and in some cases political) influence remained powerful, including massive investment and loans, allowing the perception of neocolonialism to persist for radical and nationalist critics. Inevitably this also raised the insistent questions of cultural imperialism and decolonization, most strongly perhaps in the Philippines, but by no means absent from the cultural dialogue elsewhere in the region. Secularization came into conflict with religious revival, as many reacted to destabilizing changes with enhanced religious activity and identity. There remained many chronic problems, among them political tension, socioeconomic inequalities, leftist or religion-based insurgencies, religious revivalism (or fundamentalism), overt or covert intervention by various superpowers, and dictatorship or quasi-democracy of some sort as common governmental patterns. At the same time, the mass media were expanding in reach and complexity, providing an impetus for the evolution of popular cultures and the commercial underpinning that would help shape them. Inevitably, popular culture would become involved in the dialogues of the era.

My own involvement with the subject matter developed over the course of many years. Today the Los Angeles metropolitan area, where I was raised and attended college, is considered almost a Third World city in its increasingly diverse ethnic composition, with many residents from Asia, Africa, Latin America, and the South Pacific islands. But even thirty-five or forty years ago the flavor was relatively cosmopolitan. My suburban hometown of Pasadena was multiethnic; in addition to a large African-American population, there were substantial Mexican-American and Japanese-American minorities as well as a significant number of people born in Indonesia, a notable component of the sizable migration to the United States following Indonesian independence in 1950. A curious youngster did not have to search very long to hear the exotic and ultimately captivating sounds of Mexican *ranchera*, Japanese *enka*, or Indonesian kroncong.

My recent studies of popular music were also a culmination of avocational interests developed as a teenager in the 1950s, when I adored rock and roll and rhythm and blues. These interests were honed as a college student and political activist in the 1960s. In that turbulent era I embraced folk music and also loved rock, both of which were overtly involved in and supportive of the progressive politics in which I was enmeshed. For me the 1950s and 1960s were accompanied by a constant "soundtrack" that helped me make sense of the times and my place in the overall scheme of things, while also setting a "mood" for my activities and attitudes. It seemed obvious that music and politics were—or could be—congruent forces.

Beginning in the early 1960s I also began to sojourn abroad at various times, first as a student, then as a researcher and teacher. In the mid-1980s, thanks to a Fulbright-Hays research fellowship and the hospitality of the University of Malaya's Institute of Advanced Study, I spent a year in Malaysia gathering data for a comprehensive study of popular music and its relationship to the overall social, economic, and political changes occurring in that country since the 1930s. The results of that study have been published in a monograph and various essays over the past few years.[20] The chapter on Malaysia in this volume summarizes, updates, and reformulates some of these earlier writings, while also incorporating some of my scholarship on recent Malaysian history and politics. Over the past decade I have also published a few brief essays or encyclopedia entries on American popular and folk musicians, as well as several pieces on Caribbean and African popular music.[21] While pursuing my Malaysian research I began collecting materials on popular music and politics in other Southeast Asian nations, ultimately deciding to attempt an ambitious comparative study. This work is the result.

My sporadic living experiences and travel in Southeast Asia, East Asia, East Africa, and Europe in the 1960s, 1970s, and 1980s brought me into closer contact with a wide variety of folk and popular musics and enabled me to observe the diverse and complicated interactions with Anglo-American popular culture. These experiences left me with countless treasured musical memories, many of them Southeast Asian. Among them are: tuning in to weekly Hawaiian, kroncong, and bluegrass music programs on Radio Malaysia; judging an "Elvis Presley of Kuching" contest in Sarawak; interviewing pop stars, record producers, music journalists, and pop culture magazine editors in Kuala Lumpur; uncovering old or unavailable Malay, Indonesian, and Chinese recordings in out-of-the-way shops all over Malaysia and Singapore; comparing country and western bars in Singapore; intersecting at various places in Indonesia with an American rock band attempting to incorporate gamelan instruments into their sound; seeing Rhoma Irama in concert; listening to Batak pop and folk groups in North Sumatra; absorbing nonstop recorded pop and *dangdut* songs on long distance bus trips in Indonesia; remaining enchanted through all-night temple festivals in Bali; dancing to schmaltzy love songs written by Prince Sihanouk in Phnom Penh; nightclub and coffee house hopping in Manila; sampling the variety of Filipino jazz and pop musicians working in Hong Kong clubs and bars; discussing the merits and demerits of American rock and folk stars with Thai university students; encountering a vibrant Chinese opera performance in a Bangkok back alley; and (although not truly Southeast Asian) discovering a living folk music tradition but also many recordings from Hong Kong, Malaysia, and the United States in a Hakka town located in the remote northeast of China's Guangdong Province.[22]

It is well to remember that culture is inevitably a political matter, as is its analysis. Personal biases, approaches, and experiences always have some bearing on a scholar's interpretation (whether covertly or overtly), while the prevailing intellectual climate helps frame the goals and methods of a study. Although I have lived in five countries on four continents, traveled widely, favor a cosmopolitan outlook in the best sense of the term, and have devoted my career to teaching intercultural understanding and combating ethnocentrism, I am also rooted to some degree in a particular culture and have pronounced political views. No doubt these influence my coverage and the decision to focus on the sociopolitical dimensions of cultural forms. I also am an avid collector of recordings (a major challenge to my family's need for capital accumulation) and enjoy most of the musics I write about. Indeed, I must confess to a particular love of several Indonesian styles (fashionable or not) such as dangdut, kroncong, pop country, and *irama hindustan*, Malaysian folk rock and *asli* (modernized folk), as well as Chinese torch singers of the 1940s and 1950s (artists from China, Taiwan, and Hong Kong have been widely popular among Southeast Asian Chinese). Furthermore, I maintain a keen interest in and appreciation for many African, Latin American, and Caribbean musics. This "fandom" can facilitate a sympathetic portrayal—but also pose a barrier to more critical understanding.

Perhaps now we are beginning to have enough information to assess the broad role of popular musics in Southeast Asia, including politics. This book attempts a preliminary examination of the relationship between various popular musics and political change and protest in several nations. No comparative study of the relationship between popular music and politics in Southeast Asia currently exists. The chapters focus on particular styles of music that have been conducive to political protest, and on the leading exponents of these styles, performers who often achieved superstar status in their own countries (and sometimes abroad) because of—or despite—the fact that they offered clear political messages.

The first chapter offers an introduction to the field of popular music studies in the Third World generally and Asia in particular, summarizing material on the nature and significance of both popular culture and popular music. These pages explore such topics as the relationship with sociocultural identity, intercultural and transnational patterns, the political role of music, cultural imperialism, and decolonization. There follow chapters on Indonesia (kroncong, dangdut, pop country), the Philippines (various incarnations of *pinoy*), Thailand (*luktoong*, "songs for life"), and Malaysia-Singapore (pop, rock). Finally, I draw some comparisons from these cases and try to ascertain the role these developments have played in the modern world. A survey of popular music in Southeast Asia should confirm a relatively close relationship to major sociopolitical trends found elsewhere, although the precise parameters may necessarily differ from those in other parts of the world as a result of the unique historical circumstances and cultural traditions of each nation.

Throughout the chapters I am concerned with the historical framework of musical and cultural developments—with the sociopolitical context analyzed as the necessary background for musical parameters. Hence the emphasis is more on sociocultural and political history than on ethnomusicology or even cultural studies. Some attention is paid, however, to the nature and evolution of the popular music traditions and industries, as well as to the theoretical issues punctuating the debate on mass culture. Although I am not formally trained in these fields, research for this book required me to peruse and thus gain some familiarity with the growing literatures on cultural studies and ethnomusicology. Cultural studies have been concerned with the interface between the local and the national within global circuits. I hope that this work adheres to that spirit, if not necessarily the same methodology.

I have also been influenced by some of the writings on popular music in other parts of the world. Among many others, I owe much to Gerard Behague, Wolfgang Bender, Billy Bergman, John Collins, David Coplan, Steven Davis, R. Serge Denisoff, Veit Erlmann, Jan Fairley, Steve Feld, Paul Friedlander, Simon Frith, Reebee Garofalo, Juan-Pablo Gonzalez, Jocelyne Guilbault, Dick Hebdige, Gail Holst, Charles Keil, Andrew Jones, Helen Kivnick, Edward Larkey, George Lewis, George Lipsitz, Peter Manuel, Richard Middleton, Manuel Pena, Charles Perrone, Ray Pratt, Gordon Rohlehr, Timothy Ryback, Claus Schreiner, Martin Stokes, John Street, Keith Warner, Christopher Waterman, Anita Waters, and Peter Wicke. The study also quite clearly crosses a number of disciplinary and regional boundaries but can probably be most accurately described as comparative history, I trust with some relevance to social scientists as well as those interested in questions of contemporary culture. In my view, since art is necessarily social and situated in cultural, political, economic, and historical settings, interdisciplinarity is an essential component of popular music analysis.[23]

I have visited Indonesia, Thailand, and the Philippines several times, traveling widely and collecting a few recordings, but have not done sustained field research in these countries—this in contrast to Malaysia-Singapore, where I lived and carried out research projects for four years. Hence this is (except for Malaysia-Singapore) a work of synthesis based mostly on secondary materials. These sources include both scholarly and (where available) popular books, periodicals and magazines, as well as recordings (sometimes with helpful liner notes) and discussions with specialists on, and students from, the relevant countries. The library of the University of Wisconsin–Green Bay was most helpful in obtaining sources, but I also benefited from use of, and staff cooperation at, the University of Wisconsin–Madison, Cornell University, University of California–Berkeley, U.C.L.A., Ohio University, Northern Illinois University, University of

Kentucky, and University of Malaya libraries. My arguments and ideas were challenged and improved by colleagues at Cornell and Northern Illinois, where I served as visiting lecturer in the Southeast Asia programs, as well as at several academic conferences where I offered some preliminary findings. The translations of Malay lyrics are my own, aided by Azlina Ahmed (to whom I owe considerable thanks for embellishing the nuances). Other translations are taken from the secondary source or sources cited in the appropriate footnote.

In pursuing various aspects of this study over a period of fifteen years I have inevitably "picked the brains" of many knowledgeable sources. David Walls and John Stephenson, both then at the Appalachian Center of the University of Kentucky (where I enjoyed a summer fellowship), contributed to my understanding of American folk music specifically but also of musical culture in a larger sense and its relationship to society. In Malaysia there were many helpful experts; I should single out Rehman Rashid, M. Shahabullah, Errol DeCruz, Zainal Kling, and especially Wan Abdul Kadir Wan Yusoff for special mention. I am also indebted for a deeper understanding of popular culture to conversations with George Lipsitz, John Fiske, Paul Buhle, Stuart Ewen, Fred Inglis, Michael Parenti, E. P. Thompson, George Rudé, Tom Bender, Stephanie Coontz, and Allen Hunter—all of whom spent several days at the University of Wisconsin–Green Bay as part of my department's visiting lecture series—as well as Victor Greene; they have been priceless resources. Martin Hatch, Russell Middleton, Patricia Henry, and Donna Amoroso kindly supplied me with tapes of important recordings.

Various ethnomusicologists specialized on Southeast Asia have provided inspiration and information as well as friendship; these include Martin Hatch, Jim Chopyak, Pat Matusky, Fred Lau, Deborah Wong, Margaret Sarkissian, and Andy Sutton. Among others, Ron Provencher, John Lent, Bob McKinley, Thongchai Winichakul, Bill Frederick, Dan Doeppers, and Lian-The and Kent Mulliner have aided me in understanding Southeast Asian popular culture as well as encouraging my own work. Several anonymous readers for the University of Hawai'i Press and my insightful editor, Pam Kelley, offered helpful advice for improving the manuscript. My colleague at UWGB, Terry O'Grady, a musicologist who has written on popular music, kindly read and critiqued an earlier version of Chapter 1. His suggestions helped me overcome various problems. I am also grateful to Bill Frederick and Marty Hatch for the photographs of Indonesian pop stars. Finally, my colleagues in the Social Change and Development Department, especially Harvey Kaye and Tony Galt, have provided a continuous inspiration and support for my studies, supplying source materials and helping me shape my arguments. None of those mentioned should, of course, be held responsible for any problems in the manuscript; I am perfectly capable of making my own mistakes.

Dance of Life

1

If you come down
from the [*Singapore*] *causeway to Johor Baru*
You are going to meet a lot of people
Who appreciate the rhythm and blues . . .
I got Malaya blues
Each and everyday I choose.

The Blues Gang, a Malaysian rock group.[1]

The literature on popular musics has grown enormously in recent years. This is true for North America and Europe, of course, but also for Africa, the Caribbean, parts of Latin America, and China. Perhaps now we are finally beginning to have enough information to assess the broad role of popular music in various Southeast Asian nations, including its role in politics. But first we need a broader perspective as background. This chapter examines various aspects of popular culture and popular music generally, with particular attention to Asia and the Pacific, in order to provide a larger context for the comparative assessment of the relationship between various popular musics and political expression in Southeast Asia. First we explore the meaning of popular culture and its relationship to modern society—in particular, the implications of mass mediation. We then analyze popular music as a phenomenon, including the overall parameters of the genre. The remainder of the chapter looks at the relationship between popular music and various aspects of society, history, culture, and politics.

Some Basic Data (1991)[2]

Gramophone/Phonograph Record Units Produced: Asia 1,495,000; Africa 736,000; Latin America and Caribbean ca. 30,000,000; Europe 538,590,000; United States ca. 54,000,000; World Total 696,414,000.

World Record Sales (1988): singles/EPs 370,000,000; LPs 510,000,000; tapes 1,390,000,000; CDs 400,000,000.[3]

Sound Recorders Produced (incl. cassette tape recorders/players): Asia 104,575,000; Africa 267,000; Europe 8,192,000; United States 831,000 (1990); World Total 116,096,000.

Sound Reproducers Produced (incl. gramophones, record players, compact disc players): Asia 10,737,000; Africa 56,000; Latin America and Caribbean 215,000; Europe 8,634,000; United States 933,000 (1984); World Total 19,935,000.

Radio Receivers Produced (incl. radio-cassette tape players): Asia 97,530,000; Africa 1,526,000; Latin America and Caribbean 5,582,000; Europe 12,725,000; United States 2,600,000; World Total 128,933,000.

Television Receivers Produced: Asia 75,388,000; Africa 3,161,000; Latin America and Caribbean 4,991,000; Europe 19,196,000; United States 13,267,000; World Total 125,256,000.

Popular Culture and Modern Society

In societies around the world the artifacts of popular culture and mass media have become a part of everyday life for billions of people:

> Take a walk down any street, in any city or village, as the twilight fades and the darkness comes over the scene. Whether you are in London or Tokyo, Cairo or New York, Buenos Aires or Singapore, a small blue light will flicker at you from the unshuttered windows. Take a stroll down any small town, Fussa-Machi or . . . Luxor, at the threshold of darkness, and you will find the flickering blue light shimmering in the distance. These lights are the tiny knots in the seamless web of modern media, fluttering their messages inexorably at the natives of the post-modern global village.[4]

Popular culture can be deplored, celebrated, or merely enjoyed while also functioning as a vehicle for politics, personal expression, or entertainment. As a result it challenges and changes the way people spend their leisure hours, communicate, and perhaps even think about themselves and the larger context in which they must exist.

Yet popular culture remains a nebulous concept with contested definition. In some languages, such as Japanese, there is no proper word that even corresponds to the English word *popular* (particularly in its American usage), with Japanese equivalents conveying the sense of ephemerality ("temporarily widespread" or "soon obsolete" songs), a discovery that should not surprise fans of Japanese haiku poetry or painting. As one Japanese scholar concludes, "the term 'popular' is not popular in Japan."[5] Does popular culture mean simply the products designed for mass consumption, or something more than that? Does the "popular" pertain to a mode of production and consumption, a style, a method of distribution, a form, a strategy? Could it be that popular culture functions in some respects as a form of folk culture for urban industrial societies? But popular culture is not restricted to industrialized nations, given the transformation or displacement of folk cultures in recent decades even in mostly agrarian societies. Surely researchers should be wary of applying assumptions based on Western experience to societies in other parts of the globe.[6]

Perhaps one major key is perceiving popularity as the sine qua non of popular culture. It is a "majority" culture involving aspects of culture (ideological, material, social) that are widely spread, believed in, or consumed by large numbers of people (generally on a leisure basis). In the twentieth century, popular culture became equated with the great variety of broadly intellectual-aesthetic products and activities to which the vast majority of the population has turned for recreation and enjoyment. This variety has been created and distributed chiefly by the mass media of communications, which include both electronic and print categories. Among the electronic media have been radio, television, cinema, stereos, and tape recorders. Hence popular culture consists of both spoken and printed words, pictures, activities, and the like.[7]

Popular culture has had an enormous influence on our lives. But what kinds of influence? And who has shaped popular culture? A major role of popular culture has always been communication. American sociologist George Lewis summarizes well the impact of popular culture and its relationship to communications: "For most people, the great majority of . . . communication comes in the form of popular culture; the television they watch, the music they listen to, the clothes they buy, the food they eat, the games they play."[8] Modern popular culture emerged in tandem with the development of modern technology, especially mass communications—including much more efficient means of production and distribution—to serve an audience possessing spending money and increased leisure. The predominantly oral popular cultures of early modern Europe (the carnivals, fairs, minstrels, etc.) were, beginning in the 1700s, changed forever by the growth of literacy and the spread of print media, harbingers of the enormous cultural changes generated by the Industrial Revolution (from railroads to universal education, broadsheets to cinema).[9] Yet while change was clearly a driving force, there have often been strong elements of continuity between past and present. Scholars of Japan, for example, emphasize a persisting tradition dating from the early Tokugawa period in the seventeenth century.[10]

Over the past century urbanization, commercialization, and standardization contributed to the evolution of a mass culture for a mass society, with radio, television, VCRs, and recordings bringing nationally produced amusements into our very homes. Indeed, the same technologies spread Anglo-American cultural artifacts around the globe, generating fears of cultural imperialism as part and parcel of "coca-colazation." A Malaysian observer concluded that "popular culture is thus a dynamic, revolutionary force breaking down old barriers of class, tradition, taste, and dissolving all established 'cultural' distinctions . . . generating autonomous values for itself."[11] The mass media have progressively expanded in reach and complexity over the past five decades. By the 1950s most people in Southeast Asia had access to radios, and the recording industry developed greatly during the 1960s. Videocassette recorders and televisions were common possessions in the 1980s among urbanites. Many Asians could comprehend the experience of the average American, who came to spend some three thousand entire days—almost nine years—watching television during his or her life, leading to what anthropologist Conrad Kottak has termed "teleconditioning" (TV-conditioned behavior).[12]

The pattern is widespread. A recent study of Singapore reports that "televiewing is a full evening's activity," with citizens finding it difficult to switch their sets off.[13] In much of Asia mass communications have more recently reached the villages, so that a mass culture is still in formation. In pluralistic nations like India, with many substantial linguistic groups and pronounced regional differences, it must compete with deeply entrenched folk cultures based on regional and linguistic particularism; hence the imported cultural forms are mainly enjoyed by urbanites and the more affluent. Popular culture can be crucial to the morale of a population. For example, in Mogadishu, Somalia, a radio station run by Italian military forces—Radio Ibis—has offered one of the few diversions from the terrible conflict that has ripped the city and nation apart. It provides a comforting mix of Western rock and Somali pop and folk songs (many by musicians who have fled the country). The only alternative cultural escape is found in the Western action films shown in the few remaining (and usually crowded) movie theaters.[14]

Popular culture has also been a product of social process and cannot be separated from society, politics, and the time period in which it exists. It has no fixed forms; historical circumstances can change the meaning. Hence individual artifacts also have no necessarily permanent meanings. They must compete within a changing multiplicity of discourses. No cultural moment exists, concludes American scholar George Lipsitz, within a "hermetically sealed cultural present."[15] Amidst the controversy in 1991 over Oliver Stone's attempt to rewrite official history in his film *JFK*, it was hardly noticed that Americans have for many years learned far more of their history from TV, films, and historical fiction than from academic historians. A case can be made that much of what Americans understand about slavery derived from Hollywood presentations like *Roots*, about Westward expansion from

"Westerns" like *High Noon*, and about East Asians from ethnocentric films such as the Charlie Chan series. Popular culture superstars can enjoy spectacular fame. In the same way that Michael Jordan or Michael Jackson are household names in the United States, cinema idol Amitabh Bachchan is probably a more significant and familiar figure to North Indians than most of their major political or historical figures.[16]

Observers from different cultures (or from different mindsets in the same society) can look at the same phenomenon and draw directly opposite conclusions. Elvis Presley's swiveling hips, Jim Morrison's boozy genital exposing, Michael Jackson's apparent "crotch-grabbing," and Madonna's entire arsenal of music, film, and "books" have been seen by some as smut and by others as art. Indeed, there has been a lively debate among feminists about Madonna: Should she be seen as a feminist icon of female independence (sexual and otherwise)—perhaps even a constructor of a coalition of the disenfranchised to relentlessly attack the hierarchies of power—or as a blatant self-promoter who panders to (and thus reinforces) male stereotypes for her own commercial gain?[17]

But popular culture's significance goes beyond surface manifestations; it expresses social cosmology, worldviews, class and gender relations, conceptions of good and evil, and other sociocultural phenomena. People's imaginative pictures of the world, their plans and role playing, indeed their whole lives, are deeply affected by popular culture. Life not only imitates art but makes it a part of our individual lives, a process that creates a valuable resource for coping with everyday existence. The mass media mold perceptions, fixing events in space and time. Detective writer Ross MacDonald asserted that "we learn to see reality through the popular arts we create and patronize. That's what they're for. That's why we love them."[18] Popular culture as a form of discourse can serve as a potent force for both persuasion and value building, as well as for the perception of consciousness.

People also learn about politics from popular culture. The play worlds of popular culture convey ideas and images about politics that people find useful in their effort to understand something of their "political selves" and the nature of the political world around them. They also dramatize cultural myths. Hence popular culture involves political socialization: the acquisition of ideas and images about the political world and the individual citizen's role in it. This understanding augments what people learn from their schools and families. Most of the power and effectiveness of popular culture to teach lies in its impressive ability to dramatize messages that can be retained and used in individual and group lives.[19]

Literature has long been viewed as a window on a society, telling us much about culture, social structure, and politics and conveying special insights into how culture and history intersect with the lives of people. Fiction is an active influence shaping the way people think about their social and political order. Hence the novel may become an agent of political culture, and the novelist a political philosopher. In Brazil, for example, novels about the impoverished northeast have emphasized drought, poverty, banditry, plantations, and escapist religious cults.[20] Art (highbrow or otherwise) may always be inseparable from the real world in many respects. Nigerian novelist Chinua Achebe argues that no novel is ever politically neutral, because "even the attempt to say nothing about politics is a big political statement. You are saying, then, that everything is O.K."[21] John Downing has set forth some arguments on the impact of Third World film that could equally be applied to popular music:

> Filmic political imagination is a spark which can smolder in its audiences over long periods, which can carry across nations, continents, even class-experiences. It can serve to ignite debate, self-understanding, solidarity, within and on the edges of political movements. It offers a recolorization of the scenery, a pulse in the memory.[22]

As an example, political philosophies, group behavior, social values, dress, speech, societal dilemmas, and personal dreams may be reflected to such a degree in the Indian cinema that, in South Asian society, it becomes difficult to "distinguish between art and life," a situation that allowed film stars to cross over into politics from the fantasy world of cinema. Hence, Indian cinema provides a legitimate metaphor for the society it portrays, defines, and entertains.[23] In the 1940s and 1950s, the film songs composed by Sahir Ludhianvi addressed nationalist or socially reformist themes. Indeed, in that period the Bombay film industry produced music that was modern, eclectic, and yet fundamentally Indian in flavor, with much continuity from the past and well in tune with the national identity. The late Guru Dutt became a master at giving the film song an aesthetic and artistic validity. The lively film industry of the Tamil-speaking region of southern India—with its emphasis on "pageants for the peasants"—also played a key role in sustaining

Films have been an immensely significant element in the popular culture of most nations. In Asia, with the exception of major film producing nations such as India, Japan, and the Philippines, imported films have generally dominated. This theater featuring a Western film with an African theme is in Kuching, Sarawak, Malaysia. 1966 photo by author.

linguistic and cultural nationalism as a counterweight to the political and economic dominance of the Hindi-speaking north, while also conveying meaning to the impoverished majority.[24]

Yet the films and their soundtrack songs also portray a fantasy world, unsullied by controversial perspectives, that enables viewers to forget the problem-filled real world (and also what they might do to change it). As one fan explained: The films "make me forget all my troubles. I love to sit in the dark and dream about what I can never possibly have. I can listen to the music, learn all the songs and that way I can forget about my troubles."[25] It has been estimated that the average Indian peasant knows at least fifty film songs by heart. But the reality is that film production has been closely related to the real world. In 1994 India was rocked by the arrest of star actor Sanjay Dutt (who specialized in violent action movies) for alleged involvement in a series of bombings related to communal tensions. The Bombay ("Bollywood") film industry has been partly financed by criminal syndicates, and Dutt maintained ties to underworld figures suspected in the attacks.[26] Films have occupied such a significant role in modern life that in 1978 North Korea even kidnapped two leading South Korean figures, a director and actress, reportedly on the orders of dictator Kim Il-Sung, in order to develop a film industry. In 1984 they finally escaped and returned to the south.[27]

Sometimes popular culture and political careers merge. The United States is not the only country to have elected film stars (e.g., Ronald Reagan, California senator George Murphy, Carmel mayor Clint Eastwood) or pop musicians (e.g., Palm Springs mayor and now Congressman Sonny Bono) to office. Voters in southern India have long favored stars of the local regional-linguistic film industry as state leaders, and by the 1980s that trend had even spread to parts of northern India. The most successful south Indian star-politician, M. G. Ramachandran (M. G. R.), most of whose films shaped his image as a hero to the poor and powerless, was said to perfectly embody the cultural idioms in Tamilnadu. In 1991 Filipinos installed a film star as vice president. Several popular musicians in Thailand and the Philippines have, at various times, expressed an interest in pursuing political careers. Cultural figures, especially from the realm of literature, have also gained (or contested for) higher office in Latin America (Peru, Venezuela, Dominican Republic). Indeed, popular musicians like Venezuelan romantic balladeer Jose Luis Rodriguez and Panamanian-born salsa star Ruben Blades (a U.S.-based law graduate from Harvard) publicly expressed interest in political careers; in 1994 Blades ran unsuccessfully for the presidency of Panama.[28] In 1995, dissatisfied with Japan's increasingly chaotic political party system and perceived bureaucratic ineptitude, voters in Tokyo and Osaka elected former professional comedians to their governorships. And in 1996 a wide variety of singing, film, and television stars, including action movie hero Shin Song Il, ran for office in South Korea's first elections under a civilian democratic government.[29]

Popular culture can perhaps be viewed as both a mirror and a lamp: a mirror that reflects society and a lamp that illuminates the picture (and hence facilitates the changing) of political reality. John Lennon hinted at the relationship between popular culture and the sociopolitical structure of society when he claimed, to much controversy, that in their prime the Beatles were more popular than Jesus. He presumably meant that the artifacts of popular culture created by the Beatles had more impact on shaping contemporary Anglo-American life than Christian teachings—a dubious assertion, but perhaps not to be dismissed too lightly. Later Lennon and his wife, Yoko Ono, even attempted to use the mass media to "sell" peace to the world while promoting the notion of "making love, not war" with their famous "bed-in" (which, alas, failed to generate the mass turning of swords into plowshares). Lennon always preferred to be remembered more for his peace activities than his music. Many would not distinguish between the two.[30] Observers have recognized the power of the popular arts for centuries. Plato wrote that musical forms and rhythms are never changed without producing changes in the most political forms and ways, a major reason why authoritarian societies have attempted quite overtly to control popular culture and mass communications.[31]

Popular Culture Controversies and American Society

Popular culture cannot be divorced from other sociopolitical realities. In American society, there were major controversies in the late 1980s and early 1990s about the censorship, sometimes even the banning or prosecution, of certain children's books (by Judy Blume), films *(The Last Temptation of Christ),* "over-the-edge" musicians (2 Live Crew, Jello Biafra), and rap records (by Ice Cube, Ice-T, NWA, Tupac Shakur, Snoop Doggie Dogg), indicating the interrelationships of popular culture and politics. Even earlier, the FBI maintained extensive files on politically active cultural figures like composer-conductor Leonard Bernstein and harassed John Lennon for his unorthodox views after he moved to New York.[32] Nor should we ignore the infamous blacklist of filmwriters and actors during the Cold War hysteria of the McCarthy era in the 1950s. An even more ludicrous incident came in the early 1960s, when the FBI conducted a thirty-month investigation of the alleged obscenity and immorality of the Kingsmen's hit "Louie Louie," a famous party song with garbled lyrics. After endlessly playing the song forward and backward at 33, 45, and 78 revolutions per minute, they concluded that the song was unintelligible at any speed.[33] Popular culture has even been debated in presidential elections; two examples are Vice President Dan Quayle's criticism of the sitcom *Murphy Brown* in 1992 (a program he had not actually viewed) and Senator Bob Dole's frontal assault on Time Warner films and recordings in 1995.

For decades it was considered unrespectable for scholars to study popular culture—that is, the entertainment, leisure, and art forms created for (and often by) the general population rather than the sociocultural and intellectual elite. The popular forms were considered "lowbrow" in comparison to "highbrow" or "serious" culture. There was an implicit notion of cultural hierarchy. For example, American literary critic Dwight MacDonald once distinguished between "High Culture" and what he derisively termed "Midcult" and "Masscult," the counterparts to "high brow," "middle brow," and "low brow." More recently Allen Bloom, a conservative American English scholar, earned notoriety for his attacks on rock music as "junk food for the soul . . . gutter phenomenon" that transforms young lives into a "commercially prepackaged masturbational fantasy" removed from true culture.[34]

The elite biases against popular culture developed in many societies around the world, from Indonesia to Russia. Indonesian cultural critic Ignas Kleden reports that in Indonesia

> the word "pop" is understood to mean something not very serious. Therefore if one talks about pop culture, one appears to refer to the cultural products and cultural behavior which are thought not to belong to the cultural establishment. Pop culture, created not necessarily in accordance with the formal criteria of "high culture" is denied recognition by the cultural elite. . . . In Jakarta . . . people distinguish between serious literature and pop literature, serious magazines and pop magazines, serious writing and pop writing, serious music and pop music.[35]

In the nonindustrialized world, including most Asian societies, there were also distinctions between urban and rural cultural hierarchies. The cultural landscape of the countryside usually lacked the "high culture" pretensions of the cities and courts, and was seen as a reciprocal of the "national cultures" or "mass cultures" being devised by the political and economic elites. For example, in Laos the arts of the "Great Tradition" such as the Ramayana dance *(pha lak pha lam)* and the lowland Lao classical music *(dontril Lao deum)* were contrasted favorably by the middle and upper classes with lowly "Little Tradition" styles such as plays based on narrative songs *(lam luang)*, which were never performed in the royal palace but enjoyed huge peasant audiences.[36]

Pop culture generally accords greater emphasis to the communicative capacity of its performances and products than to their critical appreciation; it follows the aesthetics of reception more than of creation, hence normally producing cultural products designed and made less from the creative drives within the artist than for the tastes and needs of the audience. Beauty is defined chiefly by mass satisfaction. High culture pretends to become perpetual, to win time at the expense of space, while pop culture tends to be instant culture. Sociologist Herbert Gans employed the term "taste cultures" to designate the level of aesthetic appreciation while also noting that much of "high culture" (books, records, films, painting reproductions) is as mass-produced as the popular arts. He believed that all taste cultures were of equal value and that popular culture reflected and expressed the aesthetic and other wants of multitudes, hence enjoying many dimensions other than the commercial.[37] This is a debatable view open to criticism from those who can point to the widespread appreciation of, for example, Western classical music by sophisticated audiences around the world, suggesting to many a certain universality despite the clear roots in Western culture. In any case, pop culture may be less elegant and more exuberant, less urbane and more urban than high culture, but it remains closer to human reality—the hopes and fears, dreams and desires of everyday life. In countries like Indonesia, India, Brazil, and Nigeria, pop culture provides an effective way for communicating urban influences, ideals, lifestyles, and expectations to the villages.

The denigration of popular culture by scholars has moderated in recent years and there is now an enormous theoretical, analytical, and descriptive literature (some of it interdisciplinary) on such fields as music, films, television, sports, and fiction. This redefinition of popular culture studies has made earlier views about a degraded mass culture and elevated elite culture problematic. Now studies recognize the power of the ordinary, view the commonplace as a legitimate object of study, challenge arbitrary divisions, and ask serious questions about the role of popular culture in sociopolitical life. One study concludes that popular culture "has found legitimacy for the very reasons it was originally derided: the scale of its social impact and its attractiveness to unschooled audiences. This has made it central to any understanding of Western societies and thought."[38] It also provides one of the most effective entries for studying non-Western peoples.

Mass Mediation and the Meaning of Popular Culture

But who has ultimately controlled the production of popular mass-mediated culture? Corporate elites? Political powers? Creative artists? The mass audience? Can popular culture forms such as music ever have a potentially revolutionary and liberating influence? Or, contrarily, have they been more likely to play a conservative, institution-maintenance role in the sociopolitical order? Or has popular culture perhaps provided an arena for negotiation and expression of conflicts and tendencies within societies, with elites, artists, and the public influencing the form and content? Some musicians and filmmakers have consciously tried to use their art to generate sociopolitical change or to comment on or criticize prevailing policies or patterns, but have they really had much impact?

One way of understanding the meaning of popular music and culture is through the concept of mass mediation. Michael Real, an American social critic, describes the situation negatively: "People may pray for daily bread, but for many millions in advanced industrial states and, increasingly, throughout the world, cultural sustenance is delivered by the mass media of communications in a form more like burnt toast." By "mass-mediated culture," Real means "culture in the form of widespread symbols, rhythms, beliefs, and practices available through media in the form of television, radio, records, films, books, periodicals, and other means of communication that transmit in a mass manner from a single source to many anonymous receivers."[39]

This culture has been both immediate and pervasive, intellectual and lightweight. But whatever the content and appeal, many observers believe that mass-mediated culture has chiefly served the interests of the political-economic power elite dominating the social pyramid. It has done this by programming mass consciousness through a form of infrastructural authoritarianism, hence belying its apparent superstructural egalitarianism. Mass-mediated culture has also expressed and determined human descriptions of life and definitions of reality while spreading specific values and ideologies; it has not been a value-neutral force. The concept of "the mediazation of modern culture" refers to a general process whereby the transmission of symbolic forms (including ideology) is increasingly mediated by the institutional and technical apparatuses of the media industries, which are transnational in their scope.[40]

The argument about the nature of mass society and popular culture is an old and heated one, particularly but by no means exclusively waged among Marxian scholars. There has also been a tendency for Third World observers to take a different view than many Western ones.[41] One prominent approach in the West is the Frankfurt School. Theorists operating in this tradition, such as Adorno and Horkheimer, saw capitalist culture necessarily leading to social and political disintegration exemplified by an impersonal mass culture, including a banal and trite pop music that stood in contrast to "art." Their analysis emphasized the commodification of musicians and their music. Jim Collins summarizes the Frankfurt School approach: "Popular culture is so contaminated by mechanization and commodification that it cannot be seen as a genuine expression of anything other than the corporations that standardize it for their own ends."[42] Hence, leisure was converted into consumption and the corporations commodified the public into submission.

A leading Frankfurt theorist, Theodore Adorno, likened pop music to "'Aunt Jemima's ready-mix for pancakes,' extended to the field of music."[43] American critic Dwight MacDonald took up the charge: Since mass culture is a manufactured commodity rather than an art form, it moves downward. Imposed from above, it "is fabricated by technicians hired by businessmen; its audiences are passive consumers, their participation limited to the choice between buying and not buying."[44] The work of Adorno and his followers was culturally elitist and pessimistic about mass culture; they implied that the only authentic culture rested on a specific kind of art that required much effort by the audience. Hence, writing in the Frankfurt tradition, Filipino historian and social scientist Renato Constantino bemoans the "standardization" of pop culture that "provides the dominant classes with happy, exploited people whose minds are sedated with entertainment . . . that distort[s] reality and ignore[s] the basic problems of society . . . because the emphasis is on individualistic solutions."[45] The effects have been characterized by a British scholar, paraphrasing an American song:

The rich get rich and the poor get poorer.
In the meantime, in between time,
Ain't we got fun.[46]

It is hard to dismiss these trenchant critiques. Even American ethnomusicologist Peter Manuel, a renowned specialist on popular styles around the globe whose views are far more nuanced than those of the Frankfurt School, castigates the manipulative U.S. media industry for its "reduction of all content to the level of entertainment, its glut of wanton violence." Such programming overloads the audience with media messages that leave them in "a state of confusion or apathy" discouraging political activism and critical thought; the process involves the subtle promotion of the ideologies and aesthetic values of those who control the media.[47] The commodification of culture is extolled by some enthusiasts for capitalism, indirectly supporting the Frankfurt view. Hence Mark Fowler, commissioner of the Federal Communications Commission in the Reagan administration, described television as "just like any other business . . . it is a toaster with pictures."[48]

In the Frankfurt perspective the effect of the culture industry has been to standardize taste and to give it a commodity orientation. Mass culture is defined essentially by products manufactured solely for a mass market; many kinds of music (including classical and folk) could be included in this process. Indeed, the relationship to industrial capitalism and marketing between high and popular cultures may be less clear cut in recent years. For example, in the United States corporate capitalism has also appropriated high- and middle-brow culture through its effective takeover of the Public Broadcasting System.[49] Criticism of popular (or mass) culture derives from both the right and left of the political spectrum. Conservative critics view television, rock, video games, and the like as undermining literacy, worker efficiency, social cohesion, and respect for authority, while Frankfurt Marxists focus on the stupefying influences that contribute to authoritarianism, conformity, co-optation, and escapism.

In the past several decades scholars associated with or influenced by the so-called British or Birmingham School of Cultural Studies (spearheaded by the Center for Contemporary Cultural Studies at Birmingham University) have become the most significant analysts of popular culture, presenting a more complex and multihued picture than the Frankfurt theorists. In their view, as summarized by sociologist Ray Pratt, "The human reality is conceived as a 'contested' reality in which people struggle in . . . a 'dialogic' process to create a satisfying existence out of the raw materials provided by 'culture industries.'"[50] Popular culture constitutes a locus of combat, a veritable battleground where contesting representations of how life should be battle for popular identification. But mass culture in whatever artistic form remains a deeply contradictory phenomenon. Hence popular culture is influenced by real living conditions and the experiences that spring from them, however much it is mediated through capitalist institutions.

British scholar Stuart Hall, one of the most influential theorists of the Birmingham School, believes that popular culture possesses an essentially contradictory nature:

> If the forms of provided commercial popular culture are not purely manipulative, then it is because, alongside the false appeals, the foreshadowings, the trivialization and shortcircuits, there are also elements of recognition and identification, something approaching a recreation of recognizable experiences and attitudes to which people are responding.[51]

Hall argues that popular culture should be perceived neither as popular traditions of resistance nor as forms superimposed from above, but rather as the "ground on which the transformations are worked." Neither "pure autonomy" nor "total encapsulation" of the audience is the sole reality. A continuous and necessarily uneven and unequal struggle is waged by the dominant culture to disorganize and reorganize popular culture; to enclose and confine its forms and definitions within a more inclusive range of dominant forms:

> There are points of resistance; there are also moments of supersession. This is the dialectic of cultural struggle. . . . It goes on continuously, in the complex lines of resistance and acceptance, refusal and capitulation, which makes the field of culture a sort of constant battlefield. A battlefield where no once-for-all victories are obtained but where there are always strategic positions to be won or lost.[52]

The constant dialectical cultural struggle takes many forms, including incorporation, resistance, distortion, negotiation, and recuperation. In this process the media serve to ceaselessly classify the world within discourses of the dominant ideologies, but in so doing reproduce the contradictions embedded within these contending ideologies and their relationship to social classes, allowing countertendencies to be manifested also. And the mass media are central to modern culture, the primary resource for meaningful organizing and patterning people's experience. The content of any media discourse can be interpreted ("decoded") three ways: in terms of the dominant hegemonic position; as a negotiated mix of adaptive and oppositional; and as oppositional, where the message may be "detotalized" and "retotalized" in an alternative framework. When events begin to be "given an oppositional reading, . . . the 'politics of signification'—the struggle in discourse—is joined."[53]

Some Birmingham School theorists, following the Italian Marxist Antonio Gramsci, have applied the term *hegemony* to the structure of power in a society. The term is used to describe any aspect of an ideology, culture, or set of practices through which elites have imposed their views and established the legitimacy of their power and privilege among nonelites. Hence it by no means refers narrowly to political rule but also to power exercised in less obvious ways. It can refer to both the fact of domination and the ways in which dominant classes can rule without using force by getting people to accept their position in the social hierarchy, to internalize the mainstream consciousness of governments, industry, and so on. Hegemony includes the process in which a ruling class or an alliance of class factions dominates subordinate groups and classes through the elaboration and penetration of ideology into their everyday practice and common sense. With "ideological hegemony," the interests of the capitalist class are made to seem to all segments of society as the immutable, natural order of the world. Hegemony is not necessarily monolithic or uniform.[54]

But hegemony is also a process; it does not passively exist as a form of dominance that cannot be dislodged, and must be continually renewed, recreated, defended, and modified because it will also be continually resisted, limited, altered, and challenged (counterhegemony).[55] American sociologist Todd Gitlin argues that hegemony is necessarily collaborative and requires the political-economic elites to ally with the cultural elites, with popular culture becoming an important venue for the negotiation and renegotiation that is entailed:

> Popular culture is one crucial institution where the rival claims of ideology are sometimes pressed forward, sometimes reconciled in imaginative form. Popular culture absorbs oppositional ideology, adapts it to the contours of core hegemonic principles, and domesticates it; at the same time, popular culture is a realm for the expression of forms of resistance and oppositional ideology.[56]

In the contested turf of popular culture, bourgeois hegemony—indirect or direct—has become limited in many respects, because popular culture embodies a conflicted mix of regressive and progressive political tendencies. To remain popular, works must fulfill authentic needs including a utopian vision of a more humane social order. Mass culture hence manages oppositional impulses by intermingling them with conventional ones:

> Mass-cultural elites and gatekeepers do not simply manipulate popular taste; they do not write on tabulae rasa. Rather, they shape and channel sentiment and taste, which churn and simmer in the larger society, and express popular desires in one form or another. . . . The genius of the cultural industry . . . lies in its ability to take account of popular aspirations, fears, and conflicts, and to address them in ways that assimilate popular values into terms compatible with the hegemonic ideology.[57]

There remains, however, the basic problem of culture under capitalism: Capital is needed to finance it. "In a society where art produces commodities," asserts one historian, "popular culture turns commodities into art."[58] High culture has mainly been targeted at a numerically limited but sophisticated and affluent audience. For popular culture the audience must be maximized and the product must then appeal to the lowest common denominator.

In industrialized societies popular culture became the meeting ground for two linked (though not identical) social processes. The cultural industry has produced goods tailored to particular markets, organizing their content so that they are packaged to be congruent with the dominant values and modes of discourse. By consuming clumps of these cultural goods, distinct social or subcultural groups have helped position themselves in the society, in the process working toward defining their status and social identity. By enjoying a particular genre of film, television program, or music, they move toward recognizing themselves as social entities. But it is a two-way street. Even when the people themselves do not actually engage in the production of mass media texts (cultural products), they inevitably articulate the texts in specific ways, therefore participating quite actively in the production of whatever meanings these texts might possess or generate as they circulate in society. The end result, then, is a fragmentation of a monolithic public into pluralistic formations that interpret the same texts in rather different ways. The "taste cultures" that emerge can be supportive of power arrangements (hegemonic); alternative (and coexisting) with the power structure; or even oppositional.[59]

Many cities developed entertainment districts with a range of nightclubs, bars, restaurants, stages, and theaters serving a primarily middle-class audience. This entertainment district is in Melaka, Malaysia. 1984 photo by author.

John Fiske, a British-born, U.S.-based leader in communication studies, extends the argument even further. Fiske asserts that the cultural artifacts of modern life—from shopping malls to tabloid newspapers to popular music—carry a multitude of messages and ways of using them, and these are often quite different from those intended by the culture industry. Popular culture thus is located at the point where people take the goods offered them by industrialized capitalism (however oppressive they may seem) and turn them to their own creative and even subversive uses, rather than mindlessly consuming every product that they are offered. In his formulation, "popular culture" is not the artifacts themselves (produced by a commodified industrial process) but the way people use, abuse, and subvert these products to create their own meanings. Hence,

> a text that is to be made into popular culture must . . . contain both the forces of domination and the opportunities to speak against them, the opportunities to oppose or evade them. . . . Popular culture is made by the people at the interface between the products of the culture industries and everyday life. Popular culture is made by the people, not imposed upon them; it stems from within, from below.[60]

But the reading is selective, with the same person being at times resistant, at times hegemonically complicit. Individuals reinterpret these things in a form of guerrilla warfare in order to achieve some degree of empowerment. In stable times the purpose is not the destruction of the system in which they are subordinated or fostering radical socioeconomic change; it is the micropolitical negotiation of unequal power relations in everyday life (jobs, families, classrooms, etc.). For these purposes, Fiske argues, the music and behavior of Madonna, the crude posturing of wrestlers, or the convoluted roles of soap opera characters can convey meanings oppositional to the values of the dominant society. Some sympathizers of the Fiske approach even contend that popular culture offers a highly democratic prospect for appropriating and then transforming daily life. In certain instances consumption itself becomes an important ground of class conflict and identity making, such as the creation of a "perpetual weekend" with the extravagant clothes, pop music, and hedonism of a Saturday night revel, in the process resisting subordination.[61]

Frankfurt-influenced observers remain unimpressed with the Birmingham arguments. Hence, according to American communications scholar Herbert Schiller:

> Audiences do, in fact, interpret messages variously. They also may transform them to correspond with their individual experiences and tastes. But when they are confronted with a message incessantly repeated in all cultural conduits, issuing from the commanders of the social order, their capacities are overwhelmed.[62]

If the seminal Frankfurt theorists were too far removed from mass culture to understand it, some of their opponents are too enmeshed in it to maintain critical distance, hence exaggerating the freedom of the consumer to create their own meanings. In any case it is quite possible to be oppositional locally without necessarily being oppositional globally; for example, to resist parental authority but not the patriarchal family system.[63]

Schiller to the contrary, popular culture may contain the possibility of its own transformation, perhaps even the transformation of the society. It contains these possibilities both by including them and limiting them. And oppositional thought can survive in popular culture because the subtle nuances of cultural moments (such as a band's public performance or a film by an independent director) are often too small for either censorship or co-optation. Cultural forms like rock music can promote both revolution and conformity, because culture simultaneously offers alternative visions and reinforces the socioeconomic order. Lawrence Grossberg, an American pioneer in cultural studies, summarizes the contradictory patterns:

> To argue that people are often "empowered" by their relations to popular culture, that they may in fact seek such empowerment, and that such empowerment sometimes enables people to resist their subordination is not the same as arguing that all of our relations to popular culture constitute acts of resistance or that such relations are, by themselves, sufficient bases for an oppositional politics. . . . Moreover, to argue that people are not cultural dopes is not the same as arguing that they are never duped; it merely says that the success of such efforts is never guaranteed.[64]

The debate about the nature of mass or popular culture will not be resolved in this study. But clearly any analysis of popular culture must examine both the creators and the receivers, as well as the power relationship between them. Furthermore, the dynamics of capitalist (or, for that matter, socialist) socioeconomic frameworks have obviously impinged on the evolution and parameters of the popular and mass-mediated cultures including music, and hence the broader social, economic, and political forces must be addressed.

The Scope and Significance of Popular Music

One of the major forces bubbling out of the cauldron of change and tension in the modern world has been popular music. The pervasiveness of these musics is not restricted to Western society; writing of Istanbul and other Turkish cities, Martin Stokes notes that music "is an omnipresent, almost atmospheric, property of public space in the city, in cafes, nightclubs, baths, brothels, shops, buses, taxis . . . providing a continual counterpoint to the rhythms of everyday life."[65] One Filipino scholar summarizes—somewhat ruefully, it seems—the ubiquity of often imported popular music as follows: "Like most advertised consumer goods and other articles . . . there is a corresponding music. . . . This music—from jazz to rock, roll and beat—permeates the whole area, in cities as well as remote villages . . . just like the advertisements of consumer goods."[66]

Any attempt to distinguish popular music from other types reveals much variation and disagreement. Indeed, almost any criterion to clearly differentiate "serious" (art and classical), "folk," and "popular" music breaks down on close inspection for many societies. For example, several studies have questioned whether the dualistic categories of classical–popular have any relevance for the Islamic Middle East in the middle and late twentieth century.[67] Until recent decades art, folk, and popular songs in Japan were closely intertwined and not easily distinguished from each other, with performance styles, composition patterns, and poetic lyrics that crossed genre lines.[68] Several strands of Brazilian popular music intersect with art music and both have been deeply influenced by folk traditions. Some believe "serious" music is not subject to commercial pressures and hence reflects pure creativity and heterogeneity, while pop cannot be creative and is characterized by standardization, manipulation, and the like. Yet the art or classical musics of India, such as the raga tradition, have since the 1920s been disseminated largely through broadcasting. This has modified the music, with musicians complaining they must shorten their performances and stress a faster tempo to meet the needs of mass mediation.[69] Many Southeast Asians are more likely to hear their "classical" musics on cassettes than in live performances.

Some would employ numerical and statistical criteria to determine "popularity," defined as the most listened to or purchased musical pieces. Here the key is commercial success: the number of people who buy the recordings or attend the performances.[70] The term "popular music" could also refer to a particular genus of music loosely bound to the mechanisms of production, distribution, and consumption. But commercial success as a prerequisite eliminates a lot of music that failed in the marketplace. Some consider popular music to be any music that is not art or folk; hence it does not constitute one genre or even group of genres—perhaps not even a separate fixed form. Others posit that it can perhaps be identified by the range of functions it carries—from jingles to film music, from dance music to hit songs, and so on.[71]

Various scholars argue that a purely quantitative definition would never suffice, as it could not explain the role of industrial mass production, distribution via the laws of commodity exchange, acquisition as semiluxury purchase, or its musical, aesthetic, or political potential.[72] According to Peter Manuel, one of the most astute American specialists, popular music can be distinguished from other types of music by two essential features: It is disseminated largely by the mass media, and it is the by-product of the mass basis for marketing commodities. Thus the media connection has influenced the evolution, production, definition, and meaning of the styles.[73] For our purposes we will accept Manuel's formulation. Popular music, then, has been clearly commercial, rooted in the music industry (including production and distribution) and a clientele able and willing to purchase the commodity.

Popular musics also include subdivisions that sociologist Phillip Ennis terms *streams*. These have a loose structure that includes the artistic system, economic arrangements, and attendant social movement—as well as a distinct ethos. The streams (such as rock, country, and jazz) have central cores and are divided by fluid boundary zones. Streams can also contain diverse genres within them (such as punk, folk rock, and heavy metal in rock).[74] For many places, including Brazil, Japan, and Indonesia, it is

Vong Co and the Vietnamese Soul

Vong co has been the favorite of all the styles of traditional Vietnamese music, among both Vietnamese musicians and audiences alike. This assertion can be substantiated by pointing to the continued development of vong co, including its frequent and widespread performance in recent years throughout Vietnam as well as the dispersed Vietnamese enclaves abroad. Vong co (literally, "longing for the past") evolved from a simple melody into the lengthy and complex-structured vocal and instrumental pieces that exist in a wide variety today. The song that originated vong co was first composed by Cao Van Lau between 1917 and 1920, during the formative period of the *cai luong* (reformed theatre). It was initially entitled "In Hearing the Sound of Night Drums I Am Thinking of My Husband"; the title was later changed to "Longing for the Past":

Since the day you, my husband
Received the king's sword and left on duty
I am constantly looking forward to hearing from you
At night I dream of you . . .
My heart grieves . . .
Every night I am in sorrow.
When will we be together
In a marital life again . . .
Be safe and return home soon to join me.

The development of diverse vong co variants owes much to a performer's skill in improvising on the melody. The singing of vong co occurs both within cai luong plays or independent of them. In the cai luong it is part of a heterogeneous collection ranging from traditional songs to Western-style popular songs, all connected with the story. Vong co is sung in traditional style several times during the play, normally as a solo by the chief character or as a duet during scenes involving serious or sad emotions.[75]

undoubtedly more accurate to speak of popular *musics* because so many different styles—streams—have wide followings.[76]

Cultural geographers have noted that popular musics can also convey a sense or an image of place, as in the psychedelic "San Francisco Sound" and California beach culture "surf" rock of the 1960s or "down home" country music.[77] A Malaysian study identifies popular songs as one of the most useful reflections of the society and culture.[78] The sense of nostalgia and sadness that permeates many folk traditions such as the Vietnamese *vong co* and the Portuguese folk songs imbued with *saudade* (a bittersweet, melancholic feeling) may reflect the painful trials and tribulations of their societal histories.[79] It has been argued that karaoke became so popular in Japan and other Asian countries (as well as among Asian immigrants in the United States) precisely because it reinforces group harmony and promotes a relaxed atmosphere, as all must eventually perform in front of the group.[80] Music constitutes a form of symbolic expression that can be enjoyed alone or in a group. Pleasure is also an important component. Perhaps the essence of rock is fun, including sensuality, grace, vigor, joy, exhilaration, and energy. Hence, music must be viewed as much more than entertainment. It becomes a cultural resource of great value, a window into the soul of a society.

Music never exists in a vacuum; it has always reflected the larger social, economic, and political relationships within a particular society. Rebels against accepted norms earn notoriety. This may be particularly true for female artists who challenge patriarchal systems, such as African singers Miriam Makeba of South Africa, Angelique Kidjo of Benin, and the Algerian Djura; the latter in particular has faced strong family and societal sanctions for pursuing a music career and emphasizing songs about real-life issues.[81]

Perhaps popular music can empower audiences when it creates dimensions of "free space," a complex variety of enclaves and autonomy involving an alternative psychological reality. As a "substitute imagery" the music mediates experience, including community, place, and time (the shaping of memory and the organizing of a sense of time). Hence the Woodstock myth about "being there" and the contemporary sense of an anti-Establishment (alternative) community might constitute a "utopian prefiguration." Music that empowers, including the cathartic emotional high of concerts, releases human energies that are energized rather than depressed. In a society characterized by imposed discipline, pleasure becomes subversive.[82] This may explain the substantial popularity in puritanical Pakistan of Munni Begum, whose poetic songs often address prohibited pleasures such as drinking alcohol (in her songs, a form of escape from life's troubles).[83]

Popular music inevitably invokes a multiplicity of meanings. The production of overall meaning occurs at the intersection between the works musicians produce (the musicians' own meaning) and the interpretations and uses audience members have for those works (the listener's meaning). This interaction occurs within the layers of surrounding social context, adding to the overall meaning. For both musicians and users, then, meaning construction constitutes a socially embedded process. Hence the intent and interpretation may differ; the overall meaning becomes an amalgamation of the work (lyrics, style, etc.), the audience's understanding of it, and the social context that surrounds it (including production and distribution). As one specialist states (surveying karaoke): "I'm interested not in what mass-mediated musics do *to* people, but what human consumers can do to such musics. . . . The ground level reception of mass-mediated musics can be a site of real contestation and redefinition."[84]

Ethnomusicologists employ the notion of the "music-culture," noting that music is universal but its meaning is not. Components include the belief system (ideas on the nature and purpose of music are related to sociocultural values and structures), aesthetics (the definition of beauty), context (when and how music is performed and for what purposes), and history (changing musical styles, preferences, meanings, etc.). Music-cultures are socially organized so that music behavior may resemble the social divisions or go against the broad grain, and musicians have particular roles and functions within the society.[85] For example, among the Shona of Zimbabwe songs have constituted a major component of the process of locating oneself; through singing, individuals learn the facts of their social location and reaffirm the basic contours of their world.[86] In his study of the Venda people in South Africa, ethnomusicologist John Blacking concludes that music constitutes a metaphorical expression of feelings derived from the actual structure and values of the society, a "reflection and response" to circumstances of daily life including work and community.[87]

Much renegotiation and mediation occurs in popular music. Most theorists argue that popular music functions as a site of struggle between dominant and dissenting interests, but disagree on the nature of the struggle, the interests that energize it, and the ultimate meanings it poses for musicians and audiences. Hence popular music has an essentially dialogic nature. Its texts have provided many with the means of understanding and enduring their circumstances because they "resonate with the tensions of the time."[88] Musical meanings become established through a process of dialogue over the "text" involving the performer and the audience. The lyrical content is not always key; many other factors influence the popularity of a song. While the vagueness and ambiguity of musical meanings can be reduced by lyrics, the meaning is defined by the code the listener applies.[89] For example, a study in Taiwan shows that teenage girls prefer a certain type of tender, romantic music (in Mandarin or English) because it articulates their life experiences; the audience defines the genre.[90]

In surveying the varied roles of popular music, Ennis concludes:

> Music is one of fantasy's best helpers. . . . Music is a way of holding off time, making the present fill all space. It joins us with others yet defends our privacy. It lifts the spirit, assuages grief, and sometimes teaches us as well. Above all, music creates values, along with a social structure that nurtures, defends, and celebrates those values.[91]

While accepting the view that mass mediation and commercialization have generally been integral components of popular music, I prefer in this study to discuss not only the obvious music fitting that category. Other kinds of political music that in some manner derived from or reached a wide audience, or influenced substantial sections of a population in the direction of significant change, criticism, or protest, will also be discussed. I also utilize the Birmingham Cultural Studies argument that popular music has constituted contested terrain in which the audience helps interpret the meaning.

Popular Music and Sociocultural Affirmation

Popular musics cannot be separated from social identity because they embody (however obliquely) pervasive ideologies that contribute to their power. The relationship of music to the broader society appears to have

The Evolution and Meaning of Hawaiian Music

In the early years after Americans ended the monarchy and assumed control of the islands (in 1898), Hawaiian composers used their songs to convey veiled criticism of their declining status while also helping preserve the endangered language. Although throughout much of the twentieth century it has become commercialized as an adjunct to the tourist industry, and in the process modified into the predominantly English hapa haole ("half-white") hybrid music well known to most Americans ("My Little Grass Shack," "Sweet Leilani"), there always remained an undercurrent of cultural authenticity for the pure and part-Hawaiians who constitute a declining proportion of the Islands' population. One study summarizes the key role of musicians in sustaining the Hawaiian heritage:

> the musician, the chanter, the dancer have long been the troubadours and heralds of our people. They have drawn us together, they have helped keep our heritage alive, they have led the search backwards to find that heritage. Musicians and artists can be considered the people's historians and philosophers. They are able to translate new thoughts and experiences in a way that is accessible and understandable.[92]

Hawaiian music reached a nadir in the 1960s, with few youth showing any interest, prompting the establishment of the Hawaiian Music Foundation in 1971 to revitalize the genre as part of the quest for a renewed ethnic identity.

been exceedingly complex, with many variables. "The function of music," Blacking asserts, "is to enhance in some way the quality of individual experience and human relationships; its structures are reflections of patterns of human relationships, and the value of a piece of music is inseparable from its value as an expression of human experience."[93] These patterns can be seen in Hawaiian music, which has served to maintain cultural identity within the larger society (not only of multicultural Hawai'i but of the white-dominated United States).[94]

In the 1970s and 1980s the Hawaiian Renaissance (including cultural and political movements for restoration of ethnic Hawaiian rights) adopted music as one of its weapons, in the process producing musicians and groups who moved away from hapa haole sounds to write and perform songs more in keeping with ethnic assertion. Some of these songs employ contemporary styles such as rock and reggae but deal with issues related to the renaissance. But the renaissance has been multidimensional; for example, the hula also was revived as a major expression of Hawaiian identity, the most potent statement of island political and cultural power. The local recording industry flourished within the context of a small market. By the late 1980s some of the music had become more militant as the movement itself developed a higher activist profile. Yet while younger groups like Hokule'a, the former Sunday

Popular Music and Yoruba Cultural Assertion

The Yoruba of southwestern Nigeria have developed several distinctive popular music styles in the twentieth century that are counterparts to Southeast Asian patterns. Each found a niche among a particular Yoruba religious or class group but also gained a wider audience in Nigeria as a whole. Juju emerged in cosmopolitan Lagos, a mix of Yoruba folk musics with Afro-American and European influences. Closely tied to the animistic religious traditions still strong among many Yoruba, juju was linked with Yoruba cultural nationalism and ethnic identity in the 1950s, constituting part of a process of reindigenization; the music allowed the Yoruba to reaffirm their identity and language in a more modern guise. During the 1960s and 1970s juju became the major, highly mass-mediated musical form among urban animist and Christian Yoruba, popular among all social classes. Juju stars like King Sunny Ade, Chief Commander Ebenezer Obey, and Sir Shina Peters still enjoy a huge audience. Apala and—more recently—fuji are neotraditional styles that derive from the Muslim minority. They blend Yoruba and Islamic influences heavily based on percussion. Apala betrays little if any Western influence, eschewing electric instruments. Apala and several related styles clearly affirm anti-Western nationalism while defiantly marking off Muslims from other Yoruba. Fuji is more modernized and danceable, with a particular following among underclass youth in the slums of Lagos and other cities. Both forms draw many of their lyrics from religious themes and traditional proverbs.[95]

Manoa, and the Brothers Cazimero are a far cry from hapa haole musicians like Hilo Hattie, Webley Edwards, and Don Ho, they are also subject to commercialization and co-optation because hotels and tourist nightclubs provide most of the venues for live music. Still, the music remains an important part of a profound sociopolitical change occurring in the state and helps to define Hawaiian identity in the face of overwhelming imported culture from Asia and the mainland United States.

Similar claims to the articulation of ethnic-national identity through music could no doubt be made for such distinctive musical genres as Brazilian samba, Chilean New Song, Japanese enka, and the *juju, fuji,* and *apala* music of the Nigerian Yoruba. For example, the enka songs of Japan were once somewhat political and indeed closely connected to the Peoples' Rights movement of the Meiji era. But in recent times they became more sentimental and full of nostalgia (drenched in tears of longing and parting). Enka is based heavily on older Japanese styles and hence has a strong national flavor. These songs occupy a persistent and substantial niche in the Japanese recording industry, with a faithful audience among older and rural Japanese, and are the preferred songs in karaoke bars.[96] Brazilian samba is a vibrant music rooted in a subgroup (the Afro-Brazilian culture of Bahia and Rio de Janeiro) that later evolved into a national cultural form.[97]

Sometimes a musician can be identified with the soul of a nation or society, as seems to have been the case with the great Egyptian singer Oum Kalthoum. Singing of abandonment and love, her recordings and shows dominated Middle Eastern popular music from the 1940s through the 1960s. At her height she was considered one of the two most popular figures among the Arab masses (the other being her friend, Egypt's President Nasser).[98] Perhaps the diva of Indian film music, playback singer Lata Mangeshkar, has served a similar role during her sixty-year career, becoming a much-imitated icon and legend admired by many millions.[99] In the chaotic 1930s and 1940s of a China racked by conflict, occupation, civil war, and desperation, the bittersweet, nostalgic singing of Shanghai-based cabaret singers (and also movie actresses) such as Bai Guang, Woo Ing Ing, and especially Chou Hsuan (known as "The Golden Voice" and "the Wandering Songstress") was credited with raising spirits while also expressing the conflicted mood of the times. Their songs and recordings would remain popular for many decades among Chinese communities in Southeast Asia and around the world.[100] Similarly, singer Hibari Misora was said to symbolize Japan's postwar recovery, her nostalgic songs cheering the population during the dark days of the late 1940s and early 1950s. She remained a major star for years afterward, the "queen" of the immensely popular *kayokyoku*, a hybrid of Western and Japanese music.[101] In Vietnam during the turbulent 1950s and 1960s, the anguished and poignant songs of Pham

Duy expressed the conflicting emotions and tragedies of the era—in the process gaining him a following among all political factions.

Particular streams of music also become identified with nations or subgroups within them. Hence, reggae music developed in many ways as a vehicle for spiritual revolt against socioeconomic oppression by peoples in the African diaspora, especially Jamaica.[102] In Papua New Guinea, inhabited by dozens of ethnic groups and with an underdeveloped sense of national unity, the *lokal musik* of string and power bands utilizes imported musical styles presented in local languages and increasingly in the *tok pisin* pidgin English that is developing as a national lingua franca. Even the local reggae, a modified form known as *ailan* (Island) reggae, offers a uniquely indigenous sound.[103]

Many musics derive from powerless subgroups within a larger nation or society. For example, in Okinawa and the Ryukyu Islands the folk rock of Shoukichi Kina and his band Champloose, singing in the local dialect, offer updated versions of island folk songs that expressed Okinawan identity and cultural separateness during the 1970s and 1980s as the island passed from United States to Japanese control.[104] In South Africa, the male Zulu choirs (whose most famous example is Ladysmith Black Mambazo) singing unaccompanied *mbube* music constituted an important cultural phenomenon for the migrants to urban mines and factories. The songs express the frequently bleak realities of their lives and memories of rural life, while performances and competitions have also provided a temporary release from workaday matters.[105] Music can be a unifying force or play a role in creating a sense of community. The rock group Hongk ("Bell") was credited with helping sustain the democracy movement that ended decades of communist rule in Mongolia in 1990. Their song "The Ring of the Bell" became the opposition anthem; other songs attacked various sacred cows of local political culture.[106] Popular musics like the Anglo-South Asian fusion known as *bhangra* can also tie emigrants to their homeland.

Bhangra Music and South Asian Emigrant Society

The *bhangra* music that originated in the Punjab region of northern India as folk songs and dances for the harvest festivals followed Indian migration to Britain over the past half century. There it has been transformed from a traditional into a popular style, cross-pollinated with music from the British and West Indian migrants. The mutating bhangra flourished among South Asians in Britain, especially Sikhs, eventually incorporating the latest pop music technology. Utilizing a mix of Indian and Western instruments, it became a lively dance music, even incorporating aspects of hip hop, reggae, disco, and other influences. By the 1980s it had spread to the diaspora communities in North America as well, sustaining Indian identity (especially for teenagers) while also facilitating modernization.[107]

Perhaps popular music was part of a continuing effort to create new forms of community necessitated by social transformations (modernization and its attendant traumas). British sociologist and musicologist Simon Frith describes the relationship:

> Pop offers identities less through shared experience than through shared symbols, a common sense of style. Pop history reveals that radical pop . . . makes better sense in some sorts of collectivity than others. The most clear-cut political music . . . has been rooted in nationalist struggle (as in much black music), in the politics of leisure (as with youth cults or gay disco), or in a combination of the two (as in certain kinds of feminist music). Class consciousness . . . has, by contrast, on the whole not been amenable to pop treatment—pop celebrations of "working classness" have not created audiences along politically conscious lines.[108]

Micromusics, or "small musics in big systems," have played important roles, assisting in defining subcultural identity in multiethnic or socially variegated societies; these can be ethnically (Cajun, Mexican-American *conjunto* in Texas), regionally (Western swing, Hawaiian), class (Thai luktoong) or even gender based (gay-lesbian and "women's music"), and they operate in a complex relationship with the dominant "superculture" in which these groups enjoy little power.[109] For example, the Vietnamese refugees who flocked to the United States beginning in 1975, a population now numbering well over a million, have maintained a lively cultural life including supporting popular musicians and recordings. This "micromusic" industry, practically unknown to white Americans, has helped sustain ethnic identity and cohesion while also facilitating adaptation to the difficult circumstances of exile.[110]

The majority of Vietnamese immigrants congregate in a few "sunbelt" cities (such as San Jose and Westminster, California). In predominantly Vietnamese neighborhoods they operate most of the shops and restaurants and provide venues for live musical performances, including many small clubs. Many musicians left Vietnam in the refugee exodus and have resumed their careers in the United States or France. Most of these specialize in either traditional classical and folk music (toward which many younger people are ambivalent or indifferent) or some sort of blend of pop, rock, and modern Asian styles that was inspired by the massive American presence in South Vietnam in the 1960s. Some younger Vietnamese born or raised in the United States have also followed pop music careers, but they mostly favor a dance-oriented, new wave pop music that owes much both to imported electronic disco styles from Europe (popular with Vietnamese youth in France) and the sort of avant garde styles seen on MTV. Hard rock is unpopular; Vietnamese pop favors a softer sound. The U.S.-based bands sing in Vietnamese, English, and French, and most feature female singers.

Many of the songs popular among the Vietnamese exiles reflect the "cultural dreams" of the community, including a desire for elegance (especially in dress), the aspiration for upward mobility, emulation of the romantic style of American culture (in contrast to the reserved Vietnamese), and idealized memories of Vietnam. A number of small Vietnamese-owned companies have emerged to record and market tapes, compact discs, and music videos by Vietnamese artists. These, as well as some recordings imported from France and Vietnam, are available in many Vietnamese shops; but the potential market is much too small to attract major American companies. Hence in the United States (and France) the Vietnamese have utilized selected elements emerging from the transnational music industry to create new sounds, in the process helping to shape and support their own cultural identities. But the music is almost unknown outside of the subculture in which it flourishes.

Musicians generally represent audiences, just as politicians represent constituents. Most styles of popular music around the world originated in the *lumpenproletariat* (urban lower classes); this includes rock and roll, rhythm and blues, kroncong, dangdut (Indonesia), reggae, calypso, samba, *mbaqanga* (South Africa), *soukous* (Central Africa), luktoong (Thailand), pinoy (Philippines), and many others. Many popular singers and musicians come from urban working class or village backgrounds, especially in the Third World. For them music provides an escape from poverty, just like professional sports in the United States.[111] For example, soukous ("Congolese" music), a syncretic music that developed in the Belgian Congo (now Congo) in the 1950s and soon spread rapidly, reflected a working-class identity while providing one of the few vehicles for upward mobility in local society. Later it became a major dance music throughout Africa and among African immigrants in Europe.[112]

The social context of—and subcultural identity derived from—music, as well as the diverse backgrounds of musicians, contribute to the contested terrain. This provides a certain counterbalance to the admitted hegemony of governments and corporations, which do have an influence (or would like to) over popular music in order to channel it in desired directions for sociopolitical stability. Pop stars have usually been viewed in the West as self-seeking individuals or as mere commodities, even iconic representations of capitalist success. But celebrity and its associated characteristics may not be the whole story; popular musicians are loved not only for their abilities to write and perform songs but because they and their work "speak" to their audiences.[113]

The Political Role of Music

What precisely is the political role that popular music plays or can play in the modern world? Perhaps the relationship of politics to culture can be summed up as "who gets to say what."[114] The polar ends of the debate might be represented by German playwright Bertold Brecht, who wrote that "art is not a mirror that reflects society but a hammer that forges it,"[115] and American political scientist John Orman, who—paraphrasing Karl Marx's views on religion—calls rock music "a very entertaining opiate."[116] Popular musicians themselves have often proclaimed the political significance of their art form. Some, such as Nigerian superstar Fela and Chilean New Song proponent Victor Jara, have quite overtly seen their music as a "weapon" against established power and a tool to politicize the audience.[117]

Music (perhaps all art) can never be completely divorced from politics. Art can certainly be a tool of politics (the Orman position); it can also use politics (Brecht). Perhaps music is simply politics by other means; it never exists in a vacuum, independent of other considerations. A major debate has occupied specialists on the question of who has ultimately controlled the production of popular music, and consequently, depending on your answer, whether it can actually serve as a significant political influence in society. Manuel concludes that popular music is neither a matter of pure resistance by the people nor of superimposition by elites. Rather he understands it as an arena for negotiation, an active participant in the mediation and expression of conflicts and tendencies within societies.[118] Hence both the public and the controlling elites have influenced the music in a dialectical process. There is

Rock Music and the Burmese Establishment

Rock music had taken firm root even in socialist Burma by the early 1980s. The authoritarian ruling junta calls periodically for preventing disruptive alien cultural influence, especially "decadent" pop music. But despite religious and political opposition, rock music has become an important part of popular entertainment, especially for youth. Rock groups always command the largest crowds at any festival. Groups like The Playboy and The LPJ (Love, Peace and Joy) play to packed houses in Rangoon and provincial cities. Most of the songs they perform are Burmese adaptations of international hits. While retaining the original tunes, their Burmese words are often changed from the original versions. This homegrown Burmese rock, known locally as "stereo," emerged during the early 1960s as local youths began imitating Western rock musicians. The conservative, government-run Broadcasting Service refused air time to rock, so musicians approached private promoters. With the advent of cassette tapes and recorders in the 1970s the market for taped music greatly expanded, attracting educated youngsters to pop music. The formerly scorned rock musicians became celebrities. By the mid-1980s four well-equipped major recording studios existed; a top vocalist could sell as many as thirty thousand copies. Since "stereo" music outsells and outrecruits mainstream Burmese musics, peasant boys more likely hum rock tunes than folk songs while working in the fields. Nonetheless, conservatives severely criticize rock musicians as purveyors of cultural pollution promoting "un-Burmese sounds, un-Burmese expressions and un-Burmese stage manners."[119]

also no question that many governments attempt to control popular culture, including music.

Popular music can be perceived as a challenge to authoritarian governments as well as an unsettling influence in fragmented societies. Among others, the paranoid, military-dominated Burmese regime, which even prohibits civilians from owning fax machines, modems, or walkie-talkies, has restricted popular music as much as possible, partly because rock and folk-pop musicians were in the forefront of opposition (as during the "Rangoon Spring" of 1988). But their efforts have only been partly successful, proscribing legal recording and performance but failing to eliminate informal concerts and the considerable illicit trade in cassettes.[120] In politically pluralistic but chronically turbulent Sri Lanka, riven by class and ethnic tensions, the government has sometimes banned TV or radio performances by Nanda Malini, an immensely popular singer who has specialized in protest songs bewailing socioeconomic inequities for three decades. A crusader for controversial causes, her career has nonetheless flourished, including many best-selling recordings, because, as one observer contended, "hers is an exceptionally great talent that no government can crush."[121] In 1992 the Tibetan pop singer Dadon released an album containing songs extolling the nationalism of her people in the face of Chinese repression. The resulting government response forced her to flee the country, becoming a spokeswoman for exiled Tibetans.[122]

In politically or religiously dogmatic states, popular music can generate great controversy. The militant Islamic government of Iran has devoted considerable efforts to silencing all female singers, including especially the massively popular melancholic vocalist Googoosh; recordings, posters, and films have been rounded up and destroyed. Yet, recordings of her music reproduced abroad are smuggled in on a large scale, turning Googoosh into a (reluctant) popular symbol of opposition.[123] Similarly, the attempts by the Islamic leaders of Pakistan to prohibit the broadcasting of the pop music of singers like London-based Nazia Hassan, who maintains a wide following, generated an ongoing debate about the role of Westernized popular culture.[124]

Wary governments are not the only "gatekeepers." Radio and television, mostly government owned or regulated in many Third World nations, are usually the most conservative media and prone to stick to safe "mainstream" or officially sanctioned entertainments that promote hegemony. The recording industry itself, motivated by commercial profits, is often leery of controversial material. Music does not exist in a socioeconomic vacuum. The international industry has been shaped by the dynamics of market capitalism on a world scale. But Western interests dominate all phases of the process; this determines how the business of music production and marketing operates.

There can be little doubt that mass communications, including the music industry, play a powerful role in the modern world. As American cultural studies scholar George Lipsitz asserts:

> The powerful apparatuses of contemporary commercial electronic mass communications dominate discourse in the modern world. They supply us with endless diversion and distraction. . . . They colonize the most intimate and personal aspects of our lives [to] . . . augment our appetites for consumer goods. Culture itself comes to us as a commodity. . . . Yet mass communications also embody some of our deepest hopes and engage some of our most profound sympathies. People ingeniously enter those discourses to which they have access. . . . The same media that trivialize and distort culture . . . also provide meaningful connection to our own pasts. . . . This capacity of electronic mass communications to transcend time and space creates instability by disconnecting people . . . but it also liberates people by making the past less determinate of experiences in the present.[125]

It is not difficult to marshall evidence that much of the musical industry in most countries has been controlled by the corporate bourgeoisie. Indeed—a fact that many observers find disturbing—the five major transnational companies based in the United States or Europe have for several decades controlled large sections of the world market through their local subsidiaries, accounting for approximately two-thirds of world sales by the 1980s.[126] For example, in Malaysia during the 1970s and 1980s, EMI, Polygram, WEA, and (sometimes) CBS were the predominant companies monopolizing the import of Anglo-American music, occupying an important niche in importing Taiwan and Hong Kong recordings, and signing most of the major local stars; a fluctuating half dozen or so local companies vied for the rest of the market with local Malay and Chinese, Indonesian, and Taiwan music.[127] In Japan the market is more competitive than most countries. As of 1990 some seventy-two companies made records, with twenty-seven of them considered influential "insiders." Most of the companies were completely Japanese in ownership, but eight of the "insiders" were foreign owned (mostly affiliated with major multinational enterprises), specialized in distributing Western music.[128]

Popular musics in any country are now shaped (at least partly) by international influences and institutions, multinational capital and technology, and global pop norms. Anglo-American dominance has been increasingly reduced, both culturally and economically, with the majority of large transnational recording companies now owned by non-American interests. But it has hardly disappeared. Regardless of the Western European or Japanese corporate ownership, it is still largely the Anglo-American top-forty records that dominate the world market, in part because the United States and Britain produce nearly two-thirds of all records; Japan is actually in second place, well behind the United States but ahead of Britain. Furthermore, the U.S. industry, feeling threatened, has resorted to protectionism in the domestic market, successfully undertaking legal activity to secure trade rights and restrict the admission of foreign musicians.[129]

Various studies have stressed the power (political and otherwise) of oligopolistic corporations, with strict contractual deadlines and complex marketing strategies underlining each hit record. This often involves a gatekeeper, a tastemaker or policy through which music is filtered so that only a narrow range of proven, niche sounds would be offered to the audience (e.g., Phil Spector's "wall of sound" in U.S. pop during the early 1960s). Most of the major record companies are part of large conglomerates, some of which have had ties to the military-industrial or political establishment.

For example, several observers have charged that the commercialization of black South African music has amounted to an exploitation—even a prostitution—of that music for the benefit of white-owned corporate interests. It can hardly be disputed that whites have owned most of the major economic institutions involved with South African musics such as *marabi*, jazz, mbube, and mbanqanga. The broadcasting industry has also been completely white dominated and mostly state owned. African musicians were heavily exploited by the recording companies, both the various multinationals and several local firms.[130] The companies promoted a more "westernized" sound while offering imported Western musics as their staple. Not until the 1940s were local popular styles like marabi—and later *kwela*—recorded at all. White managers and producers were dominant and always cognizant of white tastes and marketing possibilities. The companies preferred formula-driven niches. Musicians' unions were illegal until recently and only a few extremely successful artists could achieve the stature to manipulate the companies and become wealthy in the process. Commercialization modified by white assessments of black taste remained a powerful force to homogenize the music.

Yet there is considerable evidence that companies will accommodate significant audiences, even oppositional or countercultural ones, in their quest for profits. Small companies sometimes allow musicians to outflank the major corporations. Technological change can also facilitate media democratization. The spread of music cassettes and cassette technology beginning in the early 1970s tended to reduce the role of the major companies because cassettes could be produced easily and cheaply. The evolving cassette technology provided the transnational culture industry with an excellent format to expand into remote areas; but it also facilitated production, duplication, and dissemination of local musics. It generated new profits but also decentralized control over production and consumption, in the process blurring the distinction between producer and consumer. "Cottage-industry copying is easy and relatively cheap," writes one observer, "obviating the need for expensive record-mastering and pressing technology. . . . Taxi-drivers often play locally produced cassettes in their cabs. . . . 'Boot-legging' and piracy are easy and unstoppable."[131]

In Third World countries the cassette soon became the main medium for music distribution because: "The cassette radio-recorders could work on small batteries and be taken anywhere. . . . Before roads, running water and . . . electricity, cassette recorders and amplifiers reached the most remote villages."[132] In his study of the cassette industry in India, Manuel concludes that cassettes caused a major upheaval in the popular culture, largely replacing vinyl records because of their low cost of production and consumption. By undermining the dominance of the major multinationals, fostering independents, catering to specialized audiences rather than mass commercialization, and offering the "two-way" service of home recording as well as playing, cassettes serve to "decentralize and democratize" production and consumption. Yet while this challenges the corporate-controlled film music industry's hegemony, it also sometimes accentuates sectarian differences. In terms of Indian musics, it both spreads the homogenizing commercial film music to remote villages and facilitates the promotion of regional folk and folk-pop musics.[133]

Cassette technology can present possibilities of alternative communications in societies with official limitations on media. For example, cassettes can bypass the often restricted choices presented by state broadcasting institutions. A study of Egypt showed the circumventing of radio to have been one of the most significant consequences; cassettes provide an alternative channel.[134] The contents may not necessarily be music. In China bootleg tapes of a secret and critical speech by a high government official were distributed widely, eliciting much controversy; in Malaysia and Indonesia, Islamic militants utilize the medium to spread their views.[135] This explains the occasional campaigns to prevent the import of blank cassettes and return production and listening to institutionally regulated channels.

Cassette stalls selling local and imported recordings are an important feature of the informal economy in many Asian cities. This stall is in the Chow Kit Road neighborhood of Kuala Lumpur, Malaysia. 1985 photo by author.

Although instrumental musics, the choice of musical styles, and even the lifestyles or activities of the musician can incorporate political values, lyrics are an important component of music and perhaps the easiest way to express sociopolitical sentiments. Some songs may be legitimately labeled as protest music—part of a discourse of discontent. A protest song could be defined as "a piece of music whose lyrics speak out against a specific social, political or economic injustice. It states or implies that change is needed." Songs of persuasion stress the intellectual while attempting to convince an audience that some things require alteration. The protest song tradition has used singing to serve political ends, especially the cause of social justice.[136] American folksinger Pete Seeger argues that virtually any kind of song, from the bawdy to the pious, can be controversial and propagandistic to some group of listeners. Escapist songs denying problems or extolling private pleasures, he believes, might offer the most common propaganda of all.[137]

Yet much of popular music has remained escapist in orientation, characteristically dwelling on romantic feelings and relationships. Most of the songs on the American or Brazilian or Philippine or Taiwanese hit parade have dealt with romantic themes, which may tell us something about the universality of personal alienation and insecurities. Since the bottom line of the recording industries is always financial, of course, executives also prefer the steady market for romantic songs and dance music.

Cultural studies scholars have offered the concept of "signification" as an important component of art. This involves the inclusion of coded messages that register differently with different audiences, hence allowing individuals and groups to ascribe their own meaning to the work. Clearly this would facilitate a political reading by those inclined in that direction. Political values can be conveyed in songs in two ways: the subjective, in which political content, references, and symbols are mobilized to serve the needs of group identity and aims (e.g., Rastafarian references in reggae); and the objective, involving an overt critique of assumptions (e.g., protest songs).[138] The "cultural guerrilla" has been described as a musician who

The Rock and Roll Challenge to American Society

"The first blasts of the rock 'n' roll era blew away the depression and tedium of the post–Second World War years. Here was music that was exhilarating, even dangerous, and—so it seemed—absolutely new. Here was music born in the U.S.A. that seemed to defy the Eisenhower era's desperate plea for conformity, and the paranoia at anything that was the slightest bit different. When rock 'n' roll first hit, it shocked the U.S.A., not just because it had the power to arouse and excite that could not be easily controlled, but—more importantly—because it threatened to challenge sexual and racial taboos." —Robin Denselow[139] employs cultural and artistic items in a conceptual and symbolic approach to progressive politics, with the primary objective of consciousness rather than institutional change. Guerrilla minstrels (such as John Lennon and Bob Dylan) perceive music, art, and image as political weapons, using art and notoriety to further their causes.[140]

Some musics are closely tied to counterhegemonic expression. Many observers have pointed to rock as an inherently oppositional musical form, and it certainly became highly influential in many parts of the globe. In North America and Western Europe during the 1950s and 1960s, rock was at the center of a profound cultural revolution, a fundamental challenge to some prevailing values that may have helped create a new consciousness. When it emerged in the mid-1950s, rock and roll immediately posed a challenge to established ways. Throughout the world rock would construct a battleground for serious generational conflict (not the least part of it "Elvis the Pelvis" and his imitators) while breaking down important social barriers. With its egalitarian propensities and miscegenated origins (a blend of black rhythm and blues with white country music), rock became the first truly interracial American popular music in performance and audience. It soon redefined the social covenant of American life, fostering a shift from Cold War ascetism to relative hedonism. It became a mechanism for rejecting the knee-jerk patriotism, racial segregation and rampant racism, simple piety and polarized, simplistic views of the world characteristic of the era; youth now had a dynamic and strategic alternative.

The Soviet Union and its satellites provided a case in point about the power of rock that merits more detailed examination. Historian Timothy Ryback postulates that rock music, long an underground force with substantial influence, did much to undermine the creaking, prudish, dictatorial regimes in Eastern Europe and the Soviet Union:

> Western rock culture has debunked Marxist-Leninist assumptions about the state's ability to control its citizens. . . . It has been a conflict in which the Soviet Union and its East European allies have played out a classic scenario; they have succeeded in winning nearly every battle but have ultimately lost the war. Were a monument to be erected in grand Stalinist style to the heroes of socialist rock and roll, the statue would have to depict a young man in blue jeans, head thrust defiantly upward. In his hand, where the Stalinist war hero once gripped his Kalashnikov assault gun, this long-haired warrior would clutch an electric guitar.

Ryback also perceived rock as having constituted a highly democratic force, its persistence and popularity forcing governments to gradually accept a "cultural phenomenon long decried as an outgrowth of Western capitalism."[141]

Clearly Soviet and East European authorities were often baffled by youth movements of many kinds, and considered Western rock in the aftermath of Elvis Presley as "degenerate and immoral"; rock was denounced as "spiritually deadening" (by East German leader Walter Ulbricht), to be eradicated "with a red-hot iron" (Bulgarian leader Todor Zhivkov).[142] Hence they subjected innovative musicians to various sorts of tribulations and restrictions—although, by the early 1980s, few faced arrest. Russian Vladimir Vysotski, an irreverent singer-songwriter-actor-poet on the fringe of official cultural life, provided a model for a critical art that could express political disenchantment without incurring arrest or exile, although he was frequently harassed and criticized. He explored the "breathing space" between the official line and prison that had been pioneered by anti-Stalinist poets of the 1960s such as Yevgeny Yevtushenko. From the mid-1960s until his death in 1980, the troubled poet maintained a large cult following among the urban intelligentsia for songs, usually in colloquial language, that "exposed the Russian soul" while dealing with emotions, individuals, events, corruption, incompetence, hypocrisy, labor camps, daily life realities, and sometimes, carefully, with politics:

But wait—let's have a smoke
better yet, let's drink
drink to a time
when there'll be no jails in Russia.

Cassette tapes of his unofficial concerts enjoyed wide underground distribution. Although mourners made his grave a popular Moscow attraction, it was only in the Gorbachev era that he was rehabilitated as a national hero.[143]

The spread of cassettes and tape recorders made it all but impossible to keep out Western rock music; Bill Haley's "Rock Around the Clock" was being played by Soviet Bloc bands within a few months of its issue in 1954; and "See You Later Alligator" soon became a popular youth expression; later the Beatles took Soviet youth by storm. By the mid-1960s Soviet "hippies" had appeared, "wearing jeans, bell bottoms, peace medallions, miniskirts, . . . bare feet," and listening to the Beatles and psychedelic rock (or their Soviet clones).[144] Soon a coherent "rock community" had appeared, united by lifestyles (including drug and alcohol use) and philosophies as well as music. Until the mid-1980s, for Soviet teens rock music remained virtually the only escape from an oppressive social environment. Rock music became the main art form that attracted this age group. Hence rock buttressed the refusal to embrace ideological indoctrination, forming its own alternative mentality.[145] Duplicating and disseminating the music of the Beatles as well as Soviet rock bands became a major underground industry. Rock became the only uncontrollable and informal art form, which, unlike the samizdat books and magazines for intellectuals, knew no boundaries thanks to the gigantic underground industry. In politically restless

The Soviet Rock Scene

There may have been as many as 160,000 underground bands in the Soviet Union by the 1980s, with the largest number in Leningrad and Moscow. Groups such as Alisa, Aquarium, Strange Games (which played Jamaican ska), Time Machine, and Kino, and talented musicians like the punkish Alla Pugachova, the avant-garde jazz-rock fusionist Sergei Kuriokin, and the poetic intellectual Boris Grebenschikov, survived as "unofficial" musicians, on the fringe of respectability. They gained widespread popularity through their self-recorded "albums" (cassette tapes), which were passed from hand to hand and copied many times. Melodyia, the government-run recording company, held a monopoly and only began releasing rock recordings by "underground" bands in the late 1980s. Compared to Western rock, more stress was placed on lyrics, which expressed the ideas of the rock community. Many of them mercilessly mocked the bureaucracy and Soviet life, or the meaninglessness and absurdity of existence, but were careful to avoid direct criticism of communism or the Communist Party. For example, Alisa, in their song "Experimenter of Upward-Downward Movement," offered a thinly obscured mockery of Marxist dialectics and social engineering:

Experimenter of upward-downward movement
He sees space where I see [a] wall
He knows the answer, he is sure of his idea
In every process he reaches the bottom.[146]

"captive" states like Estonia and Ukraine, rock also became a vehicle for local nationalist assertion.[147]

As in the West, rock chiefly represented rebellion against lifestyle options and values rather than governments per se. Most rock fans were not militant dissidents but instead sought liberalization. Rather than fundamentally altering the system, freedom was perceived for many rock musicians as essentially a spiritual phenomenon that could be achieved by living, as much as possible, beyond the official realm of life. The unwillingness to openly challenge the system led Jolanta Pekacz to conclude that rock functioned mainly as a "safety valve," manipulated by both the government and musicians for their own end. Governments had a difficult time adjusting to rock music and its subculture. Some never accepted or tolerated the music; others attempted various strategies to contain rock, just as the Soviets had tried in earlier years to first repress, then contain and co-opt jazz. When regimes—through censorship or banning—made a political issue out of music that may have been politically innocent in intent, it became necessarily politically charged and hence a "subversive" pleasure.[148]

When eradication failed, the Soviet government tried to "domesticate" and contain the music, tolerating a limited industry with official support and mostly ignoring or marginalizing the underground. The Hungarian authorities loosened restrictions on music policy in the 1980s to reclaim the confidence of the increasingly alienated young. But the policy was unable to control the evolution of a vibrant punk/new wave music subculture in the early 1980s. Although operating on the fringes of popular music and not overtly political, the music created an alternative social and cultural space that challenged the definitions of culture, expanded the boundaries of debate, and revealed the disjunctures of society.[149]

East Germany first tried suppressing Western popular music; soon performances by more daring bands were prohibited and some musicians (including singer-songwriter Wolf Biermann) were forced into exile. Biermann considered himself a leftist but also promoted cultural liberalization and German reunification:

The German darkness
Descends over my spirit
It darkens overpowering in my song
It comes because I see my Germany
So deeply torn.[150]

With the more politicized artists gone, the East German authorities reversed themselves and established some official (but carefully regulated and controlled) venues as well as financial support for "youth dance-music" in hopes of permanently depoliticizing the music through dependency. They tried to control and monitor the system by having both DJs and musicians pass tests on Marxist ideology. But musicians soon learned how to manipulate the system and express their political views obliquely but effectively. The tendency of the government to read political messages into even innocuous songs often influenced audiences to do the same, even where no political sentiments were intended. Despite attempts to divide the rock musicians, who enjoyed too much popularity to ban, the regime found it increasingly difficult to orchestrate popular culture. Rock groups would play a key role in the events that ultimately brought down the regime in 1989, publicly aligning themselves with antiregime movements. Hence, in East Germany musicians could talk of "political engagement through music."[151]

Neither repression nor co-optation succeeded in completely eliminating rock, in part because of increasing youth alienation from the regimes. Historian Frederick Starr summarized the persistent problem:

> The Soviet government and its cultural bureaucrats have utterly failed to provide any acceptable alternative to the Western-style popular culture they criticize. . . . At no point in its entire history has the Soviet Union ever been the successfully organized and standardized monolith depicted by many of its more ardent friends and detractors. . . . In the

> field of popular culture it has proven absolutely impossible to implement these [totalitarian] policies effectively. . . . Soviet jazz fans have shown themselves to be independent and resourceful. Those who like jazz find ways of playing or hearing it, whatever policy may be.[152]

Again and again youth forced the regime to compromise.

By the mid-1980s a wide spectrum of musicians and groups had appeared in the various Soviet republics and the East European satellites, playing a dazzling array of styles, among them hardcore punk and heavy metal as well as fusions involving folk, classical, jazz, and rock. Although some could record their more innocuous material at the government recording studios, for the most part this was not mass-mediated popular music; rather it was spread through irregular live performances and illicit cassettes, the musicians earning little from their art but also not having their music compromised by corporate guidelines.

Yet a freer political atmosphere and the ability to travel abroad and establish an international career, made possible by Soviet glasnost and the consequent collapse of communism—in other words, the replacement of Lenin with Lennon as a hero—did not necessarily stimulate musical creativity or enhance the role of rock musicians. Their work became more commercialized but also less popular, subordinated to imported Western rock. Youth culture was challenged by a world "turned upside down," with new subcultures proliferating to fill the vacuum. Many topnotch musicians who had long struggled against official scorn now saw their careers overwhelmed by an influx of

New Song and Chilean Politics

During the 1960s New Song pioneers like Violeta Parra and Victor Jara developed a folk music–based art that spoke to prevailing socioeconomic realities in a deeply divided society. In 1970 New Song musicians joined the campaign of the left-leaning Popular Unity coalition of Salvador Allende, which came to power in free elections. Under Allende, New Song became the basis for a redefined and reinvigorated Chilean popular culture based on local traditions and experiences, with New Song musicians like Jara, Angel and Isabel Parra, and the groups Inti-Illimani and Quilapayun promoting the programs of the new government at home and abroad. The U.S.-sponsored military coup against Allende in 1973 doomed not only progressive change but also New Song; most of the musicians were arrested and executed (including Jara) or deported. New Song became an underground movement, supporting the domestic resistance to the junta and campaigning against the regime and its human rights violations abroad. But New Song remained popular because it transcended trends, fads, and governments. Always it spoke to the concerns of the impoverished sections of the population, the necessity for radical socioeconomic change, and the desire for cultural assertion in a homogenizing world.

mediocre talents catering to mass taste and emulating even more closely Anglo-American models. Musicians like Grebenschikov expressed a feeling of angst as their music became more commercialized and was used by the state to certify its openness. Critics accused them of "selling out," of losing their rebellious spirit as they were appropriated by state and capital. Rock fan and critic Artemy Troitsky condemned the absence of imagination in harsh terms:

> Perestroika and glasnost killed Russian rock. . . . When the K.G.B. forced rock underground, the music wasn't great but its social and spiritual and political significance was tremendous. Now, the bands are stupid and unimaginative. They have no idea what to sing about or how to do it.[153]

It remains to be seen whether rock will remain a vital political and cultural force in these rapidly changing, turbulent societies.

Folk-tinged or -based musics can also play a vital and active role. In Latin America, the New Song movement was also closely tied to progressive politics and protest.[154] It emerged in the 1960s and would become an important part of the musical dialogue in countries including Argentina, Cuba, and Nicaragua over the next three decades. But it achieved its greatest influence in Chile during the late 1960s and early 1970s. Through its utilization of indigenous Andean cultural traditions (including instruments and tunes) rooted in the poor and dispossessed, New Song constituted an alternative to the Anglo-American popular culture favored by privileged elites. New Song would generate emulation in Asia. During the 1990s the innovative Indian singer-songwriter Suman Chatterjee, a persistent critic and hence target of the state government in his native West Bengal, was inspired partly by New Song in formulating his socially conscious lyrics and guitar-based accompaniments. In the process he created a new syncretic, poetic, and satirical Bengali music of love, anger, protest, hope, and laughter with much appeal to urban dwellers.[155]

Some Third World observers have consistently viewed rock music as a buttress of the local power structure and of cultural imperialism. Hence Renato Constantino argues that:

> Rock music with its ear-splitting volume, its empty repetitive lyrics, generates nothing more than a purely physical excitement. It is incapable of saying anything meaningful about human life. Instead it simply erects "walls of sound" behind which its consumers exist in an unreal world where the violence done to the senses becomes an opiate of the mind.[156]

There is ample evidence in Asia, however, that rock can serve other purposes as well. In Vietnam during the 1980s and early 1990s, rock groups like Black and White and Country Band (both led by the leading rocker, former soldier Tran Tien) have offered semiprotest songs with double meanings pressing at the edge of allowable debate on issues of reform and peace. This sometimes earns them official disapproval (the first group was banned). Saigon became the center of a vibrant pop music scene; as private discos replace state ballrooms, the westernized music of musicians like disco queen Ngoc Anh provides a clear counterpoint to official culture.[157] Rock played an even more pivotal role in China where, as in Eastern Europe, rock musicians were in the forefront of movements to liberalize cultural expression. In China rockers like Cui Jian became symbols of conscience and freedom for disaffected youth; one of the top stars, Taiwan exile Hou Dejian, became a leader of the student protestors in Tiananmen Square in 1989. Indeed, one scholar asserts that "Chinese popular music is less a mere adjunct to leisure than a battlefield on which ideological struggle is waged."[158]

Sometimes the relationship between music and radical politics has been completely overt. For example, liberation movements have made use of songs to instill morale and promote group loyalty. The National Liberation Front in South Vietnam employed songs in their struggle to overthrow the Saigon government and their American patrons. Songs like "The Starling," "March Into Saigon," and "Wrest Back Power to the People" were usually sung to folk melodies in collective meetings, work activities, or leisure.[159] The FREITLIN liberation movement in East Timor used folk and composed songs in their struggles, first against Portugal and then the Indonesian invaders. Indeed, the Indonesian invasion force in 1975 singled out the leading poet-musician, Borja da Costa, for execution.[160] Music has also played a key role in the Sikh resistance movement seeking autonomy or independence from India. Songs memorializing martyrs or examining current developments and realities are distributed by cassette throughout the Sikh regions of the Punjab, promoting the ideals of sacrifice for the greater cause.[161] Throughout India militant theater groups have, since late colonial times, presented revolutionary songs in the streets of cities, towns, and villages as part of the campaigns of various left-wing political parties to maintain a radical political thrust in the country.[162]

Music played an especially critical role in some of the African liberation movements, including Angola, Mozambique, Zimbabwe, and South Africa. The *chimurenga* music, a mix of Shona folk and Western popular sounds, broadcast to guerrilla fighters struggling to end white minority rule in Zimbabwe (Southern Rhodesia), played such a powerful role that, after blacks had achieved majority rule, it was converted into a popular music, with major artists such as Thomas Mapfumo becoming local and international stars.[163] The transformation from resistance artist to pop star is not unusual. In Laos Bouangeune Saphouvong, once the major revolutionary singer for the communist Pathet Lao, became a disco star in the late 1980s, specializing in dance music for the new liberalized political and economic reality. This was quite a transformation for a man who spent his formative years with his family in the communist stronghold of Sam Neua, and whose revolutionary songs once bolstered the morale of Pathet Lao troops. Radio broadcasts of his music in 1974–1975 may have been a factor in convincing many Laotians, especially in Vientiane, to accept the soon triumphant communist movement. Later Bouangeune offered a multilingual repertoire of songs in Lao, Khmer, Vietnamese, Russian, and Spanish, and his dance albums would sell as many as fifty thousand copies.[164]

While capitalistic enterprises may try (often successfully) to control the use of music, they cannot necessarily determine its meaning for an active rather than passive audience. Popular music production has remained a social, interactive process, characterized by interrelated production and use activities; sometimes there is as much conflict within these organizations as between them. It is difficult not to conclude that the overall meaning of popular music is determined by interactive relations involving the music industry, musicians, audiences, and the layers of social context within which they work and live.[165]

Patterns of Cultural Imperialism and Interaction

The concept of *culture* is one of the most debated in the social sciences. Anthropologists generally define culture as a complex that includes knowledge, belief, art, law, custom, and other features that constitute part of a society. Thai scholar Patya Saihoo suggests several other possibilities, with none of them being completely satisfactory: a "way of life," a "traditional heritage," the "creativities" of individuals and societies, and the "arts."[166] Culture could also be viewed as a system of interconnected values, perceptions, and modes of interaction or conceived essentially as an idea-system. Some assert that culture is the product of a people's history, deriving from the process of their struggle with the natural and social environment. But it also reflects that history, embodying the value systems (or collective consciousness) by which a people view themselves as well as their place in space and time.[167] As Filipino critic Renato Constantino argues, culture is a product of both social experience and social communication. "Art must be seen, literature read, music heard before any of these aesthetic products can become part of culture. The means of communication is therefore vital."[168]

Whatever the definition utilized, cultural diversity has clearly been a hallmark of the world. According to Kenyan political scientist and social theorist Ali Mazrui, culture serves seven fundamental functions in society, providing: lenses of perception and cognition (cultural paradigms condition views of the world); motives for human behavior (influence cultural response); criteria of evaluation (beauty, morality, etc.); the basis of identity (e.g., religion or race as factors of solidarity or hostility); a mode of communication (language, music, arts, ideas); the basis of socioeconomic stratification (cultural variables condition class, rank, status); and a system of production and consumption.[169] But cultures are also subject to diffusion, with aspects of one culture used or even adopted by another. Popular culture, for example, diffuses learning; people gain ideas and images about the world that affect their behavior.

A key corollary of the neocolonialism characteristic of many Third World nations is *cultural imperialism*, the process whereby the more developed countries dominate the culture of the less developed ones by producing and exporting artifacts and content that reflect their values, beliefs, and behaviors.[170] Cultural evolution within individual societies, and cultural imperialism from the West, operate within the context of a global system, or what Arjun Appadurai terms a "global cultural economy": a single market determined by the needs of the core (Western industrialized countries plus Japan). In this system the periphery (Third World) serves the function of producing raw materials and receiving manufactured goods (including perhaps rock and jazz, the "finished products" constructed from exported African rhythms). Hence, economic and cultural imperialism are linked. While interactions between cultures were common throughout history, the interactions of the last several centuries have involved a new order and intensity. Yet there are also disjunctures in the system. The flows of peoples as well as commodities, ideas, and money are uneven and not completely one-way, creating increasingly differentiated cultures in the global landscape.[171]

The relationship between the increasingly dominant West and the Third World has compelled intellectuals to try to comprehend the nature of the changes generated. The concept of cultural imperialism, which originated in the tumultuous 1960s and gradually gained intellectual currency, has provoked considerable controversy. Many Western observers would agree that Western culture, like Western political and economic models, is increasingly triumphant throughout the world, but they view this more as a by-product of modernization or the functionality or irresistible appeal of those forms rather than as an insistent, planned assault. If these forms undermine traditional and indigenous popular arts, they argue, then so be it; the essence of the modern, market-driven world is competition: may the best art form win.

Some offer the concept of *globalization* as an alternative to imperialism; it is a far less coherent and less purposeful process rooted more in interconnection and interdependency. Those who identify cultural globalization point to cultural integration and disintegration processes both occurring at an interstate level and transcending the state-society unit. The autonomy of the globalization process may even operate independently of interstate processes.[172] But many thoughtful observers take an entirely different view, seeing cultural imperialism as a prong in economic and commercial imperialism, what Kenyan writer Ngugi wa Thiong'o calls "the cultural bomb."[173] Experts are divided on whether this apparent "synchronization" results from a deliberate political or commercial strategy, is a haphazard result of cultural contact, or is inevitable given the imbalance of power in international relationships. The causes and processes may be complex, but the issue of cultural imperialism has been well integrated into the dialogue about popular culture in many Asian countries.

The term *media imperialism* is used to describe a situation where the media flow is unidirectional, and where a small number of source countries account for a substantial share of all international media influences in the world. Whatever the process, there has been much concern about the one-way information flow, including the impact of media technologies on societies that must import them to modernize, with television and advertising as special concerns.[174] The Indian scholar Govind Vidyarthi employs the term *information imperialism* to refer to a pattern where the global flow of information becomes distorted and imbalanced by the communications revolution; the Western nations flood the Third World with belittling "disinformation and propaganda," while information from the Third World to the West is held to a trickle, marginalizing its role on the world stage.[175]

Several processes have been operating in the modern world. These include cultural imperialism by *importation*, in which nonindigenous musical forms are introduced and flourish in mostly unmodified form; and cultural imperialism by *reexportation*, in which local forms (like calypso or reggae) are exported to the West but then modified at home by the attitudes and reactions of Western rather than local audiences.[176] The emphasis may be dependent on circumstances, not the least of which is the potential Western market to be tapped (sizable for reggae, tiny for Indonesian kroncong or dangdut) and the ease of access to that market. The dominant country (or cultural epicenter) may also differ. Contemporary Zairean, Sahelian, and North African popular musics have been mightily influenced by the taste of the music audience in France, where many African and Arab musicians reside and make their living. For Filipinos the United States is the everpresent influence, admired, envied, and emulated by many but lambasted and feared by others. As one prominent Filipino nationalist put it, in describing the difficulty Filipinos have had in decolonizing their mentality as well as their politics:

> In the context of the Filipino struggle, the peculiarities of American imperialism significantly add to the difficulties of cultural decolonization. For it is relatively easy to identify an adversary who openly represses you, but rather more difficult when he purports to be your "liberator" and greatest friend: when he succeeds in misrepresenting your exploitation as generous "aid" for your development and "modernization." And this is precisely how American domination prevailed over its territories, including the Philippines.[177]

The political, economic, and sociocultural context for much of the Third World has been very different from that of the Western industrialized nations, with "decolonization" an important part of the agenda. General disillusionment occupies a more central position in both public discussion and popular culture. For example, filmmakers have addressed issues of wealth, power, repression, and neocolonialism, including an interest in producing revolutionary films to further socioeconomic transformation. Patricio Guzman, a Chilean who made documentary films before being forced into exile by the 1973 coup, expressed the sense of purpose and rewards of the experience:

> The film was an incomparably intense experience for all involved, not just in its historical dimension or for whatever virtues it may have as cinema. . . . Through the lived experience of the film, we all came to understand what it means to live through a revolutionary process—what ideological struggle really means, what fascism looks and feels like, what it means for the enraged middle class to rise up against the workers, how invisible imperialism can be—because in Chile you don't see Phantom jets spewing napalm as in Vietnam; what you see is imperialism reflected in the attitudes of the middle class. The experience of making the film marked us for the rest of our lives. Everything else is merely a figure of speech.[178]

Some of the same patterns operated among Third World musicians as for writers and filmmakers. Many writers developed an obsession with "decolonizing the mind," which sometimes means abandoning the use of Western languages, themes, or frames of reference. Kenyan novelist and essayist Ngugi wa Thiong'o has been a major proponent, exchanging English for Kikuyu.[179] The quest for indigenization required coming to an understanding and appreciation of those distinctive values embedded in a society's own history rather than those borrowed or imposed from outside. In the

Rambo Conquers Asia

An American journalist of South Asian origin recorded the impact of the U.S. film *Rambo, First Blood, Part 2* as he traveled through Asia in 1985:

> Rambo had conquered Asia. In China, a million people raced to see *First Blood* within ten days of its Beijing opening. In India, five separate remakes of the American hit went instantly into production. In Thailand, fifteen-foot cutouts of the avenging demon towered over the lobbies of some of the ten Bangkok cinemas in which the movie was playing, training their machine guns on all who passed. And in Indonesia, the Rambo Amusement Arcade was going great guns, while vendors along the streets offered posters of Stallone. Silencing soldiers, toppling systems, conquering millions and making money fist over fist across the continent, Rambo was unrivaled as the most powerful force in Asia that autumn.[180]

Philippines, whose complex cultural identity was shaped by both Spanish and American colonialism, writers, artists, and popular musicians became particularly eager to confront neocolonial legacies but struggled to find the appropriate vehicle. Their own work was often derivative of American models, indicating the problems in discovering an alternative to cultural imperialism or globalization.

It is difficult to underestimate the influence of American popular culture in the postwar world—what has been characterized as the shift from the "Monroe Doctrine to the Marilyn Monroe Doctrine."[181] Hard Rock Cafes have even been established as far afield as Beijing, and Dolly Parton is reported to be much more popular in Zimbabwe than native Shona sculpture and other traditional arts, which, in contrast to American country music, are widely seen as irrelevant to modern lives (except as tourist commodities).[182] The popular culture of films, fads, foods, fashions, jeans, and music may be the U.S.A.'s number one export. Hence, many more Asians than Americans followed the fanciful, bloody, and imperialistic adventures of Rambo, the American film hero in the 1980s. Rambo was accurately characterized by an Indonesian observer as "typical of the characters of political propaganda . . . the soul of a sick America," in a film that "fanatically despises complexity."[183] Such unsettling baggage did not apparently diminish the box office receipts. Indeed, a recent study of four Asian countries (including Malaysia) found that television viewers watched many Western programs (especially movies, serials, and sitcoms) and had mostly favorable impressions of them; large majorities did not see them as a serious cultural threat and opposed restrictions on importing these programs.[184]

Perhaps American popular culture, at once both immensely entertaining and highly challenging to traditional values, has emerged as the closest thing available to a global lingua franca.[185] In the mid-1980s French philosopher and political activist Regis Debray identified the subversive power of U.S. popular and material culture in the Cold War competition with the Soviet Union:

> Unfortunately, Americans focus more on Soviet military hardware than on their limited political prestige. That is responsible for your overestimation of Soviet power, as if power in history is the same as force of arms! What myopia and short-sightedness. There is more power in rock music, videos, blue jeans, fast food, news networks and TV satellites than in the entire Red Army.[186]

And yet, by the early 1990s European interest in American pop culture showed signs of fading, as a "European consciousness" gained ground among youth. This was exemplified in the rise of rave and techno (dance musics with an electronic beat that swept Europe before gaining a North American foothold), the "Europeanization" of MTV Europe, and the strug-

American Media Imperialism in Latin America

Latin America provides a case in point of cultural imperialism. In 1969 between 50 and 90 percent of the films shown in various Latin American countries were American imports, while in 1974 an astonishing 84 percent of television programs in Guatemala were American. Latin American newspapers were also carriers of an American perspective on world affairs, as 50 percent of the world news they carried in the mid-1970s came from U.S. news agencies.[187] Perhaps the mass media must be seen as supplementing and extending the messages that the leaders of the global system want communicated. The results of the process by which national corporate elites mediate American culture in Chile and elsewhere has been termed "creolization" (a hybrid of American and local bourgeois culture).[188]

gles of EuroDisney in Paris to attract an audience. As it expanded into Asia in the early 1990s, MTV faced competition from several international and Asia-based rivals and was forced to tailor its product to individual markets, so that viewers were getting a mixed bag of Western and local musics. American pop music was far from dislodging local varieties in many nations of Asia and Africa. For example, Hong Kong youth still prefer the Cantonese-language "Cantorock," Taiwan fans favor Mandarin pop songs, Japanese overwhelmingly listen to Japanese-language pop, and Nigerians love juju, *highlife*, reggae, and other local styles. The largest film industry in the world, India's, making twice as many films per year as Hollywood, overwhelms the Indian market. Only occasionally do American films make a huge impact there (*Jurassic Park* was a massive hit). Furthermore, U.S. cultural products often face stiff transnational competition: from Taiwan and Hong Kong pop music in China, from Indian films in southern Asia and East Africa, and from Mexican and Brazilian television programs in Spanish- and Portuguese-speaking countries, as well as elsewhere. Indeed, Mexican soap operas have gained a popular following in nations as diverse as China and Russia. And some places Americanization may be feared or resented much less than, for example, "Japanization" (in Korea), "Indianization" (in Sri Lanka), "Vietnamization" (in Cambodia), and "Russianization" (in the Baltics).[189]

American suggestions that "we are the world" address multicultural issues but may be patently misleading.[190] Still, U.S. influence remains strong throughout the globe. In the early 1980s the two most popular television programs in the world were *Dallas* and *The Muppet Show; Dallas* attracted an estimated 300 million viewers in fifty-seven nations. There were also many local adaptations of the *Dallas* theme in soap operas in many nations.[191] Since the West controls the capital, markets, and infrastructure of world finance, they also control and hence shape the messages and imagery both *within* and *among* nations. Chilean critic Ariel Dorfman has examined the socio-economic—even ideological—"hidden agenda" messages embedded in pop culture exports such as Disney comics, Babar the Elephant children's books, television programs, and *Reader's Digest*. Donald Duck comic books, for example, convey American cultural values such as the benefits of capitalism and counterrevolution, while Babar fulfilled the colonialist's dream. Along with many observers, Dorfman characterizes the spread of these products as a nefarious form of "cultural imperialism" undermining the unique values of the societies they invade and spreading characteristic American attitudes in the process.[192]

Constantino characterizes the evolving world culture as a "synthetic culture," which reorders reality and in so doing creates a mediating agency that modifies indigenous cultural traits in order to standardize people into becoming acceptable citizens who refrain from questioning the system. Echoing the Frankfurt School, he charges that transnational corporations and the communications technology they control play a large part in producing "cultural commodities" that homogenize and sedate people into abandoning their social obligations. In this cultural conditioning process, the transnational corporations distort consumption patterns in poor societies through advertising and sales. Under neocolonialism the techniques of subjugation and control are no longer chiefly military; instead synthetic culture functions as a form of social control, with the audience as passive recipients.[193] Hence, in the opinion of many observers, cultural imperialism constitutes an important by-product of outward-thrusting American policies in the world, and was furthermore a field uncontested by the Soviet Union. No wonder that many governments, from the humorless, militant Islamic mullahs running Iran (aided by gun-toting civilian cultural watchdogs called "the bearded men") to the more democratic leaders of pluralistic India, have attempted to extinguish or at least control the influx of destabilizing "alien" pop culture. An Islamic political party in Pakistan even demanded the extradition of

American fast food companies like McDonald's, Pizza Hut, and Kentucky Fried Chicken have constituted one of the most obvious aspects of the spread of American culture, with outlets in many Asian cities. During the 1980s Kentucky Fried Chicken dominated the fast food market in Malaysia. This is one of many stores in Kuala Lumpur. 1984 photo by author.

Madonna and Michael Jackson in 1995 so that they could be placed on trial as "cultural terrorists" destroying humanity.[194]

There remains a constant tension in the many dimensions of contemporary cultural interactions between homogenization and heterogenization, and observers can find evidence of both processes at work. Ultimately, the process extending global cultural interrelationships leads to a global ecumene—a region of persistent cultural exchange and interaction—characterized by the contradictory tendencies and lubricated by the implicit tensions of globalization and parochialism. But while some culture flows from the periphery to the center (reggae music, Latin American novels, Buddhist-Hindu meditation), the relationship remains asymmetrical, leading ultimately to a situation of either saturation or maturation of local cultures. The complex patterns of cultural flows produce both homogeneity and disorder (as once-isolated cultures are linked together), and they produce transnational cultures (oriented beyond national boundaries). The result is a new world culture. Swedish anthropologist Ulf Hannerz argues that:

> There is now a world culture, but we had better make sure that we understand what this means. It is marked by an organization of diversity rather than a replication of uniformity. No total homogenization of systems of meaning and expression has occurred, nor does it appear likely that there will be one any time soon. But the world has become one network of social relationships, and between its different regions there is a flow of meanings as well as of people and goods. The world culture is created through the increasing interconnectedness of varied local cultures, as well as through the development of cultures without a clear anchorage in any one territory. These are all becoming sub-cultures, as it were, within the wider whole; cultures which are in important ways better understood in the context of their cultural surroundings than in isolation.[195]

The process of transnationalism hence creates in every society a sector of "cosmopolitan" people (who facilitate global coherence) as opposed to "locals" (who remain rooted in familiar sociocultural contexts). The result is two contrasting political axes that might be termed "localism" and "globalism." The new media technologies increasingly create a "global city," so that the evolving cultural synthesis overreaches the metropolitan environment, "penetrating and feeding back from the village, desert, mountain, peasant community, suburbia and shanty town," providing an opportunity for connection as well as fracture.[196] On the Indonesian island of Bali, a creative people determined to sustain their cultural values have put imperial technologies like television and VCRs to their own distinctive uses. Hence local "readings" of imported cultural forms and technologies may vary considerably from their progenitors. The field of popular music offers much material to assess the elements of cultural imperialism and globalization, homogenization and heterogenization.

Intercultural Patterns of Popular Music Change

The hypothesis of a "cultural imperialism" emanating in the powerful Western nations and inevitably influencing "non-Western" societies in various diverse ways assumes a one-way flow of cultural products, "from the West to the Rest," a Michael Jackson world takeover of musical expression. In this situation the rich local musical traditions rapidly disappear under the onslaught of Western music pop music; homogenization replaces differentiation.[197] These fears have led many countries at various times to impose restrictions on how much foreign music can be played on radio (e.g., Canada, Chile, Nigeria, Malaysia, Indonesia, the Philippines). Nations without such restrictions, however, are not always irretrievably damaged by foreign music. The cultural manifestations are multifaceted because societies can use imported music and music technology for their own purposes. It needs to be emphasized that this general Third World context, especially in the burgeoning cities, has included a great deal of mixing of diverse ethnic groups, religions, worldviews, and cultural influences. These transitions and encounters have not always gone smoothly, but they have often been creative.

Indeed, the situation is complex, including changing local tastes amidst societal transformation. While information-age economic forces are constructing an international consumership for centrally generated and distributed popular music, other factors are promoting contrary forces, encouraging an "indigenization" of popular music production and forms but also new, eclectic combinations that contradict the constraints of societal boundaries. Musicians everywhere are influenced both by internationalized music and their own local cultural traditions, personal experiences, and particular sociopolitical conditions. Inequitable cultural flows do not necessarily correspond with cultural obliteration, especially in popular music (which can be produced inexpensively compared to television or films). Hence observers can identify both some homogenization and some pluralism occurring in global culture; the patterns are not mutually exclusive.[198]

Cultural interaction often presents as many opportunities as it closes off. The flood of Anglo-American music around the world in the 1950s and 1960s influenced local musicians but did not prevent them from developing their own styles, adapted to their own cultures. The result has been *transculturation*, where individual music cultures pick up elements from transcultural music—but also some national and local music cultures contribute to transcultural music. The resulting process is characterized by

Transculturation and World Musical Fusions

Transculturation is characterized by an international blending of sounds, including the creation of local hybrids as well as truly "transnational music" with global appeal. In the West, among others, Paul Simon, David Byrne, Sting, Ry Cooder, and Peter Gabriel are masters of "transnational" music, as are many of the exponents of "world beat" in Asia, Africa, and Latin America, such as the Senegalese Youssou N'Dour and Baaba Maal, the Malian Salif Keita, the Malagasy group Tarika Sammy, South African Johnny Clegg, the Israeli Ofra Haza, the Brazilian Gilberto Gil, the Antillian zouk band Kassav, politicized Haitian group Boukman Eksperyans, and the Pakistani Najma. In Southeast Asia the jazz-rock-folk fusion group Asiabeat (including at various times Malaysian, Singaporean, Japanese, and American musicians) have been pioneers in blending diverse influences into a musically satisfying whole that has even attracted fans in North America. Ancient Future, whose membership includes Americans and Asians, has been successfully integrating Chinese, Japanese, Balinese, Indian, African, Middle Eastern, and Western music (especially jazz) since 1980 into a pattern they call "world fusion." In urban India rock musicians write original English songs (often on local themes such as political corruption, the inadequate economic infrastructure, or the vitality of Bombay life) and reject both direct imitation of Western stars and local "cover" versions of their songs.[199]

a two-way flow.[200] Quite often the outside influences strengthen a local culture, by producing vibrant hybrid musics like dangdut, salsa, reggae, *fenua* (a Tahitian mix of ancestral chants and rock), mbanqanga (black South African pop), juju, *rai* (Algerian/North African pop), *mbalax* (folk-pop fusion from the western Sahel), *MPB* (an eclectic strand of Brazilian Popular Music) and *zouk* (the lively Caribbean dance music from the French Antilles).

Two influential Sweden-based analysts, Roger Wallis and Krister Malm, identify four overlapping patterns of cultural interaction: cultural exchange (a mutual sharing between cultures); cultural domination (the imposition by a politically powerful culture of its forms and values on a weaker one); cultural imperialism (the transfer of financial and cultural resources to achieve domination); and transculturation (an intense pattern of cultural change spread by transnational corporations rather than governments, leading to an international music industry). Transculturation constitutes a two-way process in which elements of international popular styles become incorporated into national and local music cultures, and indigenous influences contribute to the formation of new transnational styles.[201]

Diffusion has been common. The spread of reggae around the world constitutes a most impressive phenomenon:

> In Papeete, Tahiti, the buses all have speakers the size of foot lockers, making them moving sound systems. Their routes are jumping with the rhythms of Steel Pulse, Black Uhuru, and Bob Marley. . . . Four thousand miles away, there is a reggae night spot called Club 69, where local youth wear dreadlocks . . . and dance ska, rocksteady, and skank to the beats of the Wailers. . . . Club 69 is in Tokyo, the dread youths are Japanese. . . . Africa has its own reggae styles and hundreds of bands.[202]

Japanese reggae groups like Banana Blue, Chinggis Chan Dread, and Ranking Soldiers enjoy a large following.[203] Sometimes music loses its effectiveness when transported from its original context: Chilean New Song became diluted in Mexico, while reggae loses much of its social marginalization in Japan, Malaysia, Australia, or Germany.[204] The imported music is sometimes transformed dramatically as it comes into contact with indigenous rhythms, creating unique (and often barely recognizable) styles such as the *disco laggi* of North India or the *dangdut reggae* of Malaysia.[205]

Borrowing and interaction are generally treated by anthropologists under the term *acculturation*. This refers to the influence of one society or cultural form on another. One result is *hybridization*: the crossing of two species. This process can be either enriching or impoverishing.[206] Some conservative critics are alarmed by these musics. Hence, Dutch musicologist Jaap Kunst fretted about the "degenerating" influence of kroncong (a guitar-based mix of Javanese gamelan and Portuguese nostalgic songs) on Indonesia's rich indigenous traditions.[207] Syncretic music was seen as dis-

Country Music as a Global Phenomenon

Sometimes the strong appeal of American culture results in imitation. Bluegrass, rooted in the states along the Mason-Dixon Line, developed an audience in many nations, with groups playing that style forming in places as diverse as Japan, Belgium, France, Russia, New Zealand, and Malaysia. Often their music has had a clear local flavor, as with the Osaka-based Bluegrass 45 (some of whose members later played with Nashville groups) and the Russian group Kukuruza. A Japanese observer has noted how the many local performers at a bluegrass festival in the southern city of Fukuoka in 1988 (many of whom could not speak English), emanating from all generations and backgrounds, "covered roughly the entire range of the Japanese people who have come to love American bluegrass music and old-time or hillbilly music."[208] On an even larger scale, country and western music gained a following in many Asian and Oceanic nations. Cities like Tokyo, Kuala Lumpur, Manila, and Singapore came to boast a myriad of nightclubs and pubs featuring local musicians specializing in the style, such as Singapore's well-known Matthew and the Mandarins, whose most famous song, "Singapore Cowboy," pleads: "Singapore cowboy, a long way from home [Nashville]; won't you 'sing a poor' cowboy another lonesome song."

tinctly lowbrow and lacking in quality—vastly inferior to indigenous classical musics and Western art or classical music.

Some of these styles go back well before World War II, but most have flourished in the postwar years. All mix indigenous and imported influences—but the imported ones are not always from North America or Europe. For example, Zairean soukous makes heavy use of Latin American dance rhythms introduced to central Africa in the 1930s, while the highlife of Ghana and Nigeria owes much to the calypso songs brought by West Indian sailors in the early part of the century. Indian film music has been a powerful influence on the popular music of Indonesia and Malaysia, as well as among some East African countries. Arab musical models have reached as far as the spread of Islam itself, which explains why the *orkes melayu* (Malay orchestra) traditions of Malaya and Sumatra so closely resemble (at least in superficial sound) the Swahili *tarabi* music of Somalia, Kenya, and Tanzania.[209] But the Western influence in most of the musics is undeniably strong.

Western-style music plays an important role in an ongoing dialectical relationship, often both symbiotic and competitive, with indigenous or syncretic forms. Sometimes it works both ways. The rapidly changing technology of musical production and reproduction in recent years is partly responsible for the heightened Western interest in global sounds, the creation of a new category variously called "world beat," "world music," or "ethnopop." A few "exotic" songs from outside the Western tradition have sometimes found their way into the American hit parade before the advent of world beat. In the 1950s an older mbube song from South Africa, "Wimoweh," gained some attention when released by the popular folk group the Weavers; later Miriam Makeba would record it as well. In 1961 the pop group the Tokens would transform the song into "The Lion Sleeps Tonight," which became a monster hit. The Indonesian freedom song "Suliram" and the Kenyan pop hit "Malaika" also gained some attention in recordings by Makeba, Pete Seeger, and others. In 1963 a Japanese song retitled "Sukiyaki" rose to the top of the U.S. charts while also achieving fame elsewhere.

And Asian musicians can sometimes find a steady North American market for their work, especially if they relocate there. Among others, the Indonesian jazz musician Indra Ledesma, the eclectic Japanese progressive rock-fusion-world musician Ryuichi Sakamoto, Japanese New Age star Kitaro, and the Indian violinist L. Subramaniam have achieved some success in the United States. On a lesser scale, Hong Kong has often served as a lucrative base for some Malaysian, Taiwanese, and Philippine musicians. This development affords the musicians a wider audience and a dynamic, creative, politically neutral environment, but also reshapes their sound for global (i.e., Western) tastes.[210] There has also been a modest musical exodus corresponding to the "brain drain" of the educated to the West. For example, several

Malaysian artists have achieved success after relocating to Western nations (e.g., Datuk Shake in France, Kamahl in Australia), and others have followed in hopes of emulating them (e.g., pop queen Fran Peter to the United States, Roy Santa Maria to Australia). In the same way various Hong Kong (Agnes Chan) and Taiwan stars (Teresa Teng) forged successful careers while based some of the time in Japan. Taiwan-born Tracy Huang became a superstar after relocating to Singapore.

The music can transcend national or ethnic origins, as exemplified by the astonishing enthusiasm within the New York Hispanic community for the Japanese salsa group Orchestra de la Luz.[211] The rising British reggae-dancehall star Apache Indian (Steve Kapur) demonstrates the reach of transnational music. Born into an East Indian immigrant family in England, idolizing both Elvis Presley and Bob Marley, and adopting a Native American performance name, Indian's politicized—and sexual—songs have been seen as articulating South Asian youth identity, challenging racism (and bridging black–South Asian hostilities) in Britain, offering a revolutionary challenge to suffocating caste and sexual attitudes in India, and reaffirming reggae tradition in Jamaica.[212]

Conclusions

In the past half century the mass media have expanded greatly in reach and complexity. All over the world, in a turbulent context of change and media development, mass-mediated and commercialized popular musics developed and new styles proliferated, including derivative imitations of Western pop and creative fusions blending indigenous traditions with diverse external influences (depending on the situation) from North America, Europe, Africa, Latin America, the Middle East, South Asia, and Eastern Asia. These popular musics gained a mass audience and helped shape local cultures. Inevitably they would develop a relationship to politics. Many questions remain to be answered in a comparative study. For example, the question as to whether popular musics challenge or reinforce the social and political order is no less relevant to Southeast Asia than it is elsewhere. The chapters that follow analyze the political role of popular music and offer several case studies to illustrate some of the patterns that may have significance for Southeast Asia.

2

Indonesia: Many Fields, Many Songs

Oppression and abuses of power
are too numerous to mention. . . .
We're fed up with greed and uncertainty.
From song by Iwan Fals, popular rock star.[1]

Popular music has become in recent decades a central feature of culture and daily life in Indonesia. Two experts describe the situation in the 1980s:

> Today, at any hour, anywhere, we can hear music, played from just one source, or from many sources, as in villages . . . or in shopping centers, or cassette shops. . . . Music can be heard in so many forms . . . in the mountains, fishing villages . . . prisons. . . . Pop music in particular, lives 24 hours a day. . . . Pop star posters are displayed in the cities and in the villages, in the rooms of teenagers and of others not so young. Shop owners and roadside traders seize any opportunity to sell posters of pop idols . . . posters duplicated on calendars, exercise book covers, match boxes. . . . Pop music has planted itself firmly in the Indonesian soil.[2]

The Indonesian context has also proved conducive for the emergence of social criticism as a prominent feature of Indonesian popular music. This chapter surveys the emergence of various musical streams and analyzes their relationship to politics. Kroncong was the earliest form to develop, becoming an important cultural expression in the nineteenth and early twentieth cen-

Basic Data[3]

Population (1994): 200,000,000
Urban Population: 32 percent
Capital: Jakarta (metro population: 10,000,000)
Life Expectancy: 62
Adult Literacy: 82 percent
Religions: Islam (87 percent); Christianity (9 percent); Hinduism (2 percent); Others (2 percent)
Economy: Per capita GNP: U.S. $670
Radio Ownership Figures n.a.; Radio Republik Indonesia (government-owned and operated); many private stations
Radio Receivers Produced (incl. radio–cassette tape players): 997,000 (1987)
Television Ownership: 9,176,000; TVRI (government owned and operated network); one private commercial station (Jakarta)
People Per Television Set: 16.3
Television Receivers Produced: 575,000 (1987)
Sound Recorders Produced (incl. cassette tape players): 177,000 (1987)
Media: Many daily newspapers in Indonesian, English, and regional languages

turies; it was then transformed into a nationalist weapon against colonialism. Beginning in the 1960s and 1970s, various musicians specializing in *pop Indonesia* addressed sociopolitical issues. But it was dangdut and its leading adherent, Rhoma Irama, that provided the most serious challenge to the political establishment. In the late 1980s and early 1990s, the folk rock of Iwan Fals joined in the dialogue.

The Roots of Politics and Music

A former Dutch colony spread over hundreds of inhabited islands, Indonesia is the colossus of Southeast Asia, stretching east-west a distance equal to that from California to New York.[4] The rapidly growing population represents a wide variety of ethnic and linguistic groups (by some estimates more than six hundred), but the Javanese from the island of Java account for well over half the total. The national language, *Bahasa Indonesia*, increasingly serves to link the various groups and contributes to a growing feeling of nationhood. But strong regional allegiances and local languages have by no means disappeared. As one observer concludes: "Insofar as it displays a pervasive temper, it is one riven with internal contrasts and contradictions."[5] A popular folk expression reflects the wide diversity of cultures: "Different fields, different cockroaches."

Indeed, given the diversity of islands, peoples, and cultures, Indonesian leaders have been obsessed with creating national unity and identity. They chose as their slogan *"Bhinneka Tunggal Ika"* ("unity in diversity"), but this has so far expressed more an aspiration than a solid reality. The motto evokes a persistent theme in the archipelago's history; it emphasizes a spirit of unity fostered in the face of multiple, often even conflicting cultural and religious traditions. Yet in practice this usually means more a permanent balance or coexistence between them than a real merging or absorption.[6]

Indonesia's diversity is a product of her long history. For two thousand years kingdoms and states arose and declined on the various islands, but no united Indonesia ever existed. Over the trade routes from India, the Middle East, and China came merchants and new religions. Beginning in the fifteenth century the people of the coastal regions, as well as most Javanese, began to embrace Islam. Many (particularly in Java) incorporated the religion into the preexisting Hinduism/Buddhism and animism, creating a syncretic mixture; others followed a more orthodox form of the religion. In central and eastern Java an increasing cultural and socioeconomic divide separated the more pious Muslims from the syncretist, animist-oriented, more nominal Muslims. That divide would widen, and the tensions between these groups would accelerate, as the twentieth century progressed. Although many influences came from outside, the Indonesian peoples demonstrated a striking ability to integrate these influences with indigenous patterns; the new rarely overwhelmed or destroyed the old. Furthermore, diversity continued. Historian J. D. Legge summarizes the general Indonesian pattern:

> These developments were gradual—not sudden, catastrophic, and revolutionary. . . . The effect in the end was to produce not a simple coherent culture, but rather a multiplicity of traditions, many of them retaining vigorous life. There is a variety of threads to be distinguished in the modern pattern, not an even blending of color. Indonesian history has been a triumph of coexistence.[7]

The traditional musical culture of the islands is rich and diversified, with each of the major ethnic or regional groups developing one or more distinctive genres. And the arts have reflected historical change. Artistic activity proved to be a major means of facilitating the assimilation of external cultures into the mainstream of tradition. Forms of cultural expression maintained their vitality by assuming new roles and functions, hence providing a framework for continuity in a changing society. Borrowing, adaptation, and transmission of cultural elements between groups were always major forces in Indonesian artistic development, resulting in unique artistic forms—including music.[8]

According to one recent study, the Javanese created some thirty-two musical or music-related art forms over the centuries, not including the various pop forms that emerged after World War II.[9] Many of these were regional or folk variations on the famous gamelan ensemble; in its classic,

The Sound of Gamelan

"[Gamelan] is comparable only to two things: moonlight and flowing water. It is pure and mysterious like moonlight, it is always the same and always changing like flowing water. It forms for our ears no song, this music, it is a state of being, such as moonlight itself which lies poured out over the land. It flows murmuring, tinkling, and gurgling like water in a mountain stream. Yet it is never monotonous. Sometimes the sounds flow faster and louder, just as water also sometimes speaks more loudly in the night only to sink back again quietly."—Jaap Kunst[10]

elite, court-centered form, the gamelan includes many percussion and occasional wind instruments playing a rather diverse repertoire. Many villages possess their own orchestras. The sound of gamelan music has been characterized as seemingly formless, but in reality it is highly complex.

In Java and neighboring Bali the *wayang kulit* (shadow play) became the main artistic medium.[11] Accompanied by gamelan music, the wayang puppeteers *(dalang)* weaved an engaging world of gods, demons, princes, and clowns, many of the stories based on the Hindu epics imported more than a millennium ago. The complex of emotions running throughout the plays is reflected, even intensified, by the expressive power of the accompanying music, which encourages both pleasure and focus. The puppeteer, at once storyteller and philosopher, gives life to the characters and develops the stories to teach manners and morals, usually with much humor. The dalang was widely perceived as able to influence invisible forces through performances mixing entertainment and socioreligious meaning. Many specialists argue that a comprehension of wayang is essential to an understanding of the Javanese and their syncretic beliefs. The figures of the wayang came to so permeate Javanese thinking that the puppet theater became unquestionably the richest source of metaphor and imagery, with the puppeteers poetically expounding the existential position of the Javanese personality, the relationship to the natural and supernatural order, and the crucial importance of maintaining harmony and stability in a world of conflicts.

A wayang performance becomes, therefore, an interplay between myth and reality. The wayang also articulates the notion of complimentary polarities; life requires accepting seemingly irreconcilable opposites as part of the cosmic balance, so that musical developments may contain clear contradictory elements that perplex Javanese far less than they would puzzle or offend less eclectic Westerners. From the awareness of the complex relationships of human existence, Javanese ethics, morality, and philosophy as expressed in the wayang promoted human dignity and legitimized a profound sense of tolerance. Historian Laurie Sears even suggests that the wayang served as a locus for renegotiating power relationships between the

The Wayang Puppeteer's Commentaries

"The deepest respect persists for the dalang, who in the many functions of his art is justly regarded as a versatile and highly educated scholar. The dalang has a sacred responsibility, for through his religious convictions he is given the spiritual strength required to bring to life the figures of wayang. He must know all the levels of the Javanese language. He must develop a wide range of voice changes in order to accommodate the appropriate personification of the different characters. He must possess a great memory in order to retain the formalities and intricacies of many plots. He must be skilled in weaving topical humor—sometimes light, sometimes ribald, but always funny—into his stories, for it is the touches of contemporary invention that make wayang kulit the most popular and liveliest of arts."—Mantle Hood[12]

Javanese and the Dutch colonizers, with intellectuals and performers retelling the contested categories (both colonial and postcolonial) through mounting allegories of resistance. In the process the wayang stories moved from the villages and palaces into nationalist journals and, later, novels, comic books, and even cassettes.[13]

But this has not been music inaccessible to the masses. The boundaries between folk music and gamelan have been indistinct. There was always a close relationship between the music of the villages and streets and that of the courts. The ubiquitous village orchestras are largely imitations of the court gamelans, and street musicians (solo or ensemble) use original or modified versions of the instruments. There are also Javanese traditions of sung poetry *(tembang)* in which the text is the crucial factor; these include chronicles and teachings, providing a fertile basis for the later development of popular music. Both gamelan and wayang kulit continue to flourish in Java and Bali among all socioeconomic classes.

A Javanese gamelan orchestra performing in Jogjakarta. 1971 photo by author.

And the arts have never been unchanging, frozen in time. For example, during the 1920s and 1930s the Balinese developed a new technique of gamelan playing and dancing known as *kebiar* that involved a new time perception of music.[14] Meanwhile, Javanese gamelan has been influenced by imported Western ideas in areas like musical notation, technological innovations, and even direct borrowing, which has subtly altered the ethos of the performances and encouraged standardization.[15] By the 1980s composers like Nano S., Suhendi Afryanto, Pande Made Sukerta, and I. Wayan Sadra, rooted in these classical traditions, were developing an astonishing original version of gamelan and kindred styles. They utilize traditional instruments and patterns but blend them with modern and Western elements to create an experimental music for aficionados of serious music (in Indonesia and the West).[16] Nor has gamelan music been necessarily divorced from political and social questions. In the decades following the Indonesian Revolution, the Javanese musician and composer K. R. T. Wasitodiningrat ("Pak Cokro") developed many pieces with political themes, to be played by standard ensembles. His most famous work, completed in 1952, was a musical presentation of the history of Java from the eleventh century to the end of Dutch rule. Some of his later works celebrated Indonesian independence, honored the government, or protested environmental degradation.[17]

There has been a long and lively debate involving both Indonesian and Western observers as to whether the traditional arts need to be conserved in a pristine form and preserved for posterity, or whether fresh but tradition-based forms capable of expressing contemporary needs should be encouraged.[18] Hence, it can be argued that the gamelan and related traditions are both traditional and modern. They also have remained in a sense popular, because today they enjoy some mass-mediated distribution through cassette sales and broadcasting as well as live performances. A survey in 1972 showed that wayang programs were the most popular radio fare among listeners in east Java. Today old and new styles coexist, both to some degree commodified, tying the audiences to the past but also addressing the present.[19] Their main heritage for politicized music lies in their close relationship to the creation and affirmation of community solidarity and values while at the same time affirming the rigid class system. Perhaps, too, the gamelan performance conveys the impression that musical expression holds deep meaning that the audience should ponder. We should also note the sometimes improvised topicality and educational function of wayang.

The coming of the West would have a substantial impact in the political, social, and economic realms. Islam proved a rallying cry for Indonesians when European adventurers and colonizers began to arrive in search of the valuable spices exported across the trade routes to Europe. The

Portuguese annexed scattered ports and islands during the sixteenth century against fierce opposition. In the seventeenth century the Dutch displaced the Portuguese from most of their enclaves and began their long process of colonizing the archipelago, often through military conquest. Most of Java was under direct or indirect Dutch control by the end of the eighteenth century. By the first decade of the twentieth century the process of annexation of the archipelago was complete, although some outlying regions resisted bravely for years and were never fully subdued. Not surprisingly, the colonization of the archipelago and subduing of once proud civilizations has generated much retrospective poetry and prose in modern times, by writers both sophisticated and amateur.[20]

The Dutch concentrated their economic exploitation in Java and Sumatra, establishing rubber plantations and compelling peasants to grow cash crops like coffee and sugar. Many Chinese immigrated to the islands during the colonial era, becoming in the process a middle-class commercial group widely resented by Indonesians despite the considerable acculturation of many. The Dutch colonizers and their collaborators prospered from these policies, but many peasants became impoverished, especially after world commodity prices collapsed during the Great Depression of the 1930s. Colonial socioeconomic policies also contributed to population explosion, particularly on Java where population numbers multiplied rapidly, creating a terrible burden for contemporary Indonesia. Today Java, with 7 percent of the land area, contains over 60 percent of the population. Unlike the Spanish in the Philippines, the Dutch put little emphasis on fomenting cultural and religious change; hence the traditional cultures remained generally unchallenged. Few Indonesians had access to formal education. Nonetheless, colonialism had contributed mightily to undermining traditional community and identity. The gradual spread of individualistic capitalism also eroded the more communal values of the traditional villages. Essentially the Dutch "created" Indonesia (the Dutch East Indies) as an interlinked political unit. But the colony remained highly regionalized and necessarily decentralized.

Nationalism, Popular Culture, and the Emergence of Kroncong

Within a context of economic dislocation, urbanization, increasing resentment, and colonial repression, nationalist forces grew. Some of this nationalism had an ethnic or regional focus, but many among the small intelligentsia group began to envision a unified and independent nation. Their goals were not only political; they also wanted to build a unifying culture and language. As a nationalist organization put it in 1928, expressing their goals: "One nation—Indonesia, one people—Indonesian, one language—Indonesian."[21] Among the fruits of nationalism was a song, "Indonesia Raya," written for a youth congress in 1928. Later, after independent Indonesia became the reality that was only a dream in the 1920s, it would become the national anthem.

The ties between nationalism and the creation of a common language were clear, as one Indonesian historian noted:

> The problem of a national language for the Indonesian people gradually changed in character. Since 1908 the Indonesian intelligentsia had struggled to create organizations to stir the consciousness of the common people and encourage their development and progress. . . . On the premise that only by uniting the entire Indonesian people could they generate a force strong enough to challenge the colonial power, they began spontaneously to look for a language which could be understood by the great majority of the people.[22]

Increasingly Bahasa Indonesia, based on the Malay marketplace lingua franca, displaced the regional languages as the language of politics, literature, and popular culture in the more densely populated regions, and especially in the cities. Gradually an Indonesian—as opposed to a strictly regional urban—culture spread through the archipelago. These developments heartened some observers, reminding them of the age-old patterns of adaptation through coexistence: "The ability to accept new influences and to add them to the existing diversity of elements in her culture lies, perhaps, at the core of the Indonesian identity."[23] The Japanese, who occupied the colony during World War II, patronized the nationalists and,

"Indonesia Raya" ("Greater Indonesia")

Indonesia, my native country.
Land which bore and nurtured me.
Here I stand now, prepared and eager.
Pledging you my fealty.
Indonesia, my nation.
You my mother, I your son.
Let us shout with voices united.
Indonesia shall be one.
Come to life, nation mine.
Come to life native land.
Oh my country, my people arise.
Let our spirit awake, let our bodies awake.
To create Indonesia raya . . .
independent and free.[24]

as the war turned against them, armed them so as to resist the return of the Dutch.

The dramatic changes of the twentieth century generated many new artistic forms. Inevitably some of the earliest changes would be theatrical, for theater is an integral part of Southeast Asian culture. It is necessary to sketch the modern history of Indonesian theater because—unlike in the West—it constituted a major component of popular culture, closely related to musical development as well as to nationalism, education, and topical comment. James Brandon summarizes the significance:

> Theatre has been more than just entertainment. In addition to providing aesthetic pleasure, emotional release through empathic response, and even a means for accomplishing communal celebration of ritual events, theatre also functions as a channel for communication . . . reaching the largely illiterate populations of the countryside and cities. . . . What is notable about the theatre in Southeast Asia, as compared with Europe or America, is the degree to which it is involved in the educative process. . . . Strong artistic patterns, or codes, make of Southeast Asian drama a rather special communication medium. Throughout Southeast Asia plays are used to communicate new ideas in similar ways. . . . It seems unlikely that we [in Western societies] shall ever in our own theatre match the subtle communication possibilities which inherently exist in Southeast Asian theatre as a result of its long artistic traditions.[25]

At the end of the nineteenth century a popular urban theatre mixing music, acting, and dancing known as *bangsawan* (or, in Java, komedie stambul) spread widely through the archipelago, particularly in Java and Sumatra. The music mixed Indonesian, Indian, Middle Eastern, Chinese, and Western influences. Hence it reflected increasing ethnic heterogeneity and promoted musical interaction. The performances contained considerable humor and were based chiefly on highly improvised versions of well-known folk stories and historical legends. A multiethnic genre, bangsawan played for all types of audiences, producing a genuinely popular theater tradition. They were equally at home performing before kings and noblemen, town fairs and village folk. The bangsawan offered not a slice of life but rather a panorama of existence. This Malay-language genre flourished from the 1920s through the 1950s, but by the 1990s it had nearly disappeared as a popular entertainment.[26]

New musical styles also began to appear.[27] In northern Sumatra and on Malaya's west coast, a type of ensemble known as orkes melayu (also known as *Melayu Deli*) became popular, playing an instrumental and vocal music heavily influenced by Arab and Indian models. The songs, often on Islamic themes, were based on traditional poems known as *pantun*. By the 1930s the ensembles had modernized their music with the use of accor-

The Kroncong Style

The term *kroncong* implies a continually changing repertoire and style of music that developed first on Java and later spread throughout the archipelago and Malaya. It employs a distinctive, string-dominated instrumental accompaniment that conveys (like reggae or juju) a well-defined musical texture of a languid vocal style married to simple harmonies. The stream derives from a guitarlike instrument first brought by the Portuguese in the 1500s. Gradually it developed as a blend of Western instruments and ideas superimposed on the intricate rhythmic patterns characteristic of the Javanese gamelan. The vocal style is reminiscent of court gamelan but the harmonic and melodic roots are definitely European, especially Portuguese in the broad sense of the music played by Portuguese descendants and mestizo (mixed Portuguese-Asian) groups settled around the Dutch colonial capital of Batavia (now Jakarta). The longevity of kroncong can be partly explained by the beautiful, melodic nature of the music; like gamelan it effectively creates a mood. Most of the famous kroncong singers were Eurasians.[28]

dions and other Western instruments. Some groups sang in Indonesian, others in Arabic. The popularity of this genre was mainly restricted to Sumatra and the slums of Jakarta. While orkes melayu groups still exist, the popularity of the genre declined considerably in the postwar years, with most fans and musicians drawn from among the elderly. All over the islands local popular styles emerged. In some of the suburbs of Jakarta a music known as *gambang kromong*, mixing Chinese and indigenous elements, became a local favorite. After World War II it was transformed by incorporating Western pop styles and, later, Indonesian dance beats.[29]

Of wider popularity has been kroncong, a highly syncretic, acculturated traditional style that emerged out of a colonial mixture of East and West. Kroncong was a product of five centuries of cultural encounter between Indonesian and European cultures in western Java. Like other similar hybrid musics with lower-class origins (reggae, blues, highlife, marabi, calypso, Portuguese *fado*), kroncong was often dismissed as lowbrow by the sociocultural elites.

Kroncong appeared in the melting pot of multiethnic Batavia and the surrounding villages as a distinctly lower-class music, popular especially with Eurasians, mestizos, and ruffians. Like fado, it often had a quality of gentle melancholy or nostalgia and frequently dealt with romantic themes. But it could also serve as a venue for lullabies, dancing, and occasionally topical commentary. Many songs celebrate scenic beauty, idyllic villages, or the sweetness of these languid, sentimental melodies themselves. One of the oldest and most famous songs, "Oud Batavia" ("Old Batavia"), recalls the bygone life of the colonial capital:

Old Batavia
I think back, yes, to those pleasant times . . .
Full moon, with a sweet girl . . .
Mixed sauced vegetables, skewered barbecue meat and spicy tripe soup.[30]

Another famous song in this genre, "Bengawan Solo," celebrates the Solo River in central Java:

Bengawan Solo, ancient your histories span.
Linking present to past, linking the life of the soil to man.
In the summer's heat, your streams are sluggish and slow.
In the rainy season's height far afield your banks overflow.
At your source the deep springs of Solo, Mount Seribu holds them fast.
Now you flow on through fertile rice fields, down to the sea at last.
Here are ships of trade and when your journey's over.
Sailors brave the ocean seeking some far distant shore.[31]

During the long period of Dutch control, the Batavian Portuguese maintained some of their identity and traditions—including kroncong—while intermarrying and intermixing with other groups. While most kroncong songs have been performed in Bahasa Indonesia in recent decades, some older musicians still use Portuguese or Dutch. In the nineteenth century kroncong began to spread from Batavia to other parts of Java, a development aided by its increasing popularity with sailors and soldiers attracted to its romantic themes. In the process it became somewhat more Javanized or gamelanized. Soon wandering minstrels adopted the style for street music. So did some youth gangs known as *buaya kroncong* ("kroncong crocodiles"). The buaya kroncong has been described as

> a young male with no visible means of support, yet who dresses well, often flamboyantly, is handsome, virile, wears a "fierce" . . . moustache, spends his time gambling . . . drinking and seducing women. . . . The buaya kroncong were usually street singers who earned a small income from handouts. Often a female who was assumed to be a prostitute joined the group as a vocalist.[32]

Only during the 1940s did kroncong finally begin to lose its déclassé, disreputable image.

During the 1890s kroncong ensembles were added to some of the bangsawan theater troupes and other popular entertainment genres. The establishment of radio broadcasting in 1925 further popularized the genre, but also heralded the split into many varieties, including some based on American or Latin American dance rhythms. A later variation, *langgam jawa*, developed as a Javanese version with a pronounced gamelan texture.

Kroncong music also was featured in some of the pioneering films made in the 1930s, furthering its reputation as a national art form. By the 1940s kroncong was viewed correctly as an essentially Indonesian rather than foreign creation. The liner notes to a local recording in the 1950s proclaimed the connection:

> Soft music and a sweet voice fill the air. Sight and sound delight the soul. . . . Medan or Padang, Jakarta or Surabaya, Bandjarmasin or Pontianak, Menado or Makassar, Ambon. . . . Wherever [Malay] peoples live, there you will find kroncong—melodious, charming kroncong, singing the warm and human sentiments of the Indonesian heart.[33]

Some nationalists within the artistic community adopted kroncong for their own purposes, using both cinema and music to reach a larger public. One nationalist music festival in 1938 attempted to elevate kroncong to a national music. Although some of these attempts failed, kroncong gradually became strongly identified in the public mind with an obviously Malay character. The spread of kroncong was aided by radio, which nationalists early perceived as a critical means of communication. In 1933 the first local station broadcasting in Indonesia had appeared. During the Japanese Occupation this and other stations were used by nationalist leaders to spread anti-Dutch, pro-independence sentiments. The Japanese banned most other types of Westernized music from the mass media, giving kroncong musicians a more national audience. Kroncong competitions continued to be held in night markets *(pasar malam)*, and along with other types of permitted popular culture, they provided a much-needed respite from the tribulations of occupation. Although the Japanese employed the medium for songs supporting their rule, protest songs in kroncong style also appeared against the harshness and exploitation of Japanese rule.[34]

The Indonesian Revolution of the late 1940s, a bitter and bloody struggle, achieved independence in 1950. Nationalists controlled several radio stations during the Indonesian Revolution and employed that advantage to spread their message. They adapted kroncong as a weapon, with many *lagu perjuangan* ("struggle songs") written in the genre and broadcast on revolutionary-controlled radio stations. Hence kroncong came to represent not just lower-class but also nationalist aspirations. Even today most of these songs are performed in kroncong style. As ethnomusicologist Judith Becker argues, "it was the kroncong composers, who . . . wrote all of the songs which are the Indonesian equivalents of 'The Star-Spangled Banner' or 'America the Beautiful.'"[35] The nationalist songs are known as *kroncong revolusi* ("revolutionary kroncong") and deal with issues of freedom and independence. One of the best-known songs was "Kroncong Merdeka" ("Freedom Kroncong"):

Freedom, freedom forever
Every struggle of the Indonesian nation
Is faced with hindrances and obstacles
But our youth will always defend it.[36]

Indonesia has been a quasi-dictatorship for most of the post-independence period. During the 1950s and early 1960s, Indonesia was led by the charismatic but quixotic President Sukarno, the father of Indonesian independence whose strength were creating national solidarity. Indeed, he was a man with a profound artistic sensibility whose personal style and political leadership were rooted in traditional artistic and cultural concepts. The multiparty system of the early 1950s proved unstable, divisive, and volatile, with constantly fluctuating cabinet coalitions. Sukarno's increasingly authoritarian but also populist government labored hard to create a sense of national unity and culture, in part through the manipulation of nationalist and religious symbols. Of those years, Dutch sociologist W. H. Wertheim writes that "the formation of a national Indonesian culture would seem to be still in its beginnings. It is very far from a new crystallized way of life."[37]

During the later 1950s and early 1960s, Brigadier General Rudi Pirngadie, a veteran of the revolution sometimes called "General Kroncong," attempted to create an updated (and somewhat westernized) version (known as kroncong beat) that could serve as "a concrete symbol of nationalist ideology." On his famous album *A Tribute to Heroes*, he called kroncong a "peoples music . . . that is expressive of the mood of man and nature," and offered soft, melodious, but patriotic-type songs extolling the heroes of the revolution. For example, "Rankaian Bunga" ("A Wreath of Flowers") lauds selfless heroism:

Go, my faithful hero, go to your nation's defense
Do not waver!
Willingly I let you go to defend our Motherland.

Other songs, such as "Gugur Bunga," lamented those who died for the cause.

President Sukarno supported Pirngadie's attempt to create a national music for international consumption. While the experiment demonstrated that virtually any song could be adapted to a broad kroncong style, the watered-down arrangements failed to perpetuate the earlier nationalist image of the music. By the 1940s many of the Jakarta elite, furthermore, developed a taste for a similar hybrid style but of clearer foreign origins: Hawaiian music. This affinity would persist into the 1980s.[38]

Kroncong appears to have been a very adaptable musical style, in part due to the improvisational nature of the music and lyrics. During the tumul-

"Gugur Bunga" ("A Flower Falls")

How can my heart not be sad?
My hero has fallen and left me lonely!
Where now is my hero, faithful defender of nation and land?
He lies dead, his duty done!
But for one that falls, a thousand rise
And great will be the Nation.
My own heart's flower lies in the garden of devotion
Adorning the land of his birth and increasing the glory of our country.[39]

tuous Sukarno era, however, kroncong gradually declined in popularity, seen by many as overly mellow (even insipid) and—ironically, given its origins—bourgeois. Contemporary kroncong ensembles include a variety of stringed instruments (such as guitar and violin) and flutes. Although declining in popularity after the 1960s, the genre has not been completely displaced by other popular styles and still retains some ardent (mostly aging) followers in many cities of Indonesia and Malaysia. Given its nostalgia value for the generation that came to power in the revolution, various governmental bodies have sponsored groups or competitions in an attempt to maintain the influence of the music. There is also a market for a variant known as *pop kroncong*, where contemporary pop songs are presented in kroncong vocal and instrumental style. Kroncong in all its variations accounted for a mere 5 percent of cassette releases in the 1980s.[40]

In the 1950s and 1960s a new form of proletarian theater called *ludruk* became widely popular in some Javan cities; the closely related *loddrok* also developed in nearby Madura.[41] The styles were considered crude compared to the elite wayang. Mixing music, comedy, and satire, the ludruk performances generally depict the problems and issues of modern society, including social criticism and the special problems of slum dwellers. According to Peacock, the plays contrast elite and commoner behavior as well as progressive and conservative attitudes toward modernization, in the process allowing the audience to confront their fears and frustrations while promoting social action and vicarious identification with the characters presented. Hence it constitutes an important rite of modernization. Many of the songs, especially those sung by transvestites and clowns, expose hypocrisy or critique Indonesian society and the deteriorating economic conditions of the modern era. The Madurese loddrok concentrates on the opposition between villages and cities.

The accompanying gamelan music has been crucial to the mood and message; the musicians, watching the stage, improvise what they feel is appropriate for the current action. In this context it could perhaps be argued

Ludruk Song (Early 1960s)

"The people defended the country when there was a revolution;
The people all worked together.
The government should remember this.
Let us remember the people's suffering now!
They need rice, sugar and oil . . .
The price of food is increasing.
Women are depressed.
The price of cigarettes is rising; many men roll their own now. . . .
People who make profits feel happy—but neglect their relatives.
Relatives may suffer, but the new rich don't care."[42]

that gamelan almost becomes a true popular music, reaching a mass audience with a message supporting the themes of the ludruk play. In 1972, one-fifth of east Javan radio listeners identified ludruk broadcasts as their favorite programs. By the 1980s ludruk rapidly faded as a commercial venture. It was generally superseded in central and eastern Java by newer genres such as the several folk-tinged "people's theaters" of Jogjakarta as well as the Surakarta- or Solo-based *Gapit* theater, a modernized Javanese-language medium related to ludruk that utilizes gamelan music in portraying the social world of the powerless. Their performances explore the ways common people confront the challenges to traditional cultural forms generated by capitalism and technological change.[43] Like other arts, theater has regional dimensions and could serve to articulate regional identity and the relationship to the nation.

By the early 1960s some outside observers believed that Indonesia badly needed a sense of unity to reverse a clear cultural disintegration resulting from her recent history. Optimists could point to the increasing centrality of Bahasa Indonesia in politics, education, and the developing popular culture, although millions of Indonesians continued to speak regional or ethnic languages. Leftist intellectuals, many of them associated with the influential Communist Party and its Institute of Peoples Culture (LEKRA), worked to create a class-conscious, anti-imperialist art based on the values of—and communicating with—the common people. That thrust necessarily included attacks on Western popular culture as decadent and escapist, but it also brought the left into conflict with other intellectuals espousing a more conservative view of national culture.[44] Sukarno's nationalistic and moderately socialistic but poorly implemented economic policies also contributed to a severe economic crisis by the early 1960s, as well as deepening divisions between and within leftist, Islamic, and military forces.

By 1965 Indonesia had become a turbulent cockpit of combustible social and political pressures.

The Changing Context of the "New Order"

In 1965–1966, Indonesia experienced her greatest crisis as an independent nation. After a failed coup attempt by a small military faction with leftist sympathies, a group of long-discontented generals from more conservative military branches seized power, launching a brutal campaign to eliminate all leftist organizations and their members. The large, powerful Communist Party (PKI), a highly influential force among many poor peasants and nominal Muslims in Java, was a particular target, although the evidence that party leaders had been involved in the coup has remained far from conclusive.[45] A bloodbath ensued that killed upwards of a half million Indonesians, mostly although by no means exclusively from communist or communist-aligned groups. Most PKI leaders were killed or arrested, with thousands of leftists kept in prison camps for many years. Communist, Marxist, and other politically progressive ideologies were eliminated as forces in the country's political and intellectual life and nominal Muslims faced an uncertain future.

Since 1966 the "New Order" Indonesian government headed by General-turned-President Suharto has mixed military and civilian leadership and allowed some dissent and opposition within limited but fluctuating parameters that exclude Marxists. These policies achieved stability and facilitated the emergence of an educated urban middle class, but at the price of some systematic repression of all social forces as well as the imposition of a highly manipulated political structure. During the 1980s a limited multiparty parliamentary system developed, but GOLKAR, a functional coalition of groups allied to the military and bureaucracy, dominates somewhat stage-managed elections and the political agenda in what has been called a "hegemonic party system."[46] The electoral campaigns, routinely but suggestively labeled "Festivals of Democracy," are ritualistic in rhetoric and orderly in intent, with large numbers of security police. But the order often breaks down in practice, providing an entertainment component in which the attentive crowds eagerly await accidents or missteps that might facilitate excess and compromise the symbols of hegemonic power.[47] Nonetheless, behind the scenes the military remains the main arbiter of power.

The authorities, concerned with limiting the potential for disorder, considerably restrict the airing of opposing viewpoints and closely monitor the mass media, most of which practices self-censorship or comes under formal or informal government supervision, becoming in the process largely a partner of the government. The government views the media largely as an unofficial "bulletin" or "conveyor belt" for government information, and most editors promote close relationships with members of the ruling elite, if only to retain their jobs. Hence the media became an instrument for legitimating the state and its policies. This has a negative impact on public discourse. Although the press has often found ways to circumvent the laws (and political cartoonists have been adept at navigating through the political currents with satire), certain topics are studiously avoided, including Suharto's family (widely believed to be using his position to blatantly enrich themselves and their cronies), separatist movements, and ethnoreligious issues. During the Suharto years those who hoped more democratization would accompany economic growth clashed with those who feared relaxing political controls would unleash destabilizing conflicts. Between 1982 and 1993, several newspapers were closed down for covering overly sensitive issues. And in 1992 two college students were arrested on the stage at a rock music concert in central Java for making puns deemed disrespectable to Islam; both were sentenced to several years in prison.[48] There has also been a tendency to "hegemonize" popular arts to serve the regime's socioeconomic ends, such as converting sometimes vulgar regional dances into more sedate tourist forms.[49]

Suharto transformed Indonesia into even more of a "bureaucratic polity" in which power and decisions in the political system are limited chiefly to state employees, including the military officer core. Bureaucratic polities need to encourage economic expansion while simultaneously preventing rapid change and instability. Lacking a strong indigenous commercial class, Indonesia increasingly developed what some observers call a "bureaucratic capitalism," with many government corporations and the heavy involvement of top leaders (including powerful members of Suharto's family) in economic activity. This bureaucratic capitalism combined with a strong Western presence has generated considerable economic development, but it has failed to solve (and in some ways has intensified) the severe problems of poverty, overpopulation, and rampant corruption. By the late 1980s business groups were becoming more assertive in policy making, lessening the monopoly of bureaucrats and officers, and increasing pressures for a more open system.[50]

Indonesia also become dangerously dependent on the fluctuating world price for oil, which by the late 1970s provided some 70 percent of the national budget. By the early 1980s oil represented 78 percent of export earnings.[51] By the late 1980s, however, the collapse of oil prices and development of other industries had greatly reduced the role of oil but also provided fewer funds for the national budget. By 1995 Indonesia had accumulated an enormous foreign debt of nearly $100 billion. The rapid development of mining, forestry, and cash crop agriculture inevitably has taken a terrible toll on the environment. Unlike the Sukarno regime, which kept on good terms with the Soviet Bloc and patronized nationalist (often left-wing) cultural activities and groups, the Suharto government shifted to a strongly pro-Western stance. This policy allied the country with the Western

Bloc and opened Indonesia to both Western investment and Western mass-mediated popular culture. Yet the government is also interested in balancing rapid change with a "national culture" to express nonmaterial aspects of life (including "values").[52]

In many respects Suharto's New Order has improved Indonesia's economic position significantly. The Western-educated technocrats who staff the bureaucracy dramatically reduced inflation, increased per capita income (to around $1,000 per capita annually) and life expectancy, and fostered an annual growth rate of nearly 5 percent, a major improvement over the "basket case" economy of the early 1960s. In 1976 some 40 percent of Indonesians were believed to live below the poverty line; by 1987 the official figure had been reduced to 17–20 percent and by 1994 to 14 percent, although the near poor raised that figure substantially (to around 30 percent). However, in urban areas generally half the population live in poverty, and the percentage of income received by the lowest 40 percent of the population dropped from 25 percent in 1964 to 10 percent in 1980. There was also wide variation among regions of the country. While official unemployment stands at under 3 percent, some 40 percent of the workforce are underemployed, many fully employed workers earn less than the official minimum wage, and the burgeoning number of school-leavers struggle to find jobs. Low wage scales attract considerable foreign investment but insure that many employed workers live in poverty. Labor union organizers and strike leaders risk firing or worse. Hence the reality for many Indonesians in the 1980s was bleak.[53]

Journalist Michael Vatikiotis described the reality for many Indonesians in the 1980s:

> Economic growth increased absolute incomes, but at the same time widened income disparities and created pockets of opulence and wealth juxtaposed with lacunae of neglect and poverty. . . . Better educated and with far greater access to the mass media than ever before, people living in poor conditions were less fatalistic about their social and economic difficulties. Slum-dwellers in Jakarta's Tanjung Priok port area spent most of their meager income buying fresh water, but just across the street from their permanently inundated hovels, better-off Jakartans were paying more than the slum-dwellers could dream of in a month on one hour with a night-club hostess. Villagers in Lombok [Island] . . . knew that their land was being appropriated by the rich and powerful from Jakarta.[54]

While most Indonesians remain either devout or nominal (usually termed "statistical") Muslims, the government discourages Islamic revivalism (or fundamentalism) and militancy as a threat to national unity and has worked hard, with considerable success, to co-opt the Muslim organizations. Political leaders have found it necessary to carefully balance the potentially conflictive ethnic, religious, and socioeconomic groups in a country that has already witnessed much turbulence. Hence they address the fears of the small but influential Christian minority, patronize the unpopular but economically critical Chinese business class, and avoid inflaming substantial non-Javanese antagonism toward the numerically dominant Javanese. In the late 1970s the several Islamic-based political parties, ranging from traditionalist to modernist in their orientation, were forced to merge into one large grouping—the Development Unity Party (PPP)—diminishing their oppositional potential and facilitating stronger government control. The other main opposition group, the small but growing Indonesian Democratic Party (PDI), maintains a nationalist and populist stance but avoids a strongly assertive posture. It enjoys considerable support from urban intellectuals and reformers, some of whom once had links to the disbanded Indonesian Nationalist Party of Sukarno. The traditional Javanese emphasis on harmony and consensus has clearly been incorporated into the national political process.

But, given the elimination of left-wing forces in 1965–1966, it is Islam that came to provide the chief oppositional force in Indonesia. The thrust can be summarized as follows:

> There is the interregional focus of resistance offered by Islam. Possessed of a coherent value system which is in opposition to the often perceived excesses in the culture of the state, and offering its own conception of modernity, "Islam" stands always in the shadow of "Indonesia," articulating resistance in the lives of individuals and in social organization.[55]

Many Muslims (especially from among the *santri*) oppose the secular policies of the government and desire a more Islamic approach to sociocultural and legal matters. Many resent the official syncretist ideology of *pancasila*, which they view as watering down Islam into a meaningless melting pot of concepts. A set of five principles established by President Sukarno in 1945 to defuse demands for an Islamic state and recognize cultural diversity, pancasila promotes tolerance and respect for all organized religions—as well as national unity. Government supporters perceive pancasila as one prong of an attempt to create an authentic and essentially secular national identity and culture. Unlike most Islamic countries, Islam was not even mentioned in the federal constitution. However, relatively few Muslims actively sought an official Islamic state. Furthermore, the missionary-oriented, highly dogmatic, culturally reactionary Islam that proves such a potent force in countries like Iran and Malaysia remains largely absent. Indeed, one strand of Islamic thought in Indonesia is progressive and democratic, attracting many intellectuals with an appeal for liberalizing social and political reform.[56]

Nonetheless, many Muslims developed a sense of unease and seek a government or social system more amenable to their needs. Islam provides for them a strong sense of identity and community. They perceive a society engulfed in corruption and (from their perspective) immorality. As anthropologist James Peacock notes, "night life . . . tends toward the lurid. . . . The Muslims protest vigorously (but sometimes view secretly) the *porno* that threatens to poison the indigenous mind."[57] Many also blame the government for poor living standards, a resentment enhanced by the widely reported cases of lavish lifestyles and massive greed and corruption among some of the elite. Some Muslims (and many intellectuals) are concerned with the high rates of poverty among urban slum dwellers and in the rural areas, where almost 80 percent of the population reside. Malnutrition constitutes a major problem, resulting in part from inefficient distribution of resources.

Many Indonesians find the changes of recent decades destabilizing socioeconomically and ideologically. There is an increasing tendency for formerly "statistical" Muslims to become more orthodox and hence sympathetic to Islamic appeals.[58] One of a group of Muslim-oriented students given public trials for oppositional activity in 1979 articulated the litany of complaints against the system:

> The lop-sided character of our society's social existence, typified by one group that gets richer by the day without having to perform any meaningful work, alongside millions of unemployed people who are forced to sell their dignity as human beings simply to avoid starvation. Social justice is far from a reality. Our present development, with its stress on economics, is of no benefit for the masses of the people, and is incapable of overcoming the danger of famine. . . . Our political life is frozen and our political dynamic is flaccid, as a result of a concentration of power which has made political bodies and state institutions incapable of functioning properly. Most people are afraid to express their opinions freely. . . . Our cultural life today is characterized by greedy opportunism, the craving to get rich quickly without doing any work, and the revival of feudalistic attitudes in a certain sector of society. . . . Because "they" want to get rich quick . . . they rip-off state funds, they sell their offices and positions to build houses, buy up company shares, etc.[59]

Tensions between Muslims and the civil administration flared in 1984 at Tanjung Priok, near Jakarta.[60] After the arrest of several Muslims protesting against a police raid on a prayer house, hundreds of demonstrators led by a popular preacher stormed a police station demanding the release of the detainees. Troops responded with gunfire, killing several protesters (eight by official count, many more according to the militants). Several hundred Muslims were detained and charged with subversion or sedition. Meanwhile other acts of violence, including bombings and vandalism of ancient pre-Islamic buildings, occurred elsewhere in Java. The government took the opportunity to arrest several intellectual dissidents who criticized the government's crackdown.

Eventually over a hundred men were tried and convicted for their connections to the Tanjung Priok activities. During the trials many detainees' disenchantment with core aspects of Indonesian political, economic, sociocultural, and religious life became clear. In particular their perception of Islam's appropriate role in contemporary Indonesia differed greatly from those of the political elite and many of the general public. From the perspective of many devout Muslims, their religion had been relegated to a "counterculture," and they had been "disinherited" because they refused to share the mostly secular or syncretic founding myths of the nation.[61] Islam seemed to have become more attractive despite (or perhaps because of) the efforts of the government to domesticate the appeal and castrate the political thrust. In an effort to defuse these tensions, Suharto attempted—with some success—to reconcile himself to more moderate Islamic groups, granting concessions in areas like education and law and even making a well-publicized pilgrimage to Mecca, with the aim of averting further Islamic activism in urban areas.[62] Given this situation, one might expect that oppositional discourse in music would necessarily contain a strong Islamic tinge.

Mass Mediation, Censorship, and the Evolving Popular Culture

Popular culture became a major feature of twentieth-century life and was increasingly commodified. Phonograph recording began in the 1920s, with

The Media and Society on Madura Island

Although still rare among the urban and rural lower classes, television has become the main cultural distraction of the middle and upper classes on Madura Island, just off Java's northeast coast. For these families—who speak Indonesian—TV offers a more modern social fantasy than that provided by a live performance, featuring romanticized stories set in the privileged circles of Indonesian or American society; these are circles with which these Madurese would like to identify. The central government's efforts at Indonesianization have strongly influenced them, so they no longer appreciate or enjoy local artistic practices. On the other hand, few in the rural areas and villages watch television regularly. While they sometimes gather around the TV in the village head's house, the commentaries in Indonesian remain to them incomprehensible. Radios can be found in households and stores having electrical power. In interior villages men often gather around the radio during daytime breaks or in the evenings. Radio broadcasts offer most of the art forms practiced in the region, but Madurese and Indonesian songs and dangdut music enjoy a large share of the time allocation. Hence urban and rural youth learn from radio about the latest hit singles and acquire cassettes from music shops or by copying. Wealthier city youth are most attracted to Western—especially American—music, while the lower classes chiefly appreciate the Indonesian or regional repertory broadcast by radio.[63]

three Chinese-Indonesian companies dominating the colonial industry. By the late 1950s new companies were being formed. The state-run recording company, Lokananta, was established in the mid-1950s primarily to provide music for the expanding radio broadcasting. By the middle 1960s private companies began to manufacture and market cassettes (mostly pirated works initially), prompting Lokananta to expand its own operations. Some recording companies were also established outside Jakarta, specializing on regional musics. Cassette technology greatly improved in the early 1970s, generating the formation of more companies producing more and cheaper recordings, hence greatly expanding the market for popular music.

Meanwhile, the oil boom gave more Indonesians purchasing power at the same time that mass mediation was popularizing new national and regional musical styles. A mid-1970s survey revealed that around half of young people in poor Jakarta neighborhoods owned their own radios. By the early 1980s perhaps half of the families in the country could afford to purchase cassettes and most Indonesians had access to a battery-powered cassette player as well as a radio. By 1980 a third of urban households also possessed television sets; by 1990 perhaps two-thirds of the entire population had regular access to broadcasts. The medium was used quite purposefully to spread developmental and nationalist ideals to villagers, while more closely connecting remote regions to the center. At the same time many traditional arts such as the *wayang golek purwa* (Sundanese rod-puppet theater) were modified by television, with practitioners adapting their length and style to broadcast needs and—through the resulting mass mediation—producing a "superstar" ethos for favored performers.[64]

The replacement of the earlier records with more cheaply produced cassettes democratized the music industry to some extent, allowing many more young musicians to record their songs, resulting in what Hatch terms an "alternative free flow of musics."[65] But this did not lead to homogenization; rather diversity has been the hallmark. "National Music" (popular music mostly utilizing Bahasa Indonesian lyrics for a national audience) increasingly dominated the output of private companies (reflecting audience tastes), while Lokananta gradually abandoned these styles to specialize on regional (especially Javanese) and traditional musics. In part this reflected economics and the intensity of market competition. But economics was not the only reason; the government record company also sought to avoid popular styles with the potential for political criticism, including the Western and Islamic-flavored mainstream of pop music. By the 1980s recording had become more centralized in Jakarta, with many of the regional companies shutting down as a result of an inadequate customer base and distribution problems. Indeed, the major distribution companies, known pejoratively as the "Glodok Mafia" because of their offices in Jakarta's Glodok Plaza, are reputed to have almost "life or death" control of popular music (including influence over lyrics and arrangements) by their decisions concerning what and who to market; they also compete fiercely for radio and television exposure as well as dominance in regional markets.[66]

These recordings reached the public chiefly through the mass media and cassette sales. In the early 1970s Indonesia had a low rate of radio ownership by world standards (perhaps twenty-five radios per thousand Indonesians), considerably less per capita than Malaysia, Thailand, and the Philippines. By the 1980s the situation had improved considerably. Somewhat over half of the population could receive radio programming, which had a large component of musical programs. The Indonesian government operated or controlled most stations until 1978, restricting or expanding exposure to musical products as policy fluctuated. By the late 1970s and early 1980s private stations appeared, and most adopted a policy of guarded openness that took into consideration local moral standards and government fears as well as commercial popularity. Television, introduced in 1962, was much less widespread, especially outside the major cities; but by the 1980s it had become a major entertainment and information medium in urban life and was also beginning to have a stronger impact on areas once culturally autonomous and remote from the metropolitan superculture. While a dynamic relationship between national and local cultural patterns developed, with reception practices strongly influenced by local experience (such as Islamic orthodoxy), nonetheless the expansion of mass media subtly supports the spread of the somewhat secular, modernist, and multiethnic national culture. The first private channel commenced broadcasting in Jakarta in 1988; by 1995, four others had been established. The gradual easing of government restrictions combined with changing public attitudes, especially in the cities, inevitably provided a fruitful context for new music, some of it with a critical tone.[67]

Some experts believe a "metropolitan superculture" developed that gradually reached out and homogenized the countryside to a considerable extent. Artistic styles, material culture, and political ideology were preeminent in the content, which was conveyed by the national language. Western cultural as well as urban influences—filtered through the prism of Jakarta—spread throughout the archipelago, although to what degree they took hold remains a matter of debate. Anthropologist Gloria Davis argues that:

> Indonesia's countryside is dependent on her cities; and hence the values to be imitated flow, for the most part, from the "culturally superior" to the "culturally inferior" and not the other way around. . . . Children in Indonesian schools sing songs selected in Jakarta, to tunes familiar in the United States. They read comic books, ride motorcycles, and wear Western dress. . . . The point I want to leave behind, however, is not just that tradition "is disappearing, and *fast*" . . . but that we might not want it any other way. If I am right, homogenization implies that people not only believe in and aspire to a richer and better life, but that they think they can get it.[68]

On the other hand, regional cities and even villages are also producing culture, allowing for some local genius and flavor in the complex interaction with the center.[69]

Popular musical tastes dramatically shifted with the transition from the Sukarno era to the New Order. For awhile the decline of kroncong corresponded to a rediscovery of the orkes melayu traditions from Sumatra and Malaya, which were also beginning to appear in local and Malayan films. Top performers like Ellya blended orkes melayu with aspects of the highly popular Indian film music to create a dynamic—even sensuous—and distinctly "Asian" sound known as irama hindustan ("Indian melody"). During the late 1960s, however, with a different political context, both kroncong and orkes melayu were overwhelmed by the massive importation of Western popular music styles, which had been prohibited during the Sukarno era. In the late 1950s, under pressure from the procommunist cultural group LEKRA, radio banned rock 'n' roll and Sukarno condemned it as decadent; indeed, local groups playing Western rock were sometimes harassed or even jailed, as with the Beatles clones Koes Bersaudara in 1965.[70] Fans had to listen to overseas radio services. For awhile, regional musics flourished as an alternative.

Ironically, the dynamics of Indonesian politics in these years led to an expatriate Indonesian influence on popular musics elsewhere. During and after the Indonesian Revolution, thousands of Indonesians who supported the Dutch forces—including Eurasians as well as some thirteen thousand South Moluccans from the Ambon Island region—emigrated to the Netherlands. Some of them (or their children) became active in the music scene, developing an audience for kroncong and Hawaiian music; the former became a staple of the émigré community's older generation, reflecting their nostalgia and homesickness for a lost homeland. Younger musicians even invented a rock kroncong sound. During the 1950s Indonesia-born musicians such as Johnny Tielman created a hybrid music known as *Indorock*, which became a major and pathbreaking component of the Dutch popular music industry. Aspects of this music later influenced the Merseybeat sound of groups like the Beatles. At the same time Indonesian musicians who settled in Australia, especially jazz-influenced Ambonese guitarist Lodewyk Nanlohy (better known as Lou Casch), became major influences in the evolution of Australian rock and roll. Little of their music was heard in Indonesia. The famous American rock group of the 1970s and 1980s, Van Halen, was founded by members of an Indonesian family who migrated to Holland and then to California.[71]

Some Western popular musical styles did infiltrate Indonesia during the later Sukarno years. During the 1950s, radio (especially a station operated by the armed forces) introduced Western popular singers like Bing Crosby and Doris Day. Indonesian singers such as Rachmat Kartolo, Titiek Puspa, and Erni Djohan developed a derivative Western-influenced pop music of romantic songs. But "tear-jerkers" such as Rachmat's "Patah

Hati" ("Broken Hearted") were sometimes banned for "weakening" the revolution. Some popular songs of that era reflected clear Western influence, such as "Si Penjaga Sapi" ("The Cowboy"):

I'm a cowboy
Yodel le yo yo yo li dei . . .
When the evening comes
And the cows go back to the corral . . .
The cowboy takes a rest.

By the mid-1960s Bill Haley and Elvis Presley were competing on the radio with Indonesian singers like Norma Sanger and Bing Slamet. Three decades later, local Elvis impersonators can still be found in Jakarta nightclubs.[72]

Under the New Order, control of the arts and media by the government has been inconsistent, but generally Indonesia enjoyed a thriving and vibrant artistic scene—including music. Between the mid-1960s and 1990s, Indonesians developed a wide variety of popular music styles, some of which proved conducive to sociopolitical comment. Indeed, the popular music scene would have to be considered as unusually dynamic and vital. These popular forms displayed fundamental divergences from earlier patterns of evolution, dissemination, social meaning, and style.[73] Western popular musical styles developed a larger following, with the songs of the Beatles, Rolling Stones, Deep Purple, and other rock groups blared over radio and television. Rock concerts became fashionable, and Western-influenced rock and pop groups like Koes Plus, D'Lloyd, and the Mercy's achieved wide popularity during the

The "Disco Way of Life"

"It is Jakarta at 2:00 A.M., any night of the year. Outside one of the capital's many discotheques is a gathering of *becak* drivers. They are singing and dancing the *joget*, the popular Malay folk-based dance. A few hundred meters away is one of Jakarta's discotheques with its glaring neon lights promising fun, amusement, and happiness at a given price. Inside, men and women are dancing the latest 'hit' in New York, London, or Paris. They are well dressed, elegant, beautiful or handsome. Becak drivers "jogeting" and cosmopolitan Jakarta 'hussling'—two human groups with a similar leisure. But an unfathomable chasm divides the naked labor force from westernized society, with all the appearances of the Western world but without its contents. Appearances in the sense of way of life, leisure, clothing. The 'disco way of life' in Jakarta describes a form of disruption of the Indonesian social and cultural fabric through an unbalanced penetration of the Western way of life. All along the road to and from disco subculture, the path is covered by traps: advertisements, big luxury cars, sophisticated electronic equipment. This social and moral pressure through goods and services leads to the desire to consume."—Irwin Ramedhan[74]

An upscale restaurant and nightclub complex on the shore near Jakarta, built in traditional style and featuring live music. 1971 photo by author.

late 1960s and early 1970s. Consequently, the influences from these mass-mediated models were extensive. There was also an urban audience for jazz, although local jazzmen such as the pop-fusion keyboardist Indra Lesmana had to spend much of their time in North American or Australia to achieve financial success and international acclaim.

Popular music became a major component of the background for daily life. It needs to be stressed that, with several exceptions based partly on local traditions, these pop styles reflect to some extent a lingering (to some critics, pervasive) cultural neocolonialism that leads to the emulation of "superior" Western models. Yet the reality has been more complex; many popular genres are only partly derivative and, in true Indonesian fashion, demonstrate a talent for syncretism—even if observers cannot agree on identifying a truly Indonesian popular music. Not all observers have applauded these patterns. Some view the process as a kind of cultural genocide. For example, in the late 1970s an Indonesian critic, journalist Erwin Ramedhan, described the impact of what he termed "the disco way of life" of the major cities, the leisure setting where the process of cultural loss begins and ends. This "discoization" is not merely the harmless diversion of a small privileged minority oriented toward Western values and standards. Rather, he claimed, it is a spreading phenomenon as both the rural and urban middle class absorb the impact of disco subculture by way of the messages conveyed through films, radio, and television, in the process uprooting traditional values of life, love, family, and community. By the 1980s, discos had to compete with another foreign import—karaoke bars.[75]

Similar opinions on the deleterious influences of popular culture accompanied most of the musical developments. In fact, the term *pop* in Indonesian often means something light rather than serious; pop culture, then, has been considered a backward and illegitimate or deviant variant of cultural development. Periodicals aimed at middle-class Indonesians have seldom discussed popular culture and when they have, as in a series of articles in the intellectual journal *Prisma* in 1977, in the middle-class magazine *Tempo* in the 1980s, and in various periodicals in 1995, the coverage tends to be shallow and ambivalent. These judgments reflect deep fears that the country's culture could be overwhelmed by externally generated influences, hence unraveling the fabric of sociocultural life and destroying the national identity. Indeed, overt or covert fear of a materialistic and corrupting cultural imperialism as reflected in derivative musics permeates many of the essays.[76]

Given these attitudes, Indonesian cultural observers, including ethnomusicologists, have for the most part demonstrated little inclination to study popular music. Some view the form as simply crude, ultracommercial, and a harness on the artistic imagination and the tradition of improvisation. Others want only to devote their attention to the fast-disappearing traditional musics and dances. Some ethnomusicology students have strongly criticized the neglect by universities and governments of indigenous music. The cartoons of graduate student Yulianus Limbeng in the ethnomusicology bulletin *Hoho* have been described by ethnomusicologist Margaret Kartomi:

> His caricatures attack . . . the promotion of popular music in the university in particular and in Indonesian society in general, which causes the "traditional music to weep". . . . One of his caricatures . . . shows an ethnomusicology student departing to record in the field while saying "No!" to a barbarian pop musician, and another shows a fat businessman getting richer through the sales of electronic sound equipment and software.[77]

The corpus of studies by Indonesian scholars concerning rock and pop, whether homegrown or imported, is therefore rather meager.[78]

Many of the emerging popular arts developed a critical awareness, with practitioners learning quickly (and often creatively) how to make their points without overtly violating government guidelines and censorship. As political scientist Bill Liddle suggests: "To read [magazines like] *Tempo*, *Kompas*, *Prisma*, or a modern novel or short story, to watch a play, a movie, or a dance performance, or to go to an art gallery, is to recognize that there is a vital and dynamic alternative to officialese in the modern culture itself."[79] These patterns have been particularly apparent in theater, literature, and art, providing a model for popular musicians. Even wayang kulit maintains a political component. In recent decades many puppeteers have addressed contemporary material, commenting on the foibles and misdeeds of leaders and nonleaders. Various political factions (communists, nationalists, royalists, and New Order adherents) have utilized both wayang and gamelan to spread their vision. The political immunity once enjoyed by dalangs, however, was eroded after 1965, with overt criticism of local luminaries being frowned upon. Indeed, government permits are required for performance, and some puppeteers experienced imprisonment for their procommunist sympathies.

Wayang could be utilized to serve the purposes of the New Order government, as it also served Sukarno's regime. Suharto has expected wayang performances to uplift the people while delivering a message of development (economic and spiritual).[80]

Beginning in the mid-1970s with the New Art Movement, a substantial group of artists devoted their work to social and environmental issues. By the late 1980s, some engaged artists lent their talents to various nongovernmental organizations seeking to transform Indonesian realities. They view their work as a vehicle to convey a message to their audiences.[81] Australian scholar Paul Tickell, reflecting the view of many specialists in literary criticism, contends that literature is the product of social process and hence cannot be separated from society and politics, particularly given the relationship between language and nationalism in Indonesia.[82] Similar arguments can be made for theater and popular music.

Literature had been highly politicized during the revolutionary era and Sukarno years, with nationalist and social change sentiments common.[83] But there was a long struggle between those advocating "engaged" and others promoting "detached" writing. By the 1970s a division between serious literature (written by and for the educated urban elite) and popular literature (for uncritical and politically apathetic readers) had grown enormously. The latter largely dealt with the triad of *isteri* ("wife," women's novels), *cinta* ("romance"), and *arjuna* ("youth"). There was also a flourishing popular literature on Islamic themes, especially studies of the Qur'an (Koran), which tended to promote religious orthodoxy and piety in an officially heterogeneous state that some Muslims mistrusted. While many serious novelists and poets avoid sociopolitical themes and stress mystical or absurdist motifs, a few others continue to publish work with historical or political implications.

The bohemian and charismatic performance poet W. G. Rendra, who received his higher education in New York, often skirts political tolerance with his provocative verse, as in his 1990 critique of development policy:

I see developed countries giving economic aid
and as a result many people from the Third World
are losing their lands so the rich can play golf,
Or so a dam can give electric power
to industries with foreign capital.
And the unfortunate people . . . get compensation
for every square meter of their land,
with money that has the same value
as a packet of American cigarettes.[84]

Sometimes, as with Pramoedya Ananta Toer, a strong proponent for socially relevant art jailed for fifteen years for his procommunist leanings, controversial writing results in a banning of the work. When Pramoedya won an international writing award in 1995 for his work (mostly unavailable in Indonesia), many of his antagonists in the literary world protested, confirming that many writers had been implicated in the political battles of the Sukarno and Suharto eras.[85]

Modern theater has long carried political messages.[86] In colonial times, playwrights utilized romantic heroes from classical mythology to symbolize the new Indonesian. During the Sukarno era, socialist realism and alienation were dominant themes. Under the New Order, some playwrights skirt the edge of accepted topics and sometimes see their work banned. For example, Rendra and his Bengkel Teater were banned between 1978 and 1986, while Norbertus Riantiarno's examination of the underclass, "The Cockroach Opera," was closed down in 1985. But many innovative theater groups have appeared, mostly in Jakarta and Jogjakarta, some of which take on the trappings of liberation theater and have the goal of politicizing or empowering peasants and workers. By the 1990s labor theater groups had emerged as one form of working-class mobilization. All had to struggle to overcome the reality that modern theater remained a rather elitist art form rooted in the urban middle class, with few roots among the dispossessed, which is one reason why some theater figures (including Rendra) were cooperating with popular music figures by the late 1980s in order to broaden their audience.

For most of its history the film industry has lacked the critical focus of literature or theater.[87] The film industry began in the 1920s, but films in Malay-Indonesian language first appeared in 1937. Film in Indonesia rarely escaped an interlinking with political pressures. During the Sukarno years communist and noncommunist filmmakers battled to define Indonesian film. In the 1950s a few directors released films with realist themes, but commercial considerations (combined with restrictive sociopolitical attitudes) soon became ascendant (including the growing popularity of imported films). After 1965 directors with leftist sympathies were imprisoned or blacklisted. Hence most Indonesian films are as escapist as those elsewhere—mostly comedies, romantic melodramas, and sex-and-violence-laced "mysticals" based on old Javanese legends; many films offer erotic or pornographic themes (including nudity). But films also convey messages about modernization, gender relations, foreign cultures, and other issues. Unlike the stress on personal autonomy in American films, they promote the more distinctly Indonesian goal of order triumphing over disorder. The films have rarely provided an accurate mirror of society or its ethnic and religious complexities. For years many films conveyed a glamorous life far removed from that of most Indonesians, and most were set in Jakarta; as one critic wrote in 1974: "When will the dilapidated huts with their cow stables enter our films? . . . Not automobiles but . . . motorcycles or bicycles in our films? Not luxurious interiors but the homes of lower-income employees? When can we see our real face in our films?"[88]

During the New Order, a Board of Censors has had the power to revise films according to their own inclinations. They use film to convey ideas favorable to the regime, such as that everyone enjoys social equality, women need to accede to male domination (fulfillment coming through dependence in marriage), the ignorance of the poor is responsible for their situation, and Javanese political ascendancy is inevitable. By and large the poor and powerless are invisible.[89] Most films end happily, with order and harmony restored. At the same time, a government film promotion council promotes Indonesian filmmaking. Sometimes realistic films with worker or peasant heroes or themes slip through the cracks (e.g., several such films appeared in 1972–1973), but these rarely include elements of social protest. Rather society is represented in a more indirect way. Most of these films struggle to make money. By the mid-1980s, however, more serious films began appearing from directors like Teguh Karya, probing issues such as the realities of family life, urban ills, and the tension between traditional and modern ways. The subject matter of these films often parallels the concerns of pop singers.

The Rise of Pop Indonesia

Modern (post-1965) Indonesian popular music can be divided into a number of categories or streams, but there has been a mainstream. For some years that was occupied by ***hiburan*** ("entertainment"), a music utilizing Western instruments and melodies in a highly derivative manner reminiscent of the 1950s in the United States. It can be sung in either Indonesian *(hiburan umum)* or regional languages *(hiburan daerah)*. Hiburan declined dramatically by the 1970s as its audience aged and newer, more vibrant styles attracted youth. According to one observer:

> Hiburan was in all important respects a Western music, shallowly rooted in Indonesia. I suggest that hiburan's importance to Indonesians lay more in its "theatre" than in its music: it demonstrated that Indonesian performers and Indonesian languages could be incorporated into a clearly Western context. When pop emerged, demonstrating the same thing with greater energy, and linking its audience to the dreamworld of Western entertainment media, hiburan dried up and blew away.[90]

The emergence of pop may have demonstrated that Indonesian performers and languages could be co-opted into global (Western) music and entertainment with greater energy. Or perhaps, like its American counterparts (sentimental, early 1950s pop), hiburan simply fell prey to changing public tastes.

Pop Indonesia, which includes several subdivisions, rapidly replaced hiburan as the most popular idiom and aimed at a national audience. It closely resembles Western rock music of the 1960s and after, but utilizes Bahasa Indonesia lyrics and offers some local content. Stars like Emilia Contessa, Eddy Silatonga, and Koes Plus thrived in the 1970s and 1980s, as did ballad-oriented singers like Grace Simon, Diana Nasution, Betharia Sonatha, and Bob Tutopoly. Indeed, the market for romantic "soft pop" of this type has remained steady. Some musicians identified with this style, such as the Minangkabau Elly Kassim (in the 1960s and 1970s) and Hetty Koes Endang (1980s and 1990s), a sometime pop kroncong singer fluent in many song styles, and also cautiously introduced some kroncong, melayu, or folk elements to localize their sound somewhat. This earned them a following among both sophisticated and unlettered audiences. The versatile and ebullient Endang, who commenced her career in the mid-1970s, can switch effortlessly from neotraditional to pop styles. She performed up to twenty-five shows a month and recorded over fifty albums in order to sustain her popularity; her concerts have been noted for the rapport she achieves with audiences.[91] Yet much of the pop music remained derivative, exemplified in the widely popular Beatles cover group Bharata, who dress and sing like their idols. Pop Indonesia developed a fanatic audience, especially among teenagers, with a plethora of accessory products (including fashions and magazines) catering to the youthful fans and their tastes. For example, the massively popular magazine *Topchords* contains song lyrics and profiles Indonesian and Western musical personalities.[92]

Cassettes are distributed all over the country, with the more affluent and sophisticated urban youth the major market. But there is much imitation and many companies look more for attractive physical features than talent in recording singers. Many regional styles have emerged, such as *pop Jawa* (Javanese pop) and *pop Batak* (the Batak peoples of northern Sumatra), which use local languages. Indeed, the proliferation of small regionally based cassette companies aimed at local markets may have perpetuated regional styles. When, as is common, a "national" singer records in a regional language (even if only a cover version of their Bahasa Indonesian hit), this probably serves to validate the regional language and hence connect its speakers to the cosmopolitan (and perhaps superior) cultural center (Jakarta). There is also a modernized version of traditional Islamic chanted poetry. *Qasidah modern* music addresses moral issues as well as contemporary concerns such as corruption, but also utilizes a pop song format including electric guitars and keyboards. In the recordings of leading exponents such as the all-woman orchestra Nasida Ria, influences from dangdut as well as Arab pop music are apparent.[93]

The various subgenres of pop Indonesia account for some 20 percent of cassette sales.[94] The least socially concerned of the subgenres is the ephemeral *pop ringin* ("light pop"), which features rather simple lyrics and straightforward, formulaic, highly Westernized instrumentation. These are escapist and tuneful ballads or danceable up-tempo rock or disco pieces mostly on romantic themes sung in Indonesian or regional languages. Light romantic songs were a mainstay of popular groups like Koes Plus and The Mercy's in the 1960s and 1970s. Later singers like Broery Marantika, Andi

Merriem, and Betharia Sonatha and composers like Rinto Harahap and A. Riyanto would be closely identified with the style. Generally the music betrays little sociopolitical awareness, as two experts charge:

> Is Indonesian pop music able to describe the face and thoughts of Indonesian society at large? Does it give a clear picture of the life and concerns of society? No. If we listen only to soft pop with its love lyrics travelling in the same old tracks, it is impossible for us to gain any idea of the thoughts or social trends in Indonesia.[95]

However, even within this genre an occasional song with more serious intentions appears. In the mid-1980s the Sundanese pop singer Arie Wibobo explored social class contradictions in his widely popular song "Singkong dan Keju" ("Cassava and Cheese"). The singer expresses his identity with working-class culture (*jaipongan* dance, cassava) as opposed to his affluent girlfriend's taste for imported goods (Paris perfume, Italian shoes, disco dancing, cheese), in the end concluding that he ("a child of cassava") prefers an "ordinary girl" rather than the corrupted, foreign-oriented tastes of the rich. The same theme of incipient class conflict and the tension between the Indonesian and the foreign is taken up by Ria Rasty Sauzi in her song "Sepatu Kulit Rusa" ("Deer Skin Shoes"). She criticizes her suitor for offering expensive imports ("U.S. dollars," "clothes from Singapore," deerskin shoes, crocodile skin handbags, silk kerchiefs) when she prefers "only goods made in Indonesia." These songs can be

"Hati Yang Luka" ("A Wounded Heart")

"Again and again I try
Always to give in
For the sake of our marriage
Although sometimes it hurts
See the red mark on my cheek
The imprint of your hand
You often do this when you are angry
To cover up your guilt
Am I like that bird over there
for sale
so you can do what you like to me
and hurt me . . .
Just send me home to my mother . . .
Once, with a handful of gold you asked me to marry you
Once, we made vows in front of witnesses . . .
Now that's all over with
swallowed up by lies . . .
Now all that's left is the story of a wounded heart."[96]

characterized as examples of working-class "cassava nationalism" aimed at the privileges and lifestyles of the elite.[97]

In 1988 the best-selling song in the country was "Hati Yang Luka" ("A Wounded Heart"), originally released by sentimental songstress Betharia Sonatha. It shot to national stardom on a television music program and was consequently released in many cover versions by artists singing in Indonesian, regional dialects, and even English.[98] There were even pop krongcong and dangdut versions. American ethnomusicologist Philip Yampolsky describes the response to the song as follows: "The song was simply everywhere. The maids were singing it in the kitchens; musicians were playing it in the streets. . . . Eight months after it was issued, I heard the original cassette version played five times on a two-and-a-half-hour bus trip." Although the song fit easily into a common mode that might be termed "weepy" (*cengceng* in Indonesian), the song and its success imply something more than garden variety, "boy wrongs girl" lyrics. "Hati Yang Luka" focuses on a married couple rather than the more usual high school students suffering teenage angst. The lyrics also deal with real problems—a wife leaving a philandering husband who also abuses her physically.

Divorced or abandoned women occupy a difficult position in Indonesian society, and the problems addressed in the song are far more common than most Indonesians acknowledge. Hence "Hati Yang Luka" generated a major public controversy after a government official recommended banning this genre of songs ("weepys") from television as corrupting, déclassé, and disruptive of national unity. Many commentators agreed, arguing that the songs reflect the crass commercialism of the recording industry or undermine the family; many others defended the songs as a necessary social safety valve, representative of free speech, and a weapon aggrieved women could use against faithless husbands. Recording companies complained that a media ban would destroy their most profitable song genre, and that the loss of cassette advertising would devastate television revenues. The result was a compromise in which only upbeat songs on love and marriage appeared on television, but cassettes could still deal with broken hearts and marital breakup. The controversy greatly expanded the market for "Hati Yang Luka," which became one of the best-selling recordings in Indonesia's history.

Indeed, Yampolsky believes the "Hati Yang Luka" controversy "showed the popular culture industry responding to what it perceived as the wishes of the audiences defined on the bases of class, region, and religion."[99] In Indonesia, then, the audience does play a role in determining what music will be produced; yet national record producers also have a stake in repackaging national pop into regional pop sounds so that they only differ in language, hence minimizing expenses in producing regional cover versions of national hits. It constitutes a two-way street. The controversy also indicates considerable government uneasiness about the discussion of social problems in popular culture. They apparently saw "Hati Yang Luka" as the tip of the iceberg that must be held in check. In this sense, "Hati Yang Luka" can be considered political music because it raised issues the government wished to conceal and forced the government to react. At the same time, it served to enhance public knowledge and discussion about serious social issues.

Pop Indonesia and Social Change

In contrast to the mostly escapist, formulaic pop ringin, another pop Indonesia substream, *pop berat* ("heavy pop"), encompasses several varieties of new popular-oriented music with a far more complex structure and serious intent. Some pop berat musicians mix Javanese or Balinese instruments or gamelan influences with synthesizers and other innovations, creating a striking hybrid with much Indonesian content and mood. Some of the music betrays a strong jazz or jazz-rock influence, reflecting the fact that jazz (both American and Indonesian) has long been popular among educated and middle-class urbanites; other musicians reflect a heavy metal orientation. Pop berat also features a much more sophisticated lyrical structure, with complex words, serious poetry, linguistic mixtures, and some social criticism.

Perhaps the best-known exponent of this genre during the 1970s and 1980s was Guruh Soekarno, the youngest son of Indonesia's founding president Sukarno, who abandoned his university studies in Holland to pursue a musical career. Confirming his syncretist *prijaji* background, the enigmatic Guruh fluently combines gamelan influences, several Indonesian languages, and Western instruments into a commercially appealing rock-oriented blend that earned him mass popularity; he has consciously sought to create a fusion between Indonesian and international styles. Guruh's work, often presented in lavish, even spectacular, productions, betrays an intense patriotism (which sometimes blinds him to social inequities), a pride in the nation's past, and a commitment to a pluralistic culture. Ethnomusicologist Martin Hatch calls Guruh's pathbreaking 1977 album *Guruh Gypsi* "the most important work in Indonesian music of the 1970s."[100] In true eclectic Javanese fashion, the album brilliantly juxtaposes a variety of musical influences (from Balinese gamelan to acid rock, old Javanese poetry to Motown). The patriotic (and to critics naive and elitist) nature of many of his songs and extravagant stage performances is well captured in "Maharddhika" ("Freedom") on his *Gypsi* album:

Clear and bright
The hope for the coming era
Harmonious, peaceful, glorious
Beloved Indonesia
Safe and prosperous . . .
The whole spirit worships.[101]

Other pop berat musicians add light social criticism to their repertoire, commenting on poverty, elite luxury, corruption, environmental devastation, and the virtues of rural life. Indeed, environmental themes became increasingly popular with musicians competing with each other to address this problem. The messages are often oblique; in the late 1970s the group Bimbo satirized the high living and deal making of the wives of New Order power holders (especially Madame Suharto) in their popular song "Tante Sun" ("Auntie Kiss"). Rocketing to popularity with extensive mass media exposure, the song was soon banned and cassettes seized, but it remained an unofficial favorite. In the 1980s, singer-songwriter-guitarist Ully Sigar addressed feminist and social themes in her albums, while broadening the roles women could play in the music industry.[102] There was also the "gamelan rock" of the group Kelompok Kampungan, who recorded an album of protest songs and then disbanded.[103] However, the music of Guruh Soekarno and his colleagues is sometimes termed *gedongan* ("skyscraper") because it appeals mainly to urban middle-class tastes.

A pop Indonesia substream sometimes termed *pop country* is heavily influenced by Western folk and country and western. It is exemplified in musicians like Leo Kristi, Ebiet G. Ade, Gombloh, and Frankie and Jane. Pop country songs have dealt frequently with issues of regional and national significance, such as rural living, poverty, environmental decay, corruption, and war. Indeed, the lyrical orientation toward national and social issues may be the defining criteria of the style. The music also tends to reflect modern, ratio-

"Tante Sun" ("Auntie Kiss")

"Auntie Sun, oh sweet Auntie Sun . . .
off to play golf until mid-day
And straight from the golf course to the beauty parlor
For her skin cream treatments . . .
Auntie Sun, oh animated Auntie Sun
Always at meetings and gaming [gambling]
Never to be outdone by day or night
Auntie Sun, oh exemplary Auntie Sun . . .
Precious metals like gold and iron rods are her bag
Chinese fixers and wheeler-dealers
Company directors and percentage operators
Cringe and kneel of course to our Auntie Sun
Auntie Sun, oh enterprising Auntie Sun
Who never experiences any miseries
Smiling always to left and to right
To entice the handsome young gentlemen"—quoted by Hanna[104]

nalistic, or westernized attitudes.[105] In some ways pop country, thoughtfully populist in spirit, seems to be a kind of popular music counterpart to the ludruk theater, although the style appeals more to an urban middle-class than a working-class audience.

Ebiet's highly poetic lyrics and pleasant sound provided a model when he shot to overnight success in the late 1970s, earning the media rubric of "Indonesia's Bob Dylan." He claims a feeling of "responsibility to mankind" to be "the medium of communication for the less fortunate people . . . to voice their inner feelings," with some of his songs addressing the problems of the poor and other "underdog" issues. In his 1977 song "Jakarta 1," he reflected on the city's sense of alienation:

Dust lies hot on streets
Clearly empty of love and pity;
It's not like my green village here.[106]

The style has been especially popular with university students, who apparently like the mix of middle-class sophistication and populist sentiments. Like Freddie Aguilar in the Philippines, some pop country artists were clearly influenced by U.S. folk singers of the 1960s like Bob Dylan and Joan Baez, and simple guitar accompaniment is a frequent mode. Other musicians show a more marked country-and-western or rock flavor.

Pop country has enjoyed its greatest following in Java, but some singers developed a wider appeal. One of the more socially conscious of the musicians, Gombloh, offers numerous songs promoting the notion of all

Gombloh, an important pop country singer of the 1970s and 1980s in Indonesia, is known for the imagery and artistry of his songs. Photo (ca. 1981) courtesy of Martin Hatch.

"Berita Cuaca" ("Weather Report")

"Everlasting, my surroundings, everlasting my village
Where my God deposited me
Children sing at the time of the full moon
Singing a prayer for the land
Peaceful my brothers, prosperous my land
I remember my mother telling a story
A tale about the glorious archipelago of old
Peaceful and prosperous then
Why is the land anxious these days
The hills stand naked
Trees and grass do not want to sprout again
Birds are afraid to sing
I want my hills to be green again
The trees and grass wait impatiently
I pray this prayer every day
And now, when will this heart be relieved . . .
Be peaceful my brothers, be prosperous my state
I remember my mother telling a story
A tale about the victory of the country long ago
It was peaceful, prosperous, then."—Gombloh[107]

Indonesians pulling together to solve problems. In "Berita Cuaca" (1981), he employs rather cryptic imagery and traditional artistic elements or references (for example, to wayang kulit) to convey a positive image of national unity while also pleading for a cleaner environment. The glorification of the premodern and often the precolonial past is a frequent theme in the songs of Gombloh and several other musicians. In Gombloh's "Hong Wilaheng Sekarang Bawono Langgeng," he sings in archaic Javanese a well-known mystical poem (tembang) by a nineteenth-century Javanese prince, with the intention apparently of conveying the power of the past, hence relating the values of that time to the present day. The song serves to link past and present.

Other pop country singers also offer social criticism. One of Leo Kristi's best-known songs "symbolically depicted Indonesia's poor, huddled sorrowful and forgotten at the feet of a cold military."[108] More widely popular than Kristi, the duo of Frankie and Jane emphasize village themes in their sentimental, often romantic folk-country music. Many of their songs contrast urban and rural living. For example, their 1979 song "Supermarket dan Petani" ("Supermarket and Village") sympathetically relates the visit of a perplexed farmer to a town supermarket, at the same time suggesting the estrangement of urbanites from the realities of village life:

A farmer climbs on a bus
Gets off in the center of the city
Outside a supermarket he looks inside
At the fruits and vegetables all neatly tied in bundles
He shrugs his shoulders in amazement
So much food in cans
Everything in the supermarket
Has become so foreign to him
City people only know
How to buy things
They've forgotten about the villagers
Patiently waiting
From season to season
For the fields to yield.[109]

Another song examined social inequality through a story of children whose parents could not afford a television, while other families drove nice cars.

Pop Indonesia and Regional Identity

There are many regional styles of pop Indonesia. The most extensive research focuses on the mountainous Sunda region of west Java. The Sundanese are related linguistically and culturally to the ethnic Javanese, who chiefly occupy the eastern two-thirds of the island. But they developed a distinctive identity as a separate ethnolinguistic group and have generally followed a somewhat more orthodox form of Islam. During the 1960s and 1970s, *pop Sunda* could be characterized as essentially a clear imitation of pop Indonesia, offering Western or westernized songs differing only in their use of the Sundanese language. By the early 1980s some musicians were beginning to add a more local touch, with the integration of traditional Sundanese instruments and tunings as well as distinctive local vocalizations; the classical Sundanese gamelan *(degung kawih)* also was adapted to popular music.

By 1986 these innovations led to a style known as *kalangkang* ("imagining"), which relies exclusively or partly on Sundanese orchestration and vocal styles.[110] The songs are mainly lighthearted, romantic—indeed, by Sundanese standards, even erotic—descriptions of teenage behavior and emotions. Due to the elite gamelan image, modern pop Sunda finds an audience among the urban middle and upper classes; it is spread mainly by cassettes. The style also greatly transformed Sundanese gamelan into a popular rather than purely elite idiom, playing a new repertoire of pop songs. Proponents of the style have worried, however, that pop Sunda might lose its Sundanese characteristics and move closer to pop Indonesia, or that its lyrics

The Origins of Jaipongan: An Insider's Account

"The Sukarno government wanted us to create new art forms based on our old traditions. I thought for a long time how? I remembered when I was a boy everybody dancing and singing Sundanese but in my school we preferred Elvis Presley and Chubby Checker. My father and mother were traditional artists so I asked them to teach me the old songs and dances. Then my father asked me to travel round West Java to see all kinds of Sundanese culture. I felt the music was too slow, so I asked the musicians to play faster. They said I must pay. OK I will pay. But I will arrange the gamelan and the terbang (drum). So they played an old song with my new arrangement. The people copied my dance steps. Everybody liked it."—Gugum Gumbira Tirasondjaja[111]

might address themes considered too adult for teenagers. The innovative and authentic nature of kalangkang-style pop Sunda led even some Jakarta-based, "national" (Bahasa Indonesia) singers to record in the idiom, an indication of its growing popularity outside the Sunda region. Regional pop styles rarely achieve such distinction. While modern pop Sunda offers few political messages, its growing popularity revealed something about the Indonesian concern for both cultural authenticity and ethnic/regional pride. Indeed, the achievement of this redefinition of pop Sunda is considered by some musicians and composers to be a step toward modernization, while at the same time preserving the essential Sundanese musical character.

The Sunda region also produced the most important completely indigenous popular music to appear in Indonesia: jaipongan. This revolutionary new style of dance music began developing in the 1960s as the innovation of multitalented Gugum Gumbira Tirasondjaja, who was determined to create a modern indigenous art form. He became inspired to shift from the Western rock of his youth in the Sukarno years to homegrown sounds.

In the new jazzed-up version based on a village dance—once considered low status because of its association with prostitutes—jaipongan became a regional, then national craze in the late 1970s, popularized by female singers like Euis Komariah, Idjah Hadidja, and Tati Saleh. Yampolsky summarizes both the style and the impact:

> It featured dance movements that were both erotic and humorous, and the accompanying music was dominated by exuberant, highly dynamic drumming. What was revolutionary about Jaipongan was that it achieved great popularity in the most modern and nationally minded of Indonesian cities [Jakarta] while remaining a thoroughly regional and traditional genre, showing little or no influence from the West.[112]

Jaipongan exclusively employs instruments and dance idioms based in the Sundanese tradition, as well as using the Sundanese language.

In part the development of jaipongan reflects the unusually flourishing nature of traditional and classical Sundanese music, whose regional popularity crosses class and age barriers. It became the first distinctly regional musical style to achieve wide popularity throughout the country, much like the juju, fuji, and apala musics of the Yoruba people in Nigeria; in many respects it has constituted, like them, a new and organic tradition with minimal acculturation. There was much public controversy as to whether the somewhat sensuous dance style encourages and reflects immorality. Jaipongan spread rapidly by way of cassettes produced by small regional companies—often established by the musicians and composers themselves. But the music also enjoyed much radio and television coverage in the 1980s. The flowering of jaipongan owes much to mass mediation. Like kroncong, jaipongan's appeal transcends class divisions. It

> was taught in schools and private dance classes, and was performed in dance-halls and nightclubs, at parties and festivals, in the streets and on TV. . . . One might find Jaipongan [in] . . . an exercise club for rich women; an open-air stage near the railroad tracks in a seedy area, where peddlers and pedicab drivers danced with prostitutes.[113]

The content of jaipongan songs is quite varied, including romantic, moral, spiritual, vulgar, and sometimes topical subjects. One of the better-known topical songs, "Mat Peci," is a narrative about the rise and fall of a notorious Sundanese bandit with a Robin Hood reputation in the 1970s. Some observers believe this type of song clearly ties the music to, and reflects the populist values of, the Sundanese grass roots rather than the elite. Hence, "Mat Peci" notes the folk hero's working-class background and emphasizes that his career was ended by a lowly civil policeman rather than a high-ranking officer:

Mat Peci ran his operation out of Bandung
Such was his fame that a movie was made about him
Even though he was a criminal, he was self-disciplined
He killed a cop . . .
He was the most wanted outlaw
Was searched for desperately
Everywhere police were getting killed
And Mat Peci became all the more famous
We must end our story here
Mat Peci met his destiny
Although feared by many
He ended up being done in by a local civil cop.[114]

Thus, while it would appear that jaipongan does not constitute a highly politicized genre, there has been an element of social criticism and commentary. Furthermore, it has clearly represented the desire of the Sundanese to modernize in order to perpetuate their own cultural traditions. During the early 1980s jaipongan dancing and attendant dance classes swept through the archipelago. By the mid-1980s the dance craze had ebbed, but jaipongan had gained a niche as sort of national stage dance. Jaipongan percussion styles also find their way into various pop Indonesia and dangdut songs.[115]

Rhoma Irama and the Dangdut Challenge

The major challenge to the popularity of pop Indonesia as a national form has come from dangdut, a media-generated, acculturated modern music, which appeared on the Indonesian popular music scene in the 1960s as a fusion between Malay ensemble music (orkes melayu), the Indian film music popular at that time, and Western pop. The use of the tabla (Indian drum) and flute from Hindi film music remains a notable feature of most dangdut groups in Indonesia and Malaysia. Early on, the style was associated with a rather restrained type of social dance, especially important at public dances and festivals. Most songs are sung in Bahasa Indonesia and have a strong Islamic flavor. By the 1970s the dangdut style was identified with singers like A. Rafiq, Mansyur S., Elvy Sukaesih, Titiek Sandhora, Ida Laila, Mus Mulyadi, and—most famous of all—Rhoma Irama. Dangdut emerged from the cultural melting pot of Jakarta, a city sometimes compared to the spicy Indonesian salad *gado gado* because of its assimilation and intermingling of

Rhoma Irama's Early Life

Rhoma Irama was born as Oma Irama on December 11, 1947, in a small village in west Java. Because his mother had gone into labor after returning from a concert, she chose the unusual name *Irama* ("rhythm") for her son. His father, an army captain and hence lower middle class in status, decided to move the family to Jakarta in the early 1950s in search of more opportunities, settling in a ramshackle suburb. While his parents hoped he would grow up to be a doctor, Oma was an indifferent student more interested in rock music and rakish behavior. His father died in 1957, undermining the family's financial status, but his determined mother continued to encourage education for her son. By his early teens Oma had learned to play the guitar and had joined a series of bands formed by schoolmates. By 1963 he had organized his own band, known as the Gayhand, playing covers of songs by such popular artists as the Beatles, Paul Anka, and Tom Jones. The band achieved only limited commercial success. Meanwhile Oma finished high school but his university studies proved short-lived. He opted instead for a musical career. Later he would embellish his childhood name by adding "Rh" to Oma—for Raden Haji—borrowing a prestigious lower-aristocratic title that also suggested his growing interest in Islam. In 1975 he made the pilgrimage to Mecca and officially became a haji.[116]

Rhoma Irama, the creator and leading exponent of dangdut, was probably the most important pop music superstar of the 1970s and 1980s. Photo (ca. 1981) by Martin Hatch.

peoples and ideas arriving from outside. Hence, like kroncong, dangdut resulted from the fertile cultural exchange characteristic of this vibrant city with its distinctive environment.

Rhoma Irama, the master of the dangdut style, has been perhaps the best-known exponent of socially conscious music in Indonesia. In the early 1970s, Rhoma and his new group Soneta exploded onto the pop charts with a gradually changing, somewhat more rock-oriented, electrified, and highly danceable dangdut style. He replaced the original melayu instruments with modern ones and restructured the arrangements into modern terms. When his style began to reach maturity in 1975 it was described as "above all an energetic style that pumped the Melayu song full of a liquid, flowing rhythm and highlighted its characteristic waves of melody."[117]

Rhoma added electric guitars, synthesizer, and a drum set to more traditional instruments in a conscious attempt to substitute a truly Indonesian music for the Western rock he had abandoned. As he explained in 1988, "We sieve what comes from the West, we don't just swallow. We take what's good and throw out the rest."[118] He seems to consider his music much closer in spirit to the melayu than the Western tradition. Rhoma articulates his goals as follows:

> It [his music] must be broadly popular, cutting across class lines and appealing to the sensibilities of Indonesians of all sorts; it must be unmistakably modern; and it must carry a message, however simple, in a language that is easily grasped by young people everywhere. Finally, this new music must neither reveal an obvious kinship with Western styles—the goal was unmistakably "Indonesian" or at least an "Eastern" sound—nor merely imitate the existing Melayu-Deli style with its Arab and Indian flourishes.[119]

Still, it had to convey significant Western flavor to really become a national as opposed to local musical form—and hence achieve mass popularity.

Rhoma remained perhaps Indonesia's premier entertainer for almost two decades, releasing over one hundred albums, of which several dozen went gold in sales. These developments energized dangdut, which accounted for nearly half of all cassette production in the 1970s and 1980s and gained a following that spanned all barriers of region and class. By the 1990s dangdut accounted for nearly 70 percent of all cassette sales in the country. Rhoma became, in historian Bill Frederick's words, "Indonesia's first true entertainment superstar."[120] Part of his popularity derived from his electrifying and theatrical stage performances (highly innovative for Indonesia), which launched a craze for dangdut dance and dress styles in urban slums and rural villages. His magic has even worked for Malaysian audiences; a 1985 report conveys the ambience of one of his concerts there:

> A fine example of synthesis . . . of assimilating without being assimilated. . . . Rhoma brought inspiration. He managed to embody in his performance an intimation of cosmic glory and power, or a delightful energy permeating all space and giving life to all beings. . . . With a little help from technology . . . Rhoma succeeded in communicating an ecstatic sense of joy, of light, of a simple happiness untouched by deviousness and malice. The sheer radiance of the music became a message in itself: the whole audience was blissfully entranced, swaying their bodies and weaving their arms to the infectious rhythm.[121]

These developments raise some interesting questions:

> One might legitimately ask how imaginative—not to say bizarre—costuming and dancing with abandon could be related to some of the objectives Oma had set for himself and [his] Soneta Group. There is no easy answer to this question, but a key point surely is that neither Oma nor his audiences viewed the various elements being melded together as anything but complementary. Reality and fantasy carried and strengthened each other, and the impetus they built together moved dangdut beyond music in a narrow sense. Theatrics seemed, in short, to fit the dynamism of dangdut and make of it a comprehensive whole that was somehow larger than its parts.[122]

Such a development also surely fits into the broader Indonesian (especially Javanese) cultural historical pattern of reconciling opposites and blending diverse influences. And the spectacular theatricality of Rhoma's performances have clear roots in the rich theater traditions of Indonesia, from wayang to bangsawan and ludruk. In addition to the stage shows and dozens of successful recordings, the charismatic Rhoma has starred in, and produced, a number of hugely popular—if offbeat—films with a social or religious orientation; his early films were influenced by ludruk models. During the late 1970s and early 1980s, his and other dangdut films easily topped the box office charts. Rhoma's activities and massive popularity sparked intense discussion about modern Indonesian culture as well as generating for Islam a more public identity. Frederick argues persuasively that "dangdut constitutes not only a legitimate part of contemporary Indonesian culture . . . but a sensitive and useful prism through which to view Indonesian society."[123]

Unlike most pop singers, Rhoma utilizes current street language and a more developed narrative style. Another major innovation appears in the themes of Rhoma's lyrics; his songs and films, especially since the late 1970s, offer a populist message on the problems of poverty, human rights abuses, the struggle of the underdog, and the betrayal of nationalistic promise. As one of his best-known songs put it, "The rich get richer and the poor get poorer."[124] Many songs deal with the ordinary lives of people but describe a wider range of behavior than in most pop Indonesia, including revenge, unemployment, jail, gambling, prostitution, and infidelity. Rhoma's social criticism has been subtle when compared to 1960s American protest rock.[125] But these songs earned him a huge following among the *kampungan*, the urban slum dwellers and rural folk who see their values reflected in Rhoma's message; they also admire his rags-to-riches career. Not all of his songs offer serious messages; some merely extol the melayu tradition or exhort his audience to dance and enjoy themselves.

Rhoma's music contains a strong Islamic quality, full of moral teaching and missionary zeal. In many ways it seems reminiscent of the fuji music popular among lower-class Muslim Yoruba in Nigeria. Rhoma's dangdut is sometimes styled "*dakwah* (Islamic message) rock" and often includes passages from the Koran. An example of these songs is "Laillạh Haillalah" from a 1977 film:

Why should you worship human beings, why do you worship material things
You shouldn't think there can be two of Him [Allah]
You shouldn't think He shares his holiness with others [Allah is unique,
unlike the Christian trinity]
He created all nature and there is nothing else like Him
Laillah haillalah, there is no other God but Allah.[126]

Rhoma was deeply affected by his pilgrimage to Mecca and began to wear more Arab-oriented clothing. His public persona is effective; one source claims that "his soft manner radiates a vibrant strength that must be the envy of the mosque muezzins who depend on shrill loudspeakers to draw their audience."[127] In his concerts he splashes his dialogue with Arabic quotes from the Koran. In 1980 he released the first Islamic rock musical motion picture. The film, *Perjuangan dan Do'a* ("Struggle and Prayer"), offers a persistent, energetic, and highly effective Islamic message. Songs defend Islamic moral prohibitions (widely ignored in Indonesia) and blame the

"Nafsu Serakah" ("Insatiable Greed")

"All over this part of the world
We hear the drumbeats answering each other.
All over this part of the world
So many dead lie scattered everywhere
It's the result of insatiable greed
People who lust, in their cunning, for power
Will do anything and think it's all right
Have we now returned to the law of the jungle
With the strong oppressing the weak?
A small group of power-hungry people
Fill the world with suffering
Stop aggression, stop tyranny,
When will we ever see justice done?
Almost everywhere in the world
We hear the cries of a restless mankind . . .
The reason is that man has forgotten the Creator
And turned religion into little more than an addendum
Men have begun to worship material things."—Rhoma Irama[128]

problems of the world on people who do not take their religion seriously. For example, "Nafsu Serakah" mixes dakwah appeals with angry social criticism. The song also suggests that his message is well within the revered spirit of the Indonesian Revolution.

Another of Rhoma's popular songs in this genre is "Al Qur'an Dan Koran" ("The Koran and Newspapers"):

Moving with the wheels of development
People are increasingly busy
So far as to ignore their [religious] duties . . .
Getting drunk with development
So that computers become God . . .
If you talk about religion
They act as if they're allergic.[129]

Rhoma also took an increasing interest in politics as the political strength of the Islamic parties expanded, concluding that dangdut's clear ability to reach a mass audience could be a potentially powerful political tool.

Some of Rhoma's songs address more political subjects. For example, "Hak Azasi" ("Basic Human Rights"), released during the 1977–1978 election campaign, promotes human rights, a reminder perhaps that the rather authoritarian government has sometimes exercised a heavy hand in these matters and restricted some militant Islamic activities:

Increasingly, Rhoma and his music were identified with the Islamic revival, and Rhoma presented a more openly Islamic persona, sometimes dressing in Middle Eastern-style clothes. 1982 photo by Bill Frederick.

Respect basic human rights
That's the duty of all mankind
We are all free to choose
How we wish to live
Even God doesn't force
His subjects to behave in a certain way . . .
Freedom of religion,
That's a basic human right
Freedom of speech
That's a basic human right
We are free to do as we wish
As long as we don't conflict
With Pancasila.[130]

Another well-known song from that period, "Rupiah" (the Indonesian currency), was prohibited from television and saw cassette distribution restricted by government pressure; it criticizes those who sacrificed their morals in the mad scramble for wealth. One of Rhoma's most popular movies, *Begadang* (1978), introduced the title song (Jakarta slang for "Stay Up All Night"), that dominated the hit parade because of its great danceability and biting social criticism about the widening gap between the few rich and many poor.

Many of Rhoma's songs reveal a somewhat more subtle form of indirect protest or criticism. For example, in "Dangdut Rock," recorded in 1978, Rhoma gently commiserates with the many working poor who need to work

"Begadang" ("Stay Up All Night")

"What good is Saturday night
To people who aren't well off
We want to have fun but got no money
End up squatting at the side of the road
Let's stay up all night
Stay up and sing
Although we don't have money
We can still enjoy ourselves
Those who have money
Go dancing at nightclubs
We who have no money
Just dance at the side of the street
Those who have money
Eat in big restaurants
We who have no money
Eat only at roadside stalls."—Rhoma Irama[131]

all night in order to make a decent living. But he also seems to be urging young people not to waste their time in partying:

Don't stay up all night if there is no reason for it
But of course you can stay up all night if there's a need to do so
If you stay up too much, your face will become pale from a weakening of circulation
If you often experience the night air, all sicknesses will come easily to you
Care for your body: don't stay up every night.[132]

Another song ponders the unfairness of the world:

Why are people not the same?
Why are the poor and rich so different?
Why does love have limits set
That say rich and poor cannot be lovers?[133]

The vast popularity of Rhoma and dangdut generated a search for explanations. Frederick summarizes the debate:

> There is a general concurrence . . . that dangdut's popularity is intimately connected to its egalitarian character. . . . The music not only gets the majority of its fans from the majority of society—the lower classes—but evinces a sympathy with and an understanding of them that is unique. Indeed, this last characteristic has been strong enough to breed a kind of

"populist chic" . . . among the elite and middle class. For these reasons some have concluded that the dangdut style, by virtue of what it reflects as well as what it imposes, matches more accurately than any other yet devised the much sought-after national character or "countenance."[134]

But many among Indonesia's political and social elite have over the years condemned dangdut in general, and Rhoma's music in particular, as loud, vulgar, déclassé, and inherently corrupting of public morals, which is why several of his songs were kept off the airwaves. One cabinet minister characterized dangdut as "caterwauling"; another detractor called it "dog crap music." These attitudes among high officials resulted in most of Rhoma's songs and films being banned from government radio and television for a decade beginning in the late 1970s; he was also prohibited from performing live shows in Jakarta. One is reminded of the earlier elite disdain for kroncong as lower class and hybrid.[135] Other more thoughtful critics consider Rhoma and his music to be little better than shallow products of mass marketing and manipulated mass communications to create a groundswell of consumer behavior. The rather extensive coverage of Rhoma in middle-class magazines like *Tempo* tended to legitimize dangdut as a music and Rhoma as a superstar, while articles praised his religious message and social concerns. But the essays also stressed the contradiction between his populist messages and his wealth and extravagant lifestyle.[136]

Hence, there have been suggestions that he exploits religion for his own success (he became a millionaire). Rhoma rejects these charges, as in a 1985 interview: "It is written in the Koran that it is the duty of every Muslim to preach and I am just doing my duty in the way I know best—through music. . . . How do you preach to people who don't go to the mosque? . . . How do you propagate Islam to the masses who like to party or disco?"[137] Some observers unfavorably contrast the kampungan-oriented, mass culture music of Rhoma with the more middle-class and sophisticated pop berat of singers like Guruh Soekarno. Certainly dangdut's market base comes from its identification with class rather than ethnicity. It is far more likely to be heard on public transport cassette players and radios than in automobiles. By 1995 some official attitudes toward Rhoma and dangdut were changing. Rhoma and the Soneta Group were prominent in massive dangdut and musical shows sponsored by government agencies to celebrate the fiftieth anniversary of the Indonesian Republic; the shows were televised on government television. And some officials praised dangdut as "part of our developing culture" and "the lawful owner of the republic." This suggests a certain co-optation, but also a realization that dangdut would not wither away; it had become a long-term, increasingly sophisticated part of Indonesian life.[138]

Whether Rhoma and his colleagues have substantially affected political attitudes—or even facilitated meaningful socioeconomic change—remains less clear. Frederick argued that his populist songs and movies as well as his ascending personal career seem to have perhaps unwittingly conveyed the message to his audience that social mobility is more common or possible than is certainly the case, hence perpetuating unrealistic fantasies.[139] Deep societal beliefs in Horatio Alger-type myths can inhibit social mobilization for change; but they can also deepen resentments about relative deprivation. Most of Rhoma's songs and films do not cut to the heart of what really ails the country because they concentrate on superficialities and largely ignore the structural causes of poverty. Moral homilies do not redistribute income and power. The songs and their messages reflect the inevitable contradictions of a mass-oriented medium dominated by a corporate entertainment industry.[140]

Rhoma's Islamic messages also dovetailed nicely with the Islamic revival that became pronounced beginning in the 1970s, with many Indonesians seeking a more Islamic identity. Rhoma did not spark that revival but perhaps played a modest role in accelerating it through his access to mass-mediated forums and consequent popularization of revivalist themes. Indeed, journalist Paul Handley, writing in the mid-1980s, called Rhoma the "most powerful Muslim leader the country has."[141] This surely overstated the case, but it does suggest his influence. Finally, Rhoma must be credited with helping to perpetuate issues of socioeconomic inequality as part of the popular culture dialogue. Musicians like Rhoma and Guruh Soekarno apparently mastered the art of assimilating and synthesizing without becoming merely imitative.

Rhoma and several other pop (especially dangdut) singers have also been politically active in favor of certain causes and political parties. Both major Indonesian groupings utilized dangdut singers in their 1982 campaigns. The ruling GOLKAR group used Rhoma's former protégé, the immensely popular Elvy Sukaesih; her sensuous performances allegedly set off riots. The governing coalition also adapted regional folk music into their campaigns; for example, in the Minangkabau region of west Sumatra, folk songs were rewritten to praise pancasila or extol government policies such as the birth control campaign. In the 1977 and 1982 campaigns, Rhoma appeared at many rallies for the opposition Islamic coalition (PPP), helping to attract large crowds. Although he claimed that his "field is music, not politics," he urged his fans to vote for the PPP and publicly decried the widening gap between rich and poor which, he argued, the Muslim parties would rectify.[142]

When the PPP, which once offered him a leadership position, temporarily fell apart in 1983–1984, Rhoma apparently despaired of party politics. Indeed, he faced several police investigations in the 1980s after the Tanjung Priok riots involving Islamic militants with whom he was believed to sympathize. He was reportedly detained for weeks. But as one respected Muslim politician states, "they could not hold him long because they knew how this would turn the masses against the government."[143] In the wake of

Islam and a Rhoma Irama Concert

"The audience, who filled the main Senayan Stadium in Jakarta, trembled. The stage was dark. And suddenly, all the lights lit up. Rhoma Irama stood handsomely, reciting prayers. The thundering of the masses broke in as a disturbance. But not for long. All of a sudden the superstar raised both his hands, and the stadium was silent. The performance began, while quoting verses from the Koran in a short introduction. Rhoma's strength above the others is that he only sings songs of love and the dreams of the common people. He shares their desires or aspirations. Even Rhoma Irama's political outlook, his campaign for the PPP seems to be a realization of his complete conception of a 'resurgence from below,' or a way of representing that class. Therefore, the factor of religion in his music is not so unusual. There is advice on morals, suggestions on piety, religious advice on a just outlook, also on social understanding—all of which later become clearer as religious teaching with the reading of the Koran in the introduction, or singing of verses. Rhoma did not start this tradition. Islamic oral poetry is generally freely composed. Rhoma's strong point is that he has strengthened an indistinct tradition into a new 'autonomous' form.—*Tempo*"[144]

these events his music became less controversial. Like the reggae artists in Jamaica after the 1980 death of Bob Marley, he seems to be seeking political harmony. Hence, his 1986 song "Stop":

Stop debating, stop arguing
Stop hostility, stop conflict
Let's love each other.[145]

Later Rhoma rather enigmatically joined the ruling party and played for some of their rallies, perplexing those who viewed GOLKAR as antithetical to Islamic resurgence. Even then he was still required to obtain police permission before a public concert. In confirmation of the persistent power and appeal of dangdut, all three political groupings (GOLKAR, the Islamic PPP, and the nationalist-populist PDI) used dangdut singers in their 1992 campaigns, with entertainment rather than issues seemingly the dominant force in politics. Rhoma is not the only politically active musician. By 1987 Guruh Soekarno was campaigning for the PDI (and the reassessment of his father's legacy). By 1992 he was considered a potential showcase PDI presidential candidate, although the PDI ultimately backed away from challenging Suharto. Nonetheless he had a strong influence on many voters in east and central Java.[146]

Rhoma's lavish lifestyle, populist underdog persona, controversial music, political agitation, and occasional skirmishes with an authoritarian government are reminiscent of Nigeria's radical pop music superstar Fela, who was frequently incarcerated and persecuted for his overt criticism of and challenges to political leaders. It was also not hard to identify many parallels between dangdut and reggae, including their déclassé origins, steady beat, folk base, religious orientation, and social criticism. No wonder some dangdut musicians began performing dangdut versions of reggae songs.[147] Indeed, dangdut continued to evolve. By 1989 some dangdut singers began taking an antimaterialist stance; a hit by Itje Trisnawati attacks the fake material pleasures of the urban elite and extols simple village pleasures.

But the music also became increasingly commodified, as commonly heard in downtown discos as in village celebrations, its major performers wealthy entertainers with fast cars. Dangdut gradually lost some of its kampungan reputation, developing a middle-class audience. The music even gained some credibility through its popularity in countries like Japan and Malaysia, as well as by the incorporation of dangdut meolodies into gamelan and wayang kulit performances. By the 1990s many dangdut songs addressed erotic and sexual topics, a fact that troubled Rhoma as moral guardian. Indeed, it may well be for this reason that female singers and dancers in the highly popular live dangdut shows have enjoyed material gains and popularity. But their often erotic—even vulgar—performances, some observers believe, have done little to improve the status of women, promoting the female body as spectacle. Even top female artists like Elvy Sukaisih earn much less than their male counterparts. In recent years a highly danceable disco-style dangdut had also emerged. Nonetheless, Rhoma preaches tolerance toward the changes as implicit in a naturally evolving musical form.[148]

Rhoma's increasingly flamboyant, charismatic public persona and lavish lifestyle brought him a vast audience but also elicited criticism from Islamic purists and entrenched powerholders as well as those who believed his success dimmed his populist message. 1983 photo by Bill Frederick.

Few Indonesian singers have explored the fringes of tolerated dissent as assiduously as Rhoma did between the mid-1970s and late 1980s. However, in West Irian, where many peoples resent what they see as Indonesian "colonialism" and resist policies of cultural assimilation, a tradition of oppositional music developed. One nationally known pop group from West Irian, the Black Brothers, went into voluntary exile in 1979 to protest Indonesian policies on their home island; they lived and worked in Vanuatu before moving to Papua New Guinea. Later the folk-based group Mambesak (formed in 1978) would articulate West Irian concerns, including opposition to environmentally destructive forestry and mining operations. Their activist leader, Arnold C. Ap, was assassinated by the army in 1984. Mambesak stimulated the formation of other West Irian bands with similar interests.[149] But otherwise, Rhoma clearly remained the most visible example of political music in Indonesia until the rise of Iwan Fals.

Contemporary Indonesian Politics and Popular Music

Beginning in the mid-1980s, a political thaw facilitated increasingly political artistic expression. In theater and literature, the so-called Jakarta Spring of cultural liberalization fostered an unprecedented freedom to convey social criticism. Anti-Establishment plays and readings, some by long-banned artists like the countercultural poet Rendra, were performed much more openly. These were often well attended by the elite. Perhaps the government could ignore the small, elitist theater audiences. Few of these developments reach beyond the sophisticated capital city, or indeed even into the lower-class slum districts. But in 1989 Rendra put on an extraordinary dramatic performance in a Jakarta stadium that attracted fifteen thousand of all social classes and backgrounds, indicating the possibilities for mass appeal. This unprecedented artistic event involved Rendra's Bengkel theater, prohibited from public shows for seven years, in an uncompromising, seven-hour wayang-influenced drama about the trauma of political succession, a fantastic feat of charisma and endurance.[150]

In 1989 a radically different film appeared extolling a female anti-Dutch warrior hero of the nineteenth century. The film challenges many social norms and gender expectations while glorifying resistance to authority. Unlike most realist films, it played before large audiences. At the same time the feminist poetry of Sarawati Sunindyo was confronting male authority and the hegemonic state power than supports it, portraying women of all classes as victims of societal norms. By 1989–1990, the regime returned to clumsy censorship, closing down several theater performances of plays with socio-political themes and restricting live musical events. Rendra, whose poetry readings were banned, charged that "cultural life . . . is being darkened by rain clouds under which there is no freedom."[151]

Human rights abuses increased. In 1994, three influential but outspoken "cutting-edge" publications (including the preeminent weekly magazine, *Tempo*), whose writers had examined corruption issues and political infighting, had their publishing licenses revoked, signaling an end to a short period of relative political openness and stunning many middle-class Indonesians who believed (or hoped) the regime was liberalizing. Rendra himself was arrested briefly for taking part in demonstrations opposing the closing of these magazines.[152] Goenawan Mohamad, the former editor of *Tempo*, explained the intellectual atmosphere:

> For the most part, [the] carnival of expression seems absent from the Indonesian language today. Our language has been ripped from the world, stripped of shape, smell, color and form, cleansed of the grit and graffiti, the rumpus and commotion, that make up real life. . . . The language that we see forms a landscape almost barren of vegetation, dotted by sparse clumps of bamboo and threatened with a blight, a landscape in which only the poorest of transmigrants might find a home.[153]

Yet young people, supposedly depoliticized by years of social engineering, keep finding more ways to express rebellion. For example, a distinctive youth dialect, *Bahasa Prokem*, evolved among the Jakarta underworld (criminals and street gangs) in the 1970s and spread to university and high school students; it employs eccentric expressions, abbreviations, and code words as sort of a secret language for the "in-group." By the 1980s it had become almost a major youth vernacular, expressing solidarity in opposition to the political, social, and cultural heritage of their parents. The generation gap was also reflected in the 1990s by the lionization of once-discredited former President Sukarno by many young people seeking a charismatic hero figure. And there remains a persistent element of protest in the songs of the musical buskers—mostly young musicians who ply the city streets. Although Islam became a less overt theme than in the 1960s and 1970s, student protesters still addressed themes of social difference, class, anticapitalism, democracy, human rights, antimilitarism, and nationalism.[154]

By the early 1990s Indonesian society was filled with increasing class tensions and insecurities surrounding the future—after Suharto passes from the scene. Many Indonesians recognized contemporary realities in a short-lived satirical play (soon closed by the authorities) in which confusion and chaos pervade a once-contented kingdom as contestants jockeyed to succeed an aging monarch: "The more one is confused," claimed a key character, "the safer we all are."[155] Popular discontent increased during the 1990s, with student protests and labor unrest erupting more frequently. Furthermore, newspapers were reporting them more openly; several magazines even ran stories about the 1991 massacres of East Timorese protestors by Indonesian troops. In early 1994 riots broke out in the northeast

Sumatran city of Medan, aimed largely at the Chinese mercantile community and involving thousands of laborers. But the unrest seemed directed as much at the affluent non-Chinese Indonesians who prospered under the New Order and became part of a multiethnic middle class, in contrast to increasingly dissatisfied, militant, and organized urban workers as well as many demoralized, often jobless lower-class men. The unrest may have foreshadowed increasing class tensions in the twilight of the Suharto era, and indeed further sporadic anti-Chinese violence broke out in 1996 and 1997.[156] The government responded with a crackdown on dissidents, including a purge of journalists whose work is deemed too investigative or critical of the government and Suharto's wealthy family. Several leaders of an association for independent journalists were arrested in 1995 (for publishing an unlicensed magazine), and two newsletters were closed down. Top officials also accused several critics of leading an alleged communist resurgence. But popular culture remains vibrant, as the attempts by the state to channel it in safe directions conflict with an increasingly diverse, multiclass audience that cannot easily be managed.[157]

Contradictions abound. Despite sporadic repression, the growing middle class, now nearly 10 percent of the population, is becoming more assertive, and issue-oriented nongovernmental organizations proliferate, while the military role in government declines—much to the chagrin of some officers. The popular "rehabilitation" of Sukarno helped the growing Indonesian Democratic Party (PDI); some intellectuals even began to openly question the "official" history of the mid-1960s turmoil that brought Suharto to power. Sukarno's daughter Megawati Soekarnoputri took over as PDI party leader in 1994 and began developing links to Islamic groups; she became the first female party leader in the country's political history. But she was also closely monitored and prohibited from visiting some troubled parts of the country. In June 1996, the most serious political crisis in three decades erupted. The conviction of a political activist for insulting President Suharto generated student protests. In the same month, a PDI faction allied with Suharto ousted Megawati from the leadership, splitting the party. The regime apparently perceived her as a potential threat to their hegemony. Her supporters both inside and outside the PDI quickly transformed her into a populist symbol challenging the political system. Perhaps against her wishes, she became a rallying icon for dissidents—the most important alternative figure to appear in opposition to Suharto in several decades. In the political theater that characterizes New Order Indonesia, symbols assume major importance. Soon police were clashing regularly with pro-Megawati protesters. A police assault on young people occupying PDI headquarters resulted in several deaths, many injuries, and hundreds of arrests, enflaming tensions. As security forces rounded up or interrogated dissidents, conditions remained volatile. Whether the opposition could sustain its momentum against overwhelming odds remained uncertain, but the regime's legitimacy had clearly been compromised to some degree, confirming considerable disaffection.[158]

If not moving toward democracy, the nation did seem in some respects to be heading toward increased liberalization and pluralization of power. Suharto, who maintains an amazing ability to absorb or co-opt his detractors, is nearing retirement or death but no clear succession has been established. There seems little doubt that the well-organized military will continue to play a prominent political role, with a pervasive political apparatus insuring stability and continuity. The business community, NGOs, and independent labor unions (mostly illegal) also hope to be factors. But many civilians, particularly among the urban middle class, would prefer a more participatory system. Indonesia seems at a crossroads, with the future unclear.[159]

These trends inevitably influence popular music, which increasingly integrated regional, national, and international forms into an innovative mix. Rock music, with groups such as Gong 2000 (led by Achmad Albar), became more prominent. Since the late 1980s and early 1980s a new, massively popular superstar, Iwan Fals, has specialized in protest songs, some of them written by disaffected poet Rendra, with whom he sometimes performs.[160] Iwan (Virgiawan Listano) began as a street busker in Jakarta night markets in the 1970s. He reportedly wrote his first protest song (about official abuse of power) as a junior high school student in Bandung in 1975. Gradually he gained an audience with songs like "Demokrasi Nasi" ("Rice Democracy"), "Th [Tahun (Year)] 2000" (a warning that overpopulation might eventually sink Java into the sea), and "Mbak Tini" (about the struggles of a truck driver laid off by the government). His songs reflected a sympathy for the casualties of socioeconomic change, such as underpaid teachers, shoeshine boys, desperate prostitutes, and unemployed graduates. But his cassette producers were careful not to directly challenge or circumvent government or military institutions in order to avoid prohibition.

Initially Iwan's style reflected a pop country (even early Dylanesque) format of acoustic guitar and harmonica; later he took on a more rockish tone with electric guitar and synthesizer. He retains a charismatic yet unpretentious image. By the early 1980s, when his first album appeared, Iwan was attracting attention from middle-class magazines like *Tempo*, which praised his social concerns and noted his growing popularity among both middle- and lower-class youth, but also saw him as unpolished and a product of the urban streets. The critical lyrics of his songs soon attracted more attention, including a twelve-day interrogation by local police in the Riau Islands in 1984, after he helped a student fundraising effort. His notoriety as a potential oppositionist may have deterred further serious media coverage.

Iwan's fame has come largely through cassette recordings, as the government has banned many performances because of the alleged threat of rioting.

Iwan Fals as Youthful Rebel

Iwan Fals, sometimes called Mr. Thongs, was accused of promoting social unrest and disturbing national stability from early in his career. He wrote his first song in 1975 while still a junior high school student; the song told the story of "The child of a government minister who caused a stir, shooting people dead without being punished." The fifth of nine children, his father was a retired colonel. But Iwan grew up angry with society's failings. "It is truly not in accordance with the laws of the country, which is said to be a democracy," he has proclaimed through his song lyrics. Most of his successful early songs offer stories filled with social imbalance. "Guru Oemar Bakri," from his first album in 1981, recounts the saga of a mathematics teacher who, even in this video age, still had to ride an old bicycle, while his wages dropped lower every month. Iwan also composed several songs about low-class prostitutes, unfortunate women always torn between sin and hunger. The singer admits to having been interrogated eleven times by authorities by the time he was 22 because of his controversial song lyrics. Persistent warnings suggested that "I can't sing certain songs." And the cassette companies themselves were becoming more careful, "taking precautions" before making new recordings.[161]

For example, in 1989 Iwan was due to begin an unprecedented hundred-city tour throughout the country; Rhoma Irama holds the old record of fifty cities. The tour was pathbreaking for other reasons. Iwan and his record company were going to sell his new cassette, *Mata Dewa* ("Eye of God"), directly at the concert, rather than through the Jakarta distributing companies (the so-called Glodok Mafia) that maintain a stranglehold on the industry. However, the first concert (a free one in Jakarta) attracted a hundred thousand fans and ended in some looting. This gave the government an excuse to cancel the tour and place a temporary ban on all rock concerts. While political considerations undoubtedly played a role, quite likely both the Glodok Mafia (which resented Iwan's independence) and a tobacco company jealous of his commercial sponsorship by a rival may have pressured the government to act. But the cassette was not banned despite its critical lyrics.[162]

Iwan's songs demand democratization and human rights, condemn corrupt power holders in government and business, sympathize with the poor, criticize the hypocrisy of the media and the blindness of parents, and extol idealism. For example, his 1988 hit "Puing" ("Ruins") conveys the following:

Nukes are like a god
The general looks proud
From the pulpit he says:
For peace, for peace . . .
Garbage![163]

One of the songs on Iwan's *Mata Dewa* album, "Pinggiran Kota Besar" ("City Margins"), attacks the impact of pollution on slum dwellers:

> *The river is filthy and poisoned*
> *Full of garbage and chemicals*
> *We bathe and wash up in it . . .*
> *will you look . . . sir.*[164]

A 1990 song that sold over a million cassette copies urges major change:

> *Oppression and abuses of power*
> *Are too numerous to mention*
> *Stop, stop, don't go on*
> *We're fed up with greed and uncertainty.*[165]

Iwan quite consciously employs music as a forum to spread his views and perceives himself as a spokesman for society; he claims that "other people talk in coffee shops. I sing."[166] Apparently his articulation of popular resentments conveys a sense of power to his fans. Iwan has achieved wide popularity among urban youth, including a big following among both kampungan and university circles. Every day dozens of youth visit the singer's home, sporting his trademark blue jeans, long hair, and bandannas. Indeed, in 1990 a magazine was banned for a survey that found Iwan (and Suharto) more popular than the Prophet Muhammad, who finished eleventh; devout Muslims were outraged.[167]

In 1990 Iwan formed a new group, Swami, which also included prominent vocalist Sawung Jabo. Their first album offered several quite overt protest songs, including "Bongkar" ("Knock it Down") and "Bento." "Bongkar" became one of his most acclaimed and widely known songs with its message that a corrupt, unresponsive system needs to be demolished. "Bento" was also considered "subversive" by many, as the satirical lyrics portray an exploitative businessman of the well-connected corporate elite in unflattering terms. The song was presented in a jazz-rock fusion style with touches of rap.

While Swami was initially able to tour, their permits sometimes proscribed songs like "Bongkar." But they often violated the ban, without repercussions. A spectacular 1990 Swami concert with Rendra and his Bengkel theater group (which acted out the arrest of poor street peddlers) attracted between 120,000 and 200,000 to a Jakarta stadium, the largest concert in the nation's history. The highlight of the extravaganza was Swami's performance of "Bento"; a report in *Tempo* noted that "Swami's strongpoint indeed is its total communication with its fans."[168] Like Rhoma Irama, Iwan tapped into and appropriated the theater tradition with great success. After 1991 Iwan has only rarely been allowed to perform concerts. But it appears

"Bento"

"My name is Bento, my house exclusive.
My cars are many, money's no problem.
People they call me an executive boss.
A figure of first ranking, a cut above the rest, that's great.
My face is handsome, my lovers many.
I just give the girls a wink and everything's OK.
My business is to win deals, whatever comes along.
Damn them if people suffer on account of me.
So long as I feel great, let me say again, that's great.
Sermons of morality, talk of justice,
That's my breakfast fare.
Scheming, lobbying, and business graft,
I'm the champ.
Petty thieves and small-time hoods,
They're just rubbish to me.
If you want to learn, just come to me.
Say my name three times, Bento, Bento, Bento,
That's great."—Iwan Fals[169]

that Iwan and Swami have attained even greater popularity, their songs favored by buskers, their names the subject of massive graffiti. Apparently the songs strike a deep chord of public discontent; they are employed to express resistance, solidarity, and involvement. Protesters, such as the taxi drivers who struck in Jakarta in 1990, sing "Bento" and wave Iwan T-shirts.

It remains a persistent possibility that government repression and public antipathy abetted by Iwan's music might collide in violence. On the other hand, there is also the danger that Iwan's close association with intellectuals (like Rendra) and sympathetic businessmen, who together represent a sort of radical chic approach fashionable among sections of the elite, might end up co-opting or compromising his message and appeal. One of Iwan's patrons has been shipping magnate Setiawan Djody, who has sponsored concerts (including the 1990 Jakarta spectacular) and even accompanied Iwan on guitar. Although Djody seems attracted to songs about the exploited masses, he has also expressed interest in integrating a more Islamic tone into Swami's music. Some observers believe Iwan has toned down his social criticism since 1990 as his musical sound became less acoustic and more high-tech. After the intense controversy, Iwan seemed to be tiring of the many perils of celebrity. In 1993 he disclaimed any intention to speak for the younger generation and ruled out a political career as requiring "too much discipline."[170]

By 1995 Iwan, although still a countercultural hero, could astound Indonesians by performing a free concert with Rendra celebrating fifty years of the Indonesian military. The crowd of 300,000 included many peasants and urban workers. The concert was performed in Solo (Surakarta), organized by Djody, and had the support of local military officials. Whether this collaboration represented a common concern for the disadvantaged or merely served as a military-sanctioned safety valve for defusing resentments remained unclear.[171] In August 1995, both Fals and Rhoma Irama joined in the government-sponsored concerts celebrating Indonesia's fifty years of independence. Rhoma presented his latest song, "185 Juta" ("185 Million"), about Indonesia's growing population.[172] Meanwhile, by the late 1980s a more westernized musical form, rap, was gaining an audience, much to the chagrin of cultural nationalists. Local rap artists like Iwa K, Igor Tamerlan, and Farid Hardja integrated their own personalities and languages into a somewhat imitative style, but their work was criticized in the middle-class press as simple grumbling or whining. Local rap could, as it develops, offer an alternative to Iwan's folk rock and Rhoma Irama's dangdut as a vehicle for sociopolitical comment, although its derivative nature may render it inherently marginal.[173]

Conclusions

What can we conclude about Indonesian popular music and politics? There has been an ongoing struggle between various groups to define the Indonesian world and hence promote particular kinds of behavior and thought. One can make a case for most pop music as an entertaining opiate, with the state and commercial interests both profoundly influencing cultural expression in many fields. Many observers report a political passivity and obsession with materialism among contemporary Indonesian youth after two decades of social engineering to repress youthful political activism. The government might have seen limited social criticism in popular music as a useful safety valve comparable to the "Jakarta Spring." They may also have hoped that dangdut and other "countercultural" forms might eventually be "domesticated" and co-opted, turned into slick and harmless urban musical forms as kroncong had been. Rhoma's membership in GOLKAR and Iwan's collaboration with the military certainly suggest some commonality of interest between musicians and officialdom. In some respects popular music, like the "proletarian dramas" of ludruk and bangsawan before it, as well as contemporary films, may constitute a "rite of modernization," a symbolic action facilitating adjustment to a changing world.[174] Furthermore, the protest of singers like Rhoma and Iwan has been, paradoxically, commercialized by the same business interests they attack or satirize. Perhaps popular music became an escape, a refuge for youth, just like the evolution of Bahasa Prokem or the hero worship of former President Sukarno, a response to conformity and a widening generation gap.

On the other hand, the social commentary and satire component of popular music is pronounced, with the music and musicians having strong roots in the common people. This provides the mostly youthful audience with a text or model for comprehending the societal changes occurring around them. Furthermore, its reach spans the archipelago, linking varied audiences together in a shared experience. Perhaps this abets the "imagining" of a new community (national or subcultural). Artists and musicians have long played a critical role in Indonesian (especially Javanese) society, including instructing the audience on sociocultural and moral expectations and setting a mood for reflection. The popularity of critical musicians like Rhoma or Iwan may have empowered the audience, raised their consciousness, and promoted political activity, with much of the audience interpreting their music as an expression of resistance on a personal level, their concerts a collective assertion of a political stance, even if no real organized political movement resulted. There is a component of "bottom-up" expression in their music, in contradiction to the "top-down" focus of the Indonesian elite and their policies. Clearly when a pop song like Iwan's "Bento" can become a widely sung protest anthem, the musician has helped spur activism. The official restrictions on Rhoma's or Iwan's use of public forums would suggest that at least some power holders indeed fear or perceive these developments. Certainly popular musicians, with their unparalleled access to a mass audience, can be credited with raising difficult issues and keeping them in the public dialogue, offering an alternative political voice in a constricted system.

3

Philippines: Pinoy, Protest, and People Power

I hope that in due time the enchantment of Western civilization shall gradually wear off and in its place a truly integrated Filipino consciousness will develop ever more richly as the spirit of a proud and sovereign people that it must be.

Felipe Padilla De Leon, Filipino critic.[1]

Few societies have been as drenched in music as the Philippines. Pop star Freddie Aguilar describes the ubiquity of singing in his country:

> It's a part of everyday life. Street vendors sing a song about the excellence of their goods; in the country the people you pass washing in a stream will be singing; a cook in his kitchen, a laundrywoman, they're always singing. . . . Even when things are bad, instead of becoming depressed and quiet, they sing to forget their problems.[2]

Visitors will note the prevalence of T-shirts with messages like "Where There Is Music There Can't Be Misery" and "Music is the Medicine of a Troubled Mind."[3] Music has also been integral to the continuous dialogue about Filipino national identity and the extent of neocolonialism in daily life. This chapter traces the rise of a politicized pop music style known as *pinoy* and examines its leading performers such as Freddie Aguilar. It then examines the role of Aguilar and pinoy in the popular agitation and mobilization leading to the end of the Marcos dictatorship. Finally it explores musical developments in the aftermath of the Marcos era.

The Roots of Politics and Music

The Philippines boasts a mixed sociocultural heritage deriving from indigenous, Spanish, and American influences.[4] American historian David Steinberg refers to the Philippines as "both singular and plural," meaning that within a distinctive society are a multiplicity of cultures, regions, religions, and ways of life.[5] The population has scattered across seven thousand islands, although the majority live on the two largest islands of Luzon and Mindanao. Except for a small but economically influential Chinese minority, most Filipinos speak one of nearly a hundred Malay languages and dialects that developed in the archipelago. Over three centuries of Spanish colonial rule, during which the Catholic religion and many aspects of Spanish culture were imposed in a process known as Hispanization, some 85 percent of the

Basic Data[6]

Population (1994): 69,000,000

Urban Population: 44 percent

Capital: Manila (metro population: 8,000,000)

Life Expectancy: 65 (63 years for men, 66 years for women)

Adult Literacy: 90 percent

Religions: Roman Catholicism (83 percent); Protestantism (9 percent); Islam (5 percent); Other (3 percent)

Economy: Per capita GNP: U.S. $770

Radio Ownership: 7,388,000; 321 commercial and noncommercial stations

Radio Receivers Produced (incl. radio–cassette tape players): 544,000 (1983)

Television Ownership: 3,399,000; 5 Manila-based commercial television channels

People Per Television Set: 20.5

Television Receivers Produced: 300,000 (1987)

Media: 20 daily newspapers (11 in English, 9 in Pilipino, regional languages)

Major Recording Companies (1995): Abel (7 local labels incl. Able, AMS, Cebuano; distributes 3); Alpha (8 local labels incl. Alpha, Fame, Kinamaham, Mayon); Dyna (2 labels; distributes 5 incl. EMI, Chrysalis); Ivory (6 labels); OctoArts (3 labels; distributes 33 incl. Blue Note, Capitol, EMI, Narada, Rap-A-Lot); PolyCosmic (3 labels; distributes 11 incl. A&M, Decca, Island, Motown, Philips, Polydor); Quantum (2 labels; distributes 5 incl. Warner); Universal (3 labels; distributes 7); Victor (1 label; distributes Victor)

Music Publishers (1995): BMG, Bayanihan, Bell, OctoArts, Polycosmic, Victor

population adopted the Roman Catholic religion. Islamic minorities occupy the southernmost islands, while hill peoples, many of whom still practice animism, live in the mountain districts.

Although the Spanish created a country—and ultimately a nationality—they did not construct a cohesive society. The Philippines came to be a cluster of groups organized along vertical lines between superiors and subordinates, patrons and clients. The colonial economic system, especially the emphasis on sugar, forged a rural society based on plantation agriculture and tenant farming, implanting a permanent chasm between the extraordinarily rich and the impoverished, a stunted economic development dependent on the international market.[7] Regional and ethnic loyalties, as well as a primary orientation toward the family, also remained dominant.

Music of all sorts has played a stronger role in Philippine life than in most other Asian societies, and this pattern can be traced back centuries, certainly predating the Spanish period. The folk tradition was a rich one, with many regional variations. Among the oldest songs are lullabies, as well as songs about wayfaring, marriage, war, sorrow, work, and love. There were many distinctive musics among the various indigenous ethnic groups, but many would be overwhelmed by the Western presence. Only beginning in the 1960s would there be serious attempts to reclaim these instruments and rhythms, most notably in the compositions and performances of classically trained ethnomusicologist Dr. Jose Maceda, composer Lucrecia Kasilag, and in "ethnic rock" musicians like Asin, Pen Pen, and Joey Ayala, to be discussed in this chapter.[8]

The Spanish introduced Western instruments such as the guitar, violin, and piano; after awhile they became part of Filipino tradition too, included in the guitar string bands known as *rondalla* (still common in the rural areas) and as accompaniment for many of the Spanish-influenced dances. Dances such as the regional *sinulog* of Cebu City changed over the decades to reflect the local sociocultural context. Perhaps the music most identified as truly Filipino in a broad sense (neither highly regional nor blatantly derivative) is the *kundiman*, a passionate romantic ballad form with much pathos that originated during Spanish colonialism. The emotionalism of the kundiman may have allowed Filipinos to express their love of country while circumventing Spanish repression of all nationalistic sentiments. But even the classic, sentimental songs of unrequited love were transformed into revolutionary meanings in the late nineteenth century, through the use of metaphors about enslavement, oppression, and the martyrdom of nationalist heroes; some songs offered more overt political messages.[9] Filipino historian Rey Ileto has also shown how average Filipinos utilized various Spanish cultural influences in a counterhegemonic way. In particular the ritual reading of the *Payson Pilapil* (a local version of the life,

Protestant evangelical group in suburban working class near Manila using music to spread their message. 1977 photo by Bill Frederick.

death, and resurrection of Christ presented during Holy Week) became something of a subversive act (Christ as a victim of political oppression) that stimulated movements for change and inspired revolutionaries in the latter half of the nineteenth century.[10]

The country came under U.S. control from 1898 to 1946. Philippine nationalist sentiment in the nineteenth century was particularly significant among writers such as the poet and novelist Jose Rizal; it has remained a preoccupation of cultural leaders. In 1898, as Filipino nationalists waged a revolutionary struggle against the economically stagnant, corrupt, and repressive Spanish regime, the United States entered the conflict as an episode of the Spanish-American War being waged in the Caribbean. After the allied American and nationalist forces defeated the Spanish, the Americans turned on the rebels, announcing that they would annex the country as a colony. As President McKinley put it, ignoring centuries of Filipino civilization and Catholicism as well as the deep desire for independence and socioeconomic change, it was America's duty "to educate the Filipinos, and uplift and civilize and Christianize them, and by God's grace do the very best we could by them."[11]

During the four years of the Philippine-American War, U.S. forces fought a fierce and bloody struggle against a mismatched but heroic nationalist military effort that ended in 1902 with the suppression of the Filipino resistance and hence the termination of what many believe to have been an authentic social revolution against colonialism. The racism of many American soldiers (who called the Filipinos "gooks" and "niggers"), and the terrorist tactics often employed in "pacification," generated longlasting resentments among some social groups. The valor of the rebel soldiers, the active participation of many peasants, and the commitment of many Filipinos to the cause of national independence may have "made this struggle one of the first wars of national liberation."[12] It is common to over-romanticize the Filipino guerrillas, who were deeply divided along sociocultural and ideological lines. Philippine nationalist historians have glorified a revolt of the lower-class masses against exploitation and imperialism, while some recent scholarship asserts that the elite rather than the peasantry provided the main support for the revolutionary forces.[13] Historian John Larkin well summarizes the complex nature of the revolution:

> It encompassed all of the varied political aspirations of the Filipino people and has supplied national heroes and patriotic ideals for future generations. It enlisted within its ranks a wide number of social revolutionaries who had hitherto operated independently. . . . [Their] diverse aims . . . became focused upon the single goal of nationhood, with little agreement on the shape the state would take.[14]

With the revolution crushed, the Philippines became the place where the United States came closest to enjoying free rein to do whatever it wished with the lives of other people, including a strong dose of social engineering. The somewhat naive American version of taking up the "white man's burden" was known as *benevolent assimilation*, during which the colonizers did sponsor much education and public welfare, raising literacy rates well above colonial standards, as well as involving (or co-opting) the Filipino elite in administration. But also, like other colonizing powers, the United States exploited the colony economically and perpetuated a land ownership system in which a powerful group of landowners controlled the lives of millions of impoverished peasant tenants. These regionally based landowning families became the basis for the powerful business, industrial, and agricultural elite that dominated Philippine politics and society throughout the century. Reflecting the consensus of historians, American journalist Stanley Karnow concludes that the American performance was flawed because they "coddled the elite while disregarding the appalling plight of the peasants, thus perpetuating a feudal oligarchy that widened the gap between rich and poor."[15] Many Filipinos, especially among the political and economic elite, collaborated with, and prospered from, the Americans and the increasingly democratic colonial system. The local population was hence manipulated by both Filipino and American elites.

Culture inevitably reflected the sociopolitical changes. A local observer emphasizes the emotive nature of Filipino music of the late nineteenth and early twentieth century: "It must be noted that Filipino music during and after the Revolution, on the whole whether patriotic or not, in fast or in slow tempo, reveals an underlying pensiveness, a certain nostalgic vein without which it would cry for completion." Furthermore, he argues that postrevolution songs reflected either active consciousness, as in clear patriotic and martial songs, or passive consciousness, as in songs truly expressive of Filipino thoughts and sentiments.[16] The folk songs generated and passed on over the centuries included many addressing the concerns of

"Ang Nuno Nating" ("All Our Forefathers")

"All our forefathers of yore
In fighting never lost courage,
That we, who are their children,
May be just as brave in battle.
They bore hardships and gave their lives
So that we, their children,
May live happy and content.
These our own fields,
Our lives and our homes,
They [the Spanish] want to steal from us.
Should we, though alive,
Act as if we were dead? . . .
Let's defend our fields
As well as our children;
We have our own weapons,
Let's risk our life and blood.
For if we should lose
These our happy homes,
Our children and our wives
Will forever weep and suffer.
Come on, let's go
And offer our lives."—Nationalist Song[17]

daily life, peasant work, and moral behavior, including humorous and satirical examinations of interpersonal relations; moralizing and folk wisdom remained a distinctive feature. The Pampangan song "Ing Bangkeru" ("The Boatman"), for example, extols the triumph of peasant wit over sophisticated snobbery. Some songs and ballads are more overtly political and steeped in national pride. For example, the long ballad "Ang Paghihimagsik Laban sa Espanya" ("The Revolt Against Spain") chronicled the struggle for independence from a peasant perspective. A Tagalog song from the revolution period, "Ang Nuno Nating," was fiercely belligerent toward foreign invaders.

Mention should also be made of the *zarzuela*, a highly popular Spanish form of musical light comedy or operetta that flourished around the turn of the twentieth century. The pioneering zarzuela companies in Manila concentrated on essentially political topics such as anticolonialism and independence, a reflection of that region's heavy participation in the emerging Philippine Revolution. Writing about the nearby Pampangan region, John Larkin notes the revolutionary origins of the vernacular genre there:

> The Capampangan zarzuela began in the midst of revolution, a fundamental fact of its existence, and at its inception represented both a gesture of protest against and a celebration of victory over Spanish domination. In cultural terms the writing and initial staging . . . came forth as a revolutionary act of defiance against the vaunted superiority of the Spanish language.[18]

The Pampangan zarzuela peaked between 1900 and 1904. With the abrupt end of the revolution and the assumption of power by the new landed elite of American-backed Filipinos, however, any progressive orientation rapidly disappeared. The regional plays had always focused mostly on the concerns of domestic life, political nationalism being a weaker force there than sociocultural nationalism (eliminating local Spanish domination and hence competition). Soon the plays mainly served the function of perpetuating the ascendancy and values of the socioeconomic new order that financed them: "The vernacular zarzuela paid tribute to the social triumph of the native elite and the immutability of the economic order while encouraging the poor to remain within their station."[19]

What had begun as a progressive popular musical theater soon became in Pampanga an essentially irrelevant entertainment favored by the local elites, with little mass base of support. But some regional zarzuelas maintained a more critical focus. Playwrights such as Juan Matapang Cruz utilized anti-imperialist themes, prompting U.S. colonial officials to suppress the plays and jail the writers and performers. The zarzuela in the southern city of Iloilo found its initial inspiration in a frustrated nationalism and aimed at the moral uplift of colonized workers. The performances came to reflect contemporary social mores and life in the early twentieth century, including ideas of social advancement, good and evil, rich and poor. Indeed, they were both a reflection of and a catalyst for mass consciousness, addressing themes of

The Perception of Americanization

"The Philippines is also perhaps the world's largest slice of the American empire, in its purist impurist form. I felt a thrill of recognition as my eye caught Open 24-Hour gas stations, green exit signs on the freeways, Florida-style license plates and chains of grocery stores called 'Mom and Pop.' The deejay patter bubbling from the radios, the Merle Haggard songs drifting out of jukeboxes, the Coke signs and fast-food joints and grease-smeared garages—all carried me instantly back home, or, if not home, at least to some secondhand, beat-up image of the Sam Shepard Southwest, to Amarillo, perhaps, or East L.A. Most of all, the Philippines took me back to the junk-neon flash of teen America, the rootless Western youth culture of drive-ins and jukeboxes, teen proms, cheap cutoffs, and custom dragsters. Small wonder, perhaps, that I felt myself living in a chrome-and-denim Top 40 world."—Pico Iyer[20] common working-class problems, values and attitudes. The zarzuela, which over time became indigenized, suggested the possible transforming and educative functions of music-based arts. Indeed, nationalist playwright Nicanor Tiongson even successfully revived the form in 1982 for a Manila audience, integrating contemporary sociopolitical ideas into the traditional romantic and comic moods.[21]

Some wags describe Philippine history as "three hundred years in a Spanish convent followed by fifty years in Hollywood," producing what some observers have perceived as a bifurcated national personality and identity, poised uneasily between East and West, conservative and progressive, pietistic and expansive. Some refer to a cultural schizophrenia.[22] But Filipinos (nationalists and otherwise) have rightly been sensitive to the notion that instead of an authentic culture, they have an imitative or received one. The Spanish influences are often overemphasized. Some Filipino historians strongly criticize reductive studies dealing with the colonial period that tend to situate Philippine history in terms either of the "Christianization" of a subject people or the "Hispanization" of indigenous cultures.[23] Various American observers view the Filipinos as essentially brown-skinned but incomplete or facsimile Americans. Hence, Karnow writes of the Filipinos as a "mirror image of America, but I soon learned that the mirrors reflected distorted images, like those at a carnival sideshow. If this was not Asia, neither was it America."[24]

Several scholars caution against such simplistic notions of acculturation, challenge, and response in regard to sociocultural patterns (including superficially American ones), pointing out the perils involved in analyzing Filipino culture and society chiefly in terms of conspicuous outside influences. Their significance is vastly exaggerated because of the colonial auspices under which they were introduced, resulting in a tendency to look at the local culture as essentially passive and rather insignificant. Hence the foreign elements are assigned the decisive role in the shaping of Filipino culture. This view leads inevitably to the conclusion that there is in reality no true Filipino culture. Reading too much westernization into the obvious influences from outside can mislead observers. While many institutions have indeed been inherited from the colonial past, their superficial resemblance to foreign models has usually masked the subtle processes in which they have been domesticated into a unique social fabric.[25]

The Marcos Dictatorship

Following a divisive and brutal occupation by the Japanese during World War II, the Philippines achieved independence in 1946 under elected civilian governments. But over the next several decades political and economic power remained concentrated in a small, rather corrupt group of landowners, industrialists, and businessmen who had prospered under U.S. rule. Personal and family rivalries, rather than ideological differences, separated the political parties. Elections, while freewheeling, often involved enough bribery, fraud, and violence that they were criticized as mainly decided by "guns, goons, and gold." By the late 1960s there was considerable loss of faith in the ability of democratic institutions to cope with the challenges, but the elites did little to make the institutions work.[26] Furthermore, many observers characterized the Philippines as essentially neocolonial, shaped by strong political, economic, and sociocultural influences from the United States, a situation symbolized by the presence of major U.S. military bases; these bases became a significant source of income and employment for a constantly cash-strapped government.

The impoverished rural areas and predominantly Islamic southernmost islands experienced various insurgencies to bring revolution or autonomy. During the late 1940s through mid-1950s, the communist-led Huks capitalized on peasant discontent to challenge for power in central Luzon. Only the promise (but ultimately not the reality) of socioeconomic reform, and heavy U.S. assistance, succeeded in suppressing the rebellion. By 1972, when President Ferdinand Marcos declared martial law and suspended liberal democracy, a new group, the communist New Peoples Army (NPA), was active in or controlled many rural districts, attracting support from many rural tenant farmers and urban slum dwellers with a promise of dramatic socioeconomic change. Marcos ruled under martial law as dictator until 1986, when a spontaneous "peoples power" movement and the loss of U.S. support forced him to leave the country.

The Marcos Dynasty and National Culture

Imelda Marcos, the First Lady, became actively involved in national affairs, including a visionary building program to construct a cultural center that would be the Acropolis of a new Athens in Asia. She also promoted a film center modeled on the Parthenon for staging film festivals, Miss Universe contests, and professional boxing matches. If Filipinos could see cleanliness and order around them, she believed, they would be orderly and clean. "Yes, the Filipinos are living in slums and hovels," she said. "But what counts is the human spirit, and the Filipinos are smiling. They smile because they are a little healthy, a little educated, and a little loved. And for me the real index of this country is the smiles of the people, not the economics index." Imelda wanted the cultural center hall inaugurated in a way that would emphasize Philippine roots. She chose a pageant-drama involving dance, pantomime, solo and choral singing, backed by an orchestra of native instruments. The story was presented in an ancient form of Tagalog, unintelligible even to the Tagalog speakers in the audience, based on a Philippine legend about a hero who visits Panay Island and cheats the local ruler out of his property—roughly the equivalent of the Marcos family pulling the wool over everybody's eyes.—Sterling Seagrave[27]

The magnificent Philippine Cultural Center near downtown Manila, built at great cost by the Marcos regime to promote high-class local and imported cultural expression. 1981 photo by author.

During the Marcos years the divisions between left and right increased, socioeconomic conditions deteriorated, rural poverty grew apace, and political opposition was limited by detentions, censorship, and rigged elections. By 1986 the economy was in a severe crisis; investment and various economic indices (such as per capita Gross Development Product) had declined dramatically while the foreign debt and capital flight had soared. American journalist Pico Iyer notes the irony, obvious to many visitors, that "across the street from the glittering pavilions of the Cultural Center of the Philippines, whose futuristic ramps and landscaped gardens were a gaudy monument to Marcos splendor, families were sleeping in bushes."[28] When asked in 1969 why her family and friends were successfully gaining control of a substantial portion of the economy, Imelda Marcos is reputed to have answered, "Some are smarter than others."[29]

Marcos, his family, and cronies looted the country for their own benefit. Thousands of dissidents were jailed or exiled and the media was largely smothered by violence, the threat of violence, or co-optation, becoming in the process sycophantic abettors of the Marcos facade. Marcos allocated considerable state support for cultural expression (to critics, mostly flashy projects), but the policies did not substantially move the country toward a national culture. It should be noted that many Filipinos did not view the Marcos regime as essentially bankrupt and ruthless during the 1970s, much to the chagrin of critics. They welcomed the reduction in political squabbling and accepted the progressive rhetoric of the "New Society" at face value, even if it all too often clashed with reality. In part this resulted from a modestly successful public relations campaign to mythologize the First Family and recreate them as cultural heroes whose lives could give less privileged Filipinos vicarious pleasures.[30] The United States backed the Marcos government until the very end, in part because the dictator permitted continuation of U.S. military bases and welcomed the powerful U.S. economic presence.

In many development indices, the country lagged well behind most of the other noncommunist nations in Southeast Asia. Despite a growing urban middle class, a substantial portion of the population remained mired in dire poverty even after the end of colonial rule. In the early 1980s the top 2 percent of the population earned over half of the national income, while the bottom 20 percent obtained only 5.5 percent; only about a third of the prospective labor force held regular jobs. By the 1990s half of the population lived in absolute poverty, and some two-thirds were malnourished. In the rural sector, only a third of the people owned the land they worked; most of the rest were tenant farmers or hired workers. By 1989 the unemployment rate hovered at over 10 percent and the underemployment rate at around 20 percent, a situation abetted by the high rate of population growth in this overwhelmingly Catholic nation. The annual growth rate of 2.5–2.8 percent (depending on the source) was expected to double the population between 1990 and 2020.[31] The situation in one of the most depressed regions—Negros—has been described as follows:

> Sugar workers idle away as many as six months a year. Hungry children latch onto their mothers' breasts in a desperate bid to suck the last drops of milk before dying. . . . Older brothers and sisters chew sugar cane to ease their stomach pains. Men and women cannot find work during the off season when sugar is neither planted and cultivated nor harvested and milled. No work means no pay and no benefits for most of the island's 250,000 sugar workers.[32]

To a significant degree the rural poor have been aware of pervasive and chronic socioeconomic inequalities; they resent being treated as less than human, and of being deprived of the resources to support their families or improve their living conditions.[33] The contrast between the few rich and many poor in Manila is particularly glaring:

> A tiny minority of the population live in palatial homes surrounded by servants, work in air-conditioned high-rise office buildings . . . and travel to foreign cities to conduct business . . . or vacation. . . . The homes of the wealthy are surrounded by gardens in neighborhoods encircled by high walls topped with bits of broken glass and barbed wire where the gates are manned by armed guards. The vast majority of the capital's people live in improvised housing, made of scrap wood, metal and cardboard, that lines the roads and highways and the slopes surrounding better-off middle class suburbs. Manila is a city of eight million people with an infrastructure designed to accommodate two million, and it is bursting at the seams.[34]

In this situation it was not surprising that, since the 1890s, many thousands of Filipinos migrated—temporarily or permanently—to the United States or, more recently, the Middle East. Many Filipinas were forced by circumstances to work at home or abroad in sex-related jobs; by 1990 UNICEF estimated that at least twenty thousand children worked as prostitutes. Many observers conclude that the problem for the Philippines, then, is not economic growth, which has proceeded steadily in the postcolonial years, but a more just distribution of wealth.[35]

Problems of National Identity and Cultural Nationalism

Given the debate about Philippine identity, critics have not focused exclusively on socioeconomic problems. Nationalists have perceived American rule and sociocultural models (that appealed to many Filipinos) as hindering, even thwarting, the creation of a truly independent Filipino identity and culture that seemed so promising in 1898. Filipinos developed an ambivalence about the United States, with cycles of "hamburgerization" alternating with surges of nationalism.[36] One of the best expressions of a radical nationalist perspective can be found in the writings of historian and social critic Renato Constantino, a proponent of cultural decolonization:

> We see our present with as little understanding as we view our past because aspects of the past which could illumine the present have been concealed from us. This concealment has been effected by a systematic process of mis-education characterized by a thoroughgoing inculcation of colonial values and attitudes—a process which could not have been so effective had we not been denied access to the truth and to part of our written history. As a consequence, we have become a people without a sense of history. Because we have so little comprehension of our past, we have no appreciation of its meaningful interrelation with the present.[37]

Because of or despite the "mis-education" many nationalists believe they received under American rule, Filipinos themselves have been among the keenest critics of their own failings. For example, in 1988 Senator Leticia Ramos Shahani called for an official study of cultural deficiencies, since the Philippines was "a sick nation gravely afflicted with the interlocking diseases of poverty, passivity, graft and corruption, exploitative patronage, factionalism, political instability, love for intrigue, lack of discipline, lack of patriotism and a desire for instant gratification."[38]

Filipinos have never fully resolved the problem of creating an integrated national identity out of the diverse mosaic of languages and regions. Cultural researcher Edilberto Alegre puts the claim bluntly: "Culturally we are not a nation. Not yet. . . . Neither is there a language with which we can successfully communicate. . . . The [national] government and culture do not coincide."[39] Even the choice of a national language is rancorous. The national language, Pilipino, is based on the Tagalog language of central

Luzon, spoken as a native tongue by about a quarter of the population. Native Tagalog speakers constitute the largest of the dozens of ethnolinguistic groups in the islands and are dominant in Manila. This inevitably became a sensitive issue because it is not easy to distinguish between Tagalog and Pilipino. While Pilipino is taught in the schools, fluency in English remains widespread among all classes and nearly universal among the middle classes and elite. Indeed, command of fluent English can help legitimize and strengthen local power holders.[40] Elite publications use English, but much of the popular mass and entertainment media publish in Tagalog or a regional language. Furthermore, "Taglish" (sometimes called "Taglese" or "Engalog"), a mixed English-Tagalog pidgin, is also widely employed in the popular press and in daily speech, particularly in Manila and other cities. The widespread use of Taglish in films aimed at nonelite audiences, it has been argued, tends to reaffirm the linguistic hierarchy and hence the social order.[41]

By the 1980s slightly over half of the population could speak Pilipino, only marginally more than could speak English; in many regions local languages still dominate daily life. Homogenizing, mass-mediated popular culture emanating from Manila in the form of films, television, comics, and music has helped spread understanding of Pilipino/Tagalog but does

"The Guerilla Is Like a Poet"

"The guerrilla is like a poet
Keen to the rustle of leaves
The break of twigs
The ripples of the river
The smell of fire
And the ashes of departure . . .
He has merged with the trees
The bushes and the rocks
Ambiguous but precise . . .
And master of myriad images
Enrhymed with nature
The subtle rhythm of the greenery
The inner silence, the outer innocence
The steel tensile in-grace
That ensnares the enemy . . .
Swarming the terrain as a flood
Marching at last against the stronghold
An endless movement of strength
behold the protracted theme:
The people's epic, the people's war."—Jose Maria Sison[42]

not eliminate regional identities. Many of the elite are uncomfortable speaking Pilipino and most disdain or maintain a condescending attitude towards Taglish, reducing the possibilities of interclass communication. Many Filipinos are bilingual or trilingual, using the local vernacular at home, Pilipino as an urban lingua franca, and English in commerce, government, and international relations. English remains the main language of secondary and university education, a neocolonial policy that angers nationalists who believe this helps explain the 80 percent of Filipinos who do not go beyond elementary school.[43]

For decades some Filipinos, including a substantial section of the intellectual elite and progressive students, have believed that their country remained a neocolony of the United States, a situation that requires cultural as well as political decolonization. For example, literary critic Patricia Melendrez-Cruz argues that the Filipino writer has an obligation to respond to popular needs, address socioeconomic problems, and escape the enchantment of the colonizer by opposing the status quo. In this way, the writer can help create a truly Filipino worldview by realizing that Filipinos are the true creators of their own destiny:

> But, before this, writers need to free themselves from colonial influences, to connect their national character with their consciousness. Only by going back to the fountain of their art—the Filipino people—by participating in the national struggle, and by basing literature on the aspirations of the Filipino people, will writers be able to fulfill their duty as communicator and giver of meaning to the Filipino experience, and voice the hope of the people for a humane, just, peaceful, progressive and free society.[44]

Indeed, literature and politics maintained a long cohabitation, including a vigorous tradition of protest poetry and humorous satire.[45] Poet Jose Maria Sison, the founder of the New Peoples Army, has even compared the guerrilla to a poet.

In the late 1960s and early 1970s, many intellectuals and youth activists joined in a call for a "cultural revolution" to produce a "mass culture" suited for Philippine conditions and in opposition to the elite culture promoted by the ruling establishment. This sparked a nationalist dialogue on culture as well as social change-oriented popular arts and music that laid the groundwork for the activism of the 1970s. Indeed, during the Marcos dictatorship some brave writers risked retribution by employing codewords and other deceptions to criticize the regime in their works. The push for the construction of a "people's culture" and the development of a national consciousness has persisted among many in the arts and culture community.[46] For example, the poet Alfrredo Navarro Salanga calls for reinterpreting Philippine history:

It's history that
Moves us away
From what we are
We call it names
Assign it origins
And blame the might
That made Spain right
And America—bite.
This is what it amounts to:
We've been bitten off, excised
From the rind of things
What once gave us pulp
Has been chewed off
And pitted—dry.[47]

Despite the strong indigenous component of Filipino culture, most observers remark on a powerful American influence in the country's popular culture even after independence. Some Filipinos celebrate this reality and admire the former colonizer. Other more nationalistic voices bemoan the situation and call for the creation of a more authentic Filipino culture and identity freed from neocolonialism. To Constantino, "The existence of a Filipino nation is a fact, but the existence of a national consciousness is only a presupposition."[48] Constantino charges that many local newspapers and magazines are essentially purveyors of neocolonialism: "Magazines and the feature sections of newspapers tranquilize their readers by focussing attention on purely personal issues, psychological problems, sex, crime and violence, astrology and the occult, fashion and personality, entertainment and sports."[49] On the other hand, innovative, experimental theater groups seeking cultural authenticity abound and some were active in the movement to overthrow the Marcos dictatorship.[50] The debate about national culture has produced some interesting paradoxes, such as the controversial anti-American nationalist, novelist, poet, and playwright Nick Joaquin, who extols the Spanish-Creole heritage but writes in English.[51]

Doreen Fernandez, perhaps the leading scholar on Philippine popular culture, represents the nationalistic approach in her attacks on cultural imperialism and satellization and the way they sap Filipino culture. To Fernandez and many other Filipino observers, local culture reflects the persistent reality of neocolonialism:

> This inquiry into Philippine-American interaction in popular culture shows that the very beginnings of mass media in the Philippines worked toward the establishment of a strong American base in local popular culture. It is not only that American films, canned TV programs, music, comics, and popular literature are so well entrenched in Philippine life

> today; but also that Philippine films, TV programs, music, comics, and popular literature are so patently built on the American plan. This interaction is an active, ongoing, multimedia, multi-sensory bombardment. It is not merely the encounter between a strong presence and one weakened by the colonial mentality. It is quite simply, and I use the term descriptively, cultural imperialism. Before most Filipinos become aware of Filipino literature, song, dance, history, education, language and the media have already made them alert to American life and culture and its desirability. They sing of White Christmases and of Manhattan. Their stereos reverberate with the American Top 40. In their minds sparkle images of Dynasty, Miami Vice and L.A. Law. They embrace the American Dream.[52]

The Emergence of Postcolonial Popular Music and Culture

However much colonized or neocolonized, Filipinos have long demonstrated a vigorous cultural expression, including much popular art. Nonetheless, as elsewhere, popular culture was generally ignored by scholars (local or foreign) until the late 1970s.[53] Filipino scholars have been divided on the values and meanings of popular culture, reflecting the argument between Frankfurt and Birmingham School theorists in the West. Critics generally decry most popular culture products as "purely escapist slop concocted by the hegemonic order and which the undereducated and the underprivileged lap up to the max." In this view most popular (or mass) culture is created by and serves the interests of the ruling elite and the intelligentsia that supports them. Others identify nationalist and populist messages, prompting one disgusted writer to cleverly attack the pop culture defenders as those who would "canonize the ***komiks*** . . . bird-brained popular films, pop songs, pop art and any other manifestations of pop pap in terms of semiotics, hermeneutics and other pedantic forms of idiotics."[54]

Advertising for the products of the large Philippine film industry is ubiquitous in Manila and other cities. 1978 photo by author.

Whatever the intensity and merits of the debate, the literature now available allows us to at least outline some of the key developments in popular music.[55] Many of the traditional musical and dance genres have declined in recent decades as popular arts, particularly in the cities, and have been replaced by more modernized forms of popular culture. Perhaps the precipitous displacement of traditional musics owes much to their highly regional rather than national character, combined with the structure of mass communication that was erected. The diverse folk cultures were so different from the popular forms that accompanied American rule that no real competition occurred. Instead, westernized film, radio, and pop music have essentially had the whole field to themselves.

Although some would argue for comic strips and especially the ubiquitous comic magazines (with some 16 million regular readers), no single cultural form rivals the impact of the film industry on Philippine social and intellectual life.[56] The first Philippine films date back to early in the American era (often employing zarzuela performers). By the 1980s the Philippines ranked in the top ten among film-producing nations, although struggling to compete against the freely imported U.S. movies. Hagiographic films have been credited with helping elect Marcos president, as well as perpetuating the dictatorship. Most producers concentrate on low-budget, high-volume entertainments—what one critic characterizes as "kiss-kiss, bang-bang, zoom, boo-hoo, song and dance flickers" that act as political opiate or oral pacifier.[57] But a few such as Lino Brocka, the doyen of the "New Cinema," have explored serious themes, bursting the myths offered by the celluloid dream factories, sometimes running afoul of government censorship for sociopolitical content. Furthermore, films have helped propagate Pilipino as the national language and contributed in some

Escapist Pop Music: A Filipino Critique

"Popular music of the sixties and seventies was characterized by derivations from American melody and rhythm which Filipinos copied in their compositions. The themes of the musical pieces of that era show no attempt to deviate from those of foreign music and romanticism. From an analysis of the philosophies expressed in their music, a seeming confusion or absence of direction in thought can be inferred. It would seem that, not knowing how to relate to what was reality, we ran away from it. Vocalist-actress Nora Aunor became a success because she symbolized the perplexed Filipino, who, at a loss to confront the meaning in life and events, sang songs that made him forget and thus provided a diversion. It was easier to indulge in fantasies about happiness or having the luxuries in life than to observe, search and discover the true form and flow of life. We readily utilized tools which were easily accessible for this purpose, being spoon-fed with imitations of foreign culture."—Eleanor T. Elequin[58]

Discos and nightclubs featuring live music of all sorts can be found all over Manila, reflective of the overt American influence but also of the strong role played by music in Philippine society. 1981 photo by author.

fashion to promoting Filipino culture and themes. Film stars have achieved massive popularity and one of them, Joseph Estrada, was elected vice president in 1992.[59]

Other media also appeared. The introduction of radio in the late 1930s brought in more American culture, including popular music and soap operas that became the mainstays. Indeed, radio became easily the top medium for pop songs. The introduction of transistor radios in 1959 facilitated a mass distribution; by 1969, 62 percent of households owned radios (87 percent in Manila). By 1980 there were more than three hundred radio stations in the country, 10 percent of them in metro Manila. Most were privately owned, generally linked to various powerful elite families or companies. Three radio networks operated many of the stations; these were controlled respectively by the government (twenty-four stations), a Christian evangelical missionary organization (nine stations), and the Catholic Church (their Radio Veritas was the only important station to air opposition programming in the mid-1980s).[60]

The local recording industry originated in 1913. By 1975 it had become a major force, with many companies. Among the five dominant labels in that period, two mainly duplicated and distributed foreign productions; the other three mixed foreign and domestic products. Generally American recordings greatly outsold Filipino efforts, in part because radio played at least 90 percent foreign music. Hence few Filipino musicians earned substantial incomes.[61] On the whole American popular styles (big band in the 1930s and 1940s, pop and rock 'n' roll in the 1950s) were faithfully reflected in the Philippines. In 1967, 100 percent of the "top ten" records in the Philippines were from the United States or Britain.[62] A Western observer in the 1960s rued the paramountcy of Anglo-American pop music:

> The lovely old Filipino orchestras, with their soft, muted, infinitely sad and subtle musics, are nowhere to be found. . . . As everywhere in the East . . . electric guitars and electric guitar combos are all the rage, and

Beatles-type groups are to be found in the remotest regions of the Philippines, often giving a fairly good imitation of the Stones or the . . . Kinks. . . . Some of the combos . . . bore names like "The Victors," "The Beavers" . . . "Mersey Sides," "The Wildcats" . . . and "The Sociables."[63]

The derivative nature of most Filipino pop music and the obsession with Anglo-American songs has led some outside observers to conclude that, of all Southeast Asian nations, the Philippines has had the least developed indigenous popular music.[64] What popular music existed in local languages during the 1960s consisted mainly of poorly produced and widely derided translations of Western pop hits aimed at working-class Filipinos unfamiliar with English, a genre known locally as *tunog lata* ("tinny sound"). There was also a highly formulaic "bubblegum" music castigated by sophisticates as *bakya* (low-class, "wooden slipper" music). Bakya referred to cultural forms (including Joseph Estrada films) that were cheap, naive, gauche, provincial, and popular with the masses—in other words, lowbrow.[65] Neither radio nor the recording industry took these styles very seriously. Most fans understandably preferred Elvis Presley or the Beatles in their original version. Most of the Filipino music was also essentially escapist until well into the 1970s, reflecting the heritage of neocolonialism.

Nonetheless, given the strong traditional links of musical culture with recreation, social identity, and community, the contemporary popular music of records, radio, television, and the countless music bars and coffee houses has constituted an extraordinarily important cultural force. A Filipino observer describes the radio culture and the impact of multinational corporations as of the late 1970s:

Switch on any radio in the Philippines and nine times out of ten, you will get a good dose of rock, soul, the hustle, the salsa and just about any other form of pop music. Tuning from station to station will get you the same results. It has been estimated that about 80 to 90 per cent of the programming of Philippine radio stations is made up of pop music in its varied forms. . . . The lopsided emphasis on pop is not without reason. Recording companies with foreign tie-ups have sufficient resources to make disc jockeys play only the records they want promoted.[66]

The disc jockeys pocketing "payola" and the companies peddling foreign recordings may have prospered, but the earnings of most musicians, composers, and singers remained marginal. Furthermore, the influence from the United States was massive in nearly all facets of life, producing something of a cultural backlash among many Filipinos. As Fernandez remarks ruefully:

It is American song . . . that they sing in the shower, at parties, at programs, to loved ones, at amateur shows, as professional performers on radio, television or in the movies. It is American song that has provided the catch phrases, the allusions, the memory lanes of these four generations, not the Filipino song.[67]

Many visitors (including the author) have been impressed at the flawless imitations of American singers one encounters in pubs and karaoke bars, the participants (whether professional or amateur) "masters of every American gesture, conversant with every Western song," with the "Stevie Wonder of the Philippines" sounding exactly like his idol. Furthermore, the Filipinos love "We Are the World," one journalist reports, because it "gives one member of the group the chance to do Michael Jackson, and another Cyndi Lauper and a third Bruce Springsteen. Some guy even gets to do Ray Charles."[68] Even the protest songs favored by university "bohemians" in the 1960s were largely American products (Dylan, Joan Baez, Peter, Paul, and Mary). The smoky coffeehouses near the campuses spawned local imitators of the American stars (some of whom, such as Florante and Freddie Aguilar, later went on to pioneer a more local sound).

Filipino entertainers have long dominated the stages of nightclubs and pubs all over Asia, playing jazz, rock, pop, country and western, and other "international" styles, but rarely Filipino music. Indeed, in recent years many Filipino bands and entertainers, generally familiar with "Americanized" international pop, have been forced by economic necessity to play the Asian music circuit from Tokyo and Seoul to the Persian Gulf. This is part of a general pattern in which thousands of Filipinos (by 1988, some 385,000) migrated to various Asian and European countries as temporary or long-term contract workers; over half are women. For many, nostalgic Filipino songs such as "Manila" (a 1970s hit for the group Hot Dog, redone by top songstress Kuh Ledesma in 1994) help them deal with homesickness: "Simply no place like Manila . . . I'm coming home." The expatriate bands have become part of the "3-D" culture of the emigrants—referring to the dirty (domestic work), dangerous (factory work), and difficult (entertainment) jobs available. As one study of the entertainers surrealistically concludes: "They leave their families for a salary deemed worthy . . . [going] to Nagoya . . . Singapore . . . Seoul for a contract that covers housing needs medical costs and extra monetary allowances sent from Bahrain . . . Oman to Manila they sing for the experience . . . in Tagalog beat Tagalog they sing in English Aloha in Korea Japan Malaysia . . . and this next song is for everybody."[69]

For decades many Filipino songwriters have concentrated on writing songs in English, to be recorded by Filipino singers; by and large the form and content remains westernized. For example, Kuh Ledesma's breakthrough hit in 1972 was her version of "Don't Cry for Me Argentina." During the 1970s and 1980s, major pop stars like Pilita Corrales, Sharon Cuneta, Hajji Alejandro, Nora Aunor, Celeste Legaspi, Didith Reyes, Victor Wood, and Nonoy Zuniga—who recorded some Pilipino material—were at least as well known for their English songs. Most specialized on romantic themes.[70] Corrales, sometimes known as "Asia's Queen of Song," has been the most adept at developing both a local and international following, traveling widely. A former DJ in her hometown of Cebu, she has recorded dozens of albums and hundreds of singles (in Spanish, Tagalog, Visayan, and English) while also starring in movies and TV specials. As one admiring profile put it: "Top composers . . . write songs designed for her. Once Pilita introduces a new song and imbues it with her own sound, other versions hardly matter. . . . Even the smallest record bars in the remotest Philippine barrio [find] it profitable to keep Pilita's records in stock."[71]

Various local music magazines, such as *Hot Tracks* and *Solid Gold*, concentrate on reprinting lyrics to popular Anglo-American songs. Many Filipino entertainers have sought to emulate Anglo-American models such as Elvis Presley or Cliff Richard. Occasionally Filipino musicians would record under American-sounding names such as Ian Hero, in hopes that this would boost their record sales. Beginning in the 1950s there was also a significant audience for country-and-western music; Fred Panopio, who mostly sings in Tagalog, remained the superstar of the genre for decades.[72]

The major multinational record labels that have maintained a powerful position in the country also influence public taste through their mass-marketing strategies and pressures on artists. Critics believe Western popular music (and its Filipino imitations) lulls the Filipino audience into inattentiveness; they castigate soporific ballads, rapacious heavy metal (controlled violence), and mindless disco for deflecting awareness of social realities and portraying women as either emotionally helpless or predatory.[73] Reflecting nationalist resentment at this situation, an innovative Manila street theater group in 1985 developed a play about the history of popular music in the Philippines in order to convey the message that the escapist, American-influenced popular culture encouraged feelings of complacency and powerlessness, hence diverting attention from Philippine realities.

"Ang Himig Natin" ("Our Music")

"If you remember in the past
Many of us did not like Filipino songs
Oftentimes everyone thought
That the beautiful songs
Were created in other countries
But if you listen to the radio . . .
You will say to yourself
We are not behind . . .
In our music, our very own creation . . .
Sing our song
So that we'll all be together."—Joey Smith[74]

The Rise of Pinoy

The rise of politicized popular music is closely linked to the development in the early 1970s of the musical style known as pinoy (or sometimes Pilipino), a deft blend of rock, folk, and ballads sung not in English but in Tagalog (Pilipino); indeed, the lyrics were often in a slang-filled Tagalog that appeals to urban youth. Pinoy music was a conscious attempt to create a Filipino national and popular culture, and some nationalist critics have praised it for reflecting social realities and problems including poverty, prostitution, injustice, and the persistent neocolonial mentality. One Filipino observer makes the case for pinoy as a significant new art form that challenges neocolonialism:

> Pinoy pop is new because it caters to a wider audience, cuts across classes A to D, and is being sung by employees in multinational firms in Makati as well as by ill-clad children in Tagbanua village. Pinoy pop is Filipino because some songs (in their limited ways) mirror the Philippine experience in underdevelopment. While it may be said that Pinoy pop is colonial and feudal, it is only so because Philippine society is neo-colonial and semi-feudal too.[75]

Perhaps inevitably, then, pinoy music would take on political overtones. Early pinoy singers such as Rico Puno (a business college dropout who specialized in "Taglish" material), folk-oriented Florante de Leon, and three stars who commenced their career with the Juan de la Cruz Band (Joey Smith, Wally Gonzalez, and the "High Priest of Pinoy Rock," Mike Hanopol) explored the meaning of Filipino identity and the importance of pinoy expression, even though much of their music superficially resembled Western rock.[76] Indeed, Western rock had an enormous influence in the 1960s and early 1970s; the breakup of the Beatles (and the lack of equally popular replacements) may have opened the way for the pinoy phenomenon. What distinguished the de la Cruz Band's pinoy music from bakya and tunog lata was the parentage of composition and audience; these were Tagalog songs written for sophisticated Filipinos. One of Smith's early songs, "Ang Himig Natin" ("Our Music") pleaded for Filipino expression. Soon groups like The Hot Dog and Cinderella responded with pathbreaking Taglish songs.[77] By 1974 recording studios were beginning to release more and better-produced pinoy music. By 1977, a local audience for this music had grown substantially enough to provide a lucrative market.

It needs to be emphasized that the term *pinoy* (an affectionate term for Pilipino) is an imprecise but (for my purposes) convenient umbrella label for a progression of popular styles that developed, linked mainly by their use of Tagalog rather than English. Some but by no means all of the songs reflected distinct Filipino sentiments as opposed to mere replicating of Anglo-American moods. Not all observers would apply the term *pinoy* to all of the songs or musicians analyzed in this study. Two experts trace the evolution of the genre as follows: The Manila Sound (1975), Pinoy Rock (1977), Pinoy Folk (1978–1979), the jazz years (early 1980s), mellow pop and folk (mid-1980s). They conclude from this that "whenever a new musical fad dominates the airwaves, Filipino pop music manages to hang on, against all odds." The unavailability of musical technology such as synthesizers and audio equipment may help explain why pinoy music repeatedly returns to a folk-based sound. Perhaps folk music is more digestible than electronic rock, and the Filipino tradition going back to the days of the kundiman might account for the affinity for the sound and melodic possibilities of the acoustic guitar. Furthermore, folk music is direct, malleable (easily fused with ethnic rhythms), and easily recorded.[78]

The checkered history of pinoy in its changing forms during the 1970s is partly explained by a lack of leadership as well as a public image that the music served a small cult clientele. A Philippine magazine described the situation in the following terms in the late 1970s:

> The movement of Pinoy Rock music badly needs leadership and the people who are qualified would not come out, in total force. For fear of burning out? Martyr complex? No organization. And no funds. No unity. Are we really that cynical about Pinoy music? Meantime, Pinoy rock . . . remains a baby. An ugly one now. . . . As long as the ego-tripping psychedelic rock displays are gross and blatant, society won't accept Pinoy Rock.[79]

The various incarnations of pinoy have always struggled to survive and were nearly crushed by the flood of imported rock and pop encouraged by both the recording industry and the government. Meanwhile, most cultural and arts organizations have considered pinoy too déclassé and controversial. For example, the "Manila Sound" was widely criticized in 1975 for desecrating the language and employing sexual innuendo, prompting the Broadcast Media Council to temporarily ban the music from the air. It should also be noted that, given the widespread poverty and hence relatively small consuming middle class, the market for recorded music has inevitably been small, with pirating or illicit taping a major challenge to the record industry. By the mid-1980s a record selling twenty thousand legitimate copies was considered to have gone "gold."[80]

Early pinoy or proto-pinoy songs were rarely overtly political and their lyrics tended to follow safe universalistic themes like brotherhood and understanding. As in many countries, however, there was considerably more social meaning below the surface. Many Filipino popular songs during the 1970s strongly reflected a distinctive Filipino worldview; they articulated the perception of life and of society, including a strong sense of fatalism. "Incorporated in the themes of the songs are the Filipinos' view of the meaning of life, fate, love, joy, and suffering."[81] Perhaps, as some believe, pinoy music became the chief way for Filipinos to confront their realities and air their grievances, and in the process it changed the consciousness of Filipinos.[82] Filipino social critic Virgilio Enriquez goes further, contending that "inasmuch as social reality shapes the Filipino world-view, the Philippine social reality interpreted through contemporary song is that of unemployment, prostitution and poverty."[83] This has even been true sometimes for more escapist genres. For example, one of country-and-western star Fred Panopio's best-known songs, "Pitung Gatang" ("Seven Litres"), is a tale of a tough Manila neighborhood known for its street markets and bulk food sales.

The atmosphere of the martial law period for progressive musicians led to an underground music for concerts, union meetings, and picket lines. Jess Santiago, pop musician and cultural activist, remembers the creative tension of the time:

> There was a long lull. You could hardly hear any songs that you could call progressive [on the mass media]. . . . So that period in our history forced our musicians, not only our songwriters, but poets as well as other artists, to be more inventive, to be more creative to circumvent the very restrictive laws during that time. Songs came about that were very poetic. Instead of sloganeering the songwriters used poetry, used metaphors. And the people were hungry for songs that talked about the concrete experiences that they met every day, like "salvaging" (assassination or disappearance) or summary executions of people, and the strikes and the militarization. . . . Slowly, more and more songwriters started writing songs about these realities. . . . It was then that poets became songwriters.[84]

Kapwa is a Filipino term connoting a recognition of shared identity, encompassing both "self" and "other." The use of the term also implies recognition in the Filipino consciousness of contemporary realities and the need to struggle together. The pinoy pioneer Florante played off this theme in one of his best-known songs of the 1970s, "Digoman" ("War"):

Though my conscience disagrees
I am ready to do battle
For the cause of our freedom
But why can't I understand
A struggle amongst kapwa.

Florante's songs also express concern for achieving a national identity, as in his song "Pinoy" ("Filipino"):

I am a Filipino in heart and spirit
Born a Filipino into our nation
I am not skilled in foreign tongues
I am a Filipino with my own language.

"Laya" ("Free")

"If you listen to my song now,
You will say that you've heard this before.
But now the words are different
They're already in Tagalog
Once my mind was only a slave
I had awakened first to alien thoughts
But I broke the chain
So that my mind would be free."—Florante[85]

Florante's best-known songs in the genre are the nationalistic "Ako'y Pinoy" ("I'm Filipino") and "Laya" ("Free"). Another is "Awiting Sariling Atin" ("Our Own Songs"):

A scratch and a peak, that's how you see us
But we're so very rich in songs.[86]

Florante's seminal role in the evolution of a more critical popular culture was later celebrated in a 1988 rock opera.[87]

Other songs in the 1970s and early 1980s addressed common social problems and conditions. Consider Hector (Heber) Bartolome's "Buhay Pinoy" ("Filipino Life"), with its evocative portrait of poverty:

Look at the beggars on the sidewalk
There they sleep, and beg with palms outstretched
I have a friend who did not go to school
And because of poverty, was driven to steal.

Bartolome is probably the most socially conscious early pinoy singer-songwriter. Jess Santiago also specializes in these themes, with songs about injustice: a striking factory worker raped and murdered; a farmer killed defending his land; a squatter family whose house was bulldozed because it was unsightly to tourists. Bartolome and Santiago both brought their reformist political attitudes to organizations of progressive musicians from across the islands. Perhaps the seminal organization was Musika, which was established in 1979 to promote a "people's music" and coordinate cultural work during the period of martial law.

But only a few pinoy songs, such as Bartolome's "Nena" (about a poor girl forced into prostitution because rapacious factory owners exploited her father's poverty), blame a specific target such as an uncaring government, privileged elites, or imperialism. Indeed, some pinoy songs suggest that there

"Awit Ko" ("My Song")

"When we were born
Our fists were clenched
While we cried? That was in protest
Against the reality in which we are born
That ours is a nation
That blindly follows foreigners . . .
I am a Filipino, I have color
I am human, I'm not a wild boar [a reference to the accidental shooting of a Filipino by U.S. soldiers]."—Heber Bartolome[88]

is little use to struggle against fate, which determines your position in society. Hence, the song "Kapalaran" ("Destiny") asked the musical question:

Why is the life of man so
Some are rich
Some are oppressed . . .
Destiny . . . just comes without notice.[89]

Some songs criticize Filipinos themselves for their pride, flamboyance, hypocrisy, apathy, and laziness, such as Freddie Aguilar's "Katamaran" ("Laziness") and Mike Hanapol's "Laki So Layaw" ("Pampered"). A few songs offer highly subtle anti-Americanism, such as Nonoy Gallardo's "Saranggola no Pepe" ("Pepe's Kite"), which seemingly blames first the Spanish and then the Americans for dashing Filipino hopes, in the process exploiting, deculturizing, miseducating, deceiving, and controlling the people. A powerful song in this vein is Bartolome's "Awit Ko" ("My Song"), with its image of babies born with clenched fists, their protest against a nation dominated by foreigners.[90] Nor was socially conscious pinoy a complete male monopoly; singer-songwriter Coritha was an important part of the movement, with songs like "Sierra Madre" and "Leandro." Mention should also be made of the free-spirited, Indonesia-born "Queen of Pinoy Rock," Sampaguita (Tessie Santos).[91]

Perhaps because of the seemingly nonthreatening and culture-affirming nature of most of the early pinoy songs, the Marcos administration decreed that each of the many mostly private radio stations was required to play at least one—and later three—Filipino language songs an hour, giving an ironic boost to the pinoy movement while angering many in the media. Indeed, the Ministry of Culture seemed to have consciously aimed at addressing growing nationalist sentiments by minimizing foreign cultural influences. In 1978 the government launched Metro Manila Popular Song

Festival, a glitzy extravaganza to encourage—but also channel along safe lines—pinoy songwriting.[92] Imelda Marcos was fond of, and often publicly sang, sentimental pop songs like the syrupy ballad "Dahil Sayo" ("Because of You"). Perhaps the resentment against mandated Filipino recordings by radio executives and deejays may have reflected a widespread colonially imposed inferiority complex, a feeling in the Philippines—indeed in many Southeast Asian countries—that their popular music cannot possibly reach the standards of international (essentially Anglo-American) pop, with its long creative tradition, sophisticated technology, and seemingly endless supply of talent.

Nevertheless, it must be kept in mind that American music dominated both broadcasting and popular taste throughout the Marcos era, and public attitudes could not be remolded easily. As Fernandez put it: "Filipino music is thus played by order; American music by choice."[93] The growing alliance between the recording industry and the broadcast media has been credited as being a crucial development in the popularization of pinoy. Records now had a guaranteed place on radio.[94] Not all observers are convinced that pinoy music demonstrated much of an attempt to create an authentic local sound. Hence, Fernandez argued in the early 1980s that:

> Today critics and musicologists rejoice in the proliferation of composers and performers breaking into the airlanes with Filipino songs, but they admit that the rhythm and style of the music is definitely and strictly Western; except for a strain here and there, usually unconscious, there are few cases of a conscious search for what can be truly Filipino pop.[95]

Music, Protest, and Political Movements

Given the importance of music in Philippine culture, songs and singing inevitably became a part of many political movements, including those seeking radical change. This pattern even stretched back to the colonial era. The rise of student activism and feminism in the predictatorship period provided a context for protest music to flourish, often with a folk music basis, especially among urban youths and labor groups. These songs followed in a long tradition of often underground musical resistance dating back through the Japanese Occupation to the Philippine Revolution. During the 1930s, radical labor and peasant organizations, often affiliated with the Communist Party or the socialist movement, employed songs to recruit members and expand political consciousness. They also encouraged songwriting by members as part of their commitment to militancy. The songs were overtly political, and ranged from martial to kundiman in form; they extolled revolutionary action, the worker-peasant alliance, and national integrity while condemning abusive government and elite oppression.[96] During the 1940s and 1950s, the radical Hukbalahap movement—

which merged communist and socialist forces—became known as the "singing army." They utilized varied types of music for recruitment and propaganda, as well as for battle hymns. As one Huk commander explained about the song "Buhay ng Gerilya" ("Life of a Guerrilla"): "The song speaks of sufferings . . . of how it feels to be separated from your family . . . [but your family] is part of your country, you forget your sufferings. Therefore, the song itself is a cadre. . . . As you keep singing it, you protect your own [revolutionary] consciousness."[97]

Many of these older songs were revived by the student movement in the 1960s, which viewed music as a cultural weapon. For example, student protesters sang songs like "Awit Ng Pakikibaka" ("Song of the Struggle"), written to commemorate the death of a student militant during a university occupation in 1971:

One who shed blood for the country
Is full of courage and will be remembered
The life that is offered to our beloved country
Is full of lessons and greatness.[98]

A feminist, anti-Japanese song written in 1940, "Babaing Walang Kibo" ("Oppressed Women, Unite and Fight), became a rallying cry for feminist meetings and demonstrations in the late 1960s and early 1970s:

My country, ever suffering
Ever longing to be free
From foreign rule, always in tears . . .
O, oppressed woman
Think and ponder
You have long been oppressed . . .
Why don't you defend yourself?
Your children are starving
Your youngest wails
Can you bear to see them suffering?[99]

Political prisoners jailed by Marcos kept their spirits up with militant songs. Often the protesters took traditional folk songs and updated the lyrics, much like 1960s student activists and folksingers in the United States. Radical songbooks like *A Free Bird* (compiled in 1981) were widely distributed and utilized by the growing anti-Marcos resistance. One of the most popular of these new folk songs originating from the underground asked the musical question: "Can there be freedom when the country reels in abject poverty, when all her wealth is held by aliens while the people go hungry?"[100]

"If Your Tears Have Dried Up, My Native Land"

"Weep, my native land. With strong-breathing sorrow cry out
Your pitiful fate, land that's almost beyond pity:
The flag that symbolizes your integral being is shrouded by a foreign flag
Even the language you've inherited is bastardized by another tongue;
This day resurrects the day when once your freedom was wrested from you,
On the thirteenth of August, American invaders raped Manila . . .
But a day will dawn when your tears will dry up completely
A day will come when tears will no longer gush forth from your swollen eyes
But fire, fire that's the color of blood will burst out and rage
While your blood seethes and boils like molten steel!
You'll shout with noble defiance amid the fires of a million torches
And the old chains you'll snap with bullets."—Amado Hernandez[101]

The development of street theater, combined with the thirst for answers among urban intellectuals, also led to the rediscovery of Amado Hernandez, a Filipino Marxist poet and labor leader who spent a decade in prison for sedition in the 1950s and 1960s. His wife, Atang de la Rama, was a notable political activist and actress, famed for her rendition of kundiman ballads. Hernandez, who died in 1970, achieved notoriety because of his passionate revolutionary beliefs and his pioneering use of Tagalog as a poetic medium. He believed Filipinos must reject a past tainted by colonialism and elite exploitation. During the 1970s and early 1980s, artists associated with street theater put some of his poems to music, creating from them a powerful protest idiom to reach the urban workers and students.[102] One of the most influential of these songs is based on his poem "If Your Tears Have Dried Up, My Native Land."

Another Hernandez poem/song, "Rice Grains," which celebrates peasant life, bears a striking resemblance to the radical Thai folk group Caravan's famous "Man and Buffalo"(See Chapter 4):

> *Man and water buffalo have been companions from the beginning*
> *Industry and strength naturally fuse; the wilderness of thorns*
> *Is cleared by the far-ranging plow, the fields are tilled*
> *The upturned soil is harrowed.*[103]

Since several friends of Caravan and the songwriters had studied in or visited the Philippines, it is quite possible that they were influenced by the Hernandez poem.

Music has played an important role in other political movements as well, sometimes in furtherance of hegemonic interests. The ruling Marcos-created political party used music to garner support during the entire period of martial law, co-opting willing popular singers and obsessively broadcasting songs praising the virtues of government policies. First Lady Imelda Marcos commissioned songs extolling Marcos' New Society, with the requirement that they be "full of tenderness, heroic and noble strains, militant, rhythmic pulsations" in order to "tame the restless hearts of some of our countrymen who have bitterness and hate in their hearts."[104] At the other end of the political spectrum, the leftist New Peoples Army guerillas and their public support groups write, distribute, and in some cases record many revolutionary songs. For them music is part of the arsenal of what they view as a cultural revolution for the hearts and minds of a people, a necessary corollary to the political and military struggle in which they have been engaged since the 1960s. As one sympathizer notes, "To struggle and to sing: this is our vocation."[105]

Frankly aimed at subverting the popular music that reflects a colonial mentality and culture, the revolutionary songs aim to uplift the peasantry and working class while supporting armed struggle and the need for radical change. The memory of earlier nationalist heroes and groups is frequently evoked in order to liken the movement to the historical struggle for self-determination. Most of the songs have roots in the folk music of the regions where NPA influence is strongest, with the guitar and flute the normal accompaniment. A typical song, "Manggagawa at Magbubukid" ("Workers and Peasants Arise!"), urges workers and peasants to combine their efforts and struggle against an unjust system:

What is the light we see? . . .
We saw the brightness
Of the sun in the East
Gradually turning red
So wake up and arise
Dear Motherland from your bed of misery!
Workers and peasants
Make up the army of toilers
With revolutionary ideals
Resist all oppressors
Our single aim is to lead
Our impoverished people from bondage
We want to expose
The roots of oppression . . .
The whole world is aflame
With the red banners of the toiling masses![106]

These songs certainly spread widely in the country, but they could not be considered part of the popular music tradition because they lack commercial intent and mass-mediated distribution.

Freddie Aguilar and the Politicization of Pinoy

Mass-mediated Pinoy music with a social concern progressed further with the emergence in 1978 of Freddie Aguilar, an eccentric folk-rock singer-songwriter who became a highly popular figure in the Philippines.[107] He also achieved wide popularity in other Asian countries, including Japan, Hong Kong, and Malaysia, and even developed a following in Europe. Raised in a poor section of Manila, Aguilar, much against his parent's wishes, abandoned electrical engineering studies to become first a street musician, then folk club and bar singer, developing in the process a persistent reputation for nonconformity and a turbulent personal life. Like many Filipinos (including former president Corazon Aquino and nineteenth-century national hero Jose Rizal), Aguilar has some Chinese blood; a great-grandfather was a Chinese immigrant.

"Anak" ("Child")

"When you were born into this world
Your mom and dad saw a dream unfurled
A dream-come-true
The answer to
Their prayer
You were to them a special child
You gave them joy every time you smiled
Each time you cried
They're at your side
To care
Child, you don't know
You'll never know
How far they'd go
To give you all their love can give
To see you through
And this is true
They'd die for you
If they must do to see you love . . .
Now what has gotten over you
Why do you hate what your parents do
Speak out your mind
Why do you find
Them wrong
Now that your path has gone astray
Child, you don't know what to say
You're so alone
No friends are on
Your side."—Freddie Aguilar[108]

Modeling himself on Anglo-American folk-rock stars like Cat Stevens and James Taylor, Aguilar began his career with covers of Western hits such as "House of the Rising Sun," but his music gradually took on a more local flavor. His first big national and international hit (translated into six languages), "Anak" ("Child"), outlines the autobiography of a prodigal son, closely resembling the singer, who came to appreciate his parents.

The single record sold an unprecedented 100,000 copies in the first two weeks, and ultimately around a million copies. One observer describes the impact of "Anak" on the capital: "Manila became a non-stop Aguilar song begun on a cigarette vendor's lips, continued on the jeepney driver's stereo tape, and finishing in the guitar-strumming and idle serenades of neighborhood jazz stand-bys."[109] The song, composed by Aguilar, soon inspired a local television drama series. Eventually the song generated fifty-four cover versions in fourteen languages around the world. According to some sources, Aguilar's record company charted his career from the start as "the man of the masses" with a hippie image, and worked hard—and successfully—to sell "Anak" in Japan and elsewhere.[110] Although soon moving into a more comfortable neighborhood, he has maintained a reputation for personal simplicity. His early songs mourn the poverty-stricken lives of the urban shantytowns he knew so well, the grief of parents with ungrateful children, the problems faced by the physically handicapped.

At the time, he was considered something of a voice in the wilderness, one of the very few musicians to address these types of themes; but his music clearly hit a responsive chord. A Filipino recording executive summarized Aguilar's importance to the resurgence of commercialized, accessible folk music in 1979: "Before Freddie, folk music was only for one cult of people. After Freddie, it became commercial. Today, Filipino folk music can earn money for Filipino singers and composers . . . not copies or remakes of foreign efforts."[111] Hence Aguilar was helping to forge a unique but modern Filipino sound with strong folk roots, enhancing his appeal to nationalist fans; in his hands pinoy constituted a musical exploration of the Filipino ethos. Aguilar has sometimes utilized native folk instruments, but he also complains that the rapidly declining folk tradition makes it difficult to obtain the instruments or find musicians who have mastered them.[112] His own humble origins add weight to his social criticism. Aguilar has never been a hardcore linguistic nationalist. Like most Filipino musicians, Aguilar is also willing to record English songs in order to reach a wider audience, although generally restricting himself to songs by himself or other Filipino composers.

The late 1970s were stimulating years for pinoy musicians in many respects. Filipina journalist Elizabeth Reyes described well the creative atmosphere in Manila and the role music played in the life of the country in that period, identifying

> the genuine cultural pulse—where it is really beating for the Filipino soul. . . . Filipinos' most flourishing art is heard, lyric and melodic, on radio wavebands across the archipelago, in smokey folk-houses and the music bars. . . . Popular music is where the Filipino creative spirit is at—alive and free, riding the crest of a . . . sound wave.[113]

Aguilar was one of the leading lights in that flourishing musical scene. As his career progressed, Aguilar skillfully mixed sentimental and reflective songs with strong challenges to injustice. For example, his 1983 album, *Magdalena*, contained such songs as "Mindanao" (about Christian-Muslim clashes in the troubled southern island) and "Magdalena" (about a girl forced into prostitution by poverty). He followed these up in 1984–1985 with "Katarungan" ("Justice," about the injustices suffered by the powerless), "Children of Negros" (about poverty), and "U.S.-Russia" (about the arrogance of the superpowers). "Mindanao" was also noteworthy for incorporating instruments and rhythms from the local cultures. These songs earned Aguilar a media rubric as the "Bob Dylan of the Philippines." His career also showed similarities to Chile's Victor Jara, the most politicized of the New Song musicians supporting radical change and, in the early 1970s, the leftist Allende government.[114] Aguilar's later music had a more rock-oriented sound.

Aguilar, Pinoy, and People Power

To understand the evolution of politically oriented popular music during the critical years of the late 1970s and early 1980s, it is necessary to explore briefly the tumult of the Marcos years and the rise of public protests. In 1983 the popular and main opposition leader, Benigno (Ninoy) Aquino, was assassinated on his return to the islands after a long exile in the United States. Most observers linked the assassination to Marcos directly or indirectly, so

Freddie Aguilar's Early Career

Aguilar found little difficulty in identifying with other Filipinos, for he went through the same experience of struggle and hardship. His childhood years were tempestuous. When he dropped out of school, he shattered his father's hopes that he might become a lawyer. Aguilar started writing songs at 14 and felt drawn toward music. His father nagged him constantly to drop his growing—but perhaps impractical—ambition of becoming a professional singer; in response he ran away from home at 16, living in cramped quarters and eating only one meal a day since that was all he could afford. Aguilar even had to borrow a guitar from his sister. Later he wrote the lyrics for "Anak"—just in time for his father to read them on his deathbed. Only then did the dying man realize the seriousness of his son's dreams. When the song topped the pop charts, a saddened Aguilar regretted that his father didn't live long enough to witness the success of his son, a one-time nobody.[115]

public opposition to the regime began to mount. Ninoy soon became transformed into a mythical martyr, an idea around which oppositional and nationalist elements could rally.[116] In some districts the NPA capitalized on military brutality and the ills of the dictatorship to build their support. In the cities, especially Manila, much of the opposition coalesced around Aquino's politically inexperienced widow, Corazon. The unprecedented anti-Marcos coalition linked Filipinos from all walks of life, including both business and labor. Street demonstrations became a regular occurrence.

American historian Claude A. Buss conveys the electric flavor of the times:

> Students, workers, and the urban poor in Manila were joined by housewives, priests, nuns, businessmen, and clerks and secretaries in massive anti-Marcos demonstrations that lasted far into the night. Emotions ran high. . . . They were not out to overthrow the government. They demanded "Justice for Aquino, Justice for all." They wanted an end to tyranny; they longed for the return of freedom. Street demonstrations were more often like fiestas or carnivals than revolutionary protests. The marchers would dance and chant such slogans as "Down with the U.S.-Marcos dictatorship!" . . . Inevitably the carnival spirit ebbed, but the demonstrations continued.[117]

Although anti-Marcos forces were deeply divided by factionalism and strategies, the protests continued and opposition parties began to reorganize and contest the somewhat rigged elections. In 1986 Corazon Aquino headed an opposition slate in presidential elections. Although independent monitors believed that she had clearly won, Marcos was declared the official winner. The flagrantly stolen election ignited far more massive protests under the banner of "peoples power;" women played a key role at the grassroots level as a revolutionary culture of sharing and community took hold. The situation rapidly deteriorated for Marcos:

> The Filipinos rose to the occasion, and their own courage—abetted by Marcos's mistakes—brought about the most spectacular non-violent revolution the world has ever seen. . . . In four short days the heart of Philippine society, from the militia to the masses, turned swiftly and nearly bloodlessly against him. Marcos himself could not believe how the mighty had fallen. Neither could the crowds who toppled him, nor the millions of people around the world who watched—live and in color—a revolution where crowds were singing, tanks were stopped dead in their tracks by nuns and housewives, and people protected the armed forces rather than the other way around.[118]

The mass media played a remarkable role in all of these events, with opposition forces taking over one or another radio or television station, creating a viable weapon against the dictatorship. Rather than the powerful elite using the media as a weapon to coerce, intimidate, and even subjugate the people, the masses turned the electronic media against a despot and his cohorts in order to bring them down, a development rare in history.[119] With a sizable majority of his population, including most of the intelligentsia, seeking his removal, and the United States finally abandoning his cause, Marcos and his family fled to ignoble exile in Hawai'i.

The complex of events surrounding the overturning of Marcos and the installation of Aquino as president is referred to in popular shorthand as "EDSA" (for Epitanio de los Santos Avenue, a main venue for the action). It represented to many observers a significant break in Philippine history, a triumph for "peoples power" that was concentrated in metropolitan Manila but ultimately involved, actively or passively, most regions of the country in the struggle for change. On the other hand, some specialists had a less romantic view, seeing the change as less a "revolution" than a transfer of power from one elite faction to another (even if the new leaders reflected a certain populism).[120] The successful EDSA uprising also sent shock waves throughout Southeast Asia, suggesting to peoples chafing under military-dominated regimes in countries like Thailand, Indonesia, and Taiwan that political change was possible.[121]

The removal of Marcos was cathartic for the Philippine public as well:

> With Marcos gone, more than a million Filipinos burst into Malacanang Palace to see what their taxes had brought for the family that had ruled them. In a country where the per capita income was $822 a year, starving people in Manila saw a 25-foot dining table on which there was still some caviar. They wandered through rooms filled with Persian carpets, authentic Chinese antiques, gold fixtures, diamond-studded statues, pools, and spas. The closets were filled with exquisite clothes and thousands of pairs of shoes which Mrs. Marcos had bought with millions spent in New York, London, and Paris. On her bed, people used to eating the food normally given to animals read her motto on a pillow: "I love champagne, caviar, and cash."[122]

During the early Marcos period, Aguilar was considered by many to have become identified with the martial law government in his quest for commercial success, but, like many Filipinos, he became disillusioned by the widening gap between elite luxury and mass poverty, by the discrepancy between the rhetorical support Marcos gave for land reform and socio-economic change and the reality of little substantial change. By the turn of the decade he adopted a more nationalist and oppositional profile, campaigning for anti-Marcos candidates in the limited elections permitted by the regime. This course of action resulted in many of his songs being prohibited from radio play or even recording as subversive; even his managers, he complained, tried to steer him toward safer, more commercial material. He was forced to concentrate on performing abroad to sustain his career.

"Bayan Ko" ("My Homeland")

"My beloved country
Philippines is your name
Pearl of the Orient
Blest with unblemished beauty
But, alas, robbed of your longed-for freedom
Always weeping in poverty and pain
My country, the Philippines
Land of gold and flowers
Love has given her grace and tranquility
And her radiance and loveliness drew rapacious foreigners
My country, they have imprisoned you
Thrown you into sorrow and despair
Even birds who freely fly
When caged will struggle to escape
What more of a country endowed with nobility
The Philippines, my cherished land
My home of sorrow and tears
Always I dream to see you truly free
How lovely it is to live in one's native land
If there is no slavery and freedom reigns supreme
A people who are now oppressed
In the morrow shall stand up
The east will turn fiery crimson
And mark the dawn of freedom."—Freddie Aguilar[123]

Blacklisting of protest music from radio and television was the norm during the Marcos years.

In 1983 Aguilar became involved with the public opposition to Marcos generated by the assassination of Ninoy Aquino. Indeed, the Aquino assassination energized many musicians; it soon became fashionable for Manila bands to include a political song or two in their performance repertoire. Aging pinoy rock star Joey Smith, among others, participated in "Musical Tributes to Ninoy."[124] In 1979 Aguilar had first recorded an improvised version of "Bayan Ko" ("My Homeland"), a song that was written in 1896 and closely identified with the Philippine revolution against Spain (a revolution aborted by U.S. intervention). Indeed, the song had long been a favorite of nationalists, part of the underground music of those who opposed or resented American rule and later neocolonialism. As the introduction to a book of songs by political prisoners jailed by Marcos proclaimed: "Every political movement gives birth to a corollary cultural upheaval."[125]

Aguilar claims he recorded the song because he "felt that foreign culture was beginning to swamp local pop music. I thought that maybe a patriotic song would jolt back those who were starting to forget who we really are."[126] The Marcos administration forced prominent anti-Establishment film director Lino Brocka to edit "Bayan Ko" out of his latest film in 1984, prompting Aguilar to publicly charge—incorrectly but understandably—that the Philippines "is the only country where they can define a song as subversive."[127] As anti-Marcos sentiments grew, "Bayan Ko" was resurrected. Aguilar sang it beside Ninoy Aquino's coffin, an event he claimed energized his participation in the opposition movement.[128] Soon it became the anthem of the anti-Marcos movement, sung at demonstrations and at rallies for opposition presidential candidate Corazon Aquino. The lyrics proved timeless and clearly appropriate.

Perhaps ironically, the co-anthem of the opposition was "Tie a Yellow Ribbon 'Round the Old Oak Tree," a 1970s American hit by Tony Orlando and Dawn, selected because it celebrated yellow, the color of Cory Aquino's campaign against Marcos. Aguilar performed "Bayan Ko" and other songs at many mass rallies, creating in the process a new audience for his own folk-oriented pinoy style. The anthem proved cathartic at rallies: "When the crowd sang "Bayan Ko" . . . you felt all the accumulated laughter and cheering of the day turn into pure emotion."[129] Aguilar claims that Marcos unsuccessfully offered him a large bribe to quit singing "Bayan Ko" and terminate his political activity.[130] Some of this music also qualified as mass mediated because radio stations that came under opposition control or influence endlessly played recordings of "Bayan Ko" and other opposition songs, in the process spreading the message of "peoples power" and activism.

Aguilar was active in the 1986 election campaign of the opposition slate, an election Marcos attempted to subvert. He also joined the demonstrations, and describes one night of the uprising:

> We were setting up [sound equipment] on top of a . . . truck. We had no lights, so people turned flashlights toward us. One foreign correspondent said: "I have never seen a revolution like this. People are dancing and singing. You see this in the movies, in fiction. This is for real." . . . We played rock. We were euphoric. A woman came to me and asked if we could play something else. So I shifted to folk music, relevant music, and we played until morning.[131]

He sang about the "peoples power" revolution in his emotional 1987 album, *Edsa*. But Aguilar's was not the only musical retrospective of those heady days; indeed, cassettes of songs spawned by or sung during the anti-Marcos drive proliferated.[132] The challenges to Marcos beginning in the early 1980s generated a spirited debate among cultural nationalists (most of them anti-

Marcos) about which type of music provided the best vehicle for protest and politicization, but no consensus was achieved.[133] The heady days of 1986, and the role of oppositional music in them, is well summarized by two Filipino journalists:

> One of these days somebody will have to write a novel about the month just past, and from this novel somebody will adapt a play, and from the play a movie—we have gone through an era too rich with stories to ignore. The movie, of course, will have to be a musical of sorts, or will have to use a lot of music from the opening credits to the final freeze or fade-out.[134]

Radio stations that came under opposition control mobilized support in part by playing the songs of the resistance. "Real media consumers in Manila will tell you," one study argues, "that the best program here in many years was the ragged but amazing cabaret that was on the air during the revolution."[135]

Politics and Popular Music in the Post-Marcos Era

The "peaceful revolution" against Marcos generated much optimism both at home and abroad that the nation could finally begin to resolve her serious problems and forge political unity. Unfortunately, many of these hopes proved illusory. Aquino had a mandate to generate change in favor of democracy, peace, and socioeconomic justice. But the coalition that toppled Marcos and supported Aquino was comprised of many disparate elements, mostly drawn from among the traditional elite. They shared no consensus on goals or common vision, and many were tied to the same business and agricultural interests that had always dominated the political process. Indeed the coalition soon fragmented as the traditional class structure was reinvigorated and market forces became reascendant after the demise of Marcos' manipulated "crony capitalism." Mrs. Aquino missed her chance to translate her personal popularity into policies to generate social change. Soon hope was replaced by cynicism about the efficacy of democratic processes or the possibilities of substantial change that might benefit the poorest sections of the population.[136]

After the departure of Marcos the Philippines returned to a somewhat turbulent democratic pattern presided over by President Aquino. Although the country became much more open to dissenting voices and divergent cultural trends, the new government, beset by factionalism and unrest in the military as well as continuing insurgency, was largely unable (or unwilling) to seriously address the pressing socioeconomic problems, including widespread peasant misery and dangerous dependence on a few agricultural exports. As one observer concluded: "Filipinos have exchanged Marcos' dictatorship for Aquino's elitism with a smiling face."[137] Aquino's tenure in power has been characterized as a "brushfire revolution," referring to a Tagalog idiom about grass fires that rage frantically but quickly burn out.[138]

A Catholic missionary notes bitterly how economic exploitation and environmental destruction by local and foreign entrepreneurs have remained characteristic for decades: "A plunder economy, that's the post World War II Philippine history . . . plunder of seas, plunder of mines, plunder of forests."[139] Access to health, welfare, and related services continues to reflect the great disparities in income distribution between classes and regions. Marcos had also saddled the country with a massive foreign debt ($27 billion in 1986) that absorbed much-needed resources just to service.[140]

The increasing desperation of some Filipinos is evident to most observers.

> Each day, hundreds of Filipinos pour into the teeming slums of Manila, refugees from a collapsing rural economy. . . . They arrive looking for housing, work and food. Many find only garbage. Early in the morning, scores of people as young as three or four swarm over Smokey Mountain, a stinking 500-foot-high trash dump spread over 80 acres in downtown Manila. They search for something to eat or sell. Those who succeed, and who survive, are among the more fortunate of the more than 3 million homeless in this burgeoning Asian capital. However, in these rapidly changing times, even their prospects are not good.[141]

But the nation is also in flux. The mass media remain largely, as always, under the control or ownership of powerful corporations and families, greatly reducing their potential for expressing alternative viewpoints. Government apathy has left reform activities largely to the NGOs (Non-Governmental Organizations) that have proliferated since the mid-1980s. These citizen or church-run groups deal with issues of poverty, legal inequalities, human rights, social welfare, labor exploitation, and environmental destruction from a grassroots perspective that offers some hope of a renewed "peoples power."[142] The Philippine Senate also took a significant step in a nationalist direction in 1991 by terminating, against Aquino's wishes, the U.S. base agreements—a historical turning point that promised a potential loss of hundreds of millions of dollars a year in revenues; as Filipino political scientist Alexander Magno describes it: "To reject this base treaty is not by any means a practical move. . . . But the emotional release, the assertion of power and independence will be great. It will be therapeutic, a national primal scream that may mature us."[143] In the 1990s the Philippines seems committed to increasing decolonization; nationalism will remain a potent (if fluctuating) force because of its strong roots in Philippine history.

But despite Mrs. Aquino's popularity with broad sections of the public, U.S. military and economic support was crucial to her survival. One observer summarized her dilemma as follows: "Responsiveness is essential to the maintenance of democratic legitimacy, but is undermined by heavy reliance on foreign support. There lies the essence of Corazon Aquino's ultimate challenge, which she is in danger of failing."[144] Critics believe that Mrs. Aquino, a leader full of contradictions, created time for societal healing but also squandered a historic opportunity to reverse the socioeconomic injustices.[145] Nonetheless, democracy has returned. Mrs. Aquino declined to run for a second term in 1992 and Filipinos elected her protégé, former General Fidel Ramos.

Ramos admits the country has deep problems but perhaps, like most elites, has underestimated the political consequences of the nation's glaring socioeconomic inequalities. Among his first moves was to hold talks with NPA leaders about ending the insurgency. The faction-ridden NPA has suffered many setbacks in the post-Marcos era and by 1992 had seen its fighting force and mass base reduced by half from 1988 levels. By 1994 the party fractured into several rival camps. The president also worked out a peace settlement with one of the armed Muslim factions that had long sought autonomy in the southern islands.[146] Ramos demonstrates some progressive tendencies and has fostered some economic dynamism, but his ruling coalition was under increasing strain by 1996. Average Filipinos suffer from high inflation, high unemployment and underemployment, occasional rice shortages, and rising crime rates. And human rights abuses against dissidents (including labor organizers and rebel sympathizers) were becoming more common in some rural areas; these included abductions and sometimes assassinations. The future of political stability and reform remains in doubt.

Vice President Estrada, the former movie star, was favored by many to succeed Ramos. Although reputedly a philanderer and heavy drinker derided by many detractors as a clown, Estrada projects the image of a tough, no-nonsense, crime-fighting crusader independent of Ramos, and this has enhanced his popularity, particularly among the working class. A longtime observer offered these thoughts germane to longterm Philippine prospects: "The Filipino people . . . have a rough road ahead. A change of government has not solved all the country's problems. The fact is that the struggle is just beginning. The stakes are enormous, and the outcome is still in doubt."[147] The discontent was reflected in the national celebrations for the tenth anniversary of the EDSA "Peoples Power" uprising, held in February, 1996. Various leaders of the movement used the occasion to blame each other for the nation's problems, even as the economy was showing signs of recovery.[148]

The transition to a new politics and a more open society had ramifications in the popular culture. With the triumph of "peoples power," folk-style pinoy did once again dominate the popular music charts in the latter part of the 1980s, in part because it corresponded so closely to topical or social commentary. Aguilar himself remained somewhat oppositional to established authority. He also sometimes hints at plans for an eventual political career

Joey Ayala's Early Career

"Life on the turbulent southern island of Mindanao, where he was born, clearly honed Ayala's talent. But he also spent his formative years in Manila, where he absorbed Western music, from American folk to classical symphonies. Ayala also listened intently to Elvis Presley, the Beatles, and to the music of classical guitarist Andrés Segovia. In the late 1960s he became a fan of James Taylor and Neil Young, the fusion jazz of Weather Report, and the mystical guitar playing of Larry Coryell and John McLaughlin. In 1973 his family migrated to Davao city in Mindanao. For the 17-year-old Ayala, the move was traumatic but also fateful. His obsession with music led to new friendships: 'I learned to socialize really in the south. . . . I did not know the dialect. I was an alien with a different culture, strange ways. Music helped me survive socially.' Living in provincial Davao rather than trend-crazy Manila radically altered his musical inclinations. When Ayala joined a theater group, he learned that audiences were receptive to the national language, Pilipino. Soon he completely abandoned writing in English. His Pilipino lyrics became more pungent and eloquent, his music more urgent and infused with ethnic influences. He began to grow more deeply aware of his social responsibility as well as his ethnic roots."—from *The Man from Mindanao*[149]

himself.[150] Some of his later songs dealt with the continuing failure to resolve the country's fundamental problems as well as issues like war ("War") and national identity ("Pinoy"). But he also offers lighter fare (including his English songs such as "Crazy" and "You're Hurting Me").[151]

Various other popular Filipino musicians, some of whom commenced their careers in the 1970s, have also concentrated on political material in recent years. Some of them endured frequent official scrutiny and commercial neglect during the Marcos era but enjoy more visibility since 1986. A prime example is Joey Ayala, a graduate of the prestigious Ateneo de Manila high school, who developed a loyal but nonmainstream following in the Marcos years, particularly among nationalist groups. The audience is attracted to his creative musical synthesis as well as his uncompromising songs detailing the neglect of—and political turbulence on—his home island of Mindanao. His songs contain militant and discomforting images of exploitation, repression, and even resistance among both peasants and city dwellers. For example, on his socially conscious *Magkabilaan (Back to Back)* album, he paints a picture of his native Mindanao racked by religious unrest, insurgency, and neglect:

There are kings without kingdoms
And slaves freer than the rest
There are soldiers fighting themselves
And those defiled who live forever.[152]

Ayala became known for songs like "Motel Joe" (a criticism of U.S. military bases), "Sta. Filomena" (about a village abandoned because of military operations), and "Agila" (about the eagle and the forest), which became the anthem for environmental activists. His music utilizes native folk instruments much as New Song groups like Inti-Illimani did in Chile, and can probably best be described as folk rock or ethnic rock. He resists the label of protest singer as that presumes an adversarial stance absent from his songs.[153] Ayala referred to himself as a "journalist of songs." He also argues that musicians, like journalists, must be critical and not accept things at face value. But they should also take sides: "It is impossible to be neutral." Indeed, he contends: "I feel the need to say things that few other songwriters are saying. . . . Artists are the mouthpiece for society's collective subconscious."[154]

Like many of the country's more politically oriented popular and folk musicians, Ayala derives from a middle-class background; his father was a journalist and his mother a published poet. He worked as a journalist himself after finishing his university degree in economics. Ayala initially composed in English but switched to Tagalog with the rise of pinoy in the early 1970s. Some of his early music was commissioned by experimental, nationalist theater groups, an activity that continued into the 1990s. One of his best-known works was the musical *Sinalimba*, which traced the history of Mindanao from precolonial times to the exploitation by multinational corporations; he also wrote the music for the powerful antinuclear (both arms race and power) rock musical *Nukleyar*.[155] During the Marcos era Ayala and his group, Ang Bagong Lumad (New Natives), had difficulty obtaining recording contracts and concentrated on underground live concerts. Even after the overthrow of Marcos, Ayala's controversial material frightened recording companies, although his several albums have sold well and are critically acclaimed.

One of Manila's most successful and commercial groups since the early 1970s, and arguably the top group of the 1980s, is the Apo Hiking Society (APO), composed of graduates of the prestigious university, the Ateneo de Manila. APO took their name from revolutionary nationalist hero Apolinario Mabini. Despite their wholesome, teen-idol (even bubblegum) reputation and many middle-of-the-road romantic hits, they campaigned against martial law beginning in 1974, sang for political detainees (some of whom were relatives), and recorded many songs of political protest, including several on the Aquino assassination. APO's leader and main composer, Jim Paredes, has even written a rock opera in honor of nationalist hero José Rizal. In keeping with their view that form is secondary to content in developing Filipino music, their sound is commercial and westernized. But APO has long integrated more serious themes into their lyrics. For example, "Batambata Ka Pa" deals with parent-child relations. But some of their more serious work was blacklisted and circulated only in privately produced cassettes during the Marcos years.[156]

Perhaps APO's best-known protest song to achieve mass fame is "American Junk" from the mid-1980s. Supported by folk instruments and rhythms, the lyrics wage a frontal assault on neocolonialism. The song also calls for a renewed commitment to Filipino music by attacking U.S. popular culture. Inevitably, the group was later recruited to publicize Aquino's "Buy Philippine-Made Movement."

Asin ("Salt of the Earth"), another top folk-rock group, has specialized on environmental issues, especially pollution, after their formation in 1977. Most of the group derive from middle-class or elite origins; lead singer Lolita Carbon's father is a doctor (and folk music enthusiast). However, none of the band members is from Manila. They all grew up in provincial districts of Luzon or Mindanao where they became familiar with ethnic music traditions as well as the problems of rural poverty and development. Although they once served as Aguilar's backing band, their music is, by their own admission, "uncommercial [and] uncompromising." They have been quite conscious of the role their music can play in propagating change and information: "We realized we had influenced a lot of people. That's what music is all about."

They gained their greatest following among university and progressive activist groups who also supported Ayala. Nonetheless, they enjoyed a major hit in 1980 with "Masadan Mo Ang Kapaligiran" ("Look Around the

"American Junk"

"Leave me alone to my Third World devices
I don't need your technology
You just want my natural resources
And then you leave me poor and in misery
Third World blues is what I got
Trouble, yes, I've got a lot
(American junk) Get it out of my bloodstream
(American junk) Get it out of my system
(American junk) I can only take so much
(American junk) Got to get back to who I am . . .
You call it new music, I call it pollution
Your music I now can see on my television (American Top 40)
Why is it now I can only sing . . .
In English language that you people bring
Why is it now that they only play
Top 40 music in TV and radio?"—Apo Hiking Society[157]

"Tayo'y Mga Pinoy" ("We Are Filipinos")

"We are Filipinos, we are not Americans
Do not be ashamed if your nose is flat
I was born in the East . . .
I have my own brown color
But I cannot show my real self
If we look for it, we shall find it
We have an identity we can be proud of
But where are the rays of the sun
Why do we look up to the West? . . .
Why did we become this way
Why do we imitate, when we have our own?
There is a dog, who is worse than rabid
He mews, he doesn't bark
Like some people who force themselves to speak English
But listen to it, it's all wrong."—Heber Bartolome[158]

City"). The band members acknowledge a strong influence from politicized American folk singers of the 1960s like Bob Dylan and Peter, Paul, and Mary. Like Ayala and some other artists, Asin mixed indigenous ethnic instruments such as the nose flute into their mix; as they put it in 1988: "We are searching for a truly Filipino music."[159] As part of this search, they have collected and recorded the music of many of the marginalized, non-Christian hill peoples. In some respects the efforts of Asin and kindred groups to discover an authentic music with indigenous roots were reminiscent of the Chilean New Song musicians.

Another politically conscious popular singer, Heber Bartolome, a poet and artist, with his folk-rock group Banyuihay, has enjoyed a substantial university following since the late 1970s. His songs reflect nationalistic themes and social commentary. For example, decolonizing sentiments are expressed in his "Ayoku Na Kay Santa Claus" ("I No Longer Care for Santa Claus"):

I no longer care for Santa Claus
He does not exist . . .
Here Christmas color is not white
We have no snow here . . .
Many children are confused . . .
When will we ever learn.[160]

One of Bartolome's most significant compositions, "Tayo'y Mga Pinoy," encourages national identity.

Bartolome consciously employs Western rock and pop forms to create his pinoy music in order to gain an audience for his ideas:

> I cannot say it is 100% Filipino music I use. . . . I deliberately use influences of foreign music in my own songs for the purpose of getting the attention of the youth who are into this kind of music. I believe I can only step forward from where we are standing right now. I cannot go back to searching for what is the true Filipino music when even the definition of that is debatable. And I cannot go forward into the avant garde music where my audience would be very few. So I select what is the music being listened to by the majority of youth and the majority of Filipino people. Then I use that as a vehicle to put my message across. In the process, when I put my own language, my own dialect, my native tongue into this kind of music, the influence of foreign music becomes lesser because the sound will be dominated by our language, which is our very own culture. The sound of the word is music. . . . The words we use are very powerful. When the people hear Tagalog . . . especially when you talk about their problems, about what they are, who they are, when you try to situate them in your song, then they listen.[161]

Furthermore, some of the politicized groups and musicians who became prominent during the "peoples power" movement, such as Inang Laya, Patatag, and Pol Galang, began to achieve some popular success and recording contracts in the post-Marcos years. Some of Inang Laya's more important songs on their 1986 debut album include an attack on the U.S. military installations and versions of Amado Hernandez poems. Later recordings emphasize feminist concerns while also attacking militarism (a Joey Ayala composition) and extolling nationalism. The group is composed of faculty members at the University of the Philippines headed by Katina Constantino-David (who later joined the Aquino government). Other groups, such as Grupo Pendong, seek to creatively combine local ethnic and folk music traditions with Western rock, in order to reintroduce folk traditions to a younger generation raised mostly on Anglo-American pop.[162]

But not all innovative and critical musicians have prospered even in the more liberal Aquino and Ramos years. For example, Pen Pen, a heavily experimental "neoethnic" rock group headed by Emil Sanglay, achieved a cult status and critical acclaim but few recording offers since their formation in the late 1970s. Their considerable following derives chiefly from performances in pubs, campuses, and parks. Pen Pen concentrates on originally composed material, often integrating folk instruments from mountain tribes into their rock style. Many of their songs promote social change; Sanglay describes his songs as "my instrument in making people aware. I realize they are not commercial."[163]

Some popular and folk musicians have continued to search for ways to create a more truly bottom-up "people's music" utilizing influences from the Filipino heritage while also fostering closer cooperation between musicians and other social activists. Musika continued to operate during the 1980s and 1990s, becoming in the process an institution providing resources and services. These included organizing music groups, sponsoring symposia, conferences, and workshops, publishing a newsletter, collecting folk songs, and encouraging the participation of many common people in music production. In 1991 an allied organization called Musicians for Peace (MFP) was formed, comprised of working musicians (some of them Musika members) interested in working more closely with activists involved in the struggles of workers, peasants, and women for empowerment. MFP also aimed to contact musicians working in small clubs and pubs around the country with the aim of improving their working conditions and musical skills.[164]

The continuing interest of Filipino folk-rock musicians in creating a distinctive national music with a folk base comparable to the Latin American New Song movement may not have been entirely coincidental. Both regions are saddled with a neocolonial heritage that includes massive importation of North American cultural models, prompting an inevitable nationalist backlash. Both regions are preoccupied by the quest for a national identity separate from powerful neighbors or former colonial masters. Furthermore, some Filipinos have been familiar with musical developments in Latin America, since Spanish is still widely spoken or understood in the islands. The much-admired nationalist intellectual Constantino also praised the Chilean New Song model in 1985. Hence, some Filipino musicians and working-class cultural groups, including Patatag, have made use of songs or tunes from Victor Jara and Violeta Parra.[165]

Cultural nationalists and antielitists eagerly supported the EDSA revolution and generated a movement by the Aquino government toward cultural renewal. An alliance of figures from literature, music, dance, theatre, education, and art, as well as from the print and broadcast media, joined together to lobby for a Ministry or Commission of Culture. Aquino responded with a Presidential Commission for Culture and the Arts, to foster the evolution of a national culture that would derive from and be for the people, in contrast to the Western "high" culture favored by the Marcos regime. The emphasis would be on democratization, decentralization, pluralism, multiculturalism, and Filipinization. There has been much more freedom of recording and concerts, with increased cassette tape production; yet radio stations as commercial ventures still practice self-censorship to avoid offending powerful groups. Many musicians believe that the post-Marcos governments have done little to foster indigenous and progressive musical forms because they do not enforce the laws requiring radio stations to play some Filipino music and have discontinued the annual pop music competitions. Just how this sometimes turbulent marriage between the mass culture community and the government will evolve remains to be seen.[166]

The post-Marcos years have seen enhanced interest in politicized cultural expression. As one observer recently noted, the most successful art forms have been those that reproduce political theater or the real world most clearly. For example, by the late 1980s feminist writings such as those by novelist Ninotchka Rosca and poet Marra Lanot began reaching a wider audience and generating less controversy than in the past.[167] Indeed, by the early 1990s a feminist pinoy folk-rock music had developed, led by singer-songwriters like Susan Magno. Their songs, often plaintive, address issues like prostitution, castigate male chauvinism, and articulate the demand for equal rights and dignity.[168] But not all cultural developments reflect militancy. In 1987, for example, Celeste Legaspi—long one of the nation's most popular romantic singers (in English and Pilipino)—founded the Organization of Filipino Singers to promote Filipino artists and a firmer (but pluralistic) national musical identity. President Aquino supported the group and signed legislating mandating that radio stations play at least four original Filipino compositions per hour.[169]

Conclusions

As the seemingly eternal quest for national identity and true decolonization continues, and as the democratic governments fail to resolve the country's many problems, the future of political music in the Philippines seems bright. While the crucial political role of popular music in the anti-Marcos ferment seems clear, there are still many questions about the relationship between music and politics, including the perceptions of the audience. Anthropologist Scott Guggenheim has shown how the main social and political processes directing Philippine history have played an integral role in structuring cockfighting, with the cockfight reflecting, reconstituting, and distorting sociopolitical processes.[170] It is premature to draw the same connections with popular music, although the pattern is suggestive.

Nonetheless, it seems that music has played a dual role in modern Philippine history, both legitimizing and maintaining imperialist or authoritarian rule on the one hand, and resisting the forces of oppression while articulating a vision of freedom on the other. Filipino literary and social critic Bienvenido Lumbera describes this dual function as follows: "Popular culture is power, and whoever wields it to manipulate minds is likely to find its literary and technological machinery turned against him when the minds it has manipulated discover its potency as a political weapon."[171] Music has been a mirror that reflects larger social, economic, and political relationships. There are also elements of "free space" and signification in the songs of Aguilar and certain other pinoy artists, allowing the audience to interpret them as they like. Some have clearly perceived an oppositional or countercultural message.

In considering the nature and impact of political music in the

Philippines, an appropriate summary of dissident sentiments was perhaps expressed in one of the most famous poems/songs of Amado Hernandez, “The Structure of Class”:

Now, when the day of judgment comes
And the mighty have been levelled;
(but only if the persecuted open their eyes
Only if they arise and sweep away the few)
The edifice of privilege will crumble,
And in the ashes a new temple will arise;
a new rampart, a new flag, a trumpet of promise
That the nation will grow, out of the people's hope,
Out of their faith in their own leaders.[172]

4

Thailand: Songs for Life, Songs for Struggle

We live like the rice
Waiting for the rain . . .
Nothing left to hope for . . .
The red sun guides our way
It shows us the way, the road to victory
To the plentiful harvest of our dreams . . .
How many have died of starvation? . . .
How few live in luxury
The many ride their buffalo
The few ride the backs of men!
Thai folk-pop group Caravan[1]

The rise of politicized popular musics in Thailand is closely tied to the political turbulence of the early and mid-1970s. But the larger context has been a traditionally conservative political and social system that has long failed to deal adequately with socioeconomic, ethnic minority, and regional equity issues. This chapter examines several streams of music that began to address some of these issues. Beginning in the 1960s the country-style luk-toong represented the sentiments of impoverished rural folk in, and urban migrants from, the northeastern region. In the 1970s the folkish "songs for life" appeared to articulate the anti-Establishment views of radical urban students. By the 1980s a smoother and widely popular folk rock had become the major vehicle for oppositional and countercultural expression. These musics and their leading practitioners have often addressed issues of national and regional identity as well as socioeconomic inequality and persisting neocolonialism.

Basic Data[2]

Population (1994): 60,000,000
Urban Population: 20–40 percent
Capital: Bangkok (metro population: 6,000,000)
Life Expectancy: 69 (67 years for men, 72 years for women)
Adult Literacy: 90 percent
Religions: Theravada Buddhism (95 percent); Islam (4 percent); Others (1 percent)
Economy: Per capita GNP: U.S. $1,160
Radio Ownership: 13,992,000; 200 commercial stations
Radio Receivers Produced (incl. radio–cassette tape players): 1,062,000 (1991)
Television Ownership: 5,893,000; 5 television channels
People Per Television Set: 9
Television Receivers Produced: 2,426 (1991)
Media: Various newspapers (in Thai, English, Chinese)
Major Record Companies (1995): EMI; Kuma (1 local label; distributes 5 labels); MGA; Sony (CBS; distributes 12 labels incl. Arista, BMG, Chrysalis, Motown, RCA)
Music Publishers (1995): Kuma

The Roots of Politics and Music

Thailand is a predominantly Theravada Buddhist country, with centuries of independent existence and a vibrant but adaptable traditional culture.[3] Thai society has been characterized by a rich blend of cultural traits, as well as an openness to new ideas and considerable adaptability to new situations. For the ethnic Thai (Siamese) majority the Buddhist religion and the monarchy serve as the glue to tie the country together. Theravada Buddhism (much mixed with animism at the peasant level) places an emphasis on the individual seeking his or her own salvation (an ending of the endless round of birth and rebirth) through the accumulation of merit. In theory, Buddhism promotes tolerance for social deviation, consensus building, and conciliation as well as peaceful and nonviolent behavior (although these values have sometimes been honored in the breech). Thai social structure has never been rigid, but it is clearly hierarchical with a strong sense of respect for aristocrats, social superiors, and those in authority. Interpersonal and societal harmony is greatly valued, discouraging "boat-rocking." Some scholars have described Thai society as constructed from the top down, with reciprocal, vertical links between the elite and their clients. Furthermore, Thai historiography glorifies the elites while leaving the masses mute. Many scholars of Thai history and society have unwittingly adopted the hegemonic, elite-centric perspective that downplays diversity and "bottom-up" dissent.[4] These patterns have impeded populism and rendered political democracy an imported (and, to many Thais, alien) concept.

During the late nineteenth and early twentieth centuries, farsighted Thai kings promoted a defensive modernization designed to insure independence while duplicating some of the socioeconomic changes occurring in colonized societies (such as the building of a Western-style public school system and a centralizing bureaucracy). The centralization also involved more closely integrating or absorbing neighboring upland peoples (many of them non-Thai) and smaller, once-independent peripheral Thai and Lao states into the Bangkok-dominated polity and identity as "Thai." This transformation helped the country successfully resist the colonizing intentions of the Western powers besides introducing moderate rather than abrupt economic and sociocultural change. Thai economic development generally kept pace with her neighbors, but under Thai direction, although Western economic pressures placed Thailand (known as Siam until the 1930s) in a somewhat neocolonial situation until World War II. Thailand's unique success in resisting colonialism and hence maintaining traditional elites and sociocultural institutions is crucial to understanding later cultural development; Thais did not face identity crisis (unlike the Filipinos), brutal challenges to cultural values and worldviews, or severe economic displacement, even if the activist Thai state and its military showed significant aspects of indirect rule by the West.

Thailand has been neither a static nor a revolutionary society—it tends to progress at an evolutionary pace. In 1932, however, the absolute monarchy was overthrown by a coup that brought middle-class military officers and politicians into power; the monarchy became largely symbolic but continued as a force for national and cultural identity. Thai nationhood and its parameters were to some degree culturally constructed and changed over time. The focus of national loyalty henceforth became a triad comprising the three pillars of Thai society: "Nation, Religion, and King"; but each of the pillars was subject to ambiguities—even contradictions—and the claimed homogeneity of the Thai nation is often overrated by observers.[5] In the decades after the establishment of constitutional government that resulted from the coup, the ethnic Thai nationalists were preoccupied with preserving the country's independence while integrating the various (and sometimes restless) minority groups into a Thai-oriented (and Buddhist) national culture. Approximately 85 percent of the population speak Thai or related dialects as their first language.

But ethnic heterogeneity has long posed political problems. The people of the impoverished northeast (known as the *Isan*) are mainly ethnic Lao, closely related linguistically and culturally to the Siamese but distinct nonetheless. The main Isan dialect is much closer to the Lao language spoken across the Mekong River in Laos than to central Thai, but the languages are mutually intelligible. The northeasterners are often denigrated as rustic and inferior by Thai from the central plains. Collectively, the Isan people account for a third of the total national population and have maintained a strong tradition of regionalism and wariness toward the centralizing Bangkok regime. Indeed the situation has been characterized as one of internal colonialism, with the northeast generally neglected by the central government and exhibiting much higher levels of poverty. In the south many Muslims (some of them Malay speaking) have chafed at Buddhist domination for decades. The mostly non-Buddhist hill peoples of the north and northwest have been less politically volatile but nonetheless pose a persistent challenge to national unity. During the 1990s some ethnic minorities began to more openly reassert their cultural claims within the Thai nation.[6]

Like most Southeast Asian peoples, the Thai developed two distinct performing arts traditions—an elite, court-centered pattern and a village folk pattern; the latter would constitute the base for the evolution of popular culture.[7] Some fifty varieties of musical instruments, including flutes, drums, gongs, percussion-melodic pieces, and stringed instruments, appeared. The court-oriented classical music, patronized by the kings, was performed for ceremonial purposes, as backing for dance drama, and for entertainment. The mood conveyed by this music is not unlike Javanese gamelan. Traditionally the court tradition was passed on by memory. The invention of indigenous notation to preserve the music can be traced back to around 1913; in 1930 there were attempts to employ Western notation. These moves reflected a new Western-derived sense of time, a growing nationalist sentiment, diminishing royal patronage, and a concern with the inroads of Western culture.[8]

Some traditional music perhaps laid a groundwork for later political forms. In particular the formalized music to accompany the classical dance dramas such as the *khon* (performed before royal audiences) and the various puppet theatres should be noted; a wind and percussion band (the *piphat*) is employed for this purpose. After 1932 these orchestras supported a popularized dance drama with singing known as *like' (likay)*, performed by itinerant troupes in provincial towns. The mainly historical plots contain much spontaneous, witty, and risqué dialogue. Later, in the 1950s and 1960s, the government would use

Thai Classical Music

"The sound of the traditional Thai ensemble music might be likened to a stream or river; the main current, the main melody, flows relentlessly onward surrounded by secondary currents that meander in and out of the main flow; here and there little eddies and swirls come suddenly to the surface to be seen momentarily, then to disappear as suddenly. There are no high points and no low points to the ear not educated to this kind of music; it flows onward in a steady non-differentiated band of sounds, almost hypnotically, the various threads of seemingly independent melodies of the individual instruments bound together in a long never-ending wreath."—David Morton[9]

The Thai classical tradition includes various courtly dances such as this one as well as musical dramas and orchestral music. 1971 photo by author.

like' to convey anticommunist and patriotic messages.[10] Other ancient traditions have also been adapted to modern times. For example, the *lakhon chatri* dance drama, perhaps the oldest form of Thai theater, is a lavish spectacular integrating music, dance, and storytelling. Performances today celebrate the nostalgia for older, less hectic and corrupted times while also encouraging a reexamination by the audience of their idealized views of the past. In the past two decades the electronic media has taken audiences away from the live theater.[11]

There are many regional musical folk traditions. The Isan peoples developed a particularly unique style quite different from the courtly traditions of the central Thai. Their music earned a reputation as fun and danceable, but also sad. The local singing style, *lam (mawlum, maolam)*, draws from a wide repertoire including Lao historical epics, Buddhist stories, comic male-female interplay, courting songs, and wordplay. The lam form transcended mere entertainment; the musicians *(mo lam)* were expected to exercise spiritual power in local animism and utilize the strong tradition of improvisation to comment on current affairs. Since the mo lam represented local peasant attitudes vis-à-vis the center, and the musicians could even at times become protest singers, as early as the mid-nineteenth century the Bangkok government sometimes prohibited their performances.[12]

Folk music remained relatively strong in rural districts (especially among the Isan) but increasingly competed with popular mass-mediated music emanating from the major city, cosmopolitan Bangkok. Some Western musical influence can be identified as early as the 1890s, and westernized compositions were utilized to accompany dramas in the 1920s and 1930s.

Rural Song Festivals

"At almost any large gathering of Thai, and in particular at village festivals, boatloads of men prowl the canals and rivers supposedly seeking to engage boatloads of women in song contests. The soloists in each boat sing their verses accompanied by the rhythmical chanting of the others. The lines are bawdy and humorous, utilizing the play on words which is so popular with the Thai. Often the chorus sings some sort of nonsensical background, the last syllable of which the soloist must utilize in his verse. It is a quick, spontaneous affair much loved by the people. Itinerant minstrel troupes still thrive, visiting *wat* [temple], village, and family festivals to provide music and song for the celebrations. Their number and popularity reflect the Thai love for music."—Wendell Blanchard[13]

Some date the birth of Thai popular music to 1931, when a local play utilized a Western jazz band to accompany a new style of "completely worded" songs *(pleng neua tem)*. By 1932 a Thai film industry had emerged, and film-inspired songs were being recorded.[14] American film musicals achieved wide popularity at mid-century, and jazz developed a following among the elite (especially those with a Western education); the present Thai king, Bhumipol Adulyadej, is an accomplished jazz clarinetist and composer (even once accompanying a visiting Benny Goodman in a Bangkok concert). But folk arts never died; song festivals including dancing continued in the provinces.

Postwar Society and Politics

In the decades following World War II, Thailand has had to labor under what the leading American historian of the country, David Wyatt, termed "an inherently conservative political and social structure."[15] This contributed mightily to persistently authoritarian political tendencies as well as bureaucratic inertia. Thailand's postwar political history was characterized by long periods of military rule interspersed with short-lived democratically elected or quasi-democratic governments. Like many nations, Thais strove to find a balance between order and stability on the one hand and the desire for democracy—or at least personal or collective self-determination—on the other. Between 1932 and 1996 the nation experienced nineteen coups d'état by various military factions, an average of one every three years. In the same period, seventeen elections were held.[16]

Ultimately Thailand developed what has been labeled a "demi democracy" or "semidemocracy," a characteristic series of compromises that combine traditions of aristocracy, monarchy, and feudalism with Western notions of representative government and accountability.[17] Until recently politics was chiefly dominated by rival military-bureaucratic cliques with few discernible ideological differences; most civilian governments generally served as mere facades for military domination. Some observers characterize Thai politics as a "moving equilibrium" with several power centers balancing each other so that none could permanently dominate. These centers included the military, the political parties, and the king (mostly as a mediating force), joined more recently by the big business community; by 1986 some 38 percent of members of the House of Representatives and of the cabinet were businessmen.[18]

Until the 1980s there were few ideological differences among the political parties. Money lubricated elections, with most successful candidates coming from wealthy and influential families (including rural landlords). A network of patronage through the *chai por* (political godfathers) linked the citizen to the political system. In rural areas especially, electoral politics revolved around vote buying and obtaining services for the local areas, a system of corruption that reflected the failure of the political system to consistently deliver higher living standards to many rural people. The system has operated particularly in the north, northeast, and central plains regions but is much less important in sophisticated Bangkok. Journalist Rodney Tasker describes the common pattern:

> Many legislators are reelected because of the patronage they have dispensed, rather than anything they have done for the country. . . . Voter coercion through hand-outs of money or goodies by candidates has been going on in Thailand since elections were first held. The time-honored way is for money to be passed to corrupt local Ministry of Interior officials, district leaders or village headmen. They, in turn, make sure voters vote as they are paid, checking poll results against numbers paid. . . . Poor farmers and villagers need money badly, and the center of political power is very remote from their understanding, let alone any concept of real democracy. So why not take the money and vote for any candidate seen to be the source of the generosity? Maybe the candidates elected in this way will provide a bonus by returning the favor in terms of new roads, irrigation and bridges. But then again, maybe not.[19]

From the 1950s through the 1970s the political system attempted with only modest success to deal with mounting problems of inflation, high unemployment, skyrocketing energy costs, rural insurgency, and unrest among various minorities. A leftist insurgency backed by China emerged in the northeast in 1965, with the guerrillas capitalizing on local resentment of the national government and its neglect of the region's underdevelopment. In the south various leftist and Islamic insurgent groups also operated during the 1960s and 1970s. These movements forced the Bangkok elite to recognize and cater to regional distinctions (such as radio programming in local vernaculars).[20]

During the past three decades, Thailand has enjoyed high rates of economic growth that considerably expanded the urban middle class. A large share of the wealth nonetheless remains in the hands of a substantial Chinese minority. Over the centuries intermarriage has been common, and many Thais—including the king and various powerful politicians—have some Chinese blood. Despite losing many members to assimilation, the ethnic Chinese community still accounts for nearly 10 percent of the national population (the percentage is higher in Bangkok). The top of the economy tends to be dominated by Chinese-origin (known as Sino-Thai) and Western or Japanese companies, with foreign investment playing an important economic role. Some observers argue that the substantial state role in capitalist development has benefited the domestic bourgeois classes at least as much as it has foreign capital, enabling them to become more deeply involved in industrial and financial operations.[21]

Despite a growing manufacturing sector, the country has remained somewhat dependent on the export of (and hence fluctuating world prices for) extractive commodities such as rice, rubber, tin, and timber. Bangkok, the capital, contains nearly 6 million people and produces over half of the nation's Gross Domestic Product. But some 70 percent of the population still live in rural areas, mostly as peasants. Standards of public health, education, and per capita income are high by Third World standards but inequitably distributed between ethnic groups and regions. By the early 1990s the per capita annual income stood at $1,200; but, while the highest 20 percent of the people earned over half the national income, the lowest 20 percent earned only 5 percent. The import-substitution industrialization policy adopted in the early 1960s did increase the size of the industrial sector but generally had a negative effect on income distribution. Between 1962 and 1986, income inequality grew substantially (especially in the rural areas).

But the years of liberalization between 1973 and 1976 constituted a break from that pattern, with a trend toward equalization due to more democratic and welfare-oriented policies. Bangkok residents enjoy some three times the wealth of people in the northeast. About a quarter of the population now live below the official poverty line, but the great majority are rural dwellers. Between 1963 and 1973 average farm size in the north fell by half. By 1971 an estimated 63 percent of northern and 74 percent of northeastern rural households lived in poverty, and tenancy levels even in some districts of the central plains approached 90 percent. By 1986 even official statistics showed 60 percent of rural northeasterners remaining below the poverty line. Only a small minority of primary school graduates in the provinces (an estimated 10–15 percent) is able to obtain a secondary school education, and only 20 percent of the Thai labor force boast more than a primary school education.[22]

Although the Thais have long earned a well-deserved reputation for flexibility and adaptability, some of the changes have been destabilizing. Nearly a million women (and girls) work as prostitutes, many of them servicing the "sex tours" of Western men attracted by Bangkok's uninhibited rep-

The Chronic Reality of Rural Poverty in the Northeast

"Across the large, arid plateau millions of villagers still barely scratch a living growing rice, tapioca or a handful of other crops. In many places, except for the planting and harvest periods, villages are empty of all but the elderly and children. Everyone else has moved to the central plains, Bangkok or even southern rubber plantations, looking for work. Massive migration, and encroachment into protected forests to find land for cultivation, has hardly slowed. Malnutrition, landlessness, and children being forced to cut short education to go to work are also nagging signs. Rural poverty is a classic vicious cycle. Families are brought up owing money to rapacious local moneylenders. Poor land and frequent droughts mean the debts are never paid off. Social services, such as education and health, are thin. Children rarely get more than four year's schooling. In the worst times, things are sold—sometimes land, sometimes daughters. And the price is too high to get either back."—Paul Handley[23]

utation. AIDS became a skyrocketing problem, with as many as half a million Thais believed carrying the HIV virus by 1992. An organized labor movement has existed for decades but it remains relatively weak, factionalized, and subject to state manipulation or repression; less than 3 percent of the growing industrial workforce is unionized.[24] Furthermore, underneath the image of the carefree Thai peasant, increasingly inequitable landowning patterns, low rice prices, and corruption fuel rural frustrations. There is a long history of resistance by many rural villages *(ban)* to domination by the city *(muang)*, including the intrusive central government and the privileged local elites it co-opts, especially through evasion, affirmation of village community and peasant values, and migration—but also occasionally violence.[25] Even some popular comic strips, such as those of Chai Rachewat, address the frequent disconnection between villages and government officials.[26] Thais often define their personal goals as *sanuk* (a multipurpose word that can mean "easygoing," "fun," "carefree activity," "pleasant milieu"). But it became increasingly difficult to find sanuk amidst the problems and tensions spawned by modernization.

Not the least of the problems are environmental. Bangkok, the rapidly growing home to nearly a sixth of the nation's population, gained a reputation as one of the most polluted cities in Asia, its air drenched in toxic matter, while the nation's once abundant rain forests disappeared at a rapid rate with probable negative consequences. Bangkok has been a troubled city. Yet migrants fleeing rural poverty continue to flock there on a temporary or permanent basis. American sociologist David Elliott described Bangkok in the late 1960s:

> There is severe crowding in Bangkok, where construction has not kept up with the pressure of workers coming in from the rural areas in [often

> fruitless] search of employment. . . . Living conditions in the poorer urban areas are appalling by Western standards. . . . Child labor laws continue to be abused. From time to time the Western press reports the discovery of conditions even of veritable slavery . . . when impoverished parents have indentured their children to ruthless factory-owners who would literally work the children to death. Indeed, in 1969, approximately 5 million persons, about 31% of the labor force, were children and young people aged 11–19.[27]

The Brief Mid-1970s Cultural and Political "Blossoming"

Not until the 1970s would a true mass politics develop. Oppositional forces arose in response to the persistent problems; these forces struggled within as well as outside the political arena to change the direction of the country and address socioeconomic inequalities. Oppositional and dissident forces were particularly strong during the 1970s, a time when the country was undergoing some important transitions. The long-entrenched and repressive military regime had grown corrupt; by the early 1970s the two top leaders or their families held 150 company directorships and bribery was rampant.[28] Furthermore, they seemed unwilling or unable to address the increasing demands for better welfare and higher living standards. Yet the economy was expanding rapidly, creating stresses in the dictatorial system. Martial law had been imposed in 1971, making the military rule unusually harsh by Thai standards.

Between 1960 and 1970 the administrative, executive, and managerial segments of the economically active population grew tenfold. The growing middle class sought increased influence. Literacy rates and university enrollments grew apace; the five universities enrolling fifteen thousand students in 1961 grew to seventeen with a hundred thousand students in 1972. An urban working class also developed in Bangkok. During the 1960s and early 1970s, rural-to-urban migration had accelerated; many peasants became aware of new ideas as they settled in Bangkok. Even those who stayed behind in villages were exposed to often destabilizing modern (Thai and Western) influences through radio and television as well as city-bred schoolteachers, Buddhist monks, and government officials; these newcomers promoted the national culture and the accompanying urban bias that devalued village life. Unemployment was increasing for university and vocational school graduates as well as displaced peasants and unskilled workers. The U.S. presence also facilitated the spread of Western political and cultural ideas.[29]

Meanwhile, the dissident groups worked to shift Thailand's foreign policy away from slavish capitulation to American demands predicated by a Cold War mentality. Eight major American military bases were located in the country, employed in part for bombing campaigns in Indochina; by 1968 nearly fifty thousand U.S. troops were stationed in Thailand. Thailand contributed troops and moral support to the U.S. war effort in Indochina. Indeed, between 1959 and 1971 the United States contributed over a billion dollars of assistance to the Thai military.[30] Many Thais viewed this as an unacceptable compromise of their sovereignty as well as incurring the enmity of Vietnam. The presence of many free-spending American soldiers created a false prosperity while also posing a challenge to Buddhist morality. Many business, military, and bureaucratic elites prospered from and hence welcomed the U.S. presence, supplying goods and services or collecting bribes and political backing. Many of the thousands of Thais employed by or servicing the Americans earned far more than the average Thai of comparable occupations; but U.S. withdrawal rendered many of them unemployed. The presence of so many U.S. soldiers on "rest and recreation" resulted in whole sections of Bangkok and some up-country towns "being transformed into strings of gaudy nightclubs and brothels thinly disguised as massage parlors."[31]

Intellectuals and students also began to take more interest in Marxist and sometimes even Maoist approaches to both analyzing the Thai situation and rectifying the problems. Some of this understanding came from a reappraisal of long-suppressed Thai Marxist thinkers. Radical discourse has a more distinguished history in Thai intellectual life than usually thought in the West, with radical thinkers like Jit Poumisak challenging many fundamental aspects of Thai society, culture, and politics:

> The legitimacy of the Thai state rests on a web of meanings that are articulated in law, in public ceremony, and in symbolism. . . . These meanings inextricably associate the military, the monarchy, and the Buddhist monkhood as a triad that stands for "Thailand." . . . Sedition might be defined as an effort to unravel the web of meanings.[32]

Radical thinkers have either been persecuted or ignored. Some in their frustration end up joining communist insurgencies. By the early 1970s some students were finding their views relevant. This radical discourse corresponded to a move toward social consciousness in literature, although many of these writers were imprisoned for their fiction. Some of these writers (of what is sometimes termed the "literature for life" movement) sought to break down the wall between the urban and rural worlds. Jit Poumisak himself was an ardent proponent of what he termed "art for life, art for the people." Furthermore, some of the oppositional groups worked increasingly in unison, alarming conservative forces but helping to create a popular consensus.

Students played a particularly large role in this process, especially student groups from the universities in Bangkok. Occasional student activism had been a feature of Thai life since the 1930s, aimed chiefly at foreign domination, martial law, heavy-handed dictatorial policies, or educational deficiencies. This

"Art for Life" Poetry

"Each time you grab a fistful of rice
Remember it is my sweat you swallow
To keep on living.
This rice has the taste
To please every tongue of every class,
But to grow rice is the bitter work
That only we farmers must taste.
From my labor the rice becomes stalks
It takes a long, long time
From spout to grain
And it is full of misery.
Every drop of my sweat
Reflects this hard life.
My veins strain and bulge
So you can eat.
The red sweat of my labor
Is really my life's blood
That delights your teeth."—Jit Poumisak[33]

activism accelerated during the late 1960s and early 1970s. During 1973 student demonstrators sang marching songs they had written:

> *Fight without retreat, for the masses are waiting for us . . . We have joined together to fight for democracy.*[34]

Some of the students' frustrations arose from the difficulty in finding suitable employment as a result of overproduction of university graduates. Many Thais sought a more open and democratic system, but not all of these people would be sympathetic to more systematic socioeconomic transformation.

During 1973 the regime was overthrown after mass demonstrations, generating the return to democracy and political liberalization and well as the energizing of new social forces. Sparked by the arrest of thirteen professors and students distributing leaflets calling for a new constitution, massive student demonstrations broke out in October 1973, involving several hundred thousand (perhaps even a half million) students and their sympathizers; as one leader noted, "student activism can change society."[35] With public support for the demonstrators swelling, the military government, charging communist subversion, followed with repression, arresting student leaders, then beating many demonstrators, and finally opening fire, killing many (estimates range from 75 to over 350) and wounding many (perhaps thousands of) others.[36]

The public outrage, and the loss of support among the military and bureaucratic elite, forced the strongman and his closest associates to resign and flee the country. One historian concludes that "here, perhaps, was the closest thing Thailand ever had to a 'revolution,' for it was mass power mobilized on a far greater scale than any Thai had seen before."[37]

As part of this contribution, they ended one-man, authoritarian rule and signaled a new consciousness about the necessity of sharing political power more widely than ever before. Some employ the term *people power*, because for the first time in Thai history a government dominated by *phuuyai* ("men with power") had been changed by the student *phuunooj* ("little people without power").[38] One student expressed the feeling of elation: "For the first time in my life . . . I sense freedom in my native land. Like many other Thais, I have wanted it for a long time; but now that we seem to have it, I feel bewildered. I don't quite believe it yet."[39]

For Marxists and others on the political left, "the blossoming," as they called it, brought an unprecedented and exhilarating sense of promise for community and labor organizing, as well as political recruitment and education on a scale never before possible. Well-organized groups representing students, peasants, workers, teachers, and others who previously felt marginalized pressed their demands, some of them calling for a more socialist, redistributive economic approach. Progressive students saw themselves as the "conscience" of society, charged with leading the way in resolving society's problems. These were attempts, which gained broad public support, to achieve permanent enfranchisement. Democratic forces sought to integrate the rural districts into the political arena in order to reverse the always powerful trends promoting military dictatorship. This sometimes involved cultural weapons such as the film *Tongpan*, made in 1976, which depicted student activists from Bangkok assisting an Isan village in combating the corruption and inequality of the entrenched sociopolitical system.[40] A prominent intellectual expressed the hopes of the young progressives in 1974:

> In my ideal society . . . there should be unity without forced conformity; there should be room for the non-conformist, the unique, the idealist, even the crank; members of the society should be able to discern truth, beauty and goodness and cherish them and discard superficial and false values; material and spiritual welfare should be available to all, not for the few; human dignity and freedom are each individual's sacred due, however humble he be.[41]

Student militancy did not end with the installation of a democratic system, for activists still sought substantial structural and policy changes for the country as well as an end to American political and Japanese economic domination. Some also sought "cultural revolution" to change elite attitudes. One student leader described how Thai society became more politically aware:

A Literary View of Student Activism

"There was only one thing she couldn't stop him doing—when he broke the news to her that he probably wouldn't be able to finish college in four years because he had to devote part of his time to 'activities'. Mother later came to understand that these 'activities' meant politics. 'Politics aren't what I'm really after. I'm using my time to study and learn about the problems of the poor, who are so much poorer than we, who don't eat three meals a day, and who have to do heavy work as manual laborers, hiring themselves out for low wages. When they demand fair pay, and appeal for help, how could we stand idly by, Mother? Or when the peasants demand justice, sometimes to the point of having to make demonstrations, I can't possibly rest comfortably through it all. I'm concerned about our poor, not about politics. But politics concerns itself with me. So we can't escape it.' The very word 'demonstration' pierced her to the quick. She couldn't bear to look at the photos of the young men and women gunned down on the streets during October 1973. If there was a mass demonstration, and someone threw even a single bomb, rows of people would be killed or wounded. She urged him to hurry up and finish his studies, hurry and get a job like his older brothers and sisters, so she could stop worrying about him."—Wat Wanlayangkun[42]

"Hyde Parks and panel discussions are being held in nearly every province and books on social problems are selling better than all the others."[43] The students worked increasingly closely with labor, farm, and other grassroots activists and groups, becoming increasingly radical in the process. In an opening political process that was unprecedented, the new feeling that entrenched powerholders could be challenged spread even to small towns and villages. These activities alarmed conservatives in the military and bureaucracy. Some radical groups even openly called for the establishment of a socialist system, increasing ideological polarization and isolating liberals who wanted more moderate change.[44]

It is important to note that labor groups, including unions, played a crucial role in all of these developments, although students received the most attention. As one labor leader claimed in 1974: "It wasn't all students; whatever they may say, the students didn't drive the buses at the time of the demonstrations and confrontations—workers did."[45] It can also be argued that there were two revolts in the 1970s: the well-known one against the monopoly of power by a corrupt military, and a second by the rural villages against the city and centralized power. The latter revolt involved politicized peasant organizations as well as communist-led insurgents.[46] Most likely the students, many of them idealists favoring worker and peasant causes, overestimated their popular base of support, just as student militants did in the United States during the 1960s. Indeed, Thai politics did not shift very far to the left, with politicians protecting the status quo still dominant in the newly elected Parliament.

But the fragile civilian governments (all of them coalitions), torn between the political extremes and ever wary of military intervention, were unable to satisfy these demands. The ruling alliance of royalists, businessmen, and bureaucrats, while all opposing military dictatorship and favoring a more open parliamentary system, was divided on other goals and often unsympathetic to student and intellectual radicals. And the powerful bureaucracy proved typically unresponsive to new directions. Indeed, the "liberal era" was progressive only in contrast with the preceding regime; many traditional elite figures remained in power. As was true throughout modern Thai history, the political changes were somewhat superficial. Furthermore, political violence, including murders and bombings, became more common as left-wing militants and police-supported right-wing paramilitary groups struggled for influence. The rightist groups, some with links to Thai and American intelligence agencies, broke up strikes, harassed left-wing leaders, bombed political party offices, and were allegedly responsible for the murder of thirty-five leaders of the farmer's organization and three left-leaning academics, among others. Army-controlled radio and television stations began broadcasting a barrage of invective aimed at the "communist threat" represented by the progressive student organizations and leading politicians (including the civilian prime minister, a longtime royalist).[47]

Political scientist Benedict Anderson describes the growing polarization:

> The cultural and ideological consequences of October 1973 took two diametrically opposite forms. On the left, an almost giddy sense of exhilaration, iconoclasm and creativity was born. For a time it seemed that one could say, sing or do almost anything. On the right, the illusion rapidly took root that the newly established liberal regime was the cause of the sudden epidemic of subversive ideas. Democracy was quickly blamed for the consequences of the dictatorship and its complicity with American and Japanese capitalism.[48]

Finally, in October 1976, bloody clashes between leftist students and right-wing thugs precipitated a military coup and martial law. In the process hundreds of students were killed or wounded and thousands arrested. At Bangkok's prestigious Thammasat University, rightist thugs lynched or beheaded many students. As two scholars concluded, "the carnage was almost unbelievable."[49]

Radical Thai poet Khomthuon Kanthanu, who had memorialized the uprising of 1973, summarized what he perceived as the destruction of the nation in 1976:

Misfortune and disaster . . .
Deserted the whole of Thailand
Everybody living in abject poverty
Depressed and oppressed.
Too much blood spilled.

Sweat running down,
Maimed limbs, broken bones. . . .
People shed tears, those speaking out,
Will have to suffer if acting openly
If contradicting, they will be killed;
If courageous, they will be arrested.
They suffer many pains, their hearts break
Without justice and without a voice.[50]

Many Thais welcomed the end of the turmoil, strikes, and inflation of the civilian years, but the repressive atmosphere became chilling. Between 1976 and 1979 the government ruthlessly repressed the various activist groups and assassinated group leaders. Among their first acts was the public burning of thousands of "subversive" books, including many Western classics. In the decade following the coup some forty-seven journalists were murdered, sometimes by the police. The bloodbath and coup were an attempt by the traditional ruling elites to turn back the wheels of history in order to resist the rising forces of social change. The universities quieted but many activists escaped to the northeast to join the communist-led guerrillas. The influx of some three thousand students led to rapid growth for the Communist Party of Thailand (CPT), which had been waging a struggle against the Bangkok government for years in the fringe areas of the kingdom. With communist forces in ascendancy next door in Indochina, communism must have seemed the wave of the future and the only realistic alternative to fascist authoritarianism. At its height the CPT could field some fourteen thousand guerrillas and controlled hundreds of villages.[51]

And yet, by the mid-1980s the insurgency and the CPT were moribund. Most of the always practical peasants in the central plains and northeast, however dire their poverty, cared less for revolution than improving their living standards, which required government assistance. Nearly all the surviving students, disillusioned with revolutionary existence, abandoned the jungles and returned to civilian life. Many students found the CPT ideologically incompetent and rigid as well as bureaucratically inefficient and undemocratic; old guard leaders mistrusted the students. The cut-off of Chinese aid combined with a new government strategy emphasizing political ("hearts and minds") rather than military defeat of the insurgency soon rendered guerrilla life unacceptable for most of the former students, many of whom had been traumatized or angered by their experiences.[52] Many of the former guerrillas later became successful in business and the professions, the academic world, or democratic politics. Some became involved in the nongovernmental organizations promoting issues like environmental protection and women's rights that became increasingly active and influential in the 1980s.

Australian political scientist J. S. Girling posed the dilemma facing the Thai leaders in the early 1980s and still somewhat relevant today:

> The fundamental *political* problem (in the broad sense) is whether the regime is capable of creating new conditions for rebuilding consensus . . . thus gaining a grudging acceptance by the currently excluded and alienated groups. If the regime will not or cannot do so, its only alternative is to continue to rule by repression. The fundamental *social* problem is whether even political consensus is sufficient to carry out, through the existing machinery of government, those rural reforms (notably land redistribution, tenancy laws, availability of credit, and so on), combined with administrative reforms (putting an end to "feudal" attitudes and abuses, subjection to "influence," and bias in favor of the rural and urban elite) that the situation demands.[53]

Beginning in 1979 the political situation stabilized, allowing a return to a quasi-democratic system and a resurgence of student activism—albeit on a modest scale. The political system of the 1980s can be viewed as a "halfway" or "demi" democracy, a temporary accommodation to realities but transitional should a full democracy eventually emerge.[54] During these years the military had to tolerate an expansion of political participation. Military officers, bureaucrats, and political party politicians all played a role and an elected House of Representatives became an increasing (but still limited) venue for debate. The press, historically closely tied to those in power, became more important but there was considerable self-censorship; forty-seven journalists were murdered in the 1980s (many of them investigative reporters). Only a few dared to criticize prevailing patterns openly, in the process earning the enmity of their frightened colleagues. Press freedom remains partial; in 1996 a popular and aggressive current affairs show was pulled from television because of its criticism of prominent government leaders, fostering timidity.[55] Nonetheless, civil liberties have largely been respected in recent years.

The Development of Popular Music and Culture

The origins of contemporary Thai popular music can be traced back to the late 1940s, when a modernizing government opened state radio to musical currents from the West.[56] Over the next decades Thai classical music lost some (but by no means all) of its popularity, although a market remains for classical cassettes. Many musicians specializing in the classical genres have tended to become conservative, longing nostalgically for a past when their work was more valued. Ethnomusicologist David Morton laments that the traditional classical music may become more of an anachronistic museum piece than a vital force in contemporary Thai culture.[57] Some folk music genres are endangered because, thanks to social change,

> the circle of teachers and students is shrinking with every generation. . . . There is the danger that once a master passes away, his skills may be lost

forever. . . . Folk music lacks the socioeconomic strength to compete with the siren songs of extensively promoted pop music.[58]

Writer Sujit Wongthet's short story, "Second Nature," bemoaned the increasing vulgarization of classical dance forms in rural festivals, expressing horror at the extremely short skirts worn by dancers and the bawdy songs:

> The whole lot of them were dancing to the tempo of pigs or dogs scalded with boiling water. Alas and alack! . . . Two of the girls . . . danced together on the stage, complacently bumping and grinding their hips—oblivious to their fellow countrymen, oblivious to the *Chronicles of Si Ayuttaya* [the most famous Thai historical chronicle], oblivious to the inscription of the Kingdom of Sukhothai [a great early Thai kingdom] . . . oblivious of King Chulalongkorn [a great Thai king who reformed the nation].[59]

There are some contrary trends. The Fong Naam classical ensemble has attempted with some success to revitalize and reinterpret classical music, and in the process they have gained an international audience. Indeed, Thailand has a long history of creatively incorporating outside influences to her own advantage, and this has helped enrich musical traditions over the centuries. Nonetheless, by the 1990s classical music and other arts in Bangkok are confined largely to little-watched television specials and tourist hotels, but folk arts are emphasized on many rural radio stations.

By the 1960s Western and Thai popular music dominated radio, clubs, and the recording industry; indeed, in 1967, Anglo-American recordings monopolized the nation's "top ten."[60] Eventually, ten important recording companies emerged in Thailand, three of them multinationals and the majority of the rest owned by Sino-Thai families; most offered a diversified assortment of styles. The industry became an important part of daily life:

Musicians playing classical Thai music in Bangkok. Performances such as this of live music for local audiences have become rarer in the past few years, but they remain popular with tourists and older Thais. 1971 photo by author.

> Popular music thrives in Bangkok. Street vendors and small storefronts selling inexpensive cassette tape recordings are abundant, and the market for new singers—who often coin names for their own "subgenres" under commercial pressure to appear original and draw an audience—is fierce. . . . The Thai recording business is notorious for favoring certain performers, while others, eager for careers in show business, wait for a lucky break to get started.[61]

Successive governments recognize the advantages of controlling broadcasting. According to an official publication from the 1960s, the authorities regarded radio as a "powerful instrument of information and enlightenment . . . [which is] implicitly . . . subserving the policy of the government."[62] Indeed, radio had been used for blatantly propagandistic purposes since the 1930s, controlled mostly by right-wing forces. For years Radio Thailand propagated both nationalism and modernization through patriotic songs and plays. Only in the early 1950s was a second radio network (government-controlled but commercially financed) established, giving listeners a wider choice. By 1973 there were some two hundred radio stations, 80 percent controlled by the military. Already at that time Thailand had about double the radio ownership per capita as Indonesia, with some seventy-nine radios for every thousand citizens. A decade later, Thailand boasted 265 radio stations, many of them controlled by the government public relations department, as well as two military-operated and two quasi-commercial television stations. By 1992 there were 462 radio stations throughout the country. Since commercial services must obtain licenses from the state, political elites can exert some control over the product. By law, radio and television are required to provide programs strengthening national unity and identity.[63]

Radio programming has been primarily oriented toward local audiences and even the most remote villages possessed radio receivers by the 1980s. From the 1970s into the 1990s, commercial criteria dominated programming decisions for most stations. As one radio producer admitted in 1986: "I have to constantly prove to the sponsors that my (music magazine) programme is very popular. If I do not deliver the audience expected, the contract is lost at short notice. . . . We are always scrambling for sponsors to keep the programming going."[64] Even the liberal government between 1973 and 1976 attempted no serious reform of broadcasting, much to the chagrin of activists. The radical left had a broadcasting venue only through the clandestine radio of the CPT guerrillas; this unprecedented oppositional broadcasting was closed down in 1979. Censorship of some sort remains chronic, although the parameters have ebbed and flowed with the political winds. In 1985, for example, the song "One Night in Bangkok" by the British group WHAM was proscribed because it extolled the sexual attractions of the Thai capital, a matter of embarrassment for many Thais.[65]

The Perception of American Influence on Bangkok Society

"The best introduction to Bangkok was a pilgrimage to the heart of Patpong Road, a mess of more than fifty look-alike bars designed with nothing in mind but the bodily pleasure of foreigners. I had, I felt, been transported back to some B-movie image of Saigon, 1968. Behind me, a jukebox with a throbbing bass pounded out 'Do It to Me' and 'Slow Hand' and 'Da Ya Think I'm Sexy.' In Bangkok the Western influence was pronounced. The locals had come to the weekend market to savor the real exotica: bright orange toy guitars; a bowling shirt that read 'Rick's Carpet Center, Granada Hills'; and posters of Jennifer Beals and Phoebe Cates—the newly canonized goddesses of the Orient—sitting in Mustangs, showing off UCLA letter jackets or simply carrying themselves as embodiments of the Promised Land. Down every puddle-glutted lane in Bangkok lay pizzas, pizazz and all the glitzy razzmatazz of the American Dream, California style: video rental stores, Pizza Hut and Robinson's and trendy watering holes with Washington Redskins decals on the window and tapes of 'This Week in the NFL' inside."—Pico Iyer[66]

Television broadcasting commenced in 1955 and became national in 1979. By the 1980s there were four commercial companies (two of them controlled by the military), screening variety shows, weekly series (many from the United States), sports events, and immensely popular locally produced "soap opera" serial dramas *(lakhon)*. By 1990 television reached over 90 percent of urban and 70 percent of rural households. Stations controlled by the military or government have unabashedly promoted the political hierarchy and mainstream values. The first truly independent television station appeared only in 1996, but it had to combat government red tape and attempts at censorship. Although originating in Bangkok, these influences reach far into the countryside, as one Thai observer notes:

> Even in the rice field one may hear the Western music of the Beatles, or [westernized] . . . Thai songs. The music naturally comes from a transistor radio hung over the back of water buffaloes or a tree branch. . . . Thai music still remains popular but Western music has made some inroads.[67]

The first composed Thai songs accompanied by Western musical instruments appeared in 1933; this type of popular music came to be known as *phleng thai sakon* (Western Thai or international songs).[68]

The Western ideological and consumerist impact on the Thai, especially Thai youth, accelerated in the 1960s, with a profound effect on the society and culture. Benedict Anderson explains the situation:

> The impact of all this was as much cultural as social: decay of traditional arts in the face of American films and their imitators; decline in the legitimacy

> of the monkhood as television sets and Mercedes-Benzes entered the temples, while young men stayed away from them; deracination of youth and their partial absorption into the orbit of Atlantic consumer culture.[69]

Inevitably these trends were bound to produce a response. Initially this was expressed in cultural terms among a small group of Bangkok intellectuals. It then spread through university students to the wider society. Anti-Americanism became a more pronounced pattern. Among the early signs was a political theater movement that commenced around 1970 with the goal of using drama to educate peasants; they flourished in the liberal mid-1970s. By the 1980s the theater included both urban companies and a grassroots theater of liberation aimed at the peasantry.[70]

A more critically aware art became particularly apparent in literature. Thai writing developed a pattern of introspection and daring:

> Thai do not subscribe to a belief in the inherent goodness of the innovative or creative. Rather, what is important from a Thai point of view is that literature clarify or reveal that which is obviously real but unrecognized; that it make people think about what previously was improper (or dangerous or irrelevant) to think about; that it give shape, meaning and identities to things.[71]

Beginning as early as the 1950s, Thai writers were not reticent to critique the nation and its ills (including urbanization, privilege, the underclass, development priorities, U.S. imperialism, and Western influence), although few dared to subject the monarchy and Buddhism to the same analytical examination.

Khamsing Srinawk, born in the northeast of peasant stock, was a pioneer in writing satires that skewered Bangkok life and the pretensions of politicians while extolling ("warts and all") the simple farmers preyed upon by urban hucksters. The mid-1970s proved a particularly productive period, with the emergence of a "literature for life" social relevance movement based on the ideas of Jit Poumisak and the establishment of many new magazines and newspapers. Populist authors like Samruam Singh wrote about the agony of the rural areas under the assault of socioeconomic change. Even in these liberal times, however, writers often published under pseudonyms or made their points obliquely enough to escape possible censorship.[72] These writers would provide a model for political musicians.

Thailand's most popular poet in the 1970s and 1980s, Angkhan Kalayanaphong, was among the more courageous writers. In his long poem, "Bangkok, Thailand," he directly confronts the degradation of the nation's capital while also criticizing environmental exploitation:

Bangkok—rubbish, corpses, fragments of the gods.
In the holy city people congregate to commit evil.

. . . foreigners hope to sponge on whores.
They make love in coffee-shops.
Hippies shout hi, hae, hae,
Their songs are projected as far as Chiang Mai . . .
At the university they study in like manner . . .
Evil is done, the open forest is killed.
The dense jungle is thoroughly destroyed
Until all streams have dried out.[73]

The large film industry reflects many of the patterns that have characterized popular music. Thai filmmaking began in 1936 but Western-style sound films appeared only in 1971. Most of the films produced in Thailand were escapist, low-budget entertainments for a mass audience with a persistent "boy-meets-girl" theme that conveyed sanuk feelings. Between 1965 and 1970, the most popular films were love story musicals, often starring pop singers whose careers could skyrocket from such exposure; these were especially popular in the provinces. One local arts critic dismissed these films in the early 1970s as follows:

> I confess to rarely seeing Thai films, but the products seen lack even the semblance, even the glossy appearance of quality. . . . The plain truth is that . . . Thai films have remained static. The same maudlin, platitudinous themes, the same awkward and sentimental acting, the same sloppy direction.[74]

In 1972 much stricter government censorship was imposed, under police and military control. Nonetheless, Thai films emphasize local context and hence have generally reflected sociocultural conditions in the nation. The liberal period of 1973–1976 spawned a "new wave" of films reflecting the idealism, experimentation, and confusion of the times, some of them by women filmmakers like Patravdee Sritrairat; they explored social problems, war, and rural desperation. With the return of more conservative regimes, despite the restrictions, a few directors over the years have produced films with social messages, exploring overlapping social values, societal divisions, social failings (such as discrimination), and poverty. Only a few of these films are financially successful, however.

Varieties of Popular Music and Political Discourse

Thai *sakon* pop music of the 1960s and early 1970s tended to be highly imitative of Western models, although vocalization styles reflected Thai singing traditions. Many songs were taken from the Anglo-American pop charts, with the original English translated into Thai lyrics. The most urban-oriented type of pop music came to be known as *phleng lukkroong* ("child of the city"). Favored by state radio, it features slower rhythms and concentrates on

A Thai Punk Rocker

" 'At first I wanted to be a doctor,' recalls 26-year-old Anchalee Chongkhadikij, 'but things changed.' They certainly did. Instead of sedating people, Anchalee, now Bangkok's hottest young rock singer in her punk incarnation as 'Pooh,' is working them into a lather night at the posh Casablanca Disco. With her spiked hair and street-thug image, Pooh cuts a fearsomely different figure from your average Thai damsel on the street or stage. But when she isn't glaring balefully for the camera, Pooh delights her fans by wailing out Linda Ronstadt numbers ('She's my favorite') and other toe-tapping tunes with the Barracudas, her back-up band. As a result, she's now the talk of the town—perhaps not least because Daddy happens to be editor-in-chief of the [English language] *Bangkok Post.* Anchalee has studied in the U.S., where she took a master's degree in finance ('There's really not much of a future doing this for life')."—*Asiaweek*, 1982[75]

schmaltzy, romantic themes. Winai Panturang is credited as the "father" of modern *lukkroong*, with songs like "Lotus Flower" ("Young Girl"); in the 1980s singers like Jumras Sawate Taporn and groups like Char Tree came to the fore. Lukkroong and a related, more rock-oriented genre (known as *string*) have been particularly popular among the urban middle classes and elite and hence have long enjoyed a reputation as high, modernistic culture. Musicians in these streams tend to emulate the latest Anglo-American fads such as hard rock, disco, or rap.

Lukkroong songs rarely deal with social issues and problems; rather the mood is often overtly hegemonic, as in the massive hit "Happy, No Problem." Those few musicians who do address issues like justice, democracy, or class differences can find their work banned from the airwaves. For example, Chai Muangsing recorded a song called "Democracy" in the early 1980s criticizing legal favoritism for the privileged and corruption, but radio and television refused to play it. String, a highly commodified music that closely follows trends in Anglo-American rock, became highly popular in the 1980s. Some of the songs express popular frustrations and resentments, such as Billy Ogan's "Resign," which criticizes government officials, and his "Hun" ("Robot"), about the way urban life transforms people into soulless machines. The music can also pose other types of challenges to accepted norms. In the mid-1980s the popularity among teenagers (especially girls) of openly lesbian pop star Anchalee Chongkhadikij, whose sakon songs emphasized longing and loneliness, sparked a public debate about the controversial role of homosexuality in Thai culture.[76]

There has also been a sort of Thai country music known as *phleng luktoong*[77] ("child of the fields"), popular in the rural areas (especially in the northeast) and among rural migrants to Bangkok. It is considered crude and déclassé by urban elites—much like early country-and-western music in the United States—and is based heavily on the folk music of the impoverished northeast, including use of traditional instruments. Indeed, the music grew out of the village environment and the increasing problems faced by rural peoples as urban political and economic power becomes more pronounced. These often fast-paced songs have a simpler style and utilize the northeastern vernacular for easy communication with the target audience. Many musicians come from backgrounds in folk music such as mo lam. This allows them to clearly reflect Isan identity in contrast to the central Thai plains and Bangkok. The songs describe life in the countryside, including both romantic nostalgia and the difficult realities facing many peasants. The popularity of luktoong has been based on various factors, including the song style, the quality of the musicians, the role of the music in rural living, and the relationship of the themes and content to real life situations.

Most of the major stars come from the northeast and offer a unique singing style difficult for non-Isan peoples to emulate. Luktoong takes on a major entertainment role in the provinces, with bands visiting villages. These visits have gradually displaced traditional art forms such as the like' drama and the shadow play. Naowarat Pongbaiboon, a renowned poet and specialist on folk music, has commented on the popularity of the form:

> It is so popular that, if there were a temple fair where there happened to be both a Luk Thung band and a Western movie showing, the vast majority would rather pay to stand and watch the Luk Thung than sit for free and watch the movie. I should add that this standing often means waiting for an hour for the show of three hours to begin.[78]

Isan folk music has had a significant influence on Thai pop generally, and luktoong in particular. Indeed, the maolam style continues to flourish in two forms in both the northeast and Bangkok: as a collaboration with luktoong and as an alternative to it. Modern maolam songs are adapted by rock bands, or played with electronic keyboards and a funky beat; Isan youth become heavy metal heroes after hooking up their instruments to amplifiers. In Laos, the maolam has also been used for political purposes, to spread the messages desired by the government. The major folk instruments utilized include the *kaen* (a large bamboo-tube mouth organ) and *pin* (a three-stringed "guitar"). An old proverb demonstrates how closely Lao/Isan identity is tied up with folk music: "He who inhabits a pile house, eats sticky rice, and plays the kaen [bamboo windpipes], he is a true Laotian."[79]

Some observers suggest that the folk songs resemble a murky version of psychedelic rock. Although utilizing traditional instruments and tunes, many folk musicians write new lyrics reflecting contemporary interests. Many

The Evolution of Luktoong

Luktoong derived from an earlier rustic style known as "market songs," popular in the 1940s and 1950s. Some observers identify the first song in the idiom as "Oh, the Vegetable Grower's Bride," recorded in 1937. Kamrot Samboonanon, who began recording in the mid-1940s, is often considered the first major performer. Luktoong emerged as a popular, mass-mediated, widely recorded music in the early 1960s, receiving considerable radio play; Jamnong Rangsitkuhn is credited with inventing the term in 1962. By the late 1970s it had become a staple of television as well. The expanding cassette industry was crucial in developing a market among lower-income groups, especially in rural areas. Expanding road networks allowed entertainers to spread the more elaborate and glitzy luktoong to once remote towns. In its basic form the style clearly resembles traditional folk songs (such as the maolam of the Isan) and the like' theater, and it utilizes many folk tunes. But luktoong musicians have also incorporated Western musical instruments into the mix. By the 1980s luktoong divided into distinct substreams: a string-influenced electrified pop sound and regional folk-oriented sounds. Luktoong accounted for about 40 percent of the recording market share in the 1980s, with lukkroong (20 percent) and string (30 percent) garnering most of the remainder.[80]

songs deal with romantic or religious themes, but some address social issues. For example, "Lam Phloen" calls on people to face economic hardships and the problems of modernization with courage. The music continues to lubricate festive occasions in the northeast:

> On Saturday night the town comes alive with music as wandering bands with any combination of instruments roam the streets or set up amplifiers in storefronts. Mostly it's just singers and percussionists, and they'll sing anything! That FM radio is filled with overproduced, inane, rootless Thai-language pop-rock. Here it returns as rough music of the people. It's the purest roots-rock I've ever heard in Thailand, putting any recorded band to shame for pure energy. . . . No one records this music. Recording . . . is almost always seen as a stepping-stone to slickness, or at least codification. . . . These same slick recordings are subsequently distorted to death on P.A. systems at the village wat and villager's scratchy AM radios.[81]

The precise nature of luktoong seems to be a matter of considerable debate among Thai scholars, with some viewing it as a syncretic, popularized, and commercialized blend of various influences and others considering it a modestly updated version of folk music. The most recent analysis, by one of the foremost Thai scholars of popular culture—Ubonrat Siriyuvasak—describes the music as "a synthesis of western pop/rock, folk and ballad, Thai folk music and a range of traditional popular art forms," with a modern subgenre recently appearing that incorporates disco and other dance musics.[82] There is a distinctive vocal style, full of ornamentation, that requires a wide vocal range. Most of the major artists have come from rural backgrounds with little formal education.

They find a ready-made audience among the millions of rural folk (many from the Isan) who have flocked to the cities, some permanently but many temporarily, where they face economic hardship as well as discrimination that stems from their rustic ways. Luktoong, which addresses homesickness for the simpler village life while dealing with the sometimes conflictive relationship between the city and the countryside, proves attractive. This large migrant community in Bangkok inevitably influences radio playlists, giving luktoong major broadcasting time. Over time the recordings and stage shows became more commercialized, elaborate, and often bawdy, with orchestras and a bevy of dancing girls. The added expenses increased the necessity for mass exposure; as one luktoong singer laments in song: "A singer's popularity depends on the mercy of the musical program announcer."[83] Some luktoong stars have been financially linked with organized crime figures in order to support their flamboyant lifestyles, and a few developed reputations for prolific love lives. The top star of the 1960s, Surapon Sumbatcharon, was murdered by gangsters in 1967, reportedly at the behest of a discarded mistress.

Major luktoong performers develop a massive audience. When Pompuang Duangjan, the illiterate but innovative superstar exponent of a dance-oriented electronic version, died of a treatable blood disorder in 1992 at the age of 31, over two hundred thousand attended her funeral in a provincial town and the news dominated the media for days, pushing aside a major political crisis. The life of the "queen" of luktoong mirrored that of many rural young people seeking a better life in the cruel city in order to support their families back in the village, and this no doubt contributed to her massive following. After only two years of primary school she had worked as a cane cutter, beginning a singing career at the age of eight. Throughout her short life she was exploited and abused by lovers, husbands, managers, recording companies, and promoters. Her music often analyzed themes relevant to, and attitudes shared by, villagers. Some of her songs explored the gap between people from urban and rural backgrounds, as in "AM Girl"; the lyrics contrast the radio listening habits of a rural girl (who favors AM) and a sophisticated city boy (a fan of FM).

Some of Pompuang's songs dealt graphically with the harsh reality facing many female migrants:

So lousy poor, I just have to risk my luck
Dozing on the bus, this guy starts chatting me up
Says he'll get me a good job, now he's feeling me up . . .
For better or worse, I'm following my star
What will be, will be, I'm just risking my luck.[84]

"AM Girl"

"In the village we wear sarong,
Carry a basket on our shoulder out to the paddy field,
Speak just simple Thai words,
And listen to AM radio all the time
The radio set costs only 100 baht . . .
You are a city man, you will lure me in vain
We are not compatible. You listen to FM radio!
You think you can fool me because I'm a country bumpkin . . .
As a city guy, you are suitable for a city girl.
You only want my youth
You would drop me like a stone for a city girl."—hit sung by Pompuang Duangjan[85]

As in all Thai music, the genre could support national pride and established power, as in the song "Siam, the Land of Smiles":

Be proud you are a Thai
Uncolonized and generous
Siam is the Land of Smiles
We should be proud . . .
We Thais love our nation and religion
Adore the virtuous King.[86]

Yet luktoong seems to have developed a considerable element of social commentary and social criticism, addressing issues of village exploitation, poverty-induced rural-to-urban migration, and the traditions of village resistance to the center (indeed, it can be seen as a contemporary version of that tradition). One of the leading singers, Surachai Sumbatcharon (the son of Surapon Sumbatcharon), has described the social concerns of the genre in the following terms:

> *Luk tung* songs are usually made up from folk tunes or some old Thai melody. . . . Most of the lyrics . . . are about real life and real events that have happened, rather than about imaginary things or dreams. *Luk tung* is not a music for escapism. Most of the people who listen . . . live in the countryside; some of them have problems which correspond closely to the lyrics of the songs. For example, they leave their villages or their sweethearts and try to find work in the city because they are penniless. When they listen to *luk tung* they feel they are experiencing their own lives through our music. . . . Mostly our songs are about love, melancholy and grief, but they are not sentimental. They are too realistic for that. When there is a flood and the crops are destroyed, there is nothing

left. People starve and have to go to Bangkok to find work. Tens of thousands do every year. So our *luk tung* songs tell their story: about how people live and work in the countryside.[87]

One of his biggest hits, "Cry for Rain," deals with the effects of a drought then ravaging the northeast.

A content analysis of 730 luktoong songs popular between the late 1960s and mid-1980s found that 34 percent of the songs dealt with personal messages (especially the desire for love); 8 percent concerned traditional beliefs and practices (religion, folklore, the supernatural); and 37 percent explored disappointments in love (broken affairs, unrequited feelings). About 10 percent of the latter songs, however, blamed the broken heart on problems related to poverty, including migrating to join the army or become a prostitute. Indeed, songs about prostitutes accounted for an increasing proportion, reflecting perhaps the growing role of female singers and their concern with problems faced by women from rural backgrounds. The final category of social, economic, and political factors affecting the individual comprised 20 percent of songs. These included analyses of family affairs and daily life (e.g., husbands wasting family funds on dissolute living); economic survival (oil and rice prices, poverty-induced behavior such as crime or prostitution); politics and laws (bureaucratic hassles, lawbreaking, political developments, nationalism); natural calamities (floods, fires, rapes); and criticism (of acquaintances, deceptive or spendthrift women, local or national leaders). By and large, the sociopolitical points were made indirectly, through metaphor or satire; the lively rhythm and tone often masked the serious commentary. Many songs reflected rural beliefs such as the supernatural, closeness to nature, and disregard for material wealth.[88]

Ubonrat argues that luktoong has functioned to articulate class resentment against the elite by deliberately utilizing lower-class language, consciously opposing the elite's romantic view of the world (represented by lukkroong) with a more earthy sexuality, and criticizing or parodying official attitudes and policies as well as the socioeconomic class system. But, she notes, the composers and musicians must be cautious or face possible state retribution: "To avoid state censorship artists cautiously synthesize humor and satire in their lyrics. This strategy has not only produced some of the classic social commentaries but continues to set the tradition for everyday contestation."[89] Hence, luktoong reflects a peasant viewpoint while simultaneously assenting to the dominant national imagery; it is rarely openly defiant. In this sense it is both hegemonic and counterhegemonic.

The indirect approach to criticism was particularly necessary during the long periods of military dictatorship, but even during more tolerant administrations the state exercises some censorship over radio and television.

The most politically pointed songs are blacklisted but often still enjoy wide cassette circulation. An examination of the lyrics of a popular luktoong song conveys some of the flavor of the genre:

This year it's very cold and the rice has failed
The rice is dead and there is no rain
The sky is red like a fever
My love, you must be crying, and so am I
You starve for rice and the buffalo starves for grass
There is no money to spend.[90]

Songs like this lament the decline of the rural economy, the major factor in compelling many to migrate to Bangkok and other cities.

An example of how satire conveys social protest can be seen in a popular song, "Village Head Li," from the era of the dictatorship in the 1960s. The song parodies a village meeting through clever wordplay (for which the tonal Thai language offers many possibilities), in the process revealing the power relationships between villagers and hierarchical authority (the co-opted village leader) that discourages dissent. The song cryptically mocks authority while also criticizing an unpopular government agricultural scheme.

Sometimes the lyrics are more direct, though reflecting a distance as well as a pronounced cynicism about government and politics. For example, one song in the 1970s skewered unresponsive local politicians mainly interested in securing wealth and power:

The candidates' adverts tell all about their good deeds
They bring along movies to entertain us in the villages
They say they can solve all kinds of problems . . .
There will be lots of roads and canals
You won't have to raise buffaloes
Because we will provide you all with tractors
We are all so pleased at this news
But they have become MPs for many years now
We are still using buffaloes
And they have become very rich.[91]

The love songs that provide a prominent component of the genre also raise questions of social differentiation and the material poverty of the peasantry, in addition to frankly expressing sexual desire. Hence they too have made luktoong culturally and politically controversial while linking it to oppositional discourse. Ubonrat also believes that, while luktoong has continuously tried to challenge the institutions of sociopolitical power, the musicians must make pragmatic accommodations to political and commer-

"Village Head Li"

"In the year 1961, Village Head Li called a meeting
The villagers all assembled at Village Head Li's house
Now Village Head Li will tell you what he was told
The state ordered, they ordered that peasants
Must raise ducks and sukorn [a polite term for pig, the peasant colloquial mu being considered a vulgarity]
Ta Si the drunkard asked
'What is a sukorn?'
Village Head Li stood up right away and said,
'Sukorn is nothing but a ma noi' [a vulgar colloquial for a dog, indicating he also did not understand the government's high Thai language]."—song popular in the 1960s[92]

cial reality. Hence the political thrust attacks not the military (many songs in fact extol military heroes or machismo) but rather vulnerable, corrupt politicians or uncaring, oppressive bureaucrats and their regulations.[93] The songs do not seem to have openly challenged established authority or placed the blame for rural problems directly on an uncaring elite or an inequitable socioeconomic system. Rather the protest has been more indirect—and possibly not even apparent to many urban Thais. The affirmation of establishment views coexists with the ample possibilities for contestation of the meaning by audiences.

Furthermore, despite its more authentic Thai identity, rustic flavor and often sparse instrumentation, luktoong could probably not serve as a model for musicians interested in more overt protest music owing to its frequently lavish, almost circuslike stage productions (often involving elaborately clothed dancing girls), its progressive commercialization (and perhaps increasing co-optation), and the conspicuous consumption of its wealthy superstars. Moreover, the déclassé image of the music compromises its appeal for the urban middle classes, even sympathetic students, in much the same way perhaps that country-and-western music in the United States, closely identified with a conservative, rural, white southern but also essentially déclassé audience, did not and probably cannot become a model for student protesters or other progressives despite its folkish, antielite base. Perhaps luktoong essentially performs a mediating function between urban and rural cultures.[94]

Both the highly westernized styles (lukkroong, string) and luktoong have remained quite popular into the 1990s while modifying their sounds to incorporate new trends from abroad. Significantly, radio and television are generally under the control of various government departments or the military, giving them a strong right-wing character. In this context the cassette industry became increasingly important and more open to diverse

Although traditional music has lost considerable popularity, some young people continue to learn the forms. This is a dance class near Chiengmai. 1966 photo by author.

perspectives. Ethnomusicologist Deborah Wong describes the immense vitality and impact of this highly commercialized industry as follows:

> The cassette industry in Thailand is a high-powered, fast-moving, risky business which, if anything, becomes more competitive every day. Cassettes began to dominate the recording industry around 1975, and at this point [1989] they have literally flooded the country. Cassettes are everywhere. They have made music accessible to Thais in a totally new way, and vividly reflect changing musical and social values. . . . Cassettes revitalized the Thai music industry in a remarkably short time, taking it over and enlarging it. Part of the reason for the rapid spread is that Thailand has no national apparatus for the administration of music media as do some countries.[95]

The recording industry is centered in Bangkok, although companies in both Chiengmai in the north and Ubon in the northeast have produced cassettes of local music for regional sales. By 1985 Bangkok had also become the Southeast Asian center for cheap pirated cassettes of Western popular music. By the late 1980s an estimated 95 percent of all non-Thai tapes sold in Bangkok were pirated.[96]

Caravan and the Florescence of "Songs of Life"

The initial revitalization of the recording industry seems to have corresponded to the major political liberalization between 1973 and 1976. With censorship lifted and a free intellectual atmosphere, this period saw a flowering of overt politically oriented music. Rock groups with a Western folk influence emerged in the universities to sing about rural problems and social injustice; many of their members came originally from remote, poverty-stricken villages but had migrated to Bangkok for higher education. These groups called their music "Songs for Life" *(phleng phuachiwit)*. They incorporated into their compositions words and phrases from the dialect of the economically depressed northeast, an area where a communist-led insurgency had long capitalized on the inequitable socioeconomic conditions and resentment of the comparative wealth of the capital, Bangkok. But this was more to establish the voice of the peasant, because the songs as a whole remained intelligible to the urban audience.[97]

In their styles and the sociopolitical context for the music, the Songs for Life groups demonstrated many parallels to the New Song musicians of Chile and the politicized folksingers of the United States during the 1960s. However, the clear class analysis in their songs resembled the Chileans but differed substantially from the ideology of all but the most militant U.S. protest singers. No doubt the still-evolving luktoong tradition exercised some influence on the Songs for Life, but the new music was much more politically militant and intellectual in approach. The social and political protest expressed by these groups, one specialist argues, "served as a marker of group identity among progressive students, and symbolically represented

The Formation of Caravan

Surachai Jantimaton and Virasak Suntornsii, the founders of Caravan, were both students who helped mobilize the antidictatorship student movement at Ramkamhaeng University. After the 1973 student uprising hundreds of students were sent by progressive organizations to remote rural districts to help prepare the villagers for the forthcoming democratic elections. Surachai and Virasak, both reared in the northeast, used their guitars to enliven many of the public gatherings. The gap between students and peasants was wide; both groups frequently felt reticent and awkward as they huddled around evening campfires. Often students would begin to sing, one song after another, to break the ice. After awhile the assembled peasants might acknowledge acceptance of the students and confirm that the songs discussed the problems and lives of villagers. Surachai and Virasak were leading activists in this work. Both at first reflected the influence of Bangkok's westernized environment. Surachai Jantimaton, a native of Surin Province, was the son of a schoolteacher and had been a student at Silapakorn University. Virasak Suntornsii, born in Nakorn Rachasima Province, was a law student before devoting himself to political and cultural work. Both were nonprofessionals who picked up ideas from musical films and juke boxes as well as nightclub performers catering to the thousands of American GIs and civilians involved with the wars in Vietnam, Laos, and Cambodia. Both became particularly attracted to the antiwar and satirical songs of American folksingers Bob Dylan, Pete Seeger, Joan Baez, and Arlo Guthrie. Later, while performing in the northeast, they added three new Isan-bred members. Two were from vocational colleges: Tonggraan Taanaa, a founder of the United Artists of Thailand and the Cultural United Front, and Pongtep Kradonchamnana; both hailed from Nakorn Rachasima Province. The other new member, Mongkol Utok, was a native of Roi-et Province in the northeast and a recent graduate of the University of Technical Arts.[98]

the ethos of the student movement."[99] For one student supporter in 1975, "these songs are about life as it really is. It's not about life as politicians promise it will be, or as ordinary people wish it could be."[100]

Caravan, the most important of these groups, coalesced around the unrest leading to the reestablishment of a liberal democracy. Its members were all from rural backgrounds but were university students when the group began to tour in rural areas. Later their popularity would reach into—perhaps even became concentrated among—the urban university communities. Closely identified with the student movement, they became musical heroes to radical students and others interested in fundamental change. Caravan's music, relying heavily on acoustic guitars, sounds much like Bob Dylan or Peter, Paul, and Mary singing in Thai—but embellished by the use of Thai folk instruments (especially the bamboo flute) and occasionally melodies. Indeed, Caravan members acknowledge a strong influence from anti-Vietnam War U.S. folksingers like Joan Baez and Pete Seeger.

Many of their songs have been overtly political in content, emphasizing the conditions of the peasantry, the struggle for a more equitable society, the counterproductive presence of U.S. military bases, and the courage to work for change. Some songs were written by group members while others were composed by other student activists or adapted from poems by Jit Poumisak. Given the democratic situation in the mid-1970s, there was seemingly little need to mask their messages, but it must be kept in mind that military-backed right-wing groups and unsympathetic bureaucrats often harassed and sometimes assassinated dissidents. But radio and television ignored Songs for Life except briefly in early 1976; those involved in that program were investigated.[101]

Their music was and remains too controversial for most Thai elites, even liberal ones. For example, "Yellow Bird," perhaps their best-known song, honors those heroes who sacrificed their lives to overthrow the military dictatorship in 1973; it was written by journalist Vinai Ukrit (whose satirical, anti-American book *Caravan* inspired the group's name) after he walked the streets surveying the carnage of October:

Spreading your wings, fleeing the city
Yellow bird, you are leaving us now
You are flying to freedom
Now that your life has been ended . . .
What color is the world you fought for
Do you remember
The October 14 bloodshed
When your brothers and sisters
Were crushed in a hailstorm
Of bullets and teargas?

Do you remember? Brutally run down
Teargassed and shot
As they raised empty hands
Demanding freedom?
Let us pause
To honor their souls
Let us give courage
To those who push on
In the struggle.[102]

"Man and Buffalo" criticizes the exploitation of peasants by capitalists while extolling peasant values. The plight of the peasantry is a subject that Somkit Singson, the coauthor of "Man and Buffalo," knows well; he had grown up in the rural north and organized farmers' cooperatives after the overthrow of the dictatorship (even escaping an assassination attempt by right-wing forces). Another song memorializes Jit Poumisak, a leftist intellectual much respected by radical students, who had promoted the creation of a "people's art"; his writings, especially his 1957 book *The Art for Life, the Art for the People*, indeed had helped generate the concept of Songs for Life in 1972. He was a fierce critic of the Hollywood films popular in Thailand, which he viewed as products of monopoly capitalism and aimed at manipulating local minds to support U.S. imperialism. Jailed for many years, Jit was killed while fighting for the communist guerrillas in 1966.[103]

Caravan recordings and songbooks conveying these messages reached a wide and receptive audience. Other Songs for Life groups such as

"Man and Buffalo"

"Man working with buffalo
Is rooted deep in our history.
They've worked together for ages.
But it works out alright.
Come, let's go, now, let's go!
Carry our plows and guns to the fields!
Poverty and weariness endured too long!
Bitter tears held back too long!
Hardships and troubles so heavy
But whatever the burden, we will not fear . . .
The rich eat our labor
Set one against the other
As we peasants sink deeper into debt . . .
We must destroy this system!"—Caravan[104]

Kammachon (Workers), Komchai (Torchlight), and Kurochon (People Who Teach) helped spur the revolt against the saccharine romantic themes of most Thai folk and pop music. Their music expressed the political protest and progressive ethos of the student movement. For example, Kammachon emphasized the divisions between producers and merchants:

Look at the rice in the fields
And with sadness
See the interest pile up
It's the capitalist who takes it
Weak and weary laborers
Toil for meager income . . .
With our body and soul
Let's create
Only the power of labor
Can build a beautiful world
Workers, farmers, join hands
To build a new world.[105]

Their call for an alliance of workers and farmers coincided with the various community and union organizing pursued by student militants. In seeking to explain the phenomenal success of Caravan in particular, American ethnomusicologist Pamela Myers-Moro believes that the structural features, sounds, and symbolism of their songs were crucial in conveying meaning to the audience: "Caravan's music was a model of the experience of Thai progressive students."[106]

Songs for Life were only one prong of a cultural struggle waged between left and right in the democratic years, with music becoming a key arena of political debate. Right-wing forces retaliated against the Songs for Life through the use of nationalistic and patriotic songs *(phleng plukchai)* that had been utilized since the 1930s in support of governmental and elite policies. These hegemonic songs, many of them written by military officers or members of the royal family, had long occupied an important niche on radio and in historical dramas. In 1975 new laws made radio and television even more important avenues for combating "subversive" ideas, including a commission to examine the content of programs.

The lyrics of the nationalistic songs extol the nation and king. For example, "King Naresuan's Knights" proclaims:

Without the nation, the land, the king
We cannot survive
No matter, whether dead or alive
We will protect with our utmost.

Another popular song was "Burden on the Land," which calls on the nation to root out traitors:

Those who are called Thai.
Who look like Thai
Who live on the land under the holy benevolence of His majesty
But whose minds contemplate its destruction . . .
They are Burden on the Land
Those rabble-rousers
Who cause disunity among the people
Agitating the masses, creating chaos . . .
Those who sell their soul, betray their country
Taking every chance to help the enemy . . .
Those who have dangerous thoughts
Who do not want Thai-ness . . .
They are Burden on the land.[107]

Both Songs for Life and the nationalistic songs represented different discourses on the Thai nation. Songs for Life emphasized the underside of corruption, inequality, suffering, and Western imperialism, and advocated common struggle to rectify the wrongs; it looked to the future. The rightist music glorified and romanticized the nation and its history, portraying a prosperous land of contented people who owed much to the sacrifices of their ancestors; it was past-oriented. The symbolism and rhetoric of the two opposing factions appealed to different constituencies and competed for influence among those in the middle.[108]

In 1976, after increasing social unrest, ineffective government, and a widening gap between the political left and right, the Thai military launched a coup, reimposing harsh authoritarian rule. Parliament was suspended and political parties outlawed. As troops and right-wing thugs massacred students at Bangkok's Thammasat University, cheered on by the military's radio station as it played nationalistic songs, the clandestine communist station suspended regular programming to play Caravan's "Yellow Bird" throughout the day. Along with thousands of progressive students, many Songs for Life musicians, including all the members of Caravan, fled to the northeast and joined the communist-led guerrillas in the jungles. As happened in Chile under the Pinochet junta, media distribution or even singing of Songs for Life was officially prohibited, with severe punishment meted out to violators.

Caravan now transformed their musical message into one of violent resistance to an oppressive, illegitimate government. Some participated in the armed struggle while others worked in propaganda. However, life underground proved difficult, with the insurgency burdened by factional

Caravan as Guerrillas

Caravan was performing in the northeast, at the university in Khon Kaen, when they heard the news of the October 6 bloodshed at Thammasat. Because they were closely identified with the student movement and also musical heroes to the left, they were encouraged by supporters to "go underground" for their safety. To the rigid new right-wing government, the Caravan members, along with thousands of other young intellectuals and dissenters, were no different than communist insurgents and sympathizers. And although they never became hardcore communists, they joined the Communist Party of Thailand, following the rules and trying hard to believe that its promises for a better future might materialize. Mongkol spent three years in China but became quite bored, editing programs and playing music for the underground radio station. He also taught music and art to children. Band leader Surachai spent most of his time at the front lines in the north and northeast. Disillusioned with the communist cause, three group members resurfaced in 1981. Surachai left the jungle in 1982. Because of government amnesty, none of them was prosecuted.[109]

disputes, reliance on foreign support, meager rations, and an inability to spark a mass uprising; many students and musicians became disillusioned. None of the Caravan members had been members of the Communist Party before joining the guerrillas and they found the rigid discipline stifling. Several who sojourned in China were unimpressed with the socialist society they encountered. By 1981 many of the musicians began taking advantage of government amnesty offers and a less repressive political atmosphere to resurface.

Caravan reformed in Bangkok in 1983 and condemned armed struggle as unrealistic and futile. But they have continued to use their music to promote democracy and social change; as one member put it: "We know we can't make disco-type music and we don't want to play in nightclubs. We simply want our songs to reflect the reality of suffering and the struggle of various groups of people for a decent life. . . . All we want is a better life for the poor and the unfortunate—that's our ultimate goal."[110] They have made several successful international tours and retain a hard core of admirers both at home and abroad. Furthermore, some of their post-amnesty albums (such as *Blacksmith* in 1983 and *Live at the Fiftieth Anniversary of Thammasat University* in 1984) gained them considerable attention. Their most political album, *U.S. J. Pan* in 1987, maintained their stance against both American and Japanese imperialism; it features a cover illustration of a water buffalo clad in stars and stripes. Their music also has taken on a more international tone, incorporating rhythms and instruments from both Western (folk and rock) and Asian nations. In 1990 they led a Woodstock-style benefit concert in Cambodia to promote peace and reconciliation in that turbulent, wartorn country.[111]

Contemporary Thai Politics and Popular Music

During the 1980s, as the various insurgencies waned, Thailand gradually returned to a more tolerant quasi-democratic system. By the late 1980s student activism reappeared, with demonstrations seeking social justice attracting sympathetic musicians. But the scale, popularity, and degree of anger of student militancy was modest compared to 1973.[112] Undoubtedly the depoliticization had much to do with a booming economy (which grew by nearly 10 per cent per year in the 1980s); between 1986 and 1990 the per capita GDP doubled. Such dramatic economic growth strengthened nonbureaucratic forces, among them business and the media. These developments, including a maturing urban economy, created a rapidly expanding white-collar salariat of professionals, executives, administrators, technicians, and managers, many of whom promoted a civil society based on democratic principles. Indeed, the growth of a substantial, development-oriented middle class may have been the most important factor in diminishing bureaucratic power and discouraging military interventions. Many adopted individualistic attitudes and supported a more open society. While some preferred the stability of a strong state, others supported the growing number of nongovernmental organizations working for human rights, social change, and personal freedom. The growing Bangkok middle class even spawned "yuppies" who increasingly developed their own urban social institutions such as pubs. An economy characterized largely by cautious pragmatism and private enterprise, and open to both world markets and foreign investment, had grown so rapidly that by the early 1990s some optimistic observers were forecasting Thailand as the next "Little Tiger."[113]

Thailand's increasing role in the global economy as well as the burgeoning domestic communications and transportation infrastructure sparked a vigorous debate among intellectuals (including many former left-wing activists from the 1970s) as to the consequences of globalization and cosmopolitanism for Thai society. Those favoring global influences believed they would help liberalize Thailand and perhaps even empower local cultural producers by providing modern technologies. Some celebrated free markets, material progress, and multinational capital, others the collaboration with external environmental, human rights, and social reform organizations. Pessimists pointed to the alarming possibilities that Thailand's culture and environment would be standardized to international norms and overwhelmed by outside forces, pointing to, for example, the commercialization of sex. Hence both corporate elites and grassroots activists were forced to confront the dialectic between the local and the global.[114]

Nonetheless, the government has been unable to substantially resolve many of the long-standing socioeconomic and communal problems. There are clear downsides to both economic growth (the consequences of industrialization and the spread of capitalism) and democratization (the ascendancy of money politics). Furthermore, many, including devout Buddhists, became alarmed by the corruption, greed, environmental destruction, and pollution these developments had generated. Urban and rural development planning has proven insufficient, and industrial development—largely concentrated in Bangkok—encourages continued rural flight. Activist leaders of farmers' organizations formed to protest low commodity prices and increasing debts found their lives in danger. Tourism, the single biggest source of foreign exchange, is viewed by many as undermining Thai cultural values and heavily exploiting the thousands of women and girls who work as prostitutes and hostesses. Drug and alcohol abuse has been a growing trend among youth.

Many observers also criticize what they see as rampant materialism, which is enhanced by the media, especially television. Hence, according to Thai social worker and AIDS counselor Ben Sawadiwat:

> Children growing up in modern Thailand are confused about values. . . . The traditional lessons in social behavior they receive at home, at school or at the Buddhist temple conflict with the images they absorb from television—not necessarily Western programs but local dramas, too. "Television is causing a lot of the confusion because the image it imparts is of the rich urban lifestyle of a minority. . . . This creates very strong materialist values and the illusion that it is easy to succeed." Teachers and monks work against this, but youngsters take their cues from TV.[115]

Some of these tensions generated turbulence following another military coup in 1991; military leaders claimed (with some justification) that the civilian politicians were excessively corrupt. But soon an ascetic Buddhist (and former general), who had gained a reputation as an incorruptible and accessible Bangkok governor, led a protest movement challenging a new constitution that facilitated continued military control of the elected government, including the appointment of the top general as an unelected prime minister. In May 1992 as many as 150,000 protestors demonstrated peacefully in Bangkok in a move reminiscent of 1973, with many shops and businesses closing in sympathy. The state-controlled media ignored the activities, in contrast to some privately owned newspapers, demonstrating to many Thais the importance of a free press. Although the protesters included some students and labor unionists, the largest number derived from the growing middle classes, leading critics to refer to a "yuppie mob." Many of the protestors were former student activists from the 1970s or had grown up in those years. There were also many blue-collar workers. Several Songs for Life musicians also campaigned for prodemocracy forces.

After several days of scuffling between police and protesters, soldiers opened fire indiscriminately; over the next several days at least 48 were killed (unofficial estimates run as high as 750) and many injured (a full year later, some 164 were still missing and presumed among the dead). Protest leaders and three thousand of their followers were arrested. The king then summoned both the military and protest leaders and worked out a compromise; the discredited prime minister resigned, protestors were released, soldiers were given amnesty, and a coalition government was formed that held new elections.[116] Some believe the military ineptness and brutal overreaction in 1992 has reduced the prospects for coups in the near future, with popular acceptance of coups much diminished and many in the military disillusioned by the recent military interventions.[117]

The September 1992 elections following the "Black May" violence proved a significant departure from the past because the parties now presented clear choices to the electorate. The political parties were mainly divided into alliances based on their views of the military role in politics and their commitment or aversion to moderate democratizing reform. Four loosely linked antimilitary parties known collectively as the "angels" won the most seats in the competition against a coalition of promilitary parties popularly called the "devils"; the "devils" had backed the military crackdown. The new government lifted censorship and generally fostered a more open political and cultural environment (including the opening of the first two private television stations). It also pledged a new emphasis on rural development, a decentralization of political power away from Bangkok, and the strengthening of constitutional democracy.

The new prime minister—Chuan Leekpai, a southerner of humble background—was respected as principled and incorruptible, but he faced severe problems in keeping his fractious coalition together and confronting the machinations of opposition parties. The reformist government, comprised of various (and often feuding) "angel" politicians, could not maintain their popularity or successfully address the burgeoning problems, not only in the rural sector but among the increasingly militant urban working class and the growing group of thrill-seeking youthful dropouts from conventional socioeconomic life. Indeed, by the 1995 elections the "angel" coalition had collapsed and a new antireform, right-wing-led alliance, dominated by old-style politicians from the provinces, swept into power. Although the generally progressive and democratic "angel" parties still enjoyed widespread support in Bangkok, especially among the intelligentsia, the more authoritarian traditional politicians successfully used their money-lubricated patronage to attract many rural voters.[118]

By late 1996, the prime minister had resigned, plagued by charges of corruption and incompetence, and his coalition government collapsed in power struggles. As new elections were called, some disillusioned critics called for reforms in the electoral system that might discourage money politics and somehow bridge the chasm between voters in Bangkok and the provinces. The elections changed little, bringing to power a reconfigured coalition of provincial-based parties mostly disinterested in serious reform that might challenge the pervasive corruption. But the coalition was fragile and still had little support in Bangkok among the middle class.[119]

Clearly, change was in the works. In 1991 many former student activists from the 1970s announced the formation of a political party to fight for change and against corruption and money politics; eventually they hoped to contest elections. In 1996 farmers, supported by student groups and guitar-strumming musicians, were protesting living conditions, perhaps heralding a new round of social activism. In October 1996, many former activists from the 1970s liberalization era held commerative events to celebrate their past and lament the decline of a popular student movement. They hoped to rekindle the nation's social conscience and reestablish antielitist ideas. Meanwhile, various ethnic and regional groups became more assertive in seeking room for their own cultures in the broader national society. But the prospects for increasing democratization remain debatable. Some observers believe that Thais have generally been better at talking about democracy than practicing it; one party leader explains that "democracy has never been a failure. . . . It is the people who have failed democracy."[120] The growing political gap between the city and countryside as well as leaders without much vision and the lack of cohesion within political parties all pose a challenge to reformers. Yet Thais have possessed a talent for compromise as well as moderation (the Buddhist "middle path") and a belief in the worth of the individual that could form the basis for a democratic spirit.

The popular music scene also changed in the 1980s, with the commercial industry developing at an unprecedented rate. Inexpensive cassette players became more widely available and string rock music gained an increasing audience. Caravan has had only modest success in recapturing their earlier Thai following. This is partly a result of competition from slicker, more commercial, somewhat more subtle protest music produced by a few popular groups, especially Carabao, whose fusion music includes folk elements but shares a stronger rock influence than Caravan's. To reach for an American parallel, if Caravan's highly oppositional and folksy sound can be compared to Peter, Paul, and Mary, Carabao's folk rock and less overt political posture might be considered the Thai equivalent to Crosby, Stills, Nash, and Young or the electrified Bob Dylan. Ubonrat believes that Carabao fits into the category of phleng phuachiwit (Songs for Life) but that this has been transformed into progressive pop.[121]

Carabao clearly linked themselves to Caravan with their choice of name: *Carabao*, the Tagalog (Filipino) term for water buffalo, suggests Caravan's famous song, "Man and Water Buffalo." Formed by a former associate of Caravan, Carabao caused the biggest sensation in the history of modern Thai music with songs emphasizing sociopolitical themes. Their "New Wave" of Songs for Life first emerged in 1981, and they had become the most popular Thai group by the mid-1980s, with appeal to a wide range of youth.

Carabao sang about the plight of Indochinese refugees, corruption, rural indebtedness, drugs, the exploitation of women, the plight of prostitutes, and unresponsive government; banning of a song from the airwaves tended to enhance sales substantially. In 1985 they spurred a public debate about prostitution with their evocation of a girl's tragic life:

Tears streaming softly down two cheeks . . .
Society is in ruins . . .
Poverty—who can stand it?
Her father is very old. Her mother is ill
Her sisters and brothers must go on living
She is the scorn of all others.[122]

In 1988 Carabao became embroiled in a long-simmering conflict between the Thai government and the Chicago Art Institute over an ancient lintel (Hindu deity) from the early Cambodian civilization, stolen from a northeastern Thai temple in the 1960s, which eventually found its way to Chicago. In 1972 the Thai government discovered its whereabouts and began demanding its return. Touring in the United States, Carabao became interested in the controversy and released a song castigating the United States for retaining a valuable artifact many Thais believed was stolen by American soldiers based in Thailand during the Vietnam War:

A block of stone—a lintel—is the hope of the Thais for America
We would like to get it back—it's ours—they took it

The Appeal of Carabao

"Americans are often startled by how familiar Carabao looks and sounds. . . . Carabao's style, image, and rhetoric . . . is strongly informed by American folk and rock singers of the 1970s. Theirs is the classic American look of social protest: long hair, army fatigues, jeans—defiantly casual clothes, especially ironic in Thailand, where dressing neatly is equated with morality. Carabao's sound is also disturbingly familiar; it's basically rock, with a heavy electric guitar sound that is often sardonic if not openly sarcastic. Indeed, Carabao's sarcasm is rarely subtle, but it is a joy to its young listeners. The band often uses its instrumental and vocal sound to wink at its audience, to laugh in the face of authority—and for an American listener, it's a bit unsettling to hear the social history of our own music, our own political turmoil, sung back at us through the mouths of the Other."—Deborah Wong[123]

They took it—it belongs to the Thai people—why did they do it?
The helicopters came to fight in Vietnam
Established bases on Thai land, took everything . . .
Thailand is a nation . . .
The hearts of every generation are bound together
and our national lineage is passed on
The Narai lintel is in Chicago . . .
Take Michael Jackson—give us back Narai! . . .
The Statue of Liberty stands there, fast asleep, with no goals
But the Narai lintel—you [Americans] despise/put down the Thais.

The song became an immediate smash hit in Thailand, with heavy airplay, and regenerated the campaign for the lintel's return; indeed, the whole issue became part of popular culture, with T-shirts and penny notebook covers. Anti-Americanism became more fashionable. The controversy may have been part of a Thai willingness to finally embrace the legacy of the ancient Angkor empire of the rival Khmers, which once ruled much of what is now Thailand, hence redefining national culture and identity. Because of the growing furor, the Art Institute finally agreed to return the lintel, which was received with great fanfare.[124]

Carabao's best-known song and giant hit, "Made in Thailand," criticizes the obsession of Thais with foreign goods specifically, but more generally critiques the rapid changes generated by the growth of the export trade and globalizing tendencies.

Carabao reached a much wider audience than Caravan through their professionalism, pragmatism, considerably diluted protest style, and more attention to romantic songs. Some critics felt they were becoming too established and predictable, perhaps even a self-perpetuating industry. They enjoyed a particular following among rural migrants to Bangkok but also appealed to many in the middle class.[125] In the early 1990s, however, Carabao disbanded. Their leader, Yuenyong "Ad" Opakil, continues on as a popular singer specializing in controversial material with songs about deforestation, the construction of dams that despoil the environment, and the negative side effects of industrialization, as in his Isan-dialect song "No Plomplam" ("No Problem") about rural decline:

We are troubled, we are poor, we must endure
Living in poverty, we would not moan . . .
Lucky we are Thais . . .
We tell our visitors we have no problems . . .
Industry in the NIC [Newly Industrializing Country] era means papaya salad in a can

Sugar palm ale in packages with pasteurized label . . .
Why do I live? Early morn to the factory I go.[126]

Opakil considered entering politics in 1990, announcing he might run for Parliament as a backer of former general Chaovalit Yongchaiyut's left-leaning New Aspiration Party (NAP), a member of the "angel" coalition that resisted military domination. While he changed his mind about a political career, his environmental activism brought him into close alliance with various progressive politicians and groups (including Chaovalit and the NAP). Carabao and Caravan remained the most openly political of the musicians during the 1980s. In the 1990s the folk-rock group Zuzu filled the vacuum left by Carabao, often using regional instruments and music. Socially conscious singer-songwriters influenced by Caravan like Pongsit Kamphee also gained an audience. Some fans have claimed to find double entendres of social criticism in the music of "New Wave" rock star Asanee Chotikul, although he denies it. Nonetheless some of his songs deal with issues like corruption, urban exploitation, and prostitution. Pop singer Tik Shiro (Thailand's version of Michael Jackson) includes an element of protest in some songs. Most other Thai pop stars such as "teeny bopper" heartthrob Nakorn Vejsupaporn and Jae (Dhanupol Keokarn) continue to concen-trate on the tried and true formulas that have been commercially successful for years.[127]

"Made in Thailand"

"Made in Thailand—our land.
We have good things in abundance from Sukhothai to Lop Buri . . .
Made in Thailand
We do it our own way
Even our singing and dancing
Are full of excellence admired by westerners
But unappreciated by Thais
Afraid that they are not up to the latest trends
Made in Thailand
We make trousers and jeans
And send them away by plane
Thais get the credit
But westerners reap the profits . . .
Made in Thailand.
As long as tags say Made in Japan things will sell.
Guaranteed to be foreign made and from the latest fashion magazines.
They don't cheat us
We only fool ourselves."—Carabao's best-known song[128]

Conclusions

Political music has continued to flourish openly in Thailand as long as political conditions permit, but it is hard to judge what influence it ultimately enjoyed beyond the small group of urban student progressives and perhaps some rural activists. Certainly it was not powerful enough to help prevent the triumph of authoritarian forces in 1976. While most authoritarian regimes have evidently attempted to repress any overt protest music, even they permitted a limited and rather oblique social criticism in luktoong, perhaps to avert more direct challenge that might facilitate contestation. More open regimes may have seen even Songs for Life as a necessary safety valve to satisfy frustrated urban youth. It would seem, as in Malaysia, that Thai governments have usually permitted more latitude in popular music than in some other venues, as long as it stays within certain parameters.

On the other hand, it is hard to deny the place of Carabao in the sociopolitical dialogue of the 1980s or of Songs for Life in the heady experiences of the mid-1970s. And the contradictory but clearly important luktoong songs obviously reflect in many respects the resentments as well as the aspirations of rural peoples, constituting a long-term commentary on the nature of Thai society. While pop music could be diversionary, it could also be educational and oppositional. Perhaps the message of some Songs for Life will endure in the consciousness of many Thais, such as Caravan's "Yellow Bird" elegy for the martyrs of 1973:

Do you remember the stain of blood and nightmares? . . .
Now let us pause and be silent
To honor those heroes
As a reminder to those who continue to fight.[129]

5

Malaysia and Singapore: Pluralism and Popular Music

Hey we equatorial people . . . [of] the Malay archipelago
United, we are strong
Divided, we are fallen
That is the practice of our life . . .
Many people go to the fun fair
Malay, Chinese, Indian, Eurasian
United in spirit, working together . . .
My friend, destroy all conflict
Let us live in harmony
Let us eat Chinese melon
The taste so sweet, like sugar . . .
We definitely cannot deny
Malaysia is advanced and prosperous.

"Khatul Istiwa" ("Equator") by the Blues Gang, 1983[1]

Highly politicized or politically engaged music certainly did not emerge in all Southeast Asian societies. Malaysia and Singapore offer some interesting contrasts to the other case studies both in the nature of the popular culture and in the more clearly ethnic-based socioeconomic framework. Hence national unity and identity—as well as communal relationships—have been overriding concerns. Hegemonic or diversionary influences are strong. The following analysis explores how popular music has nonetheless addressed (sometimes obliquely) many aspects of sociopolitical change, even though the general framework of Malaysian and Singaporean society discourages militant expression, at least in the mass-mediated music. Some musicians—most notably postwar film star P. Ramlee and 1980s rock groups like Kembara—have been able to explore the fringes of tolerated debate and integrate observations on socioeconomic problems, prevailing lifestyles, and national identity but can seldom overtly challenge

Basic Data[2]

Population (1994): 20,000,000 (Malaysia); 3,000,000 (Singapore)

Urban Population: 45 percent (Malaysia); 95 percent (Singapore)

Capitals: Kuala Lumpur (metro population: ca. 1,500,000); Singapore (city proper: ca. 2,000,000)

Life Expectancy: Malaysia 71 (69 years for men, 73 years for women); Singapore 74 (72 years for men, 77 years for women)

Adult Literacy: 80 percent (Malaysia); 87 percent (Singapore)

Religions: Malaysia: Islam (53 percent), Buddhism (19 percent), Hinduism (9 percent), Other (9 percent); Singapore: "Chinese" religions (42 percent), Islam (16 percent), Christianity (19 percent)

Economy: Per capita GNP: $2,130 (Malaysia); $10,450 (Singapore)

Radio Ownership: 445,000 (Malaysia), 128,000 (Singapore); 4 government radio networks in 4 languages (Malaysia); 1 government radio network broadcasting in 4 languages (Singapore)

Radio Receivers Produced (incl. radio–cassette tape players): 37,019,000 (Malaysia, 1991); 19,618,000 (Singapore, 1991)

Television Ownership: 1,714,000 (Malaysia), 575,000 (Singapore); 2 government and 1 private television channel (Malaysia); 3 government-controlled television channels in 4 languages (Singapore)

People Per Television Set: 6.7 (Malaysia), 2.6 (Singapore)

Television Receivers Produced: 4,838,000 (Malaysia, 1991); 3,040,000 (Singapore, 1991)

Sound Recorders Produced (incl. cassette tape recorders): 14,000,000 (Singapore, 1989)

Media: Malaysia: 19 daily newspapers, most government owned or controlled (8 Chinese, 5 English, 4 Malay, 2 Tamil); Singapore: 6 newspapers, all government influenced (2 English, 2 Chinese, 2 Malay)

Major Recording Companies in Malaysia (1995): BMG (3 labels incl. Arista, RCA; distributes 5 labels incl. Geffen, MCA); EMI (distributes 12 labels incl. Capitol, EMI, Virgin); Hup Hup (4 local labels incl. Lark Fong, Life); Pony Canyon; Rock (5 labels); Sony (9 labels incl. CBS, Columbia, Def Jam, Epic); Warner (8 labels incl. Atlantic, Elektra; distributes 2 labels)

Major Recording Companies in Singapore (1995): Kwang Sia; Naxos (distributes 9 labels); Pony Canyon (distributes 9 labels); Rock (4 labels; distributes 3 labels); Sony (distributes 3 labels incl. Columbia, Epic); Unisong (distributes 9 labels)

Recordings Sold in Singapore (1988): LPs 200,000; tapes 4,900,000; CDs 800,000

Music Publishers (1995): Malaysia: BMG, Pustaka, Rock, Sony; Singapore: BMG, EMI, Life, Peermusic, Rock, Sony, Valentine authority and policies. In the 1990s heavy metal music joined the dialogue, offering a strongly countercultural message on the fringes of national society.

The Roots of Politics and Music

Malaysia politically links the Southeast Asian mainland with the archipelago, and is characterized by geographical division.[3] The Strait of Malacca, which bisects this realm, has long served as an artery through which peoples, cultures, and trade passed or took root in the area. Influences from China, India, the Middle East, and later Europe followed the maritime trade. While Malaya, Sarawak, Sabah, and Singapore share many historical patterns, they also experienced many unique developments as well, creating a complex historical narrative. The ethnosocial framework that developed is multivaried. The strategic position and natural resources of the region have attracted sailors, traders, settlers, and conquerors from various parts of Asia for several thousand years. Most activity centered on the Strait of Malacca, through which ships carrying goods between China and the countries around the Indian Ocean had to pass. Prosperous entrepôt states linked to this flourishing international and regional commerce developed at various times along either side of the Strait. In the fifteenth century, Melaka (Malacca) became the major trade entrepôt of Southeast Asia and a linchpin in the great maturing maritime trading network of the Indian Ocean, the dominant trading zone of the premodern world. During its brief "golden age," the important economic and political influence of Melaka also facilitated the spread of both the Malay language, as the chief trading lingua franca, and Islam, which gradually became the dominant religion of the coastal zone.

In the sixteenth century, Europeans began arriving in the region with political and economic effects that would ultimately be profound. The Portuguese were the pioneers; they defeated and occupied Melaka, which rapidly declined. The centuries after the fall of Melaka saw the development of various Malay sultanates and a pattern of fluctuating power in the region as competing states struggled for ascendancy. In the late eighteenth century, the British began playing a regional role in pursuit of both strategic and commercial objectives. In 1819 they acquired Singapore Island, which became the center for both British and immigrant Chinese commercial enterprise. Chinese began immigrating in substantial numbers, settling in the ports as merchants or in the interior as miners. Singapore rapidly grew into a leading trade entrepôt, with a predominantly Chinese population. Throughout the area the Chinese and Malays increasingly became leading elements in an inadequately integrated sociopolitical structure, a framework that would produce chronic communal friction.

In the 1870s, as demand for Malayan resources increased in the industrializing West, the British began intervening in the turbulent politics of the Malay states, establishing indirect control. By 1914 the process of gradual incorporation had been completed. Britain had now achieved formal or informal colonial control over nine sultanates, but pledged not to interfere in matters of religion, customs, and the symbolic political role of the sultans. British Malaya included a variety of states divided by the level of British control and economic development. Singapore and the coastal trading cities of Penang and Melaka were administered separately from the Malay states for some decades, although integrated into the larger socioeconomic framework. Meanwhile, a British family—the Brookes—had launched a benevolent but autocratic family dynasty that would dominate Sarawak for a hundred years, while neighboring Sabah was acquired and operated as a commercial venture in the interest of its shareholders by a British chartered company.

British rule of the Malay Peninsula and northern Borneo brought profound changes, transforming the various states socially and economically. In western Malaya and Sabah, an export economy based on minerals and cash crops was developed. Sarawak was developed on a smaller scale, while the east coast of Malaya remained largely enmeshed in the traditional economy. Singapore became the economic and financial capital of the region. To work the mines and plantations, the British imported Chinese and (on a smaller scale) Indians. By World War II these immigrants constituted nearly half of the Malayan population and around a third in Sabah and Sarawak. The Chinese soon became the dominant force in commerce as well as the base for urban growth. Much economic growth occurred. British policies promoted the planting of rubber—which soon vied with tin as the major export—as well as pepper, gambier, tobacco, and oil palm. Malaya and British North Borneo developed classic extractive, plantation-based economies oriented to the resource and market needs of the industrializing West. Malays were less involved in the modern economy and maintained a more traditional social structure, but their lives were impacted by various economic policies that subjected them to global economic forces. The Malay sultans retained their symbolic status at the apex of an aristocratic social system.

In the ethnically heterogenous societies of Malaysia and Singapore, each group tended to maintain its own cultural traditions. For example, Chinese opera and other forms of musical theater (wayang) remained very popular among the Chinese. This performance was in Singapore. 1970 photo by author.

A plural society was developing, with most Malays in villages, Chinese in towns and cities, and Indians on plantations. Colonial authorities skillfully utilized "divide and rule" tactics to maintain their control. Colonial rule facilitated the establishment of Christian mission (mostly English-medium), community-sponsored Chinese, and government Malay schools; but the separate school systems also helped perpetuate the plural society. Through enterprise, organization, and cooperation many Chinese became part of a prosperous, urban middle class that controlled retail trade. The various groups generally lived in their own neighborhoods, followed different occupations, practiced their own religions, spoke their own languages, operated their own schools, and later formed their own political organizations. The general separation of the peoples was reflected in the common folk expression "raven with raven, sparrow with sparrow." Given the heterogeneous nature of the population and the incorporation of community elites in governing, pan-ethnic nationalism was slow to develop; rather some ethnic-oriented nationalist currents stirred by the 1930s. The Borneo states experienced many of the same changes. In all the colonies, the British created single states out of many local societies but tolerated little open political activity.

Before World War II, popular culture among Malays was dominated by traditional and folk arts—often with a regional or local flavor—or by more modernized or syncretic variations on traditional themes.[4] Traditional Malay music long predates the arrival of Western culture and chiefly involves gamelan-type instruments such as gongs, drums, flutes, and those with affinities to Islamic cultures. Mohammed Taib Osman, a Malaysian culture scholar, notes that "music played an important role in upholding the social structure of the time . . . the world-view of the traditional society, music and political ideology coincided. Musical instruments formed part of the royal regalia . . . [and] are believed to have supernatural powers."[5]

Musical instruments common in traditional Malay ensembles. These ensembles could be found both in royal courts and in villages. Today this music has lost much of its audience. 1970 photo by author.

Memories of Bangsawan in Sarawak

"Malaysians who were born after Independence have certainly missed the joys and excitement of attending a bangsawan. They never knew the happiness of watching some fine stage performances amidst the kampung (neighborhood) ambience, nor of enjoying the simple things of life such as the sideshows with their many attractions, something like a minicarnival. The audience was well and truly transported to the land of fantasy peopled by legendary heroes and heroines who were forever young and beautiful. As always, the good characters triumphed over the evildoers. Bangsawan was already staged in Kuching during the 1900s and earlier. After the Second World War the bangsawan was organized on a more regular basis, at various villages in and around Kuching. It is difficult to say why the bangsawan culture suddenly erupted like a meteor after the war. People were eager to seek a form of entertainment and conviviality after experiencing so much hardship. So village folk banded themselves into bangsawan committees and created fancy names for their organizations. The bangsawan culture spread and touched the life of all sectors of society. People from all walks of life and from all ethnic communities were able to get together to enjoy an evening of entertainment. Perhaps the bangsawan has been instrumental in fostering unity among the multiracial population of Sarawak? And perhaps too, its popularity can be attributed to its wholesome nature, as a healthy form of entertainment for everyone, the young and the old, the learned and the unlettered. If the drama was heavy and posing thought-provoking issues to the intellectuals or if the play depicted sorrowful scenes of death and misfortune, the comedians would enliven the atmosphere. Other attractions included the singing contest. Some of our well-known songbirds today won several titles. Other singers later became radio personalities. Several TV and radio actors and actresses today received their early training in the village bangsawan."—Hajah Maimunah Hj. Daud[6]

Among modernized genres, bangsawan troupes toured the country, combining music and drama in their performances. Bangsawan was an eclectic—even multiethnic—urban popular theater developed for purely commercial purposes in the early twentieth century, with influences derived from Western, Arab, Latin American, Turkish, Indonesian, Indian, and Chinese cultures. As one expert argues:

> Bangsawan . . . emphasized variety and heterogeneity, constantly adapting to the changing tastes of urban audiences. . . . As a product of the time, bangsawan articulated the transformations in Malayan society in the late nineteenth and early twentieth centuries. Its emphasis on variety, novelty and innovation corresponded to the social, political and cultural processes of change.[7]

In some coastal cities, kroncong orchestras and recordings attracted both Malays and Chinese with their sensuous Portuguese-Indonesian musical blend originating in Java. *Dondang sayang* is a local music popular among both Malays and Baba Chinese in Melaka and western Johor that bears some resemblance to kroncong. Originating perhaps four hundred years ago, it became a mature form in the nineteenth century combining the verbal art of complex poetry (pantun) with orchestral accompaniment.[8] Popular Malay instrumental ensembles known as orkes melayu (heavily influenced by Middle Eastern and Indian musical styles) were also popular, especially on the west coast, and often backed bangsawan performances. *Ghazal*, a similar but unique eclectic form combining Indian, Persian, and indigenous influences, became predominant in the southern state of Johor.

Throughout the country there was also *asli*, essentially a modernized or popularized folk music including folk songs, pop songs in a folk style, instrumental pieces, and dances in various styles, with the joget perhaps the best known. Asli also refers to a style of song with distinctive rhythmic characteristics, as well as to an ornamental style of singing.[9] Some types of asli were closely identified with bangsawan and often incorporated popular Western dance beats. Traditional music persists side by side with modern music but has taken on some modern influences. For example, the violin has been adopted for the *ronggeng*, joget and dondang sayang.[10]

Although many of these popular and traditional forms derived from a synthesis of the foreign and the indigenous, all are considered today to be part of the Malay cultural tradition. By the late 1940s and early 1950s, these traditions were being greatly modified or displaced completely as Western sociocultural influence poured into the country. Today kroncong, ghazal, and asli music are only occasionally performed or recorded in their earlier forms (especially in the major cities), although some modernized versions persist.

The roots of Western music in the region go back to the late nineteenth century, when the British colonizers began establishing state or constabulary bands (often staffed by imported Filipino or Goan musicians) and Western musical instruments began to spread. By the early part of the twentieth century, Western-style dance bands were becoming much more popular, with dance halls and cabarets developing in many cities and towns. Eclectic bands playing Chinese or Malay music on Western instruments also appeared.[11] But not all the influences were Western; Indian film musicals soon became hugely popular, and the recordings of stars of the 1920s and 1930s in China such as the Shanghai torchsingers Chou Hsuan and Woo Ing Ing attracted many fans.

The harsh Japanese Occupation (1941–1945) disturbed the equilibrium of colonial society and exacerbated Chinese-Malay relations. After the war the British established formal colonial control in Sarawak and Sabah while seeking to circumvent heightened political turbulence. The major generator of political organizing was a British proposal to form a unified Malayan

There have been repeated attempts by private individuals, and sometimes government authorities, to revitalize traditional cultural forms. This shows one of a series of officially sponsored concerts by traditional music groups, in this case from Trengganu, held at the Lake Gardens in Kuala Lumpur in the 1980s. 1980 photo by the author.

Union incorporating all the Malayan territories except Singapore that would diminish the autonomy of the states and accord equal political and citizenship rights to the non-Malay communities. A tremendous upsurge of Malay political feeling resulted in the creation of the United Malays National Organization (UMNO) as a vehicle for Malay nationalism and political assertiveness. UMNO-supported strikes, demonstrations, and boycotts doomed the scheme, and the British began to negotiate with UMNO about the Malayan future.

This resulted in the Malayan Federation of 1948, which unified the territories and provided special guarantees of Malay rights. These developments alarmed many Chinese. In 1948 the mostly Chinese Malayan Communist Party went into the jungles and began a guerrilla war to defeat the colonial government, sparking an eight-year period of unrest known as the Emergency. Promising independence, British officials began negotiating with the leaders of the various ethnic communities. In 1955 UMNO and moderate Chinese and Indian parties formed a coalition to successfully contest national elections, establishing a permanent political pattern of a ruling alliance that united ethnically based, mostly elite-led parties of moderate to conservative political leanings with UMNO as the major force. Political divisions of the time sometimes had repercussions in the world of music. For example, a famous drummer, long a mainstay of the royal Trengganu *nobat* orchestra, was dismissed by the sultan for his membership in a nationalist party.[12]

On August 31, 1957, the Malayan Federation became independent, under an Alliance government headed by UMNO leader Tunku Abdul Rahman as prime minister. Singapore, predominantly Chinese in population, remained outside the federation as a British Crown Colony. The arrangement tended to favor the Malays politically, with UMNO leaders holding most federal offices and the kingship rotated among the various Malay sultans. But Chinese were granted liberal citizenship rights and maintained strong economic power. Meanwhile, new currents were also appearing in Borneo. British leaders suggested the idea of a Malaysia federation as a way of terminating their now burdensome colonial rule over Singapore, Sarawak, and Sabah. The various states were historically and ethnically distinct, but shared many historical experiences with Malaya. Political activity accelerated with the mooting of the Malaysia proposal, and new parties were formed in Sabah and Sarawak in response. Statewide elections were held, with most of the parties accepting the idea of independence through merger with Malaysia. Hence, on September 16, 1963, the Malaysian federation was formed.

Malaysia was created essentially out of a "marriage of convenience." The arrangement merged Malaya with Singapore, Sarawak, and Sabah. In the years since, the nation has struggled to create national unity out of deep and in many ways enduring regional and ethnic divisions; indeed, Singapore left the federation in 1965. Malaysia's problems are complicated by the exceptionally heterogeneous composition of the population. Malaysia has been termed the archetype of the "plural society." With slightly over half of the population, Malays dominate politics and the bureaucracy, although most Malays remain concentrated in the rural areas. With a little over a third of the population, the Chinese generally monopolize commerce and the urban economy. Indians, a tenth of the population, are divided between urbanites and rural plantation workers. The great majority of Chinese and Indians concentrate in the west Malayan states, where most of the agricultural, commercial, and industrial development has been concentrated. Various indigenous peoples of Malay stock—predominantly non-Muslim in religion—live in the Malayan highlands (the Orang Asli) and—in much larger numbers—in Sabah (the Kadazan are the major group) and Sarawak (the Iban are the most numerous of the various "Dayak" peoples), where they have played a major sociopolitical role. Chinese constitute nearly three-quarters of Singapore's population, dominating both politics and the economy.

The multiethnic nature of Malaysian society is exemplified in the old port city of Penang:

> Nowhere else, it seems, has the very human trait of dividing up a common humanity been carried out with such single-mindedness. This is particularly evident in places of worship. There are not only mosques, but mosques serving congregations from the different Muslim regions of the Malay archipelago and the Indian subcontinent. Hindu and Buddhist temples reflect a similar ethnic and regional differentiation, while Chinese temples and clan halls attest to the bewildering diversity of clans and regional affiliations within a community that is often viewed, by outsiders, as homogeneous. Food stalls and restaurants, moreover, provide a kind of religious and cultural cafeteria where different dietary restrictions and preferences are carefully observed.[13]

Chinese opera remained very popular among working-class and older Chinese, with many stages available for performances in Chinese neighborhoods. This stage is in Singapore. 1986 photo by author.

The new, hurriedly formed Malaysian nation faced many political problems, including several years of Indonesian military opposition that ended only in 1966, sporadic communist insurgency in Sarawak, considerable East Malaysian disenchantment over Malayan domination and development policies, and the departure of Singapore in 1965. The latter event resulted from increasing friction between the mostly Malay federal leaders and the mostly Chinese state leaders, who disagreed on the direction the country should take. In Sarawak and Sabah, politics within Malaysia has proved a turbulent experience. The decisions to join had been made in haste, and many continued to resent the loss of their autonomy—especially control over growing oil revenues. Political crises occurred periodically in both states, usually involving federal interference with state governments or movements seeking more flexibility. Although peninsular sociopolitical patterns increasingly influenced north Borneo, the states remain unique within the Malaysian system. Since 1965, Singapore—under autocratic direction and freewheeling economic policies—has become a highly prosperous but tightly controlled city-state, maintaining relatively cordial relationships with Malaysia. Led by the visionary but autocratic Lee Kuan Yew, Singapore welcomed foreign investment and industry, in the process becoming one of the dynamic, rapidly growing "Little Dragon" economies of the Pacific Rim. But despite a parliamentary structure and electoral system, little serious internal opposition to the established leadership is permitted.

The exit of Singapore allowed UMNO to exercise more influence over federal Malaysian policies, even if it did not end political uncertainties. Given the necessity to defuse political tensions, sustain rapid economic growth, and preserve stability, Malaysia developed a political pattern in which the elites of the major ethnic groups cooperate through political parties that ally in a Malay-dominated ruling coalition (known since 1971 as the National Front). The major opposition to the National Front has come from a militant Islamic party (strong in several northern and eastern states) and a progressive party appealing to urban Chinese and Indians. Communal tensions in Malaya—following a heated election in which opposition parties did well—generated riots and a nationwide state of emergency in 1969–1970. This was a watershed, the most significant crisis of the plural society and fledgling democracy. Ever since, the government has been more wary of inflaming communal tensions and permitting unbridled freedom of speech. This seminal year generated a permanent shift to a system containing elements of both modified democracy and quasi-authoritarianism, with a purposive depoliticization that narrowed political discourse, undermined opposition parties, and generated more restrictive sociocultural policies.[14]

The Flowering of Popular Music

Given the ethnically and regionally complex nature of Malaysian society, the rapid pace of socioeconomic change, and the fluctuating pattern of sociocultural influences from outside the country, Malaysian popular music has inevitably undergone considerable transformation since the 1940s.[15] The technological growth of the mass media and consequent marketing strategies contributed greatly to the development of a new kind of popular culture. The rapid growth of the film industry, including Indian-style Malay musicals, the spread of radio, and the introduction of new musical and dance styles had a revolutionary impact on Malayan popular culture generally, and on Malay popular music in particular. Singapore became the center for a burgeoning Malay entertainment industry in the decade after World War II. Few records were produced locally until the 1960s, but recordings by singers and film stars were pressed in India for sale in Malaya. Equally important were new music venues, especially the cabarets, cafes, band contests, and stage shows associated with postwar amusement parks such as Kuala Lumpur's Bukit Bintang, Penang's New World, and Singapore's Great World. Social dancing (from samba to cha-cha to rock and roll) also became popular among youth in the 1950s.

In the late 1940s and during the 1950s, many singers achieved popularity through their films or recordings, especially in the urban areas. Among the most successful were P. Ramlee, R. Azmi, Jasni, Ahmad C. B., S. M. Salim, Saloma, Momo Latiff, and Nona Aisha. Some had backgrounds in bangsawan or kroncong. Their music now utilized many of the new styles filtering in from outside, including Latin American-flavored dance, Hawaiian, and Indian film, as well as Western popular musics. Much of it corresponded to the prevailing romantic mood of Western popular music. Indeed, what might be called the *hatimu hatiku* ("my heart, your heart") syndrome has always dominated Malaysian popular music; as one well-known record producer concedes: "No love, no sales; no romance, no chance."[16] Hence, the Malaysian hit parade has been dominated for decades by songs with *sayang* ("love"), cinta ("love"), or *gadis* ("girlfriend") in the title. But even in the 1950s a few songs dealt with sociopolitical issues such as patriotism, polygamy, Islam, and Malaya's 1957 independence from colonialism. Some singers offered material extolling village life, a reflection not only of a persistent concern with rural themes in asli music but also the increasing urbanization of Malayan society—a process generating sociocultural change and instability among the Malays. A local Chinese pop music culture also developed in these years as urban amusement parks hired female singers of Chinese sentimental songs for their cafes.[17]

In coming to any understanding of Malayan popular culture, one cannot ignore the pivotal role of P. Ramlee, whose career spanned the late 1940s through early 1970s.[18] Ramlee proved to be the greatest talent in the history of Malay entertainment: singer, musician, composer, lyricist, arranger, actor, comedian, director, scriptwriter, film producer. More than anyone else, Ramlee infused the Malay musical and film industries with an identity and energy that have never been duplicated. Ramlee was also the first Malay popular culture superstar; his second wife, the sensuous singer and actress Saloma, became the first female superstar despite (or perhaps because of) her "sex symbol," pin-up girl image in a still-conservative society. By some estimates Ramlee wrote over a thousand songs, recording around five hundred—many of which became hits all over the country. Many artists recorded his songs, including Saloma. Indeed, several dozen of his best songs

Amusement Parks and Popular Music

One of the more interesting developments in Singapore's night life after World War II was the growth of the singing cafes, colorful, open-air theaters where local Chinese relaxed after work. The cafes were found in the three big amusement parks, offering a nightly program of vocal numbers, dances, comedy sketches, and short plays. They represented glamor and romance to average people, an escape from the drabness of daily life. The night cafe as a form of popular entertainment became more popular in 1949, when former dancer and singer Madame Tai Fong formed the Fong Fong Revue at the New World Park. With drive, energy, and imagination, Madame Fong gave life and variety to what had previously been a rather monotonous song recital. During the boom years of 1951–1952, night cafes rocketed to the peak of their prosperity. Each night patrons filled every seat available, and popular singers and dancers graced the footlights. Salaries for entertainers soared. By mid-1953 the boom had ended. The career of cafe singers proved short, seldom lasting more than four years. The majority of the girls came from poorer families and were largely self-taught through attending cafe performances and listening to records. With the drop in cafe salaries, the singers branched out, singing during lunch hours at various restaurants and hotels. Chinese amusement papers and magazines devoted considerable space to stories about cafe personalities, which were followed avidly by the fans.[19]

Only remnants or modest imitations of the old diversified entertainment parks that flourished in Malayan cities and Singapore during the 1950s remain today. Most were torn down. This is the Happy Amusement Park in Ipoh. 1985 photo by author.

remain popular national treasures today, including "Joget Pahang," "Tudong Periok," "Gelora," "Di Manakan Ku Cari Ganti," and "Azizah."

Ramlee was even better known for his films; he was the first singing actor and many of his films utilized (and hence made famous) his songs. It was Ramlee more than any other figure who moved Malay films away from strict emulation of Indian models in developing a more uniquely Malayan style and content. Ramlee acted in sixty-three films and directed thirty-four; he wrote the scripts and music for many of them, demonstrating an amazing versatility. Inevitably, his prolific musical and film work varied in quality. Not all of his songs were memorable, and many of his films fell far short of the quality of his most acclaimed efforts, such as *Hang Tuah* (the great Malay hero of Melaka history), *Penarik Beca* ("Trishaw Rider") and *Antara Dua Darjat* ("Between Two Social Classes"). Yet Ramlee developed a huge mass following in both cities and villages. While his art was primarily directed at—and chiefly enjoyed by—the Malay population, it is important to note that Ramlee was probably the first Malay entertainer to achieve wide popularity among non-Malays. A considerable number of Chinese and Indians attended his films and enjoyed his songs. In every respect, Ramlee was the quintessential Malaysian entertainer.

Ramlee's art was also closely attuned to the sociocultural changes of the time. His move to bustling, predominantly Chinese Singapore provided Ramlee with the inspiration to compose his songs and create his films. Singapore was in turmoil as the population attempted to recover from the depredations of war, deal with an increasing labor unrest (and, in the peninsula, leftist revolt), and come to terms with rising (and competitive) Malay and Chinese nationalisms as well as changing social and class structures. Ideas of social reform and ethnic rivalry permeated public discussion. Yet Malayans also sought escape in romance and pleasure seeking. Money flowed in after years of hardship, while Malays became more aware of their political and economic situation.

The Early Career of P. Ramlee

P. Ramlee (whose real name was Tengku Zakariah Nyak Puteh), descended from Achenese (north Sumatran) immigrants, was born in a village in rural Penang in 1929 and attended English-medium schools. When he was a teenager he joined a big band that played in a joget (dancing) club and took the opportunity to hone his musical skills as musician, composer, and arranger. His earliest compositions were laced with the popular dance beats of the time, such as samba, rhumba, Latin, and swing. After winning a talent competition, Ramlee was recruited in 1948 by a Singapore film company. The move to cosmopolitan, fast-paced Singapore spurred Ramlee's creative talent to a higher level. Singapore was both the economic and sociocultural capital of the Malay Peninsula.

Singapore remained the center of Malay popular culture and intellectual life well into the 1960s. Ramlee's art reflected these trends and concerns, and this ensured his popularity with the public. As a Malaysian film producer noted: "P. Ramlee was a creation of his times—times of suffering, misery, and pain."[20] Soon Ramlee was the leading filmmaker, actor, and popular singer in the country. Most observers consider the period between 1955 and 1964 as Ramlee's "Golden Age"; he made his most critically acclaimed films and wrote his most enduring music. In 1964 Ramlee moved to the federal capital, Kuala Lumpur, abandoning the creative tension and close-knit film community of Singapore. His career in Kuala Lumpur between 1964 and his sudden death in 1973 did not match his earlier accomplishments, perhaps because of changing times and tastes that even the master interpreter of the public mood could not identify.

The social concerns of Ramlee's art need to be emphasized; he claimed that "my art is not for money. My art is for society. . . . As artistes we should never forget the ordinary man, the trishaw-pedaller, the laborer, or the slum-dweller," because they constituted the audience for his art, which the rich ignored.[21] His "Golden Age" films, whether social dramas, romances, historical epics, or comedies, were filled with social comments, criticisms, or satire, often laced subtly into the entertaining whole. Ramlee's work exposed the weaknesses of Malay society; he criticized sociocultural conservatism, attacked feudalism, poked fun at the aristocracy and their hypocrisies, philosophized about discrimination, showed victimization of his working-class heroes, satirized polygamy, and encouraged a more open attitude to sex.[22] In forcing Malays to recognize and laugh at their own foibles, Ramlee hoped to promote social improvement; he realized the potential influence of the artist on society and viewed films and music as serious forms of entertainment to address social problems—especially those of the Malay community.[23]

Ramlee's musical production was so vast that it becomes difficult to categorize. A master of many instruments and a natural showman, he excelled in stage shows and concerts, using his unique voice and exuberant personality to good effect. Ramlee utilized diverse musical influences, including various asli beats, ghazal, Indian, Arab, and Chinese popular music, and fashionable Western styles from samba, cha-cha, and waltz to rock and roll, twist, rhythm and blues, jazz—even the psychedelic sound of the late 1960s. Ramlee was a master at combining (often subtly) several distinct styles, such as samba and joget. Because of the frequent use of asli influences, many Ramlee songs have a distinct Malayan feel. At the same time, Ramlee made better use than many contemporaries of changing Western musical styles such as rock and roll beats, but some critics consider his efforts derivative. The difficulty he faced in successfully mastering the rock styles probably contributed to his reduced popularity with youth in the late 1960s.

But Ramlee's music changed with the times and reflected public taste. Many of his songs were comedies, designed to bring a smile. Others were ballads, usually dealing with romantic themes. A third category of songs might be labeled "advice-giving," offering suggestions on daily life, the affairs of the heart, interpersonal relations, or the connection to the spiritual realm.[24] Some of his songs did not fit into any of the above categories, including social criticisms or commentaries dealing with the desperation of poverty, human frailties, or changing social mores. One of his most popular was "Bila Mama Pakai Chelana" ("When Mama Wears Pants"), a hilarious satire on changing gender roles. Ramlee wrote the melodies for most of his songs and the lyrics for some, while generally suggesting ideas to his lyricists.

Ramlee left a prodigious heritage for others to try to emulate. More than any other musician or songwriter, he shaped the sound of Malay popular music; yet his standard of talent and energy would be difficult to reach. Largely taken for granted during his life, he is now greatly appreciated and labeled the *seniman agung* ("Supreme Artist"). Most critics and other observers agree that Ramlee has never been adequately replaced—that his death symbolized the decline of the Malay entertainment industry generally, and the film and music fields in particular. As Malaysian journalist and social critic Rehman Rashid suggests, "He may have been a freak; a mutant genius; a lightning shot of brilliance that briefly flared through the confused and clouded skies of this country's creativity."[25]

The 1980s witnessed a Ramlee renaissance, a continuous celebration of his talent and importance: streets and theaters renamed; retrospectives or festivals of his films; concerts of his works; reissues of his best-loved recordings; symposiums on his life and work; Ramlee museums. Malaysian ethnomusicologist Tan Sooi Beng contends that the recent official glorification of Ramlee constitutes part of a government policy to control popular culture, in this case by countering the increasing power within the local recording industry of the major multinational corporations (and their Western-oriented influence) through lionizing an alternative and authentic Malaysian model.[26] But, as one local critic asserts, "it is difficult to shake off the suspicion that Ramlee has been accorded so much attention simply because there is no other entertainer [of his stature] to eulogize."[27] Ramlee has remained the most influential and respected entertainment talent Malaysia ever produced, and a keen influence on many of the most interesting musicians of the present day. Undoubtedly his major legacy to contemporary musicians is as a model of a successful and versatile entertainer. Nonetheless, many of the most creative, socially concerned musicians, such as M. Nasir and Sudirman, have certainly derived considerable inspiration from Ramlee's career and concerns.

Malaysian Popular Culture and the Plural Society

Malaysian popular music and culture has inevitably reflected the reality of a plural society, a pattern that was clear by the 1950s. The Chinese minority, especially those educated in Chinese-medium schools, have tended to favor films and recordings from Singapore, Taiwan, and Hong Kong. A local Chinese recording industry developed, although it seldom flourished and has grown less important in the past decade. Indian pop culture has mostly been imported from India, especially films (chiefly musicals) and tapes (mostly of Tamil or Hindi film music); over the past several decades only a handful of Tamil- or Hindi-language records by local musicians were issued, to little acclaim. The numerically and politically predominant Malays—especially the educated Malays—have chiefly followed Malay, Indonesian, and Middle Eastern sociocultural developments, and constitute the essential but not exclusive market for Malay-medium popular music and culture.

Western (Anglo-American) cultural influence has been substantial among all of the groups, although the strongest impact has been on those

"Bila Mama Pakai Chelana" ("When Mama Wears Pants")

"When mama wears pants
Papa scratches his head!
When mama dances the cha-cha
Papa crosses his eyes
When mama hula hoops
Papa's boil pops
When mama dresses Yankee
Papa is sour with a toothache"—P. Ramlee

Imported Chinese and Indian films, many of them musicals, were vastly popular in Malaysia and Singapore. Although catering particularly to members of those ethnic groups, they attracted a multiethnic audience, especially from the 1940s through the 1970s. Like many others the National Theater in Klang, Selangor, specialized in Chinese films from Hong Kong and Taiwan. 1980 photo by author.

Chinese, Indians, and Malays who have attended English-medium schools, especially in the urban areas. Some English-educated Malaysians have followed Western popular culture developments exclusively or primarily; others maintain an interest in both Western and local ethnic varieties. The percentage of the Malaysian population who have closely or loosely followed developments in popular music is apparently high, especially in the urban areas and the more accessible rural districts of the peninsula's west coast. Indeed, popular music as disseminated through recordings, radio, television, live shows, nightclubs, and discos undoubtedly has had a larger audience than any other performing art in Malaysia, and that audience cuts across all divisions of ethnicity, class, gender, and age.[28] Some of the music is essentially derivative of Western styles—with little local flavor—but some is clearly transculturated, with a blend of indigenous and imported influences.

Music is only one component of Malaysian culture. An increasingly educated population fostered the growth of a local literature, with the government Language and Literature Bureau (founded in 1959) helping shape Malay fiction and poetry.[29] Writers utilizing English, Malay, Chinese, or Tamil have focused on their own communities as well as on larger Malaysian themes. Perhaps the best-known Malay writer is Shahnon Ahmad. His 1966 novel *Ranjau Sepanjang Jalan* ("No Harvest But a Thorn") describes the fatalistic, inarticulate world of the peasant, tied to the land and tradition while also struggling endlessly against the eternal forces of nature to sustain a meager existence. Many other writers have also emphasized rural themes: for example, poet Muhammad Haji Salleh's evocation of rural poverty and perpetual powerlessness in a rubber-tapping community, "Quiet Village":

There's lucidity and unambiguous death
in this smokeless village . . .
the inhabitants are too poor,
too desiccated to care, to talk,

and the children too hungry
to run and laugh at their games. . . .
the rubber tree is no factory,
prices come from the businessmen.
When you are poor
you can't borrow from the poor.[30]

Sometimes literature could have serious political ramifications. Shahnon's 1967 novel *Menteri* ("Minister") included speculation about a future in which Malays had been driven into the forests while Chinese controlled the rest of the country. Some critics believe the fictional story helped spark the 1969 riots. During the 1970s and 1980s, Malay writers dissected the 1969 Emergency and also analyzed the rapid changes occurring in Malay society, some of them perceived as generated by unsettling outside influences. Chinese intellectuals have bemoaned the decline of Chinese literary traditions (and of Chinese cultural forms generally) with the switch from Chinese- to Malay-medium schools. In a lighter vein, comic books, humor magazines, women's magazines, and periodicals about popular film, television, and music flourish.

Popular Music in the 1960s and Malaysia-Singapore Separation

Many changes occurred in Malay popular music and popular culture during the 1960s, some of them related to the separation of Singapore. In part these changes reflected the growing influence of the West on Malayan sociocultural life, especially in the rapidly growing cities. Western popular music was heard increasingly on the radio and records, spreading well beyond the realm of the English educated into blue-collar neighborhoods and rural villages. Many youngsters in the later 1950s and throughout the 1960s listened mostly to Anglo-American rock and roll, often to cheap portable radios or jukeboxes in local coffee shops. By the end of the decade, blue jeans and miniskirts had become increasingly common among teenagers, not only in Kuala Lumpur and Singapore but in provincial cities. Malay entertainment and general-interest magazines were becoming much more daring in their subject matter and photographs. The tight, sometimes slit skirts and form-revealing dresses that generated so much public controversy and conservative criticism for Saloma in the 1950s and early 1960s seemed rather tame by 1970. Not surprisingly, the lyrics to romantic songs sometimes reflected a more suggestive and sexy tone than had been common a few years earlier. A real youth culture was beginning to emerge, with Western social dances (such as the twist) becoming widely popular. Traditional joget halls became more lively. At the same time, the introduction of television killed off the great amusement parks. But a local Chinese recording industry also emerged, with Malaysian singers like Poon Sow Keng achieving notable popularity throughout the region and Singaporean Zhang Xiaoying becoming a superstar among Malaysian Chinese.

Beginning in the 1960s and continuing through the 1970s, a modest regional pop music industry developed in Sarawak and Sabah. In Sarawak, for example, several small local recording companies were set up in Kuching and Sibu, specializing in recording local pop singers (mostly Iban or Malay) offering their own—or recycled—songs with backing bands. Some of the songs had a folk flavor—jogets were especially popular—but most were conventional pop in style. Pop musicians like Christopher Kelly, Christopher Kerry, Michael Jemat, Stewart Tinggie, Zamry Amera, Mary Jeane, and Veronica Roni achieved some local notoriety but failed to make much of an impact outside of their own states. By the mid-1980s the local pop scenes had withered, overwhelmed by the recordings coming in from Malaya and from foreign countries. Hence, the possibilities for the sort of thriving regional pop to support local or ethnic identity that flourished in neighboring Indonesia were aborted.[31]

The mid-1960s were troubled years politically. Indonesian confrontation with Malaysia produced a generally low-level military conflict that festered during the middle years of the decade. More importantly, the new federation of Malaysia began to splinter, with Singapore leaving the federation to become independent. The implications of this change for Malayan popular culture did not become clear until the early 1970s, but one major result was the rapid growth of Kuala Lumpur as the undisputed political, economic, social, cultural, and intellectual capital of the remaining federation states.

The period between 1965 and 1971 might be termed the "Era of *Pop Yeh Yeh*." The example of the Beatles and other guitar bands attracted Malaysian musicians and music fans alike. Soon a flood of Beatles imitators appeared, singing in Malay, English, Cantonese, and Tamil; their beat-oriented style, usually involving an instrumental backing of three electric guitars and a drum set, became known as *pop yeh yeh*, after the popular Beatles song "She Loves You, Yeh Yeh Yeh."[32] M. Osman's 1964 hit "Suzanna" may have been the first local song in this genre, but he was soon followed by dozens of others. Many of the most popular singers and musicians were from or based in Singapore, which remained the center of Malay popular music into the early 1970s. But pop yeh yeh groups *(kugiran)* formed in cities and towns all over the peninsula, quickly eclipsing and then marginalizing or eliminating the combos and big bands that dominated dance music in earlier years. This was perhaps the zenith for derivative music from the West in Malaysia, although much of Malaysian pop has always been somewhat more acculturated than in Thailand or Indonesia, reflecting the stronger Western cultural influence permeating even into the countryside of this relatively small country.

Many kugiran were recorded by the new record companies that appeared in the 1960s, the largest number of them in Singapore. The rise of pop yeh yeh corresponded to the decline of the Malay film industry, now based in Kuala Lumpur. Local film companies found it increasingly difficult to compete with the influx of Western, Indian, and Indonesian films. Many singers achieved huge popularity, such as A. Ramlie, Rafeah Buang, Adnan Othman, J. Kamisah, Ahmed Jais, Zaleha Hamid, M. Osman, Jefridin, Hussein Ismael, S. Roha, and Halim Yatim. The era also saw the rise of rock and pop bands performing by themselves or as backing to popular singers; the most popular included the Rhythm Boys, Siglap Five, Wanderers, Clifters, Jayhawkers, Hook, and Orkes Nirwana. With a few exceptions, pop yeh yeh was mostly escapist or romantic in content; for many the music served generally as background for dancing. Compared to P. Ramlee, the music exhibited little social consciousness or awareness. But rural and urban motifs were frequently invoked and one could find subtle themes of youth rebellion and frustrations.

Like 1960s-style rock music in the West after Woodstock, pop yeh yeh faded by 1971. For many middle-aged Malaysians today it is nostalgia music, comparable to the "yuppie" interest in 1960s music in the United States. Hence it enjoyed a modest revival in the second half of the 1980s, with some of the original musicians regenerating their careers. However, only a few popular singers of the pop yeh yeh era were able to maintain their careers through the 1970s and into the 1980s, including A. Ramlie, Ahmed Jais, Rafeah Buang, M. Shariff, and—most notably—Zaleha Hamid; all had to adapt to new musical styles. The decline of pop yeh yeh also marked the shift of leadership in Malay popular culture from Singapore to Kuala Lumpur.

Pop Yeh Yeh And Western Cultural Influence

Some singers started local trends by stylizing themselves after, and modeling themselves on, Western pop stars. Hence, Rocky Teoh became the "Elvis" of Malaysia and Azim Chan Singapore's "Gene Vincent"; several women called themselves the local "Connie Francis." Later, other Malaysians would aspire to emulate Tom Jones, Englebert Humperdink, Bob Marley, Janice Joplin, Tina Turner, Donna Summer, WHAM, and other foreign entertainers. The pop yeh yeh stars sold thousands of records, appeared on the new television music shows and band competitions, and dominated the entertainment (including film) magazines, although most earned only modest incomes from their activity. Many sang only in Malay while others specialized in cover versions of English songs. The pop yeh yeh music was more Western in sound than much of the earlier Malay pop music, although some singers and groups utilized asli vocal influences, and a few others incorporated the sounds and instruments of Indian film music.

Although most of the best recording studios and producers remain in Singapore, and many recording companies have their headquarters there, Kuala Lumpur became the center of Malay popular music by the early 1970s. The majority of singers and musicians live and work in the fast-growing federal capital, with Penang, Johor Baru, Kota Baru (Kelantan), and Kuching (Sarawak) as secondary hubs.

Since the 1960s Singapore has increasingly moved in sociocultural as well as political directions different from those in Malaysia. Popular culture in Singapore more and more came to reflect Chinese and Western orientations, perhaps because of a very small market for local music and little possibility of foreign sales. Most Singaporeans learn to speak fluent or at least passable English, and a hybrid pidgin known as Singlish—based on English but with many local linguistic influences—has increasingly developed as the street language, even the lingua franca, of the city-state. Singlish is a hodgepodge of Chinese and Malay words grafted onto English and is distinguished by its simple grammatical structure, clipped vowels, and lilting rhythm. It is spoken at all levels of society, from civil servants and executives to taxi drivers. In cabarets, stand-up comics use the slang to make bawdy jokes or poke fun at officials. Many Singaporeans object to Singlish, concerned that it gives a bad impression of their country. But many defend it too: "Singaporeans have been searching for an identity for years," asserts an entrepreneur. "We've found it in this language. I'm not British, so why should I speak the queen's English? . . . I don't want my children to think we're still a colony."[33]

Several Singapore-based recording companies produce Chinese records, some by local singers, some by Taiwan singers; indeed, by 1980 Singapore was challenging Taipei as the Mandarin pop capital of Asia. Even so, Mandarin music probably accounts for only about a third of local sales, if that—dwarfed by Western soft rock and pop. Singaporeans have tended to denigrate or ignore the struggling Malaysian Chinese record industry (reduced to three chief companies) and Malaysian Chinese singers. Malaysian Chinese recordings utilize Taiwanese, Western, and sometimes Malay pop material as well as some local compositions. In the 1970s and 1980s Malaysian Chinese singers like Wong Shiau Chuen, Lan Yin, Donny Yap, and Lee Yee sold fairly well at home, but foreign singers such as Singaporeans Zhang Xiaoying, Sakura Ting, and Lena Lim, Hong Kong's Frances Yip, and the Taiwanese Teresa Teng, Loong Piau Piau, and Jenny Tseng developed larger followings. Teng's romantic "girl-next-door" appeal transcends all ethnic, class, and age categories and has attracted several local imitators. In the early 1980s, a mostly Chinese-language music known as *xinyao* (a shorthand for "songs composed by Singapore youth) developed in the city-state. Mostly composed by students and recorded on cassettes, it had a rough, unpolished appeal. Later it became widely popular and by the 1990s had become highly commercialized, absorbed into the pop music industry.[34]

A few Singapore singers have recorded exclusively in English, the most famous being the talented and provocative Dick Lee. But despite these innovative approaches, American and British popular music came to dominate the Singapore market. One study in the later 1980s found that over 80 percent of youth regularly listen to music programs on radio but only a third ever listen to local pop music on the medium. Two-thirds preferred Western music, especially disco and rock.[35]

Western musical taste transcends class divisions. A popular television show invites Singaporeans to participate in look-alike-sound-alike contests, where—to the delight of local audiences—senior army men, bank managers, teachers, and other sober-minded worthies dress up and apparently enjoy themselves offering passable imitations of Tom Jones, Elvis Presley, and the Bee Gees.[36]

Singapore gradually became in many respects a graveyard for Malay popular culture. Some Malay recordings continued to be produced in Singapore's well-equipped studios—by both Malaysian and Singaporean musicians—but these have been marketed mostly in much more populous Malaysia, where Singapore entertainers frequently do stage shows or television work. By 1978 only nine Malay records were issued in Singapore, as opposed to forty-nine Chinese and eight English.[37] Today the audience for Malay popular culture is very limited in the city-state. On the other hand, those Malay singers, songwriters, arrangers, and other talented people who remain in Singapore enjoy a certain creative freedom since they are basically aiming at a foreign market (Malaysia) and are therefore somewhat ignored by a powerful, paternalistic, but watchful government.

Politics and Society in Change

Malaysia has enjoyed considerable progress since 1970, including maintaining what most scholars consider a limited or quasi-democratic political system that includes regular elections, moderate political diversity, and a (sometimes lively) Parliament containing some opposition members. But civil liberties restrictions include the occasional use of the Internal Security Act to incarcerate opponents. Radical critics (including socialists, Islamic militants, and progressive intellectuals) have been politically marginalized and in some cases periodically detained. There is also a ban on public discussion of "sensitive issues," such as special protection for Malay customs and values. The government controls the election machinery and mass media, disadvantaging opposition parties. The National Front also benefits from election laws favoring Malay-dominated rural districts, handily winning federal elections. By mediating differences between constituent parties and seeking general consensus, the successive ruling coalitions limit public debate.[38]

Many Malaysians (and Singaporeans) argue that a full-fledged democratic system would be disastrous given the political tensions embedded in the plural society. The Malaysian government can best be described as a complex and sometimes ambiguous mix of democratic and authoritarian elements, with socioeconomic pressures tugging it in both directions. Money has increasingly lubricated politics, with politicians using both personal largesse and development grants to maintain electoral and factional support. There has been a persistent trend to enhance central authority at the expense of the various states. But various grassroots pressure groups also emerged in the 1970s to lobby for consumer, environmental, human rights, social, and religious issues. In many respects they constituted the democratic alternative to the government. Women also became more politically active, with the UMNO women's organization (Kaum Ibu) particularly influential.

Benefiting from manageable population size, abundant natural resources, and entrepreneurial talent, Malaysia generally enjoyed a prosperous economy from 1963 into the 1990s, leading some observers to group it among the Asian "little tigers." High annual per capita GNP growth enabled Malaysia to surpass nations like Portugal and Hungary by 1985. In the mid-1960s the government adopted a labor-intensive, export-oriented industrial model to address unemployment problems. Tax concessions and labor controls attracted investment, with foreign capital playing a more important role than domestic capital. Beginning in the 1970s free trade zones and industrial estates were established in or near major cities to attract foreign investment for manufacturing by providing duty-free access to resources and labor. A "Look East" policy stressed emulation of Japan, Taiwan, and South Korea while also encouraging Malaysians to adopt their work ethic. The mixed economy included free enterprise and an expanding state sector.[39]

Yet despite a substantial expansion of manufacturing, industrialization levels are low by international standards, a sharp contrast with the relatively high per capita income. Achievements include considerable export-oriented light industry employing cheap labor. The economy remains chiefly extractive, a substantial segment of it foreign owned and subject to fluctuations in world commodity prices caused largely by factors beyond Malaysia's control. Rubber and tin still constitute the export mainstays but have also experienced challenges, with competition from synthetic rubber and inelasticity in world demand for tin. Hence Malaysian leaders promote economic diversification. By the early 1980s timber and palm oil accounted for an increasing percentage of exports, and oil became the most valuable export commodity. Economic growth came at the price of toxic waste problems, severe deforestation, and air pollution.

The 1969 violence shocked the government into addressing more aggressively inequalities of wealth. A New Economic Policy (NEP) aimed at redistributing more wealth to, and increasing the economic potential of,

Malays was launched in 1971. Statistics consistently revealed that the household incomes of Malays, particularly in the rural areas, lagged considerably behind those of Chinese. At the same time, Tamil estate workers and many Dayaks were often poorer and there were some impoverished Chinese as well. A number of public enterprises were established to expand the Malay role in commerce and industry. The goal was 30 percent Malay ownership in the commercial and industrial sectors by 1990, with non-Malays controlling 40 percent and foreign investors 30 percent (a substantial reduction for the latter). The NEP alarmed many Chinese, and critics charge that it mainly transfers Chinese wealth to politically connected Malay entrepreneurs while fostering a culture of mediocrity. Yet it also promised for the first time to substantially restructure socioeconomic patterns deeply rooted in history, especially the colonial era. It has also facilitated unprecedented upward mobility for many Malays, creating a substantial middle class. Among the most dramatic changes was placing more of the national economy in Malaysian hands (mostly state-run corporations), although this did not prevent increasing wealth concentration. By the 1980s the NEP was being enforced more pragmatically, and a growing economy meant that many Chinese could also flourish (but Indians were marginalized). The NEP was renewed in a modified, more flexible form in 1991 amidst much controversy.[40]

Rural development policies (including land schemes and mobile clinics) have improved life for many, and official poverty rates dropped from some 50 percent in 1970 to around 20 percent by 1987. Malnutrition became rare. Public spending on health and education reached into remote areas. Yet some Malays and non-Malays have benefited little and large pockets of urban and especially rural poverty remain, with many regional inequities in wealth. Many lack adequate livelihood, land, housing, and consumer goods. Rural families are still far more likely than urban families to live below the poverty line; while less than one-tenth of Kuala Lumpur's population lived in poverty in 1976, over half of Kelantan's did so. The introduction of better irrigation systems and mechanized equipment has reduced the drudgery of farm labor and facilitated double cropping. But while well-connected, more affluent farmers enjoy enhanced consumption and benefits, poorer villagers experience declining levels of security or are forced to seek work elsewhere. Increasingly many villages have become divided between "haves and have-nots." Many young women, their economic roles marginalized, drift to towns to work in low-paying, low-status jobs, especially in electronics and textile factories located in free trade zones.[41]

Malaysia's population grew to 17 million by 1990, about one-third of them living in cities and towns. Over 10 percent of the population live in the cosmopolitan Kuala Lumpur metropolitan area, whose jammed freeways, glittering malls, and high-rise condominiums contrast with burgeoning squatter settlements and countless street hawkers. The tumult and stresses of big-city life are lubricated by the 820,000 vehicles hitting the city streets every workday. Malay writer Sri Delima describes the pervasive traffic congestion:

> If you can drive in Kuala Lumpur without strange things happening to your nerves, heart, blood pressure and stomach linings, you must have the toughest constitution east of the Persian Gulf. Or else you have learned the art of refined detachment. It consists of the right attitude towards traffic jams. Jams are not things you can avoid, and the sooner you accept this the better for your health. You choke over a hurried breakfast to beat the office-bound crowd and you run smack into the school-going one. You stay on late at the office to avoid the four o'clock Government-office exodus and you get caught in the five o'clock private-firm pile-up. Stay back even longer and you are sure to meet the early evening-outers, heading for cinemas and eating-stalls or just taking a joy ride around town. The only way you can be sure of a good clear road is to start out with the rubber-tappers and come home after the last-show cinema crowd. The thing is to accept jams as part of the Kuala Lumpur scene—like the bewildering skyline and the unbeautiful River Klang. Ours not to reason why, ours but to drive and sigh.[42]

Lack of rural employment has resulted in a steady rural-urban migration; shantytowns and underemployed migrants (as well as illegal Indonesian immigrants) increasingly mark Malaysian cities. Growing numbers of Malays gravitate to them; by 1980, 25 percent of Malays were classified as urban, most working in blue-collar occupations or petty trade. But Malaysia has also achieved high literacy rates and an impressive mass educational system that helped produce a substantial multiethnic middle class.[43]

Malay society itself is gradually becoming more diverse. In socioeconomic class terms, a burgeoning urban middle class, created in part by the controversial New Economic Policy, increasingly separates the wealthy or aristocratic elite from the working class or peasant mass. In sociocultural orientation, a wide range of views—from the militant Islamic revivalist (or fundamentalist) to the secular Western-influenced or completely nontraditional—compete for influence. Indeed, some intellectuals worry that the Malay middle class is increasingly dividing into two distinct and potentially divisive groups. One group is comprised of those who—often graduates of North American, Australian, or European universities—are cosmopolitan in taste, have non-Malay friends, and seem more comfortable with Western culture than Malay tradition. The other group is made up of those mostly locally educated, less cosmopolitan individuals who prefer to speak only Malay and often maintain a social life restricted to other Malays or Islamic groups.[44] Furthermore, some Malays became concerned about what they perceive to be the neglected state of the traditional Malay arts, seeing in their collective decline a kind of cultural suicide. Few young people (especially in the cities) show interest in folk traditions; some Islamic revivalists designate certain of these arts as essentially pre-Islamic and hence forbidden. Islamic militants also protest and sometimes shut down performances by popular musicians whose work is deemed too secular or sexy.

Since the mid-1970s Islamic resurgence increasingly intrudes into public life. Islam has played a progressively larger role in Malay identity and behavior for five centuries, in the process more closely integrating Malays into the larger Islamic world. Yet it always competes with deeply ingrained pre-Islamic patterns, enjoys an ambiguous relationship with Malay nationalism, and operates in the multiethnic, multicultural social matrix. Fragmentation and disagreement have been more common than unanimity, with purists, syncretists, and (on a smaller scale) secularists all part of Malay society. Contemporary Islamic debates and activities must be seen in the larger historical context. The missionary (dakwah) movements, part of a general Islamic revival, attract the support of many young Malays alienated by a westernized, materialistic society, and cause a deep rift between secular and devout Malays. Universities and schools have become sites for contention between militant and moderate Islamic students, a consequence of the depoliticization of universities and suppression of activist student groups in the 1970s. The militant Parti Islam persistently challenges the religious credentials of UMNO leaders and advocates a more formally Islamic state and society, prompting federal and state leaders to promote stricter practices while also trying to manipulate Islamic revivalism. Some militants denounce all popular culture and demand government restrictions. Recently one state

A performance of a Malay folk dance. While there were many regional variations, some dances were common to the Malay states generally. Today these dances have lost much of their popularity as an entertainment or activity, especially among urban youth. 1970 photo by author.

politician sought to ban a concert by Michael Jackson because of "the permissive lifestyles of foreign artists who promote outrageous haristyles, wear earrings, shabby and torn outfits and indulge in illicit sex and drugs."[45]

These trends have worried not only non-Malays but many Malays favoring a more inclusive and tolerant national society. Government attempts to spread Islamic values as "universal" and welcome conversion have raised fears of "creeping Islamization." In response to the Islamic revival, Christian, Buddhist, and Hindu fundamentalist groups attract a growing number of Chinese and Indians. Youth alienation from traditional values and disgruntlement over job prospects are common and perhaps the inevitable by-products of rapid development. But not all opt for religion as a bulwark. By the 1980s some marginalized, aimless, urban young people adopted selective features of Western popular culture, from punk hairstyles to "heavy metal" music. Increasing numbers of teenagers and young adults (especially Malays) enjoy "hanging out"; their elders call it *lepak* ("loitering") and view it as idleness. They lepak at McDonald's outlets, shopping malls, public squares, or the beach, in order to relax, listen to music, and relieve tension after work or school. Authorities worry about drugs, smoking, and vandalism. Fears about the negative influences of "grunge" and rap fashions have led to bans on ads showing teenagers wearing baseball caps backward.[46] There was also a continuous trickle of Chinese emigration to the West. Malaysian social critics could easily find targets at home and abroad, including serious socioeconomic difficulties despite a growing economy, and the problem of creating a national culture to link the people together.

Singapore has also struggled to create a cohesive and coherent national identity.[47] Although the city-state is highly oriented to the West economically and in popular culture, with English as the main language of political and economic life, Singapore's leaders have also been concerned with maintaining (and even strengthening) those aspects of Asian—especially Chinese—culture promoting hard work, social stability, responsibility, morality, and community to check the individualism and alienation inherent in a high-consumption, competitive market economy. This "no-nonsense" attitude has led to massive social engineering campaigns, a cowed or government-controlled mass media, and laws to keep public behavior and potential dissent under control. Even minor misbehavior (such as littering or sporting "punk" hair and clothing styles) is severely punished. The government closely monitors and sometimes interferes in artistic expression. For example, in 1994 several theater groups found themselves under public attack for permitting controversial performance art as well as alleged leftist sympathies; they were punished through widespread media attack, a ban on any further public funding, and prosecution. Nonetheless, some playwrights have continued to test the limits of official tolerance by addressing current problems indirectly.[48] Those who publicly challenge the government and its policies can expect sanctions, including harassment, public humiliation, financially ruinous lawsuits, prohibition from public office, and even incarceration. Although restrictive and puritanical by Western standards, Malaysia generally remains a more open society than the city-state, with a somewhat less intrusive national government.

The resulting stability, combined with a highly educated and diligent population and policies favoring economic growth, have turned Singapore into an industrializing economic powerhouse and world financial center. Picturesque and lively—though congested—Chinese commercial districts, close-knit villagelike Malay neighborhoods, and quiet rural farmsteads have been bulldozed and replaced by often charmless but clean and utilitarian high-rise apartment blocks, shopping complexes, professional buildings, luxury hotels, and multistory parking garages, eliminating much of the cosmopolitan flavor of old Singapore but creating one of the world's most modern and efficient cities. The population, increasingly middle class, by and large enjoys considerable prosperity and ever-increasing living standards, with few interested or willing to take the risks in opposing the system. It is also true that Malays are more likely to be poor than Chinese. The popular vote of the ruling party dropped from 76 percent in 1980 to 59 percent in 1991, but it still won all but a small handful of seats in Parliament. In the 1997 elections, with the opposition badly divided and off balance, the PAP rebounded, winning all but two of the eighty-three seats and 65 percent of the popular vote.

Singaporeans have adopted the view that earning a good living is the main purpose in life. Critics perceive this as an obsessive preoccupation with social climbing, but most Singaporeans consider mobility as a chief measure of success. The watchful government issues frequent and foreboding reminders encouraging everyone to remain economically vigilant at all times. Singaporeans are frequently described as *kiasu*—a Hokkien dialect word that translates as "being afraid to lose"; in recent years it has taken on a broader connotation of "always wanting to be number one" and "always seeking bargains." Kiasuism has become a topic for discussion and laughter in local television, pop music, theater, literature, in schools, comedy clubs, and cartoon strips. For example, this seemingly unattractive side of the local character is examined in the highly successful, Singlish-drenched comic books by Johnny Lau, published since 1989, featuring Mr. Kiasu and his trademark phrase: "Better grab first, later no more."[49]

The shift from the idealism and sacrifice of the colonial era to the competition for power and money of more recent years was well described in Philip Jeyaratnam's controversial novel, *Abraham's Promise*, in which an aging teacher and a youthful political activist ruminate on the past and present. Jeyaratnam is the lawyer son of a famous and much persecuted dissident, but the government (to the surprise of many) allowed the book to be distributed.[50] Still, those with views alternative to the establishment, including some Malays and Chinese bemoaning the withering of their traditional culture and religion, environmentalists and preservationists alarmed at the price of rapid development, nonconformists of various types, and human rights activists wanting a more open and participatory society, have few outlets for expressing and promoting their views. But hints of them appear in popular music.

Popular Music in the 1970s

By the early 1970s Malay popular music in Malaysia was developing several musical styles, but none showed the energy of pop yeh yeh. In some respects this was a decade of self-examination, discovery, experimentation, and eventually, growth for the Malaysian musical scene. The mood corresponded to a general societal soul searching and readjustment following the state of emergency of 1969–1970 and the unsettled interethnic relationships. It had never been easy to make a comfortable living as a Malay popular musician, and few prospered. Even film stars like P. Ramlee did not live lavishly. The 1970s proved a sluggish period; few musicians were able to achieve wide popularity or sustain their careers. Many youthful talents became disillusioned and discouraged about their prospects. But at the same time, recording technology improved, potential instrumental backgrounds increasingly varied, and more people were able to study music. Even so, the musicians who can read music or boast much musical training have constituted a distinct minority.

Television exposure increased with several regular programs devoted to popular music and annual amateur talent contests, although the government sponsorship of such activities suggests an attempt to channel popular music in particular directions. Radio ownership and listenership in Malaysia and especially Singapore increased dramatically.[51] Record piracy also became a major problem. Unscrupulous businessmen pressed and sold cheap unauthorized versions of recordings by both local and foreign singers, making it difficult for singers and legitimate record companies to prosper. By the 1980s piracy had

Social Criticism and Singapore Literature

"There is another ache, that of conscience, the yearning to do what is right and good. That pain still throbs, but indistinctly, muffled by the tiredness seeping through my bones. How can a man keep his path true? The energy of youth has become an enemy, a threat to order, an unseemly challenge to the certitudes of life: that the poor will always be with us and power in the hands of a few. Only later did I understand the great ally of authority, the enemy of change, of progress, is distrust, distrust of those around us, the man standing at the street corner, the woman hanging out her washing next door. Who can be sure that reason will prevail amongst his neighbors, or be certain even of its domination within himself? And if not, then it can only be prudent to prefer regulation to freedom, dictatorship to democracy."—Philip Jeyaratnam, *Abraham's Promise.*[52]

shifted to cassettes; by some estimates, sales of pirated cassettes outnumbered legitimate record or cassette sales by four or five to one—sometimes even eight to one. Yet recording companies in both Singapore and Kuala Lumpur became larger and more sophisticated, although there has been a high turnover in these companies as their fortunes rise or fall. Few of the important local companies of 1972 are still operating today. Indeed, during the 1970s the five major multinational recording companies in the world (CBS, EMI, Polygram, RCA, and WEA) gained an increasing and eventually dominating place in the Malaysian and Singaporean markets, both disseminating Western pop music and signing many of the most talented local musicians. Their activities included heavy promotion as well as efforts at channeling Malay popular music along the most commercial (and hence profitable) lines. This frequently resulted in musical standardization and arrangements based on successful formulas, as well as the popularization of a "transnationalized culture."[53]

Several musical trends dominated the 1970s. Guitar-based bands soon added keyboards and later even horn sections in keeping with the more jazz-influenced sounds of Western pop and rock music. Western dance fads such as a-go-go and disco found acceptance in Malaysia and influenced many local singers. Indeed, discos generally replaced the joget clubs of old; by the late 1970s pubs featuring live music were also becoming more common in the cities. The early part of the decade saw the brief flourishing of bands specializing in English songs; groups like the Strollers, Quests, and Falcons recorded their own compositions. But by the late 1970s their popularity had declined and many disbanded, although foreign musicians specializing in English songs such as the Wynners and Theresa Carpio of Hong Kong and the Singapore-based Taiwanese Tracy Huang developed a strong following.

Although some Indonesian recordings were available in Malaya and Singapore in the 1950s and 1960s, and a few Indonesian singers such as S. Abdullah, Ellya, and Elly Kassim were popular, it was in the 1970s that Indonesian influence increased dramatically, perhaps a side effect of improving Malaysian-Indonesian relations. Several Indonesian pop singers gained a large following in Malaysia, among them Emilia Contessa, Elly Kassim, Broery, Ernie Djohan, Titiek Puspa, Wiwieck Abidin, and Bob Tutopoly. In 1974 Indonesian records reportedly outsold even Malay records in Kuala Lumpur, with Western pop a distant third and Chinese last.[54] By the middle and late 1970s a market for dangdut had also developed, with the recordings of Indonesian dangdut stars such as Rhoma Irama, Elvy Sukaesih, and Muchsin widely available. Dangdut appeared on the Indonesian popular music scene in the 1960s as a fusion between popular Malay ensemble music (orkes melayu), the then-popular Indian film music, and Western pop. In the mid-1970s the charismatic Rhoma Irama exploded onto the pop charts with a somewhat more rock-oriented, electrified dangdut style strongly imbued with both Islamic moral themes and socioeconomic populism. Despite or because of his critical approach, Rhoma has remained the dominant Indonesian dangdut musician and a major superstar in that country ever since (see Chapter 2).

Although Rhoma Irama developed a following in Malaysia among urban Malays (including musicians), dangdut proved particularly popular in rural areas, especially in the west coast states.[55] By the late 1970s some local Malaysian singers had adopted the dangdut style. Some, like M. Shariff, modified irama hindustan into a more Malayan sound, maintaining tablas and flutes as important ingredients and recording local rather than imported lyrics. Local dangdut became even more popular in the 1980s, with a number of new singers successfully specializing in the style, including Zaleha Hamid (a Singaporean), Malek Ridzuan, Nas Atea, and especially Herman Tino (Malaysia's dangdut king). But dangdut has never been as important in Malaysia as in Indonesia; it attracted a following in Malaysia mostly among rural Malays and Indonesian immigrants.

Sharifah Aini proved the most successful singer of the 1970s, with a blend of ballads, asli, and sometimes Indian-flavored local music (many songs were composed by Ahmed Nawab), as well as Malay cover versions of Western hits such as "Hello Darling" and "Whatever Will Be, Will Be." In many respects—except perhaps for Sheila Majid in the late 1980s—Sharifah Aini has been the only female superstar since Saloma, who died in 1981 but recorded little after 1973. Despite (or perhaps because of) a turbulent personal life that generates conservative criticism, Sharifah Aini had few unsuccessful recordings in Malay between her debut in 1970 and the mid-1980s, when her career began to wane; even her English recordings sold moderately well (a rarity for local English recordings in Malaysia). She also made occasional film musicals.[56]

Irama hindustan, dangdut, a-go-go (dance music), and several other styles remained on the fringe of a pop music mainstream oriented to Western-style ballads, toned-down rock, and asli-influenced light pop. Much

Irama Hindustan and Indian Influence

Another prominent trend of the 1970s could be termed irama hindustan, strongly influenced by Indian film music. Such music goes back to the 1950s in Indonesia, and Indonesian proponents such as Ellya also achieved popularity in Malaysia.[57] But irama hindustan had local roots as well. Arrangements heavily influenced by Indian models characterized some of the songs by Malay singers of the 1940s and 1950s, such as Abdul Rahman, Jasni, R. Azmi, and even P. Ramlee. By the early 1970s musicians like M. Shariff (with his group The Zurah) and Ahmadi Hassan were recording irama hindustan songs. They took Indian film songs, loosely translated them into Malay (or wrote new Malay lyrics), and backed them with Indian-influenced musical arrangements.[58] New singers such as Sharifah Aini and D. J. Dave (a Punjabi) also made use of Indian influences.

Films from Indonesia increasingly competed with imports from China, India, and the West as well as Malaysian productions during the 1980s. This film ad is in Seremban, Negri Sembilan. 1984 photo by author.

of this music was basically derivative and differed rather little in sound from the Western models, although Malay vocalization betrayed asli influence. During the middle and late 1970s, singers like D. J. Dave, M. Daud Kilau, Dhalan Zainuddin, Uji Rashid, Hail Amir, Latiff Ibrahim, and Khatijah (Kathy) Ibrahim were part of an assembly line supply of popular singers whose albums outsold those of foreign artists by a considerable margin.[59] Ahmed Nawab gradually developed into the foremost songwriter and producer, putting his romantic stamp forcefully onto Malay popular music. Rock groups such as Carefree, Black Dog Bone, and the Revolvers remained popular, although their music lacked the hard edge of many Western heavy metal or punk groups. The lyrics to popular songs of the 1970s dealt chiefly with romance and broken hearts.[60]

Popular Music and Political Change in the 1980s

Datuk Seri Dr. Mahathir Muhammed, a controversial nationalist, became prime minister of Malaysia in 1980, the first nonaristocrat to hold that office. His decade and a half in power has seen many political changes that have inevitably spilled over into popular culture. Mahathir had earned enemies in earlier years for what many considered inflammatory writings critical of both the Chinese and Malay conservatism. Mahathir adroitly handled global recession and adopted an increasingly anti-Western foreign policy, but by the mid-1980s he also demonstrated a determined—or autocratic to critics—leadership style with little tolerance for opponents. Although the National Front scored a sweeping victory in 1986 elections and controlled every state assembly, UMNO and several coalition partners were experiencing internal divisions and defections. Furthermore, the opposition won nearly half the popular vote—but only a sixth of seats.[61]

Mahathir faced several major crises, including corruption scandals and a violent confrontation between police and militant Muslims that some described as a Malay "spiritual crisis." In 1987, over a hundred government critics, including politicians and intellectuals, were detained at a time of rising ethnic tensions, a deep recession that had begun in 1985, growing unemployment, increasing government centralization, and an unprecedented leadership struggle in UMNO that posed a challenge to the prime minister. Most of the detained were later released, but four independent newspapers were closed as national leaders tightened their grip on the mass media. Malay social cohesion was cracking, with the new middle class of civil servants, professionals, and businessmen clearly asserting unprecedented influence and showing less deference to UMNO leaders.[62] Poet Muhammad Haji Salleh expressed the disillusionment felt by some toward self-promoting politicians and their empty rhetoric:

> *His voice teaches with the force of repetition . . .*
> *words flow into a flood,*
> *at times with no walls . . .*
> *conscience is divorced from the verbal river,*
> *guilt hidden by success . . .*
> *he is celebrated by melodious sounds,*
> *but entombed by his empty words.*
> *I do not recognize him now.*[63]

As UMNO split into pro- and anti-Mahathir factions based on personal rivalries and policy disagreements, Mahathir dissolved the longtime Malay standard-bearer and formed a new Malay party known as New UMNO (UMNO Baru). Mahathir's strategy succeeded—at least temporarily—in recreating substantial Malay political unity, while marginalizing his opponents. Nonetheless, the elite–middle-class consensus that had dominated since 1957 was clearly fragmenting, a reflection perhaps of a changing (more urbanized) Malay identity despite the symbolism of "traditional Malay culture" brandished by political leaders. But, despite evidence for the changing nature of Malay political culture, the 1987 developments were far less dramatic than those following the 1969 disturbances, a more seminal experience because of its multiethnic ramifications. By the mid-1990s, Mahathir remained in firm control of power and had succeeded in co-opting or outmaneuvering most opponents (including Islamic militants), as well as attaining widespread popularity due to economic prosperity.[64]

Under Mahathir and his predecessors, the federal government devised a National Culture Policy to mold a unified (and mostly Malay-derived) culture in a plural society. But the policy has been much criticized, especially by non-Malays who considered it assimilationist. It is used mostly to prohibit artistic developments considered undesirable. A government effort to revive bangsawan but with a more overtly Malay orientation was widely derided and had little success. And Malay critics argue the government has actually done little to preserve the rapidly disappearing traditional arts.[65] The policy is aided by the fact that the major National Front political parties directly or indirectly control nearly all the mass media, including the major newspapers and all radio and television. Many non-Malays have resisted or resented government attempts to build national unity and identity, such as increasing emphasis on Malay language in education and public life. Yet unlike during the colonial period, increasing numbers of non-Malays became fluent in *Bahasa Malaysia*, the medium of instruction in most secondary schools; English declined to secondary importance. A mass popular culture also spread throughout the country, often at the expense of local folk traditions. By the late 1980s televisions, stereos, and even videocassette recorders became nearly universal in the urban areas and increasingly common in the rural areas.

This highly eclectic popular culture in the form of films, television programs, magazines, cassettes, and records from the West as well as Indonesia, India, the Middle East, Taiwan, and Hong Kong attracts a large following and hence poses a challenge to the frequently embattled local recording, film, and publishing industries. Yet there have always been local artists, like P. Ramlee and Sharifah Aini, whose work reached a wide and sometimes multiethnic audience. In the 1980s singers like Sudirman became national celebrities with a mass audience, while rock groups like Kembara explored social issues as they integrated local and Western influences. The flourishing Malay comic book industry specialized in satire and parody of political and social affairs; current developments such as the split in UMNO and Islamic revivalism were well covered in their pages (at least before the crackdown of 1987).[66]

The historic tendency for foreign and Malaysian observers to emphasize pluralism neglects some common patterns of behavior and style that transcend ethnicity. The Malay cartoonist Lat, a sometime country-and-western musician, made a successful career and gained a multiethnic audience

Hundreds of shops and stalls selling music cassettes, often alongside mass circulation popular magazines, make mass-mediated popular culture available throughout Malaysia. This stall is in Ipoh, Perak. 1985 photo by author.

satirizing or revealing shared transethnic experiences and outlooks. He explored the obsession with food (for over a century restaurants and coffee shops provided an essential venue for social and business relations); the passion for sports (including badminton—in which Malaysians achieved international success—and the semiprofessional national soccer league); widespread usage of a local hybrid pidgin English ("Malglish"), containing many local influences; a tendency to return to hometowns and villages for holidays *(balik kampung)*; nostalgia for the simpler village life; and a common concern for family, friendship, and local community.[67] Pluralism has never been rigid and absolute, and this has been clearly reflected in popular culture.

Some observers consider the Malaysian popular music industry of the 1980s to have been banal, derivative, insufficiently quality conscious, and obsessed with churning out a commercially successful formula; one wrote in 1983 that "the local music industry still remains trapped in the doldrums of mediocrity, seemingly doomed to remain there forever."[68] Some critics believed Malaysian music badly needed a local identity.[69] Yet there were clear signs that the 1980s did bring more interesting and innovative ideas to Malay popular music, including the renaissance of social commentary and criticism songs. Malay music in that decade was arguably richer, more diversified, better recorded, and more intelligently produced than it had been a few years earlier.

A contributing factor was a political "thaw" that occurred during the late 1970s and early 1980s. While quasi-democratic Malaysia could hardly be considered a totally open society, the government regulation of

The Impact of Television in Villages

"When Pak Ali bought the TV set, he knew he was buying it for the whole kampung [village]. Most of the kampung folk of course cannot dream of owning or even renting a set. On Hindustani film nights the front room of Pak Ali's house is packed. The audience overflows down the steps and into the garden, for the kampung's 300 families are all Hindustani-film fans. The elders talk of religion and rubber, of politics and the new *penghulu* [village chief]. Though their eyes are fixed on the TV set, they keep up a dignified discussion, for they do not quite approve of the love scenes in the film. The women, sitting on the steps with babies in their laps, are frankly enthralled. Standing far back in the shadows are the kampung's young men and girls. There are very few, for most have gone off to town to chase the dream of a better life. "Modern Drama" night is different. Elders and young people alike get involved in the issues thrashed out on the TV screen—morality, parent-child relations, marriage and divorce, poverty—all hotly relevant to their lives. When a character in the TV play proses away against the new permissiveness, the elders nod their heads and pretend not to hear the rude remarks of the young, hissed from the darkness of the garden."—Sri Delima[70] political discussion and media content relaxed somewhat in these years. Newspapers, especially entertainment sections, gained more room for critical comment—although remaining careful to avoid excessive controversy. The new privately owned but government-influenced Television 3, with its strong Western orientation in programming, allowed for the televising of current Anglo-American popular music trends as well as the first Malay musical videos. Malay popular music came to include light doses of punk, fusion, reggae, jazz, disco, synthpop (synthesizer-based pop), new wave, heavy metal, and other contemporary Western styles. Still, Radio Television Malaysia has since 1959 maintained a blacklist of proscribed songs and recordings, and the government has occasionally prohibited concerts it deems musically or morally undesirable, especially those by local or foreign rock groups (among them the Scorpions and LaToya Jackson)—a situation spurred by vandalism after several rock concerts.[71]

Multinational record companies like Polygram and EMI seemed willing to allow for some experimentation by established stars as long as this proved profitable. However, unproven talents have tended to be channeled into safe, somewhat formulaic middle-of-the-road pop, dangdut, ballads, or new wave, usually with safe lyrical themes. Many of these albums can be labeled *rojak* (a spicy Malay mixed salad)—a bit of this, a bit of that, with little overall coherence, but aimed at a pluralistic audience. Musically, synthesizers and electronic keyboards became more prominent. The new trends and their implications were assessed in Fransissca Peter's synthesizer-driven 1984 hit, "Komputer Muzik."

Malaysia in the mid-1980s could boast of nearly twenty record companies—most of them locally owned—churning out some eight hundred new songs a year. This healthy competition for a growing consumer market stimulated a certain amount of creativity. Several of the smaller companies (especially Titra) seemed to thrive on controversy. Indeed, some believe that the smaller companies offer more scope for innovation than the giant multinationalist.[72] Yet these enterprises must also be obsessed with the profit margin, and most of the major socially conscious musicians recorded for multinational companies like EMI, Polygram, and WEA. In 1981 these three companies produced fifty-four of the sixty local albums released in Malaysia.[73] The market in Malay recordings boomed (although still small), and Malay cassettes—records had mostly been phased out by 1985—greatly outsold Western, Chinese, Indonesian, and Indian ones. Sales of thirty to fifty thousand legitimate copies of an album have not been uncommon; sales over a hundred thousand occur far more rarely. Yet pirated cassettes reportedly outsold legitimate ones by four to one in 1987.[74]

Many Western musicians have sold well or enjoyed wide popularity in Malaysia and have become heroes of local popular culture. Among others,

"Komputer Muzik" ("Computer Music")

"In times past life was difficult
Playing music was not easy
These times are so prosperous
Playing music has changed
Once before I wanted to buy a guitar
But I was poor, it was very hard
Now I have become rich
Buy a computer, discard the guitar
Press the button, computer music
Hear this sound, computer music."—Fransissca Peter [75]

Elvis Presley and Michael Jackson could boast active fan clubs in Kuala Lumpur during the 1980s; Madonna dress-alike contests replaced the Elvis imitator competitions of earlier years. Some Malaysian entertainers sought to emulate Western stars like Weird Al Yankovic (Isma Aliff) and Tina Turner (Sahara Yaacob). Indeed, Kuala Lumpur remains a center for American and British music with well-stocked record stores offering good selections of rock, pop, jazz, country and western, even punk and new wave. Country-and-western music became especially popular in urban pubs, with a half dozen Kuala Lumpur establishments featuring Singapore or Filipino groups specializing in the style. Malay pop music as well as films and magazines have generally found their major market in the smaller cities and rural areas of the country. Malaysian intellectuals occasionally bemoan the powerful Western influence on local culture, as well as the marketing strength of multinational recording companies and the dominant position of the Western—especially U.S.—mass media. But their criticism has not yet generated much response among the mass of Malaysians.[76]

Western influence is only part of the popular music story. Several Indonesian singers have enjoyed a large following, including Grace Simon, Endang S. Taurina, Rhoma Irama, and especially Hetty Koes Endang. There has remained a substantial rural market for Indonesian dangdut, and several Malaysian performers specialize in the style, although their material lacks the critical focus or controversy of Rhoma; but it has never been a mainstream genre and remains far more popular in Indonesia. Indonesian songwriters and arrangers occasionally work for Malaysian musicians, and some recording is done in Jakarta's well-equipped studios. Some local and foreign Chinese singers have sold well, as have a few Japanese and Filipino stars. Indeed, sales of tapes by Japanese stars like Mayumi Itsuwa, Momoe Yamaguchi, and Kitaro, as well as groups like Loudness and Shohjotai, increased 400 percent between 1983 and 1986, a reflection in part of the Malaysian government's

"Look East" policy to emulate Japan, a policy which has seen a growing number of Malaysians study the Japanese language.[77] Many shops also specialize in recording cassette tapes from imported Indian recordings for the local Indian market.

Yet despite the varied challenges, Malay music has risen to clear dominance, allowing more entertainers to establish or maintain a career even if only a few performers achieve enough consistent success to enjoy steady, comfortable incomes; among these were Sudirman, Sharifah Aini, D. J. Dave, and the Singaporean Anita Sarawak. Throughout the 1980s, the Malaysian musicians' union complained that despite government regulations mandating equity, local hotel lounges and nightclubs favored foreign entertainers while paying Malaysians inadequate salaries; by the late 1980s, local performing venues were decreasing in number.[78] Perhaps the most important reason for the increasing growth and innovation of Malay music has been the development of a non-Malay audience.[79] During the 1970s the government began to phase out Chinese, Indian, and English secondary education and require all students to study in the national language of Malay (termed Bahasa Malaysia). Universities also switched solely to Bahasa Malaysia. Malay has increasingly dominated public life and discourse. By the early 1980s a whole generation of Chinese, Indians, Dayaks, and Eurasians had become fluent or at least conversant in Malay, a language many of their parents understood poorly or not at all. At the same time many of them have lacked literacy, fluency, or even competence in the Chinese or Tamil spoken by their parents. Hence, the market for local or foreign Chinese recordings (mostly in Mandarin or Cantonese) has declined, hurting those record companies still maintaining Chinese divisions.

The prospects for Chinese pop musicians are mixed. There still remains a substantial market, especially among middle-aged Malaysian Chinese. During the 1980s several new local talents produced successful Mandarin recordings, including Robin, Kang Chao, Yao Yee, Janet Lee, Elaine Kang, and Jennifer Yen; furthermore, Timmy Koong (singing in Cantonese) introduced a more rock-oriented style. But there seems to be an inferiority complex about local talent that penalized musicians. Indeed, a section of Singapore youth developed a mania for Hong Kong and Taiwan pop stars like Jimmy Lim, Leon Lai, and Jackie Cheung that sometimes alarmed authorities, who feared that wasteful spending and idol worship by fans could be disruptive.[80] Competition for the modest rewards is intense, as most record companies have preferred to promote albums and concerts by popular non-Malaysians such as the Taiwanese Teresa Teng and Sarah Chen and Singaporeans like Maggie Teng, Tracy Huang, and Yueh Lei. In 1985, for example, an album by Sarah Chen outsold those by any foreign artist (over twice as many as Michael Jackson's *Thriller*) or of any Malaysians except the Alleycats.[81]

Increasingly, Malaysian Chinese musicians have had to record in English or Malay to prosper—as Jennifer Yen and Elaine Kang did successfully—or move to Taiwan or Hong Kong in order to break into those markets. The use and quality of English has also declined, reducing even further the limited demand for local English recordings. Apparently, Malaysians have not considered local English recordings to be up to international standards and prefer Western imports, while companies fear that the Malaysian accent of the singers will preclude their sales abroad.

The result of this shift is that many Chinese and Indian young people became familiar with Malay pop stars and often enjoy their songs because they understand the language. This trend has probably been most common in the smaller cities and towns, and in areas where Malay sociocultural influence is strongest—but it has by no means been absent in larger urban areas. Non-Malays have also played an increasingly important role in the Malay music industry—as songwriters, arrangers, record producers, and performers. This marks a return to patterns of the 1940s and 1950s when several Malaysians of Eurasian, Portuguese, or Filipino descent such as Alfonso Soliano (the first conductor of the Radio Malaysia Orchestra in 1957) and Jimmy Boyle wrote or arranged Malay music. A few non-Malays achieved limited success singing Malay pop songs in the late 1960s and early 1970s, including Andre Goh (a Malay-speaking Baba Chinese), D. J. Dave, and Helen Velu, as well as the prominent pop yeh yeh group, the Jayhawkers. But non-Malays were so rare that Chinese singer Mary Sia caused a sensation by singing in Malay over RTM in the early 1970s. By the late 1970s more non-Malays were performing and recording in Malay, a pattern that would increase dramatically in the 1980s.

By the 1980s non-Malays accounted for a sizable proportion of popular artists. For example, the Alleycats—an Indian and Chinese soft rock group from Penang—were the dominant Malaysian group of the decade, with many hits in Malay and the most consistent record sales. Although based in Hong Kong for several years, the Alleycats made use of compositions, especially ballads, by leading Malay songwriters. Their music blends Western folk and pop elements with local asli beats, and their following has transcended all ethnic and regional divisions. Other non-Malay bands such as Sweet September, Kenny, Remy and Martin, the Flybaits, Gingerbread, the Explorers, and Streetlights have often been among the best-selling groups. The music of Streetlights might be termed "Punjabi rock," a blend of rock, Indian vocalizations, and Malay lyrics. The most popular heavy metal group of the late 1980s and early 1990s, Search, included both Malay and Chinese members. Non-Malay singers like Fran Peter, Roy Santa Maria, Chris Vadham, Edmond Prior, Linda Elizabeth, Flora Santos, and the Indian female duo Cenderawasih ("Phoenix") all became prominent in Malay pop during the 1980s. Even some successful Chinese singers who normally record in Chinese have released Malay albums, including Elaine Kang, Angela Tang, and Sakura Ting. The ethnically mixed Asiabeat became the most important local jazz group, fusing contemporary jazz and Asian idioms. Non-Malays—including some women—became increasingly common as songwriters, record producers, and back-up musicians in the Malay music industry.[82]

In addition to the almost revolutionary move of non-Malays into Malay music, several other notable achievements characterized the 1980s. Many new talents entered the industry, with the result that the musical products are more diverse. Singers like the introspective Sohaimi Mior Hassan, the melodic Razis Ismail, the well-traveled Datuk Shake, the brooding Jamal Abdillah, the energetic Jay Jay, the jazz-oriented Sheila Majid, and the sensuous Fauziah Ahmed Daud joined the company of leading recording artists. Indeed, Sheila Majid had eclipsed Sharifah Aini as the major female superstar by the mid-1980s, and was even able to establish a successful recording career in Indonesia, a rare development for a Malaysian entertainer; she also toured in Japan and the United States. Rock and pop groups like the Revolvers, Blues Gang, Kembara, and Sweet Charity also rose to the top of the pop charts. A new male superstar emerged in the person of Sudirman Haji Arshad, a talented and creative entertainer who has come closest to matching the impact of P. Ramlee in popularity and versatility. Break dancing became a popular youth activity for a time, to the chagrin of conservative observers.

Another trend has been the inclusion of local themes in song lyrics, as well as the ability of some singers and groups to infuse their music with a local musical flavor, sometimes by updating or restyling folk or pop-folk (asli) songs. The success of M. Daud Kilau's "Cik Mek Molek," the Blues Gang's "Apo Nak Di Kato," and Ally Noor and Matsura's "Apo Keno Jang," among others, attest to the asli influence; the latter two songs radiate a strong Minangkabau flavor based in the folk traditions of Negri Sembilan state—where many are descendants of Minangkabau settlers from Sumatra. Malay musicians themselves have debated for some years whether Malay popular music can or should forge a local identity, with some advocating the more systematic integration of Western pop and rock with indigenous musical patterns and influences. A few even encourage a true Malaysian synthesis of Malay, Chinese, and Indian influences.[83]

At the end of the 1980s, composers like M. Nasir, Manan Ngah, and Zubir Ali began using the phrase *muzik nusantara* ("Malay archipelago music") or *balada nusantara* to refer to a pop music that incorporates not only Western and Asian music (including the use of indigenous instruments) but also African and Hispanic influences.[84] Musicians like Shequal and Zainal Abidin soon enjoyed some success by mixing local folk instruments like tabla, flute, and accordion with rock and world beat (especially African pop) rhythms, forging a creative synthesis that addresses local issues such as the erosion of traditional villages or ethnic ways. Hang

The Malaysian Break Dancing Controversy

"On a remote estate in the back of beyond, the heart of our rural hinterland, the First Malaysian Breakdance Fatality has occurred. Zulkifli shattered his 11-year-old spine on a plantation, a victim, we are led to believe, of the evil spread of Western culture. He should never have been allowed to see those movies and listen to that music. He should never have been coerced into believing that spinning around on his head was a valid statement of youthful exuberance. But perhaps Zulkifli wasn't trying to make a statement at all. Perhaps it never occurred to him to question whose culture he was aping. Perhaps all he wanted to do was have some fun by doing something exciting and thrilling and just a little dangerous. Cool, man! The main trouble with Western culture is that it's exciting. Western culture would not be able to get so much as a look in, if only it were possible to break your neck dancing the joget. Just think what Zulkifli's life could have been without the perfidious influence of Western culture. He could have read selected [approved] books, listened to selected music, watched selected programmes on television. He could have been molded into an exemplary Malaysian boy, with a keen awareness of his cultural heritage and the roots of his ancestry. He could have been made aware of the need for Cleanliness, Efficiency and Trustworthiness. Productivity, hard work and devoted obeisance to his elders would have become his guiding creed. He would gladly have accepted that the hideous enticements of Western Culture would do him no good at all, and he would have willingly subdued the dangerous parts of his growing intellect that demanded he find some way to dream his own dreams. Secure in his cultural isolation, guarded against the infiltration of alien movies, music and fashion, Zulkifli would have grown up to be a fine Malaysian; one who regarded his country as the undoubted center of the known universe. His loyalty would have been unquestionable and his ignorance profound."—Rehman Rashid[85]

Mokhtar utilizes Chinese tunes and syntax in some of his Malay songs.[86] But it remains to be seen whether the musical products of this approach will gain support or become commercially viable for any but a few pioneering musicians.

New songwriters who were talented, musically trained, and more sophisticated also emerged, such as Aimen, Itoh Mohammed, Kenny Tay, Khairil Johari Johar, Manan Ngah, S. Atan, and M. Nasir. Some of the writers boast an instinct for social reform and criticism similar to that of P. Ramlee. For example, S. Amin Shahab, an artist as well as writer, has used his lyrics to promote Islamic values and discuss the problems of modern living. He openly criticizes "meaningless love songs." His compositions for groups like Kembara, the Alleycats, and the Ideal Sisters are filled with meaningful, poetic messages.[87] Popular music (along with popular culture generally) came to enjoy much more media attention; even the English-medium press covers Malay popular music in detail and sometimes more critically than the Malay press.

Popular Music and Sociopolitical Criticism

If the conditions of the early and mid-1980s in Malaysia favored a more diverse and creative Malay popular music, they also promoted a more socially conscious music. Middle-class sociopolitical reform movements and organizations emerged to publicly discuss the problems of poverty, inequitable distribution of wealth, corruption, environmental destruction, and deficiencies of the National Culture policy. Government toleration made criticism or public examination of prevailing policies and attitudes more fashionable. The generally self-censored press gained somewhat more confidence to probe the edges of approved discussion. This toleration seemed to diminish, however, with the closing down of several papers in 1987.

Religious organizations as well as the militant dakwah (missionary) groups and religious-based political parties brought Islam into the forefront of public discussion, generating debate on the proper role of religion in Malay life, of Islam in a plural society, and of Islamic requirements on the activities and dress of women. By the late 1980s the major Islamic opposition party as well as some Islamic officials were calling for the banning of popular music as immoral and incompatible with any Islamic state that might develop. Hence, in 1986, the Association of Muslim *ulama* (religious officials) declared all forms of pop music, especially those derived from the West, to be *haram* (forbidden), and labeled all women who sang for a living as violating Islamic requirements for female modesty. Some villages dominated by the Parti Islam, which seeks to establish an Islamic state, have prohibited the distribution of newspapers and magazines carrying stories about popular music. Stage shows by pop singers, especially Malay women like Sheila Majid, are occasionally disrupted or protested as "morally degrading," sometimes at universities where militant Islamic student groups are influential. By 1995 the Parti Islam–controlled government in the conservative east coast state of Kelantan had successfully banned public performances involving singing and dancing, as well as carnival rides and traditional Malay—but pre-Islamic—cultural forms such as shadow plays, alarming those who favor multicultural tolerance.[88] One of the ironies of this situation is that some much criticized pop stars—among them Sharifah Aini and Sahara Yaacob—began their performing careers as Koran readers or *nasyid* (chanted Islamic poetry) singers. These tendencies greatly worried sociocultural liberals.

This highly charged atmosphere set the stage for the rapid growth through the early and mid-1980s of a popular music of social commentary and criticism. In this music, the previously unimportant lyrical content of songs came to the forefront as musicians used their talent to educate and to communicate ideas.[89] The prevailing political attitude of debate within carefully limited guidelines spilled over into popular culture so that some musicians were able to explore the fringes of tolerated debate and integrate observations on Malaysia's problems, prevailing lifestyles, and national identity into their songs in a nonmilitant, often oblique fashion. But potential government censorship—perhaps even detention—was always a problem for anyone too overtly critical and with the capacity to attract a large following, engendering caution. A true protest music for mass consumption has not emerged, and probably cannot develop, in the contemporary Malaysian political environment. But during the 1980s, mass-mediated Malay popular music became more diverse and also more socially conscious, even if few directly challenged government policies or priorities, dealing rather with broader societal problems like poverty, alienation, urban pressures, job monotony, commuter headaches, environmental destruction, and the future of the Malays.

For example, the eclectic, intellectual Malay rock group Kembara ("Wander"), whose guiding force and major composer was the Singaporean M. Nasir, produced six top-selling albums between 1982 and 1985. They appealed especially to urban youth—as well as some intellectuals—who found their laconic, questing songs full of meaning on the dilemmas of modern Malay and Malaysian society. The urban background of the members was clearly reflected in their songs and preoccupations, including a concern with blue-collar workers rarely voiced since P. Ramlee. In his sociological orientations, M. Nasir reminds some of Bruce Springsteen or the early Bob Dylan—his music has also been highly commercial—while his Islamic sentiments link him with Rhoma Irama. A former college art student, Nasir described music as art and the musician as a creative artist, with limitless freedom to experiment and create. He also stressed his intentions of reaching the audience with a message. Kembara had a fluctuating membership (mostly of Malaysians), but with Nasir as the constant center.

Their folk and country rock-oriented songs, which mix traditional dance beats, rock, and country, examine the ideology of the fried banana seller ("Simple Stall"), the social meaning of long distance bus stations ("At the Puduraya Station"), the frustrations of blue-collar workers ("Ballad of the Menial Laborer," "Blue Collar"), the destruction of Malay neighborhoods in Singapore ("Bus Number 13"), the failures of government economic policies, the worship of politicians ("At a Celebration"), the meaning of Malay identity ("Nusantara [Malay Archipelago]," "We Are Malay People"), the despair of urban life, the inadequacies of local journalism ("Newspaper Sellers"), and the problems of petty traders, school dropouts, the unemployed, the alienated, and aimless youth ("We Are the Children of this Era," "One-Way Street"). There is also a pronounced Islamic theme running through their recordings, especially in songs like "Perwira (Warrior)?" (which posits the prophet Muhammad as the force who can bring peace and togetherness), "Girl Wearing the Black Purdah Dress," and "Money" (which attacks materialism).

The sophisticated superstar Sudirman Haji Arshad was educated at the University of Malaya as a lawyer, but he was raised conservatively and impoverished in a remote east coast village. Although preeminently urban in his lifestyle and outlook, and reflecting the rootlessness of city people, he also expressed a particular sympathy for rural life and people. His songs often dealt with the problems of rural Malays migrating to the city and the frequently distressing realities of urban life such as alienation ("How Are Things, Village Boy?"), loneliness ("When Alone"), the punch-card mentality in the modern economy ("Punchcard"), and the monotony of factory work ("Returning from the Factory"), as well as the pleasures of urban existence such as the cosmopolitan street life in the Chow Kit Road area of Kuala Lumpur. Some of his songs also condemn racism ("Cool It!") and environmental destruction ("This Homeland Is My Land") or extol patriotism ("August 31") and the simple village life ("Simple Life/Old Bicycle").

Sudirman's approach to social problems was more positive—even romantic—and multiethnic than Kembara's and lacked M. Nasir's despair, but there was sometimes an element of gloom. In addition, his songs resonated with average people of various ethnic groups. Most of his twelve albums (two of them in English) between 1978 and 1987 sold well; many were theme albums, an innovation for the local recording industry. Both they and his flamboyant stage shows attracted many non-Malay fans and earned him the designation as Malaysia's top entertainer—the closest parallel to P. Ramlee in his success as well as his transethnic, multiclass appeal. Sudirman's secular, multiracial approach and eclectic, pop-oriented material made him a particular target of Islamic militants. Sudirman was a versatile man of many talents, also becoming a successful cartoonist and entrepreneur.

There were other significant voices as well. dR. Sam Rasputin, the son of a Malay policeman in Sabah, once busked his way through Europe. He developed into an eclectic and flamboyant entertainer somewhat reminiscent of Indonesia's great dangdut star Rhoma Irama, introducing a sort of rock-oriented Islamic reggae music he termed dangdut reggae. The fusion includes more reggae than dangdut, but it is an exciting eclectic, hybrid sound. The music is designed to spread the Islamic message while also com-

During the 1980s and 1990s Malaysia's growing urban middle class increasingly patronized nightclubs, pubs, and restaurants, some of which featured live music or karaoke. In Kuala Lumpur the suburb of Bangsar Baru became a center for such entertainment. 1985 photo by author.

"Kolar Biru" ("Blue Collar")

"There are people comfortably working at the office
They go in the morning and go home at 5 o'clock sharp.
There are those who work for wages but they do not like that
They are more satisfied doing
business, business, business, business . . .
Work, work, work
Blue collar, I am the blue-collar worker
Machines and machinery have become my companions
I am the blue-collar worker . . .
Work, work, work."—M. Nasir [90]

menting on local society and international politics. One of his best-known songs sought support for the anti-Soviet mujahideen rebels in Afghanistan ("Ya Mujahiddin"), while another is a chauvinistic tribute to Malaysians ("I Am a Son of Malaysia"). dR. Sam's eclectic style of musical missionizing earns him the criticism of Islamic purists. There is a certain contradiction implicit in his personality and music fusing rock and Islam, and his appeal is chiefly to urban audiences, where he has developed a cult following.

In contrast, the bohemian and raunchy Blues Gang blended John Mayall–style electrified blues and indigenous rhythms into a rollicking and unique sound for Southeast Asia. The multiethnic Gang coalesced in the southern city of Johor Bahru, and their sound is profoundly urban. College-educated Itoh Mohammed became their major songwriter and leader. Some of their songs comment about communal harmony, pollution, militarism ("Together We Unite"), the frustrations of daily life ("Yes, Well, Sure"), and the problems of the common people such as distressed urban migrants ("To the Big City"), while also celebrating Malaysian progress and ethnic diversity such as in their 1983 hit, "Khatul Istiwa." Their seven albums (two in English), released between 1979 and 1986, and their electric live performances (before sometimes chaotic audiences), earned the Malay and Indian band a multiethnic cult following among alienated urban and rural youth.

In the mid-1980s, the Chinese free-spirited maverick Kit Leee (M. Eeel) produced protest music most openly, with lyrics appealing precisely to the audience worried about Malay dominance, burgeoning problems, and an officially prescribed National Culture. His songs address uncaring bureaucracy, authoritarianism, environmental destruction, and official abuse of power. His most overt protest song, "City Hall," attacks the Kuala Lumpur city government for abusing poor hawkers, but it also constitutes a frontal assault on authoritarianism in general. But he sings in English, enjoys no mass distribution, issues his own cassettes (on which he usually plays all the instruments) of complex, avant-garde music with little popular appeal, and has attracted only a limited following, mostly among westernized urban intellectuals who follow the small but vibrant alternative music scene in Kuala Lumpur. Leee (whose real name is Lee Kit Fong) developed his bohemian ways while a high school exchange student in the politically turbulent and culturally vibrant United States in 1967–1968. Returning to Malaysia, he became a multidimensional talent (as a cartoonist, photographer, writer, poet, artist, and actor) and legendary eccentric who cheerfully rejects mainstream lifestyles and steady incomes for a rustic and uncompromising life in a remote hillside shack and complete creative and personal freedom.[91]

Leee's friend and fellow avant-garde dissenter, Rafique Rashid, has maintained a political focus and small but loyal following with pointed, often witty songs like "Lobotomy" (about societal "brainwashing"), "Khalwat" (a protest against restrictive Islamic social laws), and "Shut Up" (on the Internal Security Act, which allows arrest of dissidents). But he also sings in English and enjoys few recording opportunities, mostly performing in clubs or small concerts. Although less militant than Leee and Rafique, other musicians—most of whom record for small, local companies—have also sought to tap into the market for nonmainstream songs, such as: Titra, a Malay progressive rock group whose iconoclastic, sarcastic, and philosophical songs outrage language purists; Kumpulan Harmoni, which specializes in musical adaptations of poetry by group leader and literary figure Zubir Ali; and Hang Mokhtar, whose controversial topical offerings discuss problems of common

"Ya Mujahiddin" ("Ye Warrior of the Holy War")

"Your news I have read in the papers
Broadcast on the radio and on the TV screen
Where is the justice among mankind?
What is your sin that this would happen?
Ye Warrior of the Holy War . . .
You have lost all your rights, your life taken from you, too
Forced to follow all the wishes of Satan
Like your mountain you will always stand strong
Though you may be killed, your country will always remain
Torture of your life, enduring a rain of bullets
Like Vietnam, [you are] merely their toy
Don't ever think that you are weak
For the Koran is your guide
The living will go on fighting
Ye Warrior of the Holy War."—dR. Sam Rasputin [92]

"City Hall"

"City Hall, City Hall
Everybody says you can't fight City Hall
You can phone in, you can write
You can shout till you're blue . . .
You can sit up and beg
You can grovel and crawl
You can even keep on banging your head
Against the wall—but you know you can't fight City Hall . . .
You can't relax unless you pay a tax
You need a license when you walk
Need a license just to talk . . .
Need a license for your nose
Need a license for your toes . . .
Sometimes I feel like yelling
Go to Hell, City Hall!"—Kit Leee [93]

interest such as poor roads and highway tolls. Hang has been particularly adept at utilizing local slang and multiethnic influences to satirize local officials, such as his famous criticism of the unpopular minister of transport (Samy Vellu) for raising highway tolls to the detriment of commuters:

Ayo-yo Sami [Vellu]
People are distressed at this moment
Toll here
Toll there . . .
Can't you lower the cost of tolls?
Everyday we have to pay tolls
Soon, I will have used up all my pay.[94]

Singapore also saw some creative experimentation in the 1980s and 1990s, especially among several local musicians specializing in English songs.[95] One of them, Dick Lee, emerged as the most important local singer and composer in that medium and a major figure in the republic's popular culture, with songs that often deal with the mixed cultural context and confused identity of the plural society. Flamboyant, innovative, and multitalented—musician, choreographer, fashion designer, talk show host, theater stalwart—Lee has specialized in creating a distinctively Singapore sound and mood, integrating Asian genres into his commercial mix of jazz, fusion, electropop, and classical styles. His thoughtful lyrics—some utilizing Singlish—probe the realities and mythologies of Singapore life and culture, as in "Flower Drum Song," released in 1985:

We'll bring the people home . . .
Show them the heritage they don't know they seek.

Then there was the somewhat biting social criticism of "Culture":

Culture . . . teach yourself or have it fed into you day and night . . .
After all, culture's forced down your throat.

One of Lee's best-known songs, "Internationaland," criticized the middle-class materialism so prevalent in the city-state:

We are the children of the middle class
Growing out of childhood in a final dance . . .
Here we are the product of material things
Empty-valued carelessness vanishing
A bit too late; oh well, that's fate
Overdressed, we've never had the time to feel
Overdone in our attempts at overkill . . .
We, the mindless servants of society
Mimicking the public in self-parody . . .
Complacency and satisfaction is a crime
But not today—some other time.[96]

A 1989 song, much discussed in Singapore, was Lee's "Mad Chinaman," which explores the sometimes contradictory and bewildering feelings generated by growing up in the city's cosmopolitan environment:

Traditional, International
Western feelings from my oriental heart
How am I to know, how should I react?
Defend with Asian pride? Or attack!
The Mad Chinaman relies
On the east and west sides of his life.

Lee spent four years in London studying art and understands well the dual tugs of Western and Asian cultures.

There is also much local flavor in Lee's work. Hence his "I Am Baba" memorializes the long-established Chinese Peranakan community, whose mixed culture includes many Malay features, while "Mustapha" stresses the multilingualism so apparent in daily life. In fact, several Singapore artists have produced music reflecting the multiracial context of Singapore. For example, Chris Ho's "Buddy Buddy" mixes English and Malay words, while MC Siva Choy and the Kopi Kat Klan's song, "Why U So Like Dat," satirizes but also celebrates the widespread use of the Singlish patois. Some criticize the less attractive features of capitalism-driven, competitive, and assertive local behavior, such as the Wah Lau! Gang's attack on the win-at-all-costs mentality and fear of losing in their "Kiasu King." The same group humorously questioned the rigid laws and public campaigns resulting from the government's extensive social engineering policies:

I cannot spit, cannot litter
Chew chewing gum at all
I cannot fire crackers
And have myself a ball . . .
Cannot do this ah, cannot do that ah
If you do, you'll have no money [because of heavy fines].

Given the increasingly polluted and sterile Singapore environment, some musicians also offer "green" themes in their songs, although these safely focus more on global problems—such as ozone depletion and deforestation—than on specific local problems and policies. There are also some musicians who attempt to offer an alternative sound in their quest for freedom. *Big O*, a broad, popular culture magazine begun in 1985, became the platform for youthful exponents promoting local rock music as a means of liberalizing society. Perhaps the most popular group to come out of the movement was the confrontational heavy metal band Stomping Ground, which, like heavy metal generally, appealed mostly to a Malay audience; their songs addressed drug use and the environment. By the 1990s there were many bands singing in English, most of them mainstream but with a vibrant alternative scene as well, including punk, heavy metal, and folk. But most of the alternative musicians had to record their material outside of the established companies. There was some social criticism in these musics, with songs attacking greed, materialism, censorship, falsehood, and domination by an undemocratic elite. For example, the song "Money Isn't Everything," by Global Chaos, attacked:

Uncontrolled greed
Impetuous desire to be rich
Immune to wordly issues
Addicted to worldly pleasures.

So there was considerable resistance to official mores, often signified by band names like Rotten Germs, Bands of Slaves, and Corporate Toil. The Singapore government has quite purposefully used music (including music programs on television) as a vehicle to inculcate official viewpoints and ideologies. In response some waggish musicians in 1993 issued a songbook and cassette of parodies that satirize the official campaigns and pretensions, showing how music can become a subtle form of cultural resistance to hegemonic authority.

Contemporary Malaysian Popular Music

By the late 1980s and early 1990s, the Malay music industry was changing, with a flavor different from the earlier 1980s. Kembara broke up, with M. Nasir concentrating on songwriting and record producing. Several key members left the Blues Gang. Sudirman increasingly turned to other activities, including business and cartooning; his tragic death from pneumonia in 1992 marked the end of an era. Anglo-American pop music was once again ascendant, with the international recording companies increasing their promotion budgets in Malaysia.[97] Malay recordings by some of the more popular artists sell well, particularly now that the piracy problem—although by no means eliminated—has been reduced somewhat. But there is reportedly intense competition among the major companies for market share and a reluctance to gamble on innovative but potentially noncommercial talents.[98] For example, Fran Peter long chafed at the musical conservatism of the local recording industry, which resisted her desire to present a more jazz and rhythm and blues-oriented sound in her several successful albums, and bemoaned the difficulty of breaking into the international market from a Malaysian base, especially with the local reluctance to support English records by local singers.[99] Most singers have continued to concentrate on the sentimental ballads that always find a market among rural Malays.

But a harder-edged rock music also came to the fore. By the late 1980s and early 1990s, heavy metal groups had become the chief focus for expressing youth alienation from mainstream lifestyles and values, although the groups faced sporadic restrictions on their public performances. Local bands like Gersang, Headwind, Search, Ella and the Boys, and the Singapore-based Rusty Blade produced best-selling records and won music contests. In 1989 the heavy metal-tinged Search released the first music video by Malaysian musicians and also achieved success in Indonesia; their *Fenomena* album sold an astonishing five hundred thousand copies.[100] Kembara's M. Nasir produced their best-selling recordings. The success of Search came despite the arrest of several members on drug charges and the resulting departure of their lead guitarist, Hillary Ang. Heavy metal groups proliferated, playing a mix of local compositions and cover versions of Western numbers; discos staged battles of the bands, attracting enthusiastic teenage fans.

Several local heavy metal groups attempt to produce a music with some local flavor. For example, Purnama seeks to combine Western rock and Malay feel; their first album, *Materialisme*, recorded in 1990, criticizes materialism at the expense of human values. The popular and innovative group Lefthanded mixes heavy metal with Malay folk instruments (the *gambus*) and melodies on their first album in 1987. Following unrest at a Penang concert, they recorded "Keadilan" ("Justice") to warn fans to restrain themselves.[101] By the mid-1990s many new heavy metal groups had appeared, with names such as Silent Death, Infectious Maggots, Braindead, Deflowered, Silkhannaz, and Sludge, mostly singing in English; they offer brooding lyrics about death, hatred, and negativity. Their long hair and distinctive dress flout television codes, limiting them to live performance outlets. One Malaysian critic summarized their appeal as follows: "They're voices screaming to be heard, expressing extreme frustration about life. They express the problems of urban, cultural and sexual adjustments. I'd take them seriously."[102]

Whatever the nuances, heavy metal music appealed chiefly to frustrated urban blue-collar workers and unemployed youth, among them the alienated Malay youngsters known locally and pejoratively as *kutu* ("head lice"), who congregate around malls and affect a punk lifestyle. In some ways this evolving rock subculture provides a distinct challenge to the dominant culture and socioeconomic norms promoted by the state and Islamic purists.[103] It remains to be seen whether either heavy metal or the recently arrived rap have the capacity to do much more than ratify youth alienation and promote nihilistic escapism. They would seem, like much of Western rock, to represent rebellion against lifestyle options and values rather than governments or socioeconomic elites per se.

Other trends are also apparent. Former Sweet Charity leader Ramli Sarip (a Singaporean) achieved stardom as a bluesy hard rocker, record producer, and songwriter, perhaps the successor to Sudirman. Known as Malaysia's *rock raja*, Ramli left Sweet Charity in 1986, after sixteen years and seven albums. Sweet Charity's style was loud, longhaired music; in the mid-1980s they had been a necessary inclusion in any concert because of their attraction to youth. Originally modeling himself on Rod Stewart and Led Zeppelin, Ramli continues to sport waist-length hair. But the Singapore-based Ramli believed Sweet Charity could no longer compete in the heavy metal field with newer, hipper bands like Search and needed to change their sound toward a more moderate rock that might appeal to an aging audience. His solo albums are more in the tradition of M. Nasir, offering material for a wider audience. The songs are concerned with humankind's sins, making him a modern-day preacher attacking pretentiousness and self-delusion.[104]

Controversial "bad boy" Jamal Abdillah also returned to the top after several highly publicized incarcerations for cocaine use and a trial on immorality charges, developments that led to the periodic banning of his music from radio and television. By the mid-1990s the top male singer and musician was Zainal Abidin, a former member of the cutting-edge 1980s rock band

Headwind. Zainal's earliest solo recordings at the beginning of the 1990s utilized local instruments and stressed rural themes and the erosion of traditional culture. Later his music became notable for its world beat flavor, integrating African and Brazilian influences—unusual in Malaysia. His albums have also offered songs on environmental and nature themes, although he denies any commitment to the small and beleaguered local environmental movement.[105]

New female ballad singers have emerged to challenge Sheila Majid as female pop queen, including Fairuz Hussein, the first Malaysian to record a compact disc in 1988, Siti Fairuz, and especially Ramlah Ram, who rocketed to fame after winning a TV talent contest in 1985. Her second album sold an unprecedented 110,000 units in Malaysia, the most ever for a local singer.[106] Fairuz Hussein, the daughter of a director and an actress, began her career performing in pubs. A sophisticated singer in the mold of Sheila Majid, she was even able to record an English album heavy on rhythm and blues, a rare

Heavy Metal and Malay Youth Rebellion

"Their procession begins every Wednesday after the sun sets. Up the hill to a dusty outdoor stage behind the government television station they come by the hundreds, mostly young, mostly male, mostly Malay. They are called kutus and they have come to listen to loud rock music. 'Rock is our life,' a young man yells after the music begins. 'This is our music.' These Wednesday night concerts in the open air promise an escape for Kuala Lumpur's young and restless. With the strictures of Islamic fundamentalism pressing in on one side and, on the other side, the drudgery of working or looking for work in a place where the unemployment rate is more than 35% among 15–24 year olds, rock music offers relief: membership in the club of the kutus, Malaysia's version of punk rockers. Kutus and their music are the flip side of the resurgence of Islamic fundamentalism, a contrast to young men in Arab-style robes and young women in veils. Kutus emerged as the underbelly of this revival. Dakwahs [missionary Muslims] inhabit the universities and kutus inhabit the shopping malls. When being young and Malay means choosing sides between the club of the dakwahs at one extreme and the club of the kutus at the other, popular culture becomes a partisan pastime. Kutu culture, a provocative, challenging alternative, is a convenient target for what is at the root a debate over national identity. Banishment has not worked. Despite the restrictions on concerts and television appearances, rock—particularly heavy metal—music is more popular than ever. About 12 of the 15 albums released every month are by local heavy-metal rock bands. According to M. Nasir: 'We are all searching for what it means to be Malay in the modern world.' But why heavy metal? Because it's loud and it's got minor chords and it's offensive and it's a badge of distinction and it's got clothes to go along with it and it's only for young Malays and because dakwahs don't like it. The popular music scene is a mirror of some of the contradictions of modern Malaysia. According to one songwriter: 'We write about love but never about making love. We find a way to live with the contradictions.' "—Margaret Scott[107] treat for a Malaysian artist. She also enjoyed a hit song in Indonesia in 1988.[108] Little of this music betrays much local flavor, a trend reflected in television and radio programs emphasizing Western or Western-type pop.[109]

Most musicians still struggle to earn a living; they face a declining number of public performing venues, modest recording contracts, sojourning foreign competition, and the difficulty of breaking into foreign markets (local English recordings are still discouraged as unmarketable). This situation has led some musicians to move to the United States (Fran Peter, Anita Sarawak, Datuk Shake) or Australia (Roy Santa Maria) to seek wider opportunities and creative challenges. Peter, a bona fide star, attributed her 1989 migration to persistent frustration with the rigid formulae and modest pay of the local record industry.[110]

The status of Malay pop at the beginning of the 1990s was symbolized by Sheila Majid's 1990 album tribute to P. Ramlee, *Legenda*. The Ramlee songs are presented in an engaging, fresh, and technically proficient style but without much local soul; the rendition is too westernized to bring Malay music full circle from the pioneering days. Ramlee had borrowed heavily from abroad, but his music always retained a distinct Malaysian flavor; the indigenous and imported now seem increasingly incompatible. It could be said that the only truly "Malaysian" entertainers in recent years were those like Sudirman, Jennifer Yen, and Kathy Ibrahim who could sing passably in Malay, Chinese, and English; or Hang Mokhtar, whose music and slang-filled lyrics integrate many local influences. These performers demonstrated an inclusive vision that enhanced their shows. But there was only modest praise for these efforts, and they have not created a hybrid musical form mixing the varied influences.

In the 1990s rap came to Malaysia. The groups 4U2C and KRU developed a large following and successful tape sales among the young—especially teenage girls—despite a government ban on radio or television performances. An all-female group, Feminin, has also achieved some renown. The Malay-language music of these groups is value laden, attacking pollution, abandoned children, alcoholism, smoking, bad dietary habits, and other social ills, even though they carefully avoid more controversial topics that might result in increased government interference. But critics perceive them as too westernized and hence "un-Islamic."[111] Rap groups also appeared in Singapore, mostly offering material in English or Singlish that pokes fun at or explains Singapore life, like MC Silva Choy and the Kopi Kat Klan.[112] Compared to American gangsta rap, or even to the hard-edged rap popular among the underclass in Rio de Janeiro or Capetown, this seems pretty tame stuff, but it doesn't take much to raise hackles in Malaysia and Singapore's fragmented, delicately balanced societies.

The stagnation of mainstream Malay pop music paralleled the decline of the Malaysian film industry, which had been temporarily revitalized in the late 1970s and early 1980s. One of the highlights of that renaissance was Malaysia's first rock musical, written by M. Nasir. But official censorship has been a persistent barrier to creativity in films and television, although there was some easing of tolerated expression by the mid-1990s.[113] Excessive caution has had the same effect in popular music. While some of the contemporary artists record sophisticated albums characterized by instrumental innovation, talented songwriting, vocal prowess, and technical advances, the creativity and social consciousness of the earlier 1980s appears to be waning and Malaysian music, like Malaysian society, still seems in search of a viable, distinctive identity. Perhaps the same thing could be said for Singapore.

Conclusions

Many patterns deeply rooted in history, such as cultural resilience, a genius for adaptation, and the incorporation of foreign peoples and ideas, remained salient as Malaysians addressed the accelerating pace of change over the past few decades. Since 1963, their ability to create considerable national unity and an unusual degree of sociopolitical stability out of the complex divisions—while gradually shifting from a commodity-based agricultural economy to a newly industrializing one—has been impressive. The achievements are considerable, but often bitter disagreements over national priorities persist. It remains to be seen whether Malaysians can meet the challenge of continued development and stability through maintaining a diversified economic growth benefiting all ethnic groups, alleviating the causes of rural poverty, creating a stronger sense of common Malaysian consciousness, and fostering communal tolerance so that all Malaysians feel they have a continued place in one of Asia's most promising nations. But, as an ancient Malay proverb affirms, "it takes a long time to build a mountain." Similarly, Singapore must find better ways to balance rapid economic growth, increasing prosperity, and the perceived need for stability with enhanced personal expression and interpersonal tolerance.

A true mass-mediated—as opposed to informal street-based or underground—protest music for mass consumption has not emerged, and probably cannot develop in the contemporary Malaysian and Singaporean political environments. Much interesting music has addressed—sometimes obliquely—aspects of sociopolitical change, but the general framework of society discourages overt militant expression. Musicians like Kembara, Sudirman, the Blues Gang, Kit Leee, dR. Sam Rasputin, Dick Lee, and Hang Mokhtar, like P. Ramlee before them, were able to explore the fringes of tolerated debate and integrate observations on Malaysia's problems, prevailing lifestyles, and national identity but never overtly challenge authority and policies. Instead their songs address broader societal problems like poverty, alienation, urban pressures, job monotony, commuter headaches, environmental destruction, confused identity, and the future of the Malays. While some of these musicians have gained a substantial and sometimes multiethnic audience, they could not generate or help sustain the sort of politicization that a Rhoma Irama, Iwan Fals, or Caravan could. The heavy metal groups, although expressing a real anger, are even less able to play an activist political role since their music and audience are marginalized, alienated, and defined by lifestyle concerns rather than political commitments. Thus they lack connections to broader constituencies that might support progressive causes.

The Malaysian and Singapore cases illustrate that highly politicized music is certainly not universal, although musicians offering social commentary have been common. There was a relationship between popular music and sociopolitical change in Malaysia over the past four decades, especially in the 1980s. But the socially oriented music of groups like Kembara and entertainers like Sudirman and P. Ramlee constituted only one strand of Malaysian popular music in recent years, albeit an innovative and important one. Formulaic, light romantic songs have remained the norm. It should also be remembered that even the entertainers profiled here mixed their social commentary and criticism with romantic or introspective material such as Kembara's lyrical, melancholy 1983 commentary on the passing of time, "Musim" ("Season"), and dR. Sam Rasputin's 1984 hit, "Sayang, Oh Sayang" ("Love, Oh Love"). Compared to its neighbors, Malaysia has had relatively relaxed political conditions, especially between the mid-1970s and the mid-1980s. This, combined with a fairly high level of public satisfaction with—or apathy concerning—political and economic developments in an ethnically plural society, has meant that Malaysia would not produce militant or fearless counterparts to a Rhoma Irama, Freddie Aguilar, Caravan, Cui Jian, Bob Dylan, Bob Marley, or Fela, who emanated from more politically turbulent and economically fragmented societies. Nonetheless, the significance of popular music to Malaysians remains substantial. As the Singapore heavy metal group Rusty Blade notes in a song inviting their fans to "rock" their sufferings away:

Hey friends, don't be gloomy . . .
Let us sing together
Accompanied by our rock beat
Rock! Rock! Rock! Rock!
Forget what has happened.[114]

6

Conclusions

Rock is not art. But it is a culture,
a culture representing a way of life.
Possibly 99 percent of rock is rubbish, but maybe
in the 1 percent remaining can be found
the means to accomplishing rock's historical
mission—to promote the development and
evolution of Chinese culture. Anyhow, China needs
the spirit of rock—persistent, rebellious, critical.
China needs rock to push the actualization of
the people's true expression.

Underground samizdat essay in China.[1]

Music of sociopolitical commentary, criticism, and protest has played an important role in the popular culture of many Third World societies over the past several decades, and Southeast Asia is no exception. This was part of the broader process by which the mass media expanded in reach and complexity over the past half century. Most Southeast Asians had access to radios by the 1950s, if not earlier; by the 1990s, videocassette recorders and televisions were common possessions in the cities. The recording industry, a marginal influence before the 1950s, developed greatly during the 1960s and 1970s, with a proliferation of private and (in Indonesia) government-operated companies. The multinational giants soon became a powerful force in several countries, signing many top stars.

In this context of turbulent change and media development, mass-mediated popular musics developed and new styles proliferated, including derivative imitations of Western pop (Thai string and lukkroong, mainstream Malaysian and Philippine pop, much of pop Indonesia) and creative fusions blending indigenous traditions with external influences from the

West, India, the Middle East, or even the Caribbean (Indonesian dangdut, Malaysian dangdut reggae and balada nusantara, some types of Philippine pinoy, Thai luktoong and Songs for Life). Much popular music from North America, Western Europe, South Asia, the Middle East, Taiwan, and Hong Kong gained a mass audience and helped shape local styles, fostering a large amount of transculturation. Just as Southeast Asians always borrowed models from outside, selectively adapting desired influences into their own distinctive styles and beliefs to create a merging of the old and new to varying degrees, contemporary popular cultures—including musics—inevitably became a hybrid mix.

Popular music with a political focus emerging in modern Southeast Asia can therefore be seen in historical perspective as a response to the changes brought about by new forces such as colonialism, neocolonialism, capitalism, industrialization, and development. These broke up traditional cultural collectives and destabilized the social, economic, and political life of societies. At the same time, they introduced new forms of exploitation, sociocultural patterns, technologies, and mass-marketing techniques, all of which produced distress and hence dissatisfaction or protest among those not sharing in the fruits. As one of the most accessible media, the popular music industry inevitably became one of the few possible venues in which this protest and criticism could be presented, and the major practitioners inevitably became important voices in their own right. Music was always a social tool in many traditional and colonized societies of the region (e.g., the Indonesian wayang kulit and Malay bangsawans), playing a crucial role in fostering community cohesion while promulgating values and spreading information. Hence the rise of modernized forms should be seen in that context.

"Popular culture may be trivialized, often tasteless, and largely ephemeral," writes one observer, "but it is not meaningless. Obviously, its manifestations strike responsive chords in the populace; that's what makes it popular."[2] In some cases music has been profoundly political and militant, most clearly perhaps outside of Southeast Asia, in the songs of Nigeria's provocative Fela, reggae stars like Bob Marley, the Chilean New Song artists, and most notoriously among the African American rappers of the past decade, whose profane bitterness, antisystemic radicalism, and overt sexual warfare would be considered excessive by most Southeast Asians. The politics in the music of "cultural guerrillas" like Rhoma Irama, Iwan Fals, and Caravan can be easily perceived, but their work is less aggressive, angry, and direct. In many other cases popular music has been characterized by more subtle or less militant and localized lyrics but represents a political thrust nonetheless. Musicians like Carabao, Freddie Aguilar, and Kembara have simply been less confrontational and more circumspect, preferring to let the audience interpret the music in a critical manner; their music contains elements of signification.

The context is always a factor. Hard times, radicalism, anger, and alienation do not necessarily result in the same sort of response in different societies: "London in a recession produced the Sex Pistols. Kansas City in a depression produced Count Basie. Unemployment statistics do not explain the difference."[3] There may be some relationship between the severity of political repression and the militancy of the music, but the cases do not necessarily substantiate this. Indeed, militant music has thrived in relatively congenial political conditions (Thailand during the 1973–1976 thaw) and in repressive ones (the Philippines under Marcos).

In most cases the critical popular music clearly reflected the prevailing social, economic, and political conditions of a society and hence achieved a mass audience responsive to commentary on these conditions. Sometimes it was the only public expression of dissatisfaction tolerated or allowed by authoritarian governments (hence the debatable thesis that Rhoma Irama was the most significant spokesman for oppositional Islam). The argument that sociologist Jerome Rodnitzky makes for politically oriented music in the United States during the 1960s may also be relevant for Southeast Asia:

> Our best protest songs have indeed been a cleansing force. The songwriters have had the revivalist's faith that to hear of evil is to hate it. Their songs constitute a radical influence, but more importantly, they supply examples of conscience and principle to a society which has increasingly been unable to provide its youth with credible examples of either conscience or principle.[4]

Local, often derivative versions of Western rock have appeared, sometimes to express a particularly alienated reality and challenge the power of transculturated styles in the 1980s, particularly in authoritarian Indonesia and quasi-democratic Malaysia. These forms of national rock, like their counterparts in Latin America, China, and Eastern Europe, have inevitably played a political role in questioning the legitimacy of mainstream values and authority. Some Western observers have argued that rock music can generate a certain sense of empowerment, even if the feeling may be misleading and contrary to reality.[5] The evidence from Indonesia (Iwan Fals), Malaysia (heavy metal), and elsewhere would suggest that in some cases this does happen. Perhaps the fans of these musicians and musical styles gain some sense of empowerment that allows them to exercise control of their lives; it also enables them to "thumb their noses" at an Establishment that derides or fears that music.

Music as a form of symbol can also assist people in adapting to situations of powerlessness.[6] Undoubtedly the fans who copy the clothing styles of Iwan or Aguilar do so to make a statement, expressing their allegiance to the music and its message. It might be postulated that, in some respects, the popular music of social criticism and alienation functions as one of the "weapons of the weak" available to the disenfranchised or powerless, part of the constant and circumspect struggle of evasion and resistance waged ideologically and materially against the powerful.[7] Popular culture becomes the terrain of contestation, a dialogic process, with various forms of culture serving as means of expressing and embodying conflict between different classes and groups. The musical streams become commodified (sometimes heavily), but some of the audience clearly negotiate their own set of defiant or countercultural meanings from even seemingly nonpolitical music. People become active consumers. Perhaps as symbols the musicians express the collective power and energy of those who have perceived them as spokesmen, with their audience "decoding" their music to meet their own needs and expectations. Musicians present themselves as both observers of and participants in events.

Of course, popular music cannot be insulated from broader aspects of society and the ways in which socioeconomic change affects people. Musicians operate in a social context affecting their creativity. In some respects, as we suggested for Indonesia, their work becomes a rite or symbolic action of "modernization," inevitably resulting in social consequences.[8] Elsewhere I have argued that the attempt from the 1920s to 1990s by South African musicians (black and white, jazz and pop) to create an expanded sense of community across ethnic and even racial barriers suggests an effort at "imagining" new arrangements that could serve to bind this fragmented land where cultural boundaries constantly shifted. Hence music could potentially help "create" a new kind of society combining indigenous and foreign, black and white cultural elements.[9] Perhaps the same argument could be made for some of the pluralistic countries of Southeast Asia, with some popular musics linking the varied segments of nations still under construction. Attempts at nation building and forging national or sociocultural unity can be perceived in some of the songs of the Blues Gang, Sudirman, and P. Ramlee in Malaysia, Carabao in Thailand, and Aguilar and the Apo Hiking Society in the Philippines.

Many fear that westernization and commercialization gradually tend to undermine cultural diversity in popular music, a reflection of the real changes and processes occurring in most societies over the past several decades.[10] But these tendencies are probably more marked in some countries (Malaysia) than in others (Indonesia), and more common among the urban middle classes than the rural and urban poor, who will continue to constitute the great majority of the population in most Southeast Asian countries for the foreseeable future. Both globalization and particularism are at work, generating contradictory patterns.

Musicians, like writers, have had a role to play as active critics of society—as "guerrilla minstrels." In this role, popular music serves as a critical commentary on the processes of modernization, including the resulting trials and tribulations as well as achievements and promises. The leading proponents of politically oriented music in Southeast Asia and elsewhere have had many things in common. Some of them have been internationalists, propounding a theme of pan-Islamic, pan-African, or world proletarian solidarity against exploitation, although the universalistic themes are more common in Africa, Latin America, and the Caribbean than in Southeast Asia. Globally, musicians often addressed events beyond their borders such as the Vietnam War, South African Apartheid, the war in Afghanistan, or Central American revolution. This may be a necessary perspective in a world where the sun never sets on McDonald's. There is surely no unified "Third World outlook" spanning this diverse group of countries. But artists like Fela, Bob Marley, Trinidad's calypso stars Mighty Sparrow and David Rudder, Brazilians Caetano Veloso and Gilberto Gil, Chilean Victor Jara, dR. Sam Rasputin, and Rhoma Irama have all been able to view themselves as part of a larger, interconnected world. Even their songs on local or national themes often have broader relevance.

Perhaps the more intensely images express local reality and experience, the more global they seem to become. This may be not only because the matters they deal with have wide relevance and can be understood anywhere, but also because of the changed relationship between the local and the global at a time when the means of mass destruction are targeted from thousands of miles away—when a decision made in New York or Tokyo can put people out of work in Malaysia or the Philippines. Suffering is localized while responsibility for it dissipates or escapes into the intangible global systems of capitalism and imperialism. No longer can most societies be seen as self-contained, authentic, meaning-making communities; rather most cultures are partly derivative and mutually entangled, enmeshed in the complex, power-laden relations between local worlds and larger systems.

Transnationalism has become an influential force in the world, enveloping both material forces and social space. Because of the deterritorialization of culture, people widely separated in geography can be linked by shared cultural or consumer experiences, many of them provided or constructed by the mass media. The interplay between the local, national, and global hence becomes highly complex and dynamic, with the village or city, nation-state, and world economy interlinked. In this reality, as Guy Brett has argued, the old norms of geography and nationhood are broken through.[11] Nobody is marginal anymore.

There are other patterns that link political musicians in Southeast Asia with each other and their counterparts around the world. Many of them have been motivated by some sort of religious vision, whether it be the Rastafarian faith of Marley, Fela's Yoruba gods, the Christianity of Nigerian juju artist Chief Commander Obey, the Afro-Catholic syncretic cults of Brazilian artists, or the Islam of Rhoma, Kembara, dR. Sam Rasputin, and the Nigerian fuji/apala stars. This religious underpinning has contributed to their political goals. In some cases the faith is a minority belief, well out of the societal mainstream and hence persecuted, marginalized, or derided. For some (Rhoma and dR. Sam), their personal and musical identity was closely tied to Islam as a global force. Several reflected a Marxian-inspired worldview or activist agenda (Caravan, Fela, Joey Ayala, Heber Bartolome, Inang Laya). Some of the musicians have paid for their political activism or commentary with jail or detention (Fela, Rhoma), physical assault (Fela, Marley), assassination (Jara and Jamaica's reggae star Peter Tosh), enforced exile (the New Song survivors, Fela, the Songs for Life groups with the rural-based insurgency), official harassment (Rhoma, Fals, Malaysian heavy metal bands, Chinese rocker Cui Jian, many East European rockers), political persecution (Fela, Caravan, Rhoma), or censorship.

Most of them appealed to populist anger against a corrupt, unresponsive, or exploitative establishment. They came to symbolize for millions of fans political independence from or opposition to established political or socioeconomic power. Most came from humble socioeconomic backgrounds, with Guruh Soekarno and Joey Ayala notable exceptions. Some were well educated (Fela, Jara, Ayala, Apo Hiking Society, M. Nasir, Sudirman, Dick Lee). Their music has appealed to a largely disadvantaged population, although some (Jara, Caravan, Aguilar, Ayala, Fals, Kembara, Kit Leee, Dick Lee) achieved popularity with the middle classes, especially university students. Some were influential in the development of particular musical styles, but these styles (whether pop, rock, or folkloric) held little appeal for political or socioeconomic elites. Rather they found their mass audience in the poverty-stricken slums or on the campuses of Jakarta, Bangkok, and Manila, just as their peers elsewhere developed followings in Kingston, Santiago, Lagos, and other large cities.

Much of their music is also danceable, despite the political themes, raising the question about how much of the political message actually reached the audience. The ultimate political impact is certainly debatable. Fela's provocative fulminations, far more militant than anything in Southeast Asia, have not visibly undermined Nigerian governments—although his travels had made him an international cause célèbre who challenged government legitimacy. Chilean New Song and the Songs for Life musicians could not prevent a right-wing backlash that destroyed their causes; indeed, it could be argued that their activities helped polarize society and hence generate the counterrevolution. At best the political impact has been indirect: contributing to the subversion of an unpopular government (Philippines), fomenting or accelerating public disillusionment (Indonesia, Vietnam, China, Russia, Nigeria), rallying support for progressive movements (Chile, Philippines, China, Burma), electing a reformist government (Jamaica, Philippines), or simply calling attention to unpopular or "sensitive" issues (Malaysia, Thailand, Indonesia).

Although the musicians sometimes failed to fulfill expectations and perhaps enjoyed a certain power or prestige based more on hope than achievement, they helped to clear away the stereotypes and have created a new image of the people. Music, like art, became a means of communication in which facts are not separated from feeling, in which musicians present themselves as connected to events both as observers and participants. Their music gives structure and coherence to the intangible or inchoate. It is hard to accept the Frankfurt argument that their music should be perceived largely as a mass-mediated, diversionary reinforcer of the power structure that is chiefly neocolonial in form, shaped mostly by the imperatives of cultural imperialism.

Pop music has also played an important role in shaping, sustaining, or articulating subcultural identity in many countries (e.g., Sundanese jaipongan, Pop Batak, Isan-based luktoong, Iban pop, Hawaiian, Vietnamese emigrant, Nigerian juju, fuji, and apala). Some musics represent particular socioeconomic classes (e.g., kroncong in its early phase, dangdut, luktoong) in contrast to and even defiance of the westernized musics and values of the urban middle classes. Indeed, the class identity of a music sometimes transcends ethnicity, as with dangdut. Political and social conflicts have resulted from the fact that there exist multiple views of what the national identity or culture ought to encompass and how it should be defined. Diverse social actors promote their own cultural representations, some more powerfully than others (e.g., the Malaysian National Culture policy). On a broader scale, pop musics can also support ethnic-national identity (Brazilian samba, Trinidadian calypso, New Song, pinoy, Malaysian heavy metal).

All over the world, music has been increasingly used as a vehicle for social and political comment since the 1950s, becoming a widespread voice of protest and resistance (e.g., Jamaican reggae, calypso, New Song, Brazilian MPB and samba, Nigerian juju and Afrobeat, South African mbaqanga and township pop, dangdut, Songs for Life, pinoy). Rock became a major force for resistance to authority at various times in the Anglo-American realm, the Soviet Bloc, China, Malaysia, and Burma, among other places. There is always the potential for progressive politics even though the dominant component of popular music concerns romantic or other themes that divert attention from sociopolitical realities. The music apparently has had a dual function: sometimes as a hammer that forges society, and sometimes as an entertaining opiate; sometimes as a challenge to the system, sometimes as a diversionary reinforcer of it. It can stimulate and educate—but also pacify and inculcate. Many times it does these simultaneously, as can be seen in the way the Marcos regime exploited the cultural nationalism of pinoy for their own benefit, Thai authorities exploited Carabao for nationalist purposes, and the New Order eventually co-opted Rhoma Irama into supporting GOLKAR. Some would argue that dissent in pop music is usually illusory, at best a safety valve that defuses and diffuses resistance tendencies. Cultural studies scholars (as in the approach of John Fiske) may sometimes be too anxious to identify resistance to hegemony, to read everyday activities as examples of resistance or even rejection. Their approach runs the danger of uncritically romanticizing the oppressed and demonizing the powerful.

In Southeast Asia as elsewhere, commodification and commercialization have been significant forces, with the music industry (and careers of musicians) greatly influenced by the recording companies—whether it be the powerful transnationals in Malaysia or the monopolistic "Glodok Mafia" in Indonesia. Formulaic conventions with commercial appeal (the Malaysian "no love, no sales" principle) can constrict musical possibilities. These forces helped shape but have not completely controlled musical production. Nor were industry efforts always reactionary and uncreative (e.g., major multinationals released Kembara's, Dick Lee's, and Aguilar's pathbreaking work). There has always been something more than commodification at work, or the music could not touch or stimulate audiences to the degree that it clearly has. And the spread of cassette technology holds out some hope for increased democratization or at least decentralized diversity of popular musics. Time and again musicians and their audiences find some room to maneuver, while some profit-motivated companies are often willing to support popular antimainstream music and artists, suggesting that hegemony can never be completely enforced.

At times the potential for change was certainly significant enough that power holders cracked down, as has happened sometimes in Indonesia and Thailand. The military-dominated Burmese regime has restricted popular music as much as possible, but their efforts have been only partly successful. Similarly, the communist government in Vietnam alternately tolerates and prohibits the plethora of rock musicians that have emerged in the past decade to offer a critical commentary on the failures of the nation and society. In Malaysia, Singapore, and the Philippines, potential government censorship—even detention—has been a constant or at least occasional threat to those too publicly critical, engendering caution and self-censorship among artists and their recording companies. The state or political-economic elites have attempted, with some success, to co-opt musical forms like pinoy or dangdut. Songs that support nationalist aims ("American Junk," "Made in Thailand") or exhort patriotism ("I Am a Son of Malaysia") can be construed as somewhat hegemonic in that they buttress some power holders (public or private) and political policies. But while this compromises the independence of the musicians involved, it has not necessarily defused them as critical—even oppositional—forces. There are always gatekeepers of some sort—in the recording industry, the broadcast media, or government—even if they are not necessarily decisive in channeling popular culture along desired lines. Hence the practices of musical production are always political, with the potential to deflect or defuse criticism but also to subvert authority or raise consciousness.

Politics and popular music have related to each other in many ways, both profound and subtle. In Southeast Asia the music of superstars like

Rhoma, Fals, Aguilar, Caravan, and Carabao inevitably reflected and articulated the views of substantial segments of society. In many respects they also provided an oppositional discourse on national or international affairs, sometimes in conjunction with powerful sociopolitical movements such as the agitation for Thai or Philippine democracy. It would seem that the contested turf of popular music does reflect a complex interplay between corporate elites, governments, musicians, and the audience to establish meaning. Certainly many of the musicians discussed here have consciously attempted to use music as a political tool, with some success; but their songs may also at times have unwittingly served regime and elite ends as well. Their music has dealt with both national and subnational concerns within the broader international context, as well as with particular domestic problems and issues, but their musical styles were invariably held in contempt by the elites.

The influence of these musicians can easily be overemphasized. In no Southeast Asian society did politicized popular musicians have anything like the impact of their counterparts in Jamaica, Trinidad, Chile, Brazil, or Nigeria. Aguilar's songs contributed to the "peoples power" mobilization but were hardly among the most crucial factors in forcing Marcos into exile. Nor could Songs for Life groups do much to prevent the repression of 1976. And Rhoma's support may have boosted but hardly guaranteed the success of Islamic political groups. Most likely the Malaysian government could safely ignore pop musicians (seldom more than a minor irritant), but it never seemed able to adopt a consistent policy of "benign neglect" because of the delicate balances in the society. Ultimately, more than music is necessary to generate fundamental change; it can establish an atmosphere favorable to change, but organized political action is the necessary catalyst.

In surveying various radical cultural movements throughout Western history (from Dadaists to Leninists to Garveyites to "beatniks" and "hippies"), Jerold Starr has summarized the crucial interface necessary for democratizing lifestyles, relationships, forms of aesthetic expression, and other aspects of society:

> Despite important gains, such movements have failed to produce the deep and lasting transformation needed. It has become apparent that the complete revolution must be one that takes place both in the sphere of culture and in the sphere of politics, one that is concerned with personal relationships and morals as well as power and wealth. Movements that have aimed for only cultural change have been vulnerable to co-optation by the corporations or repression by the state. Movements that have aimed for only political change have sometimes seized power, but have failed the revolution by reproducing the established culture of domination.[12]

These movements were considerably more "countercultural," purposive, and challenging than anything emerging in the nations surveyed in this study. Furthermore, the simultaneous political and cultural revolution that transformed China and Vietnam under communism did not ultimately push aside the entire weight of tradition, even if some significant modifications were made in social hierarchies and values. Indeed, revolutionary values have been visibly crumbling in recent years, challenged by new cultural and economic currents. In countries experiencing evolutionary rather than revolutionary change, pop music can be significant but is rarely decisive in stimulating resistance and rebellion; co-optation or diversion is just as likely. But without the music, the task of promoting change might be much more difficult.

It is tempting to speculate that some of these popular musics and musicians will collectively confront and perhaps even diminish Western cultural domination, helping decolonizing people to discover their own musical roots while simultaneously concocting new musical hybrids. Such a process might help them to redefine and reaffirm their own cultures. Yet the processes at work are complex, the extent of cultural imperialism, globalization, and hybridization differs among the cases, and—except perhaps for dangdut and luktoong—none of the musical streams with strong traditional roots seems to have established any endurance as a popular art. There is a danger, of course, in making the links between music and musicians in different societies and realities, for it threatens to dilute what is powerful, significant, and unique in each. The differences are many, not the least of which may lie in the intentions of the artists.

But, as a general proposition, the evidence would seem to suggest that popular musics and some leading musicians have played a notable political role, interacting with political forces, and have constituted a major vehicle for political commentary—sometimes even of criticism and protest—in societies that lack a myriad of other outlets open to all. A popular song by Kembara, "Kami Anak Zaman Ini" ("We Are the Children of This Era"), offered the fiery spirit of resolution and concern that seemed to motivate them and many of their musical colleagues in the region:

We are the children of this era
Inheriting a spirit so pure
Working with determination
For peace . . .
This is the time for us
To unite and succeed.[13]

Notes

The note references are in a concise form, with abbreviated titles. The complete details of each reference can be found in the relevant section of the bibliography. The bibliography is divided into five sections. The first lists general and regional works (including national studies on countries not receiving chapter-length coverage); the other four sections cover Indonesia, the Philippines, Thailand, and Malaysia-Singapore.

Introduction

1. From the song "Tarian Hidup" ("Dance of Life") in Kembara's album *1404 Hejira* (Philips 822826, 1984). Translation by Craig Lockard, with help from Azlina Ahmed.
2. See " 'Get Up, Stand Up.' "
3. See Handler, "High Culture," 818–824.
4. There are a few exceptions. For example, see Hill, ed., *Indonesia's New Order;* Hooker, ed., *Culture and Society in New Order Indonesia;* Kahn and Loh, eds., *Fragmented Vision: Contemporary Malaysia;* Peacock, *Indonesia;* Pasuk and Baker, *Thailand.*
5. See Manuel, *Popular Musics*, 10.
6. *Window on Hongkong*, iii.
7. For example, see Dissanayake, ed., *Cinema and Cultural Identity.*
8. *Music for Pleasure*, 1.
9. Iain Chambers, "Review of Frith, *Music for Pleasure*," 322.
10. *You Say You Want Revolution*, 5.
11. Quoted in Marre and Charlton, *Beats of the Heart*, 9.

12. From Jara's song "Manifiesto" ("Manifesto"), translated in liner notes to *Chile Vencera! An Anthology of Chilean New Song, 1962–1973* (Rounder Records 4009/4010).
13. From the album *Cry of Vietnam* (Fellowship of Reconciliation).
14. For more on the cases summarized here, see Lockard, " 'Get Up, Stand Up.' "
15. "Kerontjong and Komedi Stambul," 41–50.
16. Ramedhan, "Disco Way of Life," 16–19; Becker, "Kroncong, Indonesian Popular Music," 14–19; Kornhauser, "In Defence of Kroncong," 104–177.
17. Frederick, "Rhoma Irama and the Dangdut Style," 103–130. The literature on African popular music is vast; some of the major books include: Barlow and Eyre, *Afropop!;* Bender, *Sweet Mother;* Bergman, *Goodtime Kings;* John Collins, *Musicmakers of West Africa* and *West African Pop Roots;* Coplan, *In Township Tonite!;* Erlmann, *African Stars* and *Nightsong;* Ewens, *Africa O-Ye!;* Graham, *Da Capo Guide to Contemporary African Music* and *World of African Music;* Kivnick, *Where Is the Way: South Africa;* Roberts, *Black Music of Two Worlds;* Stapleton and May, *African Rock;* Stewart, *Breakout: Profiles in African Rhythm;* Thomas, *History of Juju;* Waterman, *Juju: African Popular Music.*
18. *Popular Musics*, 198–220.
19. Steinberg et al., *In Search of Southeast Asia, 460.*
20. See *Reflections of Change: Malaysian Popular Music*, 1–112; "From Folk to Computer Songs: Malaysian Popular Music," 15–40; " 'Hey We Equatorial People': Popular Music in Malaysia," 11–28; "Popular Musics and Politics in Modern Southeast Asia," 149–199.
21. See "Woody Guthrie," 237–244; essays on Miriam Makeba, Theodore Bikel, Ramblin' Jack Elliott, and the Limelighters in the *New Grove Encyclopedia of Music in the United States* (New York: Grove, 1987); essays on the Almanac Singers, Harry Belafonte, Calypso, Bill Haley, Buddy Holly, and Pete Seeger in Ray Browne, ed., *Encyclopedia of American Popular Culture* (ABC–Clio, forthcoming).
22. I wrote about this experience and the folk tradition in "Letter from Meixian."
23. For a recent expression of this point, see Shepherd, "Music, Culture and Interdisciplinarity," 127–142.

Chapter 1: Popular Culture and Music in the Modern World

1. "Malaya Blues," from their album *Living It Up* (WEA 2292-50398, 1984).
2. Based on United Nations, *Industrial Statistics 1991,* 774–783.
3. *World Record Sales*, 71.
4. McLeod, "Seamless Web," 69.
5. Kato, "Some Thoughts Japanese," xvii–xviii.
6. For example, see Levine, "Folklore," 1369–1400; King, "Popular Culture," 26–34; Lewis, "Commercial," 142–156.
7. See Hinds, "Popularity," 1–13; Abdul Majid, *Popular Culture*, 112–113; Lewis, "American Popular Culture," 3.
8. Lewis, *Sociology of Popular Culture*, 1.

9. For example, see Burke, *Popular Culture.*
10. See some of the essays in Powers and Kato, eds., *Handbook of Japanese Popular Culture.*
11. Abdul Majid, *Popular Culture,* 117. On India see, for example, the essays by B. Ramesh Babu, Issac Sequira, and Indra Deva in *International Popular Culture,* 2/1 (Spring-Summer 1981), 2–21. Some other Malaysian scholarly views on popular culture generally include: Wan Abdul Kadir, "Kebudayaan Popular," 14–16; Abdul Majid, "Popular Art," 60–79.
12. *Prime-Time Society,* 2–5. See also Irwin, *Communicating with Asia,* 123–128.
13. See Heidt, *Mass Media,* 232.
14. See Associated Press, "Italian Radio Station"; Lorch, "To Find Happy Ending."
15. *Time Passages,* 13.
16. See Manuel, *Cassette Culture,* xiii.
17. For example, see Schwichtenberg, ed., *Madonna Connection*; James, "Empress," 7; Wilson and Markle, "Justify My Ideology," 75–83; Holden, "Selling Sex."
18. Quoted in Browne, "Popular Culture," 17. See also Combs, *Polpop,* 8; McLeod, "Seamless Web," 69–75: Cushman, "Rich Rastas," 23; D. Fernandez, "Philippine Popular Culture," 41.
19. See Combs, *Polpop,* 10–11, 33.
20. See Diamond, "Fiction," 435; Wagley, *Introduction to Brazil,* vii, 247–253, 259–262, 266–270; Dickenson, *Brazil,* 185–190; Weil et al., *Area Handbook Brazil,* 192–193.
21. Quoted by Gerald Graff in *New York Times,* December 9, 1990.
22. "Afterword," 316.
23. Ahmed, "Bombay Films," 289.
24. See the following works on India: Coppola, "Politics," 897–902; Arnold, "Aspects," 122–135; Arora, "Popular Songs," 143–166; Hunt, "Romance Film," 44–45; Skillman, "Songs," 149–158; Barnouw and Krishnaswamy, *Indian Film,* 172–191; Hardgrave, "Politics," 288–305; Dickey, *Cinema*; Singh, "Indian Cinema," 16–18; Cooper, "Hindi Film Song," 49–65; Chakravarty, *National Identity.*
25. Quoted in Marre and Charlton, *Beats of Heart,* 150. See also Manuel, *Cassette Culture,* 40–47, 258.
26. See Thayil, "Mob," 39–45; Cooper, "Hindi Film Song," 50.
27. See *Far Eastern Economic Review,* May 10, 1984 and April 10, 1986.
28. On Indian film stars in politics see, for example, Pandian, *Image Trap*; Marre and Charlton, *Beats of Heart,* 150; Hardgrave, "Politics," 288–305; Das Gupta, "Painted Faces," 127–148; H. McDonald, "Double Features," 46–48; Ahmed, "Bombay Films," 289–320; Forrester, "Factions," 283–296; Crossette, "Star-Studded India." For the Philippines see Tasker, "Real-Life Drama," 48–50. On Latin American cultural figures and politics see Associated Press report in *Green Bay Press-Gazette,* November 20, 1988.
29. See, for example, Sakamaki, "Bring on Clowns," 16; Shim, "Politics as Unusual," 24.

30. See Lewis, "Preface," xi; "The Press Conference: John Lennon"; and Wiener, *"Give Peace a Chance,"* 11–26.
31. On Plato's views of music see Pratt, *Rhythm and Resistance*, 2–3, 9–10.
32. See, for example, Wiener, *Come Together*.
33. See J. R. McDonald, "Censoring Rock Lyrics," 294–313; Jefferson, "Real Dirt"; Marsh, *Louie Louie*.
34. *Closing*, 68–81.
35. Kleden, "Pop Culture," 3–4.
36. See Rattanavong, "Lam Luang," 189–191; Boyd and Pathammavong, "Contexts," 131–148.
37. *Popular Culture*, vii–xi, 20–27. See also Kleden, "Pop Culture," 5–6.
38. Mukerji and Schudson, "Introduction," 53, 2–4.
39. *Mass-Mediated Culture*, viii.
40. Thompson, *Ideology*, 3–4. See also Real, *Mass-Mediated Culture*, xi; Parenti, *Make-Believe*.
41. See, for example, Hinds, "Popularity," 3. For a recent dialogue on power relationships and the meaning of popular culture in the United States, see the essays by Lawrence Levine, Jackson Lears, Natalie Zemon Davis, and Robin Kelley in the *American Historical Review*, 97/5 (December 1992), 1369–1430.
42. *Uncommon Cultures*, 7.
43. Quoted in Robinson et al., *Music at Margins*, 11. For a brief summary of the "Frankfurt school," see Bennett, "Theories of Media," 30–55.
44. Quoted in Vulliamy, "Re-Assessment," 131.
45. *Synthetic Culture*, 36.
46. Inglis, *Popular Culture*, 238.
47. *Cassette Culture*, xv, 9.
48. Quoted in Angus and Jhally, "Introduction," 3.
49. See Brennan, "Masterpiece Theatre," 373–383.
50. *Rhythm and Resistance*, vii.
51. "Notes on Deconstructing," 233.
52. "Notes on Deconstructing," 228.
53. S. Hall, "Notes on Deconstructing," 236; S. Hall, "Culture, the Media," 340–341, 346; S. Hall, "Encoding/Decoding," 128–138.
54. Mukerji and Schudson, "Introduction," 15; Gitlin, "Television's Screens," 240; Lazere, "Introduction: Entertainment," 7; Slobin, *Subcultural Sounds*, 27.
55. On this point see R. Williams, *Marxism and Literature*, 112.
56. "Television's Screens," 241–242.
57. Gitlin, "Television's Screens," 243. See also Lazere, "Introduction," 233–234.
58. Weber, "PC?" 13.
59. Collins, *Uncommon Cultures*, 18; Levine, "Folklore"; R. Williams, *Marxism and Literature*, 108–114. See also Lewis, "Who Do You Love?" 145.
60. Fiske, *Understanding*, 25. Fiske's views are summarized from *Reading* and *Understanding*.
61. See, for example, Chambers, *Popular Culture*.
62. *Culture, Inc.*, 156. See also Cushman, "Rich Rastas," 17–62.

63. See Modleski, "Introduction," xi–xii, xvi; Gendron, "Theodor Adorno," 34–36; Tetzlaff, "Divide and Conquer," 23.
64. *We Gotta Get Out*, 2. See also Ramet, "Rock: Music of Revolution," 3–4.
65. *Arabesk Debate*, 1.
66. Maceda, "Music in Southeast Asia," 88.
67. See, for example, H. Powers, "Classical Music," 5–39; Racy, "Music in Cairo," 4–23.
68. Isaku, *Mountain Storm*, 1–5.
69. See Ranade, "Popular Culture," 22–27.
70. See, for example, Robinson et al., *Music at Margins*, 10; Cooper, *Images*, 4–5.
71. See, for example, Cutler, "What Popular Music," 3–12; Fiori, "Popular Music," 13, 15.
72. See, for example, Wicke, "Popularity in Music," 47.
73. Manuel, *Popular Musics*, 2–4; Manuel, *Cassette Culture*, xvi. See also Wicke, *Rock Music*; Frith, *Sound Effects*, 11.
74. Ennis, *Seventh Stream*, 17, 22–27, 369. See also Frith, ed., *World Music*, 9–11.
75. Summarized and condensed from Dujunco, "Vong Co," 37–58.
76. See, for example, Fujui, "Popular Music," 197–220.
77. See, for example, Carney, ed., *Sounds of People;* Jarvis, "Truth," 96–122. See also Marcus, *Mystery Train*.
78. See Chan, "Gambaran Budaya."
79. On vong co see Dujunco, "Vong Co," 36–66; Pham, *Musics of Vietnam;* Manuel, *Popular Musics*, 198–204. On Portugal see Manuel, *Popular Musics*, 115–121; Broughton et al., eds., *World Music*, 144–148.
80. See Fujui, "East Asia/Japan," 366–368; Wong, "At Microphone."
81. See, for example, Burr, "From Africa;" Taylor, *Global*, 88–94, 136–142.
82. On these points see Pratt, *Rhythm and Resistance*, 22–39, 131.
83. See *Asiaweek*, August 17, 1991, 24.
84. Wong, "At Microphone," 1–2. See also Robinson et al., *Music at Margins*, 15.
85. Slobin and Titon, "Music-Culture," 1.
86. See Bessant, "Songs of Chiweshe," 45.
87. *How Musical*, 104. See also Blacking, "Ethnography," 384.
88. Lipsitz, *Time Passages*, x. See also Robinson et al., *Music at Margins*, 257.
89. See Pratt, *Rhythm and Resistance*, 8; Middleton, *Studying Popular Music*, 228, 241.
90. Yang, "Genre Analysis," 83–112.
91. *Seventh Stream*, 3.
92. Burlingame and Kasher, *Da Kine Sound*, 6.
93. Blacking, "Value of Music," 33–71.
94. Information on Hawaiian music taken from Lewis, "Don't Go Down Waikiki," 171–183; Lewis, "Beyond the Reef: Role," 189–198; Lewis, "Beyond the Reef: Cultural," 123–135; Lewis, "Da Kine Sounds," 38–52; Lewis, "Storm Blowing," 53–68; Lewis, "Music, Culture," 47–53; Kanahele, ed., *Hawaiian Music*, esp. xxiii–xxx, 106–107, 115–120; Kanahele, *Hawaiian Renaissance;* Burlingame and Kasher, *Da Kine Sound*, 6; Friedman, *Cultural*, 174–181; Stillman, "Sound," 5–22; Broughton et al., eds., *World Music*, 648–652; Keali'inohomoku, "Hula."

95. The literature on Yoruba pop is considerable. See especially the writings of Waterman, including *Juju*, and T. A. Thomas, as well as the various surveys of African popular music such as Barlow and Eyre, *Afropop!* 48–49; Bender, *Sweet Mother;* Bergman, *Goodtime Kings;* John Collins, *Musicmakers* and *West African Pop Roots;* Ewens, *Africa O-Ye!;* Graham, *Da Capo Guide* and *World of African Music;* Stapleton and May, *African Rock;* Stewart, *Breakout.* See also Chapter 6 in Lockard, " 'Get Up, Stand Up.' "
96. See, for example, Fujui, "East Asia/Japan," 360–370; Fujui, "Popular Music," 207–212; Maki, "Musical Characteristics," 283–304: Heard, "Trends," 75–96; Heard, "Songs," 12–17; Yano, "Shaping Sexuality"; Marre and Charlton, *Beats of Heart*, 242–245; Broughton et al., eds., *World Music*, 459–463. See also Patrick Patterson's submission on protest songs circulated on H-Asia, May 31, 1996.
97. The literature on Brazilian samba is vast. For good summaries see Schreiner, *Musica Brasileira*, 102–130; McGowan and Pessanha, *Brazilian Sound*, 26–51; Perrone, *Masters of Brazilian Song;* Manuel, *Popular Musics*, 64–68; Marre and Charlton, *Beats of Heart*, 215–228; Lockard, " 'Get Up, Stand Up,' " Chapter 5.
98. See "Empress of Arabic Song"; Manuel, *Popular Musics*, 141–158; Sweeney, *Virgin Directory*, 5, 14–15, 118–128; Broughton et al., eds., *World Music*, 180–181.
99. For a flawed biography see Bharatan, *Lata Mangeshkar.*
100. The general background to this music can be found in Sweeney, *Virgin Directory*, 153–154; Manuel, *Popular Musics*, 222–227; A. Jones, "Women in Discursive"; Stock, "Reconsidering," 11. Specific profiles of these singers come from the liner notes to various of their recordings that I have collected.
101. See "Japan's Voice of Hope"; Kitagawa, "Some Aspects," 305–316; Fujui, "Popular Music," 197–220; Broughton et al., eds., *World Music*, 460–462.
102. On reggae see, for example, Bergman, *Hot Sauces;* Clarke, *Jah Music;* Davis, *Reggae Bloodlines;* Davis and Simon, *Reggae International;* Ellison, *Lyrical Protest;* Hebdige, *Cut 'n' Mix;* Manuel, *Popular Musics*, 74–79; Marre and Charlton, *Beats of Heart*, 155–166; Lockard, " 'Get Up,' " Chapter 2.
103. See Webb, *Lokal Music;* Philpott, "Developments in Papua New Guinea's Popular Music Industry," 87–114.
104. See, for example, Hosokawa, liner notes to *The Music Power from Okinawa;* Sweeney, *Virgin Directory*, 160–161; Broughton et al., eds., *World Music*, 461–465.
105. On mbube see M. Anderson, *Music in the Mix;* Bender, *Sweet Mother*, 172–186; Bergman, *Goodtime Kings*, 108–121; Erlmann, *African Stars* and *Nightsong;* Ewens, *Africa O-Ye!* 254–281; Kivnick, *Where Is the Way;* Marre and Charlton, *Beats of the Heart*, 34–50; Manuel, *Popular Musics*, 106–111; Stapleton and May, *African Rock;* Lockard, " 'Get Up,' " Chapter 7; Taylor, *Global*, 69–82.
106. See Kristof, "Mongolian Rock Group."
107. On bhangra see, for example, Sweeney, *Virgin Directory*, 144–145; K. Hall, "Not in Bombay"; *The Beat*, 13/4 (1994), 68; Pareles, "Niche Music"; Manuel, *Popular Musics*, 184–185; Lipsitz, *Dangerous Crossroads;* Broughton

et al., eds., *World Music*, 228–232; Taylor, *Global*, 147–172; Sharma, *Dis-Orienting Rhythms.*

108. "Art Ideology," 475.
109. For a detailed discussion see Slobin, *Subcultural Sounds*, 11–36. See also Pareles, "Niche Music." On feminist music see, for example, Bayton, "Feminist Musical," 177–192; Rodnitzky, "Songs of Sisterhood," 77–85.
110. The discussion of Vietnam is based on Lull and Wallis, "Beat of West Vietnam," 297–236; Schramm, "From Refugee to Immigrant," 91–102.
111. Several notable films have revolved around this theme, including the Jamaican film *The Harder They Come* and the Zairian film *La Vie Est Belle.*
112. On soukous see Barlow and Eyre, *Afropop!* 26–32; Bender, *Sweet Mother;* Bergman, *Goodtime;* Collins, *West African;* Ewens, *Africa O-Ye!;* Manuel, *Popular Musics*, 97–101; Stapleton and May, *African Rock;* Stewart, *Breakout;* Lockard, " 'Get Up, Stand Up,' " Chapter 6.
113. See McRobbie, "Introduction," 2.
114. See B. Williams, "Introduction," 2.
115. Brecht quoted in John McCutcheon, liner notes to *Guitara Armada: Music of the Sandinista Guerrillas* (Rounder Records 4022, 1987).
116. Orman, *Politics of Rock*, 175.
117. See Lockard, " 'Get Up, Stand Up,' " Chapters 4 and 6.
118. *Popular Musics*, 10.
119. Summarized and condensed from a 1984 article by Burmese journalist Maung Tin Mya, "Politics and Religion," 45–46.
120. See Lintner, "Politics of Pop," 40; Maung, "Politics and Religion," 45–46; *New York Times*, November 10, 1996.
121. "Sri Lanka's Voice of Protest," 51.
122. See Pareles, "Honoring Tibet."
123. Hedges, "Beloved Infidel."
124. Rashid, "Pop Star Wars," 62; Sweeney, *Virgin Directory*, 148–149.
125. *Time Passages*, 4–5.
126. Manuel, *Popular Musics*, 6–7; Garofalo, *Rockin' the Boat*, 5–6; Robinson et al., *Music at Margins*, 17; Laing, "Music Industry," 333–334.
127. See Lockard, *Reflections of Change: Malaysian Popular Music*, 38–39.
128. See Kawabata, "Japanese Record Industry," 327–346; Fujui, "Popular Music," 197–220; Mitsui, "Japan in Japan," 107–120; De Launey, "Not-So-Big Japan," 203–225.
129. See, for example, Frith, "Anglo-America," 263–269; Rutten, "Local Popular Music," 294–305; Garofalo, *Rockin' the Boat*, 5–6; Powell, "Blockbuster Decades," 57; Denisoff, *Tarnished Gold*, 79–156; Nogus, *Producing Pop*, 7–14; Jones, "Who Fought the Law," 83–95; *New York Times*, March 19, 1990; White, " 'World Beat Stay Home,' " 17; Kawabata, "Japanese Record Industry," 327–329.
130. On South Africa see Coplan, *In Township Tonite!* 135–139, 158–160, 166–168, 178–179, 185, 194–195; Anderson, *Music in Mix*, 37–41, 45–105; Erlmann, *Nightsong*, 243–250; Ewens, *Africa O-Ye!* 186–187, 198–199; Lockard, " 'Get Up, Stand Up,' " Chapter 7.

131. Middleton, *Studying Popular Music*, 87. See also Garofalo, "Introduction," 11; Garofalo, "Whose World, What Beat," 23.
132. Malm, "Music Industry," 352.
133. *Cassette Culture*, xiii–xv, 1–36; Manuel, "Cassette Industry," 189–204; Manuel, "Popular Music in South Asia," 91–99.
134. Castelo-Branco, "Some Aspects," 32–45.
135. On China see WuDunn, "Bootleg Jab."
136. Rosen, *Protest Songs*, 22. See also Denisoff, *Sing a Song*, x.
137. Liner notes to Seeger's album, *Dangerous Songs* (Columbia 9303, n.d.). For more on Seeger's views of music and politics, see Lockard, "Pete Seeger."
138. See Middleton, *Studying Popular Music*, 253–255.
139. Extracted and condensed from a study by British observer Robin Denselow, *When Music's Over*, 1.
140. See Hampton, *Guerrilla Minstrels*, xii, 7, 9.
141. *Rock around the Bloc*, 5–6, 233. See also Cushman, *Notes.*
142. Rauth, "Back in U.S.S.R.," 3; Ryback, "Raisa Gorbachev," B1. See also the various essays in Ramet, ed., *Rocking the State;* Bright, "Soviet Crusade," 123–147.
143. Ryback, *Rock around Bloc*, 34, 46–49; Unger, " 'Voice from Russia,' " 10; Quinn-Judge, "Soviets Revere Poet," 9; Cushman, *Notes*, 53, 71–74.
144. Stites, *Russian Popular Culture*, 132, 161. See also Rauth, "Back in U.S.S.R.," 4; Ramet and Zamascikov, "Soviet Rock Scene," 150–151; Rapaport, "Negotiating Identity."
145. Dobrotvorskaja, "Soviet Teens," 150. See also Easton, "Rock Music," 46; S. F. Starr, *Red and Hot*, 297; Rapaport, "Negotiating Identity"; Hayes, "Rock," 12–13.
146. See Ryback, *Rock around Bloc*; Troitsky, *Back in USSR;* Stites, *Russian Popular Culture*, 132 ff; Rauth, "Back in U. S. S. R.," 9; Easton, "Rock Music," 45–83; S. F. Starr, *Red and Hot*, 289–315; S. F. Starr, "Rock Inundation"; Bright, "Soviet Crusade," 123–147; Ramet and Zamascikov, "Soviet Rock Scene," 149, 154–164; Pond, "Soviet Rock Lyrics," 75–91; Riggs, "Up from Underground," 1–23; Petrov, "Age of Aquarium"; Bookbinder et al., *Comrades*, 158–171; Cushman, "Rich Rastas," 38–47; Hayes, "Rock," 12–13.
147. See Riggs, "Baltic Rocks," 56–67; Bahry, "Rock Culture," 243–296.
148. Pekacz, "Did Pop Smash: Role," 41–49; Pekacz, "Did Pop Smash: Utopia." See also Easton, "Rock Music Community," 59–60; S. F. Starr, *Red and Hot;* Bright, "Pop Music," 357–369; Bright, "Soviet Crusade," 123–147; Ramet, "Rock: Music of Revolution," 1–12.
149. Kurti, "Rocking State," 483–513; Kurti, "How Can I Be," 73–102; Szemere, "I Get Frightened," 174–189; Szemere, "Pop Music in Hungary," 401–411; Szemere, "Some Institutional Aspects," 121–142; Szemere, "Politics of Marginality," 93–114; Mitchell, "Mixing Pop and Politics," 187–203.
150. Quoted in Mensh and Mensh, *Behind the Scenes*, 313. On Biermann's songs see Biermann, *Wire Harp.*
151. Wicke, "Role of Rock Music," 203. See also ibid., 196–206; Wicke, " 'Times They Are A-Changin,' " 81–92; Wicke and Shepherd, " 'Cabaret is Dead,' " 25–36; Meyer, "Popular Music in GDR"; Leitner, "Rock Music in GDR," 17–40.

152. *Red and Hot*, 319–320.
153. Quoted in Gittins, "Has Glasnost." See also Cushman, "Rich Rastas," 42–47; Cushman, *Notes*, 263–327; Shuman, "In the East Bloc"; Keller, "For Soviet Rock"; "Soviet Rock," 10–11; Vamos, "Hungary," 374–376; Pekacz, "On Some Dilemmas," 205–208; Mitchell, "Mixing Pop and Politics," 187–203; Rapaport, "Negotiating Identity."
154. On New Song see especially Manuel, *Popular Musics*, 68–72; Broughton et al., eds., *World Music*, 569–577; Canepa, "Violeta Parra," 235–240; Carrasco, *La Nueva Cancion;* Carrasco, "Nueva Cancion," 599–623; Fairley, "La Nueva Cancion," 107–115; Fairley, "New Song," 88–97; Gonzalez, "Hegemony and Counter-Hegemony," 63–75; Jara, *Unfinished Song;* Manns, "Problems of Text," 191–196; Matta, " 'New Song,' " 447–460; Moreno, "Violeta Parra," 108–126; Morris, *Canto Porque;* Pring-Mill, *"Gracias a la vida";* Tumas-Serna, " 'Nueva Cancion,' " 139–157; Lockard, " 'Get Up,' " Chapter 4.
155. See the documentary film about Chatterjee, *Free to Sing? The Music of Suman Chatterjee*. My discussion of Chatterjee is based on an entry entitled "Free to Sing?" by Sudipto Chatterjee, distributed on H-Asia, May 19, 1996.
156. *Synthetic Culture*, 37.
157. See Hiebert, "Singing Between Lines," 31–32; *Asiaweek*, April 13, 1990, 64; Schmetzer, "Vietnam Changes"; Broughton et al., eds., *World Music*, 450–452; Asiaweek, May 9, 1997: 53.
158. Jones, *Like a Knife*, 3. On Chinese rock music see also "Born in the PRC: China's New Voices of Rock," 38–43; "Born in the PRC," 34; Brace, "Popular Music," 43–66; Brace and Friedlander, "Rock and Roll," 115–128; Broughton et al., eds., *World Music*, 452–457; Delfs, "Controversial Fame," 40; Friedlander, "China's 'Newer Value,' " 43–66; Friedlander, "Rockin' the Yangtze," 63–73; Hamm, "Music and Radio," 1–42; Lee, "The 'East Is Red,' " 95–110; Lee, *Troubadours*, esp. 149–178; Lull, *China*, 127–169; Manuel, *Popular Musics*, 221–235; Peters, "Rock 'N' Revolt," 30–31; Riggs, "Up from Underground," 1–23; Sweeney, *Virgin Directory*, 154–155, 157; Terrill, "Rocking Old Guard," 24–28; "X," "China's Sidelined Generation," 16–19; Mihaica, "Chinese Rock Stars," 34–35; Mihaica, "Cultural Spring"; "Rock Rolls on in China," 51; Samson, "Music as Protest," 35–64; Schell, *Mandate of Heaven*, 311–325, 400–401; Zha, *China Pop*. See also Gold, "Go with Feelings," 907–925.
159. See liner notes to the album *Vietnam: Songs of Liberation* (Paredon 1008, 1971).
160. See Martin, "Music of East Timor," 14–17.
161. See Pettigrew, "Songs of Sikh," 89–102.
162. See Reynolds, "Revolutionary Songs," 38–39.
163. On chimurenga see Lockard, " 'Get Up, Stand Up,' " Chapter 7, as well as some of the general sources on African popular music noted above.
164. See *Asiaweek*, July 5, 1988, 27; Broughton et al., eds., *World Music*, 448–449.
165. See, for example, Robinson et al., *Music at Margins*, 13, 277; Frith, *Sound Effects*, 264–265, 270–271; Nogus, *Producing Pop*.

166. "Problems in Cultural Development," 111–112.
167. Mazrui, *Cultural Forces*, 205; Wallerstein, "Culture," 38; Ngugi, *Moving the Centre*, 26–27, 42.
168. *Synthetic Culture*, 15.
169. Mazrui, *Cultural Forces*, 7–8.
170. See, for example, Tomlinson, *Cultural Imperialism;* Regis, "Calypso, Reggae," 63.
171. "Disjuncture and Difference," 2. See also Slobin, *Subcultural Sounds*, 13–16, 34.
172. See, for example, Tomlinson, *Cultural Imperialism*, 175; Featherstone, "Global Culture," 1, 5; Featherstone, *Undoing*, 86–125; Friedman, *Cultural*, 102–116; Robertson, *Globalization;* Jameson, *Postmodernism*, 343; Kearney, "Local and Global," 547–565; van Elteren, "Conceptualizing," 54–60.
173. *Decolonizing the Mind*, 3.
174. See Boyd-Barrett, "Media Imperialism," 117–119; Lull, "Popular Music," 14; Mattelart, *Multinational Corporations.*
175. *Cultural Neocolonialism*, 1–19.
176. Regis, "Calypso, Reggae," 63, 68.
177. Constantino, *Neocolonial Identity*, 7.
178. Guzman and Burton, "Politics and Film," 243–246.
179. See, for example, his *Decolonizing the Mind.*
180. Extracted and condensed from Iyer, *Video Night in Kathmandu*, 3–4. See also Neuharth, *Nearly One World*, 10–11; Barnet and Cavenaugh, "Sound of Money," 12–16; van Elteren, "Conceptualizing," 47–81.
181. Wagnleitner, "Irony of American Culture," 286.
182. See Zilberg, "Why Zimbabweans Love Dolly."
183. See G. Mohamad, *Sidelines*, 219–220.
184. Goonasekera, "Asian Viewers," 217–221. See also Lull, *China*, 147–150.
185. See Gitlin, "World Leaders."
186. Quoted in Reeves, "Jerry Brown Lives." See also Barnett and Cavenaugh, "Sound of Money," 12–16.
187. Paterson, "Defining and Doing," 51. For a different view, see Buckman, "Cultural Agenda," 134–155.
188. The term is from Michelle and Armand Mattelart, reported in Lazere, "Introduction," 477.
189. See Schmidt, "In Europe"; Stanley, "Russians"; Hinds, "Life After Donald Duck," 272; Appadurai, "Disjuncture and Difference," 5–6; Sen, "Impact of American," 208–209, 212–217, 223; Levinson, "Rock around World," 65.
190. See Yudice, "We Are *Not* the World," 202–216.
191. Combs, *Polpop*, 138; Neuharth, *Nearly One World*, 11. On American television in Latin America see Turnstall, "Media Imperialism," 540. For Egypt see *"Layali al-Helmiya,"* 36.
192. See, for example, Dorfman and Mattelart, *How to Read Donald Duck;* Dorfman and Mattelart, *Emperor's Old Clothes.* See also Schiller, *Communication*, 1; Mattelart, *Multinational Corporations.*
193. Constantino, *Synthetic Culture*, 1–2, 7, 37–38.
194. See, for example, Hedges, "Tehran Journal"; Sarkar, "India Reacts," 33–34.
195. "Cosmopolitans and Locals," 237. See also Hannerz, "Notes on Global," 66–75; Featherstone, "Introduction," 6.

196. Middleton, *Studying Popular Music*, 292. See also Ngugi, *Moving the Centre*, 26.
197. See Hamelink, *Cultural Autonomy*, 2; Robinson et al., *Music at Margins*, 3.
198. See Robinson et al., *Music at Margins*, 4; Manuel, *Popular Musics*, 23; Garofalo, "Whose World," 16–30; Erlmann, "Politics and Aesthetics," 3–15; Toop, "Into the Hot," 123.
199. Lull, "Popular Music," 17–18; Hazarika, "India Plays;" Taylor, *Global.*
200. Wallis and Malm, *Big Sounds*, 301–302. See also Garofalo, "Introduction," 22–23.
201. Wallis and Malm, *Big Sounds*, 297–311; Malm, "Music on Move," 339–352.
202. Bergman, *Hot Sauces*, 18.
203. For a recording of the Tokyo reggae festival featuring Japanese groups, see the album *Tokyo Reggae Clash* (Blackstar Line Records 25RL0003B, 1973).
204. Lull, "Popular Music," 146–147. See also the album *MNP: Reggae From Around the World* (Ras 3050, 1988), which includes reggae musicians from countries like Ethiopia, Israel, Italy, Ivory Coast, New Zealand, Poland, Soviet Union, Sweden, and Uruguay.
205. See Booth, "Disco *Laggi*," 61–82.
206. Tran, "Traditional Music," 204–208; Manuel, *Popular Musics*, 19–22; Mitchell, "World Music," 311–314.
207. Kunst quoted in Kornhauser, "In Defence of Kroncong," 104–105. See also Powne, *Ethiopian Music*, vii–viii.
208. Mitsui, "Reception of Music," 276–277.
209. On Swahili music see John Storm Roberts, liner notes to *Songs the Swahili Sing* (Original Music Records, 103); Manuel, Popular Musics, 102–103. On Malay music see Chopyak, "Music in Modern Malaysia," 111–138.
210. See Stapleton, "Paris, Africa," 10–23; Glanvill, "World Music Mining," 58–67.
211. See, for example, Watrous, "Japanese Band"; Hucker, "Far East," 28; Lipsitz, *Dangerous Crossroads*, 14; Sweeney, *Virgin Directory*, 159.
212. I am indebted to George Lipsitz for this material. See also Lipsitz, *Dangerous Crossroads* 14–16, 129–131; Broughton et al., eds., *World Music*; 232, 538; Sharma, *Dis-Orienting Rhythms;* Taylor, *Global*, 155–165.

Chapter 2: Indonesia: Many Fields, Many Songs

1. From the song "Bongkar." Quoted in Hatley, "Cultural Expression," 261–262.
2. Piper and Jabo, "Indonesian Music," 35.
3. Based largely on Neher and Marlay, *Democracy: Southeast Asia*, 76; Robison, "Indonesia," 40; Robison, "Middle Class," 77–78; Greenwood, ed., *Asia Yearbook 1992*, 6; *The Asia & Pacific Review 1993/94*, 83; United Nations, *Industrial Statistics 1991*, 774–783.
4. Unless otherwise cited, the major works utilized on Indonesian history, society, and politics included: Abeyasekere, *Jakarta;* Alisjahbana, *Indonesia;* Aspinall, *Student Dissent;* Branigin, "Indonesia Booming," A13; Bourchier and Legge, eds., *Democracy in Indonesia;* Brown, *The State*, 112–157; Budiardjo, "Militarism," 1219–1238; Budiman, "Emergence," 110–129; Budiman, *State and Society;* Bunge, ed., *Indonesia;* Burns, "Post Priok Trials,"

61–88; Cady, *History;* Cohen, "Born," 38–40; Crouch, "Indonesia," 121–145; Crouch and Hill, eds., *Indonesia Assessment 1992;* Dahm, *Indonesia;* "Defense of the Student Movement," 11–16; Djamas, "Behind Tanjung Priok"; Drake, *National;* Errington, "Continuity," 329–353; Foulcher, *Social Commitment;* Frederick and Worden, eds., *Indonesia;* C. Geertz, *Religion;* Hefner, "Islam, State," 1–35; Hefner, "Islamizing Java," 533–554; Hill, ed., *Indonesia's New Order;* Holt, ed., *Culture;* Hill, *Indonesian Economy;* Hooker, ed., *Culture and Society;* Jackson and Pye, eds., *Political Power;* K. C. Lee, *Indonesia;* Liddle, "Islamic Turn," 613–634; Liddle, "National," 4–20; Andrew MacIntyre, *Business;* McKendrick, "Indonesia in 1991," 103–110; McVey, ed., *Indonesia;* Mulder, *Individual and Society;* Neher, *Southeast Asia;* 87–102; Neher and Marlay, *Democracy: Southeast Asia;* 75–95; Osborne, *Southeast Asia;* Pabottingi, "Indonesia," 224–256; Peacock, *Indonesia;* Peacock, *Rites of Modernization;* Polomka, *Indonesia;* Ramage, "Indonesia at 50," 147–165; Ramage, *Politics in Indonesia;* Rasyid, "Indonesia," 149–163; Robison, "Indonesia," 39–74; Robison, "Middle Class," 77–101; Robison, "Toward Class Analysis," 17–39; Robison, "Transformation," 48–68; Schiller, *Developing Jepara;* Schwarz, *Nation;* Steinberg et al., *In Search of Southeast Asia;* Vatikiotis, *Indonesian Politics;* Vreeland et al., *Area Handbook;* Warshaw, *Southeast Asia;* Wertheim, *Indonesian Society;* Winters, *Power;* Winters, "Suharto's Indonesia," 420–424; Young, ed., *Trends;* Wilhelm, *Emerging Indonesia.*

5. C. Geertz, "Afterword," 323. See also Kuipers, "Society," 71–74, 99–123, 134.
6. See Legge, *Indonesia*, 3; Bunge, "Introduction," in Bunge, ed., *Indonesia*, xxiii; Liddle, "National," 5; Brown, *State*, 112–113, 118.
7. *Indonesia*, 171. See also Alisjahbana, *Indonesia*, 2.
8. See Sutherland, "Kerontjong," 41, 48; Vreeland, *Area Handbook: Indonesia*, 137. There are many available studies of Indonesian classical and traditional musics. Good brief introductions can be found in Arps, ed., *Performance;* Brandon, *Theatre;* Brinner, "Cultural," 433–456; Broughton et al., eds., *World Music*, 417–425; Capwell, "Music," 134–164; Geertz, *Religion*, 278–287; Hood et al., "Indonesia," 167–220; Hood, "Enduring," 438–471; Kartomi, "Musical Strata," 111–133; Kartomi, " 'Traditional Music,' " 227–241; Lindsay, *Javanese;* Malm, *Music Cultures*, 34–49; Miettinen, *Classical*, 75–139; Mohd. Taib Osman, *Traditional Drama;* Purcell, *Introduction*, 8–9; Salvini, "Performing Arts," 49–63; Sunanto, liner notes; Sutton, "Asia/Indonesia," 266–310; Vickers, ed., *Being Modern*, esp. Chapters 3, 5–6. For more detailed studies see Becker, *Traditional Music* and *Gamelan Stories;* Brinner, *Knowing Music;* Kunst, *Indonesian Music;* Sumarsam, *Gamelan;* Sutton, *Traditions* and *Variations;* Tanzer, *Balinese Music;* Brakel-Papenhuyzen, *Classical Javanese Dance.*
9. Yampolsky, *Lokananta*, 39–49.
10. Dutch ethnomusicologist Jaap Kunst, quoted in Hood, "Enduring," 449.
11. The material that follows is based largely on Anderson, *Mythology;* Geertz, *Religion*, 261–278; Hanna, "Magical-Mystical," 5–10; Hatley, "Cultural," 216–266; Hood, "Enduring," 448; Keeler, *Javanese Shadow Puppets* and

Javanese Shadow Plays; Lee, *Indonesia*, 137, 138, 140; Matusky, *Malaysian Shadow Play;* Perry, "Review," 153–157; Salvini, "Performing Arts," 49–54; Seebass, "Co-ordination," 162–173; Siegel, *Solo*, 87; van Groenendael, *Dalang;* Wibisono, "Wayang," 53–59; Yousof, *Dictionary*, esp. 280–309.

12. Excerpted and condensed from a study by ethnomusicologist Mantle Hood, "Enduring," 441.
13. See Sears, *Shadows*, esp. xiii–xvi, 1–33, 269–301. See also Anderson, *Mythology*, 30.
14. See Seebass, "Change in Balinese," 71–91.
15. See Hood et al., "Indonesia," 196; Becker, "Western," 3–9; Liddle, "Improvising," 30–32.
16. See the albums *Asmat Dream: New Music Indonesia, Volume 1* (Lyrichord 7415, 1989); *Man 689: New Music Indonesia, Vol. 2 (Central Java)* (Lyrichord 7420, 1993); *Karya: New Music Indonesia, Vol. 3* (Lyrichord 7421, 1993). See also Subagio, *Apa Itu*, 22–30.
17. See liner notes to the compact disc "The Music of K. R. T. Wasitodiningrat," performed by Gamelan Sekar Tunjung (CMP 3007, 1990).
18. See, for example, Kartomi, " 'Traditional Music,' " esp. 381–382.
19. On this point see Sears, *Shadows*, 234–265. 269–274. See also Susanto, "Mass Communication," 236–237; Widodo, "Stages of State," 23–27.
20. For a good example of amateur writing, see the poem by Soejono, "Before the Time of the Coming of the Barbarians," quoted in Williams, *Five Journeys*, 22–23.
21. Quoted in Steinberg, *In Search of Southeast Asia*, 307.
22. Alisjahbana, *Indonesia*, 63. See also Drake, *National*, 61–64.
23. Legge, *Indonesia*, 173.
24. Translation adapted from Zainu'ddin, *Lagu-Lagu*, 42–43.
25. *Theatre*, 277–278, 323–324.
26. Yassin, "Malay 'Bangsawan,' " 151. See also Sutherland, "Kerontjong," 41–50; Yousof, *Dictionary*, 13–19. On Malaysian bangsawan see S. B. Tan, *Bangsawan*.
27. Unless otherwise cited, information on Indonesian popular musics throughout the study has been taken from: Becker, "Kroncong," 14–19; Broughton et al., eds., *World Music*, 425–432; Capwell, "Music," 158–163; Cohen, "Born," 38–40; Davis, ed., *What is Modern;* Frederick, "Dreams," 54–89; Frederick, "Rhoma Irama," 103–130; Geertz, *Religion*, 303–305; Handley, "Dancing," 55–57; Hardjo et al., *Sepuluh;* Harsono, "Star is Banned," 14–15; Hatch, "Popular," 49–67; Hatley, "Cultural Expression," 216–266; Hefner, "Politics," 75–94; Heins, "Kroncong," 20–32; Henschkel, "Perceptions," 53–71; Kartomi, "From Kroncong to Dangdut," 277–292; Kartomi, ed., *Studies;* Kartomi, " 'Traditional Music,' " 386–390; Kleden, "Pop Culture," 3–7; Kornhauser, "In Defence," 104–177; Leee, "Not Like"; Manuel, *Popular Musics*, 205–220; Manuel and Baier, "Jaipongan," 91–110; Moedjanto, *Tantangan*, 195–224; Murray, "Kampung Culture," 1–16; Pemberton, "Musical"; Pioquinto, "Dangdut," 59–90; Piper, "Performances," 37–58; Piper and Jobo, "Indonesian," 25–37; Ramedhan, "Disco," 16–19; "Rhoma Irama," *Asiaweek*,

June 24, 1988, 28; M. Sahabullah, "Man Who Gave Dangdut" and "Show Was 'Cukup Bagus' "; Sedyawati, *Seni Dalam,* 137–159; Siegel, *Solo,* 203–231; Subagio, ed., *Apa Itu;* "Superstar With a Message"; Sutherland, "Kerontjong," 41–50; Sutton, "Asia/Indonesia," 310–314; Sweeney, *Virgin Directory,* 170–173; "The Poor Man's Superstar," 31; Weiss, "Musical Revelations," 147–154; Wibisono, "Wayang," 53–59; Widodo, "Stages," 1–36; S. Williams, "Current Developments," 105–136; Yamashita, "Listening," 105–120; Yampolsky, *Lokananta* and "Hati Yang Luka," 1–17; Yampolsky, liner notes to *Tonggeret;* Yampolsky, *"Music of Indonesia 2."*

28. See Manuel, *Popular Musics,* 207–210; Heins, "Kroncong," 29; Frederick, "Dreams," 54–89; Geertz, *Religion,* 303–305; Kartomi, "From Kroncong to Dangdut," 280–281; Abeyasekere, *Jakarta,* 28, 64. On the history of the kroncong "guitar," see Grooss, *De Krontjong Guitaar.* For a discussion of another Portuguese-influenced music on the west coast of Sumatra, see Kartomi, "Minangkabau," 19–36.
29. See Yampolsky, liner notes to *Music from Outskirts;* Kartomi, "From Kroncong to Dangdut," 283; Abeyasekere, *Jakarta,* 143–144.
30. Kornhauser, "In Defence," 128.
31. Translation adapted from Zainu'ddin, *Lagu-Lagu,* 34–35. For the history of this song see Kartomi, "From Kroncong to Dangdut," 281–282.
32. Becker, "Kroncong," 14–15. See also Kartomi, "From Kroncong to Dangdut," 280; Frederick, "Dreams," 60; Abeyasekere, *Jakarta,* 48–87.
33. From liner notes to the album *Songs from the Peninsula in Krontjong Beat,* arranged and directed by Brigadier General R. Pirngadie (Evergreen TTS-568, n.d.).
34. See Frederick, "Rhoma Irama," 106; Frederick, "Dreams," 60–63; Sutherland, "Kerontjong," 42; Wild, "Indonesia," 15–40; Wild, "Radio Midwife," 34–42; Kornhauser, "In Defence," 125; Kartomi, "From Kroncong to Dangdut," 281; Abeyasekere, *Jakarta,* 143–144.
35. "Kroncong," 16. See also Wild, "Indonesia," 30–33; Kartomi, "From Kroncong to Dangdut," 282. In 1990, popular star Hetty Koes Endang released a commercially successful cassette of nationalist kroncong songs from the 1940s. See her album *Keroncong Masa Revolusi* (Musica 7776, 1990).
36. Kornhauser, "In Defence," 136.
37. *Indonesian Society,* 308. On Sukarno's artistic sensibility, see Angus McIntyre, "Sukarno," 161–210. For a recent assessment of the Sukarno era, see Bourchier and Legge, eds., *Democracy,* 3–114.
38. See Piper and Jabo, "Indonesian Music," 26.
39. See liner notes to Pirngadie's album, *A Tribute to Heroes* (Evergreen records, 573, n.d.). See also Kornhauser, "In Defence," 136–137; Kartomi, "From Kroncong to Dangdut," 282.
40. See Yampolsky, "*Music of Indonesia 2*"; Hatch, "Popular Music," 56; Broughton et al., eds., *World Music,* 426; Kartomi, "From Kroncong to Dangdut," 281.
41. The most extensive study is Peacock, *Rites of Modernization,* especially 6–11, 39–59, 131, 175–181. See also Brandon, *Theatre;* Geertz, *Religion,* 289–295; Hatley, "Cultural Expression," 253; Hatley, "Ludruk and Ketoprak," 38–58;

Hatley, "Theatre and Politics," 1–18; Hatley, "Theatre as Cultural Resistance," 321–348; Siegel, *Solo*, 87–116; Yousof, *Dictionary*, 113–117. On Madurese loddrok see Bouvier, esp. 121, 127.

42. Quoted in Peacock, *Rites of Modernization*, 178.
43. See Weix, "Gapit Theatre," 17–36; Hatley, "Theatre as Cultural Resistance," 339–344; Susanto, "Mass Communication," 236–237.
44. On LEKRA see Foulcher, *Social Commitment*, 83–103; Foulcher, "Construction," 301–320; Grant, *Indonesia*, 109; Hatley, "Cultural Expression," 229–230. On the national culture controversy, see also Soemardjan, "Development of Culture," 151–156.
45. The literature on the coup is heated and conflictive. For a listing of some of the major studies, see Neher, *Southeast Asia*, 101.
46. See Gaffar, *Javanese Voters*, 36–37; Budiardjo, "Militarism," 1219; Hooker and Dick, "Introduction," 2–3; Robison, "Indonesia," 41–47.
47. See Pemberton, "Disempowerment," 83–88.
48. See, for example, Mahasin, "Discourse," 1; Hooker and Dick, "Introduction," 5–6; Heider, *Indonesian Cinema*, 17–25; Vatikiotis, *Indonesian Politics*, xv–xix, 107, 191–205; Robison, "Indonesia," 68–77; Schwarz, *Nation*, 230–263; Hill, *Press*, esp. Chapt. 3; Aznam, "Contested Closure," 20–21; Makarim, "Indonesian Press," 259–281; Hatley, "Cultural Expression," 216–266; Heryanto, "Introduction: State Ideology," 289–300; Crouch, "Indonesia," 121–130; Rasyid, "Indonesia," 149–163; Neher and Marlay, *Democracy*, 85–87; "Anatomy of Press Censorship," 1–6; "Indonesia: Students Jailed," 1–4. For a general background and history of the Indonesian press, see Crawford, "Indonesia," 158–178. On cartoons see Anderson, "Cartoons," 282–321; Hanna, "Indonesian *Komik*."
49. See Widodo, "Stages," 1–36.
50. See, for example, Neher, *Southeast Asia*, 91–92; Neher and Marlay, *Democracy: Southeast Asia*, 82–91; Jackson and Pye, eds., *Political Power*, esp. 3–42, 395–398; Budiman, "Emergence," 110–128; Robison, "Toward," 17–39; Robison, "Transformation," 57–68; Robison, "Indonesia," 43–47, 55–68; MacIntyre, *Business;* Hill, ed., *Indonesia's New Order*, 1–122; Rasyid, "Indonesia," 149–163; Pabottingi, "Indonesia," 246–256; Winters, *Power*, 142–191.
51. Bunge, "Introduction," xxiv; Neher, *Southeast Asia*, 96.
52. See Hooker and Dick, "Introduction," 1–5; Rasyid, "Indonesia," 158–160.
53. Neher, *Southeast Asia*, 89–90, 97; Hill, *Indonesian Economy*, esp. 1–8, 191–238; Winters, "Suharto's Indonesia," 420–424; Budiman, "Emergence," 125; Vatikiotis, *Indonesian Politics*, 114, 165–180; McKendrick, "Indonesia in 1991," 106–107; Branigin, "Indonesia Booming"; Kuipers, "Society," 82–84; Marshall, "Economy," 164–167; Evers, "Growth," 165–167; Gargan, "Indonesian Asset"; Cohen, "Twisting Arms," 25, 28; Santoso, "Democratization," 39–41.
54. *Indonesian Politics*, 114.
55. Keith Foulcher, quoted in Hooker and Dick, ed., "Introduction," 11.
56. See, for example, the essays by Anwar Nasir in *Far Eastern Economic Review*, July 2, 1987, 41–43; Mackie and MacIntyre, "Politics," 25–32; Pabottingi,

"Indonesia," 232–256; Aspinall, *Student Dissent*, 32–34. See also Schwarz, *Nation*, 162–193: Ramage, *Politics in Indoneia*, 1–74.

57. *Indonesia*, 136.
58. See, for example, Hefner, "Islamizing Java?"; Hefner, "Islam, State."
59. "Defense of the Student Movement," 12–13. See also Wilhelm, *Emerging Indonesia*, 91–99.
60. This account of the Tanjung Priok affair follows Burns, "Post Priok Trials." See also Djamas, "Behind Tanjung Priok," 24–59; Kolstad, "Enemy Others," 357–378; Abeyasekere, *Jakarta*, 247–248.
61. See Burns, "The Post Priok Trials," especially 73–78.
62. See Crouch, "Ageing President," 55–57; Hefner, "Islam, State," 1–35.
63. Summarized from a study by French anthropologist Helene Bouvier, in "East Madurese," 125.
64. Hatch, "Popular Music," 52; Piper and Jobo, "Indonesian Music," 27–28; Drake, *National Integration*, 88–92; Sutton, "Commercial Cassette," 23–43; Karamoy and Sablie, "Communication," 63; Yamashita, "Listening," 110; Yamashita, "Manipulating," 69–82; Soemardjan, "Development," 157–158; Caldarola, *Reception*, 33–41, 49–53; Frojen, " 'Uncle Country' "; Chu and Alfian, "Indonesia's Uncommon," 27–31; Weintraub, "Mass Media"; Hughes-Freeland, "Balinese 'Culture'," 253–270.
65. "Popular Music," 52. See also Sutton, "Commercial," 25–43; Manuel, *Cassette Culture*, 32.
66. See Yampolsky, *Lokananta*, 14; Harsono, "Star"; Piper and Jobo, "Indonesian Music," 33–35; Hatley, "Cultural Expression," 257; Widodo, "Stages of State," 23–27.
67. On radio see especially Wild, "Indonesia," 33–38; Susanto, "Mass Communications," 230–243; Jackson and Pye, eds., *Political Power*, 24–25. On television see Kitley, "Tahun Bertambah," 71–109; Sumardjan, "Social and Cultural," 15–19; Yamashita, "Listening," 110; Caldarola, *Reception*; Chu and Alfian, "Indonesia's Uncommon," 27–31; Susanto, "Mass Communication," 243–249; Hughes-Freeland, "Balinese 'Culture'," 253–270; Holaday, "Social," 100–106.
68. "What Is Modern?" 316–317; Sen, "Changing Horizons," 116–124; Holaday, "Social Impact," 100–106; Schiller, *Developing Jepara*, 99–124.
69. See H. Geertz, "Indonesian Cultures," 33–38; Davis, "What is Modern," 316; Halina, "Culture," 2; Kleden, "Pop Culture," 3–7; Hooker and Dick, "Introduction," 7; Bruner, "Modern," 301–302; Schiller, *Developing Jepara*, 99–124.
70. See Piper and Jabo, "Indonesian Music," 28–29; Sedyawati, *Seni Dalam*, 139–140, 153.
71. See Mutsaers, "Indorock," 307–320; Mutsaers, "Recognition," 65–81; Cox, "Ambonese Connection," 1–16; Kartomi, "From Kroncong to Dangdut," 282.
72. Piper and Jabo, "Indonesian Music," 27–29; *Asiaweek*, June 23, 1989, 52; Sedyawati, *Seni Dalam*, 151–153, 156–158.
73. See Manuel, *Popular Musics*, 206.
74. Excerpted and condensed from Ramedhan, "Disco Way of Life," 16–17, 19.
75. Ramedhan, "Disco Way of Life," 16–17, 19. On karaoke see Dotulong, "Jakarta," 48–50.

76. See Kleden, "Pop Culture," 3–4; Henschkel, "Perceptions," 53–71; Wibisono, "Wayang," 59; Piper, "Performances," 37–58. On *Tempo* see especially Liddle, "Improvising," 6–8. For stimulating debates on the future of traditional Indonesian artistic cultures, see Davis, ed., *What is Modern;* Hooker, ed., *Culture.*
77. Kartomi, " 'Traditional Music,' " 386.
78. See, for example, Gombloh, "Musik Rock," 59–86; Emka, *Thrash Metal;* Hardjo, *Sepuluh Tokoh Showbiz;* Sedyawati, *Seni Dalam*; Moedjanto, *Tantangan.*
79. "National," 18. See also Hooker and Dick, "Introduction," 5–6; Yamashita, "Listening," 117–118; Hatley, "Cultural Expression," 216–219, 229–263; Heryanto, "Introduction: State Ideology," 289–300; G. Mohamad, *Sidelines.*
80. Pemberton, "Musical," 22; Wibisono, "Wayang," 53–59; Perry, "Review," 153–157; Hatley, "Cultural Expression," 230–232, 235–236, 252–253; Sears, *Shadows*, 218–235.
81. See Wright, "Contemporary," 47–66; Wright, *Soul;* Hatley, "Cultural Expression," 222–223, 248–249; Lee, "From National," 17–32.
82. "Writing Indonesian," 29–43. See also Foulcher, "Construction," 301–320.
83. On literature see Abdullah, ed., *Literature;* Aveling, "Literature," 1–5; Federspiel, *Popular;* Foulcher, "Literature," 221–256; Foulcher, "Politics," 83–103; Foulcher, "Post-Modernism," 27–47; Foulcher, "Sastra Kontekstual," 6–28; Foulcher, "Construction," 301–320; Hatley, "Cultural Expression," 216–263; T. Hellwig, *Shadow;* G. Mohamad, *Sidelines*, esp. 91–99; Mulder, "Individual Thailand Java," 312–327; Oemarjati, "Isteri, Cinta," 82–96; Tickell, "Writing Indonesian," 29–43; Tickell, "Writing the Past," 257–287; Wicks, *Literary;* "Indonesia's Great Debate," 64–65; special issue of *Prisma*, 29 (September 1983), 1–65.
84. Quoted in Lucas, "Land Disputes," 79. For a brief profile of Rendra see "W. S. Rendra," 34–35.
85. On this affair see Mohamad, "Indonesia's Prize," 39.
86. On theater see Bodden, "Grass Roots," 33–46; Foley, "Tree of Life," 66–77; Hatley, "Constructions," 48–69; Hatley, "Theatrical Imagery," 177–207; Hatley, "Cultural Expression," 216–263; Hatley, "Theatre as Cultural Resistance," 321–347; Heryanto, "Class Act," 30; Jensen, "Poet," 15; Jit, "Modern," 50–62; Murray, "Kampung Culture," 1–16; Siegel, *Solo*, 87–116; Van Erven, *Playful Revolution*, 184–206; "A Saucy Feast from the Slums," 61; Zurbuchen, "Images."
87. Information on films is taken from: Armes, *Third World Film*, 150–151; Buruma, "Formula," 40–41; Heider, *Indonesian Cinema;* Heider, "National Cinema," 162–173; Mohamad, "Introduction," 75–82; Hanan, *"Nji Ronggeng,"* 87–115; Hatley, "Cultural Expression," 216–263; Lent, "Historical Overview"; Lent, *Asian Film*, 201–212; Said, "Film," 65–72; Said, "Man and Revolutionary," 111–129; Said, "Rise of Indonesian," 99–115; Sen, "Image of Women," 17–29; Sen, *Indonesian Cinema;* Sen, "Politics of Melodrama," 67–81; Sen, "Power and Poverty," 1–20; Sen, "Repression," 116–133; Anwar, "Indonesian Films," 148–152; Braginsky, "Gentleman," 175–182; Caldarola, *Reception;* Salvini, "Performing Arts," 60–62.

88. Quoted in Mohamad, "Introduction," 75. See also Heider, *Indonesian Cinema;* Sen, *Indonesian Cinema;* Frederick, "Dreams," 68–69.
89. See following, all by Sen: "Image of Women," 17–29; "Power and Poverty," 1–20; *Indonesian Cinema*, esp. 105–156; "Repression," 116–133.
90. Yampolsky, *Lokananta*, 14. See also Susilo, "Review," 358–360.
91. Al-Attas, "Hetty's Still at Top"; *Asiaweek*, June 9, 1989; Murthi, "Hetty Shares." See also Sedyawati, *Seni Dalam*, 144–159.
92. See Siegel, *Solo*, 203–231; Henschkel, "Perceptions," 55–56.
93. See Piper and Jabo, "Indonesian Music," 33–36; Manuel and Baier, "Jaipongan," 99; Yampolsky, "Hati Yang Luka," 15–17; Siegel, *Solo*, 203–215; Kartomi, "From Kroncong to Dangdut," 288. On the regional pop industry see also Subagio, ed., *Apa Itu Lagu.* On nasidah modern and related Arab-influenced Islamic styles, see Bass, liner notes to *Keadilan;* Capwell, "Music of Indonesia," 158–159.
94. Hatch, "Popular Music," 58.
95. Piper and Jabo, "Indonesian Music," 36; Kartomi, "From Kroncong to Dangdut," 277. On styles and changes of romantic music see also "Dicari, Romantisme yang Tidak Cengeng," 62–65; "Jeritannya Masih Seksi," 50–51; Sedyawati, *Seni Dalam*, 144–159.
96. Quoted in Yampolsky, "Hati Yang Luka," 2–3.
97. Yamashita, "Listening," 114–116.
98. The following discussion is based on Yampolsky, "Hati Yang Luka," 1–17. See also "Dicari, Romantisme," 62–65; Kartomi, "From Kroncong to Dangdut," 287.
99. "Hati Yang Luka," 16.
100. "Popular Music," 62. See also Hatley, "Cultural Expression," 243, 245.
101. Sutton, "Indonesia," 312–313. On Guruh Soekarno see also Hardjo, *Sepuluh Tokoh Showbiz*, 23–38. On Guruh's performance style and message see Hooker and Dick, "Introduction," 7, 21.
102. See her album *Pengakuan* (Jackson Records, n.d.). See also Hanna, "Indonesian *Komik*," 10; Sedyawati, *Seni Dalam*, 147.
103. See Piper and Jabo, "Indonesian Music," 32; Sutton, "Indonesia," 312–314.
104. Quoted in Hanna, "Indonesian *Komik*," 10–11.
105. See Hatch, "Popular Music," 63–64.
106. Quoted in Zieman, "People's Representative." See also Sahabullah, "Putting Gift"; Abeyasekere, *Jakarta*, xv.
107. Hatch, "Popular Music," 65. On Gombloh see also Piper and Jabo, "Indonesian Music," 31–32; Siradj, *Gombloh.*
108. Frederick, "Rhoma Irama," 126.
109. Frederick, "Rhoma Irama," 127.
110. The information on kalangkang is taken from S. Williams, "Current Developments," 105–136.
111. Extracted and condensed from quoted material from Gugum Gumbira Tirasondjaja in Broughton et al., eds., *World Music*, 428–429.
112. Liner notes to *Tonggeret.* See also J. Hellwig, "Jaipongan," 47–57; Kartomi, "From Kroncong to Dangdut," 287–288; Sweeney, *Virgin Directory*, 172–173; liner notes to the album by Euis Komariah and Yus Wiradiredja, *The Sound of Sunda: Degung Music from Java* (Globestyle 060, 1989).

113. Yampolsky, liner notes to *Tonggeret.* See also Manuel and Baier, "Jaipongan," 91; Hellwig, "Jaipongan," 51–56; Subagio, *Apa Itu.*
114. Manuel and Baier, "Jaipongan," 106–107. The song text (although not the musical style) is very reminiscent of the Mexican and Texas-Mexican *corrida*, which often recounts the deeds of desperadoes and Robin Hood characters. See Claes af Geijerstam, *Popular Music in Mexico* (Albuquerque: University of New Mexico Press, 1976); Americo Paredes, *A Texas-Mexican Cancionero: Folksongs of the Lower Border* (Urbana: University of Illinois Press, 1976); Chris Strachwitz, liner notes to *Texas-Mexican Border Music Vol. 2: Corridos, Part 1: 1930–1943* (Arhoolie records, 9004, 1974) and *Texas-Mexican Border Music Vol. 3: Corridos, Part 2: 1929–1936* (Arhoolie Records, 9005, 1974).
115. Liner notes to Idjah Hadidjah's album, *Tonggeret;* Broughton et al., eds., *World Music*, 429–430.
116. This profile is based on Frederick, "Rhoma Irama," 108–109.
117. Frederick, "Rhoma Irama," 110. See also Manuel, *Popular Musics*, 210; Pioquinto, "Dangdut," 59; Kartomi, "From Kroncong to Dangdut," 284; Moedjanto, *Tantangan,* 195–224, Sedyawati, *Seni Dalam,* 137–143.
118. Quoted in "Rhoma Irama," *Asiaweek*, June 24, 1988, 28. See also Sutton, "Indonesia," 311.
119. Paraphrase of Rhoma's interviews, in Frederick, "Rhoma Irama," 109.
120. "Rhoma Irama," 103. See also "Superstar with a Message"; Hatch, "Popular Music," 57–58; Pioquinto, "Dangdut," 86.
121. Leee, "Not Like."
122. Frederick, "Rhoma Irama," 112.
123. "Rhoma Irama," 104. See also Siegel, *Solo*, 215–218, 225–226.
124. From the song "Indonesia." See Yampolsky, "*Music of Indonesia 2*"; Kartomi, "From Kroncong to Dangdut," 284.
125. See Yampolsky, "*Music of Indonesia 2*"; Hatch, "Popular Music," 58.
126. Frederick, "Rhoma Irama," 116. See also Henschkel, "Perceptions," 58–59, 67–70; Piper, "Performances," 43–45; Moedjanto, *Tantangan,* 195–224.
127. Handley, "Dancing with Rhoma," 55.
128. Quoted in Frederick, "Rhoma Irama," 119, 121. See also Yamashita, "Listening," 113.
129. Handley, "Dancing with Rhoma," 57. See also Yampolsky, *"Music of Indonesia 2";* Taylor, *Global Pop,* 82–88.
130. Frederick, "Rhoma Irama," 115, 117.
131. Quoted in Yamashita, "Listening," 111–113; Frederick, "Rhoma Irama," 118; Yampolsky, "*Music of Indonesia 2.*"
132. Hatch, "Popular Music," 58.
133. Frederick, "Rhoma Irama," 118.
134. "Rhoma Irama," 124. See also Siegel, *Solo*, 215–218.
135. Frederick, "Rhoma Irama," 124. On the blacklist see "Rhoma Irama," *Asiaweek*, June 6, 1988; Handley, "Dancing with Rhoma." See also Frederick, "Dreams," 69.
136. See Henschkel, "Perceptions," 58–59, 67–70.
137. Quoted in Sahabullah, "Man Who Gave Dangdut."
138. See Piper, "Performances," 37–47.

139. "Rhoma Irama," 128.
140. See Manuel, *Popular Musics*, 212.
141. "Dancing with Rhoma," 55. See also Piper, "Performances," 45–47.
142. The quote is from Frederick, "Rhoma Irama," 129. See also Pemberton, "Musical Politics," 17; Piper and Jabo, "Indonesian Music," 25–26; Kartomi, "Minangkabau," 27; Kuipers, "Songs"; Yamashita, "Listening," 112.
143. Quoted in Handley, "Dancing with Rhoma," 57.
144. Excerpted and condensed from an article in *Tempo*, 1983, translated in Henschkel, "Perceptions," 67–68. See also Piper, "Performances," 45–47; Moedjanto, *Tantangan,* 195–224.
145. Handley, "Dancing with Rhoma," 57.
146. See Sutton, "Indonesia," 312; Aznam, "Pop Politics," 20; Aznam, "More of the Same," 28; McBeth, "Third Time," 25; *Asiaweek*, May 3, 1987, 33.
147. On these comparisons see Lockard, " 'Get Up, Stand Up.' " See also Murray, "Kampung Culture," 11; Broughton et al., eds., *World Music*, 426–427.
148. Hatley, "Cultural Expression," 261; Pioquinto, "Dangdut," 59–89; Frederick, "Dreams," 72, 77–78.
149. On the Black Brothers, see "Mostly Moral Support," 18. On Mambesak and Ap, see various issues of the Jakarta journal *Oikoumene:* 92 (January 1984), 20–22; 97 (June 1984), 12–13; 99 (August 1984), 27–30. I wish to thank George Aditjondro for supplying this information, including the articles.
150. See Kaye, "Early Dawning," 41–43; Murray, "Kampung Culture," 1–16; Hatley, "Constructions," 48–50, 56–66; Hatley, "Cultural Expression," 226–228, 243–245, 261; Jit, "Poet Extraordinaire"; "A Swashbuckler Mellows," 35; "W. S. Rendra," 34–35.
151. Quoted in Jensen, "Poet," 15. See also "Making History with History," 43; Murray, "Kampung Culture," 9; Foulcher, "Construction," 311–315.
152. See Shenon, "Indonesia Shuts"; McBeth, "Rude Awakening," 18–19; McBeth, "Stop Press," 17; McBeth, "Widening Ripples," 17–18; Winters, "Suharto's," 423–424; "Rights Groups Reports Increase"; Ramage, *Politics in Indonesia*, 111–112; Santoso, "Democratization," 26–28.
153. Quoted in Schwarz, *Nation*, 230. For a more detailed examination of his views, see G. Mohamad, *Sidelines;* Liddle, "Improvising," 1–53.
154. See Chambert-Loir, "Prokem," 80–88; Cohen, "Born to be Meek," 39; Aspinall, *Student Dissent*, 22–34.
155. Quoted in Vatikiotis, *Indonesian Politics*, 114, xv.
156. See, for example, Shenon, "Rioters"; Heryanto, "Class Act," 30; "Revolt in Medan," 43–44; "Indonesia: Medan Demonstrations," 1–13; McBeth, "Tinderbox," 14–15; Cohen, "Driven," 14–15; Cohen, "Under Volcano," 42–47.
157. See "Indonesia Ridding Press"; McBeth, "Troublesome," 28; McBeth, "Red Menace," 18, 20; McBeth, "Heavy Hand," 28; Cohen, "My Word," 30–31; Winters, "Suharto's," 423–424; Frederick, "Dreams," 54–89.
158. On the PDI crisis see Cohen, "New Zeal," 19–20; Heryanto, "Shedding Light," 32; McBeth, "Far from Over," 17, 20; McBeth, "The Gloves Are Off," 16; McBeth, "Hunting Season," 14–15; McBeth, "Political Engineering," 14–15; McBeth, "Streets of Fire," 14–16; McBeth,

"Temperature Rising," 22; Mydens, "Anti-Government Protesters" and "Indonesian Opposition"; McBeth, "Tinderbox," 14–15; Cohen, "Driven," 14–15; Winters, "Uncertainty," 428–430.

159. On the general developments discussed in the preceding paragraphs, see Vatikiotis, *Indonesian Politics*, 114–115, 191–205; MacIntyre, *Business and Politics*, 244–262; McKendrick, "Indonesia in 1991," 103–109; Crouch and Hill, "Introduction," 1–2; Hill and Mackie, "Introduction," xxiv–xxxv; Branigin, "Indonesia Booming"; Aznam, "Contested Closure," 20–21; Bourchier and Legge, eds., *Democracy*, 243–247, 272–312; Crouch, "Indonesia," 121–145; Schwarz, *Nation*, 264–307; Rasyid, "Indonesia," 154–162; McBeth, "Third Time," 24–25; McBeth, "Containment," 18–19; McBeth, "Unifying Force," 24; McBeth, "Next New Order," 22–24; Cohen, "Total Correction," 22–23; Ramage, *Politics in Indonesia*, especially 184–202; Ramage, "Indonesia at 50," 147–165; Winters, "Uncertainty," 428–431.
160. The main sources on Iwan Fals include Cohen, "Born to be Meek," 38–40; Harsono, "Star Is Banned," 14–15; Murray, "Kampung Culture," 1–16; "Poor Man's Superstar," 31; "Gugaran Bencana," 11; *Asiaweek*, June 16, 1993, 46; Hatley, "Cultural Expression," 243, 261–262, 264; Henschkel, "Perceptions," 53–71; Kartomi, "From Kroncong to Dangdut," 284–287.
161. Summarized from a report in *Tempo*, translated in Henschkel, "Perceptions," 65–66.
162. On this affair see Harsono, "Star Is Banned," 14–15; Murray, "Kampung Culture," 11–13.
163. Harsono, "Star Is Banned," 14–15.
164. Murray, "Kampung Culture," 12.
165. Cohen, "Born to be Meek," 38–39.
166. Quoted in "Poor Man's Superstar," 31.
167. See Adam Schwarz, "Charismatic Enigma," 35.
168. Quoted in Henschkel, "Perceptions," 61.
169. Translated by Suzan Piper, quoted in Henschkel, "Perceptions," 71. See also Kartomi, "From Kroncong to Dangdut," 286.
170. Quoted in *Asiaweek*, June 16, 1993, 46. See also "The Poor Man's Superstar," 31; Murray, "Kampung Culture," 11–14; Hatley, "Cultural Expression," 261–262; Harsono, "Star Is Banned," 14–15; Kartomi, "From Kroncong to Dangdut," 285–286; Kartomi, " 'Traditional Music Weeps,' " 389.
171. See "Rebel Rockers," 42–43.
172. See Piper, "Performances," 37–43.
173. On rap see Henschkel, "Perceptions," 55–56; Piper, "Performances," 40, 57.
174. On this point see Yamashita, "Listening," 116–118. The concepts are taken from Peacock, *Rites of Modernization*, 5–6.

Chapter 3: Philippines: Pinoy, Protest, and People Power

1. F. De Leon, "Poetry," 266–282.
2. Aguilar, "Introduction," 151.
3. See, for example, Iyer, *Video Night in Kathmandu*, 166.

4. Unless otherwise cited, the material on Philippine history, society, and modern politics is based on the following: Agoncillo, *Short History;* Bello, "Aquino's Elite," 1020–1030; Boyce, *Philippines;* Brisbin, "Electronic Revolution," 49–63; Bunge, *Philippines;* Buss, *Cory Aquino;* Cady, *History;* Chapman, *Inside;* Constantino, *Neocolonial Identity* and *The Filipinos;* Coronel, "Dateline," 166–185; Corpuz, *Philippines;* Dolan, ed., *Philippines;* Enriquez, ed., *Philippine World-View;* Goertzen, "Agents," 20–21; Goodno, *Philippines;* Guillermo and Win, *Historical Dictionary;* Hawes, *Philippine State;* Hutchcroft, *Philippines;* Hutchcroft, "Unravelling Past," 430–434; Hutchison, "Class," 191–212; Ileto, "Outlines," 130–159; Karnow, *In Our Image;* Jones, *Red Revolution;* Kerkvliet, *Everyday Politics;* Kerkvliet and Mojares, eds., *From Marcos;* Lardizabal and Tensuan-Leogardo, eds., *Readings;* Larkin, "Philippine History," 595–628; Larkin, *Sugar* and *The Pampangans;* Lightfoot, *Philippines;* May, *Social Engineering;* Mahar Mangahas, "Distributive Justice," 80–108; Marlay, "Democracy"; Mercado, ed., *Eyewitness History;* Muego, *Spectator Society;* Mulder, *Inside;* Neher, *Southeast Asia*, 55–86; Neher and Marlay, *Democracy: Southeast Asia*, 52–74; Nelson, *Philippines;* Osborne, *Southeast Asia;* Pinches, "Philippines'," 105–136; Putzel, *Captive Land;* Rafael, *Contracting Colonialism;* Reid and Guerrero, *Corazon Aquino;* Rivera, *State;* E. San Juan, *Crisis;* Schirmer and Shalom, eds., *Philippines Reader;* Seagrave, *Marcos Dynasty;* Stanley, *Nation;* Steinberg, *The Philippines;* Steinberg et al., *In Search of Southeast Asia;* Thompson, *Anti-Marcos Struggle;* Timberman, *Changeless Land;* Villacorta, "Philippine," 39–40; Vreeland et al., *Area Handbook: Philippines;* Warshaw, *Southeast Asia;* Wurfel, "Change or Continuity," 424–429; Wurfel, *Filipino Politics.*
5. *The Philippines*, xiii.
6. Based largely on Hutchison, "Class," 192; Neher and Marlay, *Democracy: Southeast Asia*, 53; Pinches, "Philippines'," 103–104; Greenwood, ed., *Asia Yearbook 1992*, 7; *The Asia & Pacific Review 1993/94*, 215; United Nations, *Industrial Statistics 1991*, 774–783; *Billboard International 1996*, 256.
7. See, for example, Vreeland et al., *Area Handbook: Philippines*, 3; Larkin, *Sugar;* Owen, *Prosperity.*
8. See Maria Mangahas, "Music Acculturation," 56–64; R. Santos, "Philippines," 157–175; Joaquin, "Legacy." 20–21; "Queen 'King' "; Hila, "In Forefront," 16–21. On traditional and folk music in the Philippines, see Lardizabal and Tensuan-Leogardo, *Readings*, 156–168; Maceda et al., "Philippines," 631–652; Malm, *Music Cultures of Asia*, 28–33; FE B. Mangahas, "The State of Philippine Music," 62–64; Mohd. Taib Osman, ed., *Traditional Drama*, 172–175, 246–289; Pfeiffer, *Filipino Music;* Merino, *Popular Music;* Nelson, *Philippines*, 107; Lightfoot, *Philippines*, 51.
9. See comments by Teresita Maceda in Tiongson, *Politics of Culture*, 77–78; Lardizabal et al., *Readings*, 160; Ileto, *Payson*, 98, 106–108; Ness, "When Seeing," 8–13; Guillermo and Win, *Historical Dictionary*, 13–14, 27.
10. See Ileto, *Payson*, esp. 1–74.
11. Quoted in Steinberg, *In Search of Southeast Asia*, 274.
12. Steinberg, *The Philippines*, 64. The points made in this section on the Philippine Revolution and American colonial policies in the Philippines are elaborated in Lockard, "Gunboat Diplomacy," 35–57.

13. The nationalist argument is made in Agoncillo, *Revolt*. For an alternative view see May, *Battle*.
14. "Philippine History," 623.
15. *In Our Image*, 198. On the powerful families see McCoy, ed., *Anarchy*.
16. De Leon, "Poetry," 272–274.
17. Quoted in Sta. Maria, *Philippines in Song*, 56–69, 132–133; Ileto, *Payson*, esp. 118–119, 181–184.
18. "Capampangan Zarzuela," 186.
19. Larkin, "Capampangan Zarzuela," 189.
20. Excerpted and condensed from a 1988 study by Indian-American journalist Pico Iyer, *Video Night in Kathmandu*, 168–169. See also Mulder, *Inside Philippine Society*, 3–4.
21. See Fernandez, *Iloilo Zarzuela*, 96; McCoy, "Culture," 161, 171, 201–203. On the zarzuela generally, see Fernandez, "Zarzuela to Sarswela," 320–343; Fernandez, *Palabas*, esp. 74–94; *Filipino Heritage*, 1640–1648; N. Tiongson, *Filipinas Circa* 1907, 1–9; J. Roces, "Traditional Theatre," 174–175; Yousof, *Dictionary: Southeast Asia*, 320–327; Brandon, *Theatre in Southeast Asia*, 78, 284. See also Fernandez, "Contemporary Theatre," 65–77; Lacanico-Buenaventura, "Theatre in Manila," 50–66; Guillermo and Win, *Historical Dictionary*, 258–259; San Juan Jr., *Philippine Temptation*, 227–230.
22. See Sacerdoti, "Hamburgerization," 45–46.
23. See, for example, Rafael, *Contracting Colonialism*, 4.
24. *In Our Image*, 361. Karnow's book has been much criticized. See, for example, San Juan Jr., *Philippine Temptation*, 5–6.
25. See, for example, Corpuz, *Philippines*, 5; Steinberg, *The Philippines*, xiii–xiv.
26. See Tiglao and Tasker, "Options," 16; Timberman, *Changeless Land*, 71.
27. Summarized from the account by journalist Sterling Seagrave in *Marcos Dynasty*, 189, 199.
28. *Video Night in Kathmandu*, 162. See also Jayasuriya, "Structural Adjustment," 51–53.
29. Quoted in Schirmer and Shalom, *Philippines Reader*, 169.
30. See Rafael, "Patronage," 49–81.
31. See, for example, Steinberg, *Philippines*, 126–147; Boyce, *Philippines*, 1–5; Coronel, "Dateline," 167–168; Timberman, *Changeless Land*, 322–369; Neher, *Southeast Asia*, 74; McBeth, "Crusade," 24–25: Hunt, "Society," 70, 112–115; Lindsey, "Economy," 119–120; Rivera, *State*, 48.
32. Goodno, *Philippines*, 1.
33. See Kerkvliet, *Everyday Politics*, 271.
34. Putzel, *Captive Land*, xix.
35. See, for example, Goodno, *Philippines*, 1; Wetherall, "Sexual Capitalists," 105–107; Mahar Mangahas, "Distributive Justice"; Rivera, *State*, 32–35; Gonzalez and Holmes, "Philippine," 300–317.
36. See, for example, Sacerdoti, "Hamburgerization," 45; Roces, "Filipino Identity," 279–315.
37. *Neocolonial Identity*, 1. See also Guillermo, *Covert Presence*, 11–64; Eric San Juan, "Making Filipino," 1–11; Roces, "Filipino," 282–283.

38. Quoted in *Newsweek*, February 1, 1988, 36. For a more nuanced view, see "Culture, Development and Democracy," esp. 28–34. See also Mulder, *Inside Philippine Society*, 75–80.
39. *Pinoy Forever*, 58.
40. On this point see Sidel, "Philippines," 158. See also Teodoro, "Toward," 12–16.
41. On this last point see Rafael, "Taglish," 101–126. On "Taglish" see also *Asiaweek*, October 15, 1986, 39; Cristobal, "Philippines' Elite."
42. Poem by Jose Maria Sison, excerpted from Francia, ed., *Brown River*, 242–243.
43. See Vreeland et al., *Area Handbook: Philippines, 95; Asiaweek*, November 4, 1988, 52; Alegre, *Pinoy Forever*, Cristobal, "Philippines' Elite"; Edgerton, "Society," 106–107; Gonzalez, *Language*, 175: Teodoro, "Toward," 12–15; Guillermo and Win, *Historical Dictionary*, 5, 80.
44. "From Philippine Revolution," 126. See also Teodoro and San Juan, *Two Perspectives;* San Juan Jr., *Philippine Temptation.*
45. See, for example, Medina, "Pagbabago!" 125–144; B. Lumbera, *Revaluation*, 3–177; Salanga and Pacheco, eds., *Versus; Poetry of People's War;* Rafael, "Fishing, Underwear," 2–7; Encarnacion, "Social Consciousness," 1–14; E. San Juan, Jr., ed., *Introduction;* Francia, ed., *Brown River;* Roces, "Filipino," 279–315.
46. See, for example, Fajardo, "Decolonization," 92–111; Fernandez, "Mass Culture," 492; B. Lumbera, "Commodity," 273–280; Guillermo, *Covert Presence*, 30–40; Montanez, *New Mass Art;* E. San Juan, *Towards a People's Literature;* N. Tiongson, "Filipinicity," 3–11; N. Tiongson, *Politics of Culture;* Casper, *Opposing.*
47. From his poem, "A Philippine History Lesson," in Francia, ed., *Brown River*, 256.
48. *Neocolonial Identity*, 25. See also Eric San Juan, "Making Filipino History," 1–11.
49. *Synthetic Culture*, 29.
50. On one of the most important of these groups, Teatro Pilipino, see "Towards a New Cultural Identity," 31. For a general study of the seminal Philippines Educational Theatre Association and the liberation theater network, see Van Erven, *Playful Revolution*, 29–94. See also Bodden, "Grass Roots," 33–46; Fernandez, "From Ritual," 389–419; Fernandez, *Palabas*, 104–153; N. Tiongson, *Politics of Culture;* Valerio, "Tendencies," 64; Castrillo, "Philippine Political Theatre," 528–538; Van Erven, "Phillipine Political Theatre," 57–78; Godinez-Ortega, *"Datu Matu,"* 238–245.
51. See, for example, Buruma, "Philippines' Multiple Heritage," 38–39; Roces, "Filipino," 301–307.
52. Excerpted and condensed from Fernandez, "Philippine-American Cultural Interaction," 28; Fernandez, "Mass Culture," 492.
53. See, for example, Constantino, *Synthetic Culture;* Fernandez, "Philippine Popular Culture," 26–44; Flores, "People, Popular Culture," 46–55; Guillermo, "Social Roots," 281–292; B. Lumbera, *Revaluation;* S. Reyes, "Introduction," 1; Lauzon, "Postmodernism," 28–37.

54. The quotes are from Flores, "People, Popular Culture," 48, 51. Perhaps the most persistent critic has been Renato Constantino. See, for example, *Synthetic Culture*. See also Lauzon, "Postmodernism," 33–37.
55. Unless otherwise cited, the major sources on the popular musics of the Philippines include: "A Taste of Filipino Salt," 47; *Book of the Philippines 1976;* Broughton et al., eds., *World Music*, 438–439; A. de Leon, "Pinoy Rock," 33–37; F. De Leon, "Poetry," 266–282; Elequin, "Appreciation," 81–99; Fernandez, "Philippine-American Cultural Interaction," 20–30; Fernandez, "Philippine Popular Culture," 27–44; Ford, "Southeasterly View," 218–228; "Freddie A. and the Joys of Pinoy," 15; Gamalinda and Pimental, "Notes," 16–23; Gimenez-Maceda, "Popular Music," 24–32; Hila, "Fusion," 34–39; Japitana, *Superstars of Pop;* Laceba, "Notes on 'Bakya,' " 212–217; Linmark, "And Next Song," 150–163; Maceda, "Philippines," 631–652; Malm, *Music Cultures*, 29–30; FE B. Mangahas, "State," 62–82; Maria Mangahas, "Music Acculturation," 56–64; Mangusad, "Pen-Pen," 49–56; Mayne, "Songs of Dissent," 67–69; Marin, "To Unite," 15–18; Mikich, "Paalam Uncle Sam," 320–329; Molina, "Philippine Pop Music," 21–24; Montanez, *New Mass Art*, 29–46; pamphlet accompanying *Philippines: Bangon!;* Pfeiffer, *Filipino Music;* Poore, "Freddie Aguilar," 16–17, 57; E. Reyes, "Pilipino Sound," 47–48; Sweeney, *Virgin Directory*, 151–153, 166–168; Tan, "Aguilar" and "Star of Anak"; "The Man from Mindanao," 34; N. Tiongson, *Politics of Culture*, 62–68; Villanueva, "Pinoy Pop," 8–10; various articles in *Asiaweek*. Although it arrived too late to be used in this study, see also Caruncho, *Punks*.
56. Lumbera, *Revaluation*, 188. On comics see Lent, "Asian Comic Strips," 47–48; Marcelo, "Komiks," 18–20; "Opiate of the Masses," 57–58; Alegre, *Pinoy Forever*, 60, 78–79; *Philippine Almanac 1986*, 494–495, 503. On the film industry see Armes, *Third World Film Making*, 151–154; David, *Fields of Vision;* Fernandez, "Philippine-American Cultural Interaction," 25–26; Film Center, "Exciting," 19–21; Flores, "By Way of Film," 45–56; Flores, "Slum and Town," 45–52; Francia, "Philippine Cinema," 209–218; Fernandez, "Philippine Popular Culture," 30–33; Lent, *Asian Film Industry*, 149–184; Lent, "Historical Overview of Southeast Asian Film," 98–102, 152–163; B. Lumbera, *Revaluation*, 181–223; Marchetti, "Four Hundred Years," 24–48; Pinga, "Cinema," 153–157; Emmanuel Reyes, *Notes on Cinema;* Santos, "Idol, Bestiary," 209–224; Silberman, "Was Tolstoy Right," 69–78; Sotto, "Notes," 1–14; Tasker, "Real-Life Drama," 48–50; N. Tiongson, *Politics of Culture*, 48–61; L. Tiongson, "Alternative Cinema," 26–30; L. Tiongson, "Filipino Film Industry," 23–61; *Philippine Almanac 1986*, 477–492; *Philippine Yearbook 1989*, 260–262, 929.
57. Lino Brocka, quoted in Ford, "Southeasterly View," 225.
58. Excerpted and condensed from a study by cultural studies scholar Eleanor T. Elequin, "Appreciation," 90.
59. On Estrada and other media personalities running for political office, see Tasker, "Reel-Life Politicians," 18. See also Lopez, "Manila's Film," 44–48; Sidel, "Philippines," 165; Sotto, "Notes," 4–6. For an extensive analysis of Lino Brocka and his work, see David, *Fields of Vision*.

60. Fernandez, "Philippine-American Cultural Interaction," 23–24; Fernandez, "Philippine Popular Culture," 33–35; B. Lumbera, "Commodity," 278; Japitana, *Superstars of Pop*, 18–25; Pagulayan, "Radio," 93–95; *Philippine Yearbook 1989*, 926–950.
61. See Fernandez, "Philippine-American Cultural Interaction," 21; *Book of Philippines*, 287–289.
62. Gronow, "International Trends," 314.
63. Kirkup, *Filipinescas*, 79.
64. Peter Manuel omits the Philippines entirely in his generally comprehensive survey of popular musics in the non-Western world. See *Popular Musics.* See also Broughton et al., eds., *World Music*, 438.
65. See Lacaba, "Notes on 'Bakya,' " 213–217; Rafael, "Taglish," 101–126; Sotto, "Notes," 13.
66. Molina, "Philippine Pop Music," 21.
67. "Philippine-American Cultural Interaction," 27.
68. Iyer, *Video Night in Kathmandu*, 153, 172–173. See also Broughton et al., eds., *World Music*, 438.
69. Linmark, "And Next Song," 150–163. On the emigrants see Marlay, "Democracy."
70. A. de Leon, "Pinoy Rock," 36. Many of these stars are profiled in Japitana, *Superstars of Pop.*
71 Japitana, *Superstars of Pop*, 72–73.
72. See *Asiaweek*, March 26, 1982; Sweeney, *World Music*, 152, 167–168.
73. FE B. Mangahas, "State," 65–66. On the recording industry of the 1970s see Japitana, *Superstars of Pop*, 10–41.
74. Quoted in Gimenez-Maceda, "Popular Music," 24–25.
75. Villanueva, "Pinoy Pop," 10. See also FE B. Mangahas, "State," 66; Gimenez-Maceda, "Popular Music," 24–32.
76. For a detailed profile of Rico Puno, see Japitana, *Superstars of Pop*, 10, 13, 33–34, 117–123. On Hanopol see *Superstars*, 79–84.
77. Gimenez-Maceda, "Popular Music," 24–26; Fernandez, "Philippine Popular Culture," 37–38; Japitana, *Superstars of Pop*, 6–8; Villanueva, "Pinoy Pop," 10.
78. See Gamalinda and Pimental, "Notes," 16.
79. Quoted in Molina, "Philippine Pop Music," 22.
80. See FE B. Mangahas, "State," 66; *Book of Philippines 1976*, 289; N. Tiongson, *Politics of Culture*, 84.
81. Elequin, "Appreciation," 84.
82. See Gimenez-Maceda, "Popular Music," 32.
83. "Introduction," in Enriquez, *Philippine World-View*, 3.
84. Quoted in Mikich, "Paalam Uncle Sam," 327.
85. Quoted in Gimenez-Maceda, "Popular Music," 27.
86. Elequin, "Appreciation," 89, 87; Gimenez-Maceda, "Popular Music," 27; E. Reyes, "The Pilipino Sound," 48.
87. Villaruz, "Florante," 24–25.
88. Quoted in Gimenez-Maceda, "Popular Music," 30–31.

89. Elequin, "Appreciation," 92, 86–87; Gimenez-Maceda, "Popular Music," 30–31; A. de leon, "Pinoy Rock," 37; Mikich, "Paalam Uncle Sam," 321–329.
90. Gimenez-Maceda, "Popular Music," 28–29, 31; Elequin, "Appreciation," 95–97; A. de leon, "Pinoy Rock," 36.
91. For a profile see Japitana, *Superstars of Pop*, 136–141; A. de leon, "Pinoy Rock," 37.
92. On this festival see Japitana, *Superstars of Pop*, 35–37.
93. "Philippine-American Cultural Interaction," 23.
94. See Reyes, "The Pilipino Sound," 47–48.
95. "Philippine-American Cultural Interaction," 28.
96. See, for example, comments by Teresita Maceda in N. Tiongson, *Politics of Culture*, 78–79; B. Lumbera, *Revaluation*, 190.
97. Quoted in Maceda's comments in N. Tiongson, *Politics of Culture*, 80.
98. See pamphlet for *Philippines: Bangon!* See also Muego, *Spectator*, 62–68.
99. From pamphlet, *Philippines: Bangon!*
100. Quoted in Mayne, "Songs of Dissent," 68.
101. San Juan, ed., *Introduction*, 76–77. This song is included in the album, *Handog Ng Pilipino Sa Mundo* (WEA Records, 94–288, 1988).
102. See Roces, "Filipino," 287–293; "Atang de la Rama," 5; "Paalam, Ka Atang," 22–33.
103 Hernandez, *Rice Grains*, 34–35.
104. The Marcos quotes are from FE B. Mangahas, "State," 64.
105. Quoted in pamphlet accompanying *Philippines: Bangon!* 4. On revolutionary NPA music see also Montanez, *New Mass Art*, 29–46; Salanga and Pacheco, eds., *Versus.*
106. See pamphlet, *Philippines: Bangon!*
107. The most detailed sketch of Aguilar and his career can be found in Japitana, *Superstars of Pop*, 11–12, 19, 44–53. See also Mayne, "Songs of Dissent," 67–69; Poore, "Freddie Aguilar," 57; E. Reyes, "Pilipino Sound," 48; "Freddie A. and the Joys of Pinoy," 15; Sweeney, *World Music*, 151–153, 166–168; Broughton et al., eds., *World Music*, 438–439.
108. See Aguilar's album, *Anak* (Polydor Records, 2427-020, 1978).
109. E. Reyes, "The Pilipino Sound," 48.
110. See Japitana, *Superstars of Pop*, 19; Broughton et al., eds., *World Music*, 438.
111. Quoted in Poore, "Freddie Aguilar," 57.
112. See "Freddie A. and the Joys of Pinoy," 15; Aguilar, "Introduction," 152.
113. "Pilipino Sound," 47.
114. On Jara and the New Song movement in Chile see Lockard, " 'Get Up, Stand Up.' "
115. Summarized from an article by Malaysian journalist Grace Poore, "Freddie Aguilar," 17, 57.
116. See Buruma, "Man and Messiah," 53–55.
117. Buss, *Cory Aquino*, 16. For a fascinating portrayal of the developments, see also Fenton, "Snap Revolution," 33–156. For a more elite-centered view, see Tasker, "Inside Story," 27–28.
118. Buss, *Cory Aquino*, 36. See also Fernandez, "Culture of Revolution," 26–29.
119. See Brisbin, "Electronic Revolution," 49; Fenton, "Snap Revolution."

120. See, for example, Kerkvliet and Mojares, *From Marcos;* Bello, "Aquino's Elite," 1020; Timberman, *Changeless Land*, 155–158, 168–169; Hutchison, "Class," 193–194, 198–209. The most extensive study of the anti-Marcos struggle is Thompson, *Anti-Marcos Struggle*.
121. See Kulkarni and Tasker, "Promises to Keep," 22.
122. Warshaw, *Southeast Asia*, 208.
123. See Aguilar's album, *Freddie Aguilar's Greatest Hits* (Ugat Records, 5289, 1979). This English translation is taken from Mayne, "Songs of Dissent," 67.
124. See Buruma, "Man and Messiah," 53.
125. Quoted in Mayne, "Songs of Dissent," 67.
126. Quoted in Mercado, *People Power*, 249.
127. Quoted in Mayne, "Songs of Dissent," 67. On this controversy, see Buruma, "Brocka," 68–69.
128. Mercado, *People Power*, 249.
129. Fenton, "Snap Revolution," 50.
130. See Mayne, "Songs of Dissent," 69.
131. Quoted in Mercado, *People Power*, 131.
132. For two useful collections, see *Handog Ng Filipino Sa Mundo* ("The Filipinos' Gift to the World"), (WEA Records, 94–288, 1988); *Mabuhay Ang Kalayaan* ("Long Live Freedom"), (G Records, 2013, 1988).
133. See, for example, the debate in N. Tiongson, *Politics of Culture*, 62–89.
134. Gamalinda and Pimental, "Notes," 16.
135. Brisbin, "Electronic Revolution," 63.
136. See, for example, Goodno, *Philippines*, 105; Reid and Guerrero, *Corazon Aquino;* Coronel, "Dateline," 166–185; Kerkvliet and Mojares, eds., *From Marcos;* Timberman, *Changeless Land*, 374–400; Hutchison, "Class," 193–194, 198–209; Lindsey, "Economy," 124–128; Rivera, *State*, 17–23.
137. Timberman, *Changeless Land*, 386.
138. See Reid and Guerrero, *Corazon Aquino*, xii.
139. Quoted in Broad and Cavanaugh, *Plundering Paradise*, xvii. See also Pinches, "Philippines'" 124–127.
140. See Boyce, *Philippines*, 4.
141. Connell, "Picking," 8.
142. See, for example, Goertzen, "Agents"; Goodno, *Philippines*, 177–183. On the Philippine mass media generally, see Lent, "Mass Communication," 233–287; Lent, "Who Owns," 1–34; Lent, "The Philippines," 191–209.
143. Quoted in Shenon, "How Subic Bay." See also Lindsey, "Economy," 185–187; Steinberg, *Philippines*, 170–175.
144. Wurfel, *Filipino Politics*, 340.
145. On this point see Reid and Guerrero, *Corazon Aquino*, 249.
146. Wurfel, "Change or Continuity," 424–429; Tasker, "Treaty," 12; McBeth, "Internal Contradictions," 16–18; Tiglao, "Fraternal Foes," 18–19; Tiglao, "Death Threat," 29–30.
147. Buss, *Cory Aquino*, 187. See also Kulkarni, "Mid-Term Blues," 16–21; Kulkarni and Tasker, "Promises," 23; Hutchcroft, *Philippines;* Hutchcroft, "Unraveling," 430–434; Marlay, "Democracy"; " 'Disappearances' in

Philippines," 1–13; Tiglao, "Open Season," 28, 30; Tiglao, "Ramos Redux," 17; Velasco, "Philippine," 106–109; Magno, "Philippines," 285–299.

148. Mydens, "Philippine Leaders."
149. Excerpted and summarized from a 1988 account, "The Man from Mindanao," 34.
150. On Aguilar's putative political plans, see *Asiaweek*, November 13, 1987.
151. See, for example, his recent albums *Child of the Revolution* (Classic 2 Records 001, 1990) and *Crazy War* (Ivory Records A754, 1987).
152. "The Man from Mindanao," 34. See also *Asiaweek*, September 16, 1988, 44.
153. See Maria Mangahas, "Music Acculturation," 62–64.
154. The quotes are in Gamalinda and Pimental, "Notes," 22; "The Man From Mindanao," 34.
155. See Maria Mangahas, "Music Acculturation," 63; Castrillo, "Philippine Political Theatre," 537; Van Erven, "Theatre and Liberation," 58; Van Erven, "Philippine Political Theatre," 72–75. On Ayala's recent activities, see Caruncho, *Punks.*
156. On APO, see the comments by group member Jim Paredes in N. Tiongson, *Politics of Culture*, 74–75, 84–88. See also *Asiaweek*, June 3, 1988, 59.
157. Quoted in *Asiaweek*, October 4, 1985. The lyrics to "American Junk" are taken from the liner notes to the album *The Best of the Apo Hiking Society* (WEA P-94075, 1982).
158. Quoted in N. Tiongson, *Politics of Culture*, 111.
159. The quotes are in Gamalinda and Pimental, "Notes," 17; "A Taste of Filipino Salt," 47. On Asin see also Japitana, *Superstars of Pop*, 48; Mikich, "Paalam Uncle Sam," 321–329.
160. See N. Tiongson, *Politics of Culture*, 111, 113; Japitana, *Superstars of Pop*, 47; Mikich, "Paalam Uncle Sam," 321–329.
161. Quoted in Mikich, "Paalam Uncle Sam," 324.
162. On Inang Laya see *Asiaweek*, August 9, 1987. I am indebted to Russell Middleton for finding me copies of cassettes by Inang Laya and Patatag. See also Mikich, "Paalam Uncle Sam," 321–329.
163. Mangusad, "Pen-Pen," 49–56.
164. Mikich, "Paalam Uncle Sam," 321–329.
165. See Constantino, *Synthetic Culture*, 37; Mikich, "Paalam Uncle Sam," 326–327. On New Song see Lockard, " 'Get Up, Stand Up.' "
166. Fernandez, "Mass Culture," 488–502; Mikich, "Paalam Uncle Sam," 328–329.
167. See Mydens, "In the Philippines"; "Manila's Women Warriors of Words," 53.
168. From a report on CNN Headline News, May 29, 1993.
169. See *Asiaweek*, January 15, 1988, 28. For a brief profile of Legaspi, see Japitana, *Superstars of Pop*, 89–91. For a useful study of pop music trends in the 1990s see Caruncho, *Punks.*
170. "Cock or Bull," 1–30. See also Emmons, "Fowl Play," 30–31.
171. *Revaluation*, 191. See also Teresita Maceda's comments in N. Tiongson, *Politics of Culture*, 77.
172. *Rice Grains*, 64.

Chapter 4: Songs for Life, Songs for Struggle

1. From Caravan's song "Rice Waiting for Rain"; English lyrics are in the booklet accompanying the record *Thailand: Songs for Life* (Paredon 1042, 1978), 11.
2. Based largely on Hewison, "Of Regimes," 160; Hewison, "Emerging," 135–136; Neher and Marlay, *Democracy: Southeast Asia*, 30; Greenwood, ed., *Asia Yearbook 1992*, 7; *The Asia & Pacific Review 1993/1994*, 246; United Nations, *Industrial Statistics 1991*, 774–783; *Billboard International 1996*, 262.
3. Unless otherwise cited, the main sources for the historical, social, and political background include the following: Anderson, "Studies," 193–247; Anderson, "Withdrawal Symptoms," 13–30; Anderson and Mendiones, eds., *In the Mirror;* Bartak, "Student"; Basche, *Thailand;* Blanchard, *Thailand;* Brown, *State and Ethnic: Southeast Asia*, 158–205; Cady, *History of Postwar Southeast Asia;* Chu, *Thailand;* Cohen, *Thai Society;* Durrenberger, "Power," 1–21; Elliott, *Thailand;* Fairclough and Tasker, "Separate," 22–31; Chutima, *Rise and Fall;* Girling, *Interpreting;* Girling, *Thailand;* Girling, "Thailand," 305–319; Grace, "Note on Thailand"; Griffin, "Notes on Thai," 1037–1061; Flood, "Thai Left," 55–67; Handley, "Rainbow Coalition," 11–12; Heinze, "Ten Days," 491–508; Hewison, "Emerging," 137–162; Hewison, "Of Regimes," 159–190; Hewison, "State and Capitalist," 73–83; Hirsch, "Thai Countryside," 320–354; Ikemoto, *Income Distribution;* Iyer, *Video Night in Kathmandu*, 287–316; Keyes, *Thailand* and *Golden Peninsula;* King, "Thai Parliamentary," 1109–1123; Kulick and Wilson, *Thailand's Turn;* LePoer, ed., *Thailand;* Likhit, *Demi Democracy;* Moore, *Thailand;* Morell and Samudavanija, *Political Conflict;* Muscat, *Fifth Tiger;* Neher, *Southeast Asia*, 23–54; Neher, "Thailand's Politics," 435–439; Neher, "Transition to Democracy"; Neher and Marlay, *Democracy: Southeast Asia*, 29–51; Ochey, "Political Parties," 251–277; Pasuk and Baker, *Thailand;* Prizzia, *Thailand;* Reynolds, ed., *National Identity;* Smith et al., *Area Handbook;* Smalley, *Linguistic Diversity and National Unity;* Steinberg, *In Search;* Suchit, "Thailand in 1995"; Suchit, "Thailand," 131–139; Suchit, *Military in Thai Politics; Thailand in the 1980s;* Surin, "Making," 141–166; Turton et al., eds., *Thailand;* Warr, ed., *Thai Economy;* Warshaw, *Southeast Asia;* Wilson, *Politics;* Wright, "Thailand's Return," 418–423; Wright, *Balancing Act;* Wyatt, *Thailand;* Zimmerman, "Student," 509–529.
4. See, for example, Wright, *Balancing Act*, 19–25; Durrenberger, "Power," 10–14; Anderson, "Studies," 193–247.
5. On this point see Cohen, *Thai Society*, 11–35; Keyes, *Thailand*, 3–5; Pasuk and Baker, *Thailand*, 3–88; Reynolds, ed., *National Identity*. See also Smalley, *Linguistic Diversity*, 277–360; Thongchai, *Siam Mapped*, 12–16; Durrenberger, "Power," 1–21.
6. See, for example, Cohen, *Thai Society*, 67–87; Brown, *State and Ethnic: Southeast Asia*, 158–205; Fairclough and Tasker, "Separate," 22–23; Smalley, *Linguistic Diversity*, 71–101, 155–175; Vatikiotis, "Out," 31–32.
7. The main sources for traditional music and culture include: Basche, *Thailand*, 62–82; Blanchard, *Thailand*, 462–478; Broughton et al., eds., *World Music*, 440–448; Chu, *Thailand Today;* Fuller, "Thai Music," 152–155; Gaston, "Thailand," 115–155; Kartomi, " 'Traditional Music'," 366–400; Landgraf,

liner notes to *Flower of Isan;* Landgraf, "Soeng," 6–8, 46; liner notes to *Musical Atlas: Thailand;* Malm, *Music Cultures: Asia*, 118–137; Mattani, *Dance, Drama;* Miettinen, *Classical Dance in South-East Asia*, 40–74; Miller, *Traditional Music of the Lao;* Miller and Chonpairot, *History of Siamese Music*, 1–192; Mohd. Taib Osman, ed., *Traditional Drama;* Moore, *Thailand*, 220–240; Morton, "Thailand," 712–722; Morton, "Music of Thailand," 63–80; Morton, *Traditional Music; Thailand in the 1980s;* Myers-Moro, "Musical Notation," 101–105; Myers-Moro, "Thai Music," 190–194; Myers-Moro, *Thai Music and Musicians;* Panya, *Thai Music;* Surapone, "Theatre," 95–104; Tapanee, ed., *Essays;* Wong and Lysloff, "Threshold," 315–339; Wright, "Dontri," 156–157.

8. Myers–Moro, "Musical Notation," 101–103.
9. Excerpted from the study by American musicologist David Morton, "Music of Thailand," 63.
10. On like' see Moore, *Thailand*, 231; Panya, *Thai Music*, 53–70; Mattani, *Dance*, 2, 6–10, 184–186; Myers-Moro, *Thai Music;* Brandon, *Theatre in Southeast Asia;* Brandon, "Theatre," 67; Yousof, *Dictionary: Southeast Asia*, 140–146.
11. See, for example, Grow, "Tarnishing," 47–67; Brandon, "Theatre," 64–65; Brandon, *Theatre in Southeast Asia;* Chua, "Traditional Dance," 165–171; Surapone, "Theatre," 104.
12. See Landgraf, liner notes to *Flower of Isan;* Landgraf, "Soeng," 6–8, 46; Miller, *Traditional Music*, 35–72, 101–188; Pasuk and Baker, *Thailand*, 70, 73; Basche, *Thailand*, 68–69; Compton, "Traditional," 149–160; Broughton et al., eds., *World Music*, 444–447.
13. Excerpted and condensed from a study by American anthropologist Wendell Blanchard, *Thailand*, 472.
14. See Myers-Moro, "Musical Notation," 103; Mattani, *Dance*, 185–189; Gaston, "Thailand," 130–132, 136–139.
15. *Thailand*, 305.
16. Neher, "Transition," 5; Kulick and Wilson, *Thailand's Turn*, 27. For a chronology of the coups, see Wright, *Balancing Act*, 320–323.
17. See Likhit, *Demi Democracy;* Neher, "Transition," 2–3.
18. See, for example, Kulick and Wilson, *Thailand's Turn*, 3; Likhit, *Demi Democracy*, 222–223; Neher, *Southeast Asia*, 34–35.
19. Tasker, "Traveller's Tales," 52. See also Ockey, "Political," 251–277; Neher and Marlay, *Democracy: Southeast Asia*, 36–43; Neher, "Transition," 3; Robertson, "Rise," 924–941; LoGerfo, "Attitudes," 904–923.
20. See Cohen, *Thai Society*, 67–87; Brown, *State and Ethnic: Southeast Asia*, 158–205; Fairclough and Tasker, "Separate," 22–23.
21. See, for example, Hewison, "The State," 73–83: Hewison, "Of Regimes" 167–180; Pasuk, "Technocrats," 10–31.
22. See Kulick and Wilson, *Thailand's Turn*, 108, 123; Neher, *Southeast Asia*, 36; Dessaint, "Thais Rising," 33; Ikemoto, *Income Distribution*, ix–xi; Handley, "Rainbow Coalition," 11; Turton, "Current," 108–113; Brown, *State and Ethnic: Southeast Asia*, 173–187; Pasuk and Baker, *Thailand*, 64–67; Fairclough and Tasker, "Separate," 22–23; Warr, *Thai Economy*, 5–9, 325–354, 401–435; Hirsch, "Thai Countryside," 320–353; Fairclough, "Missing Class," 25–26.

23. Excerpted and condensed from a report by journalist Paul Handley, "How the Other Half Live," 47–48.
24. See Kulick and Wilson, *Thailand's Turn*, 79, 127–9; Moreau, "Sex and Death," 50–51; Tasker, "Flesh Trade," 28; Tasker, "Dirty Business," 23; Fairclough, "Back to Work," 21–22.
25. See, for example, Pasuk and Baker, *Thailand*, 67–76; Durrenberger, "Power," 6–11, 15–18.
26. See Lent, "Asian Comic Strips," 49; Gesmankit, "Cartoon Techniques," 21–23.
27. Elliott, *Thailand*, 128.
28. Kulick and Wilson, *Thailand's Turn*, 13; Grace, "Note," 1–4.
29. See, for example, Likhit, *Demi Democracy*, 170–171, 177–81; Girling, *Thailand*, 177; Elliott, *Thailand*, 128; Anderson and Mendiones, eds., "Withdrawal Symptoms," 13–24; Pasuk and Baker, *Thailand*, 74–76, 299–301.
30. Anderson and Mendiones, eds., *In the Mirror*, 23; Girling, *Thailand*, 236.
31. Keyes, *Thailand*, 83. See also Girling, *Thailand*, 236; Likhit, *Demi Democracy*, 170; Elliott, *Thailand*, 129–133; Anderson and Mendiones, eds., *In the Mirror*, 23–24. For a vivid description of the tawdry "Americanization" of Thailand, see Iyer, *Video Night in Kathmandu*, 287–316.
32. Reynolds, *Thai Radical Discourse*, 13. See also Anderson, "Withdrawal Symptoms," 23; Flood, "Thai Left Wing," 55–63; Bartak, *Student Movement*, 4, 24–26; Pasuk and Baker, *Thailand*, 291, 305–306; Bowie, *Voices*, 16–22.
33. Poem by Jit Poumisak, quoted in Bowie, *Voices*, 17.
34. Prizzia, *Thailand in Transition*, 54. See also Heinze, "Ten Days," 491–494; Morell and Samudavanija, *Political Conflict*, 137–145; Bartak, *Student Movement*, 1–11; Pasuk and Baker, *Thailand*, 299–311.
35. Quoted in Prizzia, *Thailand in Transition*, 59. See also Likhit, *Demi Democracy*, 198; Wright, *Balancing Act*, 198–207; Pasuk and Baker, *Thailand*, 302; Bartak, *Student Movement*, 11–20; Grace, "Note," 5–7.
36. See Morell and Samudavanija, *Political Conflict*, 147; Keyes, *Thailand*, 84; Seekins, "Historical Setting," 43; Wright, *Balancing Act*, 207–211; Grace, "Note," 6; Surin, "Making," 148–150. For detailed accounts of the protests see Griffin, "Notes," 1037–1061; Heinze, "Ten Days," 494–507.
37. Steinberg, *In Search*, 391.
38. Zimmerman, "Student 'Revolution,' " 514. See also Wyatt, *Thailand*, 300.
39. Quoted in Griffin, "Notes," 1037.
40. See Prizzia, *Thailand*, 1; Pasuk and Baker, *Thailand*, 302; Bartak, *Student*, 22–23.
41. Puey Ungphakorn, quoted in Smalley, *Linguistic Diversity*, v.
42. Excerpted and condensed from the short story "Before Reaching the Stars," by 'Wat Wanlayangkun,' in Anderson and Mendiones, eds., *In the Mirror*, 159–160.
43. Seksen Prasertkul, quoted in Zimmerman, "Student 'Revolution,' " 524.
44. See, for example, Morell and Samudavanija, *Political Conflict*, 145–254; Kulick and Wilson, *Thailand's Turn*, 28–29; Likhit, *Demi Democracy*, 204–205.
45. Quoted in Prizzia, *Thailand in Transition*, 29.
46. See Pasuk and Baker, *Thailand*, 290–299, 320–322.
47. See Wright, *Balancing Act*, 229–230, 308; Morell and Samudavanija, *Political Conflict*, 225–228, 257–273; Kulick and Wilson, *Thailand's Turn*,

29; Elliott, *Thailand*, 136–137; Pasuk and Baker, *Thailand*, 304–311; Bartak, *Student*, 26–30.
48. Anderson, "Withdrawal Symptoms," 15.
49. Morell and Samudavanija, *Political Conflict*, 275. See also Kulick and Wilson, *Thailand's Turn*, 32–33; Pasuk and Baker, *Thailand*, 311; Bartak, *Student*, 31–35.
50. Wenk, *Thai Literature*, 109–114.
51. See Likhit, *Demi Democracy*, 175; Kulick and Wilson, *Thailand's Turn*, 11; Brown, *State and Ethnic*, 189–200; Pasuk and Baker, *Thailand*, 311–320, 372; Bartak, *Student*, 35; Surin, "Making," 150–152.
52. See Chutima, *Rise and Fall;* Brown, *State and Ethnic*, 195–199; Pasuk and Baker, *Thailand*, 311–314.
53. Girling, *Thailand*, 288.
54. See, for example, Likhit, *Demi Democracy*, xii.
55. See Suchit, *Military*, 46; Kulick and Wilson, *Thailand's Turn*, 49; Pasuk and Baker, *Thailand*, 311–366; Fairclough, "Shut Up," 20; Suchit, *State*, 1–2, 104; Hewison, "Emerging," 139–153. On the history of the Thai press see Mitchell, "Thailand," 210–233.
56. Unless otherwise cited, the main sources on the popular music of Thailand utilized include: booklet accompanying *Thailand: Songs for Life;* Broughton et al., eds., *World Music*, 440–448; Hunt, "Thai Masters," 30–31; Kartomi, " 'Traditional Music'," 390; Kobkul, "Country Folk," 151–169; Landgraf, liner notes; Landgraf, "Soeng," 6–8, 46; Malm, *Music Cultures: Asia;* Marre and Charlton, *Beats of Heart*, 198–214; Manuel, *Popular Musics*, 204–205; Morton, "Music of Thailand," 63–80; Myers-Moro, "Songs of Life," 93–114; Myers-Moro, *Thai Music*, 6–10; Pasuk and Baker, *Thailand*, 76–80, 381, 413–415; Paisal, "Pulse of Pop," 113–115; "Sad Minstrels," 27; Sweeney, *Virgin Directory*, 163–165; Thongchai, "Turning"; Ubonrat, "Commercializing," 61–77; Ubonrat, "Cultural," 45–70; Ubonrat, "Radio Broadcasting," 92–99; Ubonrat, "Environment," 298–308; "Will Caravan Toe the Line?"; Wong, "Whose Past?"; Wong, "Thai Cassettes," 78–104.
57. "Music of Thailand," 80. See also Myers-Moro, *Thai Music*, 10, 253–258; Kartomi, " 'Traditional Music'," 227–241; Gaston, "Thailand," 115–155; Surapone, "Theatre," 104.
58. Wright, "Dontri," 156.
59. Anderson and Mendiones, eds., *In the Mirror*, 98–108.
60. Gronow, "International Trends," 314.
61. Myers-Moro, *Thai Music*, 7.
62. Quoted in Moore, *Thailand*, 334. See also Wong, "Thai Cassettes," 78; Myers-Moro, *Thai Music*.
63. Ubonrat, "Radio Broadcasting," 92–93; Ubonrat, "Development," 101–113; Ubonrat, "Cultural," 45–70; *Thailand in the 1980s*, 239; Hewison, "Emerging," 141; Hewison, "Of Regimes," 169; Hamilton, "Rumours," 356–372; Pasuk and Baker, *Thailand*, 371–373; Jackson and Pye, eds., *Political Power and Communications in Indonesia*, 25.
64. Quoted in Ubonrat, "Radio Broadcasting," 95.
65. See Ubonrat, "Radio Broadcasting," 93; "Thai Ban on Song about Bangkok."

66. Excerpted and condensed from a 1988 account by India-born American journalist Pico Iyer, *Video Night in Kathmandu*, 293, 298.
67. Banphot, "Thai Society," 29. See also *Thailand in the 1980s*, 239–240; Ubonrat, "Commercializing," 62; Pasuk and Baker, *Thailand*, 314–315, 371–372; Vatikiotis, "Freeing the Waves," 20–21; Hewison, "Emerging," 152; Girling, *Interpreting*, 47.
68. See Kobkul, "Country Folk," 151–152; Myers-Moro, *Thai Music*, 7; Pasuk and Baker, *Thailand*, 77.
69. *In the Mirror*, 24.
70. See Anderson and Mendiones, eds., *In the Mirror*, 24–26; Van Erven, *Playful Revolution*, 207–227; Mattani, *Dance*, 193–203.
71. Phillips, *Modern Thai Literature*, 16.
72. On literature see, for example, Anderson and Mendiones, eds., *In the Mirror;* Bowie, ed., *Voices;* and Mendiones, eds. Keyes, *Thailand*, 192; Mulder, "Individual and Society," 312–327; Phillips, *Modern Thai Literature;* "Seven Genres of Thai Fiction," 42–43; Hamilton, "Rumours," 341–355; Srisurang, "Social Change," 206–215.
73. Wenk, *Thai Literature*, 89–93.
74. Quoted in Boonrak, "Rise and Fall," 81. On Thai films see Armes, *Third World Film*, 147–154; Boonrak, "Rise and Fall", 62–98; Boonrak, "Underside," 76; Buruma, "Thailand's Film-makers," 53–54; Fugate, "Hit or Flop?" 7; Hamilton, "Cinema," 141–161; Lent, *Asian Film Industry*, 212–220; Lent, "Historical Overview," 98–102, 152–163; Mattani, *Dance*, 186–189; Sanchanit, "Bleak Future," 63–65; *Thailand in the 1980s*, 245–247; "The New Thai Wave," 22–26.
75. Excerpted and condensed from a report in *Asiaweek*, September 3, 1982.
76. On lukkrung and string, see Kobkul, ""Country Folk," 155; Ubonrat, "Environment," 305–306; Wong, "Thai Cassettes," 78–104; Broughton et al., eds., *World Music*, 441–442.
77. The romanization of Thai terms causes some problems, and the sources are inconsistent. Hence this type of music has been spelled as *luk tung* (Manuel, Marre and Charlton), *luktoong* (Ubonrat), *luk thung* (Pasuk and Baker), and *luuk tung* (Myers-Moro). In addition, Manuel refers to *lukkroong* as *sakon*, and *phleng* (music) is sometimes romanized as *phlaeng*. My usage follows Ubonrat, except when quoting sources utilizing an alternative romanization.
78. Quoted in Gaston, "Thailand," 137. See also Kobkul, "Country Folk," 151–154; Ubonrat, "Environment," 306–307; Ubonrat, "Cultural," 61; Broughton et al., eds., *World Music*, 442, 444.
79. Miller, *Traditional Music*, 295. On modern maolam and Isan culture, see also Landgraf, "Soeng," 6–7; Landgraf, liner notes to *Flower of Isan*; Compton, "Traditional," 150–151; Sweeney, *Virgin Directory*, 164–165; Broughton et al., eds., *World Music*, 444–447; Basche, *Thailand*, 68–70.
80. See Broughton et al., eds., *World Music*, 442; Pasuk and Baker, *Thailand*, 76–77; Ubonrat, "Commercializing," 64.
81. Landgraf, "Soeng," 6–7.
82. "Commercializing," 63–64. On the debate generally, see also Kobkul, "Country Folk," 151–154; Ubonrat, "Environment," 306–307; Ubonrat,

"Cultural," 45–70; Marre and Charlton, *Beats of Heart*, 198–214; Broughton et al., eds., *World Music*, 442, 444; Pasuk and Baker, *Thailand*, 76–80, 381, 413–415.

83. Quoted in Kobkul, "Country Folk," 154. See also Pasuk and Baker, *Thailand*, 76–77.
84. Pasuk and Baker, *Thailand*, 413–415. See also Sweeney, *Virgin Directory*, 164; Broughton et al., eds., *World Music*, 442–444; Ubonrat, "Cultural," 61.
85. Pasuk and Baker, *Thailand*, 78.
86. Quoted in Hamilton, "Rumours," 370.
87. Quoted in Marre and Charlton, *Beats of Heart*, 203–204. See also Pasuk and Baker, *Thailand*, 76–80, 381, 413–415.
88. Kobkul, "Country Folk," 156–165; Pasuk and Baker, *Thailand*, 78–79.
89. "Commercializing," 68. See also Pasuk and Baker, *Thailand*, 76–80, 380, 413–415.
90. Quoted in Marre and Charlton, *Beats of Heart*, 205. See also Hamilton, "Rumours," 370.
91. Pasuk and Baker, *Thailand*, 79.
92. Ubonrat, "Commercializing," 68–69. See also Pasuk and Baker, *Thailand*, 79.
93. "Commercializing," 69–70; "Culture," 55–58.
94. See Manuel, *Popular Musics*, 205.
95. Wong, "Thai Cassettes," 78. See also Myers-Moro, *Thai Music*, 6–7, 118–119, 130–133, 256; Ubonrat, "Cultural," 53–55.
96. Wong, "Thai Cassettes," 78; Erlanger, "Thailand."
97. See Myers-Moro, "Songs for Life," 105–106; Thongchai, "Turning," 11; Hunt, "Thai Masters," 30–31; Pasuk and Baker, *Thailand*, 374.
98. Summarized from a biographical profile in a pamphlet from the Union of Democratic Thais. The pamphlet is excerpted in booklet accompanying *Thailand: Songs for Life*, 2–3; Myers-Moro, "Songs for Life," 10.
99. Myers-Moro, "Songs for Life," 93.
100. Quoted in "Sad Minstrels," 27.
101. See Thongchai, "Turning," 5.
102. See booklet accompanying Caravan's album, *Thailand: Songs for Life*, 14.
103. Thongchai, "Turning," 4–5. On Jit see Reynolds, *Thai Radical Discourse;* Boonrak, "Rise and Fall," 72.
104. See booklet accompanying Caravan's album, *Thailand: Songs for Life*, 7.
105. Text in "Sad Minstrels," 27.
106. "Songs for Life," 108.
107. Quoted in Thongchai, "Turning."
108. These three paragraphs were based on Thongchai, "Turning," 1–18.
109. Summarized from a 1983 Malaysian press report, "Will Caravan Toe the Line?"
110. Quoted in "Will Caravan Tow The Line?" See also Hunt, "Thai Masters," 30–31.
111. See Hunt, "Thai Masters," 31; Broughton et al., eds., *World Music*, 441–442.
112. On the student movement of the late 1980s, see Paisal, "Campuses," 27–28.
113. See, for example, Muscat, *Fifth Tiger;* Handley, "Growth," 34–35; Tasker, "Steady," 32, 34, 38; Kulick and Wilson, *Thailand's Turn*, 2, 177; Neher, *Southeast Asia*, 23; Warr, *Thai Economy;* Girling, "Thailand," 305–309; Pasuk

and Baker, *Thailand*, 384–391, 409–410; Suchit, *State;* Girling, *Interpreting;* Surin, "Making," 141–148, 159–165.

114. See Reynolds, "Globalisation."
115. Quoted and paraphrased in Vatikiotis, "Social Climbers," 53. See also Tasker, "Tiller's Troubles," 19–20.
116. On these developments see Kulick and Wilson, *Thailand's Turn*, 7–25, 183–7; King, "Thai Parliamentary," 1113–1118; Suchit, "Thailand in 1991," 131–139; Wright, "Thailand's Return," 418–423; Hewison, "Of Regimes," 161–184; Pasuk and Baker, *Thailand*, 355–361; Handley, "Rainbow Coalition," 11–12; Suthichai, "Bloody Catalyst," 15; Shenon, "4 Weeks"; Handley, "Still Missing," 16; Broughton et al., eds., *World Music*, 442; Ubonrat, "Development," 102–103.
117. See, for example, Neher, *Southeast Asia*, 31; Tasker, "Coups," 42–43; Tasker, "Downsized," 22; Tasker and Fairclough, "Return to Duty," 18–20.
118. See King, "Thai Parliamentary," 1118–1123; Handley, "Back to Grassroots," 21; Tasker, "Straight and Narrow," 18–19; Tasker, "Rendered Surplus," 18; Tasker, "Disloyal Opposition," 16–17; Tasker, "Enigmatic Activist," 34; Fairclough, "Bangkok's Night-Riders," 36–37; Fairclough, "Rural Reality," 15–16; Vatikiotis, "Tension Within," 14–15; Vatikiotis, "Urban Dreams," 18–19; Ockey, "Political," 256–277; Girling, "Thailand," 305–319; Neher, "Thailand's," 435–439; Neher, "Transition," 8–14; Neher and Marlay, *Democracy: Southeast Asia*, 46–48; Suchit, "Thailand in 1995."
119. On the political crisis of 1996 see, for example, Fairclough, "Criticial Mass," 16–17; Mydens, "Thai Leader" and "Thai Premier"; Tasker, "Show," 30–31; Vatikiotis and Tasker, "Anybody's Man," 22–23; Vatikiotis and Tasker, "Barnham's Cliffhanger," 14–15; Vatikiotis et al., "Democratic Dilemma," 24–26; Vatikiotis and Tasker, "Promises Promises," 22–23; Vatikiotis and Fairclough, "Spoils of Victory," 16–17; Vatikiotis and Fairclough, "Mission," 16–18; Vatikiotis, "Who Needs Democracy?" 20–21.
120. Quoted in Kulick and Wilson, *Thailand's Turn*, 32. See also Handley, "Turning Full Circle," 34; *Far Eastern Economic Review*, April 11, 1996, 13; Tasker, "Tiller's Troubles," 19–20; Fairclough, "Vox Populi," 20; Vatikiotis, "Never Again," 53–54; Vatikiotis, "Out," 31–32.
121. "Environment," 304–306. See also Myers-Moro, *Thai Music*, 9, 256; Pasuk and Baker, *Thailand*, 374; Broughton et al., eds., *World Music*, 441–442.
122. Crossette, "Strumming."
123. Excerpted from a study by ethnomusicologist Deborah Wong, "Whose Past?" 7.
124. See Keyes, "Case of Purloined," 261–292; Wong, "Whose Past?" 1–16.
125. Crossette. "Strumming"; Myers-Moro, *Thai Music*, 9; Ubonrat, "Cultural," 61.
126. Ubonrat, "Environment," 305–306. See also Pasuk and Baker, *Thailand*, 374, 389.
127. See *Far Eastern Economic Review*, September 27, 1990, 8; Broughton et al., eds., *World Music*, 442; *Asiaweek*, January 5, 1988, 27; Pasuk and Baker, *Thailand*, 374, 389.
128. Song text in Paisal, "Pulse of Pop," 113. See also Pasuk and Baker, *Thailand*, 374.
129. The song text is from Myers-Moro, "Songs for Life," 110.

Chapter 5: Malaysia and Singapore: Pluralism and Popular Music

1. From the album *Khatul Istiwa* (WEA 50284). The song was written by Itoh Mohammed.
2. Based largely on Neher and Marlay, *Democracy: Southeast Asia*, 97, 130; Crouch, "Malaysia," 134; Kahn, "Growth," 47–48; Rodan, "Class," 17–18; Rodan, "Preserving," 76; Greenwood, ed., *Asia Yearbook 1992*, 7; *The Asia & Pacific Review 1993/94*, 126, 224; United Nations, *Industrial Statistics 1991*, 774–783; *Billboard International 1996*, 252, 257–259; *World Record Sales*, 75, 77–78.
3. The material on the historical, social, and political background is based chiefly on the following works by the author: "The Historical Setting"; "Malaysia: History," 751–755, 793; *From Kampung to City;* essays on "Malaysia," "Sarawak," "Sabah," "Kuala Lumpur." Among other sources utilized in this chapter are: S. Husin Ali, ed., *Ethnicity, Class;* Andaya and Andaya, *History of Malaysia;* Bedlington, *Malaysia and Singapore;* Brookfield, ed., *Transformation;* Brown, *State and Ethnic: Southeast Asia*, 206–257; Bunge, ed., *Malaysia: A Country Study;* Crouch, *Government and Society* and "Malaysia," 135–157; Harper, "New Malays," 238–255; Hua, *Class and Communalism;* Jesudasan, "Malaysia," 199–219; Jomo K. S., *A Question of Class;* Kahn, "Growth," 47–48; Kahn and Loh, eds., *Fragmented Vision;* Kaur, *Historical Dictionary Malaysia;* Khoo, "Democracy," 46–76; Mauzy, "Democracy"; Mauzy and Milne, "Mahathir Administration," 617–648; Means, *Malaysian Politics;* Mehmet, *Development in Malaysia;* Milne and Mauzy, *Malaysia: Tradition* and *Politics and Government;* Mohammed Agus Yusoff, *Consociational Politics;* Munro-Kua, *Authoritarian;* Muzaffar, *Challenges and Choices;* Nagata, *Reflowering;* Neher Marlay, *Southeast Asia;* Neher Marlay, *Democracy: Southeast Asia*, 96–111, 129–147; Ong, "Communalism," 73–95; Rehman, *Malaysian Journey;* Steinberg et al., *In Search of Southeast Asia.*
4. The most important sources on prewar Malay culture include Wan Abdul Wan Kadir Yusoff, "Hiburan dan Masyarakat"; Mohd. Taib Osman, *Rampai;* Mohd. Taib Osman, ed., *Traditional Drama;* Chopyak, "Music," 111–138; Malm, "Music in Kelantan," 1–47; S. B. Tan, *Bangsawan* and "*Bangsawan* of Malaysia," 49–81; S. B. Tan, "From Popular," 229–274; S. B. Tan, "From Syncretism," 220–232; S. B. Tan, "Moving Centrestage," 96–118; Mohd. Anis Md Nor, *Zapin;* Mustapha, "Malay 'Bangsawan,' " 143–153; Aisha, "Evolution," 23–24; Kartomi, " 'Traditional Music Weeps'," 366–400; Broughton et al., eds., *World Music*, 433–436; Youssof, *Dictionary.*
5. "Some Observations," 310–312.
6. Extracted and condensed from a memoir by Sarawak journalist Hajah Maimunah Hj. Daud, "Bangsawan," 14–18.
7. S. B. Tan, "*Bangsawan* of Malaysia," 80–81.
8. See Thomas, *Like Tigers.*
9. See Chopyak, "Music," 114–118.
10. See Mohd. Taib Osman, "Some Observations," 318.
11. On this history see Chelliah, "Development"; Chopyak, "Music," 132–134.
12. See Sheppard, "Pa' Mat," 98–100.

13. Seekins, "Historical Setting," 40.
14. See, for example, Mohammed, *Consociational Politics*, 34–35, 69–70, 86; Andaya and Andaya, *History*, 291–292; Steinberg, *In Search of Southeast Asia*, 412–413; Brown, *State and Ethnic: Southeast Asia*, 230–243; Khoo, "Democracy," 46–76; Munro-Kua, *Authoritarian*, 26–125.
15. The discussion on popular music and culture is based chiefly on Lockard, *Reflections of Change*, 1–111; Lockard, "From Folk to Computer Songs"; Lockard, " 'Hey We Equatorial People,' " 11–28. In addition to these works, the only reasonably comprehensive study on Malaysian popular music is Ismaal Samat, "Penghibur Melayu Masakini." For useful but briefer accounts, see S. B. Tan, *Bangsawan;* S. B. Tan, "Counterpoints," 282–305; S. B. Tan, "Performing Arts," 152–160; *Cenderamata;* Broughton et al., eds., *World Music*, 433–437; Sweeney, *Virgin Directory of World Music*, 168–170; Kartomi, " 'Traditional Music,' " 382–383, 389. For some other sources see Lockard, *Reflections*, 14. On "serious" Malaysian music, including some musicians who influenced popular culture, see Daud, "Malaysia," 91–96.
16. Interview with Fauzi Marzuki of EMI Records, Kuala Lumpur, January 7, 1985.
17. See Fu Shi, "Cafe Singers," 70–71; K. S. Kong, "Songbirds."
18. There are many Malay sources on Ramlee; for a full listing see Lockard, *Reflections*, 19–20. The most comprehensive biographies include Abdullah Hussein, *Ramlee*, and Aimi Jarr, *Ramlee dari Kacamata*. See also Pelras, "Ramlee," 243–250; Lockard, *Reflections*, 19–29; Tan and Soh, *Development*, 128–129.
19. Summarized from a 1954 article by Singapore journalist Fu Shi, "Cafe Singers," 70–71.
20. Mansur Puteh, quoted in *Malay Mail*, May 13, 1984.
21. Quoted in *New Straits Times*, Dec. 19, 1988.
22. See *Utusan Malaysia*, Oct. 26, 1984.
23. This point is made by Ahmed Daud in *New Straits Times*, Dec. 17, 1988.
24. These categories are suggested in Zaleha Selamat, "Analisa Kandungan."
25. *Malay Mail*, June 14, 1983.
26. "Performing," 154–155.
27. Saw Teck Meng, in *New Straits Times*, March 3, 1984.
28. See Tan, "Performing," 152–153.
29. Material on literature taken from Banks, *From Class to Culture;* Tham, ed., *Literature and Society in Southeast Asia;* Mohd. Taib Osman, "Tema Antara," 42–49; Aveling, "Perceptions of Society," 117–124.
30. From Biddle et al., eds., *Contemporary Literature in Asia*, 152–153.
31. This information mostly comes from my own collection of recordings by Sarawak musicians and various conversations in Sarawak and Sabah.
32. It is interesting to note that the Beatles-inspired rock music of the 1960s in Brazil was also known as *ie-ie-ie* ("yeah, yeah, yeah"). See Lockard, " 'Get Up, Stand Up,' " Chapter 5.
33. Hiebert, "War of Worlds," 44. The quote is from entertainment director Paddy Chew. See also essay by Lee Gek King in Da Cunha, ed., *Debating Singapore*, 79–82; various essays in Afendras and Kuo, eds., *Language and Society*; Tan and Soh, *Development*.

34. *Sunday Times*, February 10, 1980; Wells and Lee, "Music Culture Singapore," 29–41. On the Singapore Chinese recording industry see also Lazaroo, "Singapore-'Instant Asia,' " 5–9. On *xinyao* see Kong, "Making," 99–124. On modern "serious" music see Ting et al., "Singapore," 97–114.
35. Lock and Valbuena, "Mass Media," 6.
36. See Murray and Perera, *Singapore*, 242–243.
37. *Business Times*, November 4, 1980.
38. See, for example, Milne and Mauzy, *Malaysia*, 177–180; Mohammed, *Consociational*, 10–13, 78–81; Steinberg, *In Search of Southeast Asia*, 413; Andaya and Andaya, *History*, 292; Crouch, *Government and Society*, 29–114; Munro-Kua, *Authoritarian*, 81–142.
39. See, for example, Ong, "Malaysia," 73–74; Milne and Mauzy, *Malaysia*, 145–151, 171–173; Jomo, ed., *Industrializing Malaysia*, 1–4; Welsh, "Attitudes," 882–903.
40. See, for example, Andaya and Andaya, *History*, 283–284; Hirschman, "Development and Inequality," 78–81; Rigg, *Southeast Asia*, 109–132; Brown, *State and Ethnic: Southeast Asia*, 238–250; Jayasankaran, "Balancing Act," 24–29; Jayasankaran, "Unwritten Rule," 20–21; Khoo, "Democracy," 61–62.
41. See, for example, Andaya and Andaya, *History*, 282–284; Ong, "Malaysia," 74; Steinberg, *In Search of Southeast Asia*, 458; Hong, ed., *Malaysian Women*, 1–24.
42. Extracted and condensed from Sri Delima, *As I Was Passing*, 82–84.
43. See Hirschman, "Society and Environment," 88–89; *Asiaweek*, July 14, 1995.
44. See the comments by Ungku Aziz in *New Straits Times*, October 8, 1989. See also Crouch, *Government*, 177–195; Elegant, "Between God," 58–60.
45. Quoted in Elegant and Cohen, "Rock," 51. See, for example, Nagata, *Reflowering;* Brown, *State and Ethnic: Southeast Asia*, 243–256; Elegant, "Between God," 58–60; Camroux, "State," 852–868.
46. "Watching the World Go By," 28; Harper, "New Malays," 250; Elegant and Cohen, "Rock," 51.
47. Some of the more valuable recent studies of Singapore consulted include: Afendras and Kuo, eds., *Language and Society;* Brown, *State and Ethnic Politics in Southeast Asia*, 66–111; Chew and Lee, eds., *History of Singapore;* Clammer, *Singapore;* Da Cunha, ed., *Debating Singapore;* Hassan, ed., *Singapore;* Heng, "Democracy," 113–140; Hiebert, "Ring," 16–17; Hill and Lian, *Politics of Nation Building;* Khong, "Singapore: Political Legitimacy," 108–135; Kwok, "Singapore," 291–308; Lai, *Meanings of Multiethnicity;* LePoer, ed., *Singapore: A Country Study;* Murray and Perera, *Singapore;* Neher and Marlay, *Democracy: Southeast Asia*, 129–147; J. Quah, ed., *In Search;* J. Quah et al., eds., *Government and Politics;* S. Quah et al., eds., *Social Class;* Regnier, *Singapore;* Rodan, "Class," 19–48; Rodan, ed., *Singapore Changes Guard;* Rodan, "Preserving One-Party," 75–108; Singh, "Singapore," 267–284; Tamney, *Struggle;* Y. S. Tan and Soh, *Development of Singapore's Modern Media Industry;* Tremewan, *Political Economy;* Turnbull, *History of Singapore;* Yao, "Consumption," 337–354.
48. On these developments see Kwok, "Singapore," 303–305. For general studies see Tamney, *Struggle*, 154–168; Hill and Lian, *Politics of Nation Building*, esp. 188–219; Hanna, "Culture, Yellow Culture"; Hiebert, "Acting Up,"

62–63; essays by Philip Jeyaretnam, Sanjay Krishnan, Stella Kon, Robert Yeo, Geraldine Heng and Janadas Devan, and Derek Da Cunha in Da Cunha, ed., *Debating Singapore*, 89–119.

49. See Murray and Perera, *Singapore*, 241–243; essay by David Chan Kum Wah in Da Cunha, ed., *Debating Singapore*, 71–75; Jayasankaran and Hiebert, "War of Words," 19; Yao, "Consumption," 352; Lent, "Cartooning," 2–5.
50. See Hiebert, "Family Resemblance," 62.
51. See Tan, "Performing," 154–155; Jackson, *Political Power Indonesia*, 25; Tan and Soh, *Development*, 62–66, 95–102.
52. Excerpted and condensed from Philip Jeyaratnam's novel *Abraham's Promise*, 146.
53. See Tan, "Performing," 154–155; Tan, "Counterpoints," 296–297.
54. *Malay Mail*, Sept. 11, 1984.
55. On the popularity of Rhoma and dangdut in Malaysia, see *Utusan Radio dan TV*, May 1, 1982 and July 1, 1983; *Kisah Cinta*, December 1, 1982, June 1 and December 14, 1984.
56. On Sharifah Aini as a superstar, see Fernandez, "Sharifah Aini," 36–39.
57. See Frederick, "Rhoma Irama," 103–130.
58. Interview with M. Shariff, Kuala Lumpur, Feb. 21, 1985.
59. *New Straits Times*, August 31, 1980.
60. See A. R. Ismail, "Senikata Lagu-Lagu," 15–17; Zurinah Hassan, "Lirik Lagu-lagu Pop Melayu," 23–25.
61. See, for example, Mohammed, *Consociational*, 35–41; Ong, "Malaysia," 80; Munro-Kua, *Authoritarian*, 105–125, 128–142.
62. See, for example, Milne and Mauzy, *Malaysia;* Mohammed, *Consociational*, 74–77; Andaya and Andaya, *History*, 294–295; Crouch, *Government and Society*, 106–113; Mauzy, "Democracy," 6–19; Munro-Kua, *Authoritarian*, 121–125; Khoo, "Democracy," 68–70. For a moving personal account of the crackdown see Rehman, *Malaysian Journey*, 229–242.
63. "Politician"; Muhammed Haji Salleh, *Beyond Archipelago*, 75.
64. See Means, *Malaysian Politics*, 199–265; essays by Francis Loh Kok Wah, Harold Crouch, Clive Kessler, and Joel Kahn in Kahn and Loh, eds., *Fragmented Vision*, 1–43, 133–178; Crouch, *Government and Society*, 114–129, 149–219; Mauzy, "Democracy"; Kulkarni et al., "Dr. Feelgood," 18–22; Khoo, "Democracy," 70–72; Liak, "Malaysia," 217–237; Camroux, "State."
65. On the National Culture Policy see, for example, Wan Abdul Kadir Yusoff and Zainal, *Ideologi dan Kebudayaan;* Ibrahim Said, "National Culture," 60–69; Hatch, "National Cultural Policy"; Aziz Deraman, *Masyarakat dan Kebudayaan;* Chopyak, "Role of Music," 431–454; Tan, "Performing," 3; Tan, *Bangsawan*, 165–194; Tan, "From Syncretism," 220–232; Pixie, "Whither Culture?" 108–131; Kartomi, " 'Traditional Music Weeps,' " 382–383.
66. See Provencher, "Covering Malay Humor Magazines," 1–25; Provencher, "Modern Malay Folklore," 179–188; Provencher and Jaafar, "Malay Humor Magazines," 87–99; Lent, "Asian Comic Strips," 49–51.
67. On Lat see especially Chandy, "Lat," 38–41; Lent, "A Lot about Lat," 29–34; Lent, "Asian Comic Strips," 50; Suhaimi Aznam, "Quipping Away," 42–46.

68. Rehman Rashid in *Malay Mail*, May 1, 1983.
69. See *Berita Harian*, January 14, 1985; *New Straits Times*, August 31, 1984.
70. Extracted and condensed from an essay by Sri Delima, *As I Was Passing*, 64–66. See also Granfell, *Switch On;* Karthigesu, "Broadcasting Deregulation," 73–90; Nain, "Rhetoric," 43–64.
71. See Tan, "Counterpoints," 297–298; Rehman, *Malaysian Journey*, 181–184, 199–207.
72. See Tan, "Performing," 154–157; Tan, "Counterpoints," 299–301.
73. *New Straits Times*, December 31, 1981.
74. *New Straits Times*, February 1, 1987. On the Malay recording industry generally, see Ismaal, "Penghibur," 51–96; "Sengketa Yang Menggerhanakan," 18–20.
75. From the album *Komputer Muzik* (WEA 93493, 1984). The song was written by Michael Veerapen and Rafique Rashid.
76. See, for example, Kee, "Looking Askance."
77. Tiong, "Japanese," 7, 10.
78. See *New Straits Times*, June 10, 1987 and February 16, 1990.
79. See *Utusan Radio dan TV*, July 1, 1983, 78–79; *Berita Harian*, March 3, 1985; *The Star*, April 24 and September 13, 1981; *Malay Mail*, April 5, 1981.
80. See "Just Dying to See You," 40.
81. *New Straits Times*, July 25, 1985.
82. See *New Straits Times*, March 29, 1990. See also Tan, "From Syncretism," 229–230.
83. Extracted and condensed from a 1985 essay by Malaysian journalist Rehman Rashid, "Scorpion's Tales," 33.
84. On this debate see Chelliah, "Towards an Identity"; *New Straits Times*, August 31 and December 14, 1989.
85. See *New Straits Times*, December 14, 1989; February 22, 1990; March 27 and 30, 1990.
86. See, for example, Broughton et al., eds., *World Music*, 437; Tan, "From Syncretism," 229.
87. On Amin see *Varia Pop*, January 1, 1985, 36–37; *Kisah Cinta*, June 1, 1984, 6–7; *New Straits Times*, February 20, 1984 and April 11, 1988.
88. On the Islamic hostility and protests, see, for example, *New Straits Times*, August 20, 1986; October 10 and 13, 1986; March 22, 1989; *Watan*, October 10 and 11, 1986; Mitton, "Getting Serious," 37. See also Elegant, "Between God," 58–60.
89. The discussion that follows is elaborated in, and most of this section is based on, Lockard, *Reflections*, 37–106. See also Tan, "Counterpoint," 299–302.
90. For the Malay text, see Lockard, *Reflections*, 50.
91. The Malay text can be found in Lockard, *Reflections*, 82.
92. For a recent portrait, see Jayasankaran, "Out of Bounds."
93. From Leee's cassette album, *Solitary Vice (and Other Virtues)* (1984). For the complete text see Lockard, *Reflections*, 87.
94. See Tan, "Counterpoint," 299–300.
95. The following section on Singapore owes much to L Kong, "Popular Music," 51–77; L. Kong, "Music and Cultural Politics," 447–459; Lent,

"Cartooning," 2–10; Phua and Kong, "Ideology," 215–231; Tamney, *Struggle*, 165–166; Tan and Soh, *Development*, 87–88, 95–100; the essay by Lee Gek Ling in Da Cunha, ed., *Debating Singapore*, 79, 82.

96. From the album *Life in the Lion City* (WEA 2292-50691, 1984). See also Lockard, *Reflections*, 94.
97. *New Straits Times*, December 27, 1989.
98. *New Straits Times*, December 9 and 21, 1988.
99. *New Straits Times*, January 23, 1986.
100. *New Straits Times*, May 23 and November 15, 1989.
101. *New Straits Times*, January 13, 1987.
102. Richard Dorall, quoted in "Rapping to a New Beat," 40.
103. See Tan, "Performing Arts," 158–159. On the *kutu*, see Scott, "Kutu Clash," 36–37.
104. Extracted and condensed from a 1989 article by journalist Margaret Scott, "Kutu Clash," 36–37.
105. On Ramli see, for example, *Utusan Radio dan TV*, June 1, 1985, 38; *New Straits Times*, May 29 and August 12, 1986; January 11, 1988; June 29, 1990.
106. See Broughton et al., eds., *World Music*, 436–437; Karp, "Sounding Off," 78.
107. *New Straits Times*, December 5, 1988.
108. See *New Straits Times*, March 21 and October 26, 1988; *Asiaweek*, July 29, 1988.
109. See Chelliah, "Broadcasting."
110. *New Straits Times*, April 7, 1987 and January 19, 1989.
111. On rap see Vatikiotis, "Rapping in Malaysia," 32–33; "Rapping to a New Beat," 40; Jayasankaran, "Don't Rock," 26; *Asiaweek*, July 11, 1997, 83.
112. See Kong, "Popular Music," 51–77; Phua and Kong, "Ideology," 215–231.
113. See Keenan, "Stage Fright," 24–26.
114. Tan, "Counterpoints," 301.

Chapter 6: Conclusions

1. Riggs, "Rock and Roll China," 38–39.
2. B. Shuman, "Marshall McLuhan," 256.
3. Martha Bayles, quoted in Rothstein, "Riffs on Rap, Rock."
4. "Popular Music," 31.
5. See, for example, Grossberg, "Another Boring Day," 225–257.
6. See, for example, Kaemmer, "Social Power Shona," 44.
7. See J. Scott, *Weapons of Weak*; Cushman, "Rich Rastas," 23.
8. See Yamashita, "Listening to City: Indonesia," 116–117.
9. See Lockard, " 'Get Up, Stand Up,' " Chapter 7. These ideas derive from B. Anderson, *Imagined Communities*, 9–36; Erlmann, *African Stars*, 14, 19, 180.
10. See, for example, Manuel, *Popular Musics*, 1–23; *Cassette Culture*, 11–13.
11. *Through Our Own Eyes*, 8.
12. Starr, "Introduction," xiii.
13. From Kembara's album *Generasi Ku* (Philips 812-277-1, 1983).

Bibliography

The Bibliography is divided into five sections. The first section, General and Regional Works, contains works on general, global, or theoretical subjects, as well as regional studies (including Southeast Asia) and studies on nations that fall outside the scope of this volume. The remaining four sections contain works pertaining to the chapters on Indonesia, the Philippines, Thailand, and Malaysia and Singapore, respectively, as well as general or regional studies used as sources for those chapters.

General and Regional Works

Abdul Majid. "The Popular Art Controversy." *Ilmu Masyarakat* 2 (April–June 1983): 60–79.

———. *The Popular Culture Controversy.* Penang: Research Publications, 1983.

Aguilar, Freddie. "Introduction: The Far East and Pacific." In Philip Sweeney, *The Virgin Directory of World Music.* New York: Henry Holt, 1991: 151–153.

Ahmed, Akbar S. "Bombay Films: The Cinema as Metaphor for Indian Society and Politics." *Modern Asian Studies* 26/2 (1992): 289–320.

Alagappa, Muthiah, ed. *Political Legitimacy in Southeast Asia: The Quest for Moral Authority.* Stanford: Stanford University Press, 1995.

Anand, R. P., and Purificacion V. Quisumbing, eds. *ASEAN Identity, Development and Culture.* Quezon City: University of the Philippines Law Center, 1981.

Anderson, Benedict. *Imagined Communities: Reflections on the Origin and Spread of Nationalism*, 2nd ed. London: Verso, 1991.

Anderson, Muff. *Music in the Mix: The Story of South African Popular Music.* Johannesburg: Ravan Press, 1981.

Anek Laothamatas, ed. *Democratization in Southeast and East Asia*. Singapore: Institute of Southeast Asian Studies, 1997.

Angus, Ian, and Sut Jhally. "Introduction." In Angus and Jhally, eds., *Cultural Politics in Contemporary America*. New York: Routledge, 1989: 1–14.

Appadurai, Arjun. "Disjuncture and Difference in the Global Cultural Economy." *Public Culture* 2/2 (Spring 1990): 1–23.

Armes, Roy. *Third World Film Making and the West*. Berkeley: University of California, 1987.

Arnold, Alison E.. "Aspects of Production and Consumption in the Popular Hindi Film Song Industry." *Asian Music* 24/1 (Fall/Winter 1992–1993): 122–135.

Arora, V. N. "Popular Songs in Hindi Films." *Journal of Popular Culture* 20/2 (Fall 1986): 143–166.

The Asia & Pacific Review 1993/94: Economic and Business Report. London: The World of Information, 1993.

Associated Press. "Italian Radio Station Gives Mogadishu Daily Diversion," *Green Bay Press-Gazette*, December 14, 1993.

Bahry, Romana. "Rock Culture and Rock Music in Ukraine." In Ramet, ed., *Rocking the State*: 243–296.

Barlow, Sean, and Banning Eyre. *Afropop! An Illustrated Guide to Contemporary African Music*. Edison, NJ: Chartwell, 1995.

Barnet, Richard J., and John Cavenaugh. "The Sound of Money: Pop Imperialism Moves to a Global Beat." *Sojourners* (January 1994): 12–16.

Barnouw, Erik, and S. Krishnaswamy. *Indian Film*, 2nd ed. New York: Oxford University Press, 1980.

Bayton, Mavis. "Feminist Musical Practice: Problems and Contradictions." In Tony Bennett et al., eds., *Rock and Popular Music: Politics, Policies, Institutions*. London: Routledge, 1993: 177–192.

Bender, Wolfgang. *Sweet Mother: Modern African Music*. Chicago: University of Chicago Press, 1991.

Bennett, Tony. "Theories of the Media, Theories of Society." In Michael Gurevitch et al., eds., *Culture, Society and the Media*. London: Methuen, 1982: 30–55.

Bennett, Tony, et al., eds. *Rock and Popular Music: Politics, Policies, Institutions*. London: Routledge, 1993.

Bergman, Billy. *Goodtime Kings: Emerging African Pop*. New York: Quill, 1985.

———. *Hot Sauces: Latin and Caribbean Pop*. New York: Quill, 1985.

Bessant, Leslie. "Songs of Chiweshe and Songs of Zimbabwe." *African Affairs* 93/370 (January 1994): 43–74.

Bharatnam, Raju. *Lata Mangeshkar: A Biography*. New Delhi: UBSPD, 1995.

Biddle, Arthur W., et al., eds. *Contemporary Literature of Asia*. Saddle River, NJ: Blair Press, 1996.

Biermann, Wolf. *The Wire Harp: Ballads/Poems/Songs*. New York: Harvest, 1968.

Billboard International Buyer's Guide 1996. New York: Billboard, 1995.

Blacking, John. "Ethnography of Musical Performance." In Daniel Heartz and Bonnie Wade, eds., *Report of the Twelfth Congress, Berkeley, 1977*. Barenreiter Kassel: The American Musicological Society, 1981: 383–401.

———. *How Musical Is Man?* Seattle: University of Washington Press, 1973.

———. "The Value of Music in Human Experience." In *Yearbook of the International Folk Music Council*, 1 (1969): 33–71.
Bloom, Allen. *The Closing of the American Mind: How Higher Education Has Failed Democracy and Impoverished the Soul of Today's Students.* New York: Simon and Schuster, 1987.
Bond, Katherine, and Kingsavanh Pathammavong. "Contexts of Dontrii Lao Deum: Traditional Lao Music." In Amy Catlin, ed., *Selected Reports in Ethnomusicology, Vol. IX: Text, Context, and Performance in Cambodia, Laos, and Vietnam.* Los Angeles: Department of Ethnomusicology, University of California, Los Angeles, 1992: 131–148.
Bookbinder, Alan, et al. *Comrades: Portraits of Soviet Life.* New York: New American Library, 1985: 158–171.
Booth, Gregory D. "Disco *Laggi*: Modern Repertoire and Traditional Performance Practice in North Indian Popular Music." *Asian Music* 23/1 (Fall/Winter 1991–1992): 61–82.
"Born in the PRC." *Asiaweek*, March 23, 1990: 34.
"Born in the PRC: China's New Voices of Rock." *Asiaweek*, May 19, 1995: 38–43.
Boyd-Barrett, Oliver. "Media Imperialism: Towards an International Framework for the Analysis of Media Systems." In James Curran et al., eds., *Mass Communication and Society.* Beverly Hills: Sage, 1979: 116–135.
Brace, Tim, "Popular Music in Contemporary Beijing: Modernism and Cultural Identity." *Asian Music* 22/2 (Spring/Summer 1991): 43–66.
Brace, Tim, and Paul Friedlander. "Rock and Roll in the New Long March: Popular Music, Cultural Identity, and Political Opposition in the People's Republic of China." In Reebee Garofalo, ed., *Rockin' the Boat: Mass Music and Mass Movements.* Boston: South End, 1992: 115–128.
Brandon, James R. *Theatre in Southeast Asia.* Cambridge: Harvard University Press, 1967.
———, ed. *The Performing Arts in Asia.* Paris: UNESCO, 1971.
Brennan, Timothy. "Masterpiece Theatre and the Uses of Tradition." In Lazere, ed., *American Media*: 373–383.
Brett, Guy. *Through Our Own Eyes: Popular Art and Modern History.* Philadelphia: New Society, 1987.
Bright, Terry. "Pop Music in the USSR." *Media, Culture and Society* 8 (July 1986): 357–369.
———. "Soviet Crusade against Pop." *Popular Music* 5 (1985): 123–147.
Broughton, Simon, et al., eds. *World Music: The Rough Guide.* London: Rough Guides, 1994.
Brown, David. *The State and Ethnic Politics in Southeast Asia.* London: Routledge, 1994: 112–157.
Browne, Ray H. "Popular Culture—New Notes Toward a Definition." In Christopher D. Geist and Jack Nachbar, eds., *The Popular Culture Reader*, 3rd ed. Bowling Green: Popular Press, 1983: 13–21.
Buckman, Robert. "Cultural Agenda of Latin American Newspapers and Magazines: Is U.S. Domination a Myth?" *Latin American Research Review* 25/2 (1990): 134–155.

Burke, Peter. *Popular Culture in Early Modern Europe.* New York: Harper and Row, 1978.
Burlingame, Burl, and Robert Kamohalu Kasher. *Da Kine Sound: Conversations with the People Who Create Hawaiian Music, Vol. 1.* Honolulu: Press Pacifica, 1978.
Burr, Ty. "From Africa, Three Female Rebels with a Cause." *New York Times,* July 10, 1994.
Cady, John. *The History of Postwar Southeast Asia: Independence Problems.* Athens: Ohio University Press, 1974.
Canepa, Gina. "Violeta Parra and Los Jaives: Unequal Discourse or Successful Integration." *Popular Music* 6/2 (May 1987): 235–240.
Carney, George O., ed. *The Sounds of People and Places: Readings in the Geography of American Folk and Popular Music.* Lanham: University Press of America, 1987.
Carrasco, Eduardo. *La Nueva Cancion en America Latina.* Santiago: CENECA, 1982.
———. "The Nueva Cancion in Latin America." *International Social Science Journal* 34/4 (1982): 599–623.
Castelo-Branco, Salwa El-Shawan. "Some Aspects of the Cassette Industry in Egypt." *The World of Music* 29/2 (1987): 32–45.
Catlin, Amy, ed. *Selected Reports in Ethnomusicology, Vol. IX: Text, Context, and Performance in Cambodia, Laos, and Vietnam.* Los Angeles: Department of Ethnomusicology, University of California, Los Angeles, 1992.
Chakravarty, Sumita. *National Identity in Indian Popular Cinema.* Austin: University of Texas Press, 1993.
Chambers, Iain. *Popular Culture: The Metropolitan Experience.* London: Methuen, 1986.
———. "Review of Simon Frith, *Music for Pleasure.*" *Popular Music* 8/3 (October 1989): 322–325.
Chan Phaik Hoon. "Gambaran Budaya dan Masyarakat Dalam Senikata Lagu." Unpublished B.A. thesis, University of Malaya, 1984.
Clarke, Sebastian. *Jah Music: The Evolution of the Popular Jamaican Song.* London: Heinemann, 1980.
Collins, John. *Musicmakers of West Africa.* Washington: Three Continents, 1985.
———. *West African Pop Roots.* Philadelphia: Temple University Press, 1992.
Combs, James. *Polpop: Politics and Popular Culture in America.* Bowling Green: Popular Press, 1984.
Constantino, Renato. *Neocolonial Identity and Counter-Consciousness: Essays on Cultural Decolonization.* White Plains: M. E. Sharpe, 1978.
———. *Synthetic Culture and Development.* Quezon City: Foundation for Nationalist Studies, 1985.
Cooper, B. Lee. *Images of American Society in Popular Music: A Guide to Reflective Teaching.* Chicago: Nelson-Hall, 1982.
Cooper, Darius. "The Hindi Film Song and Guru Dutt." *East-West Film Journal* 2/2 (June 1988): 49–65.
Coplan, David. *In Township Tonite! South Africa's Black City Music and Theatre.* London: Longman, 1985.
Coppola, Carlo. "Politics, Social Criticism and Indian Film Songs: The Case of Sahir Ludhianvi." *Journal of Popular Culture* 10/4 (Spring 1977): 897–902.

Crossette, Barbara. "Star-Studded India Vote Gets Mixed Reviews." *New York Times*, May 20, 1991.
"Culture, Development and Democracy—The Role of the Intellectuals." *Solidarity* 133–134 (January-June 1992): 28–72.
Cushman, Thomas. *Notes from Underground: Rock Music Counterculture in Russia.* Albany: State University of New York Press, 1995.
———. "Rich Rastas and Communist Rockers: A Comparative Study of the Origin, Diffusion and Defusion of Revolutionary Musical Codes." *Journal of Popular Culture* 25/3 (Winter 1991): 17–62.
Cutler, Chris. "What Is Popular Music?" In David Horn, ed., *Popular Music Perspectives 2.* Salisbury: May and May, 1985: 3–12.
Das Gupta, Chidananda. "The Painted Faces of Politics: The Actor Politicians of South India." In Wimal Dissanayake, ed., *Cinema and Cultural Identity: Reflections on Films from Japan, India, and China.* Lanham: University Press of America, 1988: 127–148.
Davis, Stephen. *Reggae Bloodlines: In Search of the Music and Culture of Jamaica.* Garden City: Doubleday, 1977.
Davis, Stephen and Peter Simon. *Reggae International.* New York: R & B, 1982.
De Launey, Guy. "Not-so-Big in Japan: Western Pop Music in the Japanese Market." *Popular Music* 14/2 (1995): 203–225.
Delfs, Robert. "The Controversial Fame of China's First Rock Star." *Far Eastern Economic Review*, December 26, 1985: 40.
Denisoff, R. Serge. *Sing a Song of Social Significance.* Bowling Green: Popular Press, 1972.
———. *Tarnished Gold: The Record Industry Revisited.* New Brunswick: Transaction, 1986.
Denselow, Robin. *When the Music's Over: The Story of Political Pop.* London: Faber and Faber, 1989.
Diamond, Larry. "Fiction as Political Thought." *African Affairs* 88/352 (July 1988): 435–445.
Dickenson, John. *Brazil.* London: Longman, 1982.
Dickey, Sara. *Cinema and the Urban Poor in South India.* New York: Cambridge University Press, 1993.
Dissanayake, Wimal, ed. *Cinema and Cultural Identity: Reflections on Films from Japan, India, and China.* Lanham: University Press of America, 1988.
———, ed. *Colonialism and Nationalism in Asian Cinema.* Bloomington: Indiana University Press, 1994.
Dobrotvorskaja, Ekaterina. "Soviet Teens of the 1970s: Rock Generation, Rock Refusal, Rock Context." *Journal of Popular Culture* 26/3 (Winter 1992): 145–150.
Dorfman, Ariel, and Armand Mattelart. *The Emperor's Old Clothes: What the Lone Ranger, Babar, and Other Innocent Heroes Do to Our Minds.* New York: Pantheon, 1983.
———. *How to Read Donald Duck: Imperialist Ideology in the Disney Comic.* New York: International General, 1975.
Downing, John. "Afterword." In Downing, ed., *Film and Politics in the Third World.* Brooklyn: Autonomedia, 1987: 311–317.

Dujunco, Mercedes. "Vong Co—The Development of a Vietnamese Song Style." In Phong T. Nguyen, ed., *New Perspectives on Vietnamese Music: Six Essays*. New Haven: Center for International and Area Studies, Yale University, 1991: 36–66.
Easton, Paul. "The Rock Music Community." In Jim Riordan, ed., *Soviet Youth Culture*. Bloomington: Indiana University Press, 1989: 45–83.
Ellison, Mary. *Lyrical Protest: Black Music's Struggle against Discrimination*. New York: Praeger, 1989.
Embree, Ainslee, ed. *Encyclopedia of Asian History*. New York: Macmillan, 1987.
"Empress of Arabic Song Lives on." *New Straits Times*, April 4, 1987.
Ennis, Phillip. *The Seventh Stream: The Emergence of Rock 'n' Roll in American Popular Music*. Hanover: Wesleyan University Press, 1992.
Erlmann, Viet. *African Stars: Studies in Black South African Performance*. Chicago: University of Chicago Press, 1991.
———. *Nightsong: Performance, Power and Practice in South Africa*. Chicago: University of Chicago Press, 1996.
———. "The Politics and Aesthetics of Transnational Musics." *The World of Music* 35/2 (1993): 3–15.
Ewens, Graeme. *Africa O-Ye! A Celebration of African Music*. New York: Da Capo, 1991.
Fairley, Jan. "La Nueva Cancion in Latinoamericana." *Bulletin of Latin American Research* 3/2 (1984): 107–115.
———. "New Song: Music and Politics in Latin America." In Francis Hanly and Tim May, eds., *Rhythms of the World*. London: BBC Books, 1989: 88–97.
Featherstone, Mike. "Global Culture: An Introduction." In Featherstone, ed., *Global Culture*: 1–15.
———. *Undoing Culture: Globalization, Postmodernism and Identity*. London: Sage, 1995.
———, ed. *Global Culture: Nationalism, Globalization and Modernity*. London: Sage, 1990
Fiori, Umberto. "Popular Music: Theory, Practice, Value." In David Horn, *Popular Music Perspectives 2*. Salisbury: May and May, 1985: 13–23.
Fiske, John. *Reading the Popular*. Boston: Unwin Hyman, 1989.
———. *Understanding Popular Culture*. Boston: Unwin Hyman, 1989.
Forrester, Duncan. "Factions and Filmstars: Tamil Nadu Politics Since 1971." *Asian Survey* 16/3 (March 1976): 283–296.
Friedlander, Paul. "China's 'Newer Value' Pop: Rock-and-Roll and Technology on the New Long March." *Asian Music* 22/2 (Spring/Summer 1991): 43–66.
———. "Rockin' the Yangtze: Impressions of Chinese Popular Music and Technology." *Popular Music and Society* 14/1 (Spring 1990): 63–73.
Friedman, Jonathan. *Cultural Identity and Global Process*. London: Sage, 1994.
Frith, Simon. "Anglo-America and Its Discontents." *Cultural Studies* 5/3 (October 1991): 263–269.
———. "Art Ideology and Pop Practice." In Cary Nelson and Lawrence Grossberg, eds., *Marxism and the Interpretation of Culture*. Urbana: University of Illinois Press, 1988: 461–476.
———. *Music for Pleasure: Essays on the Sociology of Pop*. New York: Routledge, 1988.

———. *Sound Effects: Youth, Leisure and the Politics of Rock and Roll.* New York: Pantheon, 1981.
———, ed. *World Music, Politics and Social Change.* Manchester: Manchester University Press, 1989.
Fujui, Linda. "East Asia/Japan." In Jeff Todd Titon, ed., *Worlds of Music: An Introduction to the Music of the World's Peoples,* 2nd ed. New York: Schirmer, 1992: 318–375.
———. "Popular Music." In Powers and Kato, eds., *Handbook of Japanese Popular Culture*: 197–220.
Gans, Herbert. *Popular Culture and High Culture: An Analysis and Evaluation of Taste.* New York: Basic Books, 1974.
Garofalo, Reebee. "Introduction." In Garofalo, ed., *Rockin' the Boat*: 1–13.
———. "Whose World, What Beat: The Transnational Music Industry, Identity, and Cultural Imperialism." *The World of Music* 35/1 (1993): 16–30.
———, ed. *Rockin' the Boat: Mass Music and Mass Movements.* Boston: South End, 1992.
Gendron, Bernard. "Theodor Adorno Meets the Cadillacs." In Tania Modleski, ed., *Studies in Entertainment: Critical Approaches to Mass Culture.* Bloomington: Indiana University Press, 1986: 18–38.
Gitlin, Todd. "Television's Screens: Hegemony in Transition." In Donald Lazere, ed., *American Media*: 240–265.
———. "World Leaders: Mickey, et al." *New York Times,* May 3, 1992.
Gittins, Ian. "Has Glasnost Tamed Russian Rock's Muse?" *New York Times,* August 22, 1993.
Glanvill, Rick. "World Music Mining—The International Trade in Music." In Hanly and May, *Rhythms*: 58–67.
Gold, Thomas B. "Go with Your Feelings: Hong Kong and Taiwan Popular Culture in Greater China." *The China Quarterly* 136 (December 1993): 907–925.
Gonzalez, Juan Pablo. "Hegemony and Counter-Hegemony of Music in Latin America: The Chilean Pop." *Popular Music and Society* 15/2 (Summer 1991), 63–75.
Goonasekera, Anura. "Asian Viewers Do Not See Western Programmes as Corrupting Their Culture." *Media Asia* 22/4 (1995): 217–221.
Graham, Ronnie. *The Da Capo Guide to Contemporary African Music.* New York: Da Capo, 1988.
———. *The World of African Music: Stern's Guide to Contemporary African Music.* London: Pluto Press, 1992.
Greenwood, Gavin, ed. *Asia Yearbook 1992.* Hong Kong: Far Eastern Economic Review, 1993.
Grossberg, Lawrence. "Another Boring Day in Paradise: Rock and Roll and the Empowerment of Everyday Life." *Popular Music* 4 (1984): 225–258.
———. *We Gotta Get Out of This Place: Popular Conservatism and Postmodern Culture.* New York: Routledge, 1992.
Guzman, Patricio, and Julianne Burton. "Politics and Film in People's Chile: The Battle of Chile." In John Downing, ed., *Film and Politics in the Third World.* Brooklyn: Autonomedia, 1987: 219–246.

Hall, Kathleen. " 'Not in Bombay, Not in UK, Not in Yuba City': Global Cultural Forms and Localized Identities in the Lives of British-Sikh Teenagers." Unpublished paper, 1994.

Hall, Stuart. "Culture, the Media and the 'Ideological Effect.' " In James Curran et al., eds., *Mass Communication and Society*. Beverly Hills: Sage, 1979: 315–348.

——— "Encoding/Decoding." In Stuart Hall et al., eds., *Culture, Media, Language*. London: Hutchison, 1980: 128–138.

———. "Notes on Deconstructing 'the Popular.' " In Raphael Samuel, ed., *People's History and Socialist Theory*. London: Routledge and Kegan Paul, 1981: 227–240.

Hamelink, Cees. *Cultural Autonomy in Global Communications: Planning National Information Policy*. New York: Longman, 1983.

Hamm, Charles. "Music and Radio in the People's Republic of China." *Asian Music* 22/2 (Spring/Summer 1991): 1–42.

Hampton, Wayne. *Guerrilla Minstrels: John Lennon, Joe Hill, Woody Guthrie, Bob Dylan*. Knoxville: University of Tennessee Press, 1986.

Handler, Richard. "High Culture, Hegemony, and Historical Causality." *American Ethnologist* 19/4 (November, 1992): 818–824.

Hanly, Francis, and Tim May, eds. *Rhythms of the World*. London: BBC Books, 1989.

Hannerz, Ulf. "Cosmopolitans and Locals in World Culture." In Featherstone, ed., *Global Culture*: 237–252.

———. "Notes on the Global Ecumene." *Public Culture* 1/2 (1989): 66–75.

Hardgrave, Robert L. "Politics and the Film in Tamilnadu: The Stars and the DMK." *Asian Survey* 13/3 (March 1973): 288–305.

Hayes, Nick. "Rock in a Hard Place." *In These Times*, September 27–October 3, 1989: 12–13.

Hayward, Phillip, ed. *Music and Popular Culture: Asia and Australia*. Clayton: Open Learning, Monash University, 1995.

Hazarika, Sanjoy. "India Plays Its Own Rock-and-Roll Despite Competition from the West." *New York Times*, September 5, 1989.

Heard, Judith Ann. "Songs and Sighs: The World of Enka." *PHP Intersect* 1/3 (March 1985): 12–17.

———. "Trends and Taste in Japanese Popular Music: A Case-Study of the 1982 Yamaha World Popular Music Festival." *Popular Music* 4 (1984): 75–96.

Hebdige, Dick. *Cut 'n' Mix: Culture, Identity and Caribbean Music*. London: Comedia, 1987.

Hedges, Chris. "Beloved Infidel." *New York Times*, July 4, 1993.

———. "Tehran Journal: Mobilizing Against Evils of Western Pop Culture." *New York Times*, July 21, 1993.

Heidt, Erhard U. *Mass Media, Cultural Tradition, and National Identity*. Saarbrucken: Verlas Breitenback, 1987.

Hewison, Kevin, Richard Robison, and Garry Rodan, eds. *Southeast Asia in the 1990s: Authoritarianism, Democracy and Capitalism*. St. Leonards, N.S.W.: Allen and Unwin, 1993:

Hiebert, Murray. "Singing Between the Lines." *Far Eastern Economic Review*, February 21, 1991: 31–32.

Hinds, Harold E., Jr. "Life after Donald Duck." *Studies in Latin American Popular Culture* 7 (1988): 272.
———. "Popularity: The Sine Qua Non of Popular Culture." *Studies in Latin American Popular Culture* 9 (1990): 1–13.
Holden, Stephen. "Selling Sex and (Oh Yes) a Record." *New York Times*, October 18, 1992.
Hosokawa, Shuhei. Liner notes to Shoukichi Kina's album, *The Music Power from Okinawa* (Music Pub. Co. 072, 1991).
Hucker, Dave. "Far East of Eden." *The Beat* 13/3 (1994): 28–29.
Hunt, Ken. "The Romance of Film." *The Beat* 11/2 (1992): 44–45.
Inglis, Fred. *Popular Culture and Political Power*. New York: St. Martin's, 1988.
Irwin, Harry. *Communicating with Asia*. St. Leonards, N.S.W.: Allen and Unwin, 1996.
Isaku, Patia R. *Mountain Storm, Pine Breeze: Folk Song in Japan*. Tucson: University of Arizona Press, 1981.
Iyer, Pico. *Video Night in Kathmandu and Other Reports from the Not-So-Far-East*. New York: Knopf, 1988.
James, Caryn. "The Empress Has No Clothes." *New York Times Book Review*, October 25, 1992: 7.
Jameson, Frederic. *Postmodernism, Or the Cultural Logic of Late Capitalism*. Durham: Duke University Press, 1991.
"Japan's Voice of Hope in Postwar Era." *Chicago Tribune*, June 25, 1989.
Jara, Joan. *An Unfinished Song: The Life of Victor Jara*. New York: Ticknor and Fields, 1984.
Jarvie, I. C. *Window on Hongkong: A Sociological Study of the Hong Kong Film Industry and Its Audience*. Hong Kong: Centre for Asian Studies, University of Hong Kong, 1977.
Jarvis, B. "The Truth is Only Known to Guttersnipes." J. Burgess and J. R. Gold, eds., *Geography, the Media and Popular Culture*. London: Croom Helm, 1985: 96–122.
Jefferson, Margo. "The Real Dirt about a Rock Hit of Ill Repute." *New York Times*, September 2, 1993.
Jones, Andrew. *Like a Knife: Ideology and Genre in Contemporary Chinese Popular Music*. Ithaca: East Asia Program, Cornell University, 1992.
———. "Women in the Discursive and Political Economy of Shanghai Popular Music and Cinema, 1937–45." Unpublished paper, 1996.
Jones, Steve. "Who Fought the Law: The American Music Industry and the Global Popular Music Market." In Bennett et al., eds., *Rock and Popular Music*: 83–95.
Kaemmer, John. "Social Power and Music Change among the Shona." *Ethnomusicology* 33/1 (Winter 1989): 31–45.
Kanahele, George. *Hawaiian Renaissance*. Honolulu: Project WAIAHA, 1982.
———, ed. *Hawaiian Music and Musicians: An Illustrated History*. Honolulu: University of Hawai'i Press, 1979.
Kartomi, Margaret J., and Stephen Blum, eds. *Music-Cultures in Contact: Convergences and Collisions*. Basel: Gordon and Breach, 1994.
Kato, Hidetoshi. "Some Thoughts on Japanese Popular Culture." In Powers and Kato, eds., *Handbook of Japanese Popular Culture*: xvii–xviii.

Kawabata, Shigeru. "The Japanese Record Industry." *Popular Music* 10/3 (October 1991): 327–346.
Keali'inohomoku, Joann W. "Hula and Hawaiian Identity." Unpublished paper, 1994.
Kearney, M. "The Local and the Global: The Anthropology of Globalization and Transnationalism." *Annual Review of Anthropology 1995* 24 (1995): 547–565.
Keller, Bill. "For Soviet Rock Musicians, Glasnost is Angst." *New York Times*, April 9, 1987.
Keyes, Charles. *The Golden Peninsula: Culture and Adaptation in Mainland Southeast Asia*. New York: Macmillan, 1977.
King, Margaret. "Popular Culture in Cross-Cultural Perspective." In Michael Hamnett and Richard Martin, eds., *Research in Culture Learning*. Honolulu: University of Hawai'i Press, 1980: 26–34.
Kitagawa, Junko. "Some Aspects of Japanese Popular Music." *Popular Music* 10/3 (October 1991): 305–316.
Kivnick, Helen Q. *Where is the Way: Song and Struggle in South Africa*. New York: Penguin, 1990.
Kleden, Ignas. "Pop Culture: Criticism and Recognition." *Prisma* 43 (March 1987): 3–4.
Kornhauser, Bronia. "In Defence of Kroncong." In Margaret Kartomi, ed., *Studies in Indonesian Music*. Melbourne: Center for Southeast Asian Studies, Monash University, 1978: 104–177.
Kottak, Conrad. *Prime-Time Society: An Anthropological Analysis of Television and Culture*. Belmont: Wadsworth, 1990.
Kristof, Nicholas D. "A Mongolian Rock Group Fosters Democracy." *New York Times*, May 26, 1990.
Kurti, Laszlo. " 'How Can I Be a Human Being?' Culture, Youth, and Musical Opposition in Hungary." In Ramet, ed., *Rocking the State*: 73–102.
———. "Rocking the State: Youth and Rock Music Culture in Hungary, 1976–1990." *East European Politics and Societies* 5/3 (Fall 1991): 483–513.
Laing, Dave. "The Music Industry and the 'Cultural Imperialism' Thesis." *Media, Culture and Society* 8 (1986): 331–342.
"*Layali al-Helmiya* or Dallas-on-the-Nile." *Courier (UNESCO)*, October 1992, 36.
Lazere, Donald. "Introduction." In Lazere, ed., *American Media and Mass Culture*, 1987: 233–236.
———. "Introduction: Entertainment as Social Control." In Lazere, ed., *American Media and Mass Culture*, 1987: 1–23.
———, ed., *American Media and Mass Culture: Left Perspectives*. Berkeley: University of California Press, 1987.
Lee, Gregory. "The 'East Is Red' Goes Pop: Commodification, Hybridity and Nationalism in Chinese Popular Song and Its Televisual Performance." *Popular Music* 14/1 (January, 1995): 95–110.
———. *Troubadours, Trumpeters, Troubled Makers: Lyricism, Nationalism, and Hybridity in China and Its Others*. Durham: Duke University Press, 1996.
Leitner, Olaf. "Rock Music in the GDR: An Epitaph." In Ramet, ed., *Rocking the State*: 17–40.
Lent, John. *The Asian Film Industry*. London: Christopher Helm, 1990.

———. "Historical Overview of Southeast Asian Film." *Media Asia* 18/2 (1991): 98–102 and 18/3 (1991): 152–163.
———, ed. *The Asian Newspapers' Reluctant Revolution*. Ames: Iowa State University Press, 1971.
Leong, Russell, ed. *Moving the Image: Independent Asian Pacific American Media Arts*. Los Angeles: UCLA Asian American Studies Center, 1991.
Levine, Lawrence. "The Folklore of Industrial Society: Popular Culture and Its Audiences." *American Historical Review* 97/5 (December 1992): 1369–1400.
Levinson, Marc. "Rock Around the World." *Newsweek*, April 24, 1995: 65.
Lewis, George H. "American Popular Culture and the Developing Nations: Innocence Abroad?" *Journal of Popular Entertainment Resources* (October 1978): 3–5.
———. "Beyond the Reef: Cultural Constructions of Hawaii in Mainland America, Australia and Japan." *Journal of Popular Culture* 30/2 (Fall 1996): 123–135.
———. "Beyond the Reef: Role Conflict and the Professional Musician in Hawaii." *Popular Music* 5 (1985): 189–198.
———. "Commercial and Colonial Stimuli: Cross Cultural Creation of Popular Culture." *Journal of Popular Culture* 15/2 (Fall 1981): 142–156.
———. "Da Kine Sounds: The Function of Music as Social Protest in the New Hawaiian Renaissance." *American Music* 3/7 (1984): 38–52.
———. "Don't Go Down Waikiki: Social Protest and Popular Music in Hawaii." In Reebee Garofalo, ed., *Rockin' the Boat: Mass Music and Mass Movements*. Boston: South End, 1992: 171–183.
———. "Music, Culture and the Hawaiian Renaissance." *Popular Music and Society* 10/3 (1986): 47–53.
———. "Preface." In Lewis, ed., *Side-Saddle on the Golden Calf: Social Structure and Popular Culture in America*. Pacific Palisades: Goodyear, 1972: xi–xv.
———. *The Sociology of Popular Culture*. Special issue of *Current Sociology* 26/3 (Winter 1978).
———. "Storm Blowing from Paradise: Social Protest and Oppositional Ideology in Popular Hawaiian Music." *Popular Music* 10/1 (January 1991): 53–68.
———. "Who Do You Love? The Dimensions of Musical Taste." In Lull, ed., *Popular Music*: 134–151.
Lim Teck Ghee, ed. *Reflections on Development in Southeast Asia*. Singapore: Institute of Southeast Asian Studies, 1988.
Liner notes to the album *Vietnam: Songs of Liberation* (Paredon 1008, 1971).
Lintner, Bertil. "Politics of Pop." *Far Eastern Economic Review*, June 22, 1989: 40.
Lipsitz, George. *Dangerous Crossroads: Popular Music, Postmodernism and the Poetics of Place*. London: Verso, 1994.
———. *Time Passages: Collective Memory and American Popular Culture*. Minneapolis: University of Minnesota Press, 1990.
Lockard, Craig A. " 'Get Up, Stand Up': Popular Music and Politics in the Third World." Unpublished manuscript, 1995.
———. "Letter from Meixian." *Far Eastern Economic Review*, November 14, 1985.
———. "Pete Seeger." In Ray Browne, ed., *Encyclopedia of American Popular Culture*. Santa Barbara: ABC–Clio, forthcoming.

———. "Popular Musics and Politics in Modern Southeast Asia: A Comparative Analysis." *Asian Musics* 27/2 (Spring-Summer 1996): 149–199.
———. "Woody Guthrie." In Mari Jo Buhle et al., eds., *The American Radical.* New York: Routledge, 1994: 237–244.
Lorch, Donatella. "To Find a Happy Ending, Somalis Take in a Movie." *New York Times*, March 8, 1994.
Lull, James. *China Turned On: Television, Reform, and Resistance.* London: Routledge, 1991.
———. "Popular Music and Communication: An Introduction." In Lull, ed., *Popular Music and Communications*: 1–32.
———, ed. *Popular Music and Communication*, 2nd. ed. Newbury Park: Sage, 1992.
Lull, James, and Roger Wallis. "The Beat of West Vietnam." In James Lull, ed., *Popular Music and Communication*, 2nd ed. Newbury Park: Sage, 1992: 297–236.
Maceda, Jose. "Music in Southeast Asia: Tradition, Nationalism, Innovation." *Cultures* 1/3 (1974): 72–93.
MacIntyre, Andrew J., and Kanishka Jayasuriya, eds. *The Dynamics of Economic Policy Reform in South-east Asia and the South-west Pacific.* Singapore: Oxford University Press, 1992.
Maki, Okada. "Musical Characteristics of *Enka.*" *Popular Music* 10/3 (October 1991): 283–304.
Malm, Krister. "The Music Industry." In Helen Myers, ed., *Ethnomusicology: An Introduction.* New York: W. W. Norton, 1992: 349–364.
———. "Music on the Move: Traditions and Mass Media." *Ethnomusicology* 37/3 (Fall 1993): 339–352.
Malm, William P. *Music Cultures of the Pacific, the Near East and Asia*, 2nd ed. Englewood Cliffs: Prentice-Hall, 1977.
Manns, Patricio. "The Problems of the Text in Nueva Cancion." *Popular Music* 6/2 (May 1967): 191–196.
Manuel, Peter. *Cassette Culture: Popular Music and Technology in North India.* Chicago: University of Chicago Press, 1993.
———. "The Cassette Industry and Popular Music in North India." *Popular Music* 10/2 (May 1991): 189–204.
———. "Popular Music and Media Culture in South Asia: Prefatory Considerations." *Asian Music* 24/1 (Fall/Winter 1992–1993): 91–99.
———. *Popular Musics of the Non-Western World: An Introductory Survey.* New York: Oxford University Press, 1988.
Marcus, Greil. *Mystery Train: Images of America in Rock 'n' Roll Music.* New York: E. P. Dutton, 1975.
Marre, Jeremy, and Hannah Charlton. *Beats of the Heart: Popular Music of the World.* New York: Pantheon, 1985.
Marsh, Dave. *Louie Louie: The History and Mythology of the World's Most Famous Rock 'n' Roll Song.* New York: Hyperion, 1993.
Martin, Rhonda. "Music of East Timor: Songs to Resist the Wind That Blows from the Sea." *Sing Out* 26/1 (1977): 14–17.
Matta, Fernando Reyes. "The 'New Song' and Its Confrontation in Latin America." In Cary Nelson and Lawrence Grossberg, eds., *Marxism and the Interpretation of Culture.* Urbana: University of Illinois Press, 1988: 447–460.

Mattelart, Armand. *Multinational Corporations and the Control of Culture.* Sussex: Harvester Press, 1979.

Maung Tin Mya. "Politics and Religion Over-Ruled as Rock Takes Root in the Ricefields." *Far Eastern Economic Review,* January 12, 1984: 45–46.

Mazrui, Ali. *Cultural Forces in World Politics.* London: James Currey, 1990.

McDonald, Hamish. "Double Features." *Far Eastern Economic Review,* December 24–31, 1992: 46–48.

McDonald, J. R. "Censoring Rock Lyrics: A Historical Analysis of the Debate." *Youth and Society* 19 (March 1989): 294–313.

McGowan, Chris, and Ricardo Pessanha. *The Brazilian Sound: Samba, Bossa Nova and the Popular Music of Brazil.* New York: Billboard, 1991.

McLeod, J. R. "The Seamless Web: Media and Power in the Post-Modern Global Village." *Journal of Popular Culture,* 15/2 (Fall 1991): 69–75.

McRobbie, Angela. "Introduction." In Angela McRobbie, ed., *Zoot Suits and Second-Hand Dresses: An Anthology of Fashion and Music.* Boston: Unwin Hyman, 1988: xi–xx.

McVey, Ruth T., ed. *Southeast Asian Transitions: Approaches through Social History.* New Haven: Yale University Press, 1978.

Means, Laurel, ed. *Cultural Environments in Contemporary Southeast Asia.* Vancouver: Centre for Southeast Asian Research, University of British Columbia, 1993.

Mensh, Elaine, and Harry Mensh. *Behind the Scenes in Two Worlds.* New York: International Publishers, 1978.

Meyer, Gunter. "Popular Music in the GDR." *Journal of Popular Culture* 18/3 (Winter 1984): 145–158.

Middleton, Richard. *Studying Popular Music.* Milton Keynes: Open University Press, 1990.

Miettinen, Jukka O. *Classical Dance and Theatre in South-East Asia.* Singapore: Oxford University, 1992.

Mihaica, Matei P. "Chinese Rock Stars: New Generation Emerging Following Political Liberalization." *Far Eastern Economic Review,* November 19, 1992: 34–35.

———. "Cultural Spring or Illusory Thaw?" *Far Eastern Economic Review,* November 12, 1992: 50.

Mitchell, Tony. "Mixing Pop and Politics: Rock Music in Czechoslovakia before and after the Velvet Revolution." *Popular Music* 11/2 (May 1992): 187–203.

———. "World Music and the Popular Music Industry: An Australian View." *Ethnomusicology* 37/3 (Fall 1993): 308–338.

Mitsui, Toru. "Japan in Japan: Notes on an Aspect of the Popular Music Record Industry in Japan" In Richard Middleton and David Horn, eds., *Popular Music 3: Producers and Markets.* Cambridge: Cambridge University, 1983: 107–120.

———. "The Reception of the Music of American Southern Whites in Japan." In Neil V. Rosenberg, ed., *Transforming Tradition: Folk Music Revivals Examined.* Urbana: University of Illinois Press, 1993: 275–293.

Modleski, Tania. "Introduction." In Tania Modleski, ed., *Studies in Entertainment: Critical Approaches to Mass Culture.* Bloomington: Indiana University Press, 1986: ix–xix.

Mohd. Taib Osman, ed. *Traditional Drama and Music of Southeast Asia*. Kuala Lumpur: Dewan Bahasa dan Pustaka, 1974.
Moreno, Albrecht. "Violeta Parra and *La Nueva Cancion Chilena*." *Studies in Latin American Popular Culture* 5 (1986): 108–126.
Morris, Nancy. *Canto Porque es Necesario Cantar: The New Song Movement in Chile, 1973–1983*. Albuquerque: Latin American Institute, University of New Mexico, Research Paper Series No. 16, July 1984.
Mukerji, Chandra, and Michael Schudson. "Introduction." In Mukerji and Schudson, eds., *Rethinking Popular Culture: Contemporary Perspectives in Cultural Studies*. Berkeley: University of California Press, 1991: 1–63.
Neher, Clark D. *Southeast Asia in the New International Era*. Boulder: Westview, 1991.
Neher, Clark D., and Ross Marlay. *Democracy and Development in Southeast Asia: The Winds of Change*. Boulder: Westview, 1995.
Neuharth, Allen H. *Nearly One World*. New York: USA Today Books, 1989.
Ngugi wa Thiong'o, [James]. *Decolonizing the Mind: The Politics of Language in African Literature*. London: James Currey, 1986.
———. *Moving the Centre: The Struggle for Cultural Freedom*. London: James Currey, 1993.
Nogus, Keith. *Producing Pop: Culture and Conflict in the Popular Music Industry*. London: Edward Arnold, 1992.
Orman, John. *The Politics of Rock Music*. Chicago: Nelson-Hall, 1986.
Osborne, Milton. *Southeast Asia: An Illustrated Introductory History*. Sydney: Allen and Unwin, 1985.
Pandian, M. S. S. *The Image Trap: M. G. Ramachandran in Film and Politics*. New Delhi: Sage, 1992.
Pareles, Jon. "Honoring Tibet in Songs." *New York Times*, February 22, 1996.
———. "Niche Music: Tejano, Rave and, Yes, Bhangra." *New York Times*, May 14, 1995.
Parenti, Michael. *Make-Believe Media: The Politics of Entertainment*. New York: St. Martin's, 1992.
Paterson, Thomas G. "Defining and Doing the History of American Foreign Relations: A Primer." In Michael J. Hogan and Paterson, eds., *Explaining the History of American Foreign Relations*. Cambridge: Cambridge University Press, 1991: 36–54.
Patya Saihoo. "Problems in Cultural Development in ASEAN." In R. P. Anand and Purificacion V. Quisumbing, eds., *ASEAN: Identity, Development and Culture*. Quezon City: University of Philippines Law Center, 1981: 109–129.
Pekacz, Jolanta. "Did Pop Smash the Wall? The Role of Rock in Political Transition." *Popular Music* 13/1 (1994): 41–49.
———. "Did Pop Smash the Wall? The Utopia of Rock Ideology Meets the Red Trap of Communism." Paper read to American Historical Association, Washington, D.C., December 30, 1992.
———. "On Some Dilemmas of Polish Post-Communist Rock Culture." *Popular Music* 11/2 (1992): 205–208.
Perrone, Charles A. *Masters of Contemporary Brazilian Song: MPB 1965–1985*. Austin: University of Texas Press, 1989.

Peters, Matt. "Rock 'N' Revolt." *Far Eastern Economic Review*, March 28, 1991: 30–31.

Petrov, Arkadi. "The Age of Aquarium." *New Straits Times*, November 23, 1989.

Pettigrew, Joyce. "Songs of the Sikh Resistance Movement." *Asian Music* 23/1 (Fall/Winter 1992): 89–102.

Pham Duy. *Musics of Vietnam*. Carbondale: Southern Illinois University Press, 1975.

Philpott, Malcolm. "Developments in Papua New Guinea's Popular Music Industry." *Perfect Beat* 2/3 (July 1995): 83–114.

Pielke, Robert. *You Say You Want a Revolution: Rock Music in American Culture*. Chicago: Nelson-Hall, 1986.

Pond, Irina. "Soviet Rock Lyrics: Their Content and Poetics." *Popular Music and Society* 11/4 (Winter 1987): 75–91.

Powell, Walter. "The Blockbuster Decades: The Media as Big Business." In Lazere, ed., *American Media*: 53–63.

Powers, Harold. "Classical Music, Cultural Roots, and Colonial Rule: An Indic Musicologist Looks at the Muslim World." *Asian Music* 12/1 (1979): 5–39.

Powers, Richard Gid, and Hidetoshi Kato, eds. *Handbook of Japanese Popular Culture*. New York: Greenwood, 1989.

Powne, Michael. *Ethiopian Music: An Introduction*. London: Oxford University Press, 1968.

Pratt, Ray. *Rhythm and Resistance: Explorations in the Political Uses of Popular Music*. New York: Praeger, 1990.

"The Press Conference: John Lennon and Yoko Ono Talk about Peace." In Marianne Philbin, ed., *Give Peace a Chance: Music and the Struggle for Peace*. Chicago: Chicago Review Press, 1983: 11–26.

Pring-Mill, Robert. *"Gracias a la vida": The Power and Poetry of Song*. London: Department of Hispanic Studies, University of London, 1990.

Purcell, William. *An Introduction to Asian Music*. New York: Asia Society, 1966.

Quinn-Judge, Paul. "Soviets Revere Controversial Poet." *Christian Science Monitor*, June 4, 1987: 9.

Racy, Ali Jihad. "Music in Contemporary Cairo: A Comparative Overview." *Asian Music* 13/1 (1981): 4–23.

Ramet, Pedro, and Sergei Zamascikov. "The Soviet Rock Scene." *Journal of Popular Culture* 24/1 (Summer 1990): 150–174.

Ramet, Sabrina Petra. "Rock: The Music of Revolution (and Political Conformity)." In Ramet, ed., *Rocking the State*: 1–14.

———, ed. *Rocking the State: Rock Music and Politics in Eastern Europe and Russia*. Boulder: Westview, 1994.

Ranade, Ashok. "Popular Culture and Music." *International Popular Culture* 2/1 (Spring/Summer 1981): 22–27.

Rapaport, Jennifer. "Negotiating Identity in a World Turned Upside Down: Russian Youth Cultural Practice in Soviet and Post-Soviet Society." Unpublished paper, 1994.

Rashid, Ahmed. "Pop Star Wars," *Far Eastern Economic Review*, May 4, 1989: 62.

Rattanavong, Houmphanh. "The Lamluang: A Popular Entertainment." In Amy Catlin, ed., *Selected Reports in Ethnomusicology, Vol. IX: Text, Context, and Performance in Cambodia, Laos, and Vietnam*. Los Angeles: Department of Ethnomusicology, University of California, Los Angeles, 1992: 189–192.

Rauth, Robert. "Back in the U.S.S.R.—Rock and Roll in the Soviet Union." *Popular Music and Society* 8/3-4 (1982): 3–12.
Real, Michael. *Mass-Mediated Culture.* Englewood Cliffs, NJ: Prentice-Hall, 1977.
Reeves, Richard. "Jerry Brown Lives—and Interviews and Publishes." *Green Bay Press-Gazette*, July 30, 1986.
Regis, Humphrey A. "Calypso, Reggae and Cultural Importation by Reexportation." *Popular Music and Society* 12/1 (Spring 1988): 63–74.
Reynolds, Juliet. "Revolutionary Songs Find Voice in the Streets." *Far Eastern Economic Review*, September 4, 1986: 38–39.
Rigg, Jonathan. *Southeast Asia: A Region in Transition.* London: Unwin Hyman, 1991.
Riggs, Peter. "Baltic Rocks: The Singing Revolution in the Soviet Union." *Whole Earth Review* 65 (Winter 1989): 56–67.
———. "Rock and Roll in China: A Samizdat Document." *Popular Music and Society* 16/4 (Winter 1992): 37–39.
———. "Up from the Underground: Sound Technologies, Independent Musicianship, and Cultural Change in China and the Soviet Union." *Popular Music and Society* 15/1 (Spring 1991): 1–23.
Roberts, John Storm. *Black Music of Two Worlds.* Brooklyn: Original Music, 1972.
———. Liner notes to the album *Songs the Swahili Sing* (Original Music Records, 103).
Robertson, Roland. *Globalization: Social Theory and Global Culture.* London: Sage, 1992.
Robinson, Deanna Campbell, et al. *Music at the Margins: Popular Music and Global Diversity.* Newbury Park: Sage, 1991.
Robison, Richard, and David S. G. Goodman, eds. *The New Rich in Asia: Mobile Phones, McDonalds and Middle-Class Revolution.* New York: Routledge, 1996.
"Rock Rolls on in China." *Asiaweek*, May 3, 1991: 51.
Rodnitzky, Jerome. "Popular Music as Radical Influence, 1945–1970." Rodnitzky et al., eds., *Essays on Radicalism in Contemporary America.* Austin: University of Texas Press, 1972: 3–31.
———. "Songs of Sisterhood: The Music of Women's Liberation." *Popular Music and Society* 4/2 (1975): 77–85.
Rosen, David. *Protest Songs in America.* Westlake Village, CA: Aware Press, 1972.
Roskies, D. M., ed., *Text/Politics in Island Southeast Asia.* Athens: Ohio University Press, 1993.
Rothstein, Edward. "Riffs on Rap, Rock, Jazz, Modernism." *New York Times*, July 3, 1994.
Rutten, Paul. "Local Popular Music on the National and International Charts." *Cultural Studies* 5/3 (October 1991): 294–305.
Ryback, Timothy W. "Raisa Gorbachev Is an Elvis Fan, and Other Reasons Why Scholars Should Study the Role of Rock in Eastern Europe." *Chronicle of Higher Education*, June 6, 1990: B1.
———. *Rock around the Bloc: A History of Rock Music in Eastern Europe and the Soviet Union.* New York: Oxford University, 1990.
Ryker, Harrison, ed. *New Music in the Orient: Essays on Composition Since World War II.* Buren, Netherlands: Frits Knuf, 1991.
Sakamaki, Sachiko. "Bring on the Clowns." *Far Eastern Economic Review*, April 20, 1995: 16.

Sakolsky, Ron, and Fred Wei-Han Ho, eds. *Sounding Off: Music as Subversion/Resistance/Revolution.* Brooklyn: Autonomedia, 1995.
Samson, Valerie. "Music as Protest Strategy: The Example of Tiananmen Square, 1989." *Pacific Review of Ethnomusicology* 6 (1991): 35–64.
Sarkar, Jayanta. "India Reacts to Cable TV." *Far Eastern Economic Review*, July 1, 1993: 33–34.
Schell, Orville. *Mandate of Heaven: A New Generation of Entrepreneurs, Dissidents, Bohemians, and Technocrats Lays Claim to China's Future.* New York: Simon and Schuster, 1994.
Schiller, Herbert. *Communication and Cultural Domination.* White Plains: International Arts and Sciences, 1976.
———. *Culture, Inc.: The Corporate Takeover of Public Expression.* New York: Oxford University Press, 1989.
Schmetzer, Uli. "Vietnam Changes, U.S. Embargo Fails." *Chicago Tribune*, December 29, 1991.
Schmidt, William E. "In Europe, America's Grip on Pop Culture is Fading." *New York Times*, March 28, 1993.
Schramm, Adelaida Reyes. "From Refugee to Immigrant: The Music of Vietnamese in the New York-New Jersey Metropolitan Area." In Phong T. Nguyen, ed., *New Perspectives on Vietnamese Music: Six Essays.* New Haven: Center for International and Area Studies, Yale University, 1991: 91–102.
Schreiner, Claus. *Musica Brasileira: A History of Popular Music and the People of Brazil.* New York: Marion Boyars, 1993.
Schwichtenberg, Cathy, ed. *The Madonna Connection: Representational Politics, Subcultural Identities, and Cultural Theory.* Boulder: Westview, 1992.
Scott, James. *Weapons of the Weak: Everyday Forms of Peasant Resistance.* New Haven: Yale University Press, 1985.
Seeger, Pete. Liner notes to Seeger's album, *Dangerous Songs* (Columbia 9303, n.d.).
Sen, Abhijit. "The Impact of American Pop Culture in the Third World." *Media Asia* 20/4 (1993): 208–223.
Sharma, Sanjay, John Hutnyk and Ashwani Sharma. *Dis-Orienting Rhythms: The Politics of the New Asian Dance Music.* London: 2ed, 1996.
Shepherd, John. "Music, Culture and Interdisciplinarity: Reflections on Relationships." *Popular Music* 13/2 (May 1994): 127–142.
Shim Jae Hoon. "Politics as Unusual." *Far Eastern Economic Review*, February 1, 1996: 24.
Shuman, Bruce. "Marshall McLuhan Burns His Library Card: Reflections on the Public Library in the Global Village." In Fred E. H. Schroeder, ed., *Twentieth Century Popular Culture in Museums and Libraries.* Bowling Green: Bowling Green University Press, 1981: 256–266.
Shuman, Michael. "In the East Bloc, It's Lennon—Not Lenin." *New York Times*, January 1, 1990.
Singh, Shanta Serbjeet. "Indian Cinema: A Huge Juggernaut on the Move." *Asian Culture* 30 (March 1981): 16–18.
Skillman, Teri. "Songs in Hindi Films: Nature and Function." In Wimal Dissanayake, ed., *Cinema and Cultural Identity: Reflections on Films from Japan, India, and China.* Lanham, MD: University Press of America, 1988: 149–158.

Slobin, Mark. *Subcultural Sounds: Micromusics of the West.* Hanover: Wesleyan University Press, 1993.
Slobin, Mark, and Jeff Todd Titon. "The Music-Culture as a World of Music." In Titon, ed., *Worlds of Music: An Introduction to the Music of the World's Peoples,* 2nd ed. New York: Schirmer, 1992: 1–28.
Southeast Asian Affairs 1991. Singapore: Institute of Southeast Asian Studies, 1991.
Southeast Asian Affairs 1994. Singapore: Institute of Southeast Asian Studies, 1994.
Southeast Asian Affairs 1995. Singapore: Institute of Southeast Asian Studies, 1995.
Southeast Asian Affairs 1996. Singapore: Institute of Southeast Asian Studies, 1996.
"Soviet Rock." *Christian Science Monitor,* July 6, 1989: 10–11.
"Sri Lanka's Voice of Protest." *Asiaweek,* October 30, 1987: 51.
Stanley, Alessandra. "Russians Find Their Heroes in Mexican TV Soap Operas." *New York Times,* March 20, 1994.
Stapleton, Chris. "Paris, Africa." In Francis Hanly and Tim May, eds., *Rhythms of the World.* London: BBC Books, 1989: 10–23.
Stapleton, Chris, and Chris May. *African Rock: The Pop Music of a Continent.* New York: Dutton, 1990.
Starr, Jerold M. "Introduction." In Jerold M. Starr, ed., *Cultural Politics: Radical Movements in Modern History.* New York: Praeger, 1985: xiii–xxiv.
Starr, S. Frederick. *Red and Hot: The Fate of Jazz in the Soviet Union.* New York: Limelight, 1985.
———. "The Rock Inundation [in the USSR]." *Wilson Quarterly* 7/4 (Autumn 1983): 58–67.
Steinberg, David J. *In Search of Southeast Asia: A Modern History.* Honolulu: University of Hawai'i Press, 1985.
Stewart, Gary. *Breakout: Profiles in African Rhythm.* Chicago: University of Chicago Press, 1992.
Stillman, Amy Ku'uleialoha. "Sound Evidence: Conceptual Stability, Social Maintenance and Changing Performance Practices in Modern Hawaiian Hula Songs." *World of Music* 38/2 (1996): 5–22.
Stites, Richard. *Russian Popular Culture: Entertainment and Society Since 1900.* Cambridge: Cambridge University Press, 1992.
Stock, Jonathan. "Reconsidering the Past: Zhou Xuan and the Rehabilitation of Early Twentieth Century Chinese Popular Music" (Summary). *Newsletter: International Council for Traditional Music, U.K. Chapter* 7 (Summer 1990): 11.
Stokes, Martin. *The Arabesk Debate: Music and Musicians in Modern Turkey.* Oxford: Clarendon Press, 1992.
Sweeney, Philip. *The Virgin Directory of World Music.* New York: Henry Holt, 1991.
Szemere, Anna. " 'I Get Frightened of My Voice': On *Avant-Garde* Rock in Hungary." In Simon Frith, ed., *World Music, Politics and Social Change.* Manchester: Manchester University Press, 1989: 174–189.
———. "Pop Music in Hungary." *Communication Research* 12 (1985): 401–411.
———. "Some Institutional Aspects of Pop and Rock in Hungary." *Popular Music* 3 (1983): 121–142.
———. "The Politics of Marginality: A Rock Musical Subculture in Socialist Hungary in the Early 1980s." In Reebee Garofalo, ed., *Rockin' the Boat: Mass Music and Mass Movements.* Boston: South End, 1992: 93–114.

Tasker, Rodney. "Real-Life Drama." *Far Eastern Economic Review*, December 24–31, 1992: 48–50.
Taylor, John G., and Andrew Turton, eds. *Sociology of "Developing Societies": Southeast Asia.* New York: Monthly Review, 1988.
Taylor, Timothy D. *Global Pop: World Music, World Markets.* New York: Routledge, 1997.
Terrill, Ross. "Rocking the Old Guard." *World Monitor*, 5/5 (May 1992): 24–28.
Tetzlaff, David. "Divide and Conquer: Popular Culture and Social Control in Late Capitalism." *Media, Culture and Society*, 13/1 (January 1991): 9–34.
Tham Seong Chee, ed. *Essays on Literature and Society in Southeast Asia.* Singapore: Singapore University Press, 1981.
Thayil, Jeet. "The Mob in the Movies." *Asiaweek*, July 27, 1994: 39–45.
Thomas, T. Ajayi. *History of Juju Music: A History of an African Popular Music from Nigeria.* New York: Thomas Organization, 1992.
Thompson, John. *Ideology and Modern Culture: Critical Social Theory in the Era of Mass Communications.* Stanford: Stanford University Press, 1990.
Titon, Jeff Todd, ed. *Worlds of Music: An Introduction to the Music of the World's People,* 2nd ed. New York: Schirmer, 1992.
Tomlinson, John. *Cultural Imperialism: A Critical Introduction.* Baltimore: Johns Hopkins University Press, 1991.
Toop, David. "Into the Hot—Exotica and World Music Fusions." In Hanly and May, *Rhythms:* 118–126.
Tran Van Khe. "Traditional Music and Culture Change: A Study in Acculturation." *Cultures* 1/1 (1973): 197–209.
Troitsky, Artemy. *Back in the USSR: The True Story of Rock in Russia.* London: Omnibus, 1987.
Tumas-Serna, Jane. "The 'Nueva Cancion' Movement and Its Mass Mediated Performance Context." *Latin American Music Review* 13/2 (Fall/Winter 1992): 139–157.
Turnstall, Jeremy. "Media Imperialism." In Lazare, ed., *American Media*: 540–551.
Unger, Arthur. " 'A Voice from Russia'—Probing the Vysotsky Enigma." *Christian Science Monitor*, September 2, 1983: 10.
United Nations. *Industrial Statistics Yearbook, 1991: Vol. 2: Commodity Production Statistics 1982–1991.* Washington, D.C.: Congressional Information Service, 1993.
Vamos, Miklos. "Hungary for American Pop." *The Nation*, March 15, 1991: 374–376.
Van Elteren, Mel. "Conceptualizing the Impact of U.S. Popular Culture Globally." *Journal of Popular Culture* 20/1 (Summer 1996): 47–81.
Van Erven, Eugene. *The Playful Revolution: Theatre and Liberation in Asia.* Bloomington; Indiana University, 1992.
Vidyarthi, Govind. *Cultural Neocolonialism.* Hyderabad: Allied Publishers, 1988.
Vulliamy, Graham. "A Re-Assessment of the 'Mass Culture' Controversy: The Case of Rock Music." *Popular Music and Society* 4/3 (1975): 130–155.
Wagley, Charles. *An Introduction to Brazil*, 2nd ed. New York: Columbia University Press, 1971.
Wagnleitner, Reinhold. "The Irony of American Culture Abroad: Austria and the Cold War." In Lary May, ed., *Recasting America: Culture and Politics in the Age of Cold War.* Chicago: University of Chicago Press, 1989: 285–302.

Wallerstein, Immanuel. "Culture as an Ideological Background of the Modern World System." In Featherstone, ed., *Global Culture:* 31–56.

Wallis, Roger, and Krister Malm. *Big Sounds from Small Peoples: The Music Industry in Small Countries.* New York: Pendragon, 1984.

Wan Abdul Kadir Wan Yusof. "Kebudayaan Popular: Satu Pembicaraan." *Dewan Budaya* 3/11 (November 1981): 14–16.

Warshaw, Steven. *Southeast Asia Emerges: A Concise History of Southeast Asia.* Berkeley: Diablo, 1987.

Waterman, Christopher. *Juju: A Social History and Ethnography of an African Popular Music.* Chicago: University of Chicago Press, 1990.

Watrous, Peter. "A Japanese Band Gains Acceptance among Salsa Fans." *New York Times,* September 11, 1990.

Webb, Michael. *Lokal Musik: Lingua Franca Song and Identity in Papua New Guinea.* Port Moresby: The National Research Institute, 1993.

Weber, Eugen. "PC? Rethinking Popular Culture." *Contention: Debates in Society, Culture, and Science* 5 (Winter 1993): 3–14.

Weil, Thomas E., et al. *Area Handbook for Brazil,* 3rd ed. Washington, D.C.: Department of the Army, 1975.

White, Timothy. " 'World Beat Stay Home' Sez U.S. Immigration Service." *Musician* (July 1990): 17.

Wicke, Peter. "Popularity in Music: Some Aspects of a Historical-Materialist Theory for Popular Music." *Popular Music Perspectives* 2: 47–51.

———. *Rock Music: Culture, Aesthetics and Sociology.* Cambridge: Cambridge University Press, 1987.

———. "The Role of Rock Music in the Political Disintegration of East Germany." In Lull, ed., *Popular Music and Communication:* 196–206.

———. "The Times They Are A-Changin': Rock Music and Political Change in East Germany." In Reebee Garofalo, ed., *Rockin' the Boat: Mass Music and Mass Movements.* Boston: South End, 1992: 81–92.

Wicke, Peter, and John Shepherd. " 'The Cabaret is Dead': Rock Culture as State Enterprise—The Political Organization of Rock in East Germany." In Tony Bennett et al., eds., *Rock and Popular Music: Politics, Policies, and Institutions.* London: Routledge, 1993: 25–36.

Wicks, Peter. *Literary Perspectives on Southeast Asia: Collected Essays by Peter Wicks.* Toowoomba: University of Southern Queensland Press, 1991.

Wiener, Jon. *Come Together: John Lennon in His Time.* New York: Random House, 1984.

———. "*Give Peace a Chance*: An Anthem for the Anti-War Movement." In Marianne Philbin, ed., *Give Peace a Chance: Music and the Struggle for Peace.* Chicago: Chicago Review Press, 1983: 11–26.

Williams, Brett. "Introduction." In Williams, ed., *The Politics of Culture.* Washington: Smithsonian Institution, 1991: 1–18.

Williams, Raymond. *Marxism and Literature.* London: Oxford University Press, 1977.

Wilson, Janelle L., and Gerald E. Markle. "Justify My Ideology: Madonna and Traditional Values." *Popular Music and Society* 16/2 (Summer 1992): 75–83.

Wong, Deborah. "At the Microphone: Southeast Asian Karaoke in Los Angeles." Unpublished paper, 1993.

World Record Sales 1969–1990: A Statistical History of the World Recording Industry. London: International Federation of the Phonographic Industry, 1990.
WuDunn, Sheryl. "Bootleg Jab of Aide's Jab Is Hit in China." *New York Times,* May 31, 1992.
"X." "China's Sidelined Generation." *World Monitor,* July 1991: 16–19.
Yamashita, Shinji. "Listening to the City: Popular Music of Contemporary Indonesia." *East Asian Cultural Studies* 27/1–4 (March 1988): 105–120.
Yang, Fang-Chih Irene. "A Genre Analysis of Popular Music in Taiwan." *Popular Music and Society* 17/2 (Summer 1993): 83–112.
Yano, Christine R. "Shaping Sexuality in Japanese Popular Song." Unpublished paper, 1994.
Yousof, Ghulam-Sarwar. *Dictionary of Traditional South-East Asian Theatre.* Kuala Lumpur: Oxford University Press, 1994.
Yudice, George. "We Are *Not* the World." *Social Text* 31/32 (1992): 202–216.
Zha, Jianying. *China Pop: How Soap Operas, Tabloids, and Bestsellers Are Transforming a Culture.* New York: The New Press, 1995.
Zilberg, Jonathan. "Why Zimbabweans Love Dolly Parton and Are Indifferent to Shona Sculpture." Unpublished paper, 1994.

Indonesia

Abdullah, Taufik, ed. *Literature and History.* Yogyakarta: Gadja Mada University, 1986.
Abeyasekere, Susan. *Jakarta: A History.* Singapore: Oxford University Press, 1987.
Al-Attas, Suraya. "Hetty's Still at the Top." *New Straits Times,* May 19, 1989.
Alexander, Paul, ed. *Creating Indonesian Cultures.* Sydney: Oceania Publications, 1989.
Alisjahbana, S. Takdir. *Indonesia: Social and Cultural Revolution.* Kuala Lumpur: Oxford University Press, 1966.
"Anatomy of Press Censorship in Indonesia: The Case of Jakarta and the Dili Massacre." *Asia Watch* 4/12 (April 27, 1992).
Anderson, Benedict R. O'G. "Cartoons and Monuments: The Evolution of Political Communication under the New Order." In Jackson and Pye, eds., *Political Power:* 282–321.
———. *Mythology and the Tolerance of the Javanese.* Ithaca: Modern Indonesia Project, Southeast Asia Program, Cornell University, 1969.
Anwar, Rosihan. "Indonesian Films—A Search for Identity." *New Straits Times,* Annual 1977. Kuala Lumpur: Berita, 1978: 148–152.
Armes, Roy. *Third World Film Making and the West.* Berkeley: University of California Press, 1987.
Arps, Bernard, ed. *Performance in Java and Bali: Studies of Narrative, Theatre, Music, and Dance.* London: School of Oriental and African Studies, University of London, 1993.
The Asia & Pacific Review 1993/94: Economic and Business Report. London: The World of Information, 1993.
Aspinall, Edward. *Student Dissent in Indonesia in the 1980s.* Working Paper 79. Clayton: Centre of Southeast Asian Studies, Monash University, 1993.

Aveling, Harry. "Literature, Politics, and Context." *Review of Indonesian and Malaysian Affairs* 21/1 (Winter 1987): 1–5.
Aznam, Suhaimi. "Contested Closure." *Far Eastern Economic Review*, November 26, 1993: 20–21.
———. "More of the Same." *Far Eastern Economic Review*, January 28, 1993: 28.
———. "Pop Politics." *Far Eastern Economic Review*, June 4, 1992: 20.
Bass, Colin. Liner notes to Nasida Ria, *Keadilan: Qasidah Music from Music.* (Piranha Records 26-1, n.d.)
Becker, Judith. *Gamelan Stories: Tantrism, Islam, and Aesthetics in Central Java.* Tempe: Program for Southeast Asian Studies, Arizona State University, 1993.
———. "Kroncong, Indonesian Popular Music." *Asian Music* 7/1 (1975): 14–19.
———. *Traditional Music in Modern Java: Gamelan in a Changing Society.* Honolulu: University of Hawai'i Press, 1980.
———. "Western Influence in Gamelan Music." *Asian Music* 3/1 (1972): 3–9.
Bodden, Michael. "Grass Roots Theatre, Conscientization, and Development in the Philippines and Indonesia." In Laurel Means, ed., *Cultural Environments in Contemporary Southeast Asia.* Vancouver: Centre for Southeast Asian Research, University of British Columbia, 1993: 33–46.
Bourchier, David, and John Legge, eds. *Democracy in Indonesia: 1950s and 1990s.* Melbourne: Centre of Southeast Asian Studies, Monash University, 1994.
Bouvier, Helene. "Diversity, Strategy and Function in East Madurese Performing Arts." In Kees van Dijk et al., eds., *Across Madura Strait: The Dynamics of an Insular Society.* Leiden: KITLV Press, 1995: 119–134.
Braginsky, Vladimir I. "The Gentleman in the Pink Hat, or the First Malay Film." *Indonesia Circle* 63 (June 1994): 175–182.
Brakel-Papenhuyzen, Clara. *Classical Javanese Dance: The Surakarta Tradition and Its Terminology.* Leiden: KITLV Press, 1995.
Brandon, James R. *Theatre in Southeast Asia.* Cambridge: Harvard University Press, 1967.
Branigin, William. "Indonesia Booming, but Problems Loom." *Washington Post*, December 30, 1992: A13.
Brinner, Benjamin. "Cultural Matrices and the Shaping of Innovation in Central Javanese Performing Arts." *Ethnomusicology* 39/3 (Fall 1995): 433–456.
———. *Knowing Music, Making Music: Javanese Gamelan and the Theory of Musical Competence and Interaction.* Chicago: University of Chicago Press, 1995.
Broughton, Simon, et al., eds. *World Music: The Rough Guide.* London: Rough Guides, 1994: 417–425.
Brown, David. *The State and Ethnic Politics in Southeast Asia.* London: Routledge, 1994: 112–157.
Bruner, Edward. "Comments—Modern? Indonesian? Culture?" In Davis, ed., *What Is Modern Indonesian Culture?*: 300–306.
Budiardjo, Carmel. "Militarism and Repression in Indonesia." *Third World Quarterly* 8/4 (October 1986): 1219–1238.
Budiman, Arief. "The Emergence of the Bureaucratic Capitalist State in Indonesia." In Lim Teck Ghee, ed., *Reflections on Development in Southeast Asia.* Singapore: Institute of Southeast Asian Studies, 1988: 110–129.

———, ed. *State and Civil Society in Indonesia.* Clayton: Centre for Southeast Asian Studies, Monash University, 1990.
Bunge, Frederica M., ed. *Indonesia: A Country Study.* Washington, D.C.: Department of the Army, 1982.
———. "Introduction." In Bunge, ed., *Indonesia: A Country Study*: xxiii–xxx.
Burns, Peter. "The Post Priok Trials: Religious Principles and Legal Issues." *Indonesia* 47 (April 1989): 61–88.
Buruma, Ian. "A Formula in Focus." *Far Eastern Economic Review*, August 11, 1983: 40–41.
Cady, John. *A History of Postwar Southeast Asia: Independence Problems.* Athens: Ohio University Press, 1974.
Caldarola, Victor J. *Reception as Cultural Experience: Visual Mass Media and Reception Practices in Outer Indonesia.* Ph.D. dissertation, University of Pennsylvania, 1990.
Capwell, Charles. "The Music of Indonesia." In Bruno Nettl et al., eds. *Excursions in World Music.* Englewood Cliffs: Prentice Hall, 1992: 134–164.
Chambert-Loir, Henri. "Prokem, the Slang of Jakarta Youth: Instructions for Use." *Prisma* 50 (September 1990): 80–88.
Chu, Godwin, and Alfian. "Indonesia's Uncommon Boob Tube." *East-West Center Perspectives* 2/1 (Spring 1981): 27–31.
Cohen, Margot. "Born to be Meek." *Far Eastern Economic Review*, October 24, 1991: 38–40.
———. "Driven by Dissent." *Far Eastern Economic Review*, December 16, 1996 and January 2, 1997: 14–15.
———. "My Word." *Far Eastern Economic Review*, September 14, 1995: 30–31.
———. "New Zeal." *Far Eastern Economic Review*, July 11, 1996: 19.
———. "Total Correction." *Far Eastern Economic Review*, October 12, 1995: 22–23.
———. "Twisting Arms for Alms." *Far Eastern Economic Review*, May 2, 1996: 25, 28–29.
———. "Under the Volcano." *Far Eastern Economic Review*, March 13, 1997: 42–47.
Collins, Jim. *The Uncommon Cultures: Popular Culture and Post Modernity.* New York: Routledge, 1988.
Cox, Peter. "The Ambonese Connection: Lou Casch, Johnny O'Keefe and the Development of Australian Rock and Roll." *Perfect Beat* 2/4 (January 1995): 1–16.
Crawford, Robert. "Indonesia." In John Lent, ed., *The Asian Newspapers' Reluctant Revolution.* Ames: Iowa State University Press, 1971: 158–178.
Crouch, Harold. "An Ageing President, an Ageing Regime." In Crouch and Hill, eds., *Indonesia Assessment 1992*: 43–62.
———. "Indonesia: An Uncertain Outlook." In *Southeast Asian Affairs 1994.* Singapore: Institute of Southeast Asian Studies, 1994: 121–145.
Crouch, Harold, and Hal Hill. "Introduction." In Crouch and Hill, eds., *Indonesia Assessment 1992*: 1–6.
———, eds. *Indonesia Assessment 1992: Political Perspectives on the 1990s.* Canberra: Research School of Pacific Studies, Australian National University, 1992.
Dahm, Bernard. *Indonesia in the Twentieth Century.* New York: Praeger, 1971.

Davis, Gloria. "What Is Modern Indonesian Culture? An Epilogue and Example." In Davis, ed., *What Is Modern Indonesian Culture?*: 307–317.

———, ed. *What Is Modern Indonesian Culture?* Athens: Center for Southeast Asian Studies, Ohio University, 1979.

"Defense of the Student Movement: Documents from Recent Trials." *Indonesia* 27 (April 1979): 11–16.

"Dicari, Romantisme yang Tidak Cengeng." *Popular* 85 (February 1995): 62–65.

Djamas, Nurhayati. "Behind the Tanjung Priok Incident, 1984: The Problem of Political Participation in Indonesia." Unpublished Master's thesis, Cornell University, 1991.

Drake, Christine. *National Integration in Indonesia: Patterns and Policies.* Honolulu: University of Hawai'i Press, 1989.

Dutolong, Corinne. "Jakarta Night Entertainment Grows More Diversified." *Indonesia Magazine* 23/4 (1992): 48–50.

Emka, Heru. *Thrash Metal dan Grindcore Sebagai Musik Alternatif.* Semarang: Medayu Press, 1992.

Errington, Joseph. "Continuity and Change in Indonesian Language Development." *Journal of Asian Studies* 45/2 (February 1986): 329–353.

Evers, Hans-Dieter. "The Growth of an Industrial Labour Force and the Decline of Poverty in Indonesia." In *Southeast Asian Affairs 1995.* Singapore: Institute of Southeast Asian Studies, 1996: 164–176.

Federspiel, Howard M. *Popular Indonesian Literature of the Qur'an.* Ithaca: Modern Indonesia Project, Cornell University, 1994.

Foley, Kathy. "The Tree of Life in Transition: Images of Resource Management in Indonesian Theatre." *Crossroads* 3/2–3 (1987): 66–77.

Foulcher, Keith. "The Construction of an Indonesian National Culture: Patterns of Hegemony and Resistance." In Budiman, ed., *State and Society*: 301–320.

———. "Literature, Cultural Politics, and the Indonesian Revolution." In D. M. Roskies, ed., *Text/Politics in Island Southeast Asia.* Athens: Ohio University, 1993: 221–256.

———. "Politics and Literature in Independent Indonesia: The View from the Left." *Southeast Asian Journal of Social Science* 15/1 (1987): 83–103.

———. "Post-Modernism or the Question of History: Some Trends in Indonesian Fiction since 1965." In Hooker, ed., *Culture and Society in Indonesia*: 27–47.

———. "Sastra Kontekstual: Recent Developments in Indonesian Literary Politics." *Review of Indonesian and Malaysian Affairs* 21/1 (Winter 1987): 6–28.

———. *Social Commitment and the Arts: The Indonesian "Institute of People's Culture" 1950–1965.* Clayton: Monash University, Centre of Southeast Asian Studies, 1986.

Frederick, Bill. "Rhoma Irama and the Dangdut Style: Aspects of Contemporary Indonesian Popular Culture." *Indonesia* 34 (October 1982): 103–130.

Frederick, William H. "Dreams of Freedom, Moments of Despair: Armijn Pane' and the Imagining of Modern Indonesian Culture." In Schiller and Martin-Schiller, eds., *Imagining Indonesia*: 54–89.

Frederick, William H., and Robert L. Worden, eds. *Indonesia: A Country Study.* 5th ed. Washington, D.C.: Library of Congress, 1992.

Frojen, Karen. " 'Uncle Country' and Radio for the Countryside: Bringing the State to the Ideal Villager in the Model Village (North Moluccas, Indonesia)." Unpublished paper, 1994.

Gaffar, Afan. *Javanese Voters: A Case Study of Election Under a Hegemonic Party System*. Yogyakarta: Gadja Mada University Press, 1992.
Gargan, Edward. "An Indonesian Asset is Also a Liability." *New York Times*, March 16, 1996.
Geertz, Clifford. "Afterward: The Politics of Meaning." In Holt, ed., *Culture and Politics in Indonesia*: 319–335.
———. *The Religion of Java*. New York: Free Press, 1960.
Geertz, Hildred. "Indonesian Cultures and Communities." In R. McVey, ed., *Indonesia*: 24–96.
Gombloh, Joko S. "Musik Rock, Sumber Brutalitas?" *Seni Pertunjukan Indonesia: Jurnal Masyarakat Seni Pertunjukan Indonesia* 6 (1995): 59–86.
Grant, Bruce. *Indonesia*. Melbourne: Melbourne University Press, 1966.
Greenwood, Gavin, ed. *Asia Yearbook 1992*. Hong Kong: Far Eastern Economic Review, 1993.
Grooss, Rosalie. *De Krontjong Guitaar*. Den Haag: Uitgeverij Tong Tong, 1972.
"Gugaran Bencana Flores: Iwan Fals." *Popular* 61 (February 1993): 11.
Halina. "Culture of the People." *Prisma* 43 (March 1987): 2.
Hanan, David. "Nji Ronggeng: Another Paradigm for Erotic Spectacle in the Cinema." In V. Hooker, ed., *Culture and Society in Indonesia*: 87–115.
Handley, Paul. "Dancing with Rhoma to the Muslim Beat." *Far Eastern Economic Review*, June 19, 1986: 55–57.
Hanna, Willard A. "Indonesian *Komik*." American Universities Field Staff, Asia No. 16, 1979.
———. "The Magical-Mystical Syndrome in the Indonesian Mentality, Part 1: Signs and Seers." American Universities Field Staff, *Southeast Asia Series* 15/5 (1967).
Hardjo, Seno M., et al. *Sepuluh Tokoh Showbiz Musik Indonesia*. Jakarta: Penerbit PT Gramedia Pustaka Utama, 1991.
Harsono, Andreas. "A Star is Banned." *Inside Indonesia* 21 (1989): 14–15.
Hatch, Martin. "Popular Music in Indonesia." In Simon Frith, ed., *World Music, Politics and Social Change*. Manchester: Manchester University Press, 1989: 49–67.
Hatley, Barbara. "Constructions of 'Tradition' in New Order Indonesian Theatre." In Hooker, ed., *Culture and Society*: 48–69.
———. "Cultural Expression." In Hill, ed., *Indonesia's New Order*: 216–266.
———. "Ludruk and Ketoprak, Popular Theatre and Society in Java." *Review of Indonesian and Malayan Affairs* (January 1973): 38–58.
———. "Theatre and Politics of National/Regional Identity: Some Sumatran Examples." *Review of Indonesian and Malaysian Affairs* 25/2 (Summer 1991): 1–18.
———. "Theatre as Cultural Resistance in Contemporary Indonesia." In Budiman, ed., *State and Society*: 321–348.
———. "Theatrical Imagery and Gender Ideology in Java." In Jane Monnag Atkinson and Shelly Errington, eds., *Power and Difference: Gender in Island Southeast Asia*. Stanford: Stanford University Press, 1990: 177–208.
Hefner, Robert. "Islam, State, and Civil Society: ICMI and the Struggle for the Indonesian Middle Class." *Indonesia* 56 (October 1993): 1–35.

———. "Islamizing Java? Religion and Politics in Rural East Java." *Journal of Asian Studies* 46/3 (August 1987): 533–554.
———. "The Politics of Popular Art: Tayuban Dance and Culture Change in East Java." *Indonesia* 43 (April 1987): 75–94.
Heider, Karl G. *Indonesian Cinema: National Culture on Screen.* Honolulu: University of Hawai'i Press, 1991.
———. "National Cinema, National Culture: The Indonesian Case." In W. Dissanayake, ed., *Colonialism and Nationalism in Asian Cinema.* Bloomington: Indiana University Press, 1994: 162–173.
Heins, Ernest. "Kroncong and Tanjidor—Two Cases of Urban Folk Music." *Asian Music* 7/1 (1975): 20–32.
Hellwig, Jean. "Jaipongan: The Making of a New Tradition." In Arps, ed., *Performance in Java*: 47–57.
Hellwig, Tineke. *In the Shadow of Change: Women in Indonesian Literature.* Berkeley: Center for South and Southeast Asian Studies, University of California–Berkeley, 1994.
Henschkel, Marina. "Perceptions of Popular Culture in Contemporary Indonesia: Five Articles from Tempo, 1980–90." *Review of Indonesian and Malaysian Affairs* 28/2 (Summer 1994): 53–71.
Heryanto, Ariel. "A Class Act." *Far Eastern Economic Review*, June 16, 1994: 30.
———. "Introduction: State Ideology and Civil Discourse." In Budiman, ed., *State and Society*: 289–300.
———. "Shedding Light on Megawati." *Far Eastern Economic Review*, October 17, 1996: 32.
Hill, David T. *The Press in New Order Indonesia.* Perth: University of Western Australia Press, 1994.
Hill, Hal. *The Indonesian Economy Since 1966: Southeast Asia's Emerging Giant.* Cambridge: Cambridge University Press, 1996.
———, ed., *Indonesia's New Order: The Dynamics of Socio-Economic Transformation.* Honolulu: University of Hawai'i Press, 1994.
Hill, Hal, and Jamie Mackie. "Introduction." In Hill, ed., *Indonesia's New Order*: xxii–xxxv.
Holaday, Duncan Alan. "The Social Impact of Satellite TV in Indonesia: A View from the Ground." *Media Asia* 23/2 (1996): 100–106.
Holt, Claire, ed. *Culture and Politics in Indonesia.* Ithaca: Cornell University Press, 1972.
Hood, Mantle. "The Enduring Tradition: Music and Theatre in Java and Bali." In R. McVey, ed., *Indonesia*: 438–471.
Hood, Mantle, et al. "Indonesia." In Stanley Sadie, ed., *The New Grove Dictionary of Music and Musicians*, Vol. 9. New York: Grove, 1980: 167–220.
Hooker, Virginia Matheson, ed. *Culture and Society in New Order Indonesia.* Kuala Lumpur: Oxford University Press, 1993.
Hooker, Virginia Matheson, and Howard Dick. "Introduction." In Hooker, ed., *Culture and Society in New Order Indonesia*: 1–24.
Hughes-Freeland, Felicia. "Balinese 'Culture' on Television." *Indonesia Circle* 70 (November 1996): 253–270.
"Indonesia Ridding Press of Critical Writers." *New York Times*, April 17, 1995.

"Indonesia: Students Jailed for Puns." *Human Rights Watch/Asia* 5/5 (March 16, 1993).

"Indonesia: The Medan Demonstrations and Beyond." *Human Rights Watch/Asia* 6/4 (May 16, 1994).

"Indonesia's Great Debate." *Asiaweek*, August 31, 1986: 64–65.

Jackson, Karl D., and Lucien W. Pye, eds. *Political Power and Communications in Indonesia*. Berkeley: University of California Press, 1978.

Jensen, Christel. "A Poet and His Plumage." *Index on Censorship* 2/16 (June 1992): 15.

"Jeritannya Masih Seksi: Nicky Astria." *Popular Music* (September 1996): 50–51.

Jit, Krishen. "Modern Theatre in Indonesia: A Preliminary Survey." *Malay Literature* 2/1 (January 1989): 50–62.

———. "Poet Extraordinaire." *New Straits Times* (Kuala Lumpur), April 2, 1989.

Karamoy, Amir, and Achmad Sablie. "The Communication Aspect and Its Impact on the Youth of Poor Kampongs in the City of Jakarta." *Prisma* 1/1 (May 1975): 60–68.

Kartomi, Margaret J. "From Kroncong to Dangdut: Indonesian Popular Music." In Hayward, ed., *Music and Popular Culture:* 277–292.

———. "Minangkabau Musical Culture: The Contemporary Scene and Recent Attempts at Modernization." In Davis, ed., *What Is Modern Indonesian Culture?*: 19–36.

———. "Musical Strata in Java, Bali, and Sumatra." In Elizabeth May, ed., *Musics of Many Cultures*. Los Angeles: University of California Press, 1980: 111–133.

———. " 'Traditional Music Weeps' and Other Themes in the Discourse on Music, Dance and Theatre of Indonesia, Malaysia and Thailand." *Journal of Southeast Asian Studies* 26/2 (September 1995): 366–400.

———, ed. *Studies in Indonesian Music*. Melbourne: Monash University, Papers on Southeast Asia, No. 7, 1978.

Kaye, Lincoln. "The Early Dawning of the Jakarta Spring." *Far Eastern Economic Review*, January 23, 1986: 41–43.

Keeler, Ward. *Javanese Shadow Plays, Javanese Selves*. Princeton: Princeton University Press, 1987.

———. *Javanese Shadow Puppets*. Singapore: Oxford University Press, 1992.

Kitley, Philip. "Tahun Bertambah, Zaman Bertambah: Television and Its Audiences in Indonesia." *Review of Indonesian and Malaysian Affairs* 26/1 (Winter 1992): 71–109.

Kleden, Ignas. "Pop Culture: Criticism and Recognition." *Prisma* 43 (March 1987): 3–7.

Kolstad, Katherine C. "Enemy Others and Violence in Jakarta: An Islamic Rhetoric of Discontent." In Mark R. Woodward, ed., *Toward a New Paradigm: Recent Developments in Indonesian Islamic Thought*. Tempe: Program for Southeast Asian Studies, Arizona State University, 1996: 357–378.

Kornhauser, Bronia. "In Defence of Kroncong." In Kartomi, ed., *Studies in Indonesian Music*: 104–177.

Kuipers, Joel C. "Songs and the State in Weyewa: Towards a Poetics of Modernity." Unpublished paper, 1991.

———. "The Society and Its Environment." In Frederick and Worden, eds., *Indonesia: A Country Study*: 69–135.
Kunst, Jaap. *Indonesian Music and Dance: Traditional Music and Its Interaction with the West.* Amsterdam: Royal Tropical Institute, 1994.
Lee, Joanna. "From National Identity to the Self: Themes in Modern Indonesian Art." In T. K. Sabapathy, ed., *Modernity and Beyond: Themes in Southeast Asian Art.* Singapore: Singapore Art Museum, 1996: 17–32.
Lee Khoon Choy. *Indonesia: Between Myth and Reality.* Singapore: Federal Publications, 1977.
Leee, Kit. "Not Like Our Own Dull Dangdut." *New Straits Times* (Kuala Lumpur), August 2, 1985.
Lent, John. *The Asian Film Industry.* London: Christopher Helm, 1990: 201–212.
———. "Historical Overview of Southeast Asian Film." *Media Asia* 18/2 (1991): 98–102 and 18/3 (1991): 152–163.
———, ed. *The Asian Newspapers' Reluctant Revolution.* Ames: Iowa State University Press, 1971: 158–178.
Liddle, R. William. "Improvising Political Cultural Change: Three Indonesian Cases." In Schiller and Martin-Schiller, eds., *Imagining Indonesia*: 1–54.
———. "The Islamic Turn in Indonesia: A Political Explanation." *Journal of Asian Studies* 55/3 (August 1996): 613–634.
———. "The National Political Culture and the New Order." *Prisma* 46 (December 1987): 4–20.
Lindsay, Jennifer. *Javanese Gamelan*, 2nd. ed. Kuala Lumpur: Oxford University Press, 1992.
Liner notes to the album by Euis Komariah and Yus Wiradiredja, *The Sound of Sunda: Degung Music from Java* (Globestyle 060, 1989).
Lucas, Anton. "Land Disputes in Indonesia: Some Current Perspectives." *Indonesia* 53 (April 1992): 79–92.
MacIntyre, Andrew. *Business and Politics in Indonesia.* Sydney: Allen and Unwin, 1990.
Mackie, Jamie, and Andrew MacIntyre. "Politics." In Hill, ed., *Indonesia's New Order*: 1–53.
Mahasin, Aswab. "The Discourse of Power." *Prisma* 50 (September 1990): 1.
Makarim, Nono Anwar. "The Indonesian Press: An Editor's Perspective." In Jackson and Pye, eds., *Political Power*: 259–281.
"Making History with History." *Asiaweek*, April 14, 1989: 43.
Malm, William P. *Music Cultures of the Pacific, the Near East and Asia*, 2nd ed. Englewood Cliffs: Prentice-Hall, 1977: 34–49.
Manuel, Peter. *Cassette Culture: Popular Music and Technology in North India.* Chicago: University of Chicago Press, 1993.
———. *Popular Musics of the Non-Western World: An Introductory Survey.* New York: Oxford University Press, 1988: 205–220.
Manuel, Peter, and Randall Baier. "Jaipongan: Indigenous Popular Music of West Java." *Asian Music* 18/1 (Fall/Winter 1986): 91–110.
Marshall, Kathryn G. "The Economy." In Frederick and Worden, eds., *Indonesia*: 137–206.
McBeth, John. "Containment Strategy." *Far Eastern Economic Review*, June 8, 1995: 18–19.

———. "Far from Over." *Far Eastern Economic Review*, August 22, 1996: 17, 20.
———. "The Gloves Are Off." *Far Eastern Economic Review*, June 27, 1996: 16.
———. "Heavy Hand." *Far Eastern Economic Review*, June 29, 1995: 28.
———. "Hunting Season." *Far Eastern Economic Review*, August 15, 1996: 14–15.
———. "The Next New Order." *Far Eastern Economic Review*, January 30, 1997: 22–24.
———. "Political Engineering." *Far Eastern Economic Review*, July 4, 1996: 14–15.
———. "Red Menace." *Far Eastern Economic Review*, November 2, 1995: 18, 20.
———. "Rude Awakening: Press Ban Shocks the Emerging Middle Class." *Far Eastern Economic Review*, July 7, 1994: 18–19.
———. "Stop Press: Media Ban Stymies Politics of Openness." *Far Eastern Economic Review*, June 30, 1994: 17.
———. "Streets of Fire." *Far Eastern Economic Review*, August 8, 1996: 14–16.
———. "Temperature Rising." *Far Eastern Economic Review*, May 23, 1996: 22.
———. "Third Time Lucky." *Far Eastern Economic Review*, January 13, 1994: 24–25.
———. "Tinderbox." *Far Eastern Economic Review*, January 9, 1997: 14–15.
———. "Troublesome Types." *Far Eastern Economic Review*, April 6, 1995: 28.
———. "Unifying Force." *Far Eastern Economic Review*, January 18, 1996: 24.
———. "Widening Ripples." *Far Eastern Economic Review*, July 14, 1994: 17–18.
McIntyre, Angus. "Sukarno as Artist-Politician." In Angus McIntyre, ed., *Indonesian Political Biography: In Search of Cross-Cultural Understanding*. Melbourne: Monash University Papers on Southeast Asia No. 28, 1993: 161–210.
McKendrick, David. "Indonesia in 1991: Growth, Privilege, and Rules." *Asian Survey* 32/2 (February 1992): 103–110.
McVey, Ruth, ed. *Indonesia*. New Haven: Human Relations Area Studies, 1974.
Miettinen, Jukka O. *Classical Dance and Theatre in South-East Asia*. Singapore: Oxford University, 1992: 75–139.
Moedjanto, G., B. Rahmanto and J. Sudarminta, eds. *Tantangan Kemanusian Universal: Antologi Filsafat, Budaya, Sejarah-Politik dan Sastra. Kenangan 70 Tahun Dick Hartoko*. Yogyakarta: Penerbit Kanisius, 1992.
Mohamad, Goenawan. "An Introduction to the Contemporary Indonesian Theatre." *Prisma* 1/1 (May 1975): 75–82.
———. "Indonesia's Prize Scars." *Far Eastern Economic Review*, September 28, 1995: 39.
———. *Sidelines: Writings from Tempo*. Translated by Jennifer Lindsay. South Melbourne: Hyland House, 1994.
Mohd. Taib Osman, ed. *Traditional Drama and Music of Southeast Asia*. Kuala Lumpur: Dewan Bahasa dan Pustaka, 1974.
"Mostly . . . Moral Support." *Far Eastern Economic Review*, August 15, 1985: 18–19.
Mulder, Niels. "Individual and Society in Contemporary Thailand and Java: An Anthropologist's Comparison of Modern Serious Fiction." *Journal of Southeast Asian Studies* 14/2 (September 1983): 312–327
———. *Individual and Society in Java: A Cultural Analysis*, 2nd ed. Yogyakarta: Gadja Mada University, 1992.
Murray, Alison. "Kampung Culture and Radical Chic in Jakarta." *Review of Indonesian and Malaysian Affairs* 25/1 (Winter 1991): 1–16.

Murthi, R. S. "Hetty Shares in Spirited Show." *New Straits Times*, May 22, 1989.
Mutsaers, Lutgard. "Indorock: an Early Eurorock Style." *Popular Music* 9/3 (October 1990): 307–320.
———. "Roots and Recognition: The Contribution of Musicians from the Indonesian Archipelago to the Development of Popular Music Culture in the Netherlands." *Perfect Beat* 2/3 (July 1995): 65–81.
Mydans, Seth. "Anti-Government Protesters Clash with Indonesian Police." *New York Times*, July 28, 1996.
———. "Indonesian Opposition Figure Removed as Party's Leader." *New York Times*, June 23, 1996.
Neher, Clark. *Southeast Asia in the New International Era*. Boulder: Westview, 1991: 87–102.
Neher, Clark, and Ross Marlay. *Democracy and Development in Southeast Asia: The Winds of Change*. Boulder: Westview, 1995: 75–95.
Oemarjati, Boen S. "Isteri, Cinta, and Arjuna: Indonesian Literature at the Crossroads." In Tham Seong Chee, ed., *Essays on Literature and Society in Southeast Asia*. Singapore: Singapore University, 1981: 82–96.
Osborne, Milton. *Southeast Asia: An Illustrated Introductory History*. Sydney: Allen and Unwin, 1985.
Pabottingi, Mochtar. "Indonesia: Historicizing the New Order's Legitimacy Dilemma." In Muthiah Alagappa, ed., *Political Legitimacy in Southeast Asia: The Quest for Moral Authority*. Stanford: Stanford University Press, 1995: 224–256.
Peacock, James. *Indonesia: An Anthropological Perspective*. Pacific Palisades: Goodyear, 1973.
———. *Rites of Modernization: Symbolic and Social Aspects of Indonesian Proletarian Drama*. Chicago: University of Chicago Press, 1968.
Pemberton, John. "Disempowerment, Not." *Public Culture* 5/1 (Fall 1992): 83–88.
———. "Musical Politics in Central Java (Or How Not to Listen to a Javanese Gamelan)." *Indonesia* 44 (October 1987): 17–29.
Perry, Jonathan. "Review Article: Two 'Images of Asia'—A Comparison." *Indonesia* 56 (October 1993): 153–157.
Pioquinto, Ceres. "Dangdut at Sekaten: Female Representations in Live Performance." *RIMA* 29/1–2 (Winter/Summer 1995): 59–90.
Piper, Suzan. "Performances at Fifty Years of Indonesian Independence: Articles from the Indonesian Press." *RIMA* 29/1–2 (Winter/Summer 1995): 37–58.
Piper, Suzan, and Sawung Jabo. "Indonesian Music from the 50s to the 80s." *Prisma* 43 (March 1987): 35.
Polomka, Peter. *Indonesia Since Sukarno*. London: Penguin, 1971.
"The Poor Man's Superstar." *Asiaweek*, July 13, 1990: 31.
Prisma (special issue), 29 (September 1983): 1–65.
Purcell, William. *An Introduction to Asian Music*. New York: Asia Society, 1966.
Ramage, Douglas E. "Indonesia at 50: Islam, Nationalism (and Democracy?)." In *Southeast Asian Affairs 1996*: 147–165.
———. *Politics in Indonesia: Democracy, Islam and the Ideology of Tolerance*. London: Routledge, 1996.
Ramedhan, Erwin. "The Disco Way of Life in Jakarta: From Subculture to Cultural Void." *Prisma* 6 (June 1977): 16–19.

Rasyid, M. Ryaas. "Indonesia: Preparing for Post-Soeharto Rule and Its Impact on the Democratization Process." In *Southeast Asian Affairs 1995*. Singapore: Institute of Southeast Asian Studies, 1995: 149–163.
"Rebel Rockers." *Asiaweek*, October 27, 1995: 42–43.
"Revolt in Medan." *Asiaweek*, May 4, 1994: 43–44.
"Rhoma Irama." *Asiaweek*, June 24, 1988, 28.
"Rights Group Reports Increase of Rights Abuses in Indonesia." *New York Times*, October 23, 1994.
Robison, Richard. "Indonesia: Tensions in State and Regime." In Kevin Hewison, Richard Robison, and Garry Rodan, eds., *Southeast Asia in the 1990s: Authoritarianism, Democracy and Capitalism*. St. Leonards, N.S.W.: Allen and Unwin, 1993: 39–74.
———. "The Middle Class and the Bourgeoisie in Indonesia." In Robison and Goodman, eds., *The New Rich in Asia*: 79–104.
———. "Toward a Class Analysis of the Indonesian Military Bureaucratic State." *Indonesia* 25 (April 1978): 17–39.
———. "The Transformation of the State in Indonesia." In John G. Taylor and Andrew Turton, eds., *Sociology of "Developing Societies": Southeast Asia*. New York: Monthly Review, 1988: 48–68.
Sahabullah, M. "Man Who Gave Dangdut Music a New Beat." *New Straits Times*, July 29, 1985.
———. "Putting Gift of God to Good Use." *New Straits Times*, August 6, 1986.
———. "The Show Was 'Cukup Bagus,' " *New Straits Times*, August 1, 1985.
Said, Salim. "Film in Indonesia." *Prisma* 43 (March 1987): 65–72.
———. "Man and Revolutionary Crisis in Indonesian Films." *East-West Film Journal* 4/2 (June 1990): 111–129.
———. "The Rise of the Indonesian Film Industry." *East-West Film Journal* 6/2 (July 1992): 99–115.
Salvini, Milena. "Performing Arts in Indonesia." In James Brandon, ed., *The Performing Arts in Asia*. Paris: UNESCO, 1971: 49–63.
Santoso, Amir. "Democratization: The Case of Indonesia's New Order." In Anek, ed., *Democratization:* 21–45.
"A Saucy Feast from the Slums." *Asiaweek*, December 6, 1985: 61.
Schiller, Jim. *Developing Jepara: State and Society in New Order Indonesia*. Clayton, Victoria: Monash Asia Institute, 1996.
Schiller, Jim, and Barbara Martin-Schiller, eds. *Imagining Indonesia: Cultural Politics and Political Culture*. Athens: Ohio University Center for International Studies, 1997.
Schwarz, Adam. *A Nation in Waiting: Indonesia in the 1990s*. St. Leonards: Allen and Unwin, 1994.
———. "Charismatic Enigma." *Far Eastern Economic Review*, November 12, 1992: 35.
Sears, Laurie J. *Shadows of Empire: Colonial Discourse and Javanese Tales*. Durham: Duke University Press, 1996.
Sedyawanti, Edi and Sapardi Damano, eds. *Seni Dalam Masyarakat Indonesia: Bunga Rampai*. Jakarta: Penerbit PT Gramedia Pustaka Utama, 1991.
Seebass, Tilman. "Change in Balinese Musical Life: Kebiar in the 1920s and 1930s." In Vickers, ed., *Being Modern in Bali:* 71–91.

———. "Co-ordination Between Music and Language in Balinese Shadow-Play, with Emphasis on Wayang Gambuh." In Arps, ed., *Performance in Java:* 162–173.
Sen, Krishna. "Changing Horizons of Television in Indonesia" *Southeast Asian Journal of Social Science* 22 (1994): 116–124.
———. "The Image of Women in Indonesian Films: Some Observations." *Prisma* 24 (March 1982): 17–29.
———. *Indonesian Cinema: Framing the New Order*. London: Zed, 1994.
———. "The Politics of Melodrama in Indonesian Cinema." *East-West Film Journal* 5/1 (January 1991): 67–81.
———. "Power and Poverty in New Order Cinema: Conflicts on Screen." In Paul Alexander, ed., *Creating Indonesian Cultures*. Sydney: Oceania Publications, 1989: 1–20.
———. "Repression and Resistance: Interpretations of the Feminine in New Order Cinema." In Hooker, ed., *Culture and Society*: 116–133.
Shenon, Philip. "Indonesia Shuts Three Outspoken Magazines." *New York Times*, June 23, 1994.
———. "Rioters in Indonesia Demanding Higher Wages Attack Chinese." *New York Times*, April 24, 1994.
Siegel, James. *Solo in the New Order: Language and Hierarchy in an Indonesian City*. Princeton: Princeton University Press, 1993.
Siradj, M. *Gombloh: Blues untuk Kim*. Surabaya: Penerbit Jawa Pos, 1988.
Soemardjan, Selo. "The Development of Culture in Indonesia and the ASEAN Region." In R. P. Anand and Purificacion V. Quisumbing, eds., *ASEAN Identity, Development and Culture*. Quezon City: University of the Philippines Law Center, 1981: 151–158.
Steinberg, David J., et al., *In Search of Southeast Asia: A Modern History*. Honolulu: University of Hawai'i, 1987.
Subagio, Drs. Gunawan, ed. *Apa Itu Lagu Pop Daerah*. Bandung: Penerbit Pt. Citra Aditya Bakti, 1989.
Sumardjan, Selo. "The Social and Cultural Effects of Satellite Communication on Indonesian Society." *Media Asia* 18/1 (1991): 15–19.
Sumarsam. *Gamelan: Cultural Interaction and Musical Development in Central Java*. Chicago: University of Chicago, 1995.
Sunanto, Raden. Liner Notes to the album *Music of Indonesia* (New York: Folkways Records, 1949).
"Superstar with a Message." *Asiaweek*, August 16, 1985: 50.
Susilo, Hardja, "Review of Yampolsky, Lokananta." *Ethnomusicology* 33/2 (Spring/Summer 1989): 358–360.
Sutherland, Heather. "Kerontjong and Komedi Stambul: Examples of Popular Music and Theatre in Colonial Indonesia." *Jernal Sejarah* 9 (1972–1973): 41–50.
Sutton, R. Anderson. "Asia/Indonesia." In Jeff Todd Titon, ed., *Worlds of Music: An Introduction to the Music of the World's People*. New York: Schirmer, 1992: 266–317.
———. "Commercial Cassette Recordings of Traditional Music in Java: Implications for Performers and Scholars." *The World of Music* 27/3 (1985): 23–43.
———. *Traditions of Gamelan Music in Java: Musical Pluralism and Regional Identity*. Cambridge: Cambridge University Press, 1991.

———. *Variations in Central Javanese Gamelan Music: Dynamics of a Steady State*. DeKalb: Center for Southeast Asian Studies, Northern Illinois University, 1993.

"A Swashbuckler Mellows." *Asiaweek*, November 10, 1993: 35.

Sweeney, Philip. *The Virgin Directory of World Music*. New York: Henry Holt, 1991: 170–173.

Tan Sooi Beng. *Bangsawan: A Social and Stylistic History of Popular Malay Opera*. Singapore: Oxford University Press, 1993.

Tanzer, Michael. *Balinese Music*. Berkeley: Periplus, 1991.

Tham Seong Chee, ed. *Essays on Literature and Society in Southeast Asia*. Singapore: Singapore University Press, 1981.

Tickell, Paul. "The Writing of Indonesian Literary History." *Review of Indonesian and Malaysian Affairs* 21/1 (Winter 1987): 29–43.

———. "Writing the Past: The Limits of Realism in Contemporary Indonesian Literature." In D. M. Roskies, ed., *Text/Politics in Island Southeast Asia*. Athens: Ohio University Press, 1993: 257–287.

United Nations. *Industrial Statistics Yearbook, 1991: Vol. 2: Commodity Production Statistics 1982–1991*. Washington, D.C.: Congressional Information Service, 1993: 115/94, 3080-S6.2, fiche 9, 774–783.

Van Erven, Eugene. *The Playful Revolution: Theatre and Liberation in Asia*. Bloomington: Indiana University, 1992: 184–206.

van Groenendael, Victoria M. Clara. *The Dalang behind the Wayang: The Role of the Surakarta and the Yogjakarta Dalang in Indonesian-Javanese Society*. Dordrecht, Netherlands: Foris, 1985.

Vatikiotis, Michael R. J. *Indonesian Politics Under Suharto: Order, Development and Pressure for Change*. London: Routledge, 1993.

Vickers, Adrian, ed. *Being Modern in Bali: Image and Change*. New Haven: Monograph 43, Center for Southeast Asian Studies, Yale University, 1996.

Vreeland, Nena, et al. *Area Handbook for Indonesia*. Washington, D.C.: Department of the Army, 1975.

Warshaw, Steven. *Southeast Asia Emerges: A Concise History of Southeast Asia*. Berkeley: Diablo, 1987.

Weintraub, Andrew N. "Mass Media and the Development of a 'Superstar' Ethos in Sundanese Wayang Golek Purwa of West Java, Indonesia." Unpublished paper, 1996.

Weiss, Sarah. "Musical Revelations from Indonesia." *RIMA* 29/1–2 (Winter/Summer 1995): 147–154.

Weix, G. G. "Gapit Theatre: New Javanese Plays on Tradition." *Indonesia* 60 (October 1995): 17–36.

Wertheim, W. F. *Indonesian Society in Transition: A Study of Social Change*. The Hague: Van Voeve, 1964.

Wibisono, Singgah. "The Wayang as a Medium of Communication." *Prisma* 1/2 (November 1975): 53–59.

Wicks, Peter. *Literary Perspectives on Southeast Asia: Collected Essays by Peter Wicks*. Toowoomba: USQ Press, 1991.

Widodo, Amrih. "The Stages of the State: Arts of the People and Rites of Hemogonization." *RIMA* 29/1–2 (Winter/Summer 1995): 1–36.

Wild, Colin. "Indonesia: A Nation and Its Broadcasters." *Indonesia Circle* 43 (June 1987): 15–40.
———. "The Radio Midwife: Some Thoughts on the Role of Broadcasting during the Indonesian Struggle for Independence." *Indonesia Circle* 55 (June 1991): 34–42.
Wilhelm, Donald. *Emerging Indonesia*. London: Cassell, 1980.
Williams, Maslyn. *Five Journeys from Jakarta: Inside Sukarno's Indonesia*. New York: William Morrow, 1965.
Williams, Sean. "Current Developments in Sundanese Popular Music." *Asian Music* 11/1 (Fall/Winter 1989–1990): 105–136.
Winters, Jeffrey A. *Power in Motion: Capital Mobility and the Indonesian State*. Ithaca: Cornell University Press, 1996.
———. "Suharto's Indonesia: Prosperity and Freedom for the Few." *Current History* (December, 1995): 420–424.
———. "Uncertainty in Suharto's Indonesia." *Current History* (December 1996): 428–431.
Wright, Astri. "The Contemporary Indonesian Artist as Activist." In Laurel Means, ed., *Cultural Environments in Contemporary Southeast Asia*. Vancouver: Centre for Southeast Asian Research, University of British Columbia, 1993: 47–66.
———. *Soul, Spirit, and Mountain: Preoccupations of Contemporary Indonesian Painters*. Kuala Lumpur: Oxford University, 1994.
"W. S. Rendra." *Indonesian Studies Newsletter* 14 (April 1992): 34–35.
Yamashita, Shinji. "Listening to the City: Popular Music of Contemporary Indonesia." *East Asian Cultural Studies* 27/1–4 (March 1988): 105–120.
———. "Manipulating Ethnic Tradition: The Funeral Ceremony, Tourism, and Television among the Toraja of Sulawesi." *Indonesia* 58 (October 1994): 69–82.
Yampolsky, Philip. "Hati Yang Luka, an Indonesian Hit." *Indonesia* 47 (April 1989): 1–17.
———. Liner notes to the album *Music from the Outskirts of Jakarta: Gambang Kromong* (Smithsonian/Folkways SF 40057, 1991).
———. Liner notes to Idjah Hadidjah's album, *Tonggeret* (Icon Records, 79173, 1987).
———. *Lokananta: A Discography of the National Recording Company of Indonesia, 1957–1985*. Madison: Center for Southeast Asian Studies, University of Wisconsin, Bibliography Series No. 10, 1987.
———. *Music of Indonesia 2: Indonesian Popular Music: Kroncong, Dangdut, and Langgam Jawa*. Pamphlet accompanying the album *Music of Indonesia 2* (Smithsonian SF 40056, 1991).
Yassin, Mustapha Kamil. "The Malay 'Bangsawan.' " In Mohd. Taib Osman, ed., *Traditional Drama and Music of Southeast Asia:* 143–153.
Young Mun Cheong, ed. *Trends in Indonesia*. Singapore: Institute of Southeast Asian Studies, 1972.
Yousof, Ghulam-Sarwar. *Dictionary of Traditional South-East Asian Theatre*. Kuala Lumpur: Oxford University Press, 1994.
Zainu'ddin, Ailsa. *Lagu-Lagu Dari Indonesia/Songs of Indonesia*. South Yarra: Heinemann, 1969.

Zarbuchen, Mary. "Images of Culture and National Development in Indonesia: The Cockroach Opera." *Asian Theatre Journal* 7/2 (Fall 1990): 127–149.
Zieman. "A People's Representative." *New Straits Times*, August 17, 1986.

Philippines

Agoncillo, Teodoro. *The Revolt of the Masses; The Story of Bonifacio and the Katipunan*. Quezon City: University of Philippines Press, 1965.
———. *A Short History of the Philippines*. New York: Mentor, 1969.
Aguilar, Freddie. "Introduction: The Far East and Pacific." In Philip Sweeney, *The Virgin Directory of World Music*. New York: Henry Holt, 1991: 151–153.
Alegre, Edilberto N. *Pinoy Forever: Essays on Culture and Language*. Manila: Anvil, 1993.
Armes, Roy. *Third World Film Making and the West*. Berkeley: University of California, 1987: 151–154.
The Asia & Pacific Review 1993/94: Economic and Business Report. London: The World of Information, 1993.
"Atang de la Rama, Queen of the Kundiman." *Asiaweek*, October 2, 1981: 5.
Bello, Walden. "Aquino's Elite Populism: Initial Reflections." *Third World Quarterly* 8/3 (July 1986): 1020–1030.
Billboard International Buyer's Guide 1996. New York: Billboard, 1995: 256–257.
Bodden, Michael H. "Grass Roots Theatre, Conscientization, and Development in the Philippines and Indonesia." In Laurel Means, ed., *Cultural Environments in Contemporary Southeast Asia*. Vancouver: Centre for Southeast Asian Research, University of British Columbia, 1993: 33–46.
Book of the Philippines 1976. Manila: Research and Analysis Center for Communications, 1976.
Boyce, James K. *The Philippines: The Political Economy of Growth and Impoverishment in the Marcos Era*. Honolulu: University of Hawai'i Press, 1993.
Brandon, James. *Theatre in Southeast Asia*. Cambridge: Harvard University Press, 1967.
Brisbin, David. "Electronic Revolution in the Philippines." *Journal of Popular Culture* 22/3 (Winter 1988): 49–63.
Broad, Robin, and John Cavanaugh. *Plundering Paradise: The Struggle for the Environment in the Philippines*. Berkeley: University of California Press, 1993.
Broughton, Simon, et al., eds. *World Music: The Rough Guide*. London: Rough Guides, 1994: 438–439.
Bunge, Frederica M. *Philippines: A Country Study*. Washington, D.C.: Department of the Army, 1983.
Buruma, Ian. "Brocka and the Controversial Film Element of Opposition." *Far Eastern Economic Review*, February 14, 1985: 68–69.
———. "Man and Messiah—Aquino in the Mythical Martyr Mould." *Far Eastern Economic Review*, December 15, 1983: 53–55.
———. "The Philippines' Multiple Heritage Remains a Theme in the Nation's Writing." *Far Eastern Economic Review*, February 2, 1984: 38–39.
Buss, Claude A. *Cory Aquino and the People of the Philippines*. Stanford: Stanford Alumni Association, 1987.

Cady, John. *The History of Postwar Southeast Asia: Independence Problems.* Athens: Ohio University Press, 1974.
Caruncho, Eric S. *Punks, Poets, and Poseurs: Reportage on Pinoy Rock & Roll.* Pasig City: Anvil, 1996.
Casper, Leonard. *The Opposing Thumb: Decoding Literature of the Marcos Regime.* Quezon City: Giraffe Books, 1995.
Castrillo, Pamela del Rosario. "Philippine Political Theatre: 1946–1985." *Philippine Studies* 42 (4th Quarter, 1994): 528–538.
Chapman, William. *Inside the Philippine Revolution.* New York: W. W. Norton, 1987.
Connell, Daniel. "Picking through Manila's Garbage. *In These Times*, February 5–11, 1992: 8.
Constantino, Renato. *The Filipinos in the Philippines and Other Essays.* Quezon City: Malaya, 1966.
———. *Neocolonial Identity and Counter-Consciousness: Essays on Cultural Decolonization.* White Plains: M. E. Sharpe, 1978.
———. *Synthetic Culture and Development.* Quezon City: Foundation for Nationalist Studies, 1985.
Coronel, Sheila S. "Dateline Philippines: The Lost Revolution." *Foreign Policy* 84 (Fall 1991): 166–185.
Corpuz, Onofre. *The Philippines.* Englewood Cliffs: Prentice Hall, 1965.
Cristobal, Adrian. "Philippines' Elite Must Learn the Language of the Poor." *Far Eastern Economic Review*, October 30, 1987.
"Culture, Development and Democracy—The Role of the Intellectuals." *Solidarity* 133–134 (January–June 1992): 28–72.
David, Joel. *Fields of Vision: Critical Applications in Recent Philippine Cinema.* Quezon City: Ateneo de Manila University Press, 1995.
de Leon, Anna Leah Sarabia. "Pinoy Rock." *International Popular Culture* 1 (1980): 33–37.
De Leon, Felipe Padilla. "Poetry, Music and Social Consciousness." *Philippine Studies* 17/2 (1973): 266–282.
" 'Disappearances' in the Philippines." *Human Rights Watch/Asia* 2/4 (May 1990): 1–13.
Dolan, Ronald E., ed. *Philippines: A Country Study.* Washington, D.C.: Library of Congress, 1993.
Edgerton, Ronald K. "The Society and the Environment." In Bunge, *Philippines: A Country Study*: 57–110.
Elequin, Eleanor T. "An Appreciation of the Filipino Philosophical Outlook through Filipino Popular Lyrics." In Enriquez, ed., *Philippine World-View*: 81–99.
Emmons, Karen. "Fowl Play," *Far Eastern Economic Review*, January 28, 1993: 30–31.
Encarnacion, Anacleta M. "Social Consciousness in Literature Vis-A-Vis the Changing Philippine Setting." *Asian Culture* 22/4 (Winter 1994): 1–14.
Enriquez, Virgilio G., ed. *Philippine World-View.* Singapore: Institute of Southeast Asian Studies, 1986.
Fajardo, Brenda V. "Decolonization through People's Art." *Asian Studies* 28 (1990): 92–111.

Fenton, James. "The Snap Revolution." *Granta* 18 (1986): 33–156.
Fernandez, Doreen. "Contemporary Theatre in the Philippines." In *Contemporary Theatre Arts in Asia and the United States.* Quezon City: New Day, 1984: 65–77.
———. "The Culture of Revolution: Tentative Notes." *Dilliman Review* 35/2 (1987): 26–29.
———. "From Ritual to Realism: A Brief Historical Survey of Philippine Theatre." *Philippine Studies* 28 (4th Quarter 1980): 389–419.
———. *The Iloilo Zarzuela: 1903–1930.* Quezon City: Ateneo de Manila Press, 1978.
———. "Mass Culture and Cultural Policy: The Philippine Experience." *Philippine Studies* 37 (4th Quarter 1989). 488–502.
———. *Palabas: Essays on Philippine Theatre.* Quezon City: Ateneo de Manila Press, 1996.
———. "Philippine-American Cultural Interaction." *Crossroads* 1/1 (February 1983): 20–30.
———. "Philippine Popular Culture: Dimensions and Directions. The State of Research in Philippine Popular Culture." *Philippine Studies* 29 (1st Quarter 1981): 25–44.
———. "Zarzuela to Sarswela: Indiginization and Transformation." *Philippine Studies* 41 (3rd Quarter 1993): 320–343.
Filipino Heritage: The Making of a Nation, Vol. 6. Manila: Lahing Pilipino Publishing, 1978.
Film Center of the University of the Philippines. "The Exciting and Excited State of Philippine Movies." *Asian Culture* 30 (March 1981): 19–21.
Flores, Patrick D. "By Way of Film: Spaces for Intervention in Pop Practice." *The Dilliman Review* 38/3 (1990): 45–56.
———. "People, Popular Culture, Criticism: Reproducing the 'Popular' in Media." *The Dilliman Review* 39/1 (1991): 46–55.
———. "The Slum and the Town: Reassessing the Brocka Paradigm in Philippine Progressive Theatre." *The Dilliman Review* 39/4 (1991): 45–52.
Ford, Aida Rivera. "Southeasterly View of Popular Culture." In C. Lumbera and Gimenez-Maceda, eds., *Rediscovery: Philippine Life*: 218–228.
Francia, Luis. "Philippine Cinema: The Struggle against Repression." John D. H. Downing, ed., *Film and Politics in the Third World.* New York: Automedia, 1987: 209–218.
———, ed. *Brown River, White Ocean: An Anthology of Twentieth Century Philippine Literature in English.* Brunswick: Rutgers University Press, 1993.
"Freddie A. and the Joys of Pinoy." *Asiaweek*, May 4, 1979: 15.
Gamalinda, Eric, and Benjamin Pimental. "Notes from the Underground: Filipino Pop Music Is Still Alive and Kicking, Despite Its Ever Changing Moods." *Midweek* (Manila), April 30, 1986: 16–23.
Gimenez-Maceda, Teresita. "Popular Music as Politics." *International Popular Culture* 1 (1980): 24–32.
Godinez-Ortega, Christine F. "Datu Matu: Mindanao History as Theatre." *Mindanao Forum* 10/1 (June 1995): 238–245.
Goertzen, Donald. "Agents for Change: NGOs Take the Lead in the Development Process." *Far Eastern Economic Review*, August 8, 1991: 20–21.

Gonzalez, Andrew B. *Language and Nationalism: The Philippine Experience Thus Far*. Quezon City: Ateneo de Manila Press, 1980.
Gonzalez, Joaquin L., and Ronald Holmes. "The Philippines Labor Diaspora: Trends, Issues and Policies." In *Southeast Asian Affairs 1996*: 300–317.
Goodno, James B. *The Philippines: Land of Broken Promises*. London: Zed, 1991.
Greenwood, Gavin, ed. *Asia Yearbook 1992*. Hong Kong: *Far Eastern Economic Review*, 1993.
Gronow, Pekka. "International Trends in Popular Music." *Ethnomusicology* 13/2 (May 1969): 313–316.
Guggenheim, Scott. "Cock or Bull: Cockfighting, Social Structure, and Political Commentary in the Philippines." *Filipinas* 3/1 (June 1982): 1–30.
Guillermo, Alice G. *The Covert Presence and Other Essays on Politics and Culture*. Manila: Kalikasan Press, 1989.
———. "The Social Roots of Philippine Popular Arts." In C. Lumbera and Gimenez-Maceda, eds., *Rediscovery: Essays in Philippine Life and Culture*: 281–292.
Hawes, Gary. *The Philippine State and the Marcos Regime: The Politics of Export*. Ithaca: Cornell University Press, 1987.
Hernandez, Amado V. *Rice Grains: Selected Poems*. New York: International Publishers, 1966.
Hila, Antonio. "A Fusion of Poetry and Music." *Kultura* 2/2 (1989): 34–39.
———. "In the Forefront: The Music of Lucrecia Kasilag." *Kultura* 4/1 (1991): 16–21.
Hunt, Chester. "The Society and Its Environment." In Dolan, ed., *Philippines*: 70, 65–116.
Hutchcroft, Paul D. *The Philippines at the Crossroads: Sustaining Economic and Political Reform*. New York: Asia Society, 1996.
———. "Unravelling the Past in the Philippines." *Current History* (December 1995): 430–434.
Hutchison, Jane. "Class and State Power in the Philippines." In Kevin Hewison, Richard Robison, and Garry Rodan, eds., *Southeast Asia in the 1990s: Authoritarianism, Democracy and Capitalism*. St. Leonards, N.S.W.: Allen and Unwin, 1993: 191–212.
Ileto, Reynaldo C. "Outlines of a Non-Linear Employment of Philippine History." In Lim Teck Ghee, ed., *Reflections on Development in Southeast Asia*. Singapore: Institute of Southeast Asian Studies, 1988: 130–159.
———. *Payson and Revolution: Popular Movements in the Philippines, 1840–1910*. Quezon City: Ateneo de Manila University Press, 1979.
Iyer, Pico. *Video Night in Kathmandu and Other Reports from the Not-so-Far East*. New York: Knopf, 1988: 151–194.
Japitana, Norma. *The Superstars of Pop*. Manila: Makati Trade Times, 1982.
Jayasuriya, Sisira. "Structural Adjustment and Economic Performance in the Philippines." In Andrew J. MacIntyre and Kanishka Jayasuriya, eds., *The Dynamics of Economic Policy Reform in South-east Asia and the South-west Pacific*. Singapore: Oxford University Press, 1992: 50–73.
Joaquin, Francoise. "A Legacy of a King." *Asia Magazine* 28 (August 3, 1990): 20–21.

Jones, Gregg R. *Red Revolution: Inside the Philippine Guerrilla Movement.* Boulder: Westview, 1989.
Karnow, Stanley. *In Our Image: America's Empire in the Philippines.* New York: Random House, 1989.
Kerkvliet, Benedict J. Tria. *Everyday Politics in the Philippines: Class and Status Relations in a Central Luzon Village.* Berkeley: University of California Press, 1990.
Kerkvliet, Benedict J., and Resil B. Mojares, eds. *From Marcos to Aquino: Local Perspectives on Political Transition in the Philippines.* Honolulu: University of Hawai'i Press, 1991.
Kirkup, James. *Filipinescas: Travels through the Philippine Islands.* London: Phoenix House, 1968.
Kulkarni, V. G. "Mid-Term Blues." *Far Eastern Economic Review*, April 27, 1995: 16–21.
Kulkarni, V. G., and Rodney Tasker. "Promises to Keep." *Far Eastern Economic Review*, February 29, 1996: 22–23.
Laceba, Joseph F. "Notes on 'Bakya': Being an Apologia of Sorts for Filipino Masscult." In C. Lumbera and Gimenez-Maceda, eds., *Rediscovery: Essays in Philippine Life and Culture.* Manila: National Book Store, 1977: 212–217.
Laconico-Buenaventura, Cristina. "The Theatre in Manila, 1846–1896: An Assessment." *DLSU Dialogue* 271 (1993–1994): 50–66.
Lardizabal, Amparo S., and Felicitas Tensuan-Leogardo, eds. *Readings on Philippine Culture and Social Life.* Manila: Rex, 1976.
Larkin, John. "The Capampangan Zarzuela: Theatre for a Provincial Elite." In Ruth T. McVey, ed., *Southeast Asian Transitions: Approaches through Social History.* New Haven: Yale University Press, 1978: 158–190.
———. *The Pampangans: Colonial Society in a Philippine Province.* Berkeley: University of California Press, 1972.
———. "Philippine History Reconsidered: A Socioeconomic Perspective." *American Historical Review* 87/3 (June 1982): 595–628.
———. *Sugar and the Origins of Modern Philippine Society.* Berkeley: University of California Press, 1993.
Lauzon, Alden Q. "Postmodernism, Cultural Studies and the Third World." *Dilliman Review* 41/1 (1993): 28–37.
Lent, John A. "Asian Comic Strips: Old Wine in New Bottles." *Asian Culture (Asia-Pacific) Quarterly* 23/4 (Winter 1995): 39–62.
———. *The Asian Film Industry.* London: Christopher Helm, 1990: 149–184.
———. "Historical Overview of Southeast Asian Film." *Media Asia* 18/2 (1991): 98–102 and 18/3 (1991): 152–163.
———. "Mass Communication Research in the Philippines." In Donn V. Hart, ed., *Philippine Studies: History, Sociology, Mass Media, and Bibliography.* DeKalb: Center for Southeast Asian Studies Occasional Paper No. 6, Northern Illinois University, 1978: 233–287.
———. "The Philippines." In John A. Lent, ed., *The Asian Newspapers' Reluctant Revolution.* Ames: Iowa State University Press, 1971: 191–209.
———. "Who Owns the Philippine Mass Media?—An Historical and Contemporary Analysis." *Filipinas* 17 (Fall 1991): 1–34.
Lightfoot, Keith. *The Philippines.* New York: Praeger, 1973.

Lindsey, Charles W. "The Economy." In Dolan, ed., *Philippines*: 117–188.
Linmark, R. Zamora. " 'And the Next Song is for Everybody': Filipino Lounge Bands in Manila and Seoul." *MUAE: A Journal of Transcultural Production* 1 (1995): 150–163.
Lockard, Craig A. "Gunboat Diplomacy, Counterrevolution and Manifest Destiny: A Century of Asian Preludes to the American War in Vietnam." *Asian Profiles* 23/1 (February 1995): 35–57.
Lopez, Antonio. "Manila's Film Scandal: The Sequel." *Asiaweek*, November 16, 1994: 44–48.
Lumbera, Bienvenido. "Commodity and Historical Event: Popular Culture as Politics." In C. Lumbera and T. Gimenez-Maceda, eds., *Rediscovery: Essays in Philippine Life and Culture*: 273–280.
———. *Revaluation: Essays on Philippine Literature, Cinema and Popular Culture.* Manila: Index, 1984.
Lumbera, Cynthia Nogales, and Teresita Gimenez-Maceda, eds. *Rediscovery: Essays in Philippine Life and Culture*, 2nd ed. Manila: National Book Store, 1982.
Maceda, Jose, et al. "Philippines." In Stanley Sadie, ed., *The New Grove Encyclopedia of Music and Musicians*, Vol. 14. New York: Grove, 1980: 631–652.
Magno, Alexander R. "The Philippines in 1995: Completing the Market Transition." In *Southeast Asian Affairs 1996*: 285–299.
Malm, William. *Music Cultures of the Pacific, the Near East, and Asia*, 2nd ed. Englewood Cliffs: Prentice Hall, 1977: 29–33.
"The Man from Mindanao." *Asiaweek*, March 25, 1988: 34.
Mangahas, FE B. "The State of Philippine Music." In Tiongson, ed., *Politics of Culture:* 62–82.
Mangahas, Mahar. "Distributive Justice in the Philippines: Ideology, Policy and Surveillance." In Lim Teck Ghee, ed., *Reflections on Development in Southeast Asia*. Singapore: Institute of Southeast Asian Studies, 1988: 80–108.
Mangahas, Maria. "Music Acculturation and Two Filipino Composers." *The Dilliman Review* 37/4 (1989): 56–64.
Mangusad, Leo Nilo C. "Pen-Pen: The Ethnic-Rock Innovators." *Kultura* 1/3 (1988): 49–56.
"Manila's Women Warriors of Words." *Asiaweek*, December 2, 1988: 53.
Marcelo, Nonoy. "Komiks: The Filipino National Literature?" *Asian Culture* 25 (January 1980): 18–20.
Marchetti, Gina. " 'Four Hundred Years in a Convent, Fifty in Hollywood': Sexual Identity and Dissent in Contemporary Philippine Cinema." *East-West Film Journal* 2/2 (June 1988): 24–48.
Marin, Leni. "To Unite and Awaken the People: Philippine Music and Its Revolutionary Role." *Sing Out* 25/5 (1977): 15–18.
Marlay, Ross. "Democracy, Human Rights, and Philippine Foreign Policy." Unpublished paper, 1996.
May, Glenn. *Battle for Batangas: A Philippine Province at War.* New Haven: Yale University Press, 1991.
———. *Social Engineering in the Philippines: The Aims, Execution, and Impact of American Colonial Policy, 1900–1913.* Westport, Connecticut: Greenwood, 1980.

Mayne, Vidda. "Songs of Dissent and the Music of Agitation." *Far Eastern Economic Review*, February 14, 1985: 67–69.

McBeth, John. "Crusade for Condoms." *Far Eastern Economic Review*, April 22, 1993: 24–25.

———. "Internal Contradictions." *Far Eastern Economic Review*, August 24, 1993: 16–18.

McCoy, Alfred W., ed. *An Anarchy of Families: State and Family in the Philippines*. Madison: Center for Southeast Asian Studies, University of Wisconsin–Madison, 1993.

McCoy, Alfred. "Culture and Consciousness in a Philippine City." *Philippine Studies* 30 (2nd Quarter 1982): 157–203.

Medina, B. S., Jr. "Pagbabago! The Conscious Commitment." In Tham Seong Chee, ed., *Essays on Literature and Society in Southeast Asia: Political and Sociological Perspectives*. Singapore: University of Singapore Press, 1981: 125–144.

Melendrez-Cruz, Patricia. "From the Philippine Revolution, 1986 to Military Rule, 1972: The Changing World-View in the Filipino Short Story." In Enriquez, ed., *Philippine World-View*: 100–127.

Mercado, Monina Allarey, ed. *An Eyewitness History: People Power and The Philippine Revolution of 1986*. Manila: James B. Reuter, S. J., Foundation, 1986.

Merino, Manuel Walls y. *Popular Music of the Philippines*. Manila: National Historical Institute, 1980.

Mikich, Tripp. "Palaam Uncle Sam: An Interview with Musika and Musicians for Peace, Philippines." In Ron Sakolsky and Fred Wei-Han Ho, eds., *Sounding Off: Music as Subversion/Resistance/Revolution*. Brooklyn: Autonomedia, 1995: 321–329.

Mohd. Taib Osman, ed. *Traditional Drama and Music in Southeast Asia*. Kuala Lumpur: Dewan Bahasa dan Pustaka, 1974.

Molina, Exequiel S. "The Philippine Pop Music Scene." *Asian Culture* 15 (January 1977): 21–24.

Montanez, Kris. *The New Mass Art and Literature and Other Related Essays (1974–1987)*. Manila: Kalikasan, 1988.

Muego, Benjamin N. *Spectator Society: The Philippines Under Martial Law*. Athens: Center for International Studies No. 77, Ohio University, 1988.

Mulder, Niels. *Inside Philippine Society: Interpretations of Everyday Life*. Quezon City: New Day, 1997.

Mydens, Seth. "In the Philippines, the Politics of Turmoil Casts a Murky Shadow Over the Arts." *New York Times*, February 7, 1988.

———. "Philippine Leaders Celebrate Freedom to Squabble." *New York Times*, February 26, 1996.

Neher, Clark D. *Southeast Asia in the New International Era*. Boulder: Westview, 1991: 55–86.

Neher, Clark D., and Ross Marlay. *Democracy and Development in Southeast Asia: The Winds of Change*. Boulder: Westview, 1995: 52–74.

Nelson, Raymond. *The Philippines*. New York: Walker and Company, 1968.

Ness, Sally A. "When Seeing is Believing: The Changing Role of Visuality in a Philippine Dance." *Anthropological Quarterly* 68/1 (January 1995): 1–13.

"Opiate of the Masses?" *Asiaweek*, November 23, 1984: 57–58.

Osborne, Milton. *Southeast Asia: An Illustrated Introductory History*. Sydney: Allen and Unwin, 1985.

Owen, Norman G. *Prosperity without Progress: Manila Hemp and Material Life in the Colonial Philippines.* Berkeley: University of California, 1984.
"Paalam, Ka Atang." *Kultura* 4/4 (1991): 22–33.
Pagulayan, Maricel. "Radio and the Third World: The Case of the Philippines." In Russell Leong, ed., *Moving the Image: Independent Asian Pacific American Media Arts.* Los Angeles: UCLA Asian American Studies Center, 1991: 93–95.
Pfeiffer, William. *Filipino Music: Indigenous, Folk, Modern.* Dumaguete City: Silliman Music Foundation, 1976.
Philippine Almanac: Book of Facts, 1986 Edition. Manila: Aurora Publications, 1986.
Philippine Yearbook 1989. Manila: National Statistics Office, 1989.
Philippines: Bangon! Arise: Songs of the Philippine National Democratic Struggle. Pamphlet accompanying album (Paredon Records, 1029, 1976).
Pinches, Michael. "The Philippines' New Rich: Capitalist Transformation amidst Economic Gloom." In Robison and Goodman, eds., *The New Rich in Asia*: 105–136.
Pinga, Ben G. "Cinema in the Philippines." In James Brandon, ed., *The Performing Arts in Asia.* Paris: UNESCO, 1971: 153–157.
Poetry of People's War in the Philippines. Manila: MAINSTREAM: People's Art, Literature and Education Resource Center, 1989.
Poore, Grace. "Freddie Aguilar: The Singing Revolutionary." *Fanfare* (Kuala Lumpur, Malaysia), November, 1979: 16–17, 57.
Putzel, James. *A Captive Land: The Politics of Agrarian Reform in the Philippines.* London: Catholic Institute for International Relations, 1992.
"Queen 'King.' " *Asiaweek*, September 9, 1988.
Rafael, Vicente L. *Contracting Colonialism: Translation and Christian Conversion in Tagalog Society under Spanish Rule.* Ithaca: Cornell University Press, 1988.
———. "Fishing, Underwear, and Hunchbacks: Humor and Politics in the Philippines, 1886 and 1983." *Bulletin of Concerned Asian Scholars* 18/3 (1986): 2–7.
———. "Patronage and Pornography: Ideology and Spectatorship during the Early Marcos Years." D. M. Roskies, ed., *Text/Politics in Island Southeast Asia: Essays on Interpretation.* Athens: Center for International Studies, Ohio University, 1993: 49–81.
———. "Taglish, or the Phantom Power of the Lingua Franca." *Public Culture* 8/1 (Fall 1995): 101–126.
Reid, Robert H., and Eileen E. Guerrero. *Corazon Aquino and the Brushfire Revolution.* Baton Rouge: Louisiana State University Press, 1995.
Reyes, Elizabeth. "The Pilipino Sound and the Musical Gold Rush." *Far Eastern Economic Review*, November 17, 1978: 47–48.
Reyes, Emmanuel A. *Notes on Philippine Cinema.* Manila: De La Salle University Press, 1989.
Reyes, Soledad S. "Introduction." In Reyes, ed., *Reading Popular Culture*: 1–10.
———, ed., *Reading Popular Culture.* Manila: Ateneo de Manila, 1991.
Rivera, Temario C. *State of the Nation: Philippines.* Singapore: Institute of Southeast Asian Studies, 1996.
Roces, J. "The Traditional Theatre of the Philippines." In Mohd. Taib Osman, ed., *Traditional Drama and Music in Southeast Asia*: 172–175.

Roces, Minas. "Filipino Identity in Fiction, 1945–1972." *Modern Asian Studies* 28/2 (1994): 279–315.
Sacerdoti, Guy. "Hamburgerization Creates a Cultural Schizophrenia." *Far Eastern Economic Review*, August 16, 1984: 45–46.
Salanga, Alfrredo Navarro, and Esther M. Pacheco, eds. *Versus: Philippine Protest Poetry, 1983–1986.* Quezon City: Ateneo de Manila Press, 1986.
San Juan, E. [Epitanio]. *Crisis in the Philippines: The Making of a Revolution.* South Hadley: Bergin and Garvey, 1986.
———. *Towards a People's Literature.* Quezon City: University of the Philippines Press, 1984.
San Juan, E., Jr. *The Philippine Temptation: Dialectics of Philippines—U.S. Literary Relations.* Philadelphia: Temple University Press, 1996.
———, ed. *Introduction to Modern Pilipino Literature.* New York: Twayne, 1974.
San Juan, Eric A. "Making Filipino History in a Damaged Culture." *Philippine Sociological Review* 37/1–2 (January–June 1989): 1–11.
Sta. Maria, Felixberto C. *The Philippines in Song and Ballad.* Manila: Cacho Hermanos, 1976.
Santos, Benilda S. "Idol, Bestiary and Revolutionary: Images of the Filipino Woman in Film (1976–1986)." In Reyes, ed., *Reading Popular Culture*: 209–224.
Santos, Ramon Pagayon. "The Philippines." In Harrison Ryker, ed., *New Music in the Orient: Essays on Composition Since World War II.* Buren: Frits Knuf, 1991: 157–176.
Schirmer, Daniel B., and Stephen Rosskamm Shalom, eds. *The Philippines Reader: A History of Colonialism, Neocolonialism, Dictatorship, and Resistance.* Boston: South End, 1987.
Seagrave, Sterling. *The Marcos Dynasty.* New York: Fawcett Columbine, 1988.
Shenon, Philip. "How Subic Bay Became a Rallying Cry for Philippine Nationalism." *New York Times*, September 15, 1991.
Sidel, John T. "The Philippines: The Languages of Legitimation." In Muthiah Alagappa, ed., *Political Legitimacy in Southeast Asia: The Quest for Moral Authority.* Stanford: Stanford University Press, 1995: 136–169.
Silberman, Robert. "Was Tolstoy Right? Family Life and the Philippine Cinema." *East-West Film Journal* 4/1 (December 1989): 69–78.
Sotto, Agustin L. "Notes on the Filipino Action Film." *East-West Film Journal* 1/2 (June 1987): 1–14.
Stanley, Peter. *A Nation in the Making: The Philippines and the United States, 1899–1921.* Cambridge: Harvard University Press, 1974.
Steinberg, David J. *The Philippines: A Singular and Plural Place*, 2nd ed., revised. Boulder: Westview, 1990.
———, et al. *In Search of Southeast Asia: A Modern History*, 2nd ed. Honolulu: University of Hawai'i Press, 1987.
Tan Gim Ean. "Aguilar the Able Artist." *New Straits Times* (Kuala Lumpur), October 30, 1985.
———. "Star of Anak Who Sings with His Heart." *New Straits Times* (Kuala Lumpur), October 28, 1985.
Tasker, Rodney. "Real-Life Drama." *Far Eastern Economic Review*, December 24–31, 1992: 48–50.

———. "Reel-Life Politicians." *Far Eastern Economic Review*, May 14, 1992: 18.
———. "Treaty of Utrecht." *Far Eastern Economic Review*, November 19, 1992: 12.
"A Taste of Filipino Salt." *Asiaweek*, July 22, 1988: 47.
Teodoro, Luis V., Jr. "Toward the Insurgent Seventies." In Teodoro and San Juan, eds., *Two Perspectives on Philippine Literature and Society:* 1–27.
Teodoro, Luis V., Jr., and Epitanio San Juan, Jr., eds. *Two Perspectives on Philippine Literature and Society.* Honolulu: Center for Asian and Pacific Studies, University of Hawai'i, 1981.
Thompson, Mark A. *The Anti-Marcos Struggle: Personalistic Rule and Democratic Transition in the Philippines.* New Haven: Yale University Press, 1995.
Tiglao, Rigoberto. "Death Threat." *Far Eastern Economic Review*, May 19, 1994: 29–30.
———. "Fraternal Foes." *Far Eastern Economic Review*, January 14, 1993: 18–19.
———. "Open Season." *Far Eastern Economic Review*, July 4, 1996: 28, 30.
———. "Ramos Redux." *Far Eastern Economic Review*, January 30, 1997: 17.
Tiglao, Rigoberto, and Rodney Tasker. "Options for Change." *Far Eastern Economic Review*, May 7, 1992: 16.
Timberman, David. *A Changeless Land: Continuity and Change in Philippine Politics.* Singapore: Institute of Southeast Asian Studies, 1992.
Tiongson, Lito. "Alternative Cinema: Development and Prospects." *Dilliman Review* 5–6 (1986): 26–30.
Tiongson, Nicanor G. *Filipinas Circa 1907: Production Script and Notes.* Quezon City: Philippine Educational Theatre Association, 1985: 1–9.
———. "Filipinicity and the Tagalog Komedya and Sinakulo." *Kultura*, 1/2 (1988): 3–11.
———. "The Filipino Film Industry." *East-West Film Journal* 6/2 (July 1992): 23–61.
———. *The Politics of Culture: The Philippine Experience.* Manila: Philippine Education Theatre Association, 1984.
"Towards a New Cultural Identity." *Asiaweek*, June 30, 1978: 31.
United Nations. *Industrial Statistics Yearbook, 1991: Vol. 2: Commodity Production Statistics 1982–1991.* Washington, D.C.: Congressional Information Service, 1993: 115/94, 3080-S6.2, fiche 9, 774–783.
Valerio, Ariel N. "Tendencies of the Middle Class in Protest Theatre." *Dilliman Review* 35/2 (1987): 61–64.
Van Erven, Eugene. "Philippine Political Theatre and the Fall of Ferdinand Marcos." *The Drama Review* 31/2 (Summer 1987): 57–78.
———. *The Playful Revolution: Theatre and Liberation in Asia.* Bloomington: Indiana University Press, 1992: 29–94.
———. "Theatre and Liberation: Political Theatre That Works for a Change." *Illusions* 3 (Spring 1986): 6–12.
Velasco, Renato S. "Philippine Democracy: Promise and Performance." In Anek, ed., *Democratization:* 76–112.
Villacorta, Wilfredo. "Philippine Nationalism Is Alive and Well." *Far Eastern Economic Review*, April 21, 1988: 39–40.
Villanueva, Rene O. "Pinoy Pop Comes of Age (Again!)." *The Dilliman Review* 27 (October-December 1979), 8–10.

Villaruz, Basillo Esteban S. "Florante at Laura: A Rock Tribute to Blow the Poet's Mind." *Kultura* 1/2 (1988): 24–25.
Vreeland, Nena, et al. *Area Handbook for the Philippines.* Washington, D.C.: Department of the Army, 1976.
Warshaw, Steven. *Southeast Asia Emerges: A Concise History of Southeast Asia.* Berkeley: Diablo, 1987.
Wetherall, William. "Sexual Capitalists Exploit the Filipino Connection." *Far Eastern Economic Review*, May 8, 1986: 105–107.
Wurfel, David. "Change or Continuity in the Philippines?" *Current History* (December 1992): 424–429.
———. *Filipino Politics: Development and Decay.* Ithaca: Cornell University Press, 1988.
Yousof, Ghulam-Sarwar. *Dictionary of Traditional South-East Asian Theatre.* Kuala Lumpur: Oxford University Press, 1994.

Thailand

Anderson, Benedict R. "Studies of the Thai State: The State of Thai Studies." In Elizier B. Ayal, ed., *The Study of Thailand: Analyses of Knowledge, Approaches, and Prospects in Anthropology, Art History, Economics, History and Political Science.* Athens: Southeast Asia Series No. 54, Center for International Studies, Ohio University, 1978: 193–247.
———. "Withdrawal Symptoms: Social and Cultural Aspects of the October 6 Coup." *Bulletin of Concerned Asian Scholars* 9/3 (1977): 13–30.
Anderson, Benedict, and Ruchira Mendiones, eds. *In the Mirror: Literature and Politics in Siam in the American Era.* Bangkok: Editions Duang Kamoi, 1985.
Armes, Roy. *Third World Film Making and the West.* Berkeley: University of California Press, 1987: 147–154.
The Asia & Pacific Review 1993/94: Economic and Business Report. London: The World of Information, 1993.
Banphot Virasai. "Thai Society in Transition." *Asian Culture Quarterly* 9/2 (Summer 1981): 28–31.
Bartak, Elinor. "The Student Movement in Thailand, 1970–1976." Clayton: Centre of Southeast Asian Studies Working Paper 82, Monash University, 1993.
Basche, James. *Thailand: Land of the Free.* New York: Taplinger, 1971.
Billboard International Buyer's Guide 1996. New York: Billboard, 1995: 262.
Blanchard, Wendell. *Thailand: Its People, Its Society, Its Culture.* New Haven: HRAF, 1958.
Boonrak Boonyaketmala. "The Rise and Fall of the Film Industry in Thailand, 1897–1992." *East-West Film Journal* 6/2 (July 1992): 62–98.
———. "The Underside of Bangkok." *Asiaweek*, November 16, 1986: 76.
Bowie, Katherine A., ed. *Voices from the Countryside: The Short Stories of Samruam Singh.* Madison: Center for Southeast Asian Studies, University of Wisconsin, 1991.
Brandon, James. *Theatre in Southeast Asia.* Cambridge: Harvard University Press, 1967.
———. "Theatre in Thailand." In James Brandon, ed., *The Performing Arts in Asia.* Paris: UNESCO, 1971: 64–69.

Brown, David. *The State and Ethnic Politics in Southeast Asia*. London: Routledge, 1994: 158–205.
Broughton, Simon, et al., eds. *World Music: The Rough Guide*. London: Rough Guides, 1994: 440–448.
Buruma, Ian. "Thailand's Film-makers Sink in a Morass of Money vs Artistry." *Far Eastern Economic Review*, October 27, 1983: 53–54.
Cady, John. *The History of Postwar Southeast Asia: Independence Problems.* Athens: Ohio University Press, 1974.
Chu, Valentin. *Thailand Today*. New York: Crowell, 1968.
Chua Sariman. "Traditional Dance Drama in Thailand." In Mohd. Taib Osman, ed., *Traditional Drama*: 165–171.
Chutima, Gawin. *The Rise and Fall of the Communist Party of Thailand (1973–1987)*. Canterbury: Centre for Southeast Asian Studies, University of Kent at Canterbury, 1990.
Cohen, Erik. *Thai Society in Comparative Perspective*. Bangkok: White Lotus, 1991.
Compton, Carol J. "Traditional Verbal Arts in Laos: Functions, Forms, Continuities and Changes in Texts, Contexts and Performances." In Amy Catlin, ed., *Selected Reports in Ethnomusicology, Vol. IX: Text, Context, and Performance in Cambodia, Laos, and Vietnam*. Los Angeles: Department of Ethnomusicology, University of California, Los Angeles, 1992: 149–160.
Crossette, Barbara. "Strumming a Lament for Thai Losers." *New York Times*, September 1, 1985.
Dessaint, Alain. "Thais Rising." *Far Eastern Economic Review*, March 18, 1993: 33.
Durrenberger, E. Paul. "The Power of Culture and the Culture of States." In E. Paul Durrenberger, ed., *State Power and Culture in Thailand*. New Haven: Southeast Asia Studies Monograph 44, Yale University, 1996: 1–21.
Elliott, David. *Thailand: Origins of Military Rule*. London: Zed, 1978.
Erlanger, Steven. "Thailand, Where Pirated Tapes Are Everywhere and Profitable." *New York Times*, November 28, 1988.
Fairclough, Gordon. "Back to Work." *Far Eastern Economic Review*, November 5, 1992: 21–22.
———. "Bangkok's Night-Riders: Tryst with Destiny." *Far Eastern Economic Review*, September 23, 1993: 36–37
———. "Critical Mass." *Far Eastern Economic Review*, September 26, 1996: 16–17.
———. "Missing Class." *Far Eastern Economic Review*, February 4, 1993: 25–26.
———. "Rural Reality." *Far Eastern Economic Review*, June 29, 1995: 15–16.
———. "Shut Up or Shut Down." *Far Eastern Economic Review*, February 29, 1996: 20.
———. "Vox Populi." *Far Eastern Economic Review*, December 19, 1996: 20.
Fairclough, Gordon, and Rodney Tasker. "Separate and Unequal." *Far Eastern Economic Review*, April 14, 1994: 22–31.
Flood, Thadeus. "The Thai Left Wing in Historical Context." *Bulletin of Concerned Asian Scholars* 7/2 (1975): 55–67.
Fugate, Christine. "Hit or Flop? Thai Films' Successes Vary with Audience." *Centerviews* 8/6 (November-December 1990): 7.

Fuller, Paul. "Thai Music, 1968–1981." *Yearbook for Traditional Music* 15 (1983): 152–155.
Gaston, Bruce. "Thailand." In Harrison Ryker, ed., *New Music in the Orient*: 115–156.
Gesmankit, Pairote, and Kullasap. "Cartoon Techniques Widely Applied in Thailand." *Asian Culture* 25 (January 1980): 21–23.
Girling, John. *Interpreting Development: Capitalism, Democracy, and the Middle Class in Thailand.* Ithaca: Southeast Asia Program, Cornell University, 1996.
———. *Thailand: Society and Politics.* Ithaca: Cornell University, 1981.
———. "Thailand: Twin Peaks, Disturbing Shadows." *Southeast Asian Affairs 1994.* Singapore: Institute of Southeast Asian Studies, 1994: 305–319.
Grace, Brewster. "A Note on Thailand: The Student Rebellion and Political Change." *American Universities Field Staff, Asia Series* 22/4 (1974).
Greenwood, Gavin, ed. *Asia Yearbook 1992.* Hong Kong: Far Eastern Economic Review, 1993.
Griffin, Robert S. "Notes on the Thai Student Revolution." *Southeast Asia: An International Quarterly* 3/4 (Fall 1974): 1037–1061.
Gronow, Pekka. "International Trends in Popular Music." *Ethnomusicology* 13/2 (May 1969), 313–316.
Grow, Mary L. "Tarnishing the Golden Era: Aesthetics, Humor, and Politics in Lakhon Chatri Dance Drama." In E. Paul Durrenberger, ed., *State Power and Culture in Thailand.* New Haven: Southeast Asian Studies Monograph 44, Yale University, 1996: 47–67.
Hamilton, Annette. "Cinema and Nation: Dilemmas of Representation in Thailand." In W. Dissanayake, ed., *Colonialism and Nationalism in Asian Cinema.* Bloomington: Indiana University Press, 1994: 141–161.
———. "Rumours, Foul Calumnies and the Safety of the State: Mass Media and National Identity in Thailand." In Reynolds, ed., *National Identity: Thailand:* 341–380.
Handley, Paul. "Back to the Grassroots." *Far Eastern Economic Review*, October 29, 1992: 21.
———. "Growth without Tears." *Far Eastern Economic Review*, July 18, 1991: 34–35.
———. "How the Other Half Live." *Far Eastern Economic Review*, July 18, 1991: 47–48.
———. "Rainbow Coalition." *Far Eastern Economic Review*, June 4, 1992: 11–12.
———. "Still Missing." *Far Eastern Economic Review*, May 27, 1993: 16.
———. "Turning Full Circle." *Far Eastern Economic Review*, December 12, 1991: 34.
Heinze, Ruth-Inge. "Ten Days in October—Students vs. the Military: An Account of the Student Uprising in Thailand." *Asian Survey* 14/6 (June 1974): 491–508.
Hewison, Kevin. "Emerging Social Forces in Thailand: New Political and Economic Rules." In Robison and Goodman, eds., *New Rich:* 137–162.
———. "Of Regimes, State and Pluralities: Thai Politics Enters the 1990s." In Kevin Hewison, Richard Robison, and Garry Rodan, eds., *Southeast Asia in the 1990s: Authoritarianism, Democracy and Capitalism.* St. Leonards, N.S.W.: Allen and Unwin, 1993. 159–190.

———. "The State and Capitalist Development in Thailand." In John G. Taylor and Andrew Turton, eds., *Sociology of "Developing Societies": Southeast Asia.* New York: Monthly Review, 1988: 73–83.

Hirsch, Philip. "The Thai Countryside in the 1990s." *Southeast Asian Affairs 1994.* Singapore: Institute of Southeast Asian Studies, 1995: 320–354.

Hunt, Ken. "Thai Masters." *The Beat* 12/5 (1993): 30–31.

Ikemoto, Yukio. *Income Distribution in Thailand: Its Changes, Causes, and Structure.* Tokyo: Institute of Developing Economies, 1991.

Iyer, Pico. *Video Night in Kathmandu and Other Reports from the Not-so-far East.* New York: Knopf, 1988: 287–316.

Kartomi, Margaret J. " 'Traditional Music Weeps' and Other Themes in the Discourse on Music, Dance and Theatre of Indonesia, Malaysia and Thailand." *Journal of Southeast Asian Studies* 26/2 (September 1995): 366–400.

Keyes, Charles. "The Case of the Purloined Lintel: The Politics of a Khmer Shrine as a Thai National Treasure." In Reynolds, ed., *National Identity: Thailand*: 261–292.

———. *The Golden Peninsula: Culture and Adaptation in Mainland Southeast Asia.* New York: Macmillan, 1977.

———. *Thailand: Buddhist Kingdom as Modern Nation-State.* Boulder: Westview, 1987.

King, Daniel E. "The Thai Parliamentary Elections of 1992: Return to Democracy in an Atypical Year." Asian Survey 32/12 (December 1992): 1109–1123.

Kobkul Phutharaporn. "Country Folk Songs and Thai Society." In *Traditional and Changing Thai World View.* Bangkok: Chulalongkorn University Press, 1985: 151–169.

Kulick, Elliott, and Dick Wilson. *Thailand's Turn: Profile of a New Dragon.* New York: St. Martin's, 1992.

Landgraf, Ginny. Liner notes to the album *The Flower of Isan/Isan Slete: Songs and Music from North East Thailand* (Globestyle 051, 1989).

———. "Soeng—All the Hard Times of Old Isaan." *Dirty Linen* 26 (Summer 1989): 6–8, 46.

LePoer, Barbara Leitch, ed. *Thailand: A Country Study.* Washington, D.C.: Department of the Army, 1987.

Lent, John. "Asian Comic Strips: Old Wine in New Bottles." *Asian Culture (Asia-Pacific Culture) Quarterly* 23/4 (Winter 1995): 39–62.

———. *The Asian Film Industry.* London: Christopher Helm, 1990: 212–220.

———. "Historical Overview of Southeast Asian Film." *Media Asia* 18/2 (1991): 98–102 and 18/3 (1991): 152–163.

Likhit Dhiravegin. *Demi Democracy: The Evolution of the Thai Political System.* Singapore: Times Academic Press, 1992.

Liner notes to the album *Musical Atlas: Thailand—The Music of Chieng Mai* (Odeon 18080, 1976).

LoGerfo, Jim. "Attitudes toward Democracy among Bangkok and Rural Northern Thais." *Asian Survey* 36/9 (September 1996): 904–923.

Malm, William. *Music Cultures of the Pacific, the Near East, and Asia*, 2nd ed. Englewood Cliffs: Prentice-Hall, 1977: 118–137.

Manuel, Peter. *Popular Musics of the Non-Western World: An Introductory Survey.* New York: Oxford University Press, 1988: 204–205.

Marre, Jeremy, and Hannah Charlton. *Beats of the Heart: Popular Music of the World*. New York: Pantheon, 1985: 198–214.
Mattani Modjara Rutnin. *Dance, Drama, and Theatre in Thailand: The Process of Development and Modernization*. Tokyo: Centre for East Asian Cultural Studies for UNESCO, 1993.
Miettinen, Jukka O. *Classical Dance and Theatre in South-East Asia*. Singapore: Oxford University Press, 1992: 40–74.
Miller, Terry E. *Traditional Music of the Lao: Kaen Playing and Singing in Northeast Thailand*. Westport: Greenwood, 1985.
Miller, Terry, and Jarernchai Chonpairot. *A History of Siamese Music Reconstructed from Western Documents, 1505–1932*. Special issue of *Crossroads* 8/2 (1994): 1–192.
Mitchell, John D. "Thailand." In John A. Lent, ed., *The Asian Newspapers' Reluctant Revolution*. Ames: Iowa State University Press, 1974: 210–233.
Mohd. Taib Osman, ed. *Traditional Drama and Music of Southeast Asia*. Kuala Lumpur: Dewan Bahasa dan Pustaka, 1974.
Moore, Frank J. *Thailand: Its People, Its Society, Its Culture*. New Haven: HRAF Press, 1974.
Moreau, Ron. "Sex and Death in Thailand." *Newsweek*, July 20, 1992: 50–51.
Morell, David, and Chai-anan Samudavanija. *Political Conflict in Thailand: Reform, Reaction, Revolution*. Cambridge: Oelgeschlager, Gunn, and Hain, 1981.
Morton, David. "The Music of Thailand." In Elizabeth May, ed., *Music of Many Cultures*. Berkeley: University of California Press, 1980: 63–80.
———. "Thailand." *The New Grove Dictionary of Music and Musicians*, Vol. 18. New York: Grove, 1980: 712–722.
———. *The Traditional Music of Thailand*. Los Angeles: University of California Press, 1976.
Mulder, Niels. "Individual and Society in Contemporary Thailand and Java: An Anthropologist's Comparison of Modern Serious Fiction." *Journal of Southeast Asian Studies* 14/2 (September 1983): 312–327.
Muscat, Robert J. *The Fifth Tiger: A Study of Thai Development Policy*. Armonk: M. E. Sharpe, 1994.
Mydans, Seth. "Thai Leader Is Having Hard Time Holding On." *New York Times*, September 1, 1996.
———. "Thai Premier Agrees to Resign." *New York Times*, September 22, 1996.
Myers-Moro, Pamela. "Musical Notation in Thailand." *Journal of Siam Society* 78/1 (1990): 101–105.
———. "Songs of Life: Leftist Thai Popular Music in the 1970s." *Journal of Popular Culture* 20/3 (Winter 1986): 93–114.
———. "Thai Music and Attitudes Towards the Past." *Journal of American Folklore* 102 (1989): 190–194.
———. *Thai Music and Musicians in Contemporary Bangkok*. Berkeley: Centers for South and Southeast Asian Studies, University of California, 1993.
Neher, Clark D. *Southeast Asia in the New International Order*. Boulder: Westview, 1991: 23–54.
———. "Thailand's Politics as Usual." *Current History* (December 1995): 435–439.
———. "The Transition to Democracy in Thailand." Unpublished paper, 1996.

Neher, Clark, and Ross Marlay. *Democracy and Development in Southeast Asia: The Winds of Change.* Boulder: Westview, 1995: 29–51.
"The New Thai Wave." *Asiaweek*, March 12, 1976: 22–26.
Ochey, James. "Political Parties, Factions, and Corruption in Thailand." *Modern Asian Studies* 28/2 (May 1994): 251–277.
Paisal Sricharatchanya. "Campuses Come To Life." *Far Eastern Economic Review*, September 1, 1988, 27–28.
———. "The Pulse of Pop Protest and a Rhythm for Life." *Far Eastern Economic Review*, April, 25, 1985: 113–115.
Panya Roongruang. *Thai Music in Sound.* Bangkok: Chulalongkorn University Printers, 1990.
Pasuk Phongpaichit. "Technocrats, Businessmen, and Generals: Democracy and Economic Policy-Making in Thailand." In Andrew J. MacIntyre and Kanishka Jayasuriya, eds., *The Dynamics of Economic Policy Reform in South-east Asia and the South-west Pacific.* Singapore: Oxford University, 1992: 10–31.
Pasuk Phongpaichit and Chris Baker. *Thailand: Economy and Politics.* Kuala Lumpur: Oxford University Press, 1995.
Phillips, Herbert. *Modern Thai Literature: An Ethnographic Interpretation.* Honolulu: University of Hawai'i Press, 1987.
Prizzia, Ross. *Thailand in Transition: The Role of Oppositional Forces.* Honolulu: Center for Asian and Pacific Studies, University of Hawai'i, 1985.
Reynolds, Craig J. "Globalisation and Cultural Nationalism in Modern Thailand." Unpublished paper, 1995.
———. *Thai Radical Discourse: The Real Face of Thai Feudalism Today.* Ithaca: Southeast Asia Program, Cornell University, 1987.
———, ed., *National Identity and Its Defenders: Thailand, 1939–1989.* Melbourne: Centre for Southeast Asian Studies, Monash University, 1991.
Robertson, Philip S. "The Rise of the Rural Network Politician." *Asian Survey* 36/9 (September 1996): 924–941.
"Sad Minstrels." *Asiaweek*, December 19, 1975: 27.
Sanchanit Bangsapan. "A Bleak Future for Good Films." *Far Eastern Economic Review*, May 3, 1984: 63–65.
Seekins, Donald. "Historical Setting." In Barbara Leitch LePoer, ed., *Thailand: A Country Study.* Washington, D.C.: Library of Congress, 1989: 1–54.
"Seven Genres of Thai Fiction." *Asiaweek*, May 18, 1979: 42–43.
Shenon, Philip. "4 Weeks after Protests for Democracy, Anguish Grows over Missing Thais." *New York Times*, June 14, 1992.
Smalley, William A. *Linguistic Diversity and National Unity: Language Ecology in Thailand.* Chicago: University of Chicago Press, 1994.
Smith, Harvey, et al. *Area Handbook for Thailand.* Washington, D.C.: Department of the Army, 1967.
Srisurang Poolthupya. "Social Change as Seen in Modern Thai Literature." In Tham Seong Chee, ed., *Essays on Literature and Society in Southeast Asia: Political and Sociological Perspectives.* Singapore: Singapore University Press, 1981: 206–215.
Steinberg, David J. *In Search of Southeast Asia: A Modern History.* Honolulu: University of Hawai'i Press, 1987.

Suchit Bunbongkarn. *The Military in Thai Politics*. Singapore: Institute of Southeast Asian Studies, 1987.
———. *State of the Nation: Thailand*. Singapore: Institute of Southeast Asian Studies, 1996.
———. "Thailand in 1991: Coping with Military Guardianship." *Asian Survey* 32/2 (February 1992): 131–139.
———. "Thailand in 1995: The More Things Change, the More They Remain the Same." In *Southeast Asian Affairs 1996*: 357–368.
Surapone, Virulak. "Theatre in Thailand Today." *Asian Theatre Review* 7/1 (Spring 1990): 95–104.
Surin Maisrikrod. "The Making of Thai Democracy: A Study of Political Alliances among the State, the Capitalists, and the Middle Class." In Anek, ed., *Democratization*: 141–166.
Suthichai Yoon. "Bloody Catalyst." *Far Eastern Economic Review*, June 4, 1992: 15.
Sweeney, Philip. *The Virgin Directory of World Music*. New York: Henry Holt, 1991: 163–165.
Tapanee Nakornthap, ed. *Essays on Cultural Thailand*. Bangkok: Office of the National Culture Commission, 1990.
Tasker, Rodney. "Coups Not a Way of Life." *Far Eastern Economic Review*, July 18, 1991: 42–43.
———. "Dirty Business." *Far Eastern Economic Review*, January 13, 1994: 23.
———. "Disloyal Opposition." *Far Eastern Economic Review*, April 14, 1994: 16–17.
———. "Downsized." *Far Eastern Economic Review*, January 18, 1996: 22.
———. "Enigmatic Activist." *Far Eastern Economic Review*, February 24, 1994: 34.
———. "Flesh Trade Options." *Far Eastern Economic Review*, April 14, 1994: 28.
———. "Rendered Surplus." *Far Eastern Economic Review*, July 22, 1993: 18.
———. "Show Time." *Far Eastern Economic Review*, December 12, 1996: 30–31.
———. "Steady as She Goes." *Far Eastern Economic Review*, August 4, 1994: 32, 34, 38.
———. "The Straight and Narrow." *Far Eastern Economic Review*, August 5, 1993: 18–19.
———. "Tiller's Troubles." *Far Eastern Economic Review*, October 19, 1995: 19–20.
———. "Traveller's Tales." *Far Eastern Economic Review*, September 17, 1992: 52.
Tasker, Rodney, and Gordon Fairclough. "Return to Duty." *Far Eastern Economic Review*, May 20, 1993: 18–20.
"Thai Ban on Song about Bangkok." *New Straits Times* (Kuala Lumpur), May 20, 1985.
Thailand in the 1980s. Bangkok: Office of the Prime Minister, 1984.
Thailand: Songs for Life—Sung by Caravan. Booklet accompanying the album (Paredon 1042, 1978).
Thongchai Winichakul. *Siam Mapped: A History of the Geo-Body of a Nation*. Honolulu: University of Hawai'i Press, 1994.
———. "Turning the Nation: Political Songs at War in Thailand, 1973–1977." Unpublished paper, 1993.
Turton, Andrew. "The Current Situation in the Thai Countryside." In Turton et al., *Thailand*: 108–113.
Turton, Andrew, Jonathan Fast, and Malcolm Caldwell, eds. *Thailand: Roots of Conflict*. Nottingham: Spokesman, 1978.

Ubonrat Siriyuvasak. "Commercializing the Sound of the People: *Pleng Luktoong* and the Thai Music Industry." *Popular Music* 9/1 (October 1990): 61–77.
———. " Cultural Mediation and the Limits to 'Ideological Domination': The Mass Media and Ideological Representation in Thailand." *Sojourn*, 6/1 (February 1991): 45–70.
———. "The Development of a Participatory Democracy: Raison D'Etre for Media Reform in Thailand." *Southeast Asian Journal of Social Science* 22 (1994): 101–113.
———. "The Environment and Popular Culture in Thailand." In *Southeast Asian Affairs 1991*. Singapore: Institute of Southeast Asian Studies, 1991: 298–308.
———. "Radio Broadcasting in Thailand: The Structure and Dynamics of Political Ownership and Economic Control." *Media Asia* 19/2 (1992): 92–99.
United Nations. *Industrial Statistics Yearbook, 1991: Vol. 2: Commodity Production Statistics 1982–1991*. Washington, D.C.: Congressional Information Service, 1993: 115/94, 3080-S6.2, fiche 9, 774–783.
Van Erven, Eugene. *The Playful Revolution: Theatre and Liberation in Asia*. Bloomington: Indiana University Press, 1992: 207–227.
Vatikiotis, Michael. "Anybody's Man." *Far Eastern Economic Review*, August 22, 1996: 22–23.
———. "Freeing the Waves." *Far Eastern Economic Review*, July 4, 1996: 20–21.
———. "Never Again." *Far Eastern Economic Review*, October 24, 1996: 53–54.
———. "Out of the Closet." *Far Eastern Economic Review*, November 21, 1996: 31–32.
———. "Social Climbers." *Far Eastern Economic Review*, May 11, 1995: 53.
July 27, 1996: 16–17.
———. "The Tension Within." *Far Eastern Economic Review*, June 29, 1995: 14–15.
———. "Urban Dreams." *Far Eastern Economic Review*, June 29, 1995: 18–19.
———. "Who Needs Democracy?" *Far Eastern Economic Review*, September 19, 1996: 20–21.
Vatikiotis, Michael, and Gordon Fairclough. "Mission Impossible." *Far Eastern Economic Review*, November 28, 1996: 16–22.
———. "The Spoils of Victory." *Far Eastern Economic Review*, July 27, 1996: 16–17.
Vatikiotis, Michael, and Rodney Tasker. "Barnham's Cliff-Hanger." *Far Eastern Economic Review*, October 3, 1996: 14–15.
———. "Promises Promises." *Far Eastern Economic Review*, October 10, 1996: 22–23.
Vatikiotis, Michael, Rodney Tasker, and V. G. Kulkarni. "Democratic Dilemma." *Far Eastern Economic Review*, October 26, 1996: 24–26.
Warr, Peter G., ed. *The Thai Economy in Transition*. Cambridge: Cambridge University Press, 1993.
Warshaw, Steven. *Southeast Asia Emerges: A Concise History of Southeast Asia*. Berkeley: Diablo, 1987.
Wenk, Klaus. *Thai Literature: An Introduction*. Bangkok: White Lotus, 1995.
"Will Caravan Toe The Line?" *Straits Times* (Singapore), January 3, 1983.
Wilson, David. *Politics in Thailand*. Ithaca: Cornell University, 1962.
Wong, Deborah. "Thai Cassettes and Their Covers: Two Case Studies." *Asian Music* 21/1 (Fall/Winter 1989–1990): 78–104.
———. "Whose Past? A Thai Song and the Great Lintel Controversy." Unpublished paper, 1992.

Wong, Deborah, and Rene T. A. Lysloff. "Threshold to the Sacred: The Overture in Thai and Javanese Ritual Performance." *Ethnomusicology* 35/3 (Fall 1991): 315–339.
Wright, Joseph J. *The Balancing Act: A History of Modern Thailand*. Bangkok: Asia Books, 1991.
———. "Thailand's Return to Democracy." *Current History* (December 1992): 418–423.
Wright, Michael. "Dontri Chao Sayam—Traditional Folk Music of Siam." *Journal of Siam Society* 81/1 (1993): 156–157.
Wyatt, David. *Thailand: A Short History*. New Haven: Yale University Press, 1984.
Yousof, Ghulam-Sarwar. *Dictionary of Traditional South-East Asian Theatre*. Kuala Lumpur: Oxford University Press, 1994.
Zimmerman, Robert F. "Student 'Revolution' in Thailand: The End of a Bureaucratic Polity?" *Asian Survey* 14/6 (June 1974): 509–529.

Malaysia and Singapore

A. R. Ismail. "Senikata Lagu-Lagu Melayu Dulu Dan Sekarang." *Dewan Budaya* 3/3 (March 1980): 15–17.
Abdullah Hussein. *P. Ramlee: Kisah Hidup Seniman Agung*. Petaling Jaya: Penerbitan Pena, n.d.
Afendras, Evangelos A., and Eddie C. Y. Kuo, eds. *Language and Society in Singapore*. Singapore: Singapore University Press, 1980.
Aimi Jarr. *P. Ramlee dari Kacamata*. Kuala Lumpur: Pustaka Romjarr, n.d.
Aisha Akbar. "The Evolution of Malay Music." *The Straits Times Annual for 1961*. Singapore: Straits Times, 1962: 23–24.
Andaya, Barbara Watson, and Leonard Y. Andaya. *A History of Malaysia*. New York: St. Martin's, 1982.
The Asia & Pacific Review 1993/94: Economic and Business Report. London: The World of Information, 1993.
Aveling, Harry. "Perceptions of Society in Some Malay Short Stories of the Early 1980s." *Solidarity* 141–142 (January-June 1994): 117–124.
Aziz Deraman. *Masyarakat dan Kebudayaan Malaysia: Suatu Pengenalan Latar Belakang dan Sejarah Ringkas*. Kuala Lumpur: Kementerian Kebudayaan, Belia dan Sukan Malaysia, 1975.
Banks, David J. *From Class to Culture: Social Conscience in Malay Novels Since Independence*. New Haven: Yale Center for International and Area Studies, Yale University, 1987.
Bedlington, Stanley. *Malaysia and Singapore: The Building of New States*. Ithaca: Cornell University Press, 1978.
Biddle, Arthur W., et al., eds. *Contemporary Literature of Asia*. Saddle River, NJ: Blair Press, 1996: 152–166.
Billboard International Buyer's Guide 1996. New York: Billboard, 1995: 252, 257–259.
Brookfield, Harold, ed. *Transformation with Industrialization in Peninsular Malaysia*. Kuala Lumpur: Oxford University Press, 1994.
Broughton, Simon, et al., eds. *World Music: The Rough Guide*. London: Rough Guides, 1994: 433–437.
Brown, David. *The State and Ethnic Politics in Southeast Asia*. London: Routledge, 1994: 66–111, 206–257.

Bunge, Frederica M., ed. *Malaysia: A Country Study*. Washington, D.C.: Department of the Army, 1984.
Camroux, David. "State Responses to Islamic Resurgence in Malaysia: Accommodation, Co-option, and Confrontation." *Asian Survey* 36/9 (September 1996): 852–868.
Cenderamata: Pameran Muzik Sepanjang Zaman. Kuala Lumpur: Syarikat Irama, 1986. (No author listed.)
Chandra Muzaffar. *Challenges and Choices in Malaysian Politics and Society*. Kuala Lumpur: Aliran, 1989.
Chandy, Gloria. "Lat—the Malaysian Folk Hero." In *The New Straits Times Annual 1980*. Kuala Lumpur: Berita Publishing, 1980: 38–41.
Chelliah, Joe. "Broadcasting a Fairer 'Musical Menu.' " *New Straits Times*, March 19, 1989.
———. "Development of Western-Style Music Making in Malaysia." *New Straits Times*, January 22, 1989.
———. "Towards an Identity in Music." *New Straits Times*, December 12, 1988.
Chew, Ernest, and Edwin Lee, eds. *A History of Singapore*. Singapore: Oxford University Press, 1991.
Chopyak, James. "Music in Modern Malaysia: A Survey of the Musics Affecting the Development of Malaysian Popular Music." *Asian Music* 18/1 (Fall/Winter 1986): 111–138.
———. "The Role of Music in Mass Media, Public Education and the Formation of a Malaysian National Culture." *Ethnomusicology* 31/3 (Fall 1987): 431–454.
Clammer, John. *Singapore: Ideology, Society and Culture*. Singapore: Chopmen, 1985.
Crouch, Harold. "Malaysia: Neither Authoritarian nor Democratic." In Kevin Hewison, Richard Robison, and Garry Rodan, eds. *Southeast Asia in the 1990s: Authoritarianism, Democracy and Capitalism*. St. Leonards, N.S.W.: Allen and Unwin, 1993: 135–157.
Crouch, Harold. *Government and Society in Malaysia*. Ithaca: Cornell University Press, 1996.
Da Cunha, Derek, ed. *Debating Singapore: Reflective Essays*. Singapore: Institute of Southeast Asian Studies, 1994.
Daud Hamzah. "Malaysia." In Harrison Ryker, ed., *New Music in the Orient: Essays on Composition in Asia*. Buren: Frits Knuf, 1991: 91–96.
Elegant, Simon. "Between God and Mammon." *Far Eastern Economic Review*, May 9, 1996: 58–60.
Elegant, Simon, and Margot Cohen. "Rock Solid." *Far Eastern Economic Review*, December 5, 1996: 50–52.
Fernandez, Joe. "Sharifah Aini—EMI Malaysia's Golden Girl." *Asian Review* 42 (October 1977): 36–39.
Fu Shi. "Cafe Singers." *Straits Times Annual for 1954*. Singapore: Straits Times, 1955: 70–71.
Granfell, Neville. *Switch On, Switch Off: Mass Media Audiences in Malaysia*. Kuala Lumpur: Oxford University Press, 1979.
Greenwood, Gavin, ed. *Asia Yearbook 1992*. Hong Kong: Far Eastern Economic Review, 1993.

Hajjah Maimunah H. Daud. "Bangsawan Down Memory Lane ..." *Sarawak Gazette* (September 1993): 14–20.
Hanna, Willard A. "Culture, Yellow Culture, Counterculture and Polyculture in Culture-Poor Singapore." American Universities Field Staff, *Southeast Asia Series* 11/2 (1973).
Harper, T. N. "New Malays, New Malaysians: Nationalism, Society and History." In *Southeast Asian Affairs 1996*: 238–255.
Hassan, Riaz, ed. *Singapore: Society in Transition.* Kuala Lumpur: Oxford University Press, 1976.
Hatch, Martin. "National Cultural Policy and New Performing Arts in Malaysia." Unpublished paper, 1985.
Heng Hang Khng. "Economic Development and Political Change: The Democratization Process in Singapore." In Anek, ed., *Democratization*: 113–140.
Hiebert, Murray. "Acting Up." *Far Eastern Economic Review*, November 21, 1996: 62–63.
———. "Family Resemblance." *Far Eastern Economic Review*, January 18, 1996: 62.
———. "Ring in the Old." *Far Eastern Economic Review*, January 16, 1997: 16–17.
———. "War of the Words." *Far Eastern Economic Review*, March 21, 1996: 44.
Hill, Michael, and Lian Kwen Fee. *The Politics of Nation Building and Citizenship in Singapore.* London: Routledge, 1995.
Hirschman, Charles. "Development and Inequality in Malaysia: From Puthucheary to Mehmet." *Pacific Affairs* 62/1 (Spring 1989): 78–81.
———. "The Society and the Environment." In Bunge, ed., *Malaysia*: 67–128.
Hong, Evelyn, ed. *Malaysian Women: Problems and Issues.* Penang: Consumers Association of Penang, 1983.
Hua Wu Yin. *Class and Communalism in Malaysia: Politics in a Dependent Capitalist State.* London: Zed, 1983.
Ibrahim Said. "National Culture and Social Transformation in Contemporary Malaysia." *Southeast Asia Journal of Social Science* 2/2 (1983): 60–69.
Ismaal Samat. "Penghibur Melayu Masakini: Tempuan kepada Penyanyi, Pelawak dan Pemusik Popular." B.A. thesis, University of Malaya, 1984.
Jayasankaran, S. "Balancing Act." *Far Eastern Economic Review*, December 21, 1995: 24–29.
———. "Don't Rock On." *Far Eastern Economic Review,* June 19, 1997: 26.
———. "Out of Bounds." *Far Eastern Economic Review*, October 12, 1995: 166.
———. "Unwritten Rule." *Far Eastern Economic Review*, March 7, 1996: 20–21.
Jayasankaran, S., and Murray Hiebert. "War of Words." *Far Eastern Economic Review*, September 26, 1996: 19.
Jesudasan, James V. "Malaysia: A Year Full of Sound and Fury, Signifying . . . Something?" *Southeast Asian Affairs 1995.* Singapore: Institute of Southeast Asian Studies, 1995: 199–219.
Jeyaratnam, Philip. *Abraham's Promise.* Honolulu: University of Hawai'i Press, 1995.
Jomo Kwame Sundaram. *A Question of Class: Capital, the State, and Uneven Development in Malaysia.* New York: Monthly Review, 1988.

———, ed. *Industrializing Malaysia: Policy, Performance, Prospects.* London: Routledge, 1993.
"Just Dying to See You." *Asiaweek,* June 15, 1994: 40.
Kahn, Joel S. "Growth, Economic Transformation, Culture and the Middle Classes in Malaysia." In Robison and Goodman, eds., *New Rich:* 49–78.
Kahn, Joel S., and Francis Loh Kok Wah, eds. *Fragmented Vision: Culture and Politics in Contemporary Malaysia.* Honolulu: University of Hawai'i Press, 1992.
Karp, Jonathan. "Sounding Off." *Far Eastern Economic Review,* June 1, 1995: 78.
Karthigesu, R. "Broadcasting Deregulation in Developing Asian Nations: An Examination of Nascent Tendencies Using Malaysia as an Example." *Media, Culture and Society* 16/1 (January 1994): 73–90.
Kartomi, Margaret J. " 'Traditional Music Weeps' and Other Themes in the Discourse on Music, Dance and Theatre of Indonesia, Malaysia and Thailand." *Journal of Southeast Asian Studies* 26/2 (September 1995): 366–400.
Kaur, Amarjit. *Historical Dictionary of Malaysia.* Methuen: Scarecrow, 1993.
Kee Thuan Chye. "Looking Askance at U.S. Media." *New Straits Times,* July 12, 1989.
Keenan, Faith. "Stage Fright." *Far Eastern Economic Review,* November 16, 1995: 24–26.
Khong, Cho-Oon. "Singapore: Political Legitimacy through Managing Conformity." In Muthiah Alagappa, ed., *Political Legitimacy in Southeast Asia: The Quest for Moral Authority.* Stanford: Stanford University Press, 1995: 108–135.
Khoo Boo Teik. "Democracy and Authoritarianism in Malaysia Since 1957: Class, Ethnicity and Changing Capitalism." In Anek, ed., *Democratization:* 46–76.
Kong, K. S. "Songbirds of the 1950s." *The Star,* June 15 and 18, 1978.
Kong, Lily. "Making 'Music at the Margins'? A Social and Cultural Analysis of *Xinyao* in Singapore." *Asian Studies Review* 19/3 (April 1996): 99–124.
———. "Music and Cultural Politics: Ideology and Resistance in Singapore." *Transactions, Institute of British Geographers* 20 (1995): 447–459.
———. "Popular Music and a 'Sense of Place' in Singapore." *Crossroads* 9/2 (1995): 51–77.
Kulkarni, V. G., S. Jayasankaran, and Murray Hiebert. "Dr. Feelgood." *Far Eastern Economic Review,* October 24, 1996: 18–22.
Kwok Kian-Woon. "Singapore: Consolidating the New Political Economy." In *Southeast Asian Affairs 1995.* Singapore: Institute of Southeast Asian Studies, 1995: 291–308.
Lai Ah Heng. *Meanings of Multiethnicity: A Case Study of Ethnicity and Ethnic Relations in Singapore.* Kuala Lumpur: Oxford University Press, 1995.
Lazaroo, Charles. "Singapore—'Instant Asia'—Varieties of Music." *Asian Culture* 15/5 (January 1977): 5–9.
Lent, John. "Asian Comic Strips: Old Wine in New Bottles." *Asian Culture (Asia-Pacific Culture) Quarterly* 23/4 (Winter 1995): 39–62.
———. "A Lot about Lat: An Exclusive Interview." *Berita* 14/4 (Winter 1987): 28–34.
———. "Singapore Cartooning: Only a Few Bright Spots." *Berita* 21/1–2 (Spring/Summer 1995): 2–9.
LePoer, Barbara Leitch, ed. *Singapore: A Country Study.* Washington, D.C.: Library of Congress, 1989.

Liak Teng Kiat. "Malaysia: Mahathir's Last Hurrah?" In *Southeast Asian Affairs 1996*: 217–237.
Lock Yut Kam and Victor T. Valbuena. "Mass Media and Teen Culture in Singapore: An Exploratory Study." *Media Asia* 15/1 (1988): 3–8.
Lockard, Craig A. [Essays on] "Malaysia," "Sarawak," "Sabah," "Kuala Lumpur." In Ainslee Embree, ed., *Encyclopedia of Asian History*. New York: Macmillan, 1987.
———. "From Folk to Computer Songs: The Evolution of Malaysian Popular Music, 1930–1990." *Journal of Popular Culture* 30/3 (Winter 1996): 15–40.
———. *From Kampung to City: A Social History of Kuching, Malaysia, 1820–1970.* Athens: Center for International Studies, Ohio University, 1987.
———. " 'Hey We Equatorial People': Popular Music and Contemporary Society in Malaysia." In John Lent, ed. *Asian Popular Culture.* Boulder: Westview, 1995: 11–28.
———. "The Historical Setting." In Andrea Savada, ed., *Malaysia and Brunei: A Country Study.* Washington, D.C.: Library of Congress (forthcoming).
———. "Malaysia: History." *The New Encyclopedia Britannica,* Vol. 27. Chicago: Encyclopedia Britannica, 1994: 751–755, 793.
———. *Reflections of Change: Sociopolitical Commentary and Criticism in Malaysian Popular Music Since 1930.* Special issue of *Crossroads* 6/1 (1991): 1–111.
Malm, William. "Music in Kelantan, Malaysia and Some of Its Cultural Implications." In *Studies in Malaysian Oral and Musical Traditions.* Michigan Papers on South and Southeast Asia No. 8. Ann Arbor: Center for South and Southeast Asian Studies, University of Michigan, 1974: 1–46.
Matusky, Patricia. *Malaysian Shadow Play and Music: Continuity of an Oral Tradition.* Kuala Lumpur: Oxford University Press, 1993.
Mauzy, Diane K. "Democracy on Hold: Malaysia in the 1990s." Unpublished paper, 1996.
Mauzy, Diane K., and R. S. Milne. "The Mahathir Administration: Discipline through Islam." *Pacific Affairs* 56/4 (1983–1984): 617–648.
Means, Gordon P. *Malaysian Politics: The Second Generation.* Toronto: Oxford University Press, 1991.
Mehmet, Ozzy. *Development in Malaysia: Poverty, Wealth and Trusteeship.* Toronto: Oxford University Press, 1986.
Milne, R. S., and Diane K. Mauzy. *Malaysia: Tradition, Modernity, and Islam.* Boulder: Westview, 1986.
———. *Politics and Government in Malaysia.* Vancouver: University of British Columbia, 1978.
Mitton, Roger. "Getting Serious about Fun." *Asiaweek*, November 10, 1995: 37.
Mohammed Agus Yusoff. *Consociational Politics: The Malaysian Experience.* Kuala Lumpur: Perikatan Pemuda Enterprise, 1992.
Mohd. Anis Md Nor. *Zapin: Folk Dance of the Malay World.* Singapore: Oxford University Press, 1993.
Mohd. Taib Osman. *Rampai: Aspects of Malay Culture.* Kuala Lumpur: Dewan Bahasa dan Pustaka, 1984.
———. "Some Observations on the Socio-Cultural Context of Traditional Malay Music." In Mohd. Taib Osman, ed., *Traditional Drama and Music of Southeast Asia*: 309–319.

———. "Tema Antara Kaum Dalam Cerpen Malayu Semenjak Rusuhan 13 Mei." *Dewan Sastra* (January 1976): 42–49.
———, ed. *Traditional Drama and Music of Southeast Asia.* Kuala Lumpur: Dewan Bahasa dan Pustaka, 1974.
Muhammad Haji Salleh. *Beyond the Archipelago: Selected Poems.* Athens: Center for International Studies, Ohio University, 1995.
Munro-Kua, Anne. *Authoritarian Populism in Malaysia.* New York: St. Martin's, 1996.
Murray, Geoffrey, and Audrey Perera. *Singapore: The Global City-State.* New York: St. Martin's, 1996.
Mustapha Kamil Yassin. "The Malay *Bangsawan.*" In Mohd. Taib Osman, ed., *Traditional Drama*: 143–153.
Nagata, Judith. *The Reflowering of Malaysian Islam: Modern Religious Radicals and Their Roots.* Vancouver: University of British Columbia, 1984.
Nain, Zaharom. "Rhetoric and Realities: Malaysian Television Policy in an Era of Globalization." *Asian Journal of Communication* 6/1 (1996): 43–64.
Neher, Clark. *Southeast Asia in the New International Era.* Boulder: Westview, 1991: 103–132.
Neher, Clark, and Ross Marlay. *Democracy and Development in Southeast Asia.* Boulder: Westview, 1995: 96–111, 129–147.
Ong, Michael. "Communalism and the Political System." *Pacific Viewpoint* 31/2 (1990): 73–95.
Pelras, Christian. "P. Ramlee: Portrait D'un Artiste Malais." *Archipel* 5 (1973): 243–250.
Phua Siew Chye and Lily Kong. "Ideology, Social Commentary and Resistance in Popular Music: A Case Study of Singapore." *Journal of Popular Culture* 30/1 (Summer 1996): 215–231.
Pixie, C. S. "Whither Culture?" *The New Straits Times Annual 1983.* Kuala Lumpur: Berita, 1984: 109–131.
Provencher, Ronald. "Covering Malay Humor Magazines: Satire and Parody of Malaysian Political Dilemmas." *Crossroads* 5/2 (1990): 1–25.
———. "Modern Malay Folklore: The Humor Magazines." In Lent, ed., *Asian Popular Culture*: 179–188.
Provencher, Ronald, and Jaafar Omar. "Malay Humor Magazines as a Resource for the Study of Modern Malay Culture." *Sari* 6 (1988): 87–99.
Quah, Jon S. T., ed. *In Search of Singapore's National Values.* Singapore: Institute of Policy Studies, 1990.
Quah, Jon S. T., et al., eds. *Government and Politics of Singapore.* Singapore: Oxford University Press, 1987.
Quah, Stella R., et al., eds. *Social Class in Singapore.* Singapore: Times Academic Press, 1991.
"Rapping to a New Beat." *Asiaweek*, June 15, 1994: 40.
Regnier, Philippe. *Singapore: City-State in South-East Asia.* Honolulu: University of Hawai'i Press, 1991.
Rehman, Rashid. *A Malaysian Journey.* Petaling Jaya: Rehman Rashid, 1993.
———. "Scorpion's Tales." *The New Straits Times Annual '85.* Kuala Lumpur: Berita, 1986: 33–35.

Rigg, Jonathan. *Southeast Asia: A Region in Transition.* London: Unwin Hyman, 1991: 109–132.
Rodan, Garry. “Class Transformation and Political Tensions in Singapore’s Development.” In Robison and Goodman, eds., *New Rich*: 19–48.
———. “Preserving the One-Party State in Contemporary Singapore.”In Kevin Hewson, et. al., eds., *Southeast Asia in the 1990s: Authoritarianism, Democracy and Capitalism.* St. Leonards, N.S.W.: Allen and Unwin, 1993: 75–108.
———, ed. *Singapore Changes Guard: Social, Political and Economic Directions in the 1990s.* New York: St. Martin’s, 1993.
S. Husin Ali, ed. *Ethnicity, Class and Development in Malaysia.* Kuala Lumpur: Persatuan Sains Sosial Malaysia, 1984.
Scott, Margaret. “Kutu Clash.” *Far Eastern Economic Review*, 144/14 (April 13, 1989): 36–37.
Seekins, Donald. “The Historical Setting.” In Bunge, ed., *Malaysia*: 1–66.
“Sengketa Yang Menggerhanakan Industri Muzik.” *Dewan Budaya* 3/3 (March 1980): 18–20.
Sheppard, Tan Sri Haji Mubin. “Pa’ Mat: Making Music for Kings.” *The New Straits Times Annual ‘84.* Kuala Lumpur: Berita, 1985: 93–100.
Singh, Bilveer. “Singapore: Change Amidst Continuity.” *Southeast Asian Affairs 1994.* 267–284.
Sri Delima. *As I Was Passing.* Kuala Lumpur: Berita Publishing, 1976.
Steinberg, David J., et al. *In Search of Southeast Asia: A Modern History.* 2nd Edition. Honolulu: University of Hawai‘i Press, 1985.
Suhaimi Aznam. “Quipping Away at Racism.” *Far Eastern Economic Review*, December 14, 1989: 42–46.
Sweeney, Philip. *The Virgin Directory of World Music.* New York: Henry Holt, 1991: 168–170.
Tamney, Joseph B. *The Struggle Over Singapore’s Soul: Western Modernization and Asian Culture.* Berlin: de Gruyter, 1996.
Tan Sooi Beng. *Bangsawan: A Social and Stylistic History of Popular Malay Opera.* Singapore: Oxford University Press, 1993.
———. “Bangsawan of Malaysia: The Creation of Tradition.” *Review of Indonesian and Malaysian Studies* 23 (1989): 49–81.
———. “Counterpoints in the Performing Arts of Malaysia.” In Kahn and Loh, eds., *Fragmented Vision*: 282–305.
———. “From Popular to ‘Traditional’ Theatre: The Dynamics of Change in Bangsawan of Malaysia.” *Ethnomusicology* 33/2 (Spring/Summer 1989): 229–274.
———. “From Syncretism to the Development of Parallel Cultures: Chinese-Malay Cultural Interactions in Malaysia.” In Margaret J. Kartomi and Stephen Blum, eds., *Music-Cultures in Contact: Convergences and Collisions.* Basel: Gordon and Breach, 1994: 220–232.
———. “Moving Centrestage: Women in Malay Opera in Early Twentieth Century Malaya.”*Kajian Malaysia* 12/1–2 (June-December 1994): 96–118.
———. “The Performing Arts in Malaysia: State, Society and the Entertainment Industry.” *Asian Music* 21/1 (Fall/Winter 1989–1990): 152–160.
Tan Yew Soon and Soh Yew Peng. *The Development of Singapore’s Modern Media Industry.* Singapore: Times Academic Press, 1994.

Tham Seong Chee, ed. *Literature and Society in Southeast Asia: Political and Sociological Perspectives.* Singapore: Singapore University Press, 1981.
Thomas, Phillip L. *Like Tigers Around a Piece of Meat: The Baba Style of Dondang Sayang.* Singapore: Institute of Southeast Asian Studies, 1986.
Ting Chu San, et al. "Singapore." In Harrison Ryker, ed., *New Music in the Orient: Essays on Composition in Asia.* Buren: Frits Knuf, 1991: 96–114.
Tiong, John. "The Japanese Are Here Again." *New Sunday Times Viewer Magazine*, October 5, 1986: 7, 10.
Tremewan, Christopher. *The Political Economy of Social Control in Singapore.* New York: St. Martin's Press, 1994.
Turnbull, C. M. *A History of Singapore, 1819–1988.* Singapore: Oxford University Press, 1989.
United Nations. *Industrial Statistics Yearbook, 1991: Vol. 2: Commodity Production Statistics 1982–1991.* Washington, D.C.: Congressional Information Service, 1993: 115/94, 3080-S6.2, fiche 9, 774–783.
Vatikiotis, Michael. "Rapping in Malaysia." *Far Eastern Economic Review*, July 22, 1993: 32–33.
Wan Abdul Wan Kadir Yusoff. "Hiburan dan Masyarakat Melayu Bandaran 1870 hingga 1940: Satu Kajian Pertumbuhan Budaya Popular." M.A. thesis, University of Malaya, 1980.
Wan Abdul Kadir Yusoff and Zainal Abidin Borhan. *Ideologi dan Kebudayaan Kebangsaan.* Kuala Lumpur: Department of Malay Studies, University of Malaya, 1985.
"Watching the World Go By." *Asiaweek*, May 25, 1994: 28.
Wells, Alan, and Lee Chun Wah. "Music Culture in Singapore: Record Companies, Retailers, and Performers." In Lent, ed., *Asian Popular Culture*: 29–41.
Welsh, Bridget. "Attitudes toward Democracy in Malaysia." *Asian Survey* 36/9 (September 1996): 882–903.
Yao Souchou. "Consumption and Social Aspirations of the Middle Class in Singapore." In *Southeast Asian Affairs 1996*: 337–354.
Yassin, Mustapha Kamil. "The Malay 'Bangsawan.' " In Mohd. Taib Osman, ed., *Traditional Drama and Music*: 143–153.
Yousof, Ghulam-Sarwar. *Dictionary of Traditional South-East Asian Theatre.* Kuala Lumpur: Oxford University Press, 1994.
Zaleha Selamat. "Analisa Kandungan Senikata Lagu-Lagu Nyanyian Allahyaram P. Ramlee." B.A. thesis, University of Malaya, 1985.
Zurinah Hassan. "Lirik Lagu-lagu Pop Melayu: Nilai Keindahannya Terabai." *Dewan Budaya* 4/3 (March 1982): 23–25.

Index

GENERAL

POP STARS AND MUSICIANS